Sea

Christine Feehan

PIATKUS

PIATKUS

First published in Great Britain in 2008 by Piatkus Books
This paperback edition published in 2008 by Piatkus Books
First published in the US in 2008 by
The Berkley Publishing Group,
A Division of Penguin Group (USA) Inc., New York

ISBN 978-0-7499-0863-8

Typeset in Times by Action Publishing Technology Ltd, Gloucester
Printed and bound by Mackays of Chatham, Chatham, Kent

Piatkus Books
An imprint of
Little, Brown Book Group
100 Victoria Embankment
London EC4Y 0DY

An Hachette Livre UK Company
www.hachettelivre.co.uk

www.piatkus.co.uk

For my parents,
Mark and Nancy King,
who taught all of us how to love

Acknowledgments

As with any book, I have many people to thank: Domini Stottsberry, who did so much research and worked hard to pull this book together; Cheryl Wilson, an amazing friend and writer even under stressful circumstances. I owe a lot to Rich Campbell, bass guitarist for the band America, who graciously took time out of his busy schedule and gave me so much help, attempting to teach me about touring and life on the road. If I have made any mistakes, they're mine alone, as he was out touring and I couldn't double-check everything. Last, but not least, Jeri Stahl, retired Aurora, Colorado, police detective, now doing consulting work for Denver, who answered all my questions patiently and worked through my scenes with astonishing clarity.

Turbulent Sea

Chapter One

Joley Drake stared in a kind of sick dread at the mob of people crowding the gates and fence. She had forgotten what after parties were like, or maybe she'd just blocked them out. Women pushed against the car windows, lifting their tops and mashing their bare breasts against the tinted panes. Some waved thong underwear in various colors. They shoved at the car, pulling on door handles and screaming. She doubted any of those women knew who was in the vehicle, but they were clearly willing to sell themselves to get an invite inside.

'My God, Steve,' Joley muttered to her driver, 'sex, drugs and rock and roll are such a cliché, but it's so true.' Even to herself she sounded jaded.

Steve Brinkley's gaze met hers in the rearview mirror. 'You stopped coming to these things years ago; what made you change your mind tonight? I was shocked when I got your call.'

That was a question she didn't want to answer, not even to herself – especially to herself. She pushed her forehead into her palm. 'I haven't been to one of these in so long, I let everything but the music just fade away. I didn't want to think about what

1

goes on, but now that I'm here, I might just throw up.' She meant to sound light, joking, but the pounding on the hood and the hands trying to yank open doors were impossible to ignore.

She felt like an animal trapped in a cage. It was surprising how often she felt that way. And if the mob knew who was inside, they would have begun dismantling the car to get at her. She hadn't wanted to remember this part of her life. Those first heady months as a megastar, when everything she wanted, or needed, or even thought of was handed to her and the band – that had been so long ago, a dream come true that had quickly turned to a nightmare she tried to forget.

She had been born with a legacy of gifts, but even she had been overtaken by the magnitude of what was offered to her in that first flush of success, being treated like a star, godlike, given anything, wanted everywhere. Like so many stars before her, she'd fallen into the trap of selfish egotism, believing she deserved to be treated differently.

Being a Drake with special gifts prevented her from using anything poisonous to her body, but her band hadn't been so lucky. She'd seen the results, and more than once had walked into a hotel room to find naked bodies writhing everywhere and drugs and alcohol flowing freely. Her boys, as she called them, were more than just friends – almost family – and the excesses of alcohol, drugs and women crawling over one another for a chance to be with a member of a band, to do anything for him, had nearly destroyed their minds and their lives.

Most of the band members lost families to that lifestyle. It hadn't taken Joley long to become disgusted with the way they were all living. She'd walked out, turning her back on music – on the band – on fame. They knew it was her voice that had taken them to the top and without her the band would topple quickly. In the end, her manager and the band members had convinced her they would set rules and abide by them.

Joley knew she couldn't dictate to the band, but she could establish guidelines she could live with. She didn't ever pretend not to have a wild streak, but that didn't include illegal substances or sexual orgies. And it certainly didn't include underage boys or girls performing sexual favors and getting totally wasted with her band. The terms had been agreed to, and Joley rarely went to parties other than with the band immediately afterward. And she never went where someone might be providing all the things she'd most objected to – until now – until tonight.

'Why do you suppose these women feel the need to service bands? What do they really get out of it, Steve?' she asked her driver. 'Because I don't understand. They line up to give the band and even the roadies blowjobs. Actually stand in line in the halls, hoping to get the chance. They don't really care if anyone knows their name.'

'I don't know, Joley. I don't really understand half of what people do or why they do it.'

The guards pushed the crowds back to make room so the car could approach the high, wrought iron gates. All of the guards were carrying guns – and not just polite police-issue handguns beneath smooth jackets either. Those were semiautomatic weapons cradled in their beefy arms, right out in the open like in some gangster film. Joley's stomach lurched as she observed the guards through the tinted glass. These weren't rented security – these men were the

3

real deal – professionals every last one of them. They didn't wear boredom on their faces; they wore masks, and their eyes were flat and cold. She knew if she were to reach out and touch one of them, even lightly, she'd feel the chill of death.

Her cell phone went off, interrupting her train of thought. Flipping it open with a little grimace, she answered. 'Gloria, I told you I'd take care of it. I'm getting Logan now. You dragged me out of bed and I said I'd do it, so give me some time and I'll have him there.' She knew she sounded bitchy, but really. Gloria Brady, the mother of Lucy Brady, psycho-stalker from hell, every band's worst nightmare come true, was once again demanding to speak with her sax player, Logan Voight. He'd had a brief encounter with Gloria's daughter, making the mistake of seeing her more than once, and now Lucy and her demented ways would haunt him forever.

Joley snapped the phone closed and shoved it into her pocket. She'd been pacing her hotel room when the first frantic call from Gloria came in. Joley had latched on to the excuse, dragging her driver out in the middle of the night, lying to herself that she was coming to the party to deliver the message to Logan and see to it personally that he took care of the problem. Now that she was here, she realized how utterly stupid she'd been. Others might look at the guards and think they were cool; she looked at them and wondered how many people they'd killed.

A guard tapped her window, making her jump, motioning for her to let him see her. Her driver objected, but she rolled down the window and peered at the guard so he could visually identify her. She saw the instant flash of recognition. Joley Drake, legendary singer known simply as *Joley*. For

4

one brief moment she thought he might ask for her autograph, but he recovered and waved her through the gates.

Sergei Nikitin had been inviting her to his parties for months, but she always made excuses not to go. Sergei was a wealthy man who ran in the in circles. He knew politicians and celebrities of every kind. He maintained the public image of a charming businessman who liked the good life and surrounded himself with household names – movie stars, race car drivers, sports figures, models, public figures and of course the most famous bands.

Very few people knew he was reputed to be a Russian mobster with a violent, bloody past and a penchant for making his enemies disappear. Most of those who had heard the rumors thought they only added to his mystique. It seemed inconceivable that the suave, charming businessman might actually order vicious, sadistic deaths to further his already abundant wealth – to everybody but those in law enforcement – and Joley – thanks to her brother-in-law, who was a sheriff.

'Just stop here,' she instructed and waited until Steve had pulled to the side of the drive, still a distance from the house, before opening the door. She remained in the seat, hesitating.

The party was in full swing. Music blasted from the house, filling the air around it. Joley could almost feel the building expanding and contracting with every boom of the bass. Even the windows vibrated. She sat in the car with the door open and studied the house. Nikitin would know she'd come. His security people would have radioed the house immediately so Nikitin could be ready to greet her. It would be a victory of sorts for him. Finally. Joley

Drake. He'd been pursuing her for months. Another celebrity he could be photographed with.

'Are you getting out, Joley?' Steve asked.

She met the driver's eyes in the rearview mirror and made a face. 'I don't know. Maybe. Do you mind just waiting, Steve? I feel bad for dragging you out tonight.'

'That's what you pay me for,' he reassured her. 'If you want to sit here for a while, it's fine by me. I was surprised you wanted to come,' he added, a note of worry in his voice.

It had surprised her too, but she'd lain awake staring at the ceiling until she'd wanted to scream in frustration. She rarely slept, was a total insomniac, and she couldn't do anything but pace back and forth in her hotel room. The frantic call from Gloria begging her to find Logan had been all the excuse she'd needed. Gloria's daughter was in the hospital having Logan's baby and had already called the media and was making a scene, threatening to kill herself if Logan didn't show up.

Joley told herself she'd come to the party to make certain Logan knew what he was doing, to send lawyers and security as well as her manager, but she could have done it all with a phone call or two. Lucy had already agreed to turn over the baby to him, and the papers had been drawn up, but everyone knew Lucy wouldn't go away that easily. There would be one scene after another.

Joley shook her head as she turned her attention to Nikitin's grounds. There were people everywhere. They milled around the rolling grass, some making certain to be seen by the mob at the fence. A few hopeful starlets and male models even signed autographs through the gate. Cries and pleas and

6

drunken laughter were every bit as loud as the booming music.

She spotted Denny Simmons, her drummer, walking in the distance with a blonde, not his current girlfriend. She bit her lip hard. She didn't want to know any of them cheated. 'Men are dogs, Steve. That's why I don't date anymore. Hound dogs.'

He sighed, watching Simmons. 'They have too much, Joley. You know they drink too much or do a few drugs and they don't have a clue what they're doing.'

'Denny's been divorced once already and he acts as if his girlfriend is his world, but look at him now.' She narrowed her eyes as Denny stopped to kiss the girl, skimming his hands over her ample breasts. The woman jerked his shirt out of his pants and her hand went to his zipper. 'Damn him for this. I really like his girlfriend, and she has a child. I'm never going to be able to look her in the eye again.'

Men were dogs – *all* of them. Not a one could be trusted. Well, maybe her sisters's men, but not the ones Joley fell for. She liked them hard-edged and dangerous and that added up to . . . 'No, not dogs, Steve. I like dogs and they're loyal. Snakes is a better word for what men are.'

'Maybe you shouldn't be here.'

She detested the compassion in his voice. Her rapid rise to fame had created this situation, and now their lives were little more than tabloid fodder. She tried to steer the other band members away from the life of excess, but it had been impossible when everything came so easy. And men like Sergei Nikitin knew how to use fame and popularity to get what he wanted. He'd supply the drugs and women and even the pictures for the tabloids if it furthered his own cause. And once he got his claws into a person . . .

'Men can be weak,' Steve said.

So could women, Joley surmised. Or she wouldn't be here, chancing ruining her life. And for what? 'That's just a cop-out, Steve. Everyone has choices. And everyone ought to know what the people in their life are worth. And men should have more self-respect – and honor – than to abuse the people who love them.'

His gaze narrowed and Joley looked away from the mirror. She couldn't bear to see the knowledge in his eyes – or in her own – that she was really talking about herself. How hypocritical was it to condemn Denny for making wrong choices when she'd probably come here for that very thing. She couldn't even bring herself to admit the truth, hedging in her mind, pretending it was to help Logan save his child when the real reason was purely selfish.

Her body was on fire. Hot. Needy. Ultrasensitive. Her nipples brushed her lacy bra and sent streaks of white lightning zigzagging through her straight to her groin. Her body pulsed with life, with need, with want . . . Oh man did she want. She brushed a hand over her face to hide her expression from Steve.

A crush of what looked like teenage girls dressed in too-tight clothing, too much makeup and heels to make them look older came rushing around the walkway toward the front door. They were giggling loudly and pulling at their clothes, trying to look as if they belonged. Joley swore under her breath as memories flooded back. Young girls servicing band members and roadies. Groupies, looking to do anything with someone famous. Drugs and alcohol to deaden their inhibitions.

In the early days she had tried to stop it. Now she knew she couldn't. What others did and what they could live with was on them. The only stipulation she'd adamantly enforced was that any groupie had to be old enough. The girls didn't look it, but she was getting older and everyone seemed to look about thirteen to her these days. Maybe she was just jaded. Her manager and certainly the band would never break that one taboo, and risk losing everything.

The rush of excitement the show had produced drained away, even the fire racing through her veins, leaving her feeling tired. As if reading her thoughts, Steve cleared his throat and leaned out the window to get a better look at the girls.

'I swear, Miss Drake, looking at those girls, I'm feeling ancient. They look like they should be home playing with dolls.'

'I must be ancient, too,' she conceded, watching as one of them broke away and dashed around the corner to hide in some bushes. The girl pulled out a cell phone and quickly made a call.

Her eyes were bright and she couldn't stop smiling, her excitement at the opportunity of mixing with the band members and all the celebrities at the party nearly palpable. She was pretty. Young. Even with the makeup she looked no more than fourteen. Innocent looking. Definitely in need of protection. The poor girl had no idea what she was getting into. Joley pushed the door open even wider and swung her feet out of the car.

'We're not supposed to tell anyone they're letting us in,' one of the other girls called out. 'You'll get us kicked out. They told us not to tell anyone.'

Joley glanced at Steve. 'That doesn't sound good. If someone told them not to tell, they have to be underage.'

The girl with cell phone hastily snapped it closed and shoved it into her purse out of sight. 'I left a message for my mother that I'd be late,' she said and ran to join the group.

Joley got out of the car, frowning. She wouldn't have her band members or even the road crew picking up young teenagers. That was the one hard-and-fast rule the band had sworn never to break, and if any of them had been a party to the invitation for the teens, they were gone. Just like that. She'd quit before she'd have this kind of thing going on, and they knew it. She'd done it once and she'd walk away again. She could only hope her own crew had no idea who had been invited to this party. In any case, the teens had to leave immediately.

She took a couple of steps toward the group just as a limousine with tinted windows pulled up between her and the girls. Even as Joley started around the large vehicle, the door to the house swung open and several men came out. Joley recognized two of her roadies as they intercepted the girls. Relief flooded her until one of them laughingly put his arm around the girl who had made the cell phone call. Fury swept through her. The girl couldn't be more than fourteen. He had to see that.

'Dean!' She shouted his name. He was so fired. If she had any clout in the industry, he would never work for anyone in the business.

Dean spun around, the smile slipping from his face. The other roadie half turned and then said something, throwing up the hood of his sweatshirt so she couldn't get a clear look at him. The girls instantly stopped laughing and ran around the corner of the house, both roadies and two other men following after them, urging them to hurry.

Brian Rigger, her best friend and lead guitarist, stepped out of the house, a frown on his face. He looked around as if a little bored and then over at her. A smile broke out in greeting. 'Joley! When did you get here?'

'Just now, Brian. I saw Dean and some friend of his with some teenage girls.' She had to shout to be heard above the noise of the music and party pouring out the open door. 'They took off that way.' She pointed, even as she tried to walk around the absurdly big car that had pulled up at an angle to her. 'And I need to find Logan.'

'He's not here. Gloria called Jerry shrieking at him to get Logan to the hospital. It's a big mess, apparently. Logan took off with Jerry.'

Joley sighed. Of course Gloria would call the band's manager, Jerry St. Ives. And being nearly as psycho as her daughter, she wouldn't stop there. Logan had given her Joley's cell number to use in an emergency. Joley was *so* having the number changed immediately. 'Well, I hope he has an attorney with him.' She hadn't really needed to come at all. Now she didn't even have an excuse to be there. 'Go find the girls, Brian, and get rid of them.'

'It's done,' Brian assured her and took off briskly in the direction she indicated. Joley took a step to follow, but the door of the limousine swung open, blocking her path. She sent one panicked glance toward her driver before she composed herself and turned a look of sheer, utter contempt on the man who emerged from the backseat.

11

'Well, well, well. If it isn't Nikitin's new play-mate. RJ the Reverend. Or should I say the preda-tor? I thought you'd be in jail by now.'

Her heart was pounding too hard, so hard she was afraid she might have a heart attack. She didn't want to step back, or show fear, but as his bodyguards surrounded him, she moved to position her feet for better defense. Up on the balls of her feet slightly, shoulder-width apart and one back, relaxed, one arm across her waist in a casual pose while the other hand was tucked under her chin where she could use it to block any incoming punches. The tallest one was the most aggressive. He'd struck her once before, weeks earlier, and she kept a wary eye on him.

RJ glared at her. She noted that he had to assure himself he was surrounded by his men. His fingers curled into fists, and maniacal hatred shimmered in the air between them. She had exposed the Reverend on national television when she'd gotten him on live tape claiming he could end Joley's wild ways by tying her down, flogging her and having sex with her to drive out her demons. The media had played the clip endlessly for weeks after, and clearly RJ hadn't forgotten that any more than she had.

'Joley Drake. Whore of the devil. I've wanted to talk to you for a long while.'

She raised an eyebrow. 'Talk? I doubt talking is on your mind. Unless it's to hear the sound of your own voice. You're cruising for women, you and your little pack of wolves, so don't even try to give me your idiotic spiel about saving souls. Save it for someone who doesn't know what a sick pervert you are.'

The taller bodyguard stepped close enough that

12

she could smell his cologne. It seemed absurd that he was wearing something spicy and nice smelling. 'You bitch.'

Joley rolled her eyes. 'Can't you come up with something a little more original?'

'Now, Paul,' RJ said in a soothing voice. 'I do want to talk with Ms. Drake. She needs our sympathy and compassion. You're right, Joley, I am a human male. And my body often betrays me, but I try to overcome the weaknesses of the flesh.' He spread his arms to take in the house. 'Wickedness and debauchery are taking place in this establishment and I mean to aid those who will listen.'

'Do people actually believe you? You're here for the sex and drugs, nothing else. At least the rest of them don't lie about it.'

'Is that why you're here?'

The question caught her by surprise and she inwardly winced, keeping her famous smile plastered on her face. She might pretend to the rest of the world that she'd come to do a great deed, but she knew better and his question had hit a little too close to home.

'I'm not doing this with you.' She glanced over her shoulder to try to see the young girls, but they were out of sight along with the roadies and Brian. Logan was already gone and she wasn't siccing the Reverend on him. If he knew Logan's unwed girlfriend was giving birth, he'd race to the hospital and try to grab headlines at Logan's expense.

'I overheard you say there were teens here. If that's true, perhaps I can be of some assistance.' RJ moved closer, crowding her personal space.

She should have shifted, stepped to the side to give herself more room, but the taller bodyguard,

Paul, blocked her path. She found herself surrounded, in a tight circle.

'Get in the car, Joley,' RJ said. 'We can discuss this without all the noise. If the young people need to be saved, I can do it. You have to believe in me. One slip only makes me human. Let my record speak for me.'

His voice had dropped a bit, and she recognized the famous charismatic note he could produce. She nearly laughed. She was a Drake, and her legacy was spell-singing, the most powerful gift of sound in the world. If the Reverend wanted to engage in a battle of sound, he had chosen the wrong opponent.

'I suppose everyone is human, RJ,' she conceded, dropping her voice into a low, sexy drawl, one designed to slide over a man's senses. She saw the Reverend's shiver of awareness, felt the rising heat in the circle of men and realized she was playing with fire. Paul crowded her even closer so that she could feel the brush of his thigh against her hip.

That was stupid, Joley! Are you trying to get your-self raped or worse?

The voice slid into her head. Male. Humming with a kind of sexual fury. Her heart jumped and her stomach did a small, crazy flip. She didn't dare take her eyes off of the men surrounding her, but in spite of herself, she felt relief along with absolute exhilaration.

She tried to retreat, to get out of the circle, realizing the back door of the limo was still open and she was only a step from it. She glanced up at Paul as his arm came sweeping around her waist. Determination to toss her onto the backseat was on his face.

She spun away from his body, shooting her elbows

14

out as weapons, trying to gain inches so she could use her feet. With her body weight behind a kick to the knee, she could easily bring him down.

Without warning, another man moved into the circle. He glided in total silence. Complete and utter confidence surrounded him. Everyone froze, including Joley.

And just like that, Joley couldn't deny the real reason she had come in person rather than make a few phone calls. *This* was what she'd come for. Ilya Prakenskii. Russian bodyguard to Sergei Nikitin. A dangerous man with a murky past, death in his eyes and a dangerous, volatile appeal that sang to every one of her senses.

That look on his face. Ilya Prakenskii was always in control, always cool and expressionless. His eyes ice-cold, and never, *never* could she just read him like she could others – unless he wanted her to, unless he opened his mind to hers deliberately and let her catch small glimpses of the real man. She had never really seen him angry other than at her. She had power over him whether he wanted to admit it or not – and maybe that was what made him angry. He wanted her. It was in the heat of his gaze, the set of his mouth, the hot lust when he looked at her, but most of all, in his mind-to-mind touch – possession and promise and a dark need that bordered on obsession.

He was why she couldn't sleep. He was why her body felt hot and tight. She wanted to claw at everything and everybody. She swallowed fear and stood still, afraid that if she moved, if he touched her, she would wrap herself around him and be lost forever.

'Paul.' Ilya said the bodyguard's name in a low voice, but one that carried the razor edge of a knife.

15

'I suggest you keep your hands to yourself.'

'I see you've come to save your boss's little pet,' Paul said.

Despite his bravado, Joley found it significant that not only did Paul move away from her, but all of the other men did as well, including RJ.

'He sent me out to save you,' Ilya corrected. 'Getting your ass kicked by a girl would be embarrassing, especially with so many people watching.' He caught Joley's wrist and tugged until she came to his side. Instead of placing her beneath his shoulder, he brought her just one step behind him so he could shield her body should he have to. 'Sergei is waiting for you, RJ.'

'He's the Reverend,' Paul corrected. 'Everyone calls him Reverend.'

Ilya merely stared at the man until he shepherded RJ and the others up the walkway to the house.

In the ensuing silence, Joley feared Ilya might be able to hear her heart beating. She tried not to notice the width of shoulders, or the heavy muscles on his chest. He wasn't obvious about his strength until you got up close, but more than his physique, more than his perfect masculine body and his tough, heart-stopping face, she was drawn to his mental strength and intellect.

Everyone gave in to Joley. Everyone wanted to please her. She was strong, smart, famous, wealthy, and she had the gift of sound. With all that, she was beautiful, with satin skin, bedroom eyes and a sexy, curvaceous body. She was also stubborn and liked her way. She could read people – except for Ilya. He was every bit as smart, every bit as strong, and he had every single psychic gift her family had, each well developed. Aside from that, he was the sexiest thing alive and she was mesmerized by him.

'Trouble?' His gaze followed the men before he turned his full attention on her. Those ice-blue eyes drifted possessively over her face and down her body, touching her breasts, sliding over the curve of her hips and down her legs with a long, slow perusal that should have struck her as rude but instead sent her pulse skyrocketing.

Her entire body reacted with scorching heat. She felt herself go damp. Even her breath came in a little rush, lifting her breasts and unsettling her even more. Her face flushed. He knew what he did to her.

He turned her hand over, the hand he had zapped with some sort of spell months ago, the hand imprinted with his touch, his scent, the hand that marked her as belonging to him. It had happened so fast – in a little place on her home turf. She'd been dancing and he'd come in with his boss. Even then she could barely breathe when she saw him. And now, thanks to the little psychic mark he'd branded her with, she could always sense where he was, and how much her body craved his. Her palm – his mark – itched. And nothing seemed to alleviate the itch but Ilya being close.

Pride demanded she pull away from him, but the pad of his thumb moved in a delicious pattern over her palm. She felt each stroke humming through her bloodstream. Her womb clenched, and she felt the flood of liquid heat begging to welcome him deep inside her where he already seemed to live.

'It's got to be said, Joley, your driver-slash-bodyguard seems a bit useless to me.' He flashed Steve, still in the car, a look of contempt and tugged on her hand until she followed him, moving out of the glare of the floodlights, into the deeper shadows where reporters might not notice that Joley Drake had come to Nikitin's party.

'You've got to stay away from the Reverend and his moronic group of badasses, Joley,' he added. 'They're capable of doing you great harm.'

'I know.' She did know. And she wanted her hand back, because if he kept it up, she was going to strip and fling herself into his arms and she'd never forgive herself.

'I'd have to kill them. You know I would. Just stay away from them.'

'No one ever *has* to kill anyone.' She wanted to cry – or scream in pure frustration. He was so matter-of-fact about it, as if killing could solve the world's problems instead of *being* the world's problem.

'You're naïve to think that, Joley,' he said softly and brought her hand to his mouth. His lips were firm and cool. His mouth was hot and moist. He nibbled on the tips of her fingers.

He knew what he was doing to her. He had to know. And he had to know she'd come there to see him. Joley tugged halfheartedly at her hand, but he merely tightened his grip and she let it go. There was no saving her self-respect.

'Why can't you let me have some peace?'

'You know why. You belong to me and I'm not willing to give you up because you're afraid.'

She felt the first flush of smoldering anger. 'I'm not afraid of you. I don't like what you are or who you work for. There's a difference.'

'Is there?' He smiled as he scraped the pads of her fingers with his teeth, sending streaks of fire racing through her bloodstream and sizzling along every nerve ending.

She jerked her hand away and wiped it on her thigh. 'You know there is. I'm not going to deny I'm physically attracted, but I have a certain weakness for jerks. Don't ask me why, but I have "losers apply here" stamped on my forehead. You're just the kind of man I want to avoid.'

His palm curled around her throat, a gentle touch, yet it seemed a flame burned against her bare skin. A faint grin touched his mouth, turned his eyes to a deep blue. 'Am I really?' The smile was gone, leaving him looking more lethal than ever.

She swallowed the sudden lump of fear before she choked on it. His thumb slid along her neck in the smallest of caresses, sending shivers of awareness down her spine. Sexually, she was very susceptible to him. She suspected him of spell casting, but when she touched him, she couldn't find evidence of it. He often whispered to her at night, urging her to come to him. And she wanted him day and night. Even her songs were beginning to reflect her need of him.

She had come here intending to sleep with him – just getting it over with – but now that she was with him, she knew it would be a terrible mistake. He would own her, she'd never be free of him. Her only hope was to hold out and hope her obsession with him passed.

'You're a hit man. It isn't glamorous or cool. It's disgusting. You kill people for a living.'

'Do I?'

He never raised his voice or seemed to take offense, even when she was being deliberately rude.

'Don't you?' She was desperate. *Desperate.* Someone had to save her from herself, because this man had her so tied up in knots she couldn't think straight. She wanted to claw at his face, rake his body with her fingernails, fight for freedom, and yet at the same time, she craved him, needed him, wanted to wrap her body around his and feel him deep inside her, possessing her, claiming her. She nearly groaned in despair.

'Kiss me, Joley.'

Her stomach somersaulted. Her gaze jumped to his mouth. He had great lips. Very defined, very masculine. Kissing would get her into more trouble and she was already in way too deep. Ilya Prakenskii seemed so cool on the outside, ice water in his veins, but inside he smoldered like a living volcano, all molten heat and roiling lava.

He leaned close, his lips inches from hers. His warm breath was against her face and he smelled of spice and mint. 'Kiss me.' The command was low, his voice soft, almost tender. Her toes were beginning to curl.

She didn't know if she moved to cover that scant inch or if he did. She only knew that his hand shifted to shape the nape of her neck and that her body went soft and pliant, molding against his incredibly hard frame. And that his mouth was on hers. His lips were firm and cool. His teeth scraped and tugged at her lower lip and then it wasn't cool anymore. Fire ignited.

He took control before she could think or breathe, the flames sweeping up and through her, consuming her, taking her over completely. She gave herself to him, wrapping her arms around him, sliding one leg around his to bring her body some relief from the terrible tension that built and built along with the firestorm his mouth created.

His hand caught her hair and held her with a

tight, ruthless grip, the bite of pain only increasing her need to be closer, to wrap herself up in him. Her hips moved, sliding her body intimately against his thigh. She needed – *needed* – release, a respite from the continual sexual pressure that never seemed to let up. Night and day her body was on fire for this man.

The heat from his mouth spread like flames licking over her skin. She heard herself moan, and he deepened the kiss, exploring her mouth, taking everything she offered and demanding more.

The world spun away for Joley until there was only his strength and his hard body and the racing fire storming out of control. Her breasts ached, felt swollen and tender, the tips sensitive as they rubbed against his chest. The junction between her legs was hot and damp, demanding release. She slid along his thigh, applying pressure, seeking the relief only his body could provide.

'No.' Ilya lifted his mouth from hers, his fingers reluctantly releasing her. 'Not like this. When you give yourself to me, it's all the way and forever. This is too easy.'

Joley flung her head back, glaring at him. 'You're saying no to me?'

'We're not doing this, not like this. You want to get off, you can come home with me and get into my bed where you belong.'

She studied his implacable expression, wanting to belong to him, knowing he would take her over, knowing she couldn't live with what and who he was. She would end up loathing herself more than she already did.

He was rejecting her. She'd flung herself at him after months of enduring his constant assault on her

21

senses, she'd given in, driven by an obsession, a craving he'd planted, and *he was rejecting her.* Humiliation fed fury. She took a deep breath and flung back her head, chin up. 'Fine. I don't need you. I can walk into that house and go home with any man I want.'

Ilya heard the complete confidence in her voice and knew she was stating the absolute truth. She looked passionate, untamed, so sexy his heart nearly stopped. Her eyes were fairly shooting sparks. Her hair was wild and disheveled, as if he had already made love to her. She looked wild and unpredictable and so beautiful he ached.

Ilya caught her wrist again, turned over her palm. 'Do you see this, Joley?' His hand slid over her upturned palm, sending shivers along already sensitized nerve endings. 'I don't care what happened before I put my mark on you, but make no mistake, Joley, ever since I put this on you, you belong to me. I don't share well with others. Do whatever you feel you have to do, but be willing to live with the consequences. Just know you're going to make things unnecessarily hard on yourself.'

'Why are you doing this to me?' Her palm, the one marked by his brand, itched to slap the tough angles and planes of his face. He led her on and then rejected her. 'You can't tell me no and then say I can't be with anyone else. Damn you to hell for this.'

'You need a man, and I don't mean some spineless wimp who is going to give in to your every whim. You need someone who can rein you in and control your tendency to act before you think.'

'That's so sexist. As if I can't take care of myself.' She gave a little sniff of disdain, furious with him. 'I'm a famous, highly successful woman who's been all over the world, Prakenskii, and I do a darned good job of taking care of myself.'

He shook his head. 'You don't and you know you don't. Everyone thinks you're tough, Joley, because that's what you want them to believe, but you're not. And you're way too impetuous. You rush in to act without thinking. The Reverend and his pathetic excuse for bodyguards are a perfect example. What did you think would happen when you exposed him for his sleazy crimes on national television? He intends to pay you back. A man like that doesn't forgive and forget. He gets even.'

'And you think I need a man to protect me?'

'Yes. Call me sexist all you want, but in the end, it won't change the truth. You're running because you know you need me and you don't want to need anyone.'

'Joley!' Brian called her name and she spun around. Denny, her drummer, was walking with him toward her, looking guilty.

Joley loathed herself in that moment. She wasn't any better than Denny. She'd come here for sex with a man she was certain was the worst kind of criminal. And he had rejected her advances, humiliated her, threatened her, and she still was on fire for him. What did that say about her? She pushed away from Ilya and ran to meet Brian and Denny, choosing to escape before she did something she couldn't take back.

23

Chapter Two

'I've done something so stupid, Hannah.' Joley paced back and forth, skirting the furniture in her hotel room as she held the phone to her ear. 'Really, really stupid.'

'I'm not going to mention that it's three in the morning and you're scaring the hell out of me,' Hannah said amid a great deal of covers rustling and her husband Jonas whispering in the background. Hannah shushed him. 'I know you're not hurt because all of us would know.'

'I *am* hurt.' Joley kicked at the bed. She'd already thrown the pillows and every other thing she could find in the room that couldn't be destroyed. 'I can't sleep. I can't eat. All I do is think about *him*.'

Hannah might be completely across the country, but she didn't have to ask who *him* was. 'What happened?' She tried to send her sister waves of reassurance, but the distance separating them was too great.

'I couldn't sleep. I ached, Hannah, inside and out. I swear I feel like I'm in heat or something. Nothing satisfies me. I don't know what to do anymore. When I do sleep, which is rare, I dream

24

about him. And they're not just any dreams, either. Total erotica. I loathe him. I despise him. How can I want him like this? What's wrong with me? I desperately want to be normal, Hannah. Make me normal.'

'You sound scared. Tell me what happened.' Hannah used her most calming voice and breathed slowly, in and out, in the hopes that her sister would follow suit.

'He's like a drug addiction,' Joley said, 'I can't get over him no matter how hard I try. I need to come home. I need to be with you. I'm drowning here.'

'Do you think your obsession for him will be better if you come home?' Hannah asked, her voice cautious. Joley was volatile when it came to Ilya Prakenskii. The connection between the two of them was strong, and seemed to be growing stronger.

Joley put her hand over her face, shaking her head, even though Hannah couldn't see her. 'No. No, it won't. I went to a party tonight. I told myself I went because I couldn't sleep and I was bored, but I really went to see him.'

'Did you go home with him?'

'No! I didn't, but I would have had sex with him.' Joley squeezed her eyes shut tight. 'He said no. He *rejected* me, Hannah, and that made me want him even more. He knows he has power over me. I feel like I'm caught in his trap and I can't get away.'

'Is it possible he used a spell on you?'

'All of you examined me. You didn't find one. There's nothing but the zap on my palm and his voice in my head. He talks to me. His voice is so sexy, it turns me inside out. Except now he isn't talking and that feels so much worse. I'm really in trouble, Hannah.' Joley knew she was talking too fast, but she couldn't stop herself. 'I have to hear his voice, or I go crazy in my head. But if I reach out to him, he's won.' She sank onto the bed. 'Hannah. Tell me what to do.'

'I'll come out.'

Joley shook her head, forcing herself to do the right thing. Hannah had been brutally attacked and nearly died just a few short months earlier. The last thing she needed to do was to fly anywhere in public when she was still trying to heal. 'No, no, we're leaving for Chicago in the morning. I can do this. I can get him out of my head.'

She rubbed her palm frantically up and down her thigh. Ilya Prakenskii was already deep inside her and he wasn't going to let go of her without a fight. 'Why do I go after men who bring out the absolute worst in me? I don't understand why I'm so different from all of you. Look at Libby. She wouldn't be attracted to a man like Ilya. Only me. Just me.'

Joley sounded so filled with despair, Hannah was alarmed. 'Look, hon, I'm catching the next plane. Hang on and I'll be there. I'll meet you in Chicago.'

Joley wanted her sister to come. She felt safer when Hannah was around, when any of her sisters were with her, but she was an adult and this was her problem. She had to learn to manage her cravings for the Russian bodyguard because she knew the need wasn't going to just disappear. Hannah would ease the symptoms, but she couldn't stay forever and then the desire would be back at full strength and Joley would be right back where she started. She took a breath in an effort to calm down.

'I don't want you to come, Hannah. I just needed to hear your voice. Tomorrow I'll be onstage and the energy carries me a long way. I'll be all right. I just need to find a good, decent man. Maybe if I'm with someone who respects me and sees the good side of me, I'll get over my weakness for really bad men.'

She'd tried being alone, refusing to date anyone, because she was attracted to the wrong sort of men, but once Ilya had come into her life, she couldn't think about anyone else, let alone the idea of someone else touching her. But she would get over that. People could change – *she* could change.

'Are you sure, Joley, because I don't mind?'

'I do. I don't want you to have to fly across the country to hold my hand.' Besides, she was already losing her mind and knew she was already lost. Joley glanced around at the amazing mess she'd made of the hotel room, throwing a fit because Ilya Prakenskii wouldn't have sex with her. He'd made her feel cheap – no – she'd made herself feel that way, throwing herself at him because she *needed* sex – not just any sex – sex with him. And he was responsible for that, talking to her day and night in that incredibly seductive black velvet voice and zapping her palm so she itched and burned. Damn him.

She lifted her chin and took another calming breath. 'I'm going to be fine.'

'Joley, you're really upset. Don't pretend you aren't,' Hannah cautioned. 'That's when you always get into trouble. Think before you do anything.'

'Why do people always say that to me?' Joley said. '*He* said I don't think. He said I needed a man to tell me what to do because I couldn't take care of myself. As if. He's stuck in the Stone Age.'

Hannah knew she'd struck a nerve and tried to recover. 'He is very dominating. I noticed that whenever he's around you and he doesn't like you to cross him.'

'Well, he can go to hell. I don't know what game he's playing, but I'm not playing it with him. I'll be glad to get out of this city.' Joley flung herself on the bed, trying not to notice that her body ached and she felt hollow and empty.

'Europe was good?' Hannah asked.

'Very good. We sold out every concert and we actually scheduled a few extra because the sales were so high and we hated turning away fans. I'm exhausted, but it was great.'

'You had fantastic write-ups in the newspapers, and even the tabloids treated you fairly well. There were only a couple of scandals.'

Joley laughed, and for the first time it was genuine. 'I told the reporters to go easy on me because my parents believe all the lies they tell.'

Hannah laughed with her. 'I read that quote and knew you'd really said it. Mom's going to have few things to say to you.'

'That's not unusual,' Joley said. 'Go back to sleep, Hannah. And tell my brother-in-law I love him, even though he's semi-friends with Prakenskii when he should be arresting him.'

'I've got news.'

There was a small silence while Joley sat up, the note in Hannah's voice tipping her off. 'What?'

'Abbey is getting married next month, as soon as you get home. They're having the ceremony on the Drake beach and the reception here at our house. They only want immediate family at the ceremony. You know how Abbey is. And I'm pregnant.'

'Oh my God! Oh my God! For real? You're going to have a baby for real?' Joley stopped, the smile fading from her face. 'Wait a minute, Hannah. What does the doctor say? Are you sure you'll be all right? You're still not completely healed.'

'Libby doesn't know if I'll be able to nurse. There's a lot of scar tissue, but we'll see. I'm so happy, Joley, and I can't wait for you to come home to share this with us.'

'Libby's the best doctor in the world,' Joley said of her sister. Libby had special healing gifts, and thanks to her, Hannah's scars were barely visible. 'Jonas must be walking around with a big balloon head. What have you gone and done, Hannah? He's going to be impossible to live with.'

'I heard that,' Jonas called.

'Well, it's made him bossier,' Hannah said, laughing.

Joley could hear the joy in her sister's voice, and deep inside, where no one could see, she wept for her own loneliness. She wanted someone to share life with, to laugh and cry and hold at night. Her life was spent moving from city to city in an endless tour of shows, living out of hotels and buses. She loved it, but she wanted someone with her. She was so happy for her beloved sister, Hannah, but Hannah's happiness only intensified her own lonely existence.

'Wasn't Abbey going to call me?' Joley asked, somewhat hurt that her sister hadn't given her the news of her impending marriage.

'Don't be silly,' Hannah said. 'You were in Europe and they just decided. They're waiting on the actual date to speak to you. You're going to stand up for her, remember? And Kate and Sarah and Libby will be married at Christmas.'

'Finally. I thought they'd never actually do it, just talk about it.'

'If you get married, Joley,' Hannah asked, 'how would you want your wedding?'

'Since it's never going to happen, I don't think about it. I'm going to be the favorite aunt,' Joley pronounced. 'The fun one who always lets the kids get in trouble.'

'You'll find someone, Joley,' Hannah reassured her. 'You just have to be more open and let it happen. You've always been so fiercely independent.'

'It's more than that and you know it. I despise men weaker than me and hate men stronger than me. That pretty much leaves me with nowhere to go.'

'I thought I wouldn't be able to live with Jonas, Joley, but when you love each other you find a way to compromise. Jonas does get bossy with me, but I've found that I have as much power in the relationship as he does.'

'I know you're perfect for each other,' Joley said. 'I think I always knew it, but Jonas is different. He's a good man and he loves you more than anything else in the world because you're you. Hannah, you deserve to be loved that way.'

'And you don't?'

Joley was silent.

'Joley.' Hannah's voice was soft with love. 'You're a great person. You sacrifice for everyone. Don't do that to yourself, don't sell yourself short.'

'I don't.' But Joley knew things about herself Hannah didn't know. Dark things she craved, maybe even needed, in a relationship. She loathed that part of herself, driven by sex and danger, suppressed most of the time, but so strong the need fought her continually. She wanted to be loved, but what decent man could ever love someone like her? Sometimes, like now, when she felt driven to the brink of madness, she wished she wasn't a Drake and she could drown herself in alcohol and drugs and not feel the pain.

'Tell everyone I love them, Hannah,' Joley said. 'I'll be home soon.'

'I really will fly out,' Hannah offered.

'No you won't. You'll stay right there and do whatever Libby tells you to do,' Joley said. 'And Jonas. Tell him I said bossing you around right now is a good thing.'

Hannah laughed. 'I'm *so* never telling him that!'

'Get some sleep. I'm much calmer now,' Joley lied, forcing cheerfulness into her voice. 'And wish me luck in Chicago.'

'You don't need luck, Joley. Your talent sells tickets. Have fun, and call me if you need me. You know I'll come. Love you lots.'

'Back at ya.' Joley hit the end button and tossed her cell phone onto the bed before sinking down on it.

Hannah would come to her, but Joley would never ask her now, not when she was pregnant, especially after the vicious attack. Hannah was special, and Joley always turned to her when she felt in crisis. Hannah dealt with everything in her own sweet way, wanting to make the world better for her sisters. She had been a success as a supermodel, but Joley knew she'd be even more of a success as a mother.

Joley was closest to Hannah, loved her dearly, and it had been Ilya Prakenskii who had saved Hannah's life. He had stopped her attacker and kept her alive until the Drakes had gathered together to help heal her, and for that alone, Joley would always feel a connection with the man.

31

'You have Jonas,' Joley murmured. Jonas was tough as nails when he had to be, and he loved Hannah. Everyone had known it but Hannah.

Joley ran her hands through her hair several times, before she flung herself backward to lie staring up at the ceiling. She'd killed an hour talking with Hannah, but she had a long way to go before the night was over. The hotel had an exercise room. She could go there. Alone ... again. If only the tabloids really knew what her life was like.

Joley. Party girl. Lovers all over the world. *Not*. It was more like Joley up all night writing songs and going to the exercise room to keep from going into sexual meltdown.

'Damn you, Prakenskii. You're punishing me now, deliberately not speaking to me. Well, you know something, I don't need you. And I don't want you.' She leapt up and grabbed her hotel key. Sexual frustration was really good for writing songs. Her best songs had come from detesting, no, loathing Ilya Prakenskii and wanting him with every breath in her body.

The workout room was deserted, and she grabbed a bottle of water and programmed the treadmill for a run up and down hills. In her head she could hear musical notes with each step she took. Fury at Prakenskii was the pounding beat of the drum. The saxophone was purely erotic, the guitar riff – the blood sizzling in her veins. The keyboard was the breath moving in and out of her body steadily, necessarily. She could hear the bass in each slap of her foot on the surface, deep notes that set her heart pumping.

There was euphoria in music, the only place she could escape who she was, what she was. She had six sisters and she admired every single one of them. She was fiercely protective of them, although she was second to the youngest and all of them had incredible gifts. They all knew she had a weakness for dangerous men, but they had no idea just how terrible her craving for Ilya Prakenskii really was. And he was the epitome of everything she stood against.

She believed in the order of the universe. She believed in good and evil, in the balance of nature. She believed in the right to defend oneself, of course, but she deeply and sincerely believed it was wrong to harm another. It was rumored that Ilya was a hit man, and she could never, under any circumstances, have a relationship with a man who was evil. The problem was, he didn't feel evil. He felt hot and sexy, with that terrible edge of danger she seemed to crave.

She had been in his mind many times. He could communicate with her telepathically, and that meant he had to open his mind to hers. She had caught glimpses of violence, terrible things that made her afraid, but she'd never seen a memory of him murdering in cold blood – and if he was as evil as a hit man would be – then why couldn't she feel it when she could tell so easily with others?

'Joley?'

She nearly jumped out of her skin, whipping her head around and gaping at her lead guitarist, Brian. 'You scared me. What are you doing here this time of the morning?' She kept running, turning her head away from him, afraid the guilt would betray her.

'You seemed so upset when you left, Joley. You barely said a word. I saw the Reverend there and I know he and his entourage are confrontational with you, so I was worried.'

'I'm fine.' She glanced at him. 'You should get some sleep. We have a show tomorrow in Chicago.'

'Stop that thing and talk to me. This is Brian, not some schmo off the street. We've been friends for years.' He held out the water bottle as an offering.

Joley let out her breath and allowed the treadmill to slow to a stop. She took the towel from Brian and wrapped it around her neck before taking the water bottle. 'I thought you were allergic to exercise. What are you doing here?'

'You're always here when you're upset.'

'I'm here to work out. And I sometimes come up with my best songs late at night.'

'Tell me what happened. What were you doing at Nikitin's party?'

She shrugged and swallowed a long gulp of water. 'I couldn't sleep and thought I'd check it out. Once I got there, I remembered why I hated those things.' She dried off her face. 'Did you manage to run down that little weasel Dean whatever his last name is and his friend? The ones hanging with the girls who couldn't have been older than fourteen.'

Brian shook his head. 'I never found them. Denny helped me look for them, but we couldn't find them anywhere. We checked the pool, the gardens, the garages, everywhere, but they must have made the girls leave.'

'If he shows up in Chicago, Brian, I'm having Jerry fire him.' Jerry St. Ives was her manager, and she was just as angry with him as she was with Dean. He had promised to oversee the parties and make certain that no young kids were taken advantage of.

'Joley, you know very well anyone could have invited those girls. For all we know Nikitin did. At

34

least talk to Dean before you give him the axe. He could have been escorting them off the property.'

'He ran when I called him.'

'Honey, come on. Joley Drake angry is a scary thing. I'll talk to him if you don't want to do it, but at least let's give him the benefit of the doubt. This is America. Innocent until proven guilty.'

She rolled her eyes. 'And what's with Denny and the blonde?'

'He was afraid you saw that.'

'You think? She was blowing him right on the grounds in front of anyone and everyone.'

'He was pretty screwed up.'

'Is that supposed to be an excuse?' She shoved her hand through her hair in agitation. 'I like his girl-friend. Lisa's a really good person and she deserves better than him.' She knew she sounded disgusted and judgmental, but it was the truth. 'I'm not going to be able to look at him.'

Brian shook his head. 'Joley, not everyone is perfect.'

She burst out laughing. 'Is that what you think I am, Brian?'

'We all do.'

'I was there for the same reason as Denny. I just didn't go through with it.' She pushed past him and threw the towel in the empty basket. Housekeeping had come and gone long ago.

'What the hell are you talking about?' Brian demanded.

'I was lonely. I went to the party with the idea of bringing someone home. I'm not perfect, but I'm also not committed to anyone. Denny is. He should be a man and tell Lisa he needs other women. That's only fair.'

Brian rubbed the bridge of his nose, narrowing his eyes and frowning in disapproval. 'I don't believe you.'

She didn't pretend to misunderstand. 'Well, it's true. The saint is really a sinner. Sheesh, Brian, you've known me for years.'

'You don't sleep around.'

'How do you know what I do or don't do while you're at the parties having a great time?'

'I don't believe any of this. You're just upset.'

'You don't believe I can get lonely, Brian?'

'Hell, Joley, if you're lonely, I'm lonely, too. Maybe we should just make all the rumors true and hit the sack together.' He wiggled his eyebrows at her.

She studied him over the bottle of water. For one, horrible moment, she even considered the idea. They were both alone. They liked each other, were best friends, maybe if they got to together . . . Prakenskii had turned her down and her pride was wounded. She'd always been able to wrap Brian around her little finger. And he was nice. A very nice guy, but she wasn't the least attracted to him, nor was he attracted to her. She sighed. 'I like you too much,' she said.

'What the hell does that mean?'

'It means I'm not going to sleep with you and ruin a perfectly good relationship. I like you, Brian. I don't like the men I want to sleep with.'

'Okay, now I'm confused, but that isn't unusual around you, Joley.' He rubbed the bridge of his nose. 'Most of the time we're all confused.'

'Me, too.' She grinned at him. 'At least we can agree on that.'

He smiled back at her. 'We've got to catch a plane

first thing in the morning and catch up with our bus. Are you going to sleep tonight?'

'You go ahead. I was in the middle of composing.'

'You were in the middle of trying to run yourself into the ground. Did seeing Denny really upset you that much, Joley?'

'That and a lot of other things. I'm tired of this life, Brian. I want a home and a family.'

'You love performing.'

She shrugged. 'Maybe I do. I love music. I lose myself in it. But in the end, no matter how good things are, I don't have anyone to share my life with me. Maybe that's why I get so upset with Denny. He's had wonderful people to share happiness with, women who love him for who he is, not what he does, and he throws it away for a few minutes of pleasure. How many chances should he have before none of it's real anymore? Until every woman who goes near him wants him just because he's in a band and not because she loves him? And then we stop playing and he grows old and he's all alone. I guess he can look back and say he counted a few thousand blow jobs and that will comfort him in his old age.'

'You're just down tonight.'

She drank more water and nodded, agreeing with him because it was what he wanted. 'Yep, that's what it is.'

He studied her face. 'You really aren't thinking about quitting, are you? We're on top. Every song we release is a number one hit. No one does that. No one. Every concert is sold out. Our albums are double, triple platinum. Come on, Joley, tell me you're just having a bad night and you're not serious.'

'Does it matter what I say?' She pushed past him toward the door.

37

He caught her shoulder and stopped her. 'Of course it matters. You always matter. I hate that you're unhappy. I'll talk to Denny.'

'He can't change who he is. But I'm not lying to Lisa for him. I'd never want you to lie to me if my boyfriend was screwing around on me, and I won't do it for or to any of you.'

'That's fair enough,' Brian said. 'It was one party, Joley, one that got a little out of hand. Nikitin's parties are notorious for excess, but we don't usually stay long. We make an appearance, have a few drinks and leave.'

'He supplies women.' She made it a statement.

'He has women on the guest list; most hosts of parties do.'

'You know what I'm saying. I know what he is, what his reputation is. He's seducing the band, don't you see that? Supply drugs and alcohol and women. Take a few blackmail pictures and hook the boys on the high and he's got you all under his thumb. That's how he operates.'

'Nikitin throws some killer parties, Joley, which is why everyone goes when he invites us, but he's not offering anything we can't get anywhere else. Hell, Jerry can get us any drug we want, any woman we want. That's not why we like hanging out with Nikitin.'

'You like him? Nikitin?'

He shrugged. 'If he isn't already a billionaire, he's close, and yet he's cool, and I hardly think he needs to supply our band with anything to get us under his thumb. What would be the point? I don't know him very well, but yes, I like him. He's personable and intellectual. You know me. I don't hit the party scene hard, but I do like conversation and he's an interesting man. We've been talking quite a bit. He doesn't do drugs that I've seen, so we hang out, have a drink or two and talk world affairs. He's very knowledgeable in a lot of areas I'm interested in.'

'Such as?' She wasn't touching him, but his aura had changed slightly, enough for her to know he was uncomfortable with the conversation.

'Well, the market for one, what are good stocks. What makes a good investment. He really knows his stuff. He has advisors, but he does a lot of his own research and makes solid choices.'

She could hear the admiration in Brian's voice and it alarmed her. 'What about his men?'

'His men?' Brian echoed, his frown deepening. Now his aura changed sharply, throwing out a mixture of colors – annoyance – disturbed – even anger. 'What men?'

Her eyebrow shot up. 'The ones with guns everywhere. Did you notice them? Those guns are real, my friend.'

'Well the threats to him are real as well. You ought to know about that. You need bodyguards. Which reminds me, where were your bodyguards when you came to the party? Why was Steve just sitting in the car like an idiot? With the Reverend there, anything could have happened. Jerry warned you that the threats against you have been escalating. And you have that nutcase fan fixating on you and trying to tell you he loves you. His letters are very disturbing. Twice he's managed to get nearly onstage.'

She sighed. 'I might have a bodyguard or two, but I sure don't have men with automatic weapons guarding my gate. What's up with that?'

He shrugged. 'It's probably a necessity.'

39

'Why, Brian?' She persisted, wanting to shake him. 'Wouldn't a bodyguard or two be enough, or some rented security? Have you taken a look at those men? And what about Prakenskii?'

Brian's head went up sharply. 'I saw you with him. Did he make a move on you? Scare you? Because I can talk to Nikitin about him.'

She gave a short laugh. 'You really have no clue what's going on there, do you? Nikitin would never fire Prakenskii. He's afraid of him, just like anyone else with a brain. And those guards you think he needs, they're all trained soldiers.'

Brian gave a growl of total frustration. 'You have no idea what his life was like in Russia. He had a lot of enemies. That's why he has a man like Prakenskii working for him.'

'A man like Prakenskii?' she echoed. 'What has he said about his bodyguard?'

'Just that he's very dangerous and not to cross him. He advised me to stay out of his way.' Brian lowered his voice as if the walls had ears. 'I think he's killed a lot of people.'

'Is that what Nikitin told you?'

Brian shook his head. 'He implied it. And the other bodyguards defer to Prakenskii over everything. I've never actually heard the man talk. He looks at people and they just jump into action without him saying a word. Frankly, he scares me and I wish Nikitin would get rid of him. I know he doesn't altogether trust him.'

Joley went on alert, radar suddenly going on with a loud warning shriek. She was instantly protective, everything in her rising up to defend Ilya – which was silly – and stupid – but she couldn't stop herself. 'What does that mean? Why would you have a bodyguard you don't trust working for you? He's the man who takes the bullet for you.'

Brian narrowed his eyes, suspicion creeping into his expression at her sudden change of attitude. 'I don't know, but a couple of times I've seen one of Nikitin's other guards, a man by the name of Pavel Demidov, come in and whisper to Nikitin. They both always look around to see where Prakenskii is. If Prakenskii is watching or is close by, Nikitin waves Demidov off. Within a couple of minutes he makes excuses to me and tells Prakenskii to watch things while he disappears for a while. Nikitin almost always goes to a phone and has a heated conversation in Russian. He definitely doesn't want Prakenskii to hear or see him. There's no question he trusts Demidov and not Prakenskii. What's Prakenskii to you?'

'I'm just curious.' Joley widened her eyes in innocence. 'What does Nikitin say?' Nikitin felt evil, unlike Prakenskii, who felt – well – sexy. She nearly groaned aloud. She was so far gone she wasn't even hiding it from Brian.

'They talk in Russian, how the hell would I know? And I can only pretend to look for a bathroom so many times before Nikitin or Demidov gets suspicious that I'm trying to eavesdrop.'

'So you *were* trying to find out what was going on.' Joley pounced on that.

Brian shrugged. 'I find those parties boring. I'm not going home with a woman; I'm not into public blow jobs or orgies. I have to watch my drinks, so what the hell is there to do other than observe people? If Nikitin isn't available to talk to, there's not much going on for me.'

'I thought you were seeing someone.'

41

'Yeah, well, that didn't last.' He made a face at her. 'I'm too nice.'

Joley laughed and poked him, using the towel to keep from making skin-to-skin contact. 'That you are, my friend. Very nice. One of my favorite people in fact, next to my sisters and Jonas. You got dumped? Cuz I'll go hunt her down and kick her ass for you if you want me to.'

'Naw, but thanks for the offer,' Brian said, laughing with her. 'But I bet you could do it. You still taking lessons from your karate man?'

'I have several trainers.' It was another way to get through the long days and even longer nights. She liked physical exercise; it was a great way to sublimate.

'You're so crazy, Joley, why do you take that stuff? You have security and a personal bodyguard, who,' he looked around him, 'never seems to be on the job.'

She grinned at him. 'The poor man has to sleep sometime.'

'His job is to guard your butt, not sleep. And he wasn't sleeping. His lazy ass was sitting behind the wheel of the car.'

'I like being alone when I'm working out. He's off the clock and he's actually a good guy, Brian. I wouldn't have him, but Jonas convinced my family I need a personal protector, so Steve pulled the short straw and ended up guarding me as well as driving.'

'I'll bet Jonas doesn't know you don't use Steve half the time.'

'I do too.'

'He wasn't guarding you at Nikitin's party.'

'He was too; he drove me there, but I didn't want him following me around at the party and told him

42

I might need a fast getaway so to stay with the car.'

Brian rolled his eyes. 'Good plan, Joley. Good use of a bodyguard. And what did happen between you and Prakenskii?'

She shrugged. 'He pulled me out of a situation with RJ and his little gang of thugs, so I think he felt entitled to lecture me.' Her palm burned. She rubbed it up and down her thigh and hoped her face didn't flame with her blatant lies.

'Nikitin is sure strange about that man.' Brian shook his head. 'He seems to rely heavily on him yet he keeps him out of the loop part of the time. I find it fascinating.'

'Why?'

Brian held open the door for her and Joley followed him out. 'Human nature fascinates me. I like people. I like to know what makes them tick.'

'Sex,' Joley blurted.

Brian laughed. 'Don't be so nasty about poor Denny. He's going to be slinking around avoiding you as it is. If you give him one of your superior, you're-a-bug-under-my-shoe looks, he'll be squashed.'

'It doesn't stop him from being such a hound dog. Seriously, Brian, what about the others? Was everyone there getting wasted and screwing around?'

'Do you really want to know?'

She considered. 'I don't want Nikitin to have any surprises for me. Have any of them done anything illegal he could get them on? Or done anything he could blackmail them with?'

Brian whistled. 'You really don't trust the man. Seriously, hon, do you think a man like Nikitin cares what any of our band members do?'

'I think I wouldn't want to find out. He isn't all he seems, Brian. I have a lot of information because

43

I have so much family and friends in law enforcement. He's not a nice guy.'

'He told me he grew up in the Russian mob. He said a lot of his men were caught up in that life, but he's broken away, gotten legit and tried to give men like him a chance to have a decent life.'

'And you believed him? Looking at the men who work for him, the guns they carry, you believed him?'

'If he did manage to break away from the mob, Joley, especially the Russian mob, with their history of retaliation and violence, I can see why he would feel he would need guns and men who knew what they were doing.'

'And how many mobsters actually get out of that world, Brian?' She gave a harsh laugh. 'Do you also believe in Santa Claus?'

'You really ought to take some time to get to know him before you judge him,' Brian said. 'I think you'd like him.'

'You've forgotten one teeny tiny, but very important fact, my friend.' Joley keyed her room and stood in the open doorway, turning back so he could see her expression. 'I'm a Drake. We're not normal. I read people through touch, which is why I'm so careful to rarely touch any of you. I don't even have to touch Nikitin to feel the violence and evil in him. Don't be dumb, Brian, stay away from him, and keep our boys away from him, too. He'll chew you up and spit you out and not even think twice about it. And you can take that to the bank.' She closed the door on his shocked expression.

Chapter Three

Her palm itched. Really itched. Joley rubbed her hand up and down her denim-clad thigh, clenching her teeth together, all the while trying not to reach out with her mind to find – *him* – Ilya Prakenskii. Looking out the open door of her dressing room backstage, she could feel the energy in the arena, swelling and rolling like waves on the sea. Ten thousand restless people, excited, waiting, anticipating her performance, yet she knew – absolutely knew – that Prakenskii was somewhere in that vast crowd.

Adrenaline raced through her system, adding to the excitement and the building waves of sheer energy the crowd produced. Heat rushed through her body at the thought of the Russian bodyguard. She couldn't get near him without sizzling chemistry arcing between them. Sometimes, like now, she swore she could still taste him in her mouth. She touched her fingers to her lips, pressing hard, trying to erase the memory of his kiss. He ran in her veins like a drug, a bad habit she couldn't kick, no matter how hard she tried.

'Joley? You up for this? It's crazy out there.' Brian shot her a grin. His eyes were shining and he looked as sexy as hell, just the way the females in the crowd liked him. Tight-fitting jeans, shirt open to his flat stomach, chest showing and black hair tousled. The women would go wild when he took the stage.

She stepped into the hall and matched his grin. The rush of the crowd was exhilarating, but it was the music that always moved her. She thought in music – actually could see in music. Sometimes she could smell and taste it. Notes and melodies floated through her mind when she was talking casually to others. She heard music in the rhythm of the world around her, and sometimes, in silence, she found the most perfect songs. But now, when the energy was so powerful, she saw musical notes dancing in front of her, in colors, like tiny fireflies flashing in the air around her.

One of seven daughters of a seventh daughter and endowed with special gifts which could be both blessing and curse, when she opened her mind, she could feel the hopes and dreams and disappointments in the lives of her audience. She rarely sought out and touched a single mind, rarely invaded privacy. But sometimes she interspersed melodies and slower ballads between the foot stomping, get-up-and-dance rhythms of the rock and roll she was so famous for, in order to bring peace and contentment to any troubled people she sensed in her audience.

'Good choice for a warm-up band,' Brian said. 'They have a way of getting the crowd going.'

'Yeah,' Joley agreed, 'I really like them. And they're not bad to travel with.'

'Chicago is great,' Rick Henderson, the bass guitar player, announced. He came up behind Joley to air hug her.

Although he hadn't even brushed against her, she moved forward, an automatic response from childhood. She rarely touched anyone other than her sisters. It was a good way to ruin friendships. Fortunately her band had been with her a long time and they respected her personal space.

She spun around and smooched the air at Rick. 'Chicago is awesome. I love it here.' To be honest, she was just a little nervous. After the Nikitin party in New York she was somewhat depressed. She had a few enemies and the threatening letters had been more plentiful than usual lately. The Reverend and his followers were protesting her concert and she knew they would be trying to cause a scene here as well.

'Chicago always has a good crowd,' Brian agreed, high-fiving Rick. He flashed another smile at Joley. 'You aren't worried are you, hon? Seriously, we have extra security everywhere.'

'That whack job Reverend RJ is here,' Joley said, and bit down hard on her lower lip, wishing she hadn't mentioned him. She'd done a stupid, stupid thing, challenging the perverted man in front of the television cameras, but worse, she'd used her voice on him. He had enough charisma to gain followers, but Joley's voice could make men obsessive. She'd been careless, and she knew it. What was worse, Ilya had seen the entire thing. That also had made her feel cheap and dirty. She certainly knew how to make a fool out of herself around him.

She didn't want to appear as if anything bothered her. That was her trademark – happy-go-lucky Joley. Laughing at life and moving through the world like quicksilver. She hid scared well – always had. So well that her sisters, able to read others with ease, never guessed that she'd embarked on her world tour with trepidation. The recent attack on Hannah had terrified her. She knew the Drake family had bitter enemies, and the threats on her life had grown numerous.

'The Reverend shows up just to get the press,' Brian said. 'I caught his act the other day for a few minutes, how repentant he is for his lustful thoughts, and how he spent a week on his knees begging the lord's forgiveness for lusting after you. He says he wants to save you as well. He's forgiven you for tempting him, you daughter of the devil, and now he only wants to reach out and pull you from hell's claws. I think he's trying to get the world to believe you're a lesbian or at least bisexual, because then he could really crucify you.'

For a moment Brian sounded bitter, but when she glanced up sharply, he shrugged. 'He's a fucking weirdo, Joley. Don't let him rattle you.'

'Well I wish he'd just disappear.'

'He got a lot of press time for his little act with you,' Rick added, threading his fingers through his long blond hair in typical Rick fashion. He had gorgeous hair and the women went wild for it. Knowing that, he used every opportunity to draw attention to the shimmering golden strands, which made the rest of the band laugh.

'Anyone near you can pretty much stay on the front pages. And now the Rev's hanging with Nikitin,' Brian added, pointing his finger at her. 'I told you it was a mistake to ignore Nikitin. If you were his friend, he'd never let the Reverend come near his parties.'

'You ought to know. You've gone to them even when I asked you not to,' Joley said and glared at Brian.

Brian looked uncomfortable. 'I didn't know about him, Joley.'

Rick shrugged, unrepentant. 'He always has the best booze and women. What can I say? His parties rock.'

She ignored him and turned her attention to the warm-up band as the rest of her band members crowded close. Denny stayed to the back looking sheepish and avoiding her gaze. Leo Meyer, on keyboard, looking good in jeans and an open vest, blew her a kiss, his eyes shining with excitement.

Logan forgot all about her personal space and picked her up, swinging her around. 'I'm a father, Joley, can you believe that? She's the cutest baby I've ever seen.'

Brian nudged him. 'That's not hard, they're all kind of squishy and sort of undercooked.'

Logan set Joley on her feet and hugged her hard. 'Man, she's got the tiniest fingers and she looks at me and I melt.' He glared at Brian, who grinned unrepentantly. 'And she's not undercooked. She's just a little squishy.'

Joley poked both of them. 'She's new, not squishy. Is she still at the hospital?'

'Under guard.' Logan nodded. 'They're letting her go home with me tomorrow. Jerry's trying to find a nanny, but I have to be careful. I don't like the idea of hiring someone we don't know.'

'What about Tish? She's a teacher and so good with kids. Have you considered her?' Joley was careful to extricate herself from Logan. His joy was overwhelming her, along with his fears of fatherhood. She couldn't afford to have those emotions inside her when she went out to perform. Her voice could affect the entire audience.

Logan rubbed at the deliberate five o'clock shadow on his chin and glanced around the tight circle surrounding him. They were all silent, watching him. 'I think I burned that bridge pretty effectively.'

When the band was first starting out, it was Logan's wife, Tish, who'd taken care of them all, sold their CDs at the bars and made their posters and even got them gigs. She was the one who had first connected with Joley, which had eventually brought their band to fame. Tish had come up the ranks with them and they all adored her. They'd known her since high school, and all of them missed her – especially Logan.

'You won't know until you try, bro,' Leo said. 'Tish isn't with anyone else and she never divorced your sorry ass. You told me that yourself the other day.'

Joley's eyebrow shot up. 'Have you been keeping tabs on her?'

Logan looked sheepish. He shrugged. 'Maybe. A little. I ask some of our old friends how she's doing, that's all.'

'Well, ask her then. She can only say no,' Joley said to encourage him. 'She knows the ropes, the way we work together. She's always fit in.'

'You really think she's going to want to take care of someone else's baby?'

'*Your* baby,' Joley pointed out. 'If Tish thinks a baby – and you – need help, she's going to come, even if it means risking her heart.' She pinned him with her dark, straight gaze. 'If she comes, because she's generous like that, see that you don't abuse her trust. I mean it, Logan. Don't ask her, flirt around with her and then throw some groupie in her face.' Her gaze strayed to Denny.

Denny ducked his head, looking miserable. With a small sigh, Joley went to stand in front of him. He offered a hesitant smile. 'I know you're angry with me.'

'Disappointed,' she corrected, 'but it's your life, Denny. You aren't married to Lisa. I just know how upset you get when you break up with someone you profess to love, and you're always the one sabotaging the relationship.'

'I get high and the women are all over me and I can't seem to say no. She was trying to kiss on Nikitin and she looked so hot. He kind of pushed her away and she crawled under the table, right in front of everyone, like she was an animal in heat, couldn't get enough, you know. One minute I was drinking with Nikitin and laughing, the next, I was so burning hot for her I couldn't think straight.' He rubbed his hand over his face as if he could wipe out the incident. 'I wish I could tell you that I'll never forget it and she was awesome, but I can't remember most of it. I threw Lisa away for something I can't even remember.' He shook his head.

He was miserable. Joley could feel desolation rolling off him in waves. His distress was genuine, not feigned to get back in her good graces. Denny had a weakness for women, but he'd made a commitment to Lisa and told the band members that he wanted to be faithful to her, because she mattered to him. Joley had believed him and now, feeling his unhappiness, she still did.

'Denny, had you been doing drugs?'

He shrugged. 'Nothing much. Less than I normally do at a party. I have no idea what happened, but I told her. I called her last night when I got back to the room.' For a moment tears swam in his eyes, and he blinked and looked away from her. 'I wanted her to hear it from me, not read it in

51

the tabloids, and I know they got my picture, the bastards. I spend my life hurting people I care about.'

Joley frowned, not liking Denny's explanation of what happened. He might be a hound dog, but he always took responsibility. If he said he was sick and dizzy and the memory was foggy, she was suspicious that someone had slipped him a drug without his knowledge. But why? 'You might have had a little help this time,' Joley said before she could stop herself. Again she glanced at Brian, whose gaze slid away from hers. Was Nikitin up to something or was she simply overreacting because she didn't trust the man?

'Whatever happened, I think I've lost Lisa, and I can't blame her.' The drummer's eyes swam with tears.

Joley's heart jumped. She'd never seen him cry over a woman. They were about to go out and perform for thousands of people and Denny was falling apart right before her eyes.

'It isn't over until it's over, Denny. You have a chance with Lisa. She's worth fighting for. We'll all help you. Is she here tonight? Did she come?'

Lisa had promised to be in Chicago for their concert, and Denny had been looking forward to seeing her. The band had been in Europe for weeks and Lisa hadn't been able to make New York, so Chicago was to have been their reunion.

'She flew in last night. I called her at the hotel, which only made it worse. I have no idea if she decided to come to the concert. If she did, she didn't pick up her backstage pass and she didn't check in with Jerry. I asked him to watch for her.' Denny sounded more miserable than ever.

'I'll do what I can to help you, Denny,' Joley promised rashly. 'Jerry can find out if she picked up her ticket or not. If she's here, I'll do what I can to persuade her to give you another chance, but if you mean what you say about her, stay away from the parties. Leave when I do. Come back with me and we'll play Scrabble or something, anything at all to keep you out of trouble.'

The other band members nodded. 'We can play that Monopoly game, the one that never ends,' Rick said. 'We'll party with Joley.'

Denny snorted his derision, but he looked much happier.

'Yeah, cuz Joley's such a partier,' Brian said. Onstage the warm-up band broke into their final number. 'That's the windup song, we're on in a few. Come on.'

He put out his arm and they huddled together with Joley in the middle of their circle as they always did before each concert. It had become a tradition and they all were superstitious now. If they didn't come together like now, arms around one another with Joley in the center, Brian giving his standard pep talk, they all knew it was going to be a terrible show, everything that could go wrong would. Joley, like a lot of performers, did one standard sound check when possible, not wanting to chance ruining her voice. They ran through their songs, but tried not to have to repeat too much.

'Let's do it,' Brian yelled and they took off running for the stage.

Joley hung back listening to the screams and booming applause as her boys took the stage. She loved to hear the way the crowd went wild when her band picked up their instruments. They worked hard, contributed so much, each a genius in his own way, and she was proud of their music. The music swelled and she heard her name. *Joley*. Just Joley. And it was enough. She ran out into the glaring lights and it sounded like thunder.

For a moment she stood there, her body absorbing the rhythms and sounds, the currents of energy coming at her. She waved and sent the crowd her famous smile, and they went wild.

Immediately she launched into the first number, her voice low and sultry, slipping in and out of the swelling music as only she could do. The rhythm had the crowd on its feet; it was impossible for them to stay in their seats, clapping, swaying, some jumping up and down, others dancing, while her voice sank into them and turned them inside out with her music.

Ilya Prakenskii looked down at his hand. It was trembling. He had fought for survival since he was a toddler. He could withstand pain and torture. He'd been shot, knifed, hit with bats, and he had remained rock steady. He had sewn his own flesh. He had killed – numerous times. Nothing shook his calm. That place inside him, that cool detachment was what kept him alive.

He could even allow a woman to service his body, as he could hers, and still remain completely detached and in control. But he couldn't stop his hands from shaking or his body from reacting just looking at – or listening to – Joley Drake.

Emotions could get a man like him killed, so he'd been very careful never to feel. It had been so long since anything touched him, he was shaken, realizing that his deep need of that one small woman

54

wasn't going anywhere anytime soon. She took his breath away. She stole all reason. He didn't get involved – *ever* – not emotionally – with anyone. People around him frequently ended up dead. Emotion was a weakness, something that could too easily be used against him. But Joley Drake ...

Ilya hit the back of his head against the wall as if he could jolt her out of his mind. But she was already wrapped inside him and he was never going to be free of her. He knew that now, knew that no matter how disciplined he'd always been, his control went out the window whenever he laid eyes on Joley. And discipline wasn't going to save either of them this time.

He couldn't take his eyes off of her as she moved across the stage. Her voice swelled with power, vibrating through his body until he couldn't think with wanting her. He could have lived with that. The chemistry between them was so damn potent he ached every minute of every day, but there was so much more than sex. He belonged to Joley Drake. Body and soul. Men like him didn't ever belong to anyone – and no one belonged to them. Worse, she was slowly stealing his heart. He could take the craving for her body. He could even live without his soul, but if he allowed her access to his heart, he would be lost.

His eyes narrowed to slits. His gaze shifted to take in the crush of people, noting automatically every small detail and storing it so his mind could process all the information even as his body absorbed Joley – everything about her – the curves of her body, her far too erotic rhythm as she moved with the pounding music. Every step, every sway, every note screamed sin and sex. She couldn't help the way she was put together or the way her voice seduced and the way her body shouted, 'fuck me.' But it still pissed him off – and kept him awake at night.

He wished a good fuck was all he wanted, but that was the least of it. He wanted to make love to her. Hard and fast, slow and easy, memorizing every sweet curve and sinful valley. He wanted to know every intimate detail of her body and mind. He wanted to tie her to him any way he could. And he'd tried. First with his magic. Always with his magic. He used his voice shamelessly as a weapon because he knew that sound was the key to Joley. He understood, in ways she still barely perceived, that they were locked in a battle for life. And he wasn't about to lose.

The roar of the crowd swelled, building until the noise was deafening. Bright lights flashed, and Joley moved across the stage, in and out of the lights, almost as if she were making love to the shadows. Nothing in Ilya's barren existence, all the training given to him, all the hard-won experience – none of it – had prepared him for Joley.

Her voice had seduced him first. That perfect pitch that slid into his body, past every defense, and stroked and caressed until every nerve ending was on fire. Then he'd seen her, all soft inviting curves, full rounded breasts, small tucked-in waist and flared hips built to cradle a man. Her skin was flawless, looking so soft it was an invitation to touch. But her face, those classic lines, large dark eyes and full pouting mouth – he hadn't been able to drag his gaze from her the first time he'd seen her. His breath nearly strangled in his lungs and his body had turned harder than a rock. He'd been that way ever since.

More than all of that, her fierce spirit had drawn him like a moth to flame, all fire and passion, a woman in need of protection who thought she could take care of not only herself, but everyone around her. He saw how vulnerable she was. He saw inside of her, to that place she kept hidden, where she thought no one could love who she really was. If there was such a thing as love, if there was truly that emotion, then he loved her, damn it, with every breath in his body.

He'd never been in a relationship, let alone a family, and the Drake family was as alien to him as trust. Joley came from such a different background – hell, she'd managed to get under his skin, make him forget the discipline that was his life, and worse, she shook his control. He needed to be in control. *Needed* it. She had no idea of what a little stick of dynamite like her could do to a man, especially a man as dangerous and as lethal as he knew himself to be.

Ilya's body tensed as a man suddenly detached himself from the crowd and rushed the stage. Joley didn't miss a beat as security swarmed around the man, stopping him before he could climb up onstage. Ilya had already moved, a big man, fast on his feet, utterly silent, ready to protect her with his life. He took a breath and resumed his place against the wall where he could monitor the rows closest to the stage.

Joley had been raised in a loving environment. She had a large family with a lot of siblings, and parents who adored their children. Ilya had no idea what a family was like. If he had parents, he sure had no memory of them, and he only had vague memories of his older brothers. He was different and he would always be different. His training had shaped him. Trained to be a spy, an assassin, to work in the shadows and endure whatever hardship was needed in order to get the job done, he had been raised in a cruel, violent environment and had no idea how to live any other way. He'd never thought of living any other way, until he'd met Joley Drake.

Ilya spotted a man in the third row who had a look of rapture on his face as he stared up at Joley. Sweat beaded on the man's forehead and he was breathing fast. Ilya shook his head. She had half the men in the audience so tied up in knots it would be a wonder if there wasn't a riot. She was using her voice shamelessly, maybe unintentionally, but it had to stop.

He reached out to her. A slow, deliberate caress that slid like so much velvet down her arm to her palm, to the brand that marked her as his. He felt the first flutter of awareness, her mind touching his. The startled, stunned effect he always seemed to have on her. He loved that – the way she responded to him in spite of herself. She didn't want to open her mind to his, but she never could quite resist his touch.

She had power over him, had turned his life upside down, and he was working his way through his anger at that, but each first time he touched her, he knew he had the same power and control over her.

And what was a relationship after all? Hell if he knew, just that melting inside, the fierce, urgent demands of his body and the terrible need to protect her, to be with her. And with him there was more – the need to dominate, to enforce his will on her, because in the end, he had to take control back.

When you're up on that stage and you're working the audience, all I can think about is slamming you against the wall and burying myself in you over and over, so deep they'll never get us apart. Deliberately he drawled each word, low and sexy, the smoldering heat slipping inside her until he saw the change on her face.

His breath strangled in his lungs as her expression turned even more sultry, the pouring out of her voice passionate, her lips a sinful invitation, her body moving with a natural sexiness that couldn't be hidden, and her eyes, heavy lidded, almost drowsy, bedroom eyes, promising paradise when a man sank his body into the soft silky heat of hers.

Stop it.

She hadn't even missed a beat, gliding across the stage, moving under the lights, which could only mean she wasn't nearly as far gone as he was. Damn her. He was crawling out of his skin. She shook him on such an elemental, *primitive* level that he knew he'd never get over her. There was no walking away. No being sated by her soft, sexy body. He would never be free of her. If any other man approached her with the same possessive obsession, he'd mark him as a stalker and end him as soon as it could be arranged, yet even with knowing that his need of her wasn't normal, he knew he was taking her for himself – because whatever he felt – she was feeling it, too.

He saw her gaze slide through the first few rows as if looking for someone – not him. Never him. Jealously was a black, empty emotion that threatened to choke the sense out of men. Who was she looking for? Her gaze touched on the man in the third row and moved on. Ilya understood she was looking for a specific person. A man?

She'd been angry enough at him last night, but he would have known if she'd turned to another man. He'd left her alone all night because he'd wanted so badly to reach out and touch her mind with his. And he'd be damned if he'd give in to that kind of obsession. He was going to be in control one way or the other. The problem was, he'd lain awake all night, his body so painful, tight and hard he knew he couldn't let things continue this way.

He slid his mind intimately into hers, once more allowing her to feel the depth of his sexual appetite for her. Her gaze jumped to his, her face flushed. He could see the rise and fall of her soft, full breasts beneath the tight shirt she wore.

Up onstage, Joley knew she sounded as desperate as she felt. Her entire body was on fire. She detested letting him know he was getting to her, but if he didn't stop the audience was going to witness spontaneous combustion.

I'm working.

Is that what you call it? Working? You're shaking your sexy little ass in front of that idiot, third seat from the middle, and he's nearly comatose. If you do it again, he'll do something stupid like run up onstage to grab you and then I'll have to kill the poor bastard and you'll be angry with me.

You can't talk to me now. I mean it. If he'd wanted to talk, he should have done it all through the long night when she couldn't sleep, when she'd lain awake on her bed waiting to hear his voice.

Her breasts ached and her nipples were hard pebbles rubbing against the lace of her bra with every movement of her body. She was on fire, throbbing and pulsing with hot desire. *He* did that to her with just his voice. A look from his eyes. A touch. He could reduce to her to pure physical need. If he wasn't all the things whispered, rumored about him, he still was a dangerous man. She could lose herself in him. There was a part of her that craved his arrogance, his domination, his complete confidence and power.

Onstage she owned the world – she had the power, but with his voice in her head, he slowly took it from her.

Stop fighting me.

She closed her eyes, wanting him. Craving him. *I can't let you win. You know I can't, Ilya. You'd take everything from me.* Her pride. Her self-esteem, not that she had much left. Her soul. He'd own her.

I won't lose. You're running, but you're not getting away from me. I'll give you everything and that's what scares you the most. Don't worry, milaya moya, I have never run away from a battle. I won't be going anywhere. The tender note in his voice scared her. Sex she could handle, but not the sheer intimacy when he dropped that caressing note into his voice.

She forced herself to sing to the audience, to sing to Lisa, concentrating, pouring her soul into the song about regrets and mistakes and a true love so deep one needed to give it a second chance. She thought of Tish and Logan, two people who belonged together and were torn apart by stupidity, how she didn't want that for Lisa and Denny.

Without warning, the drums stopped. Just stopped. The band faltered and Joley swung her head around to look at Denny. In trying to block out Ilya, she'd gone way too far, using her voice inadvertently and not sending directly to just Lisa. She sent a look of total desperation to Brian.

The crowd realized immediately that drama was in the works and quieted. Denny moved out around the drums and walked across the stage to take the microphone from Joley's hand.

'Dude, you've got your hands all over my woman

and I'm about to ask security to throw your ass out. I may have screwed up, Lisa, but there's *no one,* no one in this world I love more than you and your son. Marry me. Take me back. Tell me what you want me to do. If you want me to leave the band, I'm gone. Whatever it takes, but give me another chance and I swear you'll never regret it.'

Joley shaded her eyes to study Lisa's face. She was crying. The man with her whispered something to her and moved a little away, making Joley think he was a friend doing her a favor, rather than someone she'd picked up. Lisa looked utterly miserable, her face covered by her hands.

Denny shoved the microphone at Joley, crouched at the edge of the stage in front of her and held out his hand. 'I'll spend my life making it up to you, Lisa.'

Joley moved next to him, placing one hand on the drummer's shoulder for support in the event Lisa rejected him.

Everything inside of Ilya coiled. Joley had just placed herself in a very vulnerable position. Security lined the rope in front of the first row, but they were looking at Denny and Lisa, not at the audience or Joley. He immediately glided into a better position, his gaze taking in the first few rows, but his mind settling on the man in the third row he'd noted earlier.

In a way this was his fault. He had distracted her, knowing she would never let down her audience. Joley had continued to sing under sexual duress and had been unable to control the notes in her voice, soft and sultry and purring like a huntress for a mate. The effect on the men was obvious, in particular on the face of the man in the third row.

Denny suddenly jumped from the stage. Joley gasped and stepped closer to the edge as if to follow him. Lisa stood up. Security rushed to protect Denny. The man Ilya was watching made his move, springing over the seats, nearly kicking a woman in the head as he leapt over her to get to the deserted aisle in front of Joley. Ilya took off running, shoving security out of the way as they surrounded Denny.

He burst out of the crowd just as the man launched himself onstage, reaching for Joley. *Move, damn it.*

In his hand, Joley warned him as she tried to back away.

Ilya caught the man from behind, taking him to the floor, locking his wrist behind him in a hold that threatened to break his arm. 'Don't move,' he hissed.

Joley laughed softly into the microphone. 'He's just enthusiastic, no problem,' she said. 'Lisa, hon, come on up here and put Denny out of his misery so we can get these folks back on their feet.'

The security team already had the man who had rushed the stage surrounded and were hauling him out. The band began to play, and Lisa, somewhat reluctantly, slipped her hand into Denny's and took the stage. Joley noted that she avoided his kiss, letting his lips only skim her cheek to the wild screams of the audience. Denny led Lisa back to the drums and took up his position. Lisa slid backstage, but sat where he could see her.

Joley let her heart regain its normal beat as she swung into a song, all the while looking for Ilya. He had disappeared in that way that he could. She had no idea if the man rushing her had had a weapon and if he'd managed to injure Ilya. Security had responded immediately and Ilya was gone as quickly as he'd arrived.

The rest of the concert went fairly smoothly, with only one equipment malfunction, which no one really seemed to notice. They took the stage twice more to yells, stomping and clapping before they called it quits.

Denny disappeared immediately with Lisa, and Logan hurried to call the hospital to check on his baby, so Joley visited with Brian, Leo and Rick while the crowd thinned. They were pumped up after the performance like always, stumbling over one another to talk. No one noticed that she said very little. She couldn't think of anything but Ilya, but pride wouldn't let her reach out to him. The longer he was silent, the angrier she became at him.

In the darkened van, she sat in the passenger-side front seat and rolled down the window as Steve took her out the back way. Die-hard fans that followed her from concert to concert knew she never traveled in the limousine or the decoy car, but stayed late and came out in the nondescript van. She always signed autographs for the ones who waited so long.

Steve knew the routine and he slowed the van as he turned onto the street. The rest of the band had come outside and stood behind the gates, watching as security milled with the crowd. These fans were polite, not rushing the car, but forming a loose line as they handed over programs and pictures for Joley to sign. She knew quite a few by name and greeted them with smiles, not for a moment letting how tired she was show.

A woman shuffled up to the car and handed her a picture. Joley didn't recognize her, but smiled and said hello. When she glanced down to sign, she saw that it wasn't her picture, but that of a young teenage girl.

'My daughter,' the woman said. 'She's missing.'

Joley looked from the woman's grief-stricken face back to the picture. 'I'm so sorry,' she murmured.

'She was at your concert in New York, and afterward she was invited by your band to go to a party. She left me a message saying she was there and would be home late, but she didn't come home. I was working. I clean office buildings. She knew I wouldn't pick up the message until it was too late to stop her. Please. Have you seen her? She's only thirteen.' Tears swam in the woman's eyes.

Joley took another look at the young girl. *I know that face.* For a moment she could barely breathe. 'Steve? Does she look familiar to you?' She leaned close to him, whispering to keep the woman from hearing her. 'Isn't she the girl who made the cell phone call and seemed to know Dean?'

Steve frowned, shrugged and shook his head, but said nothing.

'Please.' The woman clutched at Joley's arm, digging her fingernails deep.

At once grief and fear overwhelmed Joley. Her stomach lurched.

Jerry St. Ives materialized from the crowd. 'Is something wrong?'

The woman was hysterical now, trying to pull Joley out of the van, clutching her arm with one hand and yanking on the door handle with the other.

'You're bleeding. What did she do to you?' Jerry demanded.

The door began to swing open, and Jerry kicked it shut while calling for backup. Security swarmed around the woman and pulled her back, yelling at

Steve to drive.

'No!' Joley protested, but Steve saw the blood on her arm and stomped on the gas, driving away from the crowd. She looked back and saw the woman struggling with the security detail. 'Stop, Steve. It's not like she was trying to hurt me; don't let them turn her over to the police.'

'Jerry says no, to keep driving. He'll fire me if I don't get you out of here. Your safety has to come first.'

'You work for me.'

'My job is to protect you.'

'From a woman whose daughter is missing?' Joley turned around in her seat. 'Get on the phone and tell Jerry we saw that girl with Dean. What if she's hiding out with him? Traveling with the band from concert to concert? We'd be liable. That should shake him up. She's *thirteen*.'

Steve shot her a quick glance.

'Do it!' Joley stared down at the picture, suddenly afraid. Had anyone in her band issued an invitation to the girl? It would be horrible if she'd run off with a crew member. Or worse, what if something had really happened to the girl? 'And tell him I want him to find that roadie tonight and deal with this. Dean whatever. Brian knows him. I want Jerry to talk to him tonight.'

'Okay, okay,' Steve said soothingly. 'I'll tell Jerry. He'll handle it, that's his job.'

Joley breathed a sigh of relief. Jerry was very good at handling things, that's why he managed the band. She rested her head against the seat and closed her eyes.

Chapter Four

Joley paced back and forth along the narrow aisle in her tour bus. 'They should have Dean here by now, Brian,' she snapped. 'Where is he? It's been two weeks since that girl's been missing, Brian, and no one has talked to him about it. Jerry said he would take care of it and I trusted him to do it. We've had two shows since Chicago when we found out the girl was missing. This should have been done already.'

'We don't even know for certain if it's the same girl, Joley. Steve said he couldn't positively say so, that she looked like maybe, but the girls look so much alike it could be anyone.'

'I said I was positive.'

'Maybe the girl's gone back home by now.'

Joley scowled at him. 'Why do you think I'm upset all over again, Brian? I called the police in New York and she's still missing. Jerry had better take this seriously. I not only want Dean questioned, but everyone else. I had Jerry make copies of the photograph to distribute to the band and crew, and he hasn't even done that yet.'

'It's not like Jerry doesn't have a million things to do, Joley. Be reasonable. The schedule's so tight the buses barely make it from one city to the next in time to set up. The crew breaks down the set and they have to roll. By the time Jerry gets things done, they're already gone.'

'And you don't think a child's life is more important than a concert? What's wrong with you that you don't think we should look into this?'

'That's a job for the police. *If* she was at the same party, big deal, and that's a pretty big if. That doesn't mean we're responsible, Joley. You always take on way too much. She's a kid. She might have run away.' Brian crossed his arms, a stubborn look on his face.

'Maybe, but she might have run away with Dean. And that makes it our problem whether you like it or not, because if a member of our crew touched her, or ran off with her, we're looking at a lawsuit that will never end, not to mention it's *wrong*.'

'Joley, give me a break here. Dean probably saw the kid for a few minutes and forgot all about her. Do you think they remember all these girls they're with? They have sex, they get blow jobs, they do drugs with them. They aren't in love.'

'That just proves my point. We can't waste any more time. I want her picture shown to everyone before they all lose their memories. And stop trying to handle me for Jerry. The coward. He knows I'm upset and he's hiding. If he doesn't get this done, he's gone right along with Dean. I mean it, Brian. I'm at the end with all of them.'

Brian held up his hand to stop her rant. 'Listen to yourself, Joley. When was the last time you slept? Or ate, for that matter? You're not taking care of yourself. And Jerry told you we should skip Red Rocks this year, it's too small, but you insisted and we have to drive all night now and set up for a back-to-back concert. Everyone's exhausted, you included. You're acting like no one but you cares about anything.'

'Well Jerry and I just don't see eye to eye anymore about much of anything, do we?' Joley dropped into a chair and covered her face with her hands. Maybe she was acting like a diva. She couldn't tell anymore. And Brian was right, she was exhausted.

'Jerry wants whatever you want. He scheduled the stop in Red Rocks because you asked him to do it.'

'Red Rocks is magical. When the sun is setting and the energy is right . . .' She trailed off. She couldn't explain it to Brian. You either felt it or you didn't. She was so tired she could barely think, but Red Rocks would recharge her, it always did, even when they had to do one concert right after the other to fit it in the schedule.

'We're going to have to get going in order to make the schedule, Joley. Try to get some sleep.'

'Is Jerry checking on this girl right now?'

Brian shoved both hands through his hair in agitation. 'You're like a bear with a sore tooth. We don't even know if it's the same girl, Joley. Calm down and think about this logically. She could have drank too much and gone to a girlfriend's house and is afraid to go home.'

'And she's still not home after a week?'

'Okay, maybe she did shack up with Dean and they think they're in love,' Brian said, exasperated. 'Although I don't think the entire crew would be protecting him.'

'But you're certain he worked the last two concerts?'

'He was there. Everyone saw him. According to a couple of his friends, he didn't realize any of the girls were underage until you yelled and they started giggling. He was stupid and ran, but he made them leave. He doesn't want to lose his job. The others said he went back to the hotel that night to catch a shower before leaving the city with the bus and he's been working hard ever since. That's as much as I know. And they certainly haven't seen the girl with him.'

'Could she have stowed away in the bus? Did anyone check their bus?'

'They're checking it now. They were already on the road, but Jerry had the driver pull over and they're searching it before continuing. He'll call if they find her. And if we don't get moving, Joley, we're not going to make it in time for our next concert. Jerry's doing everything he can to find this girl, but we've got to get out of here now. There's nothing more we can do. She'll be found.'

Joley pressed her fingertips to her eyes. The girl wasn't going to be found, not if that terrible feeling in the pit of her stomach was right – and it usually was. She couldn't exactly explain that feeling to Brian. 'Fine. I'm sorry. I know I'm getting crazy here, but the mother said someone in our band invited this girl – this thirteen-year-old child – to an after hours party. Who would do that?'

'Anyone could have issued the invitation, not necessarily a band member or one of our people. Come on, you know that. Nikitin or any of his crew could have or someone else coming to the party. We'll show the picture to everyone tomorrow, and if we're lucky, the police will tell us she turned up and is now home safe. I promise, tomorrow morning, as soon as we hit Red Rocks, I'll talk to Dean personally and so will Jerry. I'll make certain of it. In the meantime, try to get some sleep. I know you didn't get any last night.' He leaned closer to her. 'I mean it, Joley. We don't want to have to cancel due to your exhaustion, and it could happen. Go to sleep.'

'You've all been talking again.' She knew that when the band was worried, they appointed Brian to be the spokesman. 'I'll go to bed.' She would, but there would be no sleeping. 'Logan and the baby?'

'He's going to meet us in Red Rocks early in the morning. He said he'll call Tish and see if she'll take the nanny job. I think after your song, all of us believe in second chances.' Brian's gaze was steady. Maybe even a little accusing.

Joley felt the color rising in her cheeks. 'Okay, I poured a little too much into that song. It was for Lisa, but I was a little distracted. I thought Denny was going to personally kick that man with Lisa. I've never seen him like that, have you?' Brian had known Denny since they were in kindergarten.

Brian grinned. 'Denny's got it in him when you get him riled, but no, never over a woman. I think Lisa's the real thing. She slapped him though, right across the face, very hard. And she was crying. I saw him go over to her after the performance, and she just hauled off and let him have it.'

'Good for her. Then what did she do?'

'She was crying and he kept trying to put his arms around her. She didn't run away, but she belted him a couple of more times in the chest. Girlie punches though.'

'So is he on the bus?' She didn't want to lose her drummer.

'He's driving with Lisa so they can talk. I think they rented a car. He'll follow the bus.'

71

'Joley! Brian!' Steve called out from the driver's seat. 'We've got to go now. Brian, if you're riding with us, I'm taking off.'

Brian's eyebrow went up. 'I'll stay if you want me to. We can talk things out if you like, because, seriously, Joley, you've got to lay it down.'

Joley shook her head, suddenly weary. 'I'll try to sleep.' She placed the picture of the missing girl on the small built-in stand beside the couch. 'I'll see you in Red Rocks.'

Brian nodded and waved at Steve, before shutting the door between the driver and the rest of the bus, which was Joley's home on the road. At once, the vehicle rumbled to life, and Steve pulled out of the parking lot onto the road.

Joley waved to Brian and watched him sprint for the second bus before she slid the privacy screen in place and heaved a sigh. It was going to be another long night. Was she really being ridiculous over the missing girl? It was entirely possible her band and crew had nothing at all to do with the underage teens being at the party. And Brian was right, she was exhausted and fixating on the missing girl.

Maybe she was crazy and it really wasn't the same girl – Steve didn't think so, but every time she looked at the photograph, she was more convinced than ever. She was angry with Jerry and Brian because six days had gone by and Dean hadn't been questioned – but truthfully, she was angry with herself. The Columbus concert, she'd flown in, done the sound check, and the roadies had broken everything down and were on the move before she remembered. She'd been upset because Ilya hadn't been there and he hadn't talked to her since the night in New York. She'd been thinking about him instead of the girl. She was used to handing everything over to Jerry to handle and she just let herself forget.

The Auburn Hills concert she'd remembered just before going onstage, but afterward, she didn't remember again until she was about to leave, so she hadn't asked Jerry if he'd spoken with Dean. The road crew was already gone. It was easier to blame Jerry and Brian, but ultimately, it was her responsibility to make the inquiry if she wanted it done, because she was really the only person who believed it was the same girl. She was so used to everyone doing things for her, and what did that make her after all? A diva. She really was messed up, mostly because she desperately needed to hear Ilya's voice again.

She considered calling one of her sisters, but they'd compare notes with Hannah, and one – or all – would come running. She didn't want to disrupt their lives, especially when they would see her glaring character flaws. It was fine to turn it all into a family joke – 'Loser Apply Here' stamped to Joley's forehead – but it was altogether different for her sisters to witness it. And yet laughing with them, she could pretend it wasn't that bad, but when she was out on her own, alone in the bus, with no one to share either problems or laughter, she knew she could easily get into trouble.

Joley made her way to the back of the bus. Maybe if she rested, she'd manage to pull herself together. As she passed the small closet, a large hand snaked across her mouth and an arm slid like an iron bar around her waist. She was jerked back against a hard male body. Warm breath fanned her neck.

'Don't scream.'

She knew who it was instantly. His scent. His

aura of danger. His hard, masculine body, far stronger than he looked. She drew in a breath, struggled and tried to sink her teeth into his palm. He let her. She knew he let her bite him. He didn't utter a sound, or flinch, but his body crowded closer to hers, and she felt the press of his arousal, strong and full and unapologetic. She went still and waited for him to release her.

Instead Ilya Prakenskii trapped her between him and the closet door, his body pressed tight against hers. He rubbed his palm over her full lips, as if he expected her to kiss the bite better. And she was tempted. As it was, she couldn't keep her tongue from touching the small wound. He tasted masculine and sexy. The heat of his body crept into hers, a slow assault on her senses. She could feel the band of his arm sweeping up her rib cage to halt beneath her breasts. At once her skin felt too tight, her nipples hard and aching, and between her legs, already, the first flush of dampness signaled her response to him. It didn't help that the bus swayed as it rolled over the asphalt and his body brushed against hers intimately with every movement.

'How did you get on the bus?' Her voice sounded breathy. Her heart hammered and her stomach did a slow somersault. 'How did I not see you?'

He bent to her neck, his teeth scraping over her skin, tugging at her earlobe before his mouth settled leisurely on the side of her neck. She closed her eyes, leaning into the heat of his body, feeling his thick shaft nestled tight against her. 'That's what I do,' he replied, in between bites along her neck. 'It's my job not to be seen. Bodyguards are supposed to fade into the background.'

'Really?' Self-preservation demanded she move.

Self-respect demanded she feign shock. She did neither. His arms made her feel safe when she should have felt threatened. His mouth on her skin sent little flames darting through her bloodstream. Her brain said to move, but her body refused to acknowledge the command. 'I think you're too much of a presence to fade into the background.'

'You never notice I'm around unless I want you to notice,' he pointed out. He turned her into his arms so that she was crushed against the broad expanse of his chest. 'Look at me.'

'If I do, you'll kiss me,' she said, her voice muffled by his shirt.

He laughed softly, and she was instantly aware it was something he did rarely. 'I've been craving the taste of you ever since I kissed you in New York. A week is a long time, and I don't think I can wait any longer.'

She inserted a hand between them in an effort to get space, but his body was immovable and his arms had locked her tight against him. She lifted her face, and his lips were inches – *inches* – from hers. His breath was warm with the promise of temptation and sin. She wanted both.

His mouth settled on hers, teeth tugging at her lower lip insistently, until, without much resistance, she opened for him. Lost in his intoxicating, sensual taste, all male and sex and urgent demand, Joley went pliant, melting against him, hands sliding around his neck to press even closer.

His mouth didn't just promise sex and sin – it tasted of it, delivered it, sent fire streaking through her body like lightning, and somewhere music played, vibrating through her entire body, singing in her veins. She melted into him, skin to skin, sharing breath until her toes curled. She gripped the front of his shirt for support as her knees turned to rubber and every nerve ending in her body caught fire.

Ilya didn't give her time to think or breathe. He simply took her body over, stealing her soul with scorching kisses, his hand sliding up to cover hers, to pry her fingers from his shirt, his thumb sliding in a caress over her palm.

Her entire body clenched in need. Her womb pulsed and throbbed. Joley gasped and tore herself out of his arms. How could he do that? One touch of the pad of his thumb across her palm and her body was scorched and trembling, so in need she could barely think.

Joley blinked back the tears glittering in her eyes. 'You have to go, Ilya. I'm going to call Steve and tell him to let you off someplace you can call for a car.' Even her voice trembled.

He shook his head and caught her chin, tilting her face up so she was forced to look at him. His hands were incredibly gentle, but his fingers were firm, keeping her from pulling away. 'Not tonight. I'm staying with you. Just relax, *lyubimaya moya*, I'm not going to hurt you.'

She took a breath and laid her palm against his chest, over his heart. 'Yes, you will, Ilya, and I don't think I'll recover. So, no, you can't stay with me tonight or any other night.'

'Why would you think I would hurt you?'

She blinked up at him – seeing him – seeing his aura – seeing inside of him. Each person, through individual experiences, created his or her own symphony, and she 'saw' it when she looked at them. It was the reason she could pour compulsion toward a specific person into her song. She could pull out a

short thread of his melody and match the exact pulsa-
tions. She could 'feel' the vibrations of each musical
note running in his brain, registering as various
instruments and creating pieces both complex and
simple, pieces filled with joy or sorrow, compassion
or driving ambition – everything passionate, and
especially the passions of good or evil.

She didn't see Ilya as evil – he didn't have that
sick taint to his color – but neither was there light.
There was power, far too much of it. Power
corrupted, and he overflowed with control and
authority. Strength and violence swirled around him,
almost interchangeably. Where most people were a
blend of light and dark and shades of all colors, Ilya
was all shadow, and most of that was impenetrable
and murky, so dark she couldn't see through the
unrelenting blackness.

'Joley, answer me. Why would you think I would
hurt you?'

His melody was wild and turbulent with the guitar
riffs, fiery and passionate with the keyboard, so
controlled with the percussion instruments, yet
splashed with the violence of cymbals. There was
smooth harmony accompanied by blasts of wind,
streaks of lightning as guitars warred, and interludes
of the tripping notes of a saxophone. He was fierce
and controlled, dominant and mysterious, even in his
music, the very essence of his being. She couldn't
hope to understand his melody without examining
each note, and she didn't dare get that close, not
when her heart – her very soul – was at risk.

Joley let her breath out. 'You know why. You have
gifts.'

'It's because of those gifts that I know we belong
together.'

She pulled away from him, not wanting him touching her. She couldn't read him, but it was possible he was reading her, and that wasn't safe. She was too mixed up in her feelings for him.

'Kiss me again. We don't do so well when we talk, but when we kiss, we're a perfect match.'

She wasn't so certain of that. She'd like to think she matched him, but it was more like he took her over and she just melted into him until they shared the same skin. She shook her head. 'I think it's pretty clear that you can never be in the same room alone with me. You can't ride all the way to Red Rocks with me.' Joley wanted to weep with frustration. All she could think about was stripping and relieving the terrible ache, the emptiness that never went away, but she didn't dare take the chance, not after that kiss. She was too far gone when it came to Ilya.

He studied her for a moment then settled into the chair opposite her, more than satisfied with the flush on her face, her swollen, very kissed mouth, the rise and fall of her breasts. He'd gotten to her. And he'd marked her neck, putting another brand on her. 'You're safe enough – for a while. Sit down, Joley, before you fall down.'

'Why is it that everything you say sounds like an order? I was going to sit down . . .' Basically, she had to before her legs gave out. Just looking at Ilya made her weak, and kissing him was lethal. 'But now, because you gave a royal command, I feel like I have to defy you just to keep myself.'

'Well you don't.'

She had no idea she was within his range, but sprawled out lazily, with his legs outstretched, he simply hooked her ankle and spilled her backward into the chair. 'There. Decision made. No problem.'

She threw a pillow at him, detesting his control when her heart was still racing and her body was on fire. Mostly she was upset with herself for not being able to handle him the way she handled everyone else. He was the only man who could shake her, and she didn't like feeling so exposed and vulnerable.

He snagged the pillow out of the air and placed it behind his head. 'Thanks.' He watched her with cool blue eyes. 'Have you always had problems with authority figures?'

Joley regarded him with a kind of fury sweeping through her that gave way to sudden laughter. 'You're impossible.' How many times had she heard her father tell her she *obviously* had trouble with authority figures? She eyed him with suspicion. 'You haven't been talking to my dad, have you?'

'I don't need to talk with your father to know this about you, Joley.'

She shook her head. 'You're not an authority figure, at least not to me.'

'I don't believe you. Why do you think you fight me all the time?'

'Because you're reputed to be a hit man. I don't date men who kill for money.'

'I'm a bodyguard.'

'You're denying the rumors?'

He sighed. 'Joley, you practically live in the tabloids. Is any of what they say true? Ever? Even with photographs as evidence, it seems they make things up about you. Why would you assume what you hear about me is the truth?'

He had a point, and she was a little ashamed that she believed *everything* she heard about him. He was so dangerous looking. He carried death in his eyes.

And when she touched his mind, he *felt* deadly. He looked it, sounded it, and even inside, where she could see, darkness swirled, but ... He was right; she was guilty of believing things about him without having facts to back up the rumors.

'I don't know. You're right. So I'm asking you, are you a hit man? Do you kill people for money?'

'Do you think a sniper is a hit man?'

She frowned at him. 'It's a simple enough question, Ilya.'

'Not really. It's a complex question. But you're smart. You'll figure it out. Why haven't you been sleeping?'

If she'd had another pillow handy, she would have thrown it at him. Ilya frustrated her no end. He never seemed to answer a direct question that mattered to her. She considered denying the truth, but what would be the point? 'I don't sleep. I'm an insomniac. I have been since I was a kid.'

'So have I. You had a good childhood, Joley.'

She heard the question, or maybe he was touching her mind and she felt his sudden stirring, as if something wasn't quite as right as it should have been, as if she'd better have had a good childhood or he would take it in his hands to do something about it. His expression hadn't changed, but something dark and disturbing moved in him and frightened her. 'I did. My parents were very loving. I had my sisters and Jonas and life was great, one adventure after another. I was always in trouble.'

'I can imagine.'

But he liked the idea of her as a child doing naughty, defiant things and having loving parents who shook their heads and loved her all the more for it. She pulled that thought right out of his head and it made her feel warm inside. Even intimate. As if they already had a close, very personal relationship and he loved her childhood stories. The uneasiness inside her lessened.

She smiled at him. 'My mother had all the psychic gifts so she thought she could keep up with me, you know, always know what I was going to do before I did it. By the time I was three, I was very aware she was watching me, so I set out to prove I could get away with things. I was the child always climbing on the roof and trying to fly, or walking by myself to the store because they said no, they couldn't take me. And homework was for everyone else. I've played the drums since I was four and never went anywhere without my sticks.' She pointed to the drumsticks just inches from her hand. She'd removed them from her back pocket and tossed them on the chair when Brian came onto the bus. 'If it made noise or music, I had to have it. My dad nailed my window closed because I kept escaping.'

His eyes lit up, but he didn't smile. 'I'll bet you were a hellion growing up. I've considered tying you to a bedpost upon occasion, and more than once I've wanted to turn you over my knee.'

'I might have liked it,' she said with a saucy grin. 'But I'm so glad you restrained yourself just in case.'

His eyebrow shot up. 'In case you liked it? Knowing you, you probably would have. My punishment would have turned into a reward and then where would I be?' He reached out and snagged her hand, holding it up in the air between them. 'Wrapped around your little finger like everyone else.'

He let her go, slowly, reluctantly, the pads of his fingers stroking down her bare palm, where he had marked her before his hand dropped away. His touch was electric. She felt that caress not only over her palm, but deep inside, between her legs, so that her womb clenched and liquid fire throbbed and burned.

Joley stared at him, horrified that he could touch her *inside*, that his mark was not just a brand, but a sexual stimulant, so strong even her nipples had peaked and her breasts felt heavy and swollen. Her entire body ached for his. Her tongue touched suddenly dry lips. Did he know what he was doing? She was in way more trouble even than she'd first thought.

'You're lethal. I don't think we can stay alone in this bus together. It isn't safe for you.' But she didn't want him to leave. Just looking at him did something strange to her, filled her with a mixture of excitement and anticipation, but also peace, safety, as if she could lay everything down for a while and just let him take care of it.

This time he did smile. Her heart nearly stopped. There was a heady exhilaration in knowing he rarely smiled and she'd managed to get the genuine article.

Ilya pressed his palm over his heart. 'You amaze me, Joley, all the time. One moment you lie your sexy little butt off, and the next, you're so honest you break my heart. I am sorry, you know. You took what happened last week entirely wrong.'

Joley stiffened. 'I don't know what you're talking about.'

The smile lit his eyes – changed his entire face. He looked younger, more relaxed, still as tough as ever, but less intimidating. 'There you go lying again. I did hurt you. I thought I might have, but I've never actually been in a relationship so I have no idea how to handle certain things. It would be best if you just told me the truth and made it easier for me. When we have children, we're going to be in trouble, you know that, don't you?'

Her breath stilled in her lungs. He had never had a relationship? *Ever*? The idea was both fascinating and terrifying. 'I'm not having children. Whatever put that idea in your head? I'm not ever getting married. I'm going to be the favorite aunt and make all my sisters crazy by letting my nieces and nephews do whatever they want.'

Did she sound as scared as felt? The idea that Ilya might want more than a quick, frantic session in bed scared her to death. He was the kind of man who controlled all things in a relationship, and Joley needed freedom like she needed air to breathe. And yet, like the proverbial moth, she raced to the flame.

'I really hate ruining your plans, but your idea of your future doesn't match what I have in mind for you.'

'And that matters?'

He nodded. 'Definitely.' He not only looked completely confident and complacent, he sounded it as well.

She wasn't touching that one. Call her cowardly or smart, it didn't matter, whatever Ilya said, they were alone and she didn't trust herself with him if he started talking long-term. Men like Ilya didn't do long-term. They were one-nighters and they were gone. No commitment. No strings. He'd just admitted it. She took refuge in attack.

'How long was your longest relationship?'

His blue gaze held hers. 'I just told you, I've never had a relationship.'

'*Exactly*. Because you don't have relationships, Ilya, you have one-night stands. You have sex and you leave. Fast. You probably don't remember her

83

name or face afterward.'

'Like you planned to do last week?'

She had the grace to blush. 'I'll admit it. I thought if we had sex, it would get you out of my system and I wouldn't have to lie awake thinking about you anymore, but you said no, and I'm good with that.'

'Are you?'

His foot touched hers, the gentlest of taps, but her heart jumped in response.

'I don't think you're telling me the truth again. Are you afraid I'll forget you, Joley? Because frankly, *lyubimaya moya*, I don't think that's possible.'

'Whatever.' She bit her lip, not believing she'd said that. She'd just lost every bit of respect for her own ability to argue her way out of anything. It was just the way his voice turned husky and intimate when he spoke Russian. *Lyubimaya moya*. She translated it as 'my sweetheart.' The phrase was far more romantic in his language.

For a moment there was silence between them, filled only by the sound of traffic flowing around the bus. Ilya touched her shoe again with his. 'I want you more than I've ever wanted anything in my life, but you were hoping to have sex and walk away without ever looking back. That's not what's between us. That's how you're looking at me – at us – and I'm not willing for that to be all there is.'

He was throwing down the gauntlet with a vengeance. She looked around her bus, her home away from Sea Haven, and desperately wished herself safe within the protection of her sisters. The simple act of inhaling took him into her lungs. He seemed to dwarf everything in the bus, including her. And the last thing she wanted to talk about was how she had humiliated herself by going to a party she clearly didn't want to go to in order to throw herself at him only to be rejected. Not when he was so ready to cooperate with her now.

Abruptly she got up and yanked open the fridge, peering inside blindly. 'You want anything?'

'I don't drink alcohol.'

She turned back toward him, her eyebrow raised. 'Why not?' Was she finally finding a chink in his armor? A weakness?

He shrugged. 'In my line of business alcohol can get a man killed – and it doesn't really affect me the way it does others. As with you, I imagine, any type of drug or drink poisons my body and is rejected.'

She knew the truth when she heard it. She didn't drink either, because being a Drake made it nearly impossible to be anything but violently ill if she indulged. 'Bottled water or juice?'

'Orange juice then.'

She took a deep, calming breath. She could do this. She could handle Ilya Prakenskii. She forced a smile as she handed him the bottle of orange juice. 'Ice cold. Should be good.'

She tried not to watch him drink, not to watch his throat as he swallowed. How in the world she found it sexy, she didn't know, but even the way he held the juice bottle by the neck, his eyes on her while he drank, made her womb clench. She sank back into the chair opposite him and touched her tongue to her lips. 'What were you like as a child?'

Ilya's breath caught in his lungs, the question bringing up a time he kept hidden and refused to examine too often. *Afraid and hungry*.

His first thought was so strong he wasn't certain

he had repressed it in time to hide it from her. Ilya searched his memories to give her a piece of himself that wasn't too bad. He didn't want pity. His life had been shaped by his childhood, and if he had to give up something to her, he wanted it to be something she might be able to relate to.

'I craved knowledge of every kind. Every book I could read on any subject. Every physical ability and way of fighting, and of course the use of psychic gifts – anything and everything, I soaked up like a sponge. I needed to learn all the time.'

Because knowledge was power and it meant he would survive. It meant he would grow strong and invincible, that he could use his body as a weapon. That he could use his knives, guns, thin wire and anything else. That he could use his brain to stay alive. He needed to be stronger and faster and smarter than his enemies, and in the end he would see fear in their eyes instead of that little boy shivering in a corner, trying to make himself small so no one would notice him.

She caught glimpses of a small boy with dark curls huddled beneath a table. Terror consumed him, spread through her and left her close to tears. The memory was gone almost immediately.

To cover her reaction, Joley took a long drink of water, keeping her gaze above his head. What did she really know about him? Absolutely nothing. She had judged him mainly on rumors and his looks. She stole a quick glance.

His shoulders were wide, his chest thick and muscular. Dark hair made his blue eyes all the more startling. There was an innate toughness about him, and etched into his face were lines of hard experience. More than all that, danger clung to his aura, a dark, moody color and scent that felt violent and frightening, and where she might be able to ignore everything else, she couldn't ignore what her senses told her. He might be a bodyguard, but he was much, much more. That danger drew her like a magnet and yet repelled her at the same time.

'Do you have siblings?'

He shrugged his broad shoulders, a mere ripple of muscle, the movement casual, his gaze hot. 'I have six brothers, but I didn't grow up with them. I've never been able to find them.' And he had abundant resources all over the world – which meant they were dead – or they didn't want to be found.

'How sad for you – and for them. My family is everything to me. I can't imagine what it must be like to know you have someone but not be able to be with them.'

'As I don't know them, it doesn't much matter.'

She blinked. It made sense, but he wasn't telling the entire truth. He stayed close to her mind, sliding in and out at will and leaving behind impressions. He had wanted a family, and her family made the yearning all the more sharp. She didn't want to feel sympathy for him, or to picture him as a little boy with a mop of curls, scared and hungry. It made her all the more vulnerable to him.

'Why did you come here tonight?'

'You haven't been sleeping.' He kept his gaze fixed on her.

She had thought his gaze cold, but the piercing blue had turned into something altogether different – glittering, hungry, almost like a very cunning animal waiting to leap and devour prey. She shivered and willed her blood not to surge so hotly in her veins. 'You stopped talking to me.'

87

'Is that why you can't sleep?'

'I wasn't sleeping when you were talking to me,' she pointed out. 'And I'm too exhausted to have a battle of wits with you. What do you want?'

'I'm going to lie down with you and get you to sleep.'

She nearly snorted water out her nose. 'Are you crazy? I'm not getting in a bed with you. We wouldn't be sleeping.'

'One of us has discipline.'

'Really?' Her eyebrow shot up, and deliberately she slid her gaze over his body in a long, slow perusal. Her tongue touched her bottom lip while her fingers instinctively stroked the mark – his mark – on her hand.

He moved. It was a subtle shift, but there was no doubt in her mind he was easing the sudden tightness of his jeans. She could see the thick evidence in the front of his lap that the stroke over the mark affected more than just her. Dark lust glittered in his eyes, and the hunger grew ravenous.

'You're playing with fire,' he said softly. 'I came here to help you sleep, not for anything else. Don't force the issue before you're ready.'

She had learned a few things about Ilya from their brief encounters, and he rarely wasted words. He wouldn't warn her again. The perverse part of her wanted to see him out of control and reap the benefits of it, but the intelligent think-of-the-consequences part of her held her in check. She dropped her hand and rubbed her palm on her thigh in a reflex action, hoping to soothe the burning.

'I'm not ready,' she admitted. 'You scare me.'

'I'm always going to scare you. That isn't the issue.'

She shook her head. 'I have more than one.'

'I know. It won't be so bad, belonging to me. You'll always be safe.'

'Will I?' She doubted it. 'It's been my experience that extreme macho men are usually jealous, possessive, tend to hit women and cheat on them.'

'I've discovered I can be jealous, and there's no doubt that what belongs to me stays with me, but men who hit women and cheat have no honor, no code. They aren't men, and you should know the difference.'

The low, caressing note in his voice wrapped around her like a velvet blanket. He would take her apart, and when he put her back together, the most important pieces of who she was wouldn't be hers anymore. Ilya would own her.

'What about bossy?' He would rule her life. He was dominating, and there would be no denying that; she'd touched his mind. He would want to rule every aspect of her life, and Joley guarded her independence fiercely.

'You have to trust me with you, Joley. You don't trust anyone, you never have.'

'That's not true. I trust my family.'

He shook his head. 'You don't trust them to see inside you and love you anyway. You guard yourself from them because you don't think they would understand your needs or what drives you.'

Horror blossomed, and she pressed her hand to her suddenly churning stomach. He had been in her mind. She hadn't kept him out the way she thought she had, and Ilya was a ruthless man. He would be relentless in his pursuit of her, and now, having been in her mind, discovering her darkest secrets, he would use them against her. He had psychic gifts, and she could never forget, not for one moment, that he could use them against her.

She nearly groaned aloud. She could see his melody. She could see his aura. Could he see hers? The darkness in her? Not just shadows, but actual darkness?

'Joley.' He said her name in a low caress. 'There's no reason to be so afraid of me. I really did come here to help you get some sleep.'

'How?' Because she couldn't imagine closing her eyes when he was in her bus. It was intimate – and it would make her far too vulnerable.

'There's always hypnotism.'

She knew that utter distaste showed on her face. He laughed, and immediately her complete attention was riveted on him. The sound was husky, sexy, so low and brief it was more of an impression than reality, but all the more captivating because of that. He turned her inside out, and if he kept it up, she would melt into a puddle at his feet.

'Somehow I was fairly certain you wouldn't like that idea. We'll go back to the very simple way. You're going to lie down and close your eyes and I'm going to guard you, watch over you so you can rest.'

'I'm afraid of you. And I don't trust anyone enough to sleep in front of them.'

'I'm giving you my word nothing will happen, and my word is gold all over the world.'

Joley took a breath. She was tired, but she couldn't imagine really falling asleep with Ilya in the close confines of her bus. 'I don't know . . .'

He tapped the table beside him. 'Just try for me, Joley. I'm not asking you to give yourself to me.'

'In a way you are. You're asking me to trust you.'

'Just to keep you safe. It is my job after all.'

Chapter Five

Ilya stood up, his gaze dropping to the small end table as he pushed himself up. He picked up the photograph. 'Who is this?'

Joley braced herself against the sway of the bus as she stood up to view the photograph. Lights from oncoming cars flashed through the interior and illuminated Ilya's profile. His face could have been carved in stone. She tried not to fixate on his all too mesmerizing mouth by examining his eyes. He had long lashes. She'd never noticed that before, when she thought she'd noticed everything about him. She took the photo from his hand and studied the young face as if that could give her a clue to the girl's whereabouts.

'She's missing. She went missing at the New York concert. Not the concert, but the party – Nikitin's party. I saw her there.'

Ilya shifted, drawing her immediate attention. It wasn't a movement so much as the rippling of his muscles, the sudden focus of a predatory animal watching her with cunning intelligence. His expression didn't change, he looked exactly the same, but he was entirely different. Joley had wanted color in his aura, but not like this. Never like this. Blood-red poured into the edges of the black, mixed and swirled, darkening the shadows and turning the color to violent death.

The musical notes representing him clashed and burned with passion and darkness, feeding on violence and swirling with the need to destroy. She wanted to press her fingertips to her eyes, to keep the images from her mind, but there was no escaping the sound and sight.

Breath strangled in her throat, and her heart slammed hard in her chest. Knots formed in her churning stomach. She was looking at the grim reaper. She'd had a brush or two with the death collector, but at that moment, watching the way the colors around him changed, she recognized with a sinking heart what she was seeing.

Ilya could smell her fear. Hell, he could see it on her face. She took two steps away from him, never taking her eyes off of him. Foolish Joley, thinking those meager steps would make her safe. She turned to run toward the front of the bus and what she clearly thought was the safe harbor of her driver's presence. Ilya caught her when the bus lurched, and she almost went down. Drawing her against him, he caged her between his much larger frame and the door of the closet. He could feel tremors running through her body.

He stood for a moment in silence, absorbing the satin heat of her skin, the silk of her hair and the soft feminine curves molded against him. He inhaled her, the scent feminine and clean, yet holding a hint of spice and more than enough sultriness for ten women. She kept her head down, holding herself still, like a cornered mouse, though he knew she was a tigress when riled.

'Why are you suddenly so afraid of me, Joley?' His hand cupped the nape of her neck, his fingers sliding in the thick wealth of her hair. 'What do you see in me that frightens you?' His other hand held her wrist loosely, keeping the palm of her left hand – the one he had marked – pressed against his hip.

For a moment he thought she wouldn't answer, but Joley wasn't timid. Even afraid, she would face him. He felt her steel herself, that tremor that ran through her body, and she straightened, her back stiff, shoulders rigid. Respect and admiration rose in him. He tightened his fingers around her wrist and pressed her palm hard against his thigh. He felt his mark on her like a burning brand, right through the denim of his jeans.

'Your aura.' Joley choked getting the words out. 'Your face gives nothing away, but I see what's inside of you.' A volcano, on the verge of erupting into a violent maelstrom that would blast anything and everyone out of his path. He would mow them down as if they were straw in the wind. The truth of what and who he was terrified her, because if there was one man totally capable of death and destruction, she was standing in front of him, with his mark on her – all over her.

'She's a child. What? Thirteen? Fourteen? Do you think I shouldn't be affected by her disappearance simply because she's a stranger?' His voice was gentle, low and caressing, reassuring. 'She's a teenager at most, and she was in a place she shouldn't have been. I was there to keep an eye on things, to prevent anything like this from happening. Instead, my eyes – and my attention – were on you, and this child slipped past me.'

It was the melody in him that soothed her now. Once again his song had changed, and the notes were comforting and calm, as if that violent rendition had never been. The steady beat of his heart was strong and precise, the beat that set the rhythm for his life. Calm. Exact. Absolute. The symphony rising around him sang to her, touched her where words might not have gotten through.

'That wasn't concern I saw in you just then.' Her mouth was still dry, although her heart had calmed and the adrenaline rush was fading.

'You grew up very differently from me, Joley. In the world where I live, when young girls disappear, very unpleasant things happen to them.'

Joley let her breath out and nodded. 'Unfortunately, this time I have to agree with you. I'm afraid for her, Ilya. I have a bad feeling about this. She called her mother to tell her where she was even when she wasn't supposed to, and that speaks of someone who wasn't running away from home.'

'I'll find her.' Ilya spoke with that same absolute confidence his heart beat with. Rock-steady and deliberate.

She stared up at his face, mesmerized by the determination there. His expression was one of the same utter calm, but his eyes glowed like a fierce warrior of old. Whatever Ilya was or was not – he cared about that young missing girl. Joley didn't doubt for a moment that he was going to find her one way or another. He would never stop, never give up, until he had knowledge of what had happened to that child. He hadn't given up on Hannah when the odds of saving her had been impossible, and he wouldn't give up on the missing girl.

Joley yawned and hastily tried to cover it. She took

94

a step toward a chair as exhaustion settled back into her body. She stumbled and Ilya caught her waist.

'You're so tired you don't even know what you're doing.' He tugged on her wrist and walked her to the back of the bus, where her bed was. 'Lie down while we talk so I know you're at least resting.'

'I've never done this.' The confession felt silly. She had never closed her eyes with a man in her room. She didn't have that kind of trust. The simple act of lying on the bed made her feel vulnerable. 'I don't sleep with others in the room.'

'It's not going to hurt.'

Joley sighed and complied, crawling to the far side of the bed and lying down, feeling small and vulnerable. She was too tired to argue, and it wouldn't take all that long for him to realize she really couldn't sleep.

Ilya bent down to remove her shoes. He tossed them aside and ran his hands over her feet in a rough caress that felt like he was taking her over. His hands made one pass only, but she trembled, the blood heating instantly in her veins.

He sank down onto the mattress, sitting with his back to the headboard, his legs stretched out. The heat from his body warmed her as she lay stiff and wary beside him. 'Relax for me, Joley. We're just going to talk.'

'I feel like I'm lying down with the big bad wolf.'

He leaned over and brushed a kiss across her temple. 'What big eyes you have, *devochka moya*. Close them now.' He dimmed the light.

Joley moistened her lips, so aware of him there in the darkness. Every sway of the bus sent her body sliding against his. 'How often have you gone to sleep with someone else in the room with you?'

'Never. But I'm in a line of work guaranteed to make enemies.'

'That's a nice way of saying you have trust issues.'

He tugged at her hair, so that she felt a small bite of pain before his fingers soothed with long, caressing strokes. 'We fit.'

She wasn't certain she wanted to hear that. She still feared he could see her aura the way she could see his, but she wasn't certain she could face him knowing, so she didn't ask. 'We fight all the time.'

'That's just you running. Why do you think I'm here, Joley? You haven't slept in days and you're not at the top of your game. I want you back at your fighting weight when we do this thing, so later you can't say I took unfair advantage.'

She found herself smiling. 'Liar. You don't want me at my best; I'd kick your ass and you know it.'

'We'll see.' He leaned down and brushed a kiss across each eyelid. 'About this girl who's missing. Are you absolutely certain you saw her at the party? Maybe she just looks familiar to you.'

'Steve doesn't think it's her,' Joley answered honestly, 'but in my heart, I'm absolutely certain. She was there with a group of other young girls. I wasn't looking when they first got there, so I don't know which car brought them, but they had to come through the gate. Whoever was on guard duty should remember them. Maybe five girls. All very young. One of them, this one,' Joley opened her eyes and tapped the photograph he was once again holding, 'made a cell phone call. Another girl shouted at her that she wasn't supposed to tell anyone that she was there. That confirmed it for me that they shouldn't have been there.'

'Joley.' Ilya took her wrist again and brought her

hand to his chest. 'Did you notice anyone around? Anyone who would have observed you there at the time?'

'Sure. Dean, one of my crew, and another man who I didn't get a good look at seemed to know the girls. They all took off running together when I shouted at them.' Joley closed her eyes, replaying the scene in her head as she lay in the dark. 'Brian came out and went to find them. Denny and some blonde were a distance away, and RJ and his body-guards had driven up. I know they saw the girls and heard me talking to Brian. There were other people milling around as well. And Steve saw the girl, too. We both thought all the girls with her were too young to be there. Steve and I discussed it, but they were a distance away and we didn't get the best look at them.'

He stroked his fingers through her hair. 'You take too many chances.'

Joley frowned. 'What does that mean?'

'It means you should never have gone to that party and gotten out of that car without your bodyguard right beside you. And earlier, the moment trouble broke out in the arena, you should have backed away, not gone to the edge of the stage where someone could reach you. I don't understand your security people. They know you've been threatened . . .'

'How do you know that?'

'It's common knowledge in your family, Joley. That man was with the Reverend's demented flock, and he had a can of spray paint in his hand to mark you as the devil's harlot. Your voice really affected him, which is why he was too slow to do any damage. I was lucky I got to him before he got to you.'

She didn't think it was luck. Ilya didn't rely on

luck. 'Well, thank you for keeping me from being spray painted. It wouldn't have been pleasant.'

'It could easily have been a knife.'

'I know. I'm well aware, after Hannah, what can happen with knives and how easily they're concealed.'

He brushed back her hair again, his touch this time comforting. 'I didn't mean to bring up bad memories, *laskovaya moya*. Don't think about the attack on Hannah. Instead, tell me what you and Brian were arguing about. Your music was playing and I only caught a few sentences.'

She sighed. 'I shouldn't have yelled at him. I was really angry with myself for not inquiring about that missing girl and I took it out on him. Ever since that night, I've been wishing I'd done something. Maybe if I hadn't left it to Brian to run them down, that girl would be safe at home with her mother.'

'When did you find out she was missing?'

'After the Chicago concert, a week ago. And yes, she's still missing; I called the police department to check. After a show I often sign a few autographs for the fans who follow all my shows. The girl's mother was there and she grabbed me.' Without thinking she rubbed her arm.

Ilya pulled her sleeve back to examine the scratches in the dim light. The pads of his fingers soothed over the fading marks. 'She did this to you? Where the hell was your bodyguard? And where was Jerry? He's supposed to be watching out for you.' He brought her arm to his mouth, brushing his lips over the scratches.

Her stomach did a little somersault at the feel of his lips, soft and firm, pressing against her bare arm. She forced her mind to think when everything in her seemed to be turning to mush. 'Don't worry, everyone acted crazy and pulled her off of me. I tried to tell them I wanted to talk to her, but no one listened to me. Steve drove off and wouldn't stop even when I told him he had to. The last I saw of her, they were dragging her away.'

'Good. They at least did their jobs – after the fact. She should never have gotten close enough to do that kind of damage.'

Joley opened her eyes again and glared at him. 'I don't think you're a restful person – *at all*. The woman was scared and worried about her daughter. She wasn't trying to attack me.'

Ilya stared down at her with a long, accusatory stare. For some reason his expression made her squirm. She rolled her eyes.

'Okay, she tried to pull me out of the van, but that was because she was so upset.'

'One of these days, someone is going to get hurt, *laskovaya moya*, and life as you know it is going to be over.'

She shoved at his immovable body. 'That's exactly why we don't get along. I just go about living my life as normally as I can, and you throw out stupid statements like that. What does that mean? Is that some veiled threat?'

'I don't know how veiled it was.' His tone was mild. 'I think the threat was clear enough. Once we're permanently together, you're going to have a bodyguard who actually protects you.'

She sniffed, showing disdain for his confidence, but her wayward body reacted. 'I don't do permanent.' She glared at him. 'And neither do you.'

'All that's about to change.'

She was disgusted that she could be so physically

attracted to a man who handed out orders as if born for it. A part of her felt she couldn't come to life unless this man was dominant, and yet she had to fight him until there was no hope of any relationship. She needed emergency therapy, but she was afraid it was already too late. Everything about Ilya both drew and repelled her. She needed him to take charge as much as she needed to fight him for trying to dictate to her.

He brushed back her hair. 'Don't look so upset. You're going to be fine. You just need a little sleep and you'll be back on fighting form.'

'I don't want to be attracted to you.'

He didn't even wince. He simply nodded his head. 'I know. But we fit. We belong. I'm not willing to walk away because you're afraid.'

She closed her eyes against her own melting body – the clenching of the tight muscles in her feminine channel, the heated pulse and flip of her stomach. She betrayed herself – everything she was and believed in – for this man. It made no sense, but she was too tired to figure it out. 'You're a dictator. Why in the world would you think for one moment – even one – that someone like me with a need for control would fit with a personality like yours? You take control, you insist on your way. I'd drive you even more nuts than you'd drive me. We'd end up hating one another.'

'I don't dictate other than in matters of safety. And someone needs to do that for your protection.'

She peeped out from under her lashes to see if he'd gone up in flames for that lie. 'Even you, Mr. No Expression, can't keep a straight face. It's a wonder lightning didn't strike you dead. You're a dictator. You want every little thing your way.'

'Only with you.'

'I'll ask Nikitin sometime if that's the truth.'

Something dangerous swirled in the depths of his eyes. 'You stay far away from that man. I mean it, Joley.'

She started to sit, anger sweeping through her, but his heavy arm simply dropped across her, holding her down. Joley suppressed the childish urge to bite him. 'I'm not being soothed here. I thought you weren't going to make me crazy. I think *you* made my point for me.'

'I don't particularly give a damn if you get mad, just for once in your life listen to someone who knows more than you do. Nikitin is dangerous, particularly to you, so stay far away from him. You don't like him, so there's no reason for your childish defiance.'

Joley studied his face. Something wasn't quite right, but she couldn't put her finger on it. 'Now you're deliberately provoking me. Why? I wonder.' She reached up a hand and slid her fingers over his face, tracing the lines and shaping the bones.

He turned his face to press his mouth against her palm in a slow, burning kiss. Her entire body clenched, the demand urgent. Every nerve ending flared to life. Deliberately, his gaze holding hers, he lapped over his mark with his tongue, a long, slow lick that stole her breath as she felt it deep inside her, in her most feminine core. His tongue drew a lazy circle, and a moan escaped her throat. Her body was on fire, damp and needy, the pressure building as if his tongue was buried between her legs. She felt hot and dizzy, unable even to lift her head in protest. She couldn't think with the pleasure bursting through her.

He stroked again with his tongue, made the same

circles until the throbbing between her legs built and built. *He isn't doing anything but touching his tongue to my palm.* The thought was terrifying. She was close to an orgasm, feeling his tongue on her clit rather than on her palm. How? She and her sisters had gifts, but to her knowledge, none of them had ever experienced anything like this. She didn't understand it, or how Ilya could possibly be the one to take over her body when she was always the one in control. When she was with him, her body melted, gave itself to him like a sacrifice, and there seemed little she could do to prevent it.

'There's no giving you up,' he murmured against her palm. 'This says you belong to me, and me to you.'

Mutely she shook her head. Or maybe it wasn't mutely, maybe she was whimpering her denial. She had been so needy for so long, her body craving his to the point that she'd thrown herself at him in the hopes of ridding herself of the obsession. Now he was so close, larger than life, dominating her personal space, the scent and heat of him surrounding her. His melody suddenly took on dark erotic notes that tugged at her nipples until they were pebble-hard. Sensual notes throbbed and pulsed and moaned, licking over her skin and setting her on fire.

'You're mine,' he insisted. Keeping his gaze locked with hers, he once more bent his head to the center of her palm.

The brush of his lips sent streaks of fire rippling through the wall of muscles until she nearly spasmed with an orgasm. She was that close – so close – and she wanted more. She pressed her palm against his mouth, a low moan escaping.

His aura suddenly expanded, the darker colors swirling around her like a cloak, enveloping her colors of purple and iridescent pink and vivid orange, the jeweled tones that represented her. His darker colors bled into hers, mixing and swirling until she could feel a thousand fingers brushing over her skin, tongues lapping at her nipples and between her legs.

And then he bit down right in the center of her palm. She heard herself scream as her body convulsed, as pleasure burst through her. Her orgasm was strong and long, rippling through her from head to toe, a bright blast of rockets that sent colors and musical notes scattering like gems around her head and bursting behind her eyes.

Ilya held her to him, closing her fingers around her palm to make a fist, holding it against his heart while she fought for breath and control. He had claimed her body for his own, showed her that he could own her – he did own her – and she couldn't go back. She looked up at him with a mixture of terror and awe.

'What did you do?'

He kissed her forehead. 'Lie down and go to sleep now.' She looked so confused, beautiful and a little desperate that he gathered her closer. 'My gifts are a little different from yours and your siblings.'

She drew in her breath and tried to gather her scattered wits about her. If he could make her body explode just by kissing her palm, what the hell was going to happen to her if he ever decided he was going to make love to her? 'Ilya, don't you think that's a little scary?'

'Only if you decide to retaliate.'

'Could I?' She opened her fingers and looked at

her palm.

He caught her hand. 'Don't even think about it, because I swear, if you try anything, I'll strip you down to bare skin and you'll be under me all night. I came here to get you to sleep. Now go to sleep.'

There was steel in his voice, but she caught the uneasiness in his eyes. He wasn't as nearly in control of the situation as he wanted her to believe and that gave her some satisfaction. She let her breath out and lay down again. 'Soothe me. You said you could. And right now, I'm not feeling soothed.' On fire maybe, her body still rippling with after-shocks, and the sexual tension slowly draining away, but she wasn't soothed by a long shot.

He stroked caresses over her hair. 'Go to sleep, Joley. Just let yourself relax. You should learn meditation.'

She scowled at him. 'I know how to meditate. I've got things on my mind.'

Things like a man giving her the orgasm to end all orgasms by teasing her palm. That just wasn't right. And could she really do the same thing back? She'd like to give it a try, but knew there was no handling the consequences. She wasn't sure of him yet – not yet.

Things like young girls disappearing with members of her band – well, not the band, but her crew. And the poor mother who had been dragged away from the van when was only trying to get answers. She must have been desperate.

'You're sighing. I'm considering stronger measures than I've already taken.'

She didn't want to think what those measures might be. In any case his hand continued to brush back her hair, and the feel of it was almost mesmerizing. His voice had dropped another octave and came out a husky whisper, the sound sliding into and through her body like the sound of a beautiful musical instrument. And this time, her body responded by relaxing. She didn't question it, she was too tired.

'I don't want you to worry about anything right now except going to sleep,' he said.

'I can't help thinking about that poor woman and how upset she must be, not knowing where her daughter is,' Joley admitted, turning on her side and curling up. She was exhausted, and for the first time in a long while, in spite of his presence – or because of it – tension began to drain from her body. 'I need to talk to Dean, and then both of us should go to the police and at least tell them what we know. We may have been the last people to see her.'

'Let me handle this, Joley. I'll question your crew and make a report to the police.'

'I'm firing him if he dared invite that child to a party. Her poor mother.'

His hand moved over the back of her head, stroking silky strands. 'I'll find her. You stay out of it. It could be a very dangerous situation. Tell me about the man who was with her. Dean. What's his last name?'

'Walters. Dean Walters. And he had another member of the crew with him. Funny,' she mused, 'I used to know them all by name. I even knew their families. The same crew always stayed with us in the early days, but a couple of years ago some just up and quit. Now nothing is the same. Jerry had to tell me his last name was Walters.'

There was a small silence broken by the sound of cars on the highway. 'What happened a couple of

105

years ago to break up your crew?'

'I don't know.' She turned slightly to look over her shoulder. 'I don't know. That's a good question. Everyone seemed happy enough, but then there were all the parties and Tish got fed up with Logan and walked out on us. Maybe she was the glue that held us all together. One by one, the old crew, the sound-men and the roadies who always traveled with us just up and quit. They didn't show up for work.' She snuggled back into the coolness of her pillow. 'Since then I don't bother so much with learning who they all are because we have a big turnover.'

'Is that common?'

'It wasn't, but it seems to be now. Traveling is always hard on families. I didn't think our group would ever break up. We treated them like family and paid very well, but drugs and alcohol take their toll on everyone. And after Tish left, we all were depressed. It was hard to keep going.'

'Tish was Logan's girlfriend?'

'Wife. They were married, and still are, although we don't talk about it. Logan and Tish went to school with Rick, Leo and Denny. Brian was in a private school, but he spent summers with them. When they formed a band, Tish did their website, got their bookings and sold their CDs. I heard them play at the Caspar Inn when I was just out of high school. I talked with Tish for a long time that night and ended up giving her a recording of my voice. She was the one who brought us all together. I loved their sound and they loved mine. The road crew were friends of theirs from school as well. We all learned the business together.'

She yawned. Her eyelids were suddenly very heavy, and it was too difficult to keep her eyes open, so she curled deeper under the comforter he pulled up over her. His fingers eased the knots in the nape of her neck.

'Has Walters been traveling with your band the last two years?'

'Jerry would know. He handles everything on the road, but I've seen him often, at least enough that I recognize him and wave. He's never made an effort to talk to me, but then I haven't really talked to any of the crew other than the sound crew. And I don't know most of them very well anymore.'

'You aren't having much fun performing, are you? Why do you keep doing it?'

'I love to perform. I love the energy of the audience, being with my band and the music we make together. I even love the pressure of putting together new material.' She was lonely though. And she missed Sea Haven and her family. At least she could laugh with them and feel as if someone in the world cared about her for herself, not because she was a celebrity. 'I'm just tired. We've been keeping a grueling schedule.'

She could feel herself drifting under the influence of his massaging fingers. The motion of the swaying bus added to the dreamlike feeling pressing down on her. 'I'm going to make a list. That's what Libby does and it always works for her.'

'Libby is a brilliant woman,' Ilya said of her sister. 'And wise. What is this list for?'

'The pros and cons of being with you. I'm going to put them down on a piece of paper and then call my sisters to see if any of it makes sense.'

Her voice was a thread of sound, low and muffled by the pillow and comforter. She sounded a mixture of sexy and drowsy, and he shifted to ease the nearly permanent ache in his body. 'Are there cons to being with me?'

'You're so bossy. I hate that.'

Honesty poured into her voice like warm honey. She really was drifting in a dream, or she would never have admitted she was contemplating making a list and discussing him with her siblings. He found her drowsiness incredibly sexy. He nearly groaned, holding on to discipline and control to keep from taking what was his.

'You're always telling me what to do and you just take me over. But when you kiss, everything just goes to hell fast. I can't even think straight when you kiss me.'

He found himself smiling. 'I would think that should be put under pro.'

'No, no. You don't understand. That's not a good thing.'

He swept her hair away from her neck and bent until his lips could brush her ear. 'Kissing me is on the pro side for certain. If you're going to make a list and talk about me with your sisters, at least be honest. Kissing has got to be a huge pro.'

She gave a little sigh and her mouth curved. For one moment her eyelashes fluttered as she struggled to surface. 'Maybe both sides.'

'No way. That would cancel both entries out, and I have a feeling I'm going to need everything I can get on the pro side. What else are you putting on this list?'

She yawned and turned into him, fitting her face beneath his shoulder. 'I'm trying to think of things I like about you.'

'My charm.'

There was amusement in his voice and it captivated her. 'I wasn't aware you were charming. But you did save Abbey's Aleksandr when you could have been caught by the police.'

'I wasn't worried about the police,' he replied, 'so I'm not certain we can count that.'

'And you saved Hannah at a great cost to yourself.' She wanted to open her eyes and look at him, but her lids were too heavy and she couldn't make herself lift her head. Besides, his fingers were pure magic, melting her body so that she was boneless. Her fingers slid along his thigh, up toward his rib cage, until he caught and held her hand over his heart. 'I don't know if I really thanked you for that. Did I?'

'You can put that on the pro side,' he said and brought her hand to his mouth to tease the tips with his teeth. 'And yes, you thanked me.'

'Hannah is special.'

Ilya could barely hear her anymore. She was falling asleep, cuddling into him like a sleepy kitten. He kissed her knuckles and sat watching her face. She looked so young and innocent, angelic in her sleep, although her mouth promised paradise, a lush curve that kept his body hard with urgent demand.

The first time he'd ever heard of Joley Drake had been on the radio. Her voice had come on and his world had stopped. That voice. Pure and perfect, it had slid into his mind and lifted the shadows as if sunshine had suddenly burst through heavy layers of dark clouds. His world was violence and dirt, the dregs of society. Nothing shocked him anymore, and he had long since given up all illusions of finding good in a world of debauchery and excess indulgence. He had stopped believing in anything, and only his personal code kept him from destroying everyone around him.

He had spent two years investigating a child pornography ring that had taken him around the world, and the things he'd seen still haunted him – and he'd been hardened to the sins of man a long time ago. His orders had been to take the ring down, dispose of the guilty leaders and walk away without anyone ever knowing he'd been there. He followed leads from England to Brussels to Thailand. One by one he'd exterminated vermin until he'd found the man responsible for organizing the ring in the first place. The man had offered to share two little boys and a girl with him, but hurry, he was making a special video with these three.

By the time Ilya had worked his way through the maze, he found three dead children, killed in a snuff film of indescribable sickness and depravity. His control had slipped, always a dangerous thing. He had become a rabid animal, and he still couldn't examine too closely his behavior. For a short time his mind had shut down and the trained killer had taken over.

It was then, when he was at this darkest hour, that he heard a song on the radio. Joley's voice had given him peace for the first time in years. He hadn't believed anything could lighten his soul, but listening to her, it had been as if the sun had burst for the first time into his life and shone down on him. There was no redemption for him. He didn't expect or want it, but he craved the sun on his soul, those few moments of peace and contentment. She had saved his sanity. He would have left her alone, just collected her music, but their paths had crossed in the unlikeliest of chances. Now that he'd seen her, been in her presence and felt her warmth on his skin

110

– on his soul – there was no going back. He needed her as a barrier between him and the unrelenting shadows of his life.

His fingers tangled in the silk of her hair. She'd been a shock to him, when he thought himself impossible to shock. She wasn't a perfect angel from heaven – one he couldn't relate to – she was human. Sexy as hell. Flirty. She'd drive a man mad in seconds. She was fiercely loyal. A tigress when it came to her family, and he'd begun brooding over that trait in her, drawn to it, drawn to her capacity to protect those she loved. She knew what it was like to need to do whatever it took to protect those weaker than she was. And he desperately needed someone to save him – to love him – to be as fierce for him as Joley Drake was in the protection of her sisters.

There had been a photo in a tabloid. The headline had read *Joley Caught In Her Love Nest*. He had been furious, not disillusioned – he knew she was no angel – that her lover hadn't protected her from that kind of exposure. Then he'd found out it hadn't been her at all, but that she'd dyed her hair and taken the blame to keep her sister from nasty gossip that might have harmed her sister's career. In that moment she'd ripped out his heart and took it into her keeping for all time.

There was no getting around wanting Joley. His body ached when he thought of her. And when she sang – or talked – or just stood there in silence – he found he was more aroused than he'd ever been in his life. She brought out things in him he hadn't known were there. Tenderness. Gentleness. Emotions that had never been in his life, not even as a child. She introduced him to laughter. She made him a better person, and she'd replaced despair with hope.

Ilya bent his head again and brushed a kiss along her cheekbone. 'Life with you will never be dull.' She also brought out the worst side of his nature, the need to dominate and control, his own protective instincts honed into fighting skills and determination. Ilya always won, no matter the cost, and he would win Joley. He had marked her because he couldn't stop himself from doing so, and that had scared the hell out of him. It was rare for him to lose control, and he knew putting his mark on her was not something he could take back. They were irrevocably bound together.

He shifted a little to slide down beside her, resting the back of his head on the pillow. She stirred, eyelashes fluttering before lifting. Her eyes, large and dark and glorious, smiled up at him. She nearly stopped his heart.

'Go to sleep, Ilya. I'll make sure nothing happens to you.' She wrapped her arm around his waist and slid closer to lay her head on his chest.

His heart ached. An actual pain to rival the one in his groin. Even asleep, she'd felt his need, maybe it had registered in his voice. He was used to being alone. He didn't know any other way, had never considered anything else – he didn't know how to trust enough. But she made him want to learn – want to take a chance. She was the first person in his life who had offered to take care of him – ever. She had to be asleep and unaware.

'You talk in your sleep.' He nuzzled the top of her head with his chin.

She smiled without opening her eyes. 'I don't sleep.'

'You're sleeping now – with me. For me.'

Her smile widened and her arm tightened around him, before she relaxed completely into him again. 'Because you're such a dick – tator.'

He found himself smiling all over again.

Chapter Six

Ilya was gone. Joley kept her eyes squeezed shut tight, trying not to feel alone and panic-stricken. She hated waking up to the sound of silence. Growing up in a large family, she loved being home and hearing the comforting sounds of the household stirring to life. As strange as the night had been, she had fallen asleep and actually rested.

She sighed, opened her eyes, rolled over and stared up at the ceiling of her bus. She knew they had to be in the Red Rocks parking lot or the bus would still be in motion and Ilya would still be inside with her. Holding her arm up, she opened her fingers and stared at her palm. There was no visible mark, but she felt the faint itch that was often present, reminding her that Ilya had zapped her with something she couldn't get rid of. She hadn't realized how powerful it was, or just how the mark had tied them together. She ran the pad of her finger lightly over her palm. Nothing happened. Nothing at all.

With a little frown, Joley sat up and shoved back her hair. She needed to make her list of pros and cons. And the pros needed to outweigh the cons when she discussed it with her sisters, because she was already lost. She paced across the room to the small kitchen to put on the kettle while she got ready for the sound check. They only had a few hours to get things pulled together for tonight's concert. It was difficult to do two shows in a row, but Red Rocks was worth it to her. She already wanted to go outside and just breathe in the air. She was definitely going to go running and do a little exploring, as Red Rocks had to be one of the coolest places on earth.

She could still feel Ilya's presence in her bus while she showered. Had Steve seen him when he left? She doubted it. Ilya wasn't the kind of man to be seen when he didn't want to be, and somehow she was fairly certain Ilya would try to protect her reputation. And that was going on the pro side of her list. She was definitely making a list of pros and cons to determine if she should sleep with Ilya Prakenskii, because listing them was the only sane thing to do.

She sat down with a cup of tea, her pen between her fingers, drumming on the tabletop and trying to remember all the cons she'd thought of the day before. There had been a lot of them, but that thing he'd done with her palm had tipped the scales right back in the pro direction. In fact, the cons seemed to be permanently wiped from her mind.

Sarah. Before making up her mind one way or the other about Ilya, Joley should discuss the situation with Sarah. After all, she was the oldest and she really gave good advice – even when no one wanted to hear it.

Joley reached for her cell phone, then hesitated. She had time to do a little exploring and she definitely needed exercise. Maybe calling Sarah right now wasn't such a good idea. Everything was so crazy and she really was mixed up; nothing would make sense. There was no way she'd do more than babble and stammer, and she needed to be coherent and thinking when she talked to her sisters about Ilya. Now was not the right time. Besides, they'd talk too long, and then she wouldn't have time to go exploring before she had to do the sound check . . .

Her cell phone rang and she flipped it open. Joley held the phone away from her ear as Sarah's voice blasted her. 'Joley Elizabeth Drake, just what are you up to?'

Joley strove for complete innocence. 'I have no idea what you're talking about, I just woke up, and at this precise moment I'm drinking a cup of tea and making out an important list.'

'I'm not buying that. You were going to call me and then you decided not to and I could feel the backlash of guilt. What's going on and what do you have to feel guilty over?'

Joley rolled her eyes, thankful her eldest sister couldn't see her. Sarah knew all kinds of things before they happened. She always knew before someone called. 'Well, I did want your advice on something, but I just woke up and wasn't certain what time it was, so I didn't want to chance calling and waking everyone up if it was early.' She drummed her fingers on the table, looking for a way to distract her sister. 'How's Damon doing?'

Joley had grown very fond of Sarah's fiancé. He was a good man, quiet but brilliant, and he obviously adored Sarah, and the minute anyone mentioned him, Sarah was distracted.

'He's wonderful. Libby has spent some time trying to help his hip and leg, but the injury is old

116

enough that she's not getting the results she'd like. But Damon says there isn't as much pain. He's in San Francisco today, working on some project I'd rather not know about.'

'I'm so glad Libby's able to help him a little. He's a good man, Sarah.'

'Yes, he is. And speaking of men, I'm sensing this problem you have involves one,' Sarah said, returning like a dog with a bone to the point of her call.

Joley winced a little at the note of suspicion in her sister's voice. On the blank paper in front of her she wrote out *Pros* and *Cons* with a line separating them. Under cons she wrote, *Gets me in trouble with my sister – received lecture.* Because it was coming – and Sarah's lectures were never pleasant, because she knew exactly what to say to make a person feel guilty.

'Joley?' Sarah prompted. 'Tell me what's going on.'

'Well . . .' Joley tried to hedge, but that wasn't too smart with Sarah. 'It's just that I've been considering having a relationship and I'm trying to be practical.' She was fairly certain she heard a snort, and then Sarah was coughing. 'Did you choke on something?'

'Sorry. You're being practical – over a man?'

'Hey! I don't think that comment was strictly necessary.' Joley was indignant.

There was a small silence. 'Really? Who is he?'

Joley pressed the point of the pencil so hard into the paper it broke. Of course Sarah would ask. 'Ilya Prakenskii.'

There was a silence. Joley felt the gathering explosion and rushed into an explanation. 'I don't think he's any of the things everyone says he is. I really don't. He's just too – nice.' Even she winced

117

when she said the word. Nice wasn't a description one could use for Ilya.

'He's dangerous, Joley. *Dangerous* is not *nice*. You stay away from him.'

Her palm itched and she rubbed it over her thigh. 'He has all the same gifts that our family has, Sarah – but the gifts are little different. When my magic touches his, or our auras get close, they merge and flow together. I can feel the difference in the way he summons and uses energy.'

'I noticed that when he was holding Hannah to him,' Sarah agreed. 'And Hannah spent a lot of time connected to him, and she tried examining the way he gathered and cast energy, but he's cut off. His aura was too dark, hiding everything from her.'

'Well, it's definitely different. I know you've been studying the books our ancestors have on the ancient ways, and I wondered if you ever came across anything in our history about marks.' Joley drummed out a nervous rhythm with the pencil on the table. 'Maybe something to do with binding two people together, or claiming, or I don't know, anything, any mention at all.'

'Are you talking about your hand? Describe the mark.'

There was comfort in her sister's matter-of-fact, practical voice. That was Sarah, getting to the heart of the matter and gathering information.

'That's the problem, Sarah. There is no visible mark. I can't describe something to you I can't see. There are times when my palm itches and other times I think I see a faint color, like a bluish-purple, but it's never strong enough to be certain and it fades quickly.' With a little sigh, she took her pencil sharpener out of the drawer beneath the table and began shaving a new point on the pencil. She had the feeling she'd be doing it a lot.

'When you do see the color, is it linear? Vertical? Horizontal, or all over the place?'

'It's in the exact center of my palm and it appears almost to be two circles intertwined, but that could be my imagination. Most of the time there's nothing there at all.' She examined her palm. It looked smooth and unblemished.

'*Joley.*' Sarah bit her name out between her teeth. 'Why didn't you ever tell us about this?' She sighed when Joley didn't answer. 'I want you to describe to me how you got it again. *Exactly.* Every detail you can remember.'

Joley resisted the urge to hang up. The mark was private. Very intimate. And she felt almost as if she was betraying Ilya by describing the events to her sister – although they'd all been there when it happened. 'We were at the Caspar Inn dancing. Prakenskii was there and he made me mad. Nikitin had forced me to sing and then he wanted to meet with me. I said no and Prakenskii turned his back to me and was walking away. I pushed energy at his back. It was just a little shove and maybe I should-n't have done it, but he'd been lecturing me and disapproving of me all evening. I was sick of him. I was only trying to make him stumble, but the energy came back on me. I heard crackling and popping, like electricity, and I could see sparks all around my hand. My palm burned, for just a moment, really burned, deep inside. I remember I sort of yelped and held my hand.'

Sarah sighed heavily again. 'The girls shielded you from him, but he didn't even turn around.'

'That's right. My hand hurt so badly, and we

decided to leave. I was angry enough for a confrontation and Abbey was worried, everyone was, because he seemed to be so powerful. As I walked past him to leave, he reached out and took my hand. His thumb slid over my palm just once, and he let go, but as his skin touched mine and continued a brushing movement, it was as if he wiped away all the pain.' Even as she described the gesture to her sister, Joley felt that amazing touch all over again, the single brush of skin to skin that sent flames racing through her body, marking her inside and out.

'When did you first notice the discoloration?' Sarah's question drew Joley back from the memories.

'In the beginning, my hand just kept itching like wounds do when they're healing. Eventually that stopped – now the itching only comes back when he's near, or when I am thinking about him, or when he's talking telepathically to me. And recently I discovered that there's some connection between the mark he put on me and the two of us. It connects us . . .' She searched for the right word. Just thinking about what Ilya did with that mark and his mouth left her damp and needy all over again. 'It connects us in a physical way. I suspect it enables him to speak telepathically to me over greater distances.'

There was no way she was going to admit to Sarah that the connection was sexual, that Ilya had given her an orgasm simply by manipulating that spot on her hand.

Sarah made a little noise that alarmed Joley.

'What? Have you read about this?' She carefully drew two circles intertwined right above the words *Pros* and *Cons*.

'I've read references, pretty vague ones. There are a few entries in some of the diaries about a male line with similar gifts. Once in a while one of our ancestors crossed one of theirs.'

Joley rubbed her palm along her thigh, then realized that rather than trying to brush the mark off as she used to do, she was now brushing her palm slowly back and forth in a caressing motion. She snatched her hand back. 'That doesn't sound particularly bad.'

'Well, at one of the points when the male line clashed with our line, it was because a woman had come to the Drake women and claimed someone had marked her with a magical symbol, two circles intertwined. She claimed it bound her to this man and she suspected he was a witch or a sorcerer. She seemed frightened. Of course they took her in.'

'I don't like the tone of your voice. This doesn't have a good ending, does it?' Joley asked. She pressed her hand tighter against her body, suddenly afraid. It was one thing to contemplate having an affair by her own choice, but it was something altogether different to think she didn't have free will in the matter.

'Well, even their combined powers and skills couldn't break the bond between the man and the woman. No one knew what happened – just that she got up one night and left the house. He was waiting for her. She went off with him and they never heard of her again.'

Joley took a deep breath. 'So there is some documentation about another family having similar powers to ours, only male.'

'Yes, although I can't find anything in our time, or even Mom's. I can call Mom and ask her if she's read or heard anything more. She always studied the history of our family, and I don't have near the knowledge she has.'

Joley swept her hand through her hair, twirled strands around her finger and bit down on her lip, trying to decide. 'Ask her, Sarah, but . . .' She trailed off, not wanting to alarm her sister any more. Just the fact that she would consult her mother would elevate Sarah's warning radar.

'You're in way over your head, aren't you, Joley?' Sarah asked.

Joley rubbed her hand along her thigh again. 'I don't know. But whatever mark you read about is on my palm, and I'm fairly certain it has somehow, chemically or magically or both, tied me to Ilya Prakenskii.' On the paper in front of her, she drew a double circle on the pro side started to draw a line through it and then left it.

'And you're contemplating a relationship with him?'

Joley had known Sarah wouldn't let her off that easy. She sighed, knowing that if she wanted help she would have to confess, tell the absolute truth and hope her sisters would think of a way to save her.

'I'd have to say it's too late for contemplation. I'm obsessed. I wouldn't admit that to anyone but one of my sisters, but he's all I think about day or night. It's more than obsession. I swear, Sarah, it's like he's become the blood in my veins.' She gave a small, derisive laugh and drew her fingertip over the circles on the paper. 'How cheesy is that? He's the air in my lungs. I breathe him in and out with every breath I take.' And she was cold and lonely without him, without the heat of his body, the heat of his gaze, his voice in her head driving her crazy. 'It's like we're merging together. You know me. I may have bad taste in men, but I've never been obsessive and I've never needed a man. Ever. But I need him.'

'If Prakenskii is bothering you, Damon and I can fly out today if we have to and get you through the rest of the tour.'

'No, it isn't like that. It's more me than him.'

'I can't imagine that. You don't exactly chase men, Joley. They chase you.'

'I threw myself at him the other night and he turned me down,' Joley confessed. 'And he spent last night with me and didn't do much but get me to sleep.'

Again there was a small silence. Joley counted to ten while her words sank in. She imagined Sarah with a little frown on her face.

'You don't sleep with anyone in the room. You never did even as a child.'

'I know. But I did last night. He said he couldn't stand me not sleeping, and he was going to guard me so I could just relax and sleep all night – and I did.'

'And he didn't touch you?'

'He kissed me.'

'And?'

'Rockets. Holy cow, Sarah, he's like the greatest kisser of all time.'

'That's not good.'

'Actually I told him I was putting that in the con section of my list, but he said I couldn't.' She couldn't help the bubble of laughter in her voice. She touched her lips, tingling at the memory.

'I'm going to talk to Mom immediately.' Sarah sounded more than a little alarmed. 'Don't do anything stupid, Joley. If Prakenskii really comes from this other lineage, you could be in real trouble. In the diary, our ancestors wrote that the woman who came to them was terrified of the man who marked her. She was very religious and thought maybe he had made a pact with the devil. The house should have protected her along with all the protections the Drakes could muster for her, yet for some reason, she left the house in the middle of the night and went to him. That doesn't make sense when she was safe.'

Joley could have told her why. If the man had been like Prakenskii, he had seduced her with his voice. He had pursued her day and night, until she was in such a state of arousal, she couldn't fight him anymore. 'I'm going to be careful. Find out everything you can and call me. I hear a lot of commotion outside. They'll be setting up soon and calling me in for a sound check and I'd like to get in a run at least.'

'I love you, Joley. If you need me to help you fight him, I'll come. All of us will.'

'I'm good for now. Love you right back. Kiss Damon for me.' Joley hit the end call button and sat for a moment, pressing the cell phone to her chin. She had no idea what she was going to do. On the con side of her list she wrote, *Scares the hell out of me*.

She broke the lead in the pencil twice as she wrote out *The hand thing*. She wrote it half on the pro side and half on the con side. Frowning, she was about to add the kiss right in the middle between the two columns as well. And while she was thinking about it, she was pretty sure talking telepathically to her day and night, in an attempt to seduce her, had to go smack in the middle also. She hadn't exactly consulted Sarah over that little piece of information.

The pencil snapped in half. Joley took it as a sign she needed to go running.

It was bright outside. She hadn't pulled back the privacy sliders in the bus, and the light from the sun nearly blinded her. Whipping out her sunglasses, she pushed them onto her nose and stepped into the parking lot. Steve would have a fit that she went running without him to guard her, but he had to be tired from driving all night and she didn't want to disturb him.

She looked carefully around her, her breath catching in her throat. Red Rocks was beautiful. The bus was parked in the lot behind the amphitheater, and she looked up at the surrounding natural walls of towering rock that always took her breath. It was as if nature had created an amphitheater with a perfect acoustic sound just for the sheer love of hearing music and then had provided the most beautiful backdrop it could offer. For someone like Joley who was all about sound and nature, it was almost perfection on earth. She loved the natural rock formations, the layers and layers of sandstone that had been there millions of years, slowly rising until they were the majestical towers of red rock creating the walls of the theater.

Joley took a deep breath and let it out. Coming to Red Rocks always revitalized her. The sandstone formations, the prehistoric footprints of time rising above her like a cathedral, were inspiring on every level. It had been difficult to talk everyone into a back-to-back concert, but she was grateful she had. She walked toward the stage, where she could hear a commotion as the crew began to set up.

She noticed a couple of Nikitin's guards with dogs searching the rows of the amphitheater. He must

125

have decided to attend, and his security was doing a sweep right along with hers. Loud voices coming from behind several crates attracted her attention. A few of the crew looked uneasy when they saw her, glancing hastily away or acknowledging her with a slight nod of the head. Curious, she moved closer to the commotion.

Jerry and Brian had evidently caught up with Dean, and the discussion didn't appear to be going very well. Dean looked angry, and he was gesturing obscenely at Brian. Joley had to fight her natural inclination to go join the fray. It hadn't been fair to force Jerry and Brian to confront Dean. She was the one who had forbidden underage groupies at the parties. It was her rule and ultimately her decision to fire Dean if he had broken it. She was putting her manager and Brian, her best friend, in the position of looking like the bad guys. She really had become a diva, although, in the music business, everyone knew it was always the star's decision that carried the weight.

She had taken three steps when a woman emerged from the rocks to her left. Joley recognized Tish Voight, Logan's estranged wife. Joy swept through Joley, and she realized just how much she had missed her. Tish had been a mother hen to all of them, but especially to Joley, as she was younger than the band members.

'Joley!' Tish's face lit up and she ran across the parking lot toward her.

'Tish!' Joley, who rarely touched anyone, threw her arms around Tish and hugged her close. 'I've missed you. When did you get in? Are you staying?'

Tish hugged her back hard. 'Actually I just arrived, my car's down in the lot. You look great,

126

Joley. The band has done so well. I'm really proud of all of you.'

'We've never been the same without you. How have you been? Tell me everything.'

Joley couldn't believe how good Tish looked. She'd matured in the last few years. Medium height, she had long dark hair, which she still pulled back in a ponytail, but it looked shiny and healthy, as did her skin. She had a woman's body with lots of curves. That was Tish – no makeup, no glamour, but all beautiful. There wasn't a devious bone in her body.

'I've been working; teaching again. Love the kids, you know I do. So it's all been good.'

'But you miss us, right? Miss the road and the craziness?' Joley asked hopefully.

'I miss you and the boys, not so much the craziness.' Her eyes looked sad, although she was smiling. 'Logan called and said it was an emergency and he desperately needed me, so I came.' She shrugged. 'I didn't want to come, Joley. I can't afford the risk.'

'I know. I'm so sorry, Tish, all of us were. You and Logan . . .'

'Don't. I don't want to go there. Logan and I were childhood sweethearts. I guess that's very cliché nowadays. He outgrew me. I'm small town and I like it that way. He's uptown and he likes it that way.'

'Neither of you filed for divorce,' Joley pointed out. She couldn't tell Tish that she felt her sorrow at the loss of her marriage, and that she knew, after touching her, that Tish still loved Logan. Joley hadn't meant to invade her privacy.

Tish shrugged. 'I'm not looking for another relationship, and it seemed too much of a hassle. I

127

figured if he ever wanted to divorce me, he'd just do it. He has the lawyers and I don't care about his money. He knows that. I've made my own living without him.'

'But he sends you money, doesn't he?'

'He insisted on a joint account, and apparently he puts money in it every month. He told me once everything he had was in both our names, but I never checked and I've never accessed the bank account.'

That was total Tish. Independent and fiercely proud. Joley understood her. 'So are you going to stay and help with the baby?'

'I don't know. Logan wants me to, but you know me, I'll get attached to her and then won't be able to let go when the time comes.'

'No one would make a better mother, Tish. You were born to be a mother.'

'I can't have children – at least I can't give birth to them. I had cancer as a child. The radiation and chemotherapy saved my life, but not anything else.' She glanced toward the band's bus. 'I always wondered if that . . .'

'Tish! No! Logan was crazy about you. Drugs and alcohol and groupies throwing themselves at the boys ruined everything. You know that. It was too much, too fast, and we couldn't handle it. None of us – except you.'

Tish had always stood for them, but as their popularity grew, the band needed someone who knew the business and could handle all the details of a huge venue, and Jerry had come into their lives. With Jerry had come overnight success and all that came with it.

'I didn't handle it all that well either,' Tish

protested. 'Seeing all those girls willing to do anything with Logan – with the others – they were like brothers to me, it was overwhelming. Maybe I shouldn't have stayed away so long, but I thought our marriage could handle it.' She shook her head. 'Now look at us. I'm alone and he's got a child.'

'Logan has sole custody of the baby, Tish. Lucy gave up all rights to her and she doesn't want her at all. Neither does Lucy's mother. They wanted money. When Lucy found out Logan was married and he had dropped her, she went berserk. She has mental problems and I think she's all the mother can handle. If you're still married to Logan, I don't know the legal ramifications, but I think you should be able to adopt the baby easily. Maybe this is your chance. Talk to Logan about it.'

Tish sighed. 'That's one more tie to him.'

'Is that really such a bad thing?'

Angry voices rose, and Joley looked past Tish to the three men arguing. She had never seen Brian actually lose his temper, but he shoved Dean, his posture very aggressive. Jerry stepped in between the two men, pushing Dean away from Brian. She was still too far away to hear what they were saying, but body language suggested it was a fairly violent argument. She could see several members of the crew watching the three men while pretending to work.

'Do you know what that's about?' Tish asked.

Joley sighed and filled her in. 'I guess I should have been the one to speak with Dean, instead of making Jerry and Brian do it.'

'No, you shouldn't,' Tish said. 'Jerry's your manager and he deals with the crew. You aren't responsible for anything these people do. If Dean took advantage of a minor, Jerry will fire him. And if he knows where she is, they'll get it out of him. You can't be involved in things like that. You're the star, Joley, the band is secondary. If you got involved in a confrontation with a crew member, someone's going to videotape it and it will end up on television, the Internet and especially the tabloids. Let Jerry do his job.'

'I don't want it to come to blows. Brian almost never loses his temper. I can't imagine what would make him get so angry.'

'You can't?' Tish shook her head. 'The band looks at you as a younger sister. They're very protective and very loyal. My guess is Dean said something very ugly about you and got Brian's back up. None of them are going to let anyone say anything bad about you.'

Joley felt a tug at her heartstrings. She felt as if the band were family – brothers she loved – but their camaraderie with one another was very different than with her and she always felt the odd man out. 'Since you've been gone, I haven't felt as much a part of things as I used to,' she admitted, frowning as she watched the argument get a little more heated.

The disturbance had attracted the attention of not only the crew, but also the Russians. They paused in their work and observed the altercation. Joley's palm began to itch. She rubbed it against her thigh, and her heart began to pound. Ilya was nearby – very close. She spotted him making his way to the two Russians and her stomach did a little somersault. He moved with fluid grace, like a large jungle cat, all rippling muscle and power, yet conserving energy with every step.

'Whoa! Mama mia, who is that?' Tish asked.

'He's hotter than Hades.'

Joley considered feigning indifference, but this was Tish. 'Ilya Prakenskii, Nikitin's bodyguard.'

'He can guard my body anytime,' Tish said appreciatively. 'Have you . . .'

'No. But ask me if I want to.'

'You'd have to be dead not to want to. I think I'm having an orgasm looking at him.'

Joley pressed her palm tighter against her thigh. The center throbbed and burned, and deep inside, in her most feminine core, the same throbbing and burning began. It was going to start all over again, that terrible need, the emptiness that nothing – no one – could fill but Ilya. If she was going to suffer, it was only fair that he should. She wished she could make him feel the same relentless, merciless craving.

Lifting her palm, she studied the center. Already the discoloration was appearing. Faint marks, two circles intertwined. Joley lifted her gaze to Ilya, watching his every move as he approached the two Russian guards. She took a deep breath and ran her finger over the center of her palm, imagining touching him intimately, holding his body close to hers and claiming it for her own.

Ilya's body jerked. He looked up, his gaze locking with hers across the distance. Time seemed to stand still, and for one moment there were only the two of them locked together in the natural wonder of the amphitheater.

I'm sorry. She hadn't believed she could really give him such a jolt of physical awareness.

Be very careful playing with fire you don't understand.

She moistened her lips and turned away from him.

131

It was his magic – not hers – and she didn't understand it. But she knew how dangerous it could be.

'Is something going on between you two?' Tish asked.

'Not yet,' Joley answered honestly. 'I'm still considering the price tag.'

'For a man like that? It's going to be hefty.'

Joley laughed. 'I missed you, Tish. You're so right, about a lot of things, but especially about this.'

'But I bet he'd be worth it.'

Joley had the feeling she was going to find out. If she didn't find something huge to put on the con side of the list fast, she would allow him to seduce her, and then she'd be in way over her head. Tish wasn't like Joley's sisters. She looked at the man and saw 'hot' all over him. She didn't see the neon warning lights flashing, *danger, danger*. If Joley hung out with Tish, she could easily talk herself into an affair with Ilya, because she desperately wanted him.

'Have you seen Logan yet?' Joley asked, needing to switch the subject. She couldn't think too much about Ilya, especially with him close by. She couldn't afford for him to be reading her thoughts.

The teasing smile faded from Tish's face. 'We spoke on the phone, and I said I'd meet him here, but I haven't seen him yet. I drove all night to get here, and now I'm thinking of jumping back in the car and calling him from the safety of two or three hours away.'

Joley looked past her. Logan had just stepped out of the bus, and his radar had found Tish immediately. He was staring at her with naked longing. 'I think it's too late to run, Tish. He's coming this way.'

Tish didn't turn around. Instead, she closed her eyes briefly, as if gathering strength. Joley pressed her hand for courage. 'I hope you stay, Tish. You're family to all of us and we've never been the same without you.' She kept her voice low. 'But I understand if you can't stay.'

Tish's fingers clung to hers for a moment, and Joley felt her tremble. Instantly she felt protective and stood her ground, letting Tish hold on to her for courage.

Logan stopped a few steps short of them. 'You came, Tish.' His voice was low and gravelly, choked even.

Joley was nearly overwhelmed with the mixture of emotions pouring out of Logan. He was close to a breakdown, she realized. The pregnancy had been a nightmare, with Lucy threatening to kill herself every few days and the paparazzi dogging his every footstep. He stood directly behind Tish, his usually good looks worn and tired.

Joley watched the struggle on Tish's face as she turned to face her husband. 'I came,' she agreed. Her fingers tightened around Joley's.

'Thank you for coming, Tish. Believe me, I know what I'm asking.' Logan raked both hands through his hair and then rubbed the shadow along his jaw. 'I have the baby here. She's been crying most of the night, kept us all awake. I don't know what's wrong.' He glanced over to where Jerry and Brian were now shouting at Dean. 'Everyone's temper is a little frayed. They all took turns holding her to try to get her to sleep, but we can't keep that up.'

'The baby's in the bus?' Tish asked, obviously melting at the sheer desperation in Logan's voice. 'Show me.'

Joley took a couple of steps toward Jerry and Brian, but Tish hung on to her like a pit bull. 'It looks like it's getting out of hand over there.'

'Don't think you'll make it any better,' Logan cautioned. 'Dean was talking crap about you this morning and Brian overheard him. He was seething when he came into the bus. He's hard to rile, but when he gets going, you've got to look out. Come see the baby.'

Joley frowned, torn between hope that she could end the argument that looked like it was coming to blows and fear that she would possibly make it even worse. Dean glanced up, and his venomous gaze met hers across the distance. He spat on the ground and gestured obscenely at her. Even from where she was, Joley could feel the malevolence pouring from him to her. She shivered as waves of hatred and anger washed over her. And something else. She turned her head quickly to see Ilya straighten, his gaze on Dean, hard and cold and glittering with promise. His aura was black and swirled around the edges with blood red. She drew in her breath sharply.

Brian spun Dean around and smashed his fist into his face. Dean staggered back and then flung himself on Brian. Around them the crew sprang into action, surrounded the two men and dragging them apart.

Logan pressed Tish and Joley forward toward the band's bus. 'You don't need to be out here. Somewhere, you know someone with a camera is lurking. Let Jerry and Brian toss the bum out on his ass.'

'I feel responsible,' Joley said.

'He's right, Joley,' Tish agreed. 'You can't be involved in that. Brian shouldn't have been either.

Either the man knows something or he doesn't. If he does, he should just give them the information, and if not, he shouldn't be so resentful that they asked him. It's a perfectly legit question when some kid is missing.' She tugged at Joley. 'Let's go see the baby.'

Joley glanced back toward Ilya, but he was walking away, heading toward the front of the amphitheater, his back toward her.

Chapter Seven

Logan stepped out of the bus and put the baby into Tish's arms, standing there with a look of utter, naked, helpless love on his face, for the entire world to see. 'I named her Melissa Lacey, the one we picked out together back when we were in high school. We've all been calling her Lissa. Isn't she beautiful?'

Tish looked as if she would cry. She stared down at the little upturned face, the little waving hands with soft, perfect fingers, then pushed the baby into Joley's arms and stepped inside the bus.

Logan caught Joley's shoulders for support, leaning heavily on her, looking down at his child. 'She doesn't want her, Joley. She can't forgive me for the things I did.'

Joley patted his hand, looking up at him. 'I love you, Logan, but you're dense. She's crazy about you and desperately wants to believe she can be a family with you and the baby, but she's afraid. Take the baby and go to her, and for God's sake, eat your pride. Tish is the best in the world. They don't come better. If she accepts you back and takes Lissa as her daughter, she'll never look back. You'll never have anything thrown in your face. You don't deserve her, but if you really want her, I don't think it's going to be all that difficult to convince her. You've got Lissa, and who could resist her?' She smiled at the baby, bent her head and kissed the little forehead. 'She's so beautiful.'

'If Tish doesn't come back to me, Joley, I don't know what I'm going to do. And now she'll think I only wanted her for the baby. I got here about five in the morning, and we've been passing Lissa back and forth since then. No one's complained, but I can't ask them to help me with her, and I sure can't haul her around the country without help. I don't trust anyone but Tish.'

'Tish went into the bus, not back toward her car. Rent an RV or something larger for the three of you for the rest of the tour. We can make them comfortable. If we have to, I can bunk with the boys and the three of you can use my bus. We're family. We'll get through this together.' She handed him the baby. 'Go tell her you love her and that you're an idiot.'

'Thanks, Joley.' Logan pressed a kiss to the top of her head.

'I'm going running.' She always went jogging to clear her head. Physical exercise was a form of meditation to her.

'Where's Steve?' Logan asked.

'He drove the bus last night. He's asleep, but no one's around yet and I should be fine. Nikitin's security is already here and I noticed a few uniforms showing up.'

Logan cradled his daughter close and nodded, although he still looked worried. 'Be careful, Joley, and don't go very far.'

She glanced at her watch and then over to where

Jerry and Brian had argued with Dean. Apparently the fight had broken up and everyone had found something to do. Dean was stalking across the parking lot toward the crew's bus, and Brian was nowhere in sight. She'd have to ask them later what Dean had said about the young girl. 'I've got about an hour before this place starts filling up. Jerry told me they'd call me for the sound check around two. That sound about right with you?'

Logan nodded and went up the small steps to the bus. 'That's when everything should be ready.'

Joley waved, mouthed *good luck* and took off jogging away from the stage area toward the trail leading up into the rocks. Logan was a lucky man. In spite of everything he had done, all the mistakes he'd made, Tish loved him. Even the fiasco with Lucy had turned into something wonderful. Little Lissa would be well loved by Tish and Logan.

In the beginning the band had lived their lives together, and everything had been good. They'd been best friends and had people surrounding them who really loved them. As they'd climbed to success, everything had changed. All of them had been sucked into a life of excess, and they'd all forgotten what really mattered. As the years went by, they'd learned the hard way, and all were trying to find their way back. She hoped Logan and Tish could do it through the baby.

And Denny. She had no idea if Lisa had stuck around to forgive him. Joley hoped so. Love wasn't always forgiving, but at least he'd found it, even if he'd been stupid enough to throw it away.

Her sisters had been lucky. Sarah had found Damon. He was an odd man, brilliant and gruff, but he had embraced Sarah's family and they all had fallen in love with him. Sweet Kate had found Matt Granite, former Army Ranger and now a contractor. He was just what Kate needed. And Abbey was truly in love with her Russian, Aleksandr Volstov.

Love seemed to happen fast to everyone but her. She obsessed over Ilya Prakenskii, but she wasn't in love with him. Just because he took her breath away and set her heart pounding – that was purely physical. Chemistry. They had it in abundance, but she wanted the kind of love her sisters had. Libby and Tyson. Libby was a natural healer, Tyson a renowned researcher for pharmaceuticals, and he looked after Libby, treating her like a precious treasure. And of course there were Jonas and Hannah. Jonas adored Hannah. It was in every look he gave her, every touch of the hand. Joley wanted that. Not just hot sex – and it would be hot with Ilya – but it wouldn't be love.

And maybe no one could love her, not unconditionally, the kind of love her sisters had found, the kind that Tish felt for Logan. She feared it was her. She didn't know how to love, to give herself to someone, to put herself into someone else's keeping and take him into hers. She didn't trust anyone with her heart – or the darker places in her soul.

She picked up her pace, listening to the rhythm of her shoes hitting the trail. She wanted to enjoy being a loner, satisfied with trekking the world and singing wherever she went, in stadiums filled with crowds, but she couldn't live just for those moments. She wanted to share her life with someone else, laugh with him, stay up until all hours of the night talking with him, or just sit quietly side by side and feel at peace.

The morning sun had risen, and the beams of

lights shining on the red rock set the hillside ablaze with color. The towers of sandstone that rose up toward the sky were incredible, and she tried to find solace in nature. The trail climbed into the heart of the rock, and she felt surrounded, protected even. Trees and bushes sprang up as life found the sun and stretched toward it. It should have been impossible for her not to be happy, but with every step she took, her heart seemed to grown heavier, until it sat in her chest like a stone and dread filled her.

She didn't want to go back. She didn't want to face Jerry and Brian, or even Tish and Logan with their happy smiles. By now, Lisa might have resolved things with Denny. Joley would have to be happy for everyone. She pressed a hand to her churning stomach. The feeling of dread deepened and she felt sick. A dark shadow slid over her, played over the rocks and trail as a vulture circled lazily. Joley glanced up to see the bird gliding with languid intent in a large circle over the area.

She could see the morning sun glistening off the feathers, the dark underbelly and the fringe as the bird passed overhead. This time the shadow stretched and magnified, casting a bizarre image on the red rock. With the sun shining through, the rock looked like deep blood flowing through the vulture's blackened shadow. With the feathering wing tips and the beak and talons, Joley looked at a specter of death.

She stumbled to a halt and studied the ominous shadow. The bad feeling in the pit of her stomach grew stronger. Something was wrong. Very wrong. Her eyes scanned the area around her, and for the first time she became completely aware that she was alone, unprotected by her usual security.

140

Nerves tightening, she turned and began jogging back toward the parking lot, this time careful to stay to the center of the trail where she could see anything coming at her from either side. Trees, rocks and brush lined the winding path. An attacker could hide in any number of places. Movement caught her eye, leaves swaying against the slight wind as she ran past a sprawling rock formation. Again the bird circled above her, casting its shadow wide.

Joley kept running, hearing the rhythm of life change around her. The sound of the soles of her shoes echoed the beat of her pounding heart. She heard the wind whistling and leaves rustling. The sharp eyes of the bird seemed filled with evil malice, and the shadow spread wider against the red rock, reaching out to surround her.

She spun around in a circle, unable to shake the feeling of eyes watching her, of evil stalking her. It was a blessing and a curse to feel things, and right now she felt like a hunted rabbit. She took off running again, watching the trail, staying loose and ready, knowing the feeling could be caused by anything from one of her stalkers to a photographer watching with a long-range lens.

'Stupid, stupid, stupid,' she hissed under her breath as she rounded a turn. The trail narrowed here, and brush encroached close to the walkway, allowing anyone to conceal himself and jump out at an unwary runner. She picked up her pace, but she was heading downhill and it was dangerous to run too fast.

She was fairly certain the series of switchback bends marked about the halfway point to the bottom of the trail. Rounding the second curve with a smooth, perfect rhythm, she felt she'd managed to hit a good stride, when she ran right into a solid body. She crashed hard, her face pressed tight against a broad chest. Arms swept around her, swinging her off her feet as she lost balance. Joley screamed and brought her thumbs down hard in a stabbing motion for the person's exposed throat, but he had already dropped his chin and covered the spot.

She knew him the moment she inhaled – the moment she got past fear and felt his familiar body, the iron strength in his arms. He was covered in a fine sheen of sweat. He'd been out running, too. Ilya set her on the ground, steadying her, but keeping her close to him.

'Are you okay?'

She licked her lips, taking in his tousled hair, the raw arousal in his eyes, his heavily muscled chest and arms stretching his thin black tee. His narrow waist and hips, the thick bulge in the front of his jeans ... Her mouth went dry, and a thousand butterflies took flight in her stomach. Her body went damp in instant arousal.

His melody sang to her of heat and fire and passion. She felt the notes, heard them racing through her bloodstream, singing in her ears. Beckoning. Seducing. Whispering to her with such erotic promise she could barely think with wanting him.

'You ran into me,' she accused indignantly, trying to hide the excitement seeing him always brought. The tension was still in her from the edgy, ominous signs the shadow of the bird had brought, but it was being taken over by a completely different tension. She caught at his arms to keep contact more than to

142

keep upright, although her knees seemed a little weak. Her palm was itching like mad, burning even, to match the burning emptiness begging to be filled between her legs.

'Actually you ran into me. I heard you coming at the last moment and caught you.' He looked around as if expecting to see someone. 'Is your bodyguard having a hard time keeping up with you?'

She made a face at him. 'You know very well he isn't with me, and I don't appreciate your sarcasm at all.' She might be frowning, but as always, when he was near, her body reacted – or maybe it was her soul, because her mouth went dry, her heart beat too fast, and she could hear a strange roaring in her ears. All she wanted to do was slip her hands beneath the thin material stretching over the hard muscles of his chest and lift her face up to his to taste his hot, sinfully seductive mouth again.

His melody shifted, introducing dominant notes, needy and urgent and full of demand. The song pulsed with the same heat and smoldering fire, but this time leapt with the force of an erupting volcano, a demand she couldn't ignore, one that ignited flames in her belly until she craved his kiss beyond all imagination.

It was more than want. She *needed* to kiss him. Needed to feel his mouth on hers, his hands running over her body. She needed to be skin to skin. She licked her lips again, imagining what he might do if she knelt right there and unzipped his tight jeans. Would that famous control of his simply disappear? She desperately wanted his control to slip so she could see that he was as shaken by his reaction to her, as she was by hers to him.

Dark lust flickered and burned in the depths of his

eyes. He simply lifted her, taking her right off the trail into the shelter of the rocks. He didn't say a word, but trapped her body between his and the towering shelf of sandstone, his mouth coming down on hers. Hot. Hard. Ravaging. *Perfect*. Absolute perfection. Heat burst through her. Music hummed in her veins. Her heart drummed a tune that echoed the throbbing in her deepest core. Joley had no thought other than that she was well and truly lost.

She wrapped her arms around his neck, and his mouth still fastened to hers, he lifted her, half sitting her on a narrow shelf. Joley locked her legs around him, aligning her body with his so that she could feel the hot, hard thickness of him pressing against her. Her nipples tightened, breasts aching and swollen as she melted into him. Her hips moved in a slow, erotic swirl, rubbing her body against his heavy erection. God help her, he felt like home to her.

She gave herself up to him. Offered herself even knowing he would destroy her. There was something more than physical magic, more than pure chemistry; her soul, as stupid and as corny as it sounded, touched his. Her brain that always ran at high speed and prevented her from sleep, that horrible turmoil always raging inside of her – all of it stilled when she was near Ilya.

The moment her mouth touched his, he was inside of her, in her mind, wrapping himself in her thoughts, touching each erotic image and enhancing it with his own. She was stunned by the heat rushing through her, the flames dancing over her skin and in her belly, the tingling in her thighs and the naked longing in her feminine core.

His hand slid under her shirt, cupping the underside of her breast, sending a wave of liquid fire rushing between her legs. The silken wall of small muscles tightened in anticipation, and her song harmonized completely with his until she couldn't tell one from the other.

It was Ilya who pulled away, not putting space between their bodies, but lifting his head inches from hers and running his hands down her arms until he found her hands. His fingers tangled with hers, and he rested his forehead against hers, struggling to get his breathing under control.

'You aren't helping me at all.'

'I know.' Her voice came out a husky whisper, maybe even an invitation, but she couldn't help it. 'I'm sorry.' But she doubted if that was true.

'You aren't ready and I'm trying to be noble. Nobility isn't my strong suit, Joley, so you've got to help me out. Otherwise, we'll spend hours in bed and you'll roll over hating me and hating yourself. You have to know I'm the one. You have to accept me as your other half.'

'You've been seducing me for months,' she reminded him, trying to absolve herself of the guilt. 'With your voice. You know I'm susceptible to sound and you use that against me.' It was a pathetic accusation and she knew it. She wasn't helpless, she hadn't even tried to stop him. He'd mesmerized her so completely she hadn't even turned to her sisters for help, not seriously. She wanted him – lusted after him – was consumed by her obsession with him. She grasped at that. 'Obsession is not love.'

His blue eyes were dark with arousal. 'I don't give a damn what it is, Joley. I don't care what you call it. Love, lust, obsession, need, whatever. We belong. That's all that matters. We fit. You're mine and I'm yours, and there doesn't need to be an endless discussion on the subject. We are. Once you accept that, we'll be fine.'

'I don't tease men, Ilya, that's not what I'm trying to do.'

'I know that.'

'Why is it like this between us? We're so obviously wrong for each other.'

He pressed a kiss to her forehead. 'We're so obviously right, even our songs merge.'

That startled her. 'You do see melodies.'

'And colors. Yours are all over mine.'

She shook her head. 'No, if that were true, I wouldn't be so afraid. Your colors cover mine until I don't know where one of us starts and the other leaves off.'

He kissed her again, long and hard and heart-stoppingly slow. 'We have to get somewhere safe, Joley. If we stay here alone, this isn't going to turn out the way either of us wants. I'll race you down the mountain.'

'No way. I don't like losing, and it doesn't take a genius to see that you're in good shape. We'll go, but casually, no hurry, no competing.' She circled his neck with her arms and pulled his head back to hers, kissing him one last time, savoring the taste of him.

Ilya didn't take over. He let her direct the kiss, explore his mouth, caress the nape of his neck with her fingertips. When she pulled away, they looked at each other.

Joley smiled. 'You taste good.'

'We have to get out of here,' he reiterated, tugging at her hand to urge her back onto the trail.

Her smile widened. He definitely was as affected

by her kiss as she was his. She didn't say anything else as they took off running, side by side. Ilya allowed her to set the pace, keeping up easily. She was very aware of him beside her, the smooth way his muscles rippled beneath his shirt, the way the wind ruffled his thick hair, the swing of his arms and his steady breath. Their melodies merged, just as their auras always seemed to when they were close. Joley actually slowed her pace in order to prolong her time with him.

Ilya seemed content to jog beside her quietly. He made no attempt to talk and she was grateful. He was right. She wasn't ready to commit herself to a relationship with him, she had too many doubts about what and who he was, yet she was the one always flinging herself at him, and that was as humiliating as it was disturbing.

They were nearly walking as they rounded the last bend, which opened to a long straight stretch to the beginning of the trail below them. People milled around, and yellow tape surrounded the rocks about halfway down near the bottom and off to the left side.

Joley slowed her pace and caught at Ilya's arm. 'Something's wrong; that's a medical examiner's van.'

'It doesn't look good.' He caught her hand when she would have headed down toward the commotion. 'Don't. Let me check it out first.'

'It could be one of the band members or my crew. We're practically the only ones here.' Her mouth was dry. Something terrible had happened here. She felt violent energy swirling through the rocks. Auras were dark and subdued. The medical examiner's van was parked to one side along with several sheriff cars.

Ilya walked with her toward the officers and security people milling outside the tape. She gripped his arm tightly as a man dressed in a gray suit approached them.

'Miss Drake? Joley Drake?'

'Yes. Tell me what happened.' She couldn't stop the anxiety in her voice.

'One of your crew has been killed – murdered. My name is James Branscomb, I'm a detective. I'd like to ask you a few questions.'

She wished she could say the murder came as a complete surprise, but with the sick dread weighing so heavily on her, she had expected trouble. She glanced at Ilya. As usual, his expression was unreadable, the calm mask in place, but he had to have known, had to have felt the deep, violent disturbance permeating the amphitheater, just as she had.

'Who? Who was killed?' Unknowingly she stepped closer to Ilya.

He pulled her beneath his shoulder. 'I'm Ilya Prakenskii – bodyguard. We've been running up the trail and have no idea what's going on. If you could fill us in, we'd be grateful.' He glanced around, his eyes sharp. 'You've got several paparazzi here, Detective. Perhaps we should get Miss Drake into her bus and away from the photographers.' His voice made the suggestion a command.

The detective's eyes narrowed, but he nodded. 'We'll talk inside the bus then.'

Ilya slid his arm around Joley's waist, keeping her beneath the protection of his shoulder, his body shielding hers, sheltering her face from long-range lenses as he started her moving past the yellow tape.

'I want to know who it is,' Joley insisted.

'A man by the name of Dean Walters.' The detective watched her with shrewd eyes.

Joley's breath caught in her lungs. 'Dean? I just saw him. Before my run. He was angry with me.'

'You spoke to him?'

Ilya kept Joley moving. She seemed stunned. Ilya wanted to be able to watch the cop, to feel his emotions as he questioned Joley, but until he got her in a safe place, he couldn't do that. He didn't want to take a chance on prying eyes, or worse, a photographer, recording Joley's emotions and making money off her distress. And he didn't trust the cop, or anyone for that matter, not to take advantage of the fact that Joley was a high-profile celebrity. He yanked open the door to the bus and almost pushed Joley inside before she could answer. He kept his body between hers and the detective's.

Joley flung herself into a chair and covered her face for a moment. When she looked up, the detective was seated across from her and Ilya was pulling water bottles from the refrigerator. He handed one to her, offered one to the detective, who declined, and took one himself.

'I'm sorry, what did you ask me?' Joley said. 'I can't seem to take this in. Did someone identify the body? When did this happen? I just saw him, before I took off for my run. He was in the parking lot, heading over to his bus. Are you absolutely certain it's Dean?'

'Yes. I'm sorry,' Branscomb said. 'Several members of your band came forward and positively identified him. You said he was angry with you.'

Joley nodded and rubbed at the relentless pounding in her temples. 'I have a rule about minors partying with any band or crew member. It's actually written into the contract they sign with us when we go on the road. After the show in New York, I went out to a party to deliver a message to one of the band members, and I saw a group of girls who looked too young to be there. Dean was with one of them. He had his arm around her, and when I called out to him, they took off running.'

'How old was this girl?'

Joley sighed. 'Thirteen, I later found out. I was going to talk to him about it, but in all honesty, with the traveling and everything else going on, I didn't have a chance and even forgot about it until Chicago. A woman came up to me after the concert and said her daughter had been missing since my show in New York. She handed me a photograph, and I swear, it's the same girl.' She looked around the bus. 'It's here somewhere.'

Ilya retrieved the photograph from the stand by the bed and handed it to the detective. He didn't want to draw attention, so he did what he did best, faded into the shadows and masked his presence with a small, influential push to keep the detective from really noticing him.

'I called the police in New York, and the girl was still missing, so I asked my manager, Jerry St. Ives, and one of the band members, Brian Rigger, to find Dean and ask him about the girl when we reached Red Rocks this morning, before the crew set up. I told Jerry, if Dean had violated our agreement and invited this girl to the party, he was to be fired.'

'So they both talked to him this morning.'

Joley nodded. 'I got ready for my run and stepped off the bus. Tish, the wife of my sax player, had just arrived and I haven't seen her for some time, so I went over to say hello. I saw Brian, Jerry and Dean talking together. They were standing over by the stage. I couldn't hear what was said, but Dean was angry and he kept looking over at me. Eventually he flipped me off and walked to the parking lot. I went for my run, and the last I saw of Dean, he was alone, over by the crew bus.'

Ilya stepped out of the shadows. 'I observed them as well. He was angry and he stalked off toward his bus. I didn't hear what was said, but he was evidently quite upset at Miss Drake.'

'Did your manager fire him?'

Joley leaned her head against the back of the couch. Her headache was getting worse. 'I don't know. I haven't had a chance to talk to Jerry about it. I wanted to get in a run before the sound check, and this morning was my only opportunity.'

'Did you see the argument becoming heated?'

Joley took a deep breath and let it out. 'It got loud, yes. But if you think either Jerry or Brian could have harmed Dean, you're wrong. They just aren't like that.' She frowned at the detective, leaning forward so that he would look her directly in the eye. 'I've known Brian forever and he doesn't have a mean bone in his body. And Jerry has too much authority over everyone to have to resort to murder. You didn't say what happened. Could it have been an accident?'

'He was shot between the eyes. No, ma'am, I don't think we could call it an accident. Do you know if Rigger or St. Ives own a gun?'

'No. God, no. I'm telling you, they would never do something like that – kill Dean, I mean. Brian is incredibly gentle and Jerry just plain wouldn't bother.'

'And you never talked to Walters?'

Joley shook her head. 'No. And when I saw he was so angry, I didn't want to.' She pressed her fingers to her temples again. 'I really have a headache. I've never had one this bad.'

Ilya studied her pale face. The headache was worsening. It was essential to keep a low profile, but he couldn't stand by and watch Joley suffer needlessly, not when he could help her. With a small sigh, he moved from the shadows, sat down beside her and turned her face toward his. He rested the pads of his fingers on either side of her head. 'You're pale, Joley. Do you get migraines?'

'Not as a rule,' she admitted. 'But occasionally. This one is bad.' And getting worse by the moment. It made her feel vulnerable in front of the detective. Already, her stomach was churning and little white dots flashed in front of her eyes.

'Just close your eyes. This won't take more than a moment.'

Ilya sighed to himself. Even with the ability to fade the detective's memories, Branscomb would remember this. Joley was too famous, too beautiful and sexy not to make an impact. A bodyguard ridding her of her headache was something too intimate not to be noted. And Ilya couldn't touch her without being intimate. His hands were that little bit too gentle. His touch more of a caress than anything else. This was the reason a man like Ilya Prakenskii didn't get involved emotionally, because in the end, it was dangerous to both of them.

Inwardly he cursed, but he maintained his expressionless mask. He couldn't hide the body language warning the other man off, or the gentleness of his own touch, but his face gave nothing away as he placed his fingers at her temples and pushed healing energy from his soul to hers. Healing was intimate – giving Joley a part of himself, taking a part from her.

Better, laskovaya moya?

Joley nodded. 'Thank you, it's much better.'

Ilya glanced at the detective. Shrewd eyes. Cops eyes. Ilya recognized that look.

'You two went running,' Branscomb said, his voice almost casual.

'Running keeps me in shape,' Ilya said, 'and allows us a small measure of time alone together.' He picked up Joley's hand and ran his thumb over the back of it.

'You have an accent. Are you Russian?'

'Yes.'

Beside him, Joley stirred. 'I need to talk with Brian and Jerry. Where are they?'

The detective closed his notebook. 'Mr. Rigger and Mr. St. Ives both agreed to come down to the station and give their statements. Mr. St. Ives insisted on bringing an attorney, but stated they would both cooperate fully.'

'This sounds terrible, but we either have to do the show tonight or cancel on all these people, and we have to pull out tonight to make it to Dallas on time for that concert.'

'Our forensic people will be working as fast as they can. I've got officers taking statements from everyone. Obviously if we can allow you to go ahead with the performance, it would be better for everyone, so we'll do our best.'

'Thank you,' Joley said, 'although to be honest, it seems horrible to put on a show after someone is murdered.'

The detective rose, taking the photograph of the

missing girl with him. 'Do you know if Mr. Walters was in any way involved with the mob – specifically the Russian mob?' He asked the question of Joley, but he studied Ilya with his cop's eyes.

'No, but I didn't know him very well. He's been working with us on and off for two years, but we never had much contact. He had a couple of close friends in the crew. I couldn't tell you who they are, although I might recognize them if I saw them.' And she was going to look, because there'd been a crew member with Dean that night in New York. She hadn't seen his face, but she'd seen his aura – and fragments of his melody. 'Why do you ask about the Russian mob?'

'There were things done to him that are fairly signature mob, things warning others to play ball or else.'

Joley glanced at Ilya, took a deep breath and exhaled. 'In New York, the party was held by a man named Sergei Nikitin. He surrounds himself with armed guards, and I believe most of them are Russian.'

'Do you know Mr. Nikitin?' Branscomb asked Ilya.

'Of course. I work for him often in my capacity as a bodyguard. He's a businessman with powerful enemies.'

'Do his enemies include the Russian mob?'

'You would have to ask him that,' Ilya said.

Branscomb took a few steps down the corridor. 'Thank you for your time, Miss Drake. As for your performance tonight, hopefully we'll have an answer for you within the next hour.'

'We'll need to do sound checks,' Joley said.

'There's no reason not to. You won't be in the

crime scene area. He was killed where we found him. I do want to speak to every one of your crew.'

'I'll tell them to cooperate fully with you.'

'I would appreciate that.' Branscomb turned back, his hand on the door. 'Miss Drake. Is there a reason Dean Walters might want to harm you?'

Joley's heart jerked. She remembered the malevolent look he'd shot her as he walked toward the crew bus. There had been genuine, naked hatred on his face. 'Harm me?' she echoed, fear tugging at her.

'It looked as if he were heading up the running path after you. Several people mentioned he watched you take off running and that you were alone. They were worried about your lack of security.' His gaze flicked to Ilya. 'And he had a knife.'

Branscomb had known all along they hadn't left together. Ilya had to give him points for that. Of course suspicion would fall on him. He was Russian. He was a bodyguard and very strong. He knew that Dean's death had been a hit, and Nikitin had probably ordered it; he just didn't know why. He had known the body was there. He'd felt the dark, violent energy and gone to investigate, worried for Joley. Fortunately he'd approached the area from above, and he'd seen the body and the mess that had been made of it. Walters had died of a bullet to the head, but they'd stomped every bone in his body first.

Ilya remained silent, waiting for Joley to give him up. He prepared himself for Joley's betrayal. He shouldn't look at it that way. She would think she had to tell the exact truth, and maybe there wasn't anything else for her to do. But the thought of being handcuffed and taken in, and his past brought up to further cast doubt on him in the midst of his investigation, was doubly dangerous.

Joley flicked a glance from Ilya to the detective. It was very obvious where he was going with his questioning. She put a hand on Ilya's arm, her mouth suddenly dry, heart pounding. There was a strange roaring in her ears. Ilya couldn't have killed Dean Walters. He couldn't have. She would have known the moment she touched him. Yes, he was violent, and yes, he had killed, but under what circumstances she didn't know, and right now it didn't matter because he hadn't killed Walters. She trusted her instincts, and her instincts said, not even for her had he done this.

'It's difficult to have a relationship with someone with the paparazzi following everywhere you go and photographing your every move. The things they print – all the lies and innuendos – it ruins any chance at a real bond. We try to be careful so we have the opportunity to build a foundation before it's all over the media and we're both hounded into the ground.'

Her voice was soft, persuasive, held a note of pure truth the detective couldn't fail to respond to. Ilya didn't even know if she was aware of the compulsion buried in it. His hand slid against hers, fingers tangling and then enveloping with hers. He brought her knuckles up to his mouth. *Thank you*.

He knew she was protecting him, implying, without saying it, that he had joined her immediately. No one had ever done that for him, stood in front of him, not at their own risk – and she was risking a lot. If Branscomb discovered she was shielding Ilya by deliberately misleading the detective, there was no doubt he'd haul her into his office and make life very uncomfortable for her.

Ilya was fairly certain that strange sensation in his chest was his heart melting. She yanked emotion out of him when all feeling had been buried so deep he'd thought – he'd hoped – it was lost for all time. He loved her in that moment, yet at the same time, a part of him was terrified that she could do that to him, and that part was dangerous and cunning and hated her, because anyone who could make him that vulnerable held power over him – endless power – and he had vowed that would never happen again in his lifetime.

She turned her head and looked at him, her eyes soft and loving, twisting him up inside because she wasn't even aware of it yet. He could rule her sexually, he knew that, and he knew he could bind her to him, and that he'd always be bound to her, but this was more – way, way more than he had bargained for. Joley was more than just his – she was so deep inside of him she was a part of him – and just as she had protected him, he would protect her with his last breath.

Ilya read the cop as intelligent, and he was already cutting Joley a break. 'Nikitin sent several of his security force here to sweep the area for bombs. He's had many death threats, as has Miss Drake. And I spotted at least four photographers busily filming the argument as well as the band members from the rocks. If you can find them, they might have caught something on camera that would help.'

It was a risk – although a small one. Ilya had a way of blending into the background, making it difficult for people and lenses to spot him. As he was nearly always aware of the photographers, he found it easy enough to hide his presence from them. Branscomb deserved a little help, and in any case, he had probably already thought of it.

Branscomb nodded. 'I'll be in touch. If you think of anything more, call my number. I left my card on the table.'

Chapter Eight

The door closed behind the detective. Joley stood very still in the ensuing silence, her gaze locked on Ilya's face, her body trembling. He crossed the distance between them and put his arms around her, pulling her close. She burst into tears.

Ilya pressed her face against his chest, his fingers sliding into her hair to massage her scalp, murmuring softly to her. He didn't know where the words came from, most of it made no sense, just soothing noises, but her distress was so genuine. He hadn't known he could actually feel gentle, or tender; he'd thought those things had long ago been beaten out of him, but she brought out a softer response and he was grateful.

'You feel too much for others, Joley,' he said, pressing his lips into the soft disarray of her hair. 'This was not a good man.'

'He has family. And we don't know that he wasn't good.'

'If he had anything to do with the Russian mob, believe me, *laskovaya moya*, he wasn't good. And contrary to popular belief, members of the mob don't kill indiscriminately. If he drew their attention, he was in bed with them.' He nuzzled the top of her head, his chin sliding through the soft strands of hair. He loved holding her, and that was terrifying. She made him soft inside, different. This woman could turn him inside out with one look. And dark eyes drowning in tears were enough to turn stone into molten gold.

She sighed and turned her head so her cheek rested against him. 'Do you think he was using our band, traveling from one city to another in order to run drugs or something?'

He brushed tears from her cheeks with his fingertips. 'Or something.'

She pulled away just enough to look up at him. 'You knew he was dead, didn't you, when you came up the mountain? Did you see who did it? Do you know why?'

'If I saw who had done it, I would have told the detective and I would have called for help immediately. Do you think I had anything to do with that man's death?'

'No. No, of course not.' She wrapped one hand around the nape of his neck and rested against his solid strength. 'But the detective was suspicious, I could tell.'

'It was dangerous handing him Nikitin,' Ilya pointed out. 'Nikitin isn't kind to his enemies, and you've skated for a while on the edge of slighting him by refusing his invitations to his parties.'

'Branscomb was going to get that connection anyway,' Joley said and reluctantly pulled away from him. 'There was someone with Dean at the party. I saw him with three other men and the group of girls. One of three was another member of my crew. I recognized that I'd seen him working on the equipment, but I never saw his face. The others I'd never seen before, and I assumed they were other guests. I was hoping Dean might know the names of the other girls so the police could question them.'

'You're not thinking of finding the other man who was with Dean.' Ilya made it a statement. 'Joley, you always rush into things without thinking. You're not a cop, you're a superstar, with cameras on you every second. You can't conduct a secret investigation into a murder or a child's disappearance.'

'Well I can't just do nothing! Dean was in my crew. He worked for me. And the girl went to a party thinking she was going to party with the band. *My* band. Sarah and Elle would investigate. They'd never let it go until they found out the truth.'

'Well you aren't your sisters. Stay out of it and let the professionals handle it.' Even as he said it, her eyes flashed fire and her mouth set in a firm line. Her chin lifted a little and he cursed under his breath. Joley was a powder keg, and telling her what to do was the same as lighting a match.

'Like you? You said you were going to talk to Dean, that you were looking into that girl's disappearance.'

He had the urge to shake her. 'You're not a defiant child, rebelling against a parent. I'm telling you this is dangerous and to stay the hell out of it. What good is it going to do if you get yourself – or Brian or Jerry – killed?'

Joley paled visibly. 'Why would anyone want to kill Jerry or Brian?'

'They asked Walters questions, didn't they? Has it occurred to you that whoever killed him might not have wanted him to answer questions? He knew something and they didn't want it out, so he's dead.

This friend of his, still on your crew, is either part of what Dean was into or entirely innocent. If you question him, you could draw attention to him and the killer might think he knows something, or worse for you, if he's in on it, they might target both of you for execution.' He stepped closer to her again, catching her arm and pulling her against his body. 'You stay away from all of them. Don't ask questions and let the cops take care of it.'

Her large eyes darkened, glittering with anger, and he felt lust hit with a hard punch to the gut. His belly burned and his blood pooled hot and demanding in his groin. He bent his head, one hand anchoring in her hair, and he took her mouth, effectively stopping the protest he knew was coming. Heat spread through his body, rockets went off in his head, and colors burst behind his eyes. He pulled her closer, locking her tight against him, so that he could feel every lush curve of her soft, feminine body.

She tasted just like the honey he remembered so vividly from the beehives outside of the school where he'd spent so many years being trained. He'd stolen that, too, just as he stole his kiss from Joley. And like he'd accepted the stings he'd received as a child, he would accept whatever punishment Joley meted out, because in the end, the pleasure spreading through him at her taste, the feel of her soft skin and silky hair, the fire in her rising up to meet the fire in him made any and all retribution worthwhile.

It wasn't just sparks she gave off, it was a conflagration, and the rush was instant and consumed him. The flames devoured him so quickly he didn't have a chance for control and discipline, the two things that had been drilled – beaten – stomped into him. No woman should be able to shake his control and take over his body, but the moment he touched Joley's soft skin, felt the whisper of her warm breath against him, the touch of her lips, and tasted her, wild and addicting, he was lost.

His hands spanned her throat, tilting her head back so he could take her kiss, devour her the way he needed. Music burst through him, perfect notes he rarely heard. Fire and ice, wind and calm, sky and earth, water and rock all fused together. Joley seemed as wild and turbulent as the sea, yet beneath her fiery passion, at the very core of her, she was as forceful and strong and as constant as the deepest ocean currents. Ilya seemed as calm as a windless sea, yet beneath the surface smoldered a volcano of such explosive magnitude, his power could easily sweep everything from his path. Together they completed each other, his melody and hers merging into a single, perfect harmony.

It took him a moment to realize the odd rhythmic note was pounding on the door, not his heart or hers out of sync. The problem with them was that everything was exactly in sync. He forced himself to pull back, to breathe through the urgent demands of his body. He had to close his eyes to keep from responding to the naked need in her eyes.

'Help me here.'

'You started it.'

'Someone's at the door.' He put her from him, noting that his hands were shaking. His famous control slipped dangerously around her. He could drown in her eyes if he wasn't careful, and he definitely got lost in the taste and texture of her.

Joley nodded, her fingers touching her lips. 'I can still feel you – on my mouth – inside me. How do you do that?'

'I wish I was inside you. I ache like a son of a bitch. This has got to stop.'

Her smile flashed, just the way he'd known it would. Joley could light up the world. She certainly could chase away the shadows in his.

'If you keep·pushing me away, Ilya, we'll never get it to stop.'

'Joley!' Brian's voice insisted. 'Open up.'

Instantly her face changed. 'It's Brian. They're back from the police station.'

The anxiety in her voice was real enough to slice into Ilya like the razor edge of a knife. He wanted that anxiety for himself – not another man – not even her lead guitarist.

Joley yanked open the door and actually hauled Brian into the room and, ignoring her own long-standing rule, hugged him tight. 'I was worried about you. Are you all right? They didn't hurt you, did they?'

Ilya leaned against the wall and observed the expressions chasing across her face. She looked like a fierce angel. What did she think? That the cops had used a rubber hose on Brian? The idea was absurd that they would touch him, not as famous as he was. And had she forgotten he'd had a lawyer with him?

Damn it. He couldn't stay here smoldering and drawing even more attention to himself. With some effort he managed to look and walk normally as he slipped past them. To his annoyance, Joley didn't do more than wave as he shut the door.

Brian watched Ilya go, a slight frown on his face as he turned back to Joley. 'I'm fine. It was uncomfortable, but we got through it.'

'I'm so sorry I asked you to talk to Dean in the

164

first place. I should have done it.'

'It didn't help that we had an argument right before someone murdered him, but I've never owned a gun in my life and don't even know how to fire one.' Brian shrugged. 'I just told the truth. I told them you'd asked me to speak to him about the missing girl and inviting teens to parties and hoped they believed me.'

'The cops told Jerry we can do the show tonight,' Brian added with some relief. 'They let us both go. I got here as fast as I could to do the sound check and Jerry's ordered the crew to break everything down fast after the show so we can get on the road as soon as possible.' Brian ran both hands through his hair. 'Man, I freaked when the FBI agent showed up.'

'FBI?' Joley echoed. 'What's that about?'

'Branscomb said they were a small town and the local FBI was giving them a hand.' Brian sighed. 'I never want to do that again. They asked me the same questions over and over, and I began to think I was saying something wrong.'

'What exactly did happen between you and Dean?' Joley asked. 'Tish didn't want me going over there just in case someone was taking video. I should have though.'

'You would have made it worse. He was furious and told us we didn't have any right to tell him who he could or couldn't see. He didn't remember her name, but he said, and I'm quoting here, "She wanted it."'

Joley groaned. 'Damn that man. He had to have known she was a child. Give her alcohol and she'd say anything he wanted to hear.'

'Well, if you were looking for remorse, he didn't

165

have any, and he could have cared less that the girl was missing. Jerry's pretty hard, but Dean's cavalier attitude that the girl was still missing got to him. Jerry fired him and Dean said all kinds of things about you, which pissed me off.' Brian showed her his knuckles, looking a bit sheepish. 'I haven't hit anyone since eighth grade. I had to tell the cop I hit him, and believe me, that didn't sound so good when the guy ends up dead.'

'Did they ask you about the Russian mob?'

He nodded. 'After our conversation about Nikitin I was worried. And a few of his men have been hanging around here checking things out.'

'I was running with Ilya Prakenskii,' Joley said. 'He gets upset when I don't take a bodyguard with me.' She was careful to watch him closely just in case he'd observed Ilya leaving after her.

'That's good, at least we know he didn't do it.' Brian frowned at her. 'Your face changes when you talk about him. Do you two have something going on?'

'I don't want to talk about him.'

Brian scowled at her. 'Oh, you so have something going on with the bodyguard. Isn't that against the personal protector code or something?'

Joley knew she looked guilty. 'He's not my bodyguard and we're not in a relationship. We're just sort of dancing around the idea.'

'Look, Joley,' he said, rubbing the bridge of his nose and peering at her. 'I'll admit he's got some kind of mesmerizing cobra-before-the-strike appeal, but you can't be serious. And before you go all crazy on me, you remember you told me to say something the next time I saw you going off the deep end for a loser.' He held up his hand. 'And don't say he's not a loser. Maybe he's not a pill-popping, woman-beating asshole, but he's the kind of man who would strangle you with his bare hands if you weren't faithful to him.'

Outrage swept through her. 'I have *never* cheated on anyone. *Never*.'

'There you go, losing your mind. I knew you would. I meant to point out what kind of man he is, not what kind of woman you are.'

Joley threw her arms up into the air, signaling she'd had enough of the conversation. 'Let's go,' she said. 'We have to talk to everyone and settle them down for the show. Everyone has to be freaked.'

'Logan was afraid Tish might leave, but she's not like that. She's steady as a rock,' Brian said, stepping aside so Joley could exit the bus first.

Lights immediately blinded her as cameras went off all around them. Hands caught at her, tearing at her clothes. She was jerked off the stairs and she nearly fell, catching herself at the last moment. A hard hand shoved her in the back, propelling her forward and down. She fell hard, Brian's shout mingling with the questions coming from all around her. She caught a glimpse of the Reverend's body-guard disappearing to the back of the swarm, malicious satisfaction on his face.

Flashes went off as she pushed herself off the ground. One cameraman crouched beside her as if to help her up. 'Are you and Brian a couple? Are you seeing each other?' He thrust a recorder closer to her.

'Joley!' Brian called to her, clearly trying to get through the mass surrounding her.

More flashes went off. 'You're all such gentlemen,' she murmured under her breath, wishing she had Hannah's powers. She'd turn them all into toads – well, maybe Hannah couldn't exactly turn them into big, ugly, wart-covered toads, but she might be able to pull off the warts. She rarely went anywhere anymore, not even with her sisters, unless she was in her hometown, where the people protected her. This was her life, every second recorded and photographed until there seemed nothing left for her.

Large hands caught at her and yanked her to her feet, setting her up against a hard body. Ilya dragged her beneath his shoulder, his long arm covering her head, and caught at Brian with his other arm, pulling him in his wake as he began to walk them through the pushing and shoving photographers. His eyes were twin glittering diamond chips, hard and burning with fire. He kept moving even when photographers got in his way, wading through them as if they weren't there. He never responded to their questions or taunts, just took Joley and Brian through the mass toward the stage.

Security swarmed around them in the form of police officers, men who worked as security in off-duty hours. They began shepherding the reluctant paparazzi out of the area while Joley's crew formed a line across the entrance to the stage, blocking the cameramen off so Ilya could get the two of them to safety.

'Are you hurt?' Ilya asked, moving faster as the cops took control. He kept his voice low. 'Tell me if you're injured.'

Joley realized she was shaking. 'I'm just angry. I tore my jeans and skinned my knees and hands. RJ's bodyguard shoved me down. I'll bet he got them in.'

'What about you, Brian?' Ilya asked. 'Are you hurt?'

'Just my pride. I saw Joley go down and couldn't get to her. It's like that anywhere she goes. It's bad, but not like that for the rest of us. She can't get a cup of coffee or go out without them mobbing her. I should have been able to protect her.'

'That rotten coward set me up,' Joley bit out between her teeth. 'I'm *so* going to get him back.' She was struggling not to cry, not wanting to admit how terrifying that couple of minutes had been, lying vulnerable and exposed on the ground surrounded by a mob.

The crew opened their line and allowed the three of them onto the stage. As they made it to safety Ilya let go of Brian and turned to fully face Joley, his hands on her arms. 'You leave RJ's people to me. This is getting out of hand and you need to be safe, Joley. If RJ is trying to harm you and his people are using the paparazzi to do it, you can't give him any openings.'

His eyes swept over her, taking in the torn jeans and the smears of dirt on her clothing. She was trembling. His hands fit around her waist, and he lifted her to the platform where Denny's drums were assembled.

'He's right, Joley,' Brian said. 'That was plain scary. Anyone could have stuck a knife in you and no one would have known until it was too late. There were too many of them. You went down so fast, and their instincts weren't to help; they all wanted pictures of you on the ground. I'll bet the headlines are going to say you were drunk or doing drugs.'

Joley wanted to smash something. That was part of the problem with her life – there were aspects that were so out of control – and she had lost her sense of humor over it. She had money, lots of it, more than she could ever need in her lifetime. She had put it to good use, of course; she had Libby for a sister, and Libby made certain they were all very aware of every environmental issue as well as humanitarian one. But money didn't get her freedom; in fact, just the opposite. The higher she'd risen in fame, the narrower her world had become the fewer people she could trust.

She loved singing and she loved performing, but she hadn't been able to strike enough of a balance with the paparazzi to get them to give her some space, and she was drowning. For the second time in her career, she was considering quitting – giving it all up. She had no idea what she'd do, but the life was making her physically ill. She couldn't sleep at all anymore, and even her intense exercise was no longer helping.

Ilya's hands were warm on her knees, and she knew he was healing the small scrapes. His energy was strong. She felt his heat, and for one moment white light burst through his darkened aura. She glimpsed a multitude of colors, and then the shadows drew across him like a veil, closing his real character off to her, although she felt she was beginning to see the real Ilya through all the little glimpses.

'Thanks.' Her voice was too intimate, and she saw Brian glance at her sharply. She cleared her throat and tried again. 'Thanks for getting us out of there, Ilya, I – we really appreciate it. We've got to get moving on the sound check. We've only got a couple of hours before the performance tonight. Where's Jerry?'

'Right here.' Jerry came up behind her. 'Are you all right?'

She nodded. 'Did security clear them all out of here?'

'For now.' Jerry stuck out his hand to Ilya. 'Thanks for helping out. I'd like to talk to you later if you can spare a couple of minutes.' He waved his hand around to encompass the scene. 'I'm busy right now, but can we get together after this?'

Ilya nodded.

Joley slid off the platform, brushing at the dirt on her clothes. 'Jerry, call everyone in. We need to talk about what happened . . .' Beside her, Ilya stirred, not physically – he didn't move a muscle – but she felt the impact of his reprimand mentally. She sighed. 'To settle everyone down before the performance.'

As if I have to explain myself to you. I don't need your approval for anything. But she had explained, and that made her angry at herself. She was getting used to his domineering ways, which meant he was wearing down her defenses.

She sent Ilya a snippy look and turned back to the business at hand. 'These people have paid money to see us, and we need to be able to deliver a good show if we're going on tonight.'

Ungrateful little wretch.

He simply reached for her hand and slid his thumb across her palm. Her body nearly convulsed with pleasure. Shivers slid down her spine; her womb spasmed and her nipples tightened. He sent her the impression of a wicked smirk even though his expression remained absolutely impassive. And then he walked away.

Joley lost her train of thought. She simply stood there with her mouth open and her heart pounding and her body throbbing with urgent need. Damn him. He always seemed to get in the last word. She rubbed her itching palm against her thigh. Maybe not. She lifted her hand to her mouth, rounded her lips to press them tight against her palm, took a long slow lick right over the center and followed it with a sensuous scraping of her teeth along the skin.

Ilya stumbled. His perfectly graceful, fluid walk faltered and he nearly tripped over his own feet. He glanced over his shoulder at her, and she flashed her sweetest smile. Suddenly feeling very good about things, she turned her attention to the assembling crew and band members, leaving Ilya to think about how she could even things out.

The little minx. Ilya walked a short distance away and draped his large body in a casual pose against the wall, crossing his arms and trying to ease the aching discomfort in the front of his jeans. He'd handed her a hell of a weapon to use against him. He was sporting the biggest hard-on he'd ever had, and he'd had a few. Back in school they'd used very talented women to train him. The idea was stay in control, and when he didn't, the consequences had been immediate, painful and dire.

In one stroke of her tongue, Joley had wiped out years of brutal training. He'd felt her lips suddenly close over him, her tongue stroke down the hard length of him, teeth just barely scraping, and he'd nearly burst out of his jeans. The woman learned fast, and she was just mean enough to use her knowledge. Keeping the upper hand with her wasn't going to be as easy as he'd thought. He willed the blood in his veins to cool to a slow, simmering boil while he stood there watching with hawk eyes the crowd around her.

He could handle sex. Any kind of sex with any woman, and he would stay in complete control; his years of training had seen to that. But he was finding out – much to his horror – that emotion – real emotion – changed everything and made sex something far beyond what he'd ever been shown or taught. There was no controlling his desire or his body when his heart was involved. Damn her, she'd turned his life upside down, turned the very foundations of his life from hard rock to sand. His need for Joley had turned the pleasurable act of sex into something altogether different. Now he knew why people used the phrase 'falling in love.' The drop was long and scary.

Joley was all too aware of Ilya. He made every nerve ending in her body come alive. Her soul sang to his. It was corny, but true. And his answered. She didn't know what that meant exactly, only that she was hyperaware of him and the fact that his aura was drowning in lust – and *she'd* done that with one stroke of her tongue on the center of her palm. That palm that had plagued her for months. He had seemed stunned by her touch, even if it was through their weird connection. She turned that piece of information over in her mind, even as she addressed her crew. She wasn't exactly as powerless in her odd relationship with Ilya as she had always believed.

Everyone was subdued, some openly distraught and afraid. All had been questioned by the police, and a few were ambivalent about going on with the show. No one seemed terribly upset about Dean's death. He'd kept to himself for the most part, and the crew seemed to want to distance themselves from him. Maybe it was the nature of the murder – the suspicion that it had been a mob hit, and no one wanted any part of that.

She looked them over carefully, noting auras and melodies, unconsciously searching for the one that she'd glimpsed in New York with Dean. She spotted him toward the back of the pack, a swirling of brownish-green mud coated with speckles of dark gray and streaks of murky pink. The aura puzzled her, as every color was muddy and dirty. She glanced from him to Ilya, her unease difficult to hide.

'Let's give these people a concert. Whatever happened with Dean, the police will handle it. Thank you all for cooperating. The detective was able to clear us to perform, so let's get it done. I believe we have a sound check to conduct.'

The crew broke out into assents, nodding heads and talking all at once. She pulled Brian aside and nodded toward the man who was hastily ducking behind heavier equipment, clearly staying out of her way.

'Who is that?'

Brian shrugged. 'John or Jake or Joe, something with a "J." I don't know, why?'

She glanced around. Several of the crew, a few of the security people, as well as Nikitin's guards were still observing her. For all she knew, the long-range zoom lenses of the photo-graphers were watching – and she could feel Ilya's gaze boring into her back.

'No reason. I just thought maybe I should get to know the people traveling with us a little bit. We used to know everyone, and I think some of our crew have the wrong idea about me.' She pushed a hand through her hair, realized she was trembling, and put her fist behind her back. Ilya's warning had affected her more than she liked. She didn't want anyone thinking Brian knew anything he shouldn't. 'Never mind. I just don't like people thinking I'm a diva.'

Once more her gaze was pulled over toward the man with the muddy aura. She tried not to look, but she couldn't help it. And he was staring back at her with a mixture of fear and anger. He knew she recognized him. He straightened slowly, maintaining eye contact, obviously trying to intimidate her. Suddenly his gaze shifted from her to the three Russian security guards off to his left, and then to Ilya, who had come up behind her.

Ilya took her arm and pulled slightly away from Brian. 'Explain all this to me. What are you doing?' *Keep looking at me.*

She wasn't cut out for intrigue. Her eyes kept shifting toward the crew member she knew had hung out with Dean. Everyone had professed to the detective that Dean was a loner and rarely talked to any of them. That had taken on a sinister aspect when she realized everyone was afraid to be associated with him. She kept her eyes locked with Ilya's. He was so good at it, looking as casual as a coiled rattler, which was the way he always looked.

'Well, each venue where we perform has different acoustics.' She tried to keep her voice even, but it trembled.

She cleared her throat. Brian had walked off and was talking to the one of the sound crew, and the man with muddy aura walked over to him. Everything in her shifted. From scared she went into protective mode. She even took a step in their direction, but Ilya shackled her wrist, preventing her from moving.

'Keep talking. I'd like to understand.'

He kept his smile easy, although it never reached his eyes. Joley knew he was buffering her. She took a deep breath and tried to play along, even as she kept an eye on Brian. 'When I say different, I mean very different. You can hear a perfect pitch, so you're aware of sound quality. We have to make up

175

for the differences at each venue. The PA is tuned before each concert to get the system ready for a performance. Our sound engineer is very particular about his equipment, and he makes certain everything checks out before the band goes up. He always checks each instrument alone and then blended together. That gives us a rough idea how it's all going to sound for the show.'

Ilya watched out of the corner of his eye as the man who had been friends with Dean inched closer, all the while talking animatedly to Brian. Ilya had been investigating the band and crew for some time, and he knew the man's name was John Dylan. Dylan had been working on and off for the band for the last two years. He'd traveled to Europe twice with them and had a good reputation as a crew member. He showed up for work, worked hard and didn't party so hard he was hungover the next morning. Most of Ilya's inquiries had resulted in positive things. Dylan was somewhat of a loner, but well liked, hung out mainly with Dean and mostly smoked pot rather than did harder drugs.

Nothing about Dylan had singled him out as someone who would have a mob affiliation, but he was clearly trying to overhear what Joley was saying, and the look he'd shot her earlier had alarmed Ilya. Fear could make people do things they ordinarily wouldn't consider. And the Russian mob ruled with fear.

The sound engineer called out to the band. 'Let's get the instruments. Yours, Brian. Let's hear sound.'

The band was already loosely assembled. Joley started over to them, Ilya keeping close pace, his body between hers and Dylan's at all times. He glanced out over the amphitheater. 'The audience would change everything,' he observed. 'Don't they absorb some frequencies, and the sound would echo on the walls and ceilings of most buildings. In this case, the rocks.'

She nodded. 'That's why I have a genius for a sound engineer. The first two songs during the actual performance generally give him an immediate idea of what's going to happen, and he compensates for it. Are you staying for the check? You might find it interesting. Sometimes we get a few people who sneak in to listen so they can get an idea of what we're doing in the show. When I want to introduce new material into the show, or Brian or Rick has something they've worked on, we rehearse it several times during sound check before adding it in.'

She picked up the microphone and turned toward her sound engineer. He lifted a hand and Denny counted off with a drumbeat. The band instantly swung into a familiar song, one that had been a number one hit for weeks on end and was always in demand. Ilya listened, but his gaze was moving over the crew members, yet always keeping Nikitin's security guards in his vision as well. He wanted to know if they even went close to Dylan. The crew member appeared to be concentrating on his job, crouched down back behind the sound engineer. The last notes of the song died away.

'Everyone okay with levels? Okay with guitar, Brian?'

Brian nodded. 'Good here. Joley, let's try the new number.'

She lifted the microphone to her mouth and smiled at Ilya. His heart nearly stopped beating. She was hazardous to herself as well as to everyone around him. Any woman who could make him forget he was surrounded by danger, by cameras, by the damned Russian mob, was truly dangerous. 'I hope you like this one. I wrote it.'

She glanced at Denny, who immediately went into action, his drumsticks twirling and then pounding down in a dynamic burst of powerful rhythm. The guitar came in, the music aggressive, and then Joley's voice broke over them, passionate and intense and drowning in a sultry melody of notes. When she stopped, there was a small silence.

'Is everyone okay with everything? Are we good?' Joley turned to survey the band.

Ilya let out his breath. They were used to her, but her voice still got to all them – he could tell by the short pause.

'A little more bass,' the sound engineer finally said. 'Can you give me a little more, Rick?'

Denny picked up a glass and swallowed the contents. 'I'm having a little trouble hearing.'

Each instrument performed a long solo until it received a thumbs-up from the sound engineer. He then nodded to Joley. She swung into the next number, one, Ilya noted, that they sang often. They moved back and forth between the well-known numbers they were familiar with and the newer numbers, to ensure that everything was perfect for their audience.

The natural acoustics of the place were incredible. He watched Joley perform. Her love of music showed in the way she poured herself into every song. Joy was on her face, in her eyes, in the color of her aura. She had a loving relationship, more like siblings, with the band, and an easy, familiar relationship with her sound crew. The others she might not know so well, but those traveling with her obviously cared about her in the same way she cared for them.

'That's it,' she said, coming up to him. 'We run through our song list once and hopefully nothing goes wrong tonight. What did you think?'

He thought she was the most beautiful, vibrant woman alive, but he merely nodded his head and escorted her back to the bus.

Chapter Nine

Joley glanced around the small all-night diner where the buses had stopped. Her band and the crew were traveling together to Dallas in a caravan, and they'd all been hungry. They'd broken down the stage in record time and gotten on the road, still anxious over Dean's death in spite of the fact that the show had been good – not great – but good. Joley hoped they performed better in Dallas.

She walked to the largest round booth, where Denny was sitting, and put a hand on his shoulder. 'How'd it go with Lisa?' There was compassion in her voice.

The other band members went silent, waiting, willing things to have gone well for Denny. He had lines on his face that hadn't been there before.

Denny shrugged. 'We talked and I think it was good. At least she didn't just walk away from me like I deserved. But she has a son and she said she needed some time to think about us. She doesn't want him getting attached to me and then me walking out on them.'

Joley rubbed his arm through his sleeve. 'That's fair. She doesn't want to risk her son, and that's admirable. You just have to show her that you mean it, Denny. That you're capable of being faithful and committing to her and your relationship.'

'She flew back home after the Red Rocks concert. I didn't want her hanging around just in case it wasn't safe,' Denny added.

Joley slid into the booth. 'Surely whatever Dean was up to didn't have anything to do with us.'

'Whatever it was, I'm hoping it's a long way from us,' Rick said. 'I heard every single bone in his body was broken. Can I just say ouch?'

'He was an ass, but he didn't deserve that,' Jerry said.

Logan wedged himself into the booth, scooting close to Joley. 'Do you think his murder had anything to do with the disappearance of that girl? The cops were asking questions about the Russian mob. Maybe Nikitin is involved with them . . .'

'Shut up, Logan,' Brian admonished him. 'Nikitin isn't involved in the mob.'

'You ought to know,' Logan said. 'You hang out with him all time.' He plopped a stack of tabloids and magazines in front of Joley. 'Take a look at these, my little sister.'

Joley glanced around the diner. Few people were there at three in the morning, but several of the workers had cell phones with cameras and recorders. They were busy texting their friends. The band would be lucky if the place didn't fill up immediately in spite of the hour. She sighed. It didn't seem to matter where they went, they couldn't ever have a quiet meal.

She glanced at the stack of papers Logan put in front of her. 'What are we up to now?'

The rest of the band pushed into the booth,

making her grateful she'd chosen the largest, round one. Everyone peered at the dramatic headlines.

'We're married, Joley. A secret wedding with our secret baby.' He pulled one out of the stack and placed it on top. 'You had the baby and we've been hiding it.'

She laughed. 'You have to be kidding me. Your "love" child was splashed all over the papers a week ago. Let me see that.'

'Joley, you rock, girl,' Rick said, ripping open a cracker from the little basket on the table. 'How could you stay so slim and be pregnant? You hid it well.'

'Didn't I?' She spread the paper on the table so they could all see.

The photographs had been taken of the two of them standing with the baby in front of the band's bus. Joley was holding the baby and Logan was standing behind her, hands on her shoulders looking down at his child. The next picture showed him kissing the top of Joley's head. The third photograph showed Joley placing the baby in his arms, and in the fourth he was climbing into the bus to 'hide' their child.

She scanned the article. 'Wow. I supposedly had this baby while on tour. How cool is that? All that working out kept me from showing, although apparently once or twice they thought they saw a baby bump.' She looked down at her flat stomach. 'I need to do more sit-ups.'

Brian rolled his eyes. 'You've already got a six-pack there, Joley. Pretty soon the tabloids are going to say you swing both ways.'

'I think they did that a year or so ago,' Logan pointed out.

182

Joley looked around. 'Where's Tish? Has she seen this one?'

Long ago, Tish had told them all to either ignore the tabloids totally or assume every word in them was a lie and just enjoy the ridiculous absurdity of it. Looking back, Joley realized how truly sage her advice had been. Living in the spotlight, with no letup, was an exercise in endurance. It made them all immensely popular, but in the end, they had all begun to crack. They'd come to feel like hunted animals, stalked every moment of every day. Tish had also told them they had to find ways to live out of the spotlight when they weren't touring, which had been one of the things that saved them all. Her advice was one of many things Joley missed about her.

'She just changed the baby, but she's coming.'

'Well, make room for her. I don't want to be the only chick at the table.'

Logan pulled another paper from the stack and smoothed it out in front of them all. 'Yes, Tish has seen the tabloids, and this one is her particular favorite.'

The band members crowded closer, hovering over each other's shoulders to peer down at the magazine.

'Wow, Joley,' Denny said. 'Check it out. You've always wanted a ready-made family, and now you have one without ruining your figure.'

Brian whistled. 'I had no idea that was so important to you, but hey, it's right here in the headlines. You want children but don't want a matronly body.'

'Well I am just so vain.' Joley blew on her fingernails.

Rick pointed to another headline. 'This says child protective services are investigating you for drug and alcohol consumption, and that you left the baby in a restroom and we had to turn the buses around to go back for her. Wow, Joley, that's kind of sick.'

Leo tugged at strands of her hair. 'You were in the restroom doing one of the band members and Logan is devastated.'

'I'm sorry, Logan, but seriously, you're two-timing me with Tish, so I feel you sort of deserve it. And which band member am I doing this time?' Joley asked, leaning her chin into her hand and batting her eyes at him.

'The handsome one,' Rick said. 'Me.'

'Ooh baby,' Joley cooed and blew a kiss at him.

Laughter bubbled up as the waitress came over. She appeared starry-eyed and breathless. 'Do you think I could get an autograph? And maybe a picture with you?' she asked.

'How 'bout this, sweetheart?' Brian said. 'We'll all sign autographs for you and your crew and take pictures if the place doesn't suddenly fill up with friends, family and reporters. We'd just like a quiet meal.'

She nodded her head several times, held up a finger and ran over to the counter to whisper to the other waitress and the cook, before coming back to take their orders. The other waitress struggled with getting orders from the crew.

Joley looked around. Even with no other customers, they took up most of the room. Granted, it was a small diner, but how different this all was from how it had been in the beginning, when the band had no one but Tish traveling with them. Now there were so many ... Her gaze collided with ice-blue eyes. Her breath caught in her throat. Ilya Prakenskii stood just to the side of the booth where he could hear everything that was said. And she hadn't been aware of him. Her palm hadn't even itched – until now.

'What are you doing here?' Joley asked, trying not to stare. She didn't know whether to feel belligerent or exhilarated.

'I asked him to come,' Jerry said. 'I felt maybe we should beef security up a little around everyone until the end of the tour.'

'But he has a job,' Brian protested. 'And you should have consulted me.'

Joley ducked her head, not looking at any of them, least of all Ilya. It was scary having him around so much, because the more she saw him, the less resistance she seemed to have.

'He's on temporary loan,' Jerry said. He beckoned Ilya to sit down.

Ilya shook his head. 'I'm fine right here.'

Tish, holding the baby, squeezed in and flashed Ilya a tentative smile. 'I feel for you, trying to guard Joley. She's not the most cooperative.'

'Hey now!' Joley objected. 'I'm the epitome of cooperation.'

A groan went up around the booth.

'He's not the kind of bodyguard who needs cooperation,' Jerry said, casting Joley a hard look.

She sat up straight. 'What does that mean?'

'It means his job is to keep you safe. I'm getting gray hair reading your hate mail lately. And after Dean was murdered, I don't want to sit up nights wondering if some nut is going to kill you right in front of all of us, so I've hired him to keep you alive and told him to use whatever means it takes.'

'Umm, Jerry,' Joley said, beginning to smolder with fury. She carefully avoiding Ilya's slashing blue gaze. 'You work for me. You're supposed to clear this kind of thing with me. And it isn't cleared.'

'I had a long talk with Jonas and your sister Sarah. They both agreed we need to cover you better, especially if the Russian mob is in any way involved.'

'He's Russian,' Brian snapped. 'Nikitin probably fired him and he's been hanging around making you think we need him, Jerry. Seriously, are you crazy?'

At once Joley felt protective toward Ilya, a complete contradiction. Sometimes she felt her emotions around him were like a Ping-Pong ball, just jumping all over the place. 'Rein it in, Brian. Sheesh. The man is standing right there listening to every word you say.'

'I'm backing you up,' Brian pointed out.

'You're being mean about it. Nikitin didn't fire him, he wouldn't.' Probably for more reasons than she wanted to know, but she was certain she was right.

'Nikitin loaned him to us to keep Joley safe.'

'You know, I don't know why all of you think I'm the only one in danger. Every one of us is hanging out there.'

'Maybe because you live your life in the tabloids,' Ilya interjected, his voice low and controlled.

'That's not fair,' Brian objected. 'It's not like we ask for the paparazzi to follow us everywhere we go and make up lies.'

'It's still a choice. And this,' Ilya leaned over Joley's shoulder and snapped the paper with his finger, 'this is dangerous. There are people who believe this crap. They want to believe it and they fixate on it.'

Joley glared at him, crumpled the tabloid and

threw at him. 'You don't have to approve of my lifestyle. I don't want or need your approval.'

Brian shoved at his glass of water, spilling it on the table. 'He can't be her bodyguard, Jerry. Personal protectors can't think clearly when they're in a relationship with the protectee, and he's screwing her.'

Tish gasped audibly. The band members looked at one another. Ilya simply caught the front of Brian's shirt in his fist and hauled him over the back of the booth, bringing him up on his toes. Joley covered her face with her hands, imagining all the cells phones out, both recording and taking photos.

'You owe Joley an apology.' Ilya's voice was whisper-low, but it cut like a knife. 'You're supposed to be her friend and you're deliberately hurting her and trying to publicly humiliate her.'

Rick stood, too. 'Brian, that was way over the line.'

'Whoa, dude,' Logan added, 'if he doesn't kick your ass for that, I'm going to have to do it and I haven't kicked ass in ten years.'

Tish put her arm around Joley and glared at Brian as Ilya shoved him back to solid ground. Brian rocked back on his heels, straightened his shirt and looked at the band, who were all gaping at him in horror.

'That's not cool,' Leo weighed in.

'What the hell's gotten into you, bro?' Denny asked. 'You've been acting weird for a couple of weeks now. You pissed at Joley for something?'

Brian glared at Ilya, obviously considered trying to punch him and then changed his mind, and climbed over the booth to sit back down. 'Sorry, Joley. And I'm apologizing because it was a lousy thing to say, not because muscle man got physical.'

187

Joley didn't look at him. Other than her sisters, Tish, and Jonas, she counted Brian and the others as her best friends – more even – family. Brian had been a little off for a while now. She considered that he might be jealous of Ilya, but truthfully, Brian didn't think of her in that way. He offered, but he wasn't really attracted to her.

Tish shifted, drawing her attention. The baby was sound asleep cradled against her in an sling. Joley was grateful for the distraction. 'My sister's pregnant.'

Logan snorted and ruffled her hair. 'You have like a hundred sisters. Which one?'

'Hannah. I'm so excited for her. Jonas is walking on air, but I'll bet he's turned all bossy on her.'

Logan laughed. 'From everything you've said about him, I'm betting he was already that way.' He leaned in to the kiss the baby's cheek, his mouth very close to Tish. 'I'm never letting Lissa date. Men are pigs.' He rested his head on Tish's shoulder. She didn't look at him, but she didn't move away. 'Even the good ones can act like pigs sometimes.'

Brian gave an overly loud sigh. 'I suppose you're referring to me. Okay, fine. I deserve it.'

Everyone laughed, including Joley, although she had to force it. She wanted to forgive Brian, but part of her was still hurt, and she had never been very good at forgiveness, even with her closest friends.

The food was surprisingly good, or maybe they were all just very hungry. Joley tried not to be so aware of Ilya. He had such a powerful energy, yet he seemed to be able to blend into the background, which made no sense until she detected the subtle flow of power in the room. He used his gifts to aid him in disappearing in plain sight, which was probably how he'd kept her palm from giving away his presence earlier.

Conversation flowed around her, and Joley managed to laugh at the appropriate places, but she didn't feel like it. Outside her family and Jonas, Brian had been her closest friend. She had been always been extra careful never to intrude on his thoughts. She enjoyed his company and looked forward to their conversations. He came from a very wealthy family and had attended private school, although he'd always remained best friends with the band members, from the time they were young boys first playing sports together. He dressed a little neater and had incredible manners and definitely was more sensitive toward others. He was probably everyone's favorite. And he'd always been the most diplomatic – until now.

'Hey, Joley,' Jerry said, 'you falling asleep on us?'

'The scintillating conversation is so profound, how could I ever fall sleep?' Joley let her head droop onto the table and pretended to snore.

Ilya's gaze narrowed when Rick threw a biscuit at her and then leaned over to brush the hair from her face, his fingers staying on the silken strands of her hair. The touch held enough affection that Ilya's belly knotted up. He had observed the waitresses and cooks taking numerous pictures of the band and Joley eating. A couple of them had tried to take videos, and he was fairly certain that before dawn the videos would be playing on the Internet.

Joley looked up suddenly and her gaze collided with his. She sent him a small, sad smile that nearly tore out his heart. It was a jolt to feel such deep emotion just from one little exchange. He knew she was upset. Why didn't her friends know? How could they all sit there, joking and laughing when she wanted to cry? He had the urge to simply pick her up, cradle her close and take her out of there.

Jerry glanced at his watch. 'Let's give these folks a couple of pictures and get on the road. We have a schedule.'

Ilya moved into a better position to protect Joley as the band began to pose for photographs with the waitresses and kitchen staff. She was gracious and talked to each one of them, shaking hands when they were offered, even though he could see by her expression that she was being overwhelmed with emotion and information about each person.

More people entered the diner, and Ilya was aware of cars pulling into the parking lot. He waded through the group and took Joley's elbow, smiling politely, but distantly, making certain to look as intimidating as possible.

'Miss Drake, if you don't leave now, you won't make your next concert on time,' he reminded her, already moving her away from the growing crowd.

She went with him, staying close to his body but giving him enough room to maneuver should he have to. Twice she brushed against him, and she had to have felt the harness beneath his jacket as they walked out the door into the parking lot.

Her cell phone rang and she paused to flip it open.

'Bitch.' The voice was distorted but loud enough for Ilya to hear.

She looked up at him a little helplessly, her face pale, her gaze colliding with his. He leaned down to listen. She didn't try to pull away from him or stop him. The voice on the other end was filled with menacing hatred, even through the obvious device the person was using to distort their voice. It was impossible to tell if it was a man or a woman. The voice sounded computer-generated.

'You think your sister was fucked up? Back the hell off, or you're going to be cut into so many little pieces no one will ever be able to identify you.'

The call ended as abruptly as it had begun. Even as Ilya listened, his eyes slashed around the parking lot, noting where each member of the crew or band was, and whether or not they were using a cell phone. He put the phone in his pocket. I'll have Jerry get you another.'

'They mentioned my sister. Why did they do that? Why would they say anything about what happened to Hannah? That was the mob, Ilya. Ever since Abbey met Aleksandr, we've had nothing but problems with them.' As soon as the words were spoken aloud, she clapped her hand over her mouth, her expression horrified. Tears swam in her eyes. 'I didn't mean that. I don't know why I thought it, let alone said it. I didn't mean it.'

Say nothing, laskovaya moya, until we are out of the open.

'Joley!' Brian called. 'You want me to ride with you?'

Joley nearly choked. She was suddenly very frightened. The Russian mob had wreaked havoc on her family, nearly killing Hannah. Twice now, they'd had encounters with them, and with Nikitin following her every move, she felt trapped. Brian had been acting so strange, she didn't trust anyone at all. Sea Haven, her hometown, was the only safe place, yet if the mob was after her, she didn't dare head home and endanger her family again.

Wave to Brian. Tell him you're fine. He's feeling guilty for the way he acted and the things he said.

Ordinarily Joley would have objected to the order and tone, but this time she let Ilya take over, waving halfheartedly at Brian and blowing him a kiss as Ilya moved her toward her bus. She could hear laughter and chatter as the band and crew boarded their buses. Ilya kept his body between her and everyone else as they neared her bus.

Coming at you. Keep your head down.

It was all the warning she had. Flashes went off as the paparazzi swarmed around her. Ilya didn't slow down, wading through them without speaking, his face set in grim lines, his arm over her head. She heard her name called countless times. Once she felt the impact as someone bumped into Ilya hard and his weight shifted slightly into her, but with his large muscle mass he was nearly as immovable as a rock.

She moved with him naturally, as if they were dancing, her steps perfectly in tune to his. They could have rehearsed their walk to the bus. Ilya made it all matter-of-fact, without urgency, as if they were simply strolling through a crowd, instead of being mobbed.

She felt safe. Joley took a breath and absorbed that knowledge. In the midst of the threat, the murder, and the crush of paparazzi, Ilya made her feel completely safe. He didn't push or shove or threaten anyone. They stood in front of him and he looked through them, and then walked through them. Something about the set of his shoulders, the expressionless look on his tough features and the cold look in his eyes made even the most hardened veterans of the tabloid press move out of his way.

Ilya yanked open the door to her bus and thrust

her in and to the side. 'Stay there while I do a quick search.'

The door between her driver and the home section of the bus was already closed, which meant Steve was in a hurry to leave. The feeding frenzy of the paparazzi only made him cranky, so it didn't surprise her when the bus roared to life. Ilya moved swiftly through it, checking every conceivable hiding place, including ones she hadn't even thought of. When she would have spoken, he shook his head and walked through a second time with a small device in his hand.

'We're clear,' he said and stepped out of her way.

Joley flung herself on the couch. 'Thanks. They must have gotten wind of us stopping. Someone at the diner had to have called. They'll get their fifteen minutes of fame, telling lies about us. Or making something out of our conversations.'

'Who has your cell number?'

She shrugged. 'I have to change it all the time. Usually Jerry and the band and my family. A few friends. I always let Tish have my number, and I think I gave it to Lisa. I meant to change it recently because Logan gave it to that whack job groupie's mother.'

'That doesn't mean anything to me.'

She sighed. 'Logan had this brief fling with a groupie named Lucy Brady. She was absolutely nuts, and I mean certifiable. She caused so many scenes in public. He slept with her a few times, and then dropped her when he realized how crazy she was. She went after him with a broken bottle, which by the way is her favorite weapon, it happened more than once. She turned up pregnant and threatened to kill herself. We tried to tell Logan to just stay away from her, but he felt responsible. She was in and out of institutions the whole time she was pregnant, and in the end, Logan went through an attorney and Lucy gave up the baby. She didn't want it, but she did carry it, although once she was going to cut it out of her stomach, again with a broken bottle. That was really ugly.'

'And she has your number?'

She rolled her eyes. 'You don't have to sound like that. Her mother had the number, not Lucy. I never had anything to do with Lucy. She was very fixated on Logan, until he told her he was married.' She leaned her head back against the cushions. 'Our lives sound like a high school soap opera. Sheesh.'

'What makes you want to live like this?' Ilya asked. 'You have everything you could possibly want. And a family who loves and cares about you. What makes you want – or need – all of this?'

Joley inhaled sharply. The contempt in his voice stung. 'You don't know me, Ilya. You only think you do. I may get lost sometimes, and it can be a struggle to stay centered, but I know who I am. I love music. This is my life because it makes sense. And every now and then a letter gets through to me, or someone comes up to me after a show and tells me my songs matter to them. What about you, Ilya? You're so good at handing out judgment. Do you love what you do? Are you sure what you do is the right choice for you?'

'I didn't have a choice. I do what I have to do to survive.' He took the chair across from her and stretched out his legs. 'Your voice changed my life.'

The admission was so unexpected, it stunned her into silence for a moment. She searched his expression. As always, he gave nothing away. There was little softness about Ilya. He was hard and capable and could be counted on if he was on your side. She didn't know how she knew that about him, but the feeling in her was strong.

'How did my voice change your life?'

Ilya could see the genuine surprise on her face. Joley was so transparent, every thought that crossed her mind was telegraphed on her mobile features. He had no softer, happier memories. Grim, dark experiences, hard physical and mental labor and unrelenting pain had shaped who and what he had become – until Joley. She had unexpectedly given him back his humanity. Somewhere inside all of that calm discipline and control, she had tapped into long forgotten emotion. She had made the sun shine and taught him laughter. Maybe it was rusty in sound, and came rarely, but he now knew what true happiness felt like.

He cleared his throat, knowing he was going to give a piece of himself away. 'I was in a very bad place, an ugly place, when I first heard your voice. You sounded like an angel, and I didn't believe in them. I didn't know joy in life until the first time I listened to a song by you. I knew duty and survival, but not joy or what it meant to really live. You gave that to me. I guess if you give that same thing to others, it's well worth the sacrifices you make, although to be honest, I don't like the danger it puts you in. I suppose that's selfish of me.'

Joley's eyes softened, were almost luminous. For a moment he imagined he saw love in them. He'd never seen, or maybe recognized, love or thought much about it until he had crossed paths with the Drake family. They had a great capacity for loving – especially, Joley. She was a wild thing, impetuous and compulsive, but she knew how to love fiercely, passionately and protectively. He hadn't known he wanted that for himself until he'd first laid eyes on her.

'I wish I could be as good a person as you make me out to be,' Joley said. 'I have a temper that I spend half my life having to rein in. I'm not at all like my sisters, Ilya. They really are good people. I just can't seem to be forgiving and I have a tendency to fly off the handle when people do stupid things.' She looked away from him, ducking her head as if something about her character shamed her.

His gut tightened in reaction. 'Why are you so afraid of who you are, Joley? There's nothing wrong with you.'

Lights flashed as cars went by and the sounds of traffic filled the silence in the bus. She twisted her fingers together and shrugged her shoulders.

'Maybe. Maybe not. You never really know what's inside of people.'

'That's not true of us. We see through different eyes and hear sounds no one else hears. We touch other people's minds and thoughts all too easily. You recognize evil when you see it. So do I. Most people think evil is just a word. We know it exists and that it does terrible, vicious things and spreads as it goes. We see one another, and I don't see anything in you that you should ever be ashamed of.'

'Maybe you don't see all of me. I know I don't see all of you. I can't pierce the shadows of your aura. I've caught glimpses, but you hide yourself very well – even from me, and I've touched your mind a thousand times.'

'But you know I'm not evil.'

She bit her bottom lip and shivered a little. Ilya immediately rose and dragged the comforter from the bed to wrap her in.

'No, you're not evil,' she admitted, almost reluctantly. 'But I don't know what you are. You're not the sweet boy next door, that's for sure.'

'You don't want the sweet boy next door. If you did, you'd be with Rick.'

'Rick?' Her gaze jumped to his. 'Why Rick? Brian's my best friend.'

'You're not attracted to Brian and he isn't attracted to you. But you have some chemistry with Rick.' His blue eyes burned hot. 'I don't like it, but it's there.'

'You're nuts. He's like a brother. All the band members are. I've never had sex with any of them, nor would I. It would be gross.'

He shrugged. 'I believe you, but that doesn't negate the fact that you find Rick attractive. In any case,' he added before she could protest, 'he can't meet your needs.'

'My needs?' She stumbled over the last word. Her chin went up a little, and there was defiance in her tone as well as her expression. 'And you think you know what I need?'

He leaned toward her. 'I know exactly what you need. Why do you think you fight me so hard?

Joley scowled at him. 'You have an archaic view of relationships, Ilya. You think the man should dominate the woman, and that's so last century.'

'How do you know what I think? You've never bothered to ask me.'

That shut her up. She sat back and studied his face. 'Well then, what do you think makes a good relationship?'

'Two people who complete one another. They should each complement the strengths and weaknesses of the other person. And they should meet one another's needs, spiritually, sexually and intellectually. I can do all those things for you. I can also protect the life you want to have. If you keep going as you're doing, you'll burn out in another couple of years. You're already starting to do that. I can provide the buffer you need between you and everyone else in order to allow you to continue with your career.'

Okay, that sounded like heaven, too good to be true, but Joley knew life wasn't like that, so perfect and uncomplicated. 'Why do you have to say all the right things, Ilya? You and I both know it wouldn't be that easy.'

'It would if you let it, Joley.' His voice turned tender. 'You're exhausted and upset. Lie down and I'll get you to sleep.'

'I never sleep.'

'Unless I'm with you.' He held out his hand to her. 'You slept just fine the last time I was here. That's another item for the pro side of that list you were making.'

Joley took his hand and let him tug her to her feet. 'You got me in trouble with Sarah. That earned a lot of negative points you'll have to make up.'

He settled her on the bed and brushed a kiss across her temple. 'Fortunately I have a lot of other skills to make those points up fast.'

Joley looked alarmed – and intrigued. 'Really? Well save them for another time. I'm wiped out.'

'I know, *lyubimaya moya*, go to sleep and I'll watch over you.' He stretched out beside her. 'And this should go on the pro side of your list as well,' he muttered under his breath.

Joley curled close to him and smiling, closed her eyes.

Chapter Ten

Lying beside any attractive woman for three hours could give a man a raging hard-on, but watching Joley sleep, with her lush, curvaceous body and her soft skin, had created a monster.

In those hours she barely moved, her face young and relaxed, the fingers of her hand curled against her palm as if protecting Ilya's mark. Dawn crept in through the blinds, spilling light across her face. She looked like an angel, with her silky hair in disarray on the pillow and her long lashes curving in two thick crescents on her cheeks. And then she moved restlessly, turning toward him, whispering his name, and he lost all pretense of control.

There was nothing saintly about him, and there never would be. There was no way he could lie beside her and not need to touch her soft skin or taste her wild, honeyed flavor. He had known, when the doors of the bus had closed, that he was going to seduce her. She wanted him. The truth was in her eyes when she looked at him, in the feminine fragrance of her body and the seductive sound of her voice. She was fighting her attraction because she didn't trust him, she didn't fully believe he wasn't the bad man he was reputed to be – but she wanted him with every cell in her body, in just the same way he wanted her.

His reaction to her, the first time he'd actually laid eyes on her, had been so physical, so sharp and strong, the ache in his body becoming a permanent part of him in her presence. He'd tried to convince himself he could have her and not be emotionally touched by her. She'd dashed that ridiculous hope completely.

Joley was a strong woman with strong moral convictions. The chemistry between them flared bright and hot, but he was a man in the shadows – and he had to remain there. It would take finesse to overcome Joley's convictions, and there would be repercussions, but damn, he'd waited as long as he could wait.

He needed to touch her silken skin, stroke his hands over her lush, curvy body, sink into the fiery heat of her and bury himself deep and hard, over and over, until she could never think of another man – look at another man – feel the least chemistry with another man, as she did with Rick Henderson, her bass player. She might not acknowledge that she did, but he felt a spark each time the two were together, and that was unacceptable to him. Her emotional dependence on Brian felt like a threat as well. Ilya wasn't into sharing any part of Joley.

He was through being the gentleman and protector; he was going to stake his claim in no uncertain terms, because if he didn't – he would go quietly insane. His body was already so sensitive he couldn't stand the painful press of fabric against his skin for even one more moment. With one hand he tore his shirt over his head, then he went around to every window and slid the privacy screens in place, signaling to everyone that Joley was sleeping and to leave her alone should they stop. He took the precaution of locking the door to the outside as well as the one to the driver's compartment because he wasn't going to allow any interruptions. He left one dim light on because he had to see her face, watch her emotion as he took possession of her.

He shed his jeans, grateful for the cool air on his hot body. His erection was fierce, thick and painful, a reminder of the months of long, sleepless nights when he'd lain in a cold bed and thought of her, his hand on his shaft and emptiness surrounding him. Nothing sated his need for her, no matter how many times he relieved himself or how many cold showers he took. One thought of her, the sound of her voice, her music, a glimpse of her brought the painful lust roaring back stronger than ever.

Joley. Just Joley. She was the sexiest woman he'd ever encountered, and he'd met many trained in the art of driving men wild. Joley needed no such training. She was naturally sensual with her curvy body, her husky voice and the fluid, feminine grace with which she moved. He bent his head to hers, unable to resist that full, beautiful mouth. He'd had a lot of fantasiess about her mouth, warm and velvet soft and so perfect it could stop a man's heart.

He wasn't feeling gentle at all, he was feeling animalistic and in desperate need of taking her. He could hear his music now, not at all soft and bluesy, but wild and dominant like a heavy metal band. The pounding pulse of the music matched the way he needed to drive deep into her body. The heavy bass throbbed in his groin, and the drum beat through his veins demanding satisfaction. He caught both wrists as she came awake, stretching her arms above her head and pinning them to the mattress.

'Kiss me, Joley. Don't think. Just kiss me.'

Beneath him, she froze, her lashes lifting. She looked dazed and drowsy, a little fearful, but she wanted him. He could see instant desire flare in her eyes.

Joley's breath stilled. For a moment she couldn't think or breathe. Butterflies whirled and danced in her stomach, fluttering their wings until every muscle bunched and tightened in anticipation. Immediately her body responded to his, this one man who would be her downfall if she let him. Desire pulsed hot and wet between her legs. Her entire body vibrated, almost as if humming to his song.

She was aware instantly that he was naked, and her gaze, of its own accord, shifted to his thick, heavily muscled chest, the bulging muscles in his arms. He was lying on his stomach beside her, and his butt was tight and firm and totally sculpted the way she'd always imagined. Her heart kicked in, and her blood heated, drowning her in desire.

She heard his song, blending with hers, the wild, intoxicating timbre, roughened with lust. There were more instruments beneath that hammering beat, the soft and tender notes of a flute, a violin moaning, almost pleading – *save me* – save me – and the saxophone introducing a haunting lonely note, but all that was nearly drowned out by the relentless pounding command of the drums and the crash of cymbals making adamant demands. His song merged with hers, blending and then overtaking hers, the wild strains a fiery, passionate declaration of ownership that swept away her resistance.

The combination was heady and enticing, a powerful aphrodisiac she couldn't resist.

Arousal teased her breasts, danced over her thighs, slid into her stomach to wreak chaos. She stared up at the face only inches from hers. Strongboned, straight nose, firm mouth, eyes as deep blue as the sea itself, eyes that were too old for his years, held too much knowledge and too much pain – or nothing at all. She inhaled sharply. Right now those blue eyes glittered with arousal – with lust – with the need for her – for the heat and fire she could provide.

'Kiss me, Joley.' His voice was nearly a growl.

She recognized the command. He wouldn't close that scant inch between them; he was insisting she give herself to him.

'I'm afraid.'

'I know.' His hands framed her face, his body shifting even more to blanket hers. 'Kiss me now.'

'If I do this, there's no going back for me. You're asking me to give myself to you, and I won't ever be the same.'

One hand, warm and rough, slid down her throat, over the swell of her breast, moved with infinite slowness over her thin shirt to find the hem. Fingers bunched the material and his fist caressed her stomach, still holding her shirt. 'Kiss me.'

Molten liquid pooled low and wicked. Inner muscles rippled and heated. His voice was implacable. Imperative. Commanding. The sound sent a shiver down her spine, teased her nipples into hard pebbles. She took a ragged breath. She was so susceptible to him.

'Ilya.' His name came out a raspy whisper. A plea to save her from herself.

His head lowered, his silky hair brushing over her skin like caressing fingers. His lips brushed over her neck just below her ear, tongue licking wickedly, teeth scraping, sending her nerve endings into shock. He lifted his head again, his gaze, hot and hungry, colliding with her desperate one. 'Kiss me, Joley. Stop running and kiss me.'

Heat radiated from his body. His need for her surrounded her, enclosed her in raw sexual hunger. His song crashed around her, demanding her compliance, terrifying her even as it seduced her. Her womb contracted. Her obsession for him stole her breath. She knew what he was asking – no – demanding. He wanted surrender – complete surrender.

She touched his lips, tracing the firm, warm curves. 'Do you know what you're asking of me? Do you really know who I am?' She was really asking if she was safe, but she could see by his expression he wouldn't let her get away with that. He insisted on blind trust.

'Damn it, Joley. Fucking kiss me now.'

His voice was rough, agonized, almost a growl, but so sensual Joley felt a spasm in her deepest core. She cried out, a gasping plea, tormented with hunger for him. It seemed as if she'd needed him for so long she couldn't think of anything else but having him buried inside her. His hand slid down the slope of her belly, sending each muscle curling into a tight ball of desire. In desperation she closed that small distance, her mouth finding his, arms circling his neck, fists bunched in his hair, holding on as if to a life preserver.

Their tongues twined and danced, hot licks, desperate frenzied kisses, devouring one another, feeding on each other's passion. He kissed her as though his very life, his very survival depended on it. He kissed her as if he could never get enough of her or the taste of her.

He shifted again, throwing the cover from the bed onto the floor, his mouth never leaving hers, caging her with his body. She felt his heavy erection, thick and hard, pressed tight against her thigh, and another needy moan escaped.

Her head fell back as his mouth moved across her chin and down her throat, teeth taking small nips as if he wanted to take a bite out of her, his tongue easing each sting. His lips went to the neckline of her thin tee, and he frowned, lifting his head for a minute to look down at the cloth covering her heaving breasts. He simply caught at it with one hand and jerked hard, ripping the material from her body and tossing it aside. Her whole body clenched, her temperature shooting up at his display of impatience.

'Mine,' he growled and lowered his head to feast on the swollen, aching mounds.

The harsh sound of his voice sent a ripple of fire shooting through her veins, nearly sending her over the edge, her body pulsing with desire, the muscles of her silken sheath clenching hard. His mouth was fiery hot, closing over her nipple, suckling strongly. Joley shivered as sensations poured through her.

She was terrified he had read her mind and would take her down a seductive path from which she could never return, yet she couldn't stop, couldn't find the will to resist his dark seduction. His body was hard and hot, spreading fire through her, sending electrical currents sizzling through her veins. His mouth was rough, sensuous; his lips pulled at her breast, sending lightning to her thighs and melting her inner flesh. His hands were even rougher than his mouth, teasing and pulling at her nipples, cupping the full mounds possessively. His teeth scraped and taunted, his tongue stroking each nipple with quick hot flicks that drove the breath from her body.

His hands slid down her body, shaping her ribs, her waist, sliding beneath the waistband of her thin cotton pants to strip them from her, leaving her exposed to his hot, hungry gaze. He stared down at her body, the flushed breasts, the tucked in waist and flared hips, her thighs slightly parted to give him a glimpse of the treasure waiting, already damp with need.

He bent his head to her stomach, finding her sexy little navel, blazing a trail of fiery little bites all the way to the intriguing curls at the junction of her legs.

Joley's head tossed on the pillow and she cried out again, a soft whimper as she tried to make sense of the fire building relentlessly. She'd never experienced such a clawing need in her body, so much pleasure that it bordered on pain. She needed a moment, needed to slow down and get control.

Ilya refused to give her the time. He took her over, driving her out of her comfort zone, pushing her beyond anything she'd ever imagined – even in her darkest erotic fantasies. Her skin was hypersensitive, her inner body pulsing with a tormented need.

His hands swept her thighs open for him, one leg sliding between hers, his arms pinning her hips beneath him, locking her in place as he lifted his head. His blue gaze held stark, raw hunger, ravenous lust and absolute command. 'Mine.' His tone was raspy and harsh, a wild, arrogant Cossack claiming ownership.

She tried to catch his hair, to stop him. She needed to breathe. To control herself, control the lust crawling through her body and taking over her mind. Ilya ignored the fist jerking his hair and her thrashing body. His mouth ruthlessly covered the hot, sweet core of her, tongue plunging deep, finding her most sensitive spot and flicking hard, over and over. She tried to scream as an orgasm ripped through her, but no sound emerged. She nearly came off the bed in spite of his arms restraining her. His mouth only continued the assault, burning her from the inside out between the suckling and the hot flicks of his tongue.

The more she fought, the firmer he locked her in place, his arms enormously strong, his mouth consuming her, the sensation shattering, rocking her with its intensity. She couldn't catch her breath; her nerve endings were so tight and sensitive she thought she might die. The music was pounding through her veins, thundering in her ears, in her hammering heart, but most of all in her feminine channel, beating too hard and fast, but the crescendo would not come. The inferno built and built. She shook her head back and forth on the pillow, fingernails digging into his back as she tried to either pull him closer or push him away.

He was relentless, taking his pleasure, insisting on her going with him as high as he wanted to take her. He plunged his tongue deep, took the slick, wet offering and reveled in his ability to send her into the next level of sensual sensation. Blood pounded through the muscles of her sheath, tightening, contracting, until she nearly sobbed as his mouth drove her ever higher, and she could feel her body straining for another release. His music vibrated through her, danced against her clit, flinging her hard into another orgasm.

He rose above her like the warrior he was, his eyes fierce and filled with an insatiable lust. He jerked her thighs apart, his hands rough and insistent. She saw him then, savagely aroused, thick and hard and far too intimidating. He pushed the head of his erection against her tight sheath and stilled, holding her gaze with his.

'You're mine. Say it, Joley. Only mine. I want to hear you say it.'

He moved, a short thrust that had her biting off a scream as he pushed in a little deeper, stretching her. The burning need increased until she wanted to sob, terrified she'd never be free of it. She had known all along he was the one who would know, who would see beneath her skin, down to her very core, and once he uncovered her need for this – this taking her beyond anything she'd ever known – she'd be lost – and she was. She'd never be free of him. She was his, body and soul, locked together now by something beyond her, and it was terrifying.

She shook her head, tears swimming in her eyes.

Ilya caught her hands, laced his fingers through hers and bent over her, pressing her hands to the mattress, rocking with another short thrust of his hips, stretching her again as he sunk deeper. 'Look at me, Joley. Right now. Look at me.'

She couldn't look away. She was trapped in his heat. In his lust. His needs. She was trapped by his absolute will and his expertise. He played her body like a maestro, his sensuality beyond her ability to resist. She blinked at the tears stinging her eyes, and he leaned forward and took them with a slow caress of his tongue. Instantly her womb spasmed, convulsed, sending streaks of fire racing through her, her muscles clamping tightly around him.

'Say you belong to me, Joley.' He repeated each word in a rough, harsh voice, his hands holding hers tightly. 'Say you're mine.'

'Damn you,' she hissed. 'You want everything.'

He bent forward again, rocking his hips, forcing another inch, stretching her relentlessly, burning with her. 'Everything you are is mine.'

'Then you're mine,' she said in desperation. 'Then you belong to me.'

'With everything I am,' he agreed and slammed his body home.

He took her breath away, his body driving through her tight inner muscles, spreading fire as she arched into him, her body still fighting for more, or trying to pull away from him as she writhed under him, impaled now and gasping for breath.

'Damn, Joley, you're so tight.' His voice was a harsh gasp above her head.

Around them, the music crashed and throbbed and sent electrical currents sizzling through her veins. In some secret place in her mind, she had wanted this, a man who knew exactly what he wanted and took it, a man who dared to push her further than she'd ever been, but reality was different than imagination, and she was terrified she'd never be able to pull herself back together and be Joley. Just Joley.

Ilya easily controlled her body with his own, throwing back his head and losing himself in the heat and fire. He had been born for this moment, trained for this moment, learning from a young age to wield sex like a weapon, to dominate completely without losing himself, to exhibit absolute, utter mastery over a woman. He could ride a partner for hours, have a woman begging and pleading to tell him anything he wanted to know, but nothing in his experience had prepared him for mixing expertise with his own needs, desires and emotions, and the woman who owned him body and soul. He was lost in the absolute carnal pleasure of their bodies.

He set a harsh, demanding tempo, rocking her with streaks of fire. Her silken sheath was tight, strangling him, pulsing and throbbing, squeezing him as he pistoned again and again, hard thrusts that buried him to the hilt. Each time her muscles clamped down and sensations tore through his body, the pleasure burst through him, far more than he'd ever experienced. His strokes became harder, deeper, more rhythmic as she went wild beneath him. Her head tossed on the pillow, her hips arching into him, muscles tightening as the pressure built and built with no relief. She fought the torturous erotic pleasure, sobbing his name.

His hands clamped down on her thighs, holding them apart, shifting her so that she felt the caress of steel stroking over her sensitive knot of nerves already on fire. The more she fought, the higher he took her, biting back a growl, his teeth bared as he drove himself into her, claiming her, riding her, taking her with him into another sensual dimension.

'Stay with me, Joley,' he rasped. 'Stop fighting it.'

'I can't,' she gasped.

'You will,' he decreed.

Joley couldn't stop the shudders wracking her body, or the involuntary raking at his back with her nails. She was on fire as he rode between her thighs.

210

He felt like velvet-encased steel, driving through tight, stretched muscle already inflamed and in need of release, but the erotic torture didn't end, didn't stop, and she couldn't stand it. The fierce thrusting of his hips, the thick cock driving deep into her, stretching and burning, sending streaks of lightning flashing through her entire body, the tension inside coiling tighter and tighter as she gasped and writhed beneath him was too much. Fear skated through the haze of lust and need, heightening the sensations even more. The sounds of his fierce possession and her pleas added to the crashing music, rising to a crescendo as the firestorm swept over them, engulfing them completely.

Her breath ceased, music thundered in her ears, the room darkened around her, and colors danced behind her eyes as her body tightened unmercifully around his thick erection. And then it came. Wave after wave, multiple orgasms streaking through her womb, blazing through her stomach and breasts, burning her from the inside out, endless, vicious, without mercy, the sensation so intense she wasn't certain if it was pleasure or pain.

The fierce milking of his shaft by her fiery, slick sheath was too much for Ilya. The sensation started in his toes, ran up the column of his thighs, tightened in his balls and burned in his belly. He lost all control for this first time in his life, pouring himself into her, jet after jet of hot semen, as her body gripped him with erotic pleasure. He collapsed over her, breathing roughly, her body pulsing around his.

Joley lay under him, limp, her breathing ragged. His body shuddered from the explosive release. Never in his life had it ever been like that. Her slick, wet heat, burning around his shaft, the tight grasp of her body on his, the torturous brutal release was more pleasure than he'd ever known.

Joley had made him come alive, turning a trained bodily function, an expertise, into a secret paradise of sensation. Before her, sex, like everything else about him, had been a weapon to use, a tool for survival, but she had given him an immeasurable gift. She had surrendered herself to him, entrusted her body, her mind, all that she was to him and in doing so had staked her own claim on him.

'I don't think I'm alive anymore,' Joley whispered. 'I think you killed me.'

She looked dazed, almost uncomprehending. He nuzzled her neck, kissed the pulse beating rapidly behind her ear and rolled over, closing his eyes as he slid from the warmth of her body. 'Your body is incredible.'

Joley could hear her heart thundering in her ears. She hadn't known sex could be like that, and it was truly terrifying. On one hand to think it might happen again, and on the other to think it might never happen again. She didn't know which was worse. She turned her head to look at him. 'You're so far out of my league I can't even play.'

He dropped his hand to her bare stomach, fingers splayed wide. 'You did more than play, *laskovaya moya*, you drained me. I have never had that happen.' The pads of his fingers began slow, circular caresses along her belly, just above the damp curls.

His touch sent ripples through her body, tightening her muscles and creating delicious aftershocks.

'Since neither of us were very responsible, I'll go first. I don't have any diseases and I'd appreciate it if you confess if you have any.' She held her breath.

212

He smiled up at the ceiling, his fingers sliding into the curls, continuing the small, light movements. 'I have no disease, Joley.'

'And I'm on the pill so you don't have to worry about pregnancy,' she said, 'but you should have asked.'

His eyebrow shot up. 'And you think the pill will protect you?'

'From pregnancy, but not from an STD.' She was a little alarmed by the smirk in his voice, as if he knew something she didn't.

'I told you I have no diseases, but I did put my mark on you.' He took her hand and brought her palm to his lips.

Again she felt his kiss at her very core. The fingers of his other hand continued to weave through her damp curls until they slid into her slick heat, tracing more small circles. He enjoyed the shudders of pleasure and the arching of her restless hips, the way she responded to every touch. Her breathing changed; her breasts heaved and her body tightened on his fingers. She lost all coherent thought.

'Ilya.' She caught his wrist. 'I'm done. Totally done.'

He turned toward her, his blue eyes drifting possessively over her face . 'No, you're done when I say you're done. I'm done when you say. That's the way it works, *radost' moya*. And I say you're not done.'

'I don't understand.'

He bent his head to her breast, his tongue flicking the nipple, teeth tugging, and then his mouth settled to suckle. She gasped, and turned more into him as the flashes of fire went from nipple to sheath. Her arm cradled his head, as she held him to her.

'I'm exhausted. I want more, but I'm so tired.'

His fingers plunged deeper, stroking and caressing and circling her clit. This time her orgasm was gentle and washed over her like the receding waves of the seas. He flicked her nipple with his tongue and lifted his head to find her mouth with his. His kiss was infinitely tender.

'You have trust issues, Joley. Serious ones. You gave your body into my keeping, but you don't trust me to know that you're tired and you need to come down slowly. You were flying high and it frightened you.'

She kissed him again. He was right, her body was already calmer, the sensations like gentle waves calming turbulent seas. 'I'm still scared.'

'I don't mind you being afraid, especially if you tell me, but you know I can read you – what you want, what you like, what you need. Trust me to provide you with those things.'

'You're talking about sexually.' She lay back against her pillow, too tired to prop herself up even to look at his handsome face.

'Emotionally first, Joley. Then, yes, physically, sexually. But this isn't about sex. You still want it to be, but it's not. If you could never have sex with me again, I would still want to be with you. I would still need to be with you. I won't lie and say I don't have a very healthy sex drive. Make no mistake, I'll take from you the things I want and need, but your plea-sure, your needs always – *always* – come first, even if you don't know what they are.'

She made a face at the ceiling. 'You talk and I don't know what you mean.'

'You know exactly what I mean. I don't do anything by halves and neither do you. You committed yourself to me and you saw inside of me enough to know what kind of man I am.'

Joley inhaled sharply, her breath catching in her lungs. She did know – and yet she didn't. She had been drawn to him, mesmerized and seduced by him, by his aura and his song. By his magic – his strength. Oh, God, his strength was what she craved more than anything in the world. That absolute confidence, that aggression that pushed her out of her comfort zone, that took her places she had only dreamt of – places she craved but feared. He would take her over and she would fight him every inch of the way. He was going to make her life hell – or heaven.

She moistened her lips. 'Do you think you're going to rule me? Because if you think so, your fantasy is way beyond reality.'

He caught her face between his hands, forcing her toward him. Her startled gaze jumped to his. 'Don't start a fight with me, Joley. Not now. We've only got a few hours left together.' He leaned down and brushed kisses across her eyelids, the tip of her nose, back and forth across her mouth.

Alarmed, Joley pushed at the wall of his chest. He was stealing her heart. He'd taken her body and her soul, she wasn't handing him her heart to destroy as well. He had given her the most fantastic sexual experience of her life, and she knew she would need him again and again. Nothing would ever compare to what she had with him, but it wasn't lovemaking. She hadn't felt that he was loving her. Possessing her – claiming her – yes. Owning her even, but not loving her, and she could be addicted, she could let him rule her in bed, but she refused, absolutely refused, to hand her heart to a man who might be involved in terrible things.

215

'Yes,' he said softly, kissing her again.

Small, caressing kisses that left her feeling helpless against the onslaught of tenderness. 'I won't let you.'

He knew what she was afraid of. She could feel him in her mind, touching her inside where there was no way to stop him. He had marked her everywhere, all over her skin, and now he was leaving his mark on the inside.

'It's already too late,' he whispered, trailing kisses along her cheekbone to the corner of her mouth.

She was melting inside. Butterfly wings all over again. She wasn't just getting wet and needy, she craved his touch, his voice, the scent of him, but most of all she wanted him to feel that same frightening vulnerability that for her just seemed to grow worse around him.

His hands stroked her skin, memorizing every inch of her, and all the while he whispered to her of faraway places, of being a boy in a cold, hard land, of belonging to her and only her. She could hear the strains of his song wrapping her up in haunting notes, holding her close while she drifted – drifted – on a tide of sex and sin and the fragile beginnings of love.

She went to sleep to the soft murmur of his voice, and woke to the sensual enticement of it only an hour later. He was already hard and moving inside her, his kiss taking her breath while his hands shaped her breasts.

In the tour buses, the trip from Red Rocks to Dallas took a little over fourteen hours. Ilya woke her over and over, until Joley thought she would have to crawl to make it to the shower to relieve the aches in her sore body. He carried her and took her

216

hard and fast up against the wall. Once they rolled off the bed, and he just took her there on the floor. They tried to eat, and he put her on the small table and ate her instead, until she was sobbing for release, and then he sank into her, first with her lying on the table and then bending her over it.

When the bus finally pulled into their space and stopped, and Steve had called to tell her he was going to bed, Joley sat on the floor, her legs drawn up, head back against her mattress, clutching a blanket around her naked body. Ilya sat beside her, holding a bottle of water so she could sip it.

'Are you all right?'

Joley looked at him, his body fit, the long, thick length of him semi-hard against the strong column of his thigh. 'You're a freakin' sex machine, Ilya. Nobody can do that. Nobody. You're either downing Viagra by the bottle or you're a cyborg.'

He shrugged his shoulders, slipped an arm under her legs and lifted her back onto the bed, placing her close to the wall so he could wrap his body around hers. 'I was trained to stay hard no matter what, to ride a woman for hours if need be, to plea-sure her and never let it affect me. But in the end, angel moya, all that training is for nothing with you. No matter how many times I have you, how many ways I take you, it is never enough for me. I should be sated, unmoved by what we share, and yet I'm addicted to you and cannot get enough of you.'

She was exhausted beyond anything she'd ever known but ... 'Ilya.' She frowned, sliding her arms around his neck. 'What do you mean, trained? Sexually trained? How? How can someone train you? And where?'

He was silent, and she sensed – knew – he was

217

uncomfortable and wished he could take the revelation back. She held her breath waiting. For the first time she felt he was as vulnerable and naked as she was.

'I was trained in a lot of things, Joley.'

'They hurt you, didn't they?' She guessed.

She had seen scars on his body, felt them under her fingertips; she'd caught glimpses of a young man huddled in a corner with blood running down his back and legs. Now she knew for certain it was Ilya. The glimpses of violence, the black aura – there was so much she didn't know, but she was beginning to get small pieces that fit together forming a very ugly picture.

'Don't. We're not going there, Joley.'

Her hands framed his face and she kissed him gently, her stomach fluttering, her heart reaching for his. Ilya caught her by her shoulders and yanked her back down to the mattress. 'I said no. Don't you pity me.'

Fury flashed through her. He had spent hours – *hours* – keeping her vulnerable and forcing her to confront her own failings and needs, her own fears, but he refused to share any part of himself with her. She was so angry her body trembled. She dropped her hands immediately, fingers curling into two tight fists.

As she stared up at his handsome face, his ice-cold eyes, the anger drained away. Her breath hitched in her throat, the lump there nearly choking her. Her chest hurt, was too tight, a piercing pain tearing through her heart. He had rejected her again. She could tell herself forever that it had been just sex for her, but she knew better. She had thought he was everything, but he had pushed her away and refused to give anything of himself to her. All his talk was just that – talk. Survival counted now, more than anything she had to survive.

What if he had done what he'd been trained to do? Maybe Nikitin had ordered him to screw her. Well, he'd done a good job. He could go to the tabloids and say he'd screwed a celebrity. She had never felt so betrayed, so ashamed or so stupid. The pain was physical.

She did the only thing possible, she pulled herself back from the brink of that terrible precipice she'd almost gone over. She had to walk away now. This instant. Withdraw and hold a part of herself to her, protected and sheltered, in order to stay alive. He'd taken everything else from her, and she doubted she'd ever get it back, but she wasn't going to give him her life.

She would cry. She would be lonely. She would feel empty forever, but she could survive if she pulled away.

'Joley.'

Ilya sensed her withdrawal. Of course he would. He knew her inside and out. He couldn't help but realize she was moving away from him. She did her best to cover.

'No. You're right. I'm sorry. I shouldn't have pried.' She turned onto her side. 'I've only got a couple of hours to sleep and then I'll be working. When you leave, please don't wake me up.'

'Joley, you're angry with me.'

'No, I'm just very tired.' And she wasn't angry. She was empty. Not even sorrow could fill her emptiness. She would say whatever he needed to hear so he would go and she would be safe. She flashed a fake smile at him and closed her eyes, waiting for him to leave her.

Chapter Eleven

'Joley. Wake up. Wake up, honey.'

Joley groaned and squeezed her eyes closed tighter. 'Go away.'

There were whispers. She heard them from a distance and tried to turn her head to see who was disturbing her. Her body felt heavy and cumbersome and her eyelids barely opened. Tish and Brian huddled together over the bed. Jerry stood at her table with the shreds of two white packets in his hands.

Joley?

Ilya's voice shredded her heart. That perfect pitch. No one had such a perfect, heartbreaking tone. She closed her eyes and pulled the covers over her head. She couldn't hear him or see him. She needed to stay asleep where he couldn't get to her to destroy her further.

'Joley, what the hell did you take?' Jerry pushed Brian and Tish aside and crouched by the bed, shaking her. 'What did you take?' He dipped a finger into the envelope and tasted it, scowled and handed it to Brian.

'She doesn't do drugs,' Brian said, repeating the same action and tasting the powder.

'She took something,' Jerry snapped. 'Joley, what the fuck have you done? I swear you'd better tell me or I'm calling a fucking ambulance right now. Get her up. Walk her up and down the bus. Get some water on her face. What did you take?'

Joley frowned at them, forcing her lashes to lift. 'Go away. I'm sleeping.'

'You're getting up,' Jerry decreed. 'I don't expect this kind of drama from you, Joley. Denny maybe, but not you. What the hell did you take?'

Her mouth felt like cotton. 'I can't take drugs. You know that. They don't work on my body. They just make me sick.' She rolled over and stared at the ceiling, keeping the comforter wrapped tightly around her body.

Tish took the packet from Brian and sat on the edge of the bed. 'What is this, honey?'

'Hannah made it up for me. I'm only supposed to use one envelope, but I couldn't sleep so I took two – and it worked.' She glared up at Jerry. 'Until you decided to barge in.'

'What's in it?' Jerry demanded, relief making his voice gruff.

'I don't know. She grows all that stuff. She's like supergardener, and all her powders and creams work.' Joley put her hand over her eyes. 'Did you have to raise all the screens?'

'Only two,' Brian said. 'I'm getting you something to eat. I'll be right back.'

'Get her moving, Tish,' Jerry said and awkwardly patted Joley's head.

Tish waited until the men had left and shut the door. 'You're covered in bruises, Joley, you have marks all over your body. What happened? Do you need a doctor?'

Marks all over her? Ilya's marks. Inside and out. She could feel him touching her, whispering to her, his breath warm against her skin, his hands like magic. She pulled the comforter closer to hold the marks tight against her skin. The absolute compassion and caring in Tish's voice was her undoing. Tears burned in her eyes and clogged her throat. She shook her head. 'I'm all right. Nothing bad happened. I was just stupid, the way I'm always stupid.'

'You're never stupid, Joley. You might be attracted to the wrong men, but you're careful. You know to keep a distance.'

'Does it look like I kept my distance this time, Tish?' Joley raised her head and looked straight at the other woman, letting her see the heartache, the betrayal, the pain that wasn't going to end just because she was smart enough to walk away. She had committed herself to Ilya. She had given herself to him – all that she was, everything – and he'd stolen her heart even when she tried to protect herself. 'I'm such an idiot. I know my own weaknesses. I do, Tish. I laugh at them and guard against them. I've never allowed myself to fall in love. *Never.*'

Until now. With the wrong man. Everything about him appealed to her, even his aloofness. 'I intended to be the goddess who finally melted his heart of stone. What a crock.' She covered her face with her hands. 'I can't believe I did this.'

'Come here, baby,' Tish said.

Joley laid her head in Tish's lap and let her stroke her hair soothingly. She wasn't going to cry. She deserved this for her own stupidity. Men like Ilya Prakenskii didn't really fall in love and live happily ever after, and neither did women like Joley. 'I want to be normal.'

Tish bent and kissed the top of her head. 'You're Joley and that's enough. If he doesn't love you, he's crazy. We all love you. Every single one of us. We know you'd go to hell and back for us. Why do you think Brian's braving the paparazzi right now, getting you something to eat? With the murder, it's even crazier than normal. They've said all kinds of cruel things about him both in the tabloids and in the newspapers, implying he's guilty.'

'Oh, no.' Joley sat up with a small frown. 'Why would they think he'd have a reason to kill Dean?'

Tish sighed. 'The heaviest speculation is that you were secretly having an affair with Dean and Brian got jealous. They had words over you and Brian killed him.'

Joley swore under her breath. 'Can't they just once give us a break? Why do they have to do that?'

'I told you when you got into this business, baby, they feed off scandal and rumors. When there's nothing there, they have to make it up, and when there is, they make it a thousand times worse.' Tish pointed to the shower. 'Go. He'll be back soon and you're going to want to be on your feet. You'll need cover-up for your neck.'

Joley wrapped herself more tightly in the comforter and slid off the bed. Tears were useless, even though she couldn't stop them in the shower.

Joley.

There he was again, a stirring in her mind. A whispered caress. It didn't mean anything. This was a man admittedly trained in the art of seduction – and he had seduced her. He'd used her own dark desires against her. She had to stay focused on reality and not on what she wanted or needed from him.

I'm in a hurry. I'm late getting ready for the sound check and everyone is waiting.

There. Steady. Matter-of-fact. She took a deep breath, let it out and stepped out of the shower to rub a towel over her body. She was sore everywhere, and so sensitized that touching her breasts sent streaks of fire shooting down her thighs

She stared at herself in the mirror. Her eyes were dark, almost black, filled with pain. She'd let someone do that to her. She had known all along she felt things too deeply. She became attached. She didn't want a lover who could walk away from her, because she could never do that – love someone completely and survive intact if he left her.

Joley, before you go on tonight, we need to talk.

I'm sorry. I doubt there's time. I'm running late and Tish is here. Brian's just come with some food. Later. Much later. As in never. She was going to have to ask Jerry to find a way to get rid of him without tipping him off. Jerry was good at covering for her.

Tish handed her clothes through the door and Joley put them on. Tish knew her so well. She pressed her fingertips to her eyes. Tish knew about pain and loss. She loved Logan and he'd betrayed her. Joley detested the selfish part of her that had pushed Logan to ask Tish to come for the baby. She understood now how hard it had been for Tish. She hadn't wanted to see Logan, to speak to him, to take even his money from him. She wanted nothing to do with him, and now Joley understood.

She was careful with makeup. She rarely wore much other than during a performance, but she needed the added confidence as well as something to mask the dark circles under her eyes.

'Hey,' Brian knocked on the bathroom door. 'The food I risked my life bringing to you is getting cold. And Tish made you a cup of tea, that special blend Hannah always sends you.'

Joley smiled. It was nice to have friends who cared. People who knew you so well. She stepped out and hugged Brian. After his initial shock, he hugged her back. For the first time, she was drowning so much in her own misery, she couldn't catch more than worry and guilt flowing from him.

'Thanks for braving the crazies to get me food, Brian.' She managed to look normal as she walked to the table and sat down. She didn't even burst into tears.

'Dallas is wild, Joley. Jerry and I have been tried and convicted in most of the tabloids, and the general speculation is that I'm getting off because I'm a celebrity. It's pretty vicious stuff so don't bother reading it. The newspapers are the same. I was hiding in the bus until Jerry said there was something wrong with you.'

Tish nodded. 'Security's tight and they've got ropes up, but there's already a mob outside. We've got security going through the usual gifts and things left for you.' She glanced at Brian uneasily as she placed the tea in front of the plate of food on the table. 'We've gotten a couple more disturbing letters, Joley. Jerry had Prakenskii look at them, and he also faxed copies to Jonas. He said that was standard now, to copy Jonas on everything.'

Joley nodded. 'Jonas is more than a brother-in-law, he's also like a brother. I've known him my entire life and he's bossy when it comes to safety. All the men in my family are.'

Brian sat down and leaned his chin onto his hand

watching her eat. 'That's good.'

'I suppose,' Joley agreed.

Tish touched her hair with a gentle hand. 'I've got to check on the baby. You don't have much time for the sound check, Joley. You've only got about two hours before the performance, and you're going to have to get ready. The band did the check, but they need you.'

'I know. I'm sorry. I was just so tired. It was dumb to double up on that stuff. Next time, believe me, I'll know better. I'm sorry I scared everyone.' Joley caught at Tish's dress. 'Are you okay with taking care of the baby, Tish? I should have told Logan it wasn't a good idea. I knew he wanted you back with him, and I did, too. It was wrong of me – of all of us. We were thinking about ourselves, not you.'

'I'm taking one day at a time. I won't let Logan push me into anything before I'm ready, but I missed everyone – and him. Especially him. He's treating me like a queen right now.'

'He should, Tish. He doesn't deserve you, none of us do.'

Tish's eyes went soft, her smile gentle. 'I love all of you. And little Lissa is the sweetest, most beautiful baby in the world.'

Brian sighed as she went out. 'Lissa is the one who will get Tish back for Logan. We're all crazy about that kid already. She has too many 'uncles' who are going to spoil her rotten.' He leaned his elbows on the table and shoved his hands through his hair in agitation. 'I have to say it, Joley. I'm sorry. I really shouldn't have talked to you that way the other night. You're my best friend. I just lost it there.'

She took a sip of tea and nudged the other cup Tish had made closer to him. 'Why did you? What's going on with you? And don't say it's jealousy, because you don't think of me that way. I know we joke all the time, but I've never felt your interest, not once.'

'I love you, Joley.'

'I know that, but not like that. So what got you so upset?'

'It's that man. Prakenskii. He just irks me. And then Jerry decides to hire him without really giving any of us a choice. What the hell is that about?'

Joley's stomach knotted. She put her fork down. 'Why do you dislike him so much?' And why hadn't he told her before she made such a fool out of herself?

'It's the way Nikitin is with him.' The words burst from Brian as if he'd been holding them in forever. 'I think he's involved with him somehow.'

Joley frowned and rubbed her temples. 'I have no idea what you mean by involved. Prakenskii works for Nikitin as a bodyguard. Everyone knows that.'

Brian shook his head. 'It's more than that. Seriously, Joley, something's going on with those two. And suddenly Nikitin loans him to us. Did Nikitin send him on purpose? Does he want something? I think those are legitimate questions we have to ask.'

'You've sure changed your mind.' Joley pushed away from the table, taking her tea with her. She needed the soothing chamomile. 'You defended Nikitin before.' Although he'd never liked Prakenskii, she recalled.

'After you talked to me, I thought a lot about the time I'd spent with him, the things I saw and heard, and although I didn't want to admit it, I think there's a possibility that you're right about Sergei.'

Her eyebrows shot up at the familiar way Brian said the Russian's name. 'You've spent more time with Nikitin than I realized. I'm sorry if you thought he was a friend, Brian. I should have told you my concerns about him earlier. I just thought you all went to his parties for the benefits.'

Brian jumped up, knocking hard into the table, sending the plate skittering across it. He righted it, avoiding her eyes. 'Yeah. I spent time with him. And I don't trust Prakenskii. Nikitin is weird about him. Really weird.'

She wanted to hear but she didn't. The mention of Prakenskii sent pain crashing through her. Pain. Guilt. Shame. She hated feeling stupid. 'In what way?'

'At first I thought they had a thing – you know – a sexual thing.'

Joley spewed tea across the room, choked and coughed, gasping for air. When she managed to breathe, she scowled at him. 'Why in the world would you think Ilya Prakenskii and Nikitin are lovers?'

'You are very naïve, Joley, in a lot of ways. Prakenskii is a dominant, in every sense of the word, and very sexual. He could mesmerize someone, male or female, and keep them tied to him. Nikitin seems under his control, afraid of him, but influenced by him. He obviously won't fire him, you said so yourself. But he doesn't trust him. I saw that with my own eyes. And Nikitin is gay.'

'How would you know that?'

There was a small silence that lengthened and grew. Joley slowly put down her teacup and stared at the man she'd known for years. A man she thought of as her best friend. He met her gaze steadily, but she could see the expectance of rejection in his eyes. 'You? Brian, why didn't you ever tell me? How could I not know? Do all the guys know?'

He shook his head but remained silent.

Joley looked around for a chair, and when nothing was close by she leaned against the wall. 'Why didn't you say something to me?'

'I couldn't.'

She swallowed hard. 'You didn't trust me. You knew I loved you, but you still didn't trust me, Brian. I don't understand. Did you think it would make a difference in how I feel about you?'

'Right now, I'm just Brian, one of the band, a member of the family, and we all get along and love each other and it's all good. Everyone respects me and comes to me for advice for everything from dating to what to do when they have a problem. In an argument, they all listen to me. What do you think will happen when it comes out I'm gay? I'll be the gay guy who might cry if someone yells at him. Everything will change. My friends will treat me differently, and you can bet the paparazzi will have a field day talking about all of us traveling in the bus together, taking showers, sleeping. They'll speculate on the others, and pretty soon it won't be jokes when we read the tabloids, it will be Brian has to have his own bus because they won't be able to laugh about sleeping with a gay man. They can laugh when the paparazzi claim you're banging all of us, but it won't be so funny if it's them with me.'

He was right. She could see how it would happen. 'How could you hide this so long and no one know?' She rarely touched him, but she should have had some warning. She'd thought it was just that she felt a lack of sexual attraction toward her.

'Because the band and the music meant more to me than banging someone. I just dated a few girls and made certain we were photographed a lot, and eventually broke up with them. I went to the parties and looked like I fit in. Staying sober helped. I could think clearly and set the stage when I needed to. Our names were linked all the time and I made certain it stayed that way.'

'But now? Why are you telling me now?'

'Because Nikitin knows about me, he knows I'm gay. I fell in love with him. He was like a dream come true for me. We'd talk for hours and laugh together. We'd go up to his room and have a cognac and end up in bed. Not at first. At first we just talked, but I couldn't stay away from him, even though I knew I was risking my career. But his risk seemed just as great. He's always with beautiful women. I asked if he was bisexual and he said no, but like me, he needed to keep his image straight. He said it was better for his business. He was perfect. He understood I traveled often; he did, too. He could follow the band on the pretense of loving the music and give extravagant parties and we could be together and no one would be the wiser.'

It took a few minutes to digest what he was telling her. Everything she'd ever thought or believed about Nikitin was wrong. Everyone thought Nikitin was obsessed with her, but all along it had been with Brian. He'd followed the band because he'd been Brian's lover.

'How long has this been going on?'

Brian rubbed his forehead in distress. 'A long time. Over a year.'

'His security has to know.'

'You mean Prakenskii. Yeah. I'm pretty certain he knows. Sergei wouldn't discuss him with me. I was so jealous, Joley. So jealous and so stupid. Prakenskii is a very dangerous man. To you. To me. Maybe even to Sergei.'

Joley went to the window and stared out. People were milling everywhere, but she felt alone and empty and sad. Terribly sad. Ilya had known about Brian before she had, and Brian was her best friend. Why hadn't Ilya said anything to her? Loyalty toward his boss? Did he have other motives?

And Brian. She sighed. Brian was a good person, and he didn't deserve heartache any more than she did. 'I'm afraid for you, Brian. Sergei Nikitin heads up the Russian mob. He isn't just a little part of it, he's the top dog. If he believes you're a threat to him, he'll have you killed.'

Brian stood behind her, staring out the window as well. 'I broke it off with him, made certain he knew I had as much to lose, and he said he wasn't willing to let it go. He said he would never harm me, but the rest of the band wasn't going to be so lucky.' He covered his face with his hands and slid down to the floor. 'That kid. Dean. I think his men killed him because of me – as a warning to me. And then he sent Prakenskii here as a warning that you were next. I don't know what to do, Joley. I couldn't bear it if he had you killed, too.'

Joley slid to the floor beside him, slinging her arm around, uncaring that his sorrow and fear only compounded her own. 'You know we're going to have to go to the police.'

'That won't stop him, Joley. You should have seen him when I talked to him. And God help me, I still love him. I had no idea he was a monster. He was as lonely as I was and I think he really cared. I hope that he did. But he flew into a rage when I told him we had to end it.'

'Is he here in Dallas?'

'Yes. And he wants me to go to his party tonight after the performance. He said we have to talk, to clear things up. If I don't go, I don't know what he'll do. Logan's got the baby traveling with him and Tish. Denny we can keep from the party, but Rick and Leo will go for sure. He could do anything to them.'

'We're getting ahead of ourselves.' She pressed a hand to her churning stomach.

Was it possible that they all had it wrong? Brian insisted that Nikitin feared Prakenskii. Could Nikitin be the front man and Prakenskii be the real boss? Everyone deferred to him – everyone. She'd watched it a million times. The moment he spoke. The moment he moved. Every one of Nikitin's men stopped what they were doing to pay attention. Could he be the real head of the Russian mob? All the violence she'd seen in his memories, all the darkness clouding his aura, even his dominating personality pointed to it. Did he control others through his sexual expertise? The thought sickened her. She rubbed her face against her knees.

'Let's not panic, Brian. No one else knows about this, right?'

He nodded.

'Well, let's do the show. Say you'll go to the party. We can have something go wrong at the performance. I can fall and hurt myself. We've got a couple of hours to think of something to buy us a little more time.'

'We have to leave Dallas tonight for some reason.'

She nodded. 'We'll come up with an excuse and make it seem real. We're performers. Jonas is in law enforcement. I'll talk to him and a couple of my sisters about Nikitin. I'll do my best to cover what he's got on you.'

He shook his head. 'It's over for me. Once the fact that I'm gay is out, I've got to leave the band.'

'No, you don't.' She had to get away from him. His misery overwhelmed him. 'And you can forget the suicide crap, it's not an option.' Because she could feel him considering that as well. 'Come on, Brian, we're in this together. We're smart. We'll figure it out.' She stood up and brushed herself off. 'My family's tangled with the mob before, and we always come out on top. You tell the sound crew I'll be there in a few minutes. I'm calling Jonas.'

It had taken a lot of courage for Brian to come to her and tell her the truth. He had served himself up on a platter to her, and she was going to stand by him, by their long-standing friendship and the love she had for him. She loved him all the more for trusting her with his secret. Joley hugged him again hard.

Brian brushed a kiss against her temple. 'I'm sorry I brought this to us.'

She couldn't let him leave weighed down with so much guilt. 'Brian.' She caught his sleeve. 'Don't do anything stupid. You didn't think Nikitin was anything but a businessman. I suspected Ilya was more than he appeared, so if we're really in trouble here, I'm far more to blame than you.'

She had never understood why Denny couldn't just walk away from the groupies and the drugs. She was appalled at Logan for betraying Tish. He'd been so strong, night after night, but in the end, in spite of loving Tish, he'd succumbed to temptation. She hadn't understood how a person could be so weak that they would make the choice to do something they knew was so wrong – until now.

'You didn't do anything wrong, Brian. Of all of us, you're the only one who tried to do the right thing. None of this is your fault. And certainly Dean's death isn't. That's on whoever killed him, and we don't know that it was Nikitin.'

'Thank you for that, Joley,' Brian said.

He went out the door, leaving her standing alone in the silence. In emptiness. Because that was her life. Empty. Having spent hours of happiness with Ilya, the sheer loneliness was that much harder to take. Maybe that had been Logan's downfall. When Tish stopped traveling so much with them, he couldn't take being alone. Maybe that was the reason Denny couldn't resist the groupies and Rick and Leo partied so much. She could understand how Brian, after so many years of emptiness, had turned to someone he thought it was safe to love.

She flipped open her phone and called Jonas. When it came to her family, she knew they were rock-solid, could always be counted on, but he was going to go berserk on her. She told him the entire story. All of it. Including her downfall with Ilya. She skated over Brian, but she knew he got the gist of it, and one thing about Jonas was his absolute silence when she spoke to him in confidence – which she'd been smart enough to insist on before the conversation even got started.

She had to hold the phone away from her ear until he got done swearing and telling her to get her ass home now. Tonight. On a plane. She stood for what seemed like forever before his rant stopped and she could speak again.

'Jonas, I cannot cancel the rest of my tour. We're sold out at every single venue. In any case, if we did cancel, that would certainly tip off Nikitin that Brian told us everything.'

'I don't give a damn. You get home to the house that eats people and I know you'll be safe. Bring the band if you need to, but get where we can protect you.'

'It's not like I'm going to be poking around asking questions. I'm not stupid.' She made a face. 'Okay. I take that back, I'm stupid where men are concerned, but not about safety.'

'Nothing can happen to you, Joley. I'll fly to Dallas with Aleksandr and Jackson and we'll help provide protection. Aleksandr knows a great deal about the mob, and once Jackson puts the crosshairs on someone, they're dead.'

She sucked in her breath. 'You can't do that. I mean it, Jonas. First of all, I absolutely am not risking my family. You promised you'd be reasonable. Don't fly off the handle. If you all come down here, my sisters will come.'

'Over my dead body.'

'You know they will. Come on. Think with me. If you come to Dallas right now, my sisters will follow, and that would have the same effect as if I canceled the tour. Nikitin would know Brian gave him up and he'd have him killed. Tell me I'm wrong.'

There was more swearing on the other end. Jonas finally sighed. 'Listen to me, Joley. Really, for once in your life, listen to me. Hannah, your sisters, your parents, and me, Joley, we wouldn't survive it if anything happened to you. You're like the sunshine in this family. Nothing would ever be the same. I'll gather as much information as possible here. Aleksandr will be able to tell us more about Prakenskii, but you stay the hell away from him. My gut says he's some kind of cop, but I've been wrong before. He's sided with our family numerous times, and between you and me, I know he's the one who took out the mobster threatening Hannah. He did it to make certain the feds didn't keep him alive where he could direct reprisals from a cell.'

'That hit benefited Nikitin, though, didn't it? I heard you talking to Jackson about it.' Joley began pacing up and down the narrow corridor of the bus.

'You shouldn't have been listening.' There was an edge now to Jonas's voice, something that happened a lot with Joley.

'Sorry, I find your whispered conversations so intriguing.'

'That's not funny, Joley.'

Her fingers tightened around the phone. 'If I don't laugh, I'm going to cry. I'm counting on you to figure something out. I'm doing the concert tonight, and I'm going to have Jerry announce that we have to leave right after so no one will have a chance to go to that party.'

She could feel Ilya's presence now. He was close – very close – and her heart began to beat faster in anticipation of seeing him.

'You just remember there's already been one murder, Joley. If it's about Brian, Nikitin won't hesitate to teach him another lesson.'

'I'm scared enough, thank you very much. I've got to do the sound check. My poor sound crew is probably having fits. I've got to go, Jonas, but I'm counting on you to save us.'

'That's my specialty, honey. And I'll find out everything I can on Prakenskii, but if he's undercover, I don't want to blow it for him or raise any red flags. Stay away from him.'

She closed her eyes for a moment, wishing she had, wishing it wasn't already too late. 'Please don't tell Hannah how stupid I've been.'

'No one thinks you're stupid, Joley. Please be careful. I'll call back with information and a plan.'

'I knew you would. Thanks, Jonas.'

Joley slipped the phone into her pocket and went to the door of her bus. Taking a deep breath, she opened it, knowing Ilya would be waiting to escort her to the sound check. She was right, and the sight of him took her breath away. He was so handsome, so mesmerizing, his deep blue eyes hypnotic. She inhaled his scent, and went dizzy with wanting him, weak with need. She forced a small smile and glanced at her watch.

'Sorry. I'm so late. We're going to have to hurry.' Deliberately, before Ilya could respond, she looked beyond him to spot Logan stepping out of the other bus. She waved and beckoned him over, trying to hide her relief.

'Joley, stop it,' Ilya hissed. 'What's this going to prove?'

She flicked him a quick look from under her lashes and then shrugged her shoulders. 'I don't know what you're talking about other than I'm hours late with my sound check and my crew's had to wait on me.'

She kept walking toward Logan as fast as she could, and, thankfully, Logan hurried toward her. Before Ilya could say anything else Logan was there. Deliberately she stepped to the other side of him, putting him between Ilya and her. She should have known it wouldn't work. Ilya simply dropped a pace back smoothly, looking as stone-cold and as professional as ever.

'Baby all right?' she asked quickly.

'Lissa's great. I think everyone holds her too much. We get her down, and one of the guys will come in and pick her up right out of her little carry crib. Tish deals with it, but I think it makes it hard to keep to a schedule.'

'And you and Tish? How's that coming?' Joley prompted. She was so aware of Ilya. So aware of the rise and fall of his chest, his every breath, even his heartbeat. Her palm itched and tingled no matter how much she rubbed it against her thigh seeking relief.

'Not bad. I'm going to have to do a lot more groveling.'

She flashed him a look. 'And I hope you know you deserve to grovel. She shouldn't take you back.'

'I know that. But I'm not stupid enough to ever lose her again. I love Tish, Joley. It was a dumb mistake. I was drunk and she wasn't there and I was lonely, and if I could take it back, believe me, a million times I've thought of that moment, that one moment when I walked out of that room with that woman. I can't remember what she looks like. I don't even remember her name. I only remember Tish standing there with that look on her face, so happy to see me, and then seeing – knowing – and her smile fading. The light just died out of her eyes. Believe me, Joley, I know exactly what I lost. If I get it back, I'm not going to ever lose it again.'

She put her hand on his sleeve. 'Then I wish with all my heart that she takes you back.' They were only steps away from the door, and she wanted to run. She could barely breathe through the pain in her heart. It felt like a knife through her chest. She swore under her breath, counting the steps to safety.

Without warning, Ilya moved fast, a huge graceful tiger inserting his body with fluid grace between her and someone she couldn't see. He actually shoved her to the side and away from him. A woman screamed.

'*Bastard*! You bastard, Logan. I'm going to kill you. I'm going to destroy you.' Lucy Brady, the woman who had given birth to Lissa, lunged at Logan, swinging her fist. In her fingers, she clutched a broken bottle.

Ilya restrained her, taking her to the ground. 'Keep moving,' he ordered. 'Both of you. Get inside.'

Logan hesitated. Joley grabbed his hand and yanked him with her, running now, into the building and toward the safety of her crew. Glancing back, she saw more security guards converging on the snarling, spitting woman on the ground, and Ilya calm and cool holding her, uncaring of her threats.

Chapter Twelve

Joley flashed across the stage like quicksilver, looking so sexy Ilya found it hard to tear his gaze from her. She was all glitter and flash, sultry and dazzling, burning so hot, flying so high, he knew she would crash after the performance. He had done that. Driven her to the breaking point. To everyone else she looked strong and confident; to him she looked vulnerable and fragile. She wanted the world to think she was just fine – she wanted *him* to believe it, but he knew her too well.

He had crushed her with his careless handling. For the first time in his life his training had utterly failed him. Joley was everything he had ever dreamt of – more. She had given him back humanity, taught him to feel, to believe in hope. He had been careless for the first time in his life, stealing time for himself, forgetting that his life depended on secrecy. And he had been indiscreet, giving her a truth and then pulling back when she accepted it.

He swore and forced himself to look away from her, to study the audience in the first several rows and then slowly back farther. Her voice played over his skin, a mix of sultry heat and promise that kept his body hard when his chest felt weighed down with sorrow.

He had absolutely no experience when it came to relationships. None. His instinct, when he realized she was withdrawing, had been to pull her close to him, to force the issue, but he couldn't give her what she needed, and she would have fought him with her last breath. It would have turned into a physical confrontation, and there would have been no winner. So he'd backed off, and now he had no idea what to do to regain her trust.

He detested this feeling of inadequacy, of indecision. He was a man confident in his abilities, sure of his responses, quick to make judgment calls, and in the most important area of his life, he felt paralyzed by his lack of knowledge.

His gaze strayed back to Joley. The stage was every bodyguard's worst nightmare. The venue was a bowl with the stage in the center, surrounded by thousands of screaming fans. They had people scanning the crowd, but to find trouble was like looking for a needle in a haystack. And there was going to be trouble. The electric energy of the crowd nearly drowned out the small threads of malevolence he could feel, but he was ultrasensitive to danger and it was there, somewhere in that vast sea of faces.

'Check the south side,' he said into his radio.

He didn't like the shows in the huge venues. Joley used a rig shaped like a platform bridge that swung her out over the audience. It put her right in the midst of them, up high; she gyrated and sung on a narrow metal path in the air. And when she performed, she was giving it her all. Lights flashed, the sky rained sparkles, and fire rose from the stage. Joley ran and leapt for the platform as it began to swing out over the audience.

'South side. South side,' Ilya hissed. His gut was in hard knots now. 'Get the camera on her. Make certain there's nothing wrong with that platform.' He had inspected it himself. With his belly churning and that heaviness of dread weighing down his chest, he knew the small threads of dangerous energy were gathering fast.

There were a million tricks one learned as a personal protector, but he realized most of them went out the window when the person you were guarding was your soul. He had to keep forcing his gaze from straying toward her. His heart beat too fast, and he tasted fear in his mouth. If someone wanted her dead, it would be so easy. A gun – hell, in this crowd, whoever shot her could probably tuck the gun into his shirt and walk away.

He took a deep breath and pushed it all away, falling back on years of cool distance. He forced himself back under rigid control, knowing that if he allowed emotion to rule him, he would lose this battle. He let his senses flair out, uncaring that he would be gathering information it would take his mind months to get rid of.

The stadium was on its feet as the band swung into one of the favorites. Joley looked like mouth-watering candy as she moved over the bridge. The crowd responded with wild screams and waves, reaching up toward her, thunder filling the bowl as the people stomped feet and clapped hands to the pounding beat.

As the platform swung to the south, Ilya shut everything out of his mind but the people under her; he was watching intently for something beyond his vision, something that would register in his mind, in

242

his senses, long before his brain would recognize what his eyes were seeing. People dancing. Women on men's shoulders, arms lifted. His heart jerked and he began moving fast.

'Just under the bridge. Focus directly under the bridge.'

He raced across the stage, leapt for the stairs going up the bridge. Even as he ran, his training didn't fail him. He blurred his image to keep cameras from focusing on him. Below him he could see the man on the shoulders of another man taking his hands away from the steel. Both men ducked, hands over their heads.

Joley. Toward me!

She didn't question or hesitate. As if they had choreographed a dance together, she turned and raced toward him, still singing, still holding the microphone. The charge went off just after she passed the device. Sparks raced to the ceiling, but no more than the dazzling display of light and sound racing around the bowl. The sound of grinding metal was loud as the beam split, one side, jagged and sharp, popping up, catching Joley's arm as she flashed by. The other side dropped down toward the crowd, held only by threads.

'In the crowd. Two men. One is wearing a striped shirt, the other has on a leather jacket, a long one. Get them. I'll be there as soon as possible to question them.' He spoke low into the radio, keeping in the shadows as he moved into a better position to help Joley.

She went still, keeping control of the situation like the pro she was. 'Swing it slowly over the stage, guys, we don't want anyone hurt.' Her voice was absolute calm, and it stopped the crowd beneath her from panicking. She sent them a quick sassy grin. 'These little things happen at all shows. That's going to get a lot of play on the Internet. Oops, watch Joley fall off the platform. Maybe I'll get really lucky and become famous!'

The audience went wild cheering. As always, she carried them with her personality and her voice. No one seemed to realize that there was still danger.

He was standing behind her now, his hand on her, as the bridge moved back into position. He felt the shifting under his feet as it wanted to shred and buckle, and he tightened his hands at her waist in case he had to throw her clear. Joley kept talking, seemingly unaware that her arm was dripping blood. He got a good look at the cut as the lights played over them.

It's bad, Joley. Your arm's ripped open.

Tell me something I don't know. Can you do anything to get me through this?

He didn't hesitate. As the platform went level with the stage, he lifted her to firm ground, turning for a moment, his body blocking hers from sight, both hands wrapping around her forearm. She gasped and went pale. Blood dripped steadily. Warmth spread from him to her, and she took a breath and stepped back.

Thanks. I can work with this.

He didn't turn around but kept walking, jumping off the stage as the audience erupted into a round of applause.

'Aren't my guys great?' Joley asked, then turned and sent a mock scowl toward her band. 'Hey! I didn't see any of you rushing to be my hero.'

Denny held up a glass. 'Sorry, love, we were taking a break. Did something happen?' He burst

244

into a drum solo that had the crowd laughing and back on their feet.

The crew discreetly moved the platform back away from the audience as far as possible once it was lowered to the stage, while Joley took the towel Brian handed her and casually wrapped it around her arm.

'Joley.' His voice was broken.

'Thanks, babe,' she said and stood on her toes to brush a kiss against his cheek where she could whisper reassurances. 'I'm fine. We need to keep going here, Brian. Help me, okay?'

He nodded and backed away from her, but his face was stiff with guilt and fear. Joley straightened her shoulders, ignored the pain in her arm and moved to the front of the stage, peering down at the rows in front of her. Spotting a young girl of about ten who looked frightened, she leaned toward her, flashing her famous smile. 'Were you scared just then?'

The girl nodded.

'So was I, but not nearly as scared as the time I decided to crawl out my window to go to a girl-friend's house. I was just about your age and she was having a sleepover. My parents said I couldn't go because I'd done something that day at school to get in trouble.' She'd put a live mouse in the teacher's drawer because the teacher had yelled at her for writing notes, but she for sure wasn't confessing that. 'Well I got stuck half in and half out of that window and I heard my dad coming down the hall. I have to tell you – now *that* was a truly scary moment.'

The little girl laughed and visibly relaxed. Joley turned back to the band.

'The father has punished you for your sins.' The

voice blared over a handheld microphone, loud and commanding.

Ilya, who had been striding up to the office, paused, holding his breath. Joley could turn the crowd ugly with one tone of her voice. She slowly turned back, shading her eyes with her hand, and a small smile broke out. With Joley, that was like watching the sun break free.

'RJ. I see you're back again. You just can't seem to stay away.'

'I follow where sin and debauchery take me so I might be an instrument of good. Had you been following the path of righteousness, no evil would have befallen you.'

The crowd booed and stomped their feet. Joley held up her hand for silence. Ilya held his breath. She held them in her palm, didn't the Reverend see that? Hear it? She was magic on a stage. She probably didn't even realize how much of her gift she utilized onstage as she performed, but her voice was a powerful weapon and it definitely could incite an ugly riot. He knew the power of sound, he'd used it more than once to hypnotize, incite, or to seduce. Survival was everything, and any and all weapons were exploited.

'No, sir, that was a good old-fashioned accident. They happen all time. These people have worked all week, and they're here to have a good time and enjoy themselves, that's all. So you sit down and let's get on with the fun.'

The Reverend sat – and that more than anything showed the power Joley wielded with her voice.

As the band swung into a number, Ilya made his way into the office where security held two men. They were much younger than he'd first thought, and both looked scared. He made them even more terrified by leaning up against the desk, folding his arms and staring at them in silence. One of the security guards handed him the two IDs, showing one was eighteen and the other twenty.

Ilya nodded his head toward the door and the guards left, leaving him alone with the two kids. In silence he pulled on thin leather gloves as he deliberately glanced around the room as if looking for cameras, making certain that the two young men looked as well.

The younger of the two, Raymond Silver, was the one who had planted the charge. He cleared his throat and shifted anxiously when Ilya's cold gaze settled on him. The boy kept sending frightened looks to his friend. The silence stretched and lengthened.

'Look, man,' Raymond finally burst out with. 'I was just telling those dudes. That wasn't supposed to happen. It was only supposed to rock the platform and unbalance her, not break like that. A guy paid us a hundred a piece to put the device there. He even gave us the tickets for those seats and showed us on a drawing where to place it. He was filming it for the Internet. You know, where they play all the videos.'

The other boy, Tony Morano, grinned. 'I'll bet it turns out cool.'

Ilya reached out, his hand a blur of motion, slapping the kid hard enough to rock him back on his heels. The blow was fast, vicious and shocking, the sound loud in the small confines of the room. Tony staggered and fell against the desk.

'I guess you didn't notice that Miss Drake was injured.' Ilya kept his voice low and calm, completely at odds with the blow.

'You can't hit me,' Tony yelled, wiping the blood from his mouth. 'I could sue you. This is police brutality, man.'

Ilya caught him by the throat, again the movement so fast the boy never saw it coming. Ilya yanked him off his feet and slammed him against the door, a foot off the ground, simply holding him there by his throat, while the kid's heels drummed against the wood.

Again he used a calm, mild, unhurried voice. 'I guess you didn't hear me, Mr. Morano. I said Miss Drake was injured. A proper response would have been to say you're sorry and that you hope it isn't a bad injury.' Ilya ignored the gasping for breath, the ragged, desperate choking and gagging as the boy turned color. Ilya shifted slightly so he could look at Raymond. 'Don't you agree that would have been a better response, Mr. Silver?'

Raymond nodded desperately over and over, backing around the desk to put it between them.

Ilya allowed Tony to drop to the ground, releasing him abruptly and not at all gently. Tony fell to the floor, holding his throat, coughing and sputtering.

'Let's try again, Mr. Morano.' The voice never changed. It remained casual and matter-of-fact, almost friendly. 'I am not the police. I don't arrest people and I have no intention of turning you over to the police. They can find you all by themselves if there's anything left to find when I'm done here. I do, however, do other things besides arrest people. You don't want me to have to do those things to you. There are no cameras in this room, no recorders, and those men outside are my men. They'll walk away and disappear, just like I can make you disappear. So, with that in mind, let's try again. Miss

Drake was injured by your little stunt.'

Tony tried to get his feet under him twice, but fell back coughing.

'I have a good job. Extermination. At first I wasn't so certain it was a good thing, but after a while I realized there were people that just were never going to get it, you know? They were never going to understand the rules of living in a society.' Ilya shrugged. 'You know what I mean, Mr. Silver?' He never took his gaze from Tony's face.

Raymond nodded vigorously again.

Ilya sighed and took a step toward Tony.

Tony froze. 'I'm sorry she was injured,' he managed to blurt out, although the words were strangled and rusty sounding. 'I hope it wasn't too bad.'

'That wasn't so difficult, was it?' Ilya asked.

Tony shook his head.

'I want a description of the man who paid you money to injure Miss Drake.' He held up his hand for silence. 'Not out loud. I want separate descriptions written down. Details are important to me.' He reached down and with casual strength hauled Tony to his feet, caught a chair with the toe of his shoe, spun it around and slammed the kid down into it. 'Get started.

'Keep in mind while you're writing, I know where you both live. I know your names. My men will recover the device and trace the origins. Should you have any involvement other than sheer stupidity, I'll come back and do my job. Are we clear?'

Raymond kept nodding. Tony mumbled an affirmative reply. Both bent to the task the moment Ilya put pen and paper in front of them. The younger boy was an artist with a good memory for every facet of his subject. While Tony wrote down a description, Raymond drew the man who had paid them, and he drew him with close attention to detail. Ilya immediately recognized the emerging face. He waited until the boy finished.

'Both of you look at me. Look directly at me because I don't want you later to say you misunderstood me.'

He had already been distorting his image and feeding their imaginations another one, but with Raymond an artist, he needed to implant memories. 'I want you to draw me just as you see me, every detail so you won't forget my brown eyes, and long hair, and small dark beard. You won't forget that I'm very tall and lean. I want you to remember the sound of my voice. The pattern of my speech. Everything about me.'

The two boys set to work, and Ilya watched the drawing come to life of a security guard who looked anything but like him. He shoved the first sketch, of one of Joley's crew members, John Dylan, into the inside pocket of his jacket and walked out, nodding to his two men, who immediately disappeared into the crowd.

Ilya made his way back inside the bowl, noting that Joley still had her arm wrapped in a towel as she sang a love ballad. She hadn't slowed down at all, giving her audience everything inside of her, sending her beautiful voice to every seat in the stadium with as much energy as she'd had when the show started.

Jerry came up to stand beside him. 'Isn't she amazing?'

'She's in pain. Lots of pain.'

Jerry nodded. 'I've got a medic standing by. We'll take her straight to her bus and let him work on her there, away from cameras. There's a huge crowd of the bastards waiting for her. Ordinarily I'd be happy for the publicity, but she's running on nerves. I'm putting them all on a private plane and flying them out of here tonight. No one knows yet, not even them.'

'That's probably for the best. You might give Nikitin a heads-up. He was planning a huge party for them. He won't tip the press.'

'Good idea. Why don't you give him a call and let him know. Tell him what's happened and that we can't take any chances with the band. The show's almost over. I want to hustle her out of here fast, Ilya, so make certain we've got a clear path.'

Ilya nodded and made the call to Nikitin. The Russian had elected not to come to the night's performance, which was highly unusual, but he'd been acting strange for the last few days. He asked if all the band members were okay, and Ilya gave him the information that Joley had been injured. He wanted the flight time, to meet them at the airport and see for himself that everyone was okay. He ordered Ilya to go with them and make certain nothing more happened to them.

It was a strange conversation, and very unlike Nikitin, who would usually be upset over the cancellation of a group he'd honored with a party. Ilya turned the conversation over and over in his mind as he made his way to the stage.

Lights flashed, the music rose to a crescendo, and the band rushed from the stage. Security lined the aisle, allowing them a quick and safe retreat. Ilya fell into step with Joley, who barely glanced at him. It was obvious he wasn't going to be forgiven anytime soon, nor was she going to acknowledge that she was angry with him.

Joley was hurried straight to her bus, where the medic waited for her. The band members crowded inside, leaving Ilya blending into the shadows where she wouldn't notice him. But she noticed. He caught her irritated and somewhat fearful gaze several times.

'You have to hurry,' Jerry told the medic. 'She's got a plane to catch.'

'She needs stitches and probably some blood. She should go to the hospital.'

Joley scowled at him. 'Just get it done.'

Jerry nodded to the medic, who shrugged and unwrapped Joley's arm, ignoring the manager as he addressed the band. 'All of you are leaving tonight. I've got a plane waiting at the airport. Prakenskii called Nikitin and let him know we appreciated all the trouble he went to, but we aren't taking chances with Joley or any of the rest of you. We've lost one crew member – and that was no accident – we're not losing anyone else.'

'What about Tish and the baby?' Logan said. 'I'm not leaving without them.'

'There's room. Tell her to get ready to go.'

The medic poured something that burned like acid over Joley's arm, and she cried out and jerked away from him. 'Ow, you sadist. What was that for?'

'To clean the wound. Hold still. I'm numbing it.'

'By sticking a needle into it? Are you crazy?' She looked around. 'He's crazy. Get him out of here. I'll just wrap it up.'

Jerry leveled a look at her. 'You need that arm sewed up. Either here or the hospital.'

She made a face at him. 'It was good tonight, boys. We held it together, and I think I can safely say, that's one of the worst "gone wrong" incidents we've had.'

Rick caught her head and kissed the top of it. 'Yeah, baby, you were on fire. You rocked their world tonight. Even that preacher was probably jacking off just watching you, you little sinner you.'

'Thanks, I think,' Joley said and flashed Rick her brightest smile. 'I love that shirt on you.'

Rick dusted off his chest. 'Drives the women wild.'

Joley laughed and then quickly changed expression, glaring at the medic. 'It hurts – it hurts – it hurts – it hurts,' she repeated, wincing as the needle went in and out of her skin. 'Damn, can't you do something to make me not hurt?' Tears glimmered in her eyes. 'Brian, hit me or something. I heard somewhere you can't hurt in more than one place.'

Brian swung around, a mixture of anger, guilt and fear on his face. 'I told you not to use that platform. Why don't you ever listen to anyone? You could have been killed.'

'Stop jerking your arm away from me,' the medic said. 'You need a tetanus shot as well.'

Joley glared at him. 'I'm sure I don't. God, you're a freakin' butcher, and now you want to stab me with another needle. Everyone go away. I'm just fine. And for your information, Dr. Frankenstein, I can sew up my own arm. Jerry, make them all leave.'

'You're kicking us out?' Brian said, his gaze shifting toward Ilya.

'Yes.' She rocked back and forth. The energy high was giving way under the onslaught of nerves and pain. She needed to be alone, to pull herself back together. She was too exhausted to face any of them, let alone Ilya.

Jerry waved toward the door, and the band went out. She saw Brian glance around, and then he flipped open his cell phone. Instinct told her he was calling Nikitin. Fear skittered down her spine. 'Jerry. Call Brian back.' Jerry didn't turn around. She yanked her arm away from the medic and stood up.

Immediately the room swirled and the walls began to undulate. The floor shifted out from under her. Ilya caught her before she went down.

'I told you she needed blood,' the medic complained.

'She'll be fine,' Ilya said. 'I'll take it from here.'

'At least let me give her the tetanus shot.'

'Do it then,' Ilya suggested. 'Before I throw you out on your ear.'

'I'm not the one that did this to her,' the medic protested.

'No, but you sure don't know much about suturing wounds either,' Ilya pointed out. He waited impatiently for the man to administer the shot to Joley's arm, before placing her on the bed. The medic went out, closing the door, leaving the two of them alone.

Joley tried to say something, to stop her worst nightmare from happening, but no sound came out. She hadn't been able to bring herself to come right out and tell Jerry that she had worries about whether or not Ilya was in the Russian mob. And she certainly wasn't going to admit to sleeping with him. The best she could do was push ineffectually at him with her hand.

Ilya pretended not to notice her distress. 'Lie back. I'll get you some orange juice. You can drink that while I finish sewing you up.'

She made a face at his back, struggling into a semi-sitting position that made her feel less vulnerable. 'You're not coming near me with a needle.' She meant to sound firm, but her voice was thin and a little hoarse, as if her throat was raw.

He shot her a quelling look. 'Don't waste your energy on arguing. You couldn't fight your way out of paper bag, Joley.' He pushed the glass of juice into her hand and pulled her arm closer to him to inspect it. Swearing under his breath, he placed his hands over the wound and sent warmth to speed healing and hopefully numb the area while he worked.

Tears coursed down her cheeks, but Joley didn't complain or try to pull away from him. He was as gentle as he could be.

'John Dylan is the member of your crew who you thought was friends with Dean. Dylan paid two kids to plant the charge to bring down the platform. He told them it was only going to shake the platform and he'd record you falling on your butt for the Internet. They thought it would be "cool." Stupid kids.'

Joley let out her breath and pressed her free hand to her mouth to keep from weeping. Her arm hurt like hell, and Ilya's touch was so gentle it ripped at her heart. 'I didn't do anything to him. I didn't even talk to him.'

'He knows you spotted him. He doesn't know how, but he knows you did. He's covering something up and doesn't want you questioning him or telling anyone that he was the one you saw that night with Dean.'

'He'll figure I told you. You were with me.'

'He'll try to kill me.' Ilya was matter-of-fact. 'I'm going to give him his opportunity.'

255

She sucked in her breath sharply. 'That's stupid. You aren't a stupid man.'

He paused for a moment and waited until she looked up at him. 'In some areas, I can be very stupid, Joley. I hurt you and I'm sorry for that.'

Her stomach protested the turn in the conversation. She didn't want him to be nice. She didn't want him near her at all, because she didn't trust herself. She was weak when it came to Ilya, and just like every other person in the world, where she was weak, she could make a terrible mistake. 'Don't worry about it. I'm a big girl.'

His eyes glittered dangerously and her pulse leapt. 'Joley, whatever happened the other night . . .'

'Stop. I don't want to talk about it. I don't want to think about it. I'm tired, Ilya. And I have to catch a plane tonight. I hurt like hell and I think someone's trying to kill me. If I had any idea why, maybe I could figure it out, but I don't, so I'm screwed. I don't want you talking to me, or being nice to me, or pretending there's anything at all but sex between us, because you made it clear there wasn't. I don't like mixed signals, so don't throw them at me, especially now.'

He bent over her, forcing her across the pillow. The deep sea of his eyes went from calm to stormy. 'You're running from yourself, and the things you need in a relationship, not from me. I might not say what you want to hear, but there are no mixed signals. I'm fully committed to you. Now. Always.'

Her heart slammed hard in her chest, and as hard as she tried, her body went into meltdown from his aggression, his strength, the raw possession and hunger in his eyes. Even with one hand wrapped around her throat, his thumb tipping her face up toward him and his thick chest weighing her down, she realized he was careful of her arm, careful to keep from jarring her. 'You want sex, Ilya. You don't want to share who or what you are.' Her gaze slid from his. 'You know you can rule me in the bedroom, so yeah, it's probably a great turn-on for you.'

'Be very careful what you say to me, Joley. I know you're hurt, and you're pushing me away, but sooner or later we're going to be alone together and you're going to have to face everything you've said or done.'

Fear skated down her spine. She moistened her lips. 'We're not going to be alone.'

His eyebrow shot up. 'Really? We are now.'

He simply closed the scant inches between their lips and took her mouth. Not savagely. Not with the ravenous hunger she felt smoldering beneath the surface, but with such tenderness it nearly wrenched her heart right out of her body. Tears burned behind her eyelids, but she blinked them away. Before she could stop herself, she was kissing him back. She could try to blame it on exhaustion, but truthfully, the moment he touched her – he owned her.

Someone slammed their palm against the outside of her door. 'Car's waiting. Let's go.'

Ilya didn't hurry lifting his head. He finished kissing her thoroughly. 'We'll figure this out, Joley, give it some time.'

Pressing her hand against her burning mouth, she nodded and rushed out, Ilya following at a more leisurely pace. She didn't care if it looked to him as if she was running. She slid into the car beside Brian and closed her eyes, leaving them closed for nearly the entire ride to the airport. Around her, she could hear the others laughing and talking. Inside she wept. She hated that she had become the person she despised most. Weak and helpless against her own needs.

She watched Brian as he hurried away from the band at the airport, making his way to Nikitin's car in what had to be a previously arranged meeting. She felt for him, knew what it was like to want someone that was wrong for you. She wouldn't have understood before, but her own failings had given her a tolerance for and understanding of the weaknesses in others.

Brian returned within a few minutes, his steps heavy, his shoulders slumped. He looked as if the weight of the world was on him. Joley glanced around her to see if anyone else was watching. Tish knew. Joley could see it in her eyes when she looked at Brian as he walked back toward them. The others didn't notice, but Tish knew heartbreak, and Joley was becoming all too familiar with it, and there was no missing the pain in Brian's expression. For once, Joley didn't care about feeling another person's pain or emotion, she only cared about shielding her friend. As Brian approached, his steps heavy, she flung her arm around him and walked with him up the stairs to the plane.

'You okay?'

He shook his head. 'When I'm with him, I find it so hard to believe that he's what you say he is. Even with the evidence I've seen with my own eyes, all the little things that add up, I don't want to believe it, Joley.' He pressed his fingertips to his eyes hard.

'I'm sorry, Brian.'

'He said he didn't mean the things he said. He swore he'd never consider hurting you or anyone else I cared about. He was hurt and angry that I didn't give him a chance to tell his side of things. I should have done that. I should have listened to him.'

Joley sank into the seat beside him, noting that Logan, who was holding Lissa, and Tish had their heads close together while Rick strapped an infant seat to the chair for Lissa. Leo took a seat with Denny across from him. She knew, without looking, exactly where Ilya was at the back of the plane. She could feel his gaze on her. She was far too aware of him, every detail, so much so that sometimes she swore she knew when he took a breath. She reached over to Brian and rubbed his sleeve in an attempt to comfort him – or herself.

'If he is the head of one of the branches of mafia, or whatever they call it in Russia, he's dangerous. Being with him isn't worth dying over.' She leaned her head back against the seat. 'You know my family is different. We have other senses, gifts, magic if you will. We don't think of it that way, but we know things about people when we touch them. It's why I'm careful not to touch skin. I can feel emotions, and sometimes see things others would rather keep private.' She smiled at him. 'You hid yourself very well from me. I see auras and melodies, and yours has always been rather sad, as if you had suffered a great sorrow.'

He shrugged his shoulders. 'It's hard to be so alone all the time. I love music, Joley, and I love what we do. I looked after everyone and tried to keep us all together, which wasn't always easy, especially after Tish left Logan, but I was still alone. How can you be anything else when no one knows who you really are?'

Joley sighed. 'Strangely, my friend, I felt exactly the same way.'

'Joley, how could you? You're so beautiful and talented and easy to love. Hell, if I were straight, I'd be all over you.'

She laughed. 'There's always an excuse with you. But, seriously, I'm not all that great. I have secrets just like everyone else. We'll have to form the club for worst taste in men.'

Brian ducked his head. 'He could be good, Joley. He swears he had nothing to do with the incident to-night.'

'You know better, Brian. Deep down, you know, that's why it hurts so much.' She could feel Ilya's gaze on her and knew he was wondering what they were talking about. Sometimes she felt her palm itching, and a slight flutter of warmth in her mind, but she refused to acknowledge him. She might succumb if he touched her, but in the meantime, she was building defenses as fast as she could.

Chapter Thirteen

Ilya stood in the shadows as he normally did. The park had little lighting, and with the clouds overhead obscuring the moon, and the thick stand of trees, he doubted anyone could see him, but he wasn't taking chances with this meeting. He'd been followed. He'd lost his pursuers the moment he entered the park, but they'd find him again soon, so he had to hurry.

He watched through night glasses as Jonas Harrington came into view. Jonas wasn't alone, and Ilya recognized Aleksandr Volstov just from the way the man moved. They halted at the appointed meeting place, and with one last look around, he went to join them.

'What part of "come alone" didn't you understand?' he asked Jonas.

Joley's brother-in-law looked him up and down, his expression a mixture of wariness and respect. Jonas was a man who couldn't be bought, had intense loyalties and would charge hell with a bucket of water if need be. Ilya liked and respected him almost as much as he did Aleksandr. He knew Volstov was engaged to another of Joley's sisters. The man had been a policeman in Russia and then later worked for Interpol.

'What the hell are you doing with Joley?' Jonas demanded.

'This meeting is about our mutual problem with Nikitin, not about Joley. That subject is off-limits,' Ilya decreed.

Joley had been safely locked up in a hotel room for the last three days, away from him, and he hadn't realized until that moment how much it disturbed him that she wouldn't see him. She hadn't responded the times he'd whisper to her, shamelessly using his voice through their telepathic link, although he'd known she was awake and could hear him.

'My ass, it's off limits,' Jonas snarled. 'You're not going to hurt Joley without getting the pounding of your life. I could care less if you scare everyone on three continents, you don't scare me. Stay the hell away from my sister.'

Aleksandr put a restraining hand on Jonas's arm, giving Ilya a clue as to why he was there. Jonas was a hothead when it came to the Drake sisters. He'd been protecting them all of his life.

Ilya found Joley both maddening and endearing in her fight to stay away from him. He knew she thought she was running because of his reputation. His refusal to disclose his past had been another excuse. She feared turning her life, her body, her heart over to him. He knew what her needs were, and that embarrassed her, terrified her, because he would make certain they were met and she was fiercely independent. She didn't want to need him. She didn't even want to want him. He hoped she craved him, thought of him night and day the way he did her, because right now, that was all he had to entice her with – sex – and his voice.

Ilya shrugged. 'I'm going to marry Joley, so you'd better get used to the idea of having me around.'

'She know that?' Jonas asked, somewhat mollified.

'Not yet. She has a few issues with me.'

'Don't you hurt her.'

Ilya's eyebrow shot up, and for a moment his tough features were stamped with sheer arrogance. 'I have no intentions of hurting Joley. And we're done with the subject.'

More of the tension drained out of Jonas. 'I'm not going to ask who you work for, Ilya, but you're in a bad position. Aleksandr's been hearing rumors from a few friends at Interpol that Nikitin is one of the main traffickers of women and children into Brussels and Indochina. If that's true, and his reputation is growing throughout Europe, then you're smack in the middle of a time bomb. Nikitin is spending so much time in the States that he's in danger of losing his stronghold. They'll be a war soon, and with every side thinking you're the enemy, you're going to be the number one target.'

Aleksandr agreed. 'Nikitin is spending way too much time here; he's been doing business, and he's made a few enemies, cutting into territories. He's got trouble on two fronts.'

Ilya nodded. 'I was afraid of that. I need information fast. I can't go through my usual channels so I'm asking for help.'

Aleksandr snorted in derision at the tone of his old friend. 'That must be hard.'

Ilya sent him a look. 'Nikitin is gay. He doesn't like women or little children, never has, they represent money and power to him, nothing else. He isn't sampling his products, he just sends them down the line fast.'

'Are you sure?' Jonas asked. 'Because Joley . . .'

'Not Joley. It's never been Joley. She's his cover. We've known that for some time. He recruited at least one of her crew members to help him move young girls, but his main interest is one of the band members – he's in love. I know you have someone undercover, working the other end to find the routes and the girls. I need to know if she's safe and out of the way because this thing is going to blow up in our faces.'

Jonas and Aleksandr exchanged a long look. 'Who are you talking about? Interpol has someone inside?'

Swift impatience crossed Ilya's face. 'I'm coming clean with you at the risk of my life, not only my life, but blowing years of undercover work, not to mention taking down a major human trafficking ring. I'm asking you to do the same. If she was working for Interpol, I wouldn't need you reaching out, now would I? Where is she? Is she out yet?'

'She?' Jonas was beginning to have an idea of just who Ilya was referring to. 'Tell me Elle Drake is not in any way involved in this mess. Do you think Elle is working undercover trying to bring down this network? What have you heard?'

'You tell me. Nikitin is unstable at best, and now he's crazy. Joley tipped her band friend off, and the idiot did the noble thing and broke up with Nikitin. Nikitin knows the heat's come down on his human trafficking routes. On top of that, Joley spotted some of the young girls with a couple of her crew members. Nikitin had one of the roadies killed, and did it nice and ugly to scare the other one, but if he loses his lover, his route and everything else he considers his because of Joley, he'll try to wipe out her and everyone close to her. If he gets an inkling

Elle's anywhere near him, she'll be the first to go, and he'll make certain she suffers a long time before she's killed. I need to get her out if she isn't already gone.'

'Honestly, Prakenskii, I have no idea where Elle is or who she's working for.' Jonas swore in frustration. 'Do you have enough evidence on Nikitin to take him down?'

'I can take down his routes, and most of his people, but he's never tied directly to anything and he always, *always*, has an alibi. He's got another layer above the one I've compromised, and I need them to make sure the trafficking is closed off for good here. Otherwise, I cut off one head and another grows back. It would take years to get that one and I don't have that much time.'

'Jackson can get word to her. They've always been able to connect,' Jonas said. 'I honestly don't know what Elle's doing. I was fairly certain it involved undercover work, because Jackson's been restless and edgy lately and Elle's disappeared again.'

'See if he can get word to her to get out for a while. Any excuse. I don't care how close she thinks she is to shutting things down, she has to get clear. I can't control or guess what Nikitin will do, but he has a tendency to resolve issues with violence.'

'Joley has to come home where we can protect her,' Jonas said.

'Joley can't go home without finishing her tour. As long as Nikitin is following the band, he'll think he has a chance to put things back together with his lover. The moment she pulls out, he's going to know he's blown and it won't matter anymore. I'm not throwing away years of work, Harrington. I can protect Joley from Nikitin. If I have to, I'll kill him, but I've got to get to his first line of people or all this has been for nothing.'

Jonas exchanged another long look with Aleksandr. 'Joley only has two performances here in southern California and two in northern California before she's finished. Time's running out, Prakenskii.'

Ilya nodded. 'I'm aware of that.'

'You can't have her and keep up with this kind of work, Ilya. She's an all-or-nothing girl. She's never fallen in love before. She's wanted to, but she doesn't give her trust to anyone. If you're that man, you can't walk away from her. It would destroy her.'

Joley was afraid of giving too much of herself and not surviving if something went wrong. Jonas didn't have to tell him that. He already knew it, because he felt the same way. But he wasn't going to run from his only chance at happiness. Joley had a family; he didn't. Joley had people who made her laugh and could share her troubles. He didn't.

'I wouldn't presume to tell you how best to take care of Hannah.'

'The difference is, Joley's my sister. I've loved her since she was born.' Jonas refused to back down.

'You'll just have to trust me then,' Ilya said and pulled on a thin pair of leather gloves. He drew a very small but wicked-looking knife from a hidden sheath, palming the handle, blade up against his wrist. 'Get out of here. We're about to have company, and no one can know you were here.'

Aleksandr crouched low, pulling his weapon. 'You got any backup here, Ilya?'

Ilya shook his head. 'And you can't stay. If anyone spots you, it could tip them off. It was a risk calling you. And get me as much information on John

Dylan as you can, as fast as you can. I put it through channels, but they're going to take some time.'

'You got it,' Jonas agreed. 'But we're not leaving you to get killed.'

'I don't kill so easy,' Ilya said, his voice dropping even lower. 'Get out so I don't have to worry about you. With the two of you gone, any movement means an enemy in the field, and I don't have to worry about fucking up.'

Aleksandr nodded. 'He's always worked alone, Jonas, we'll just be in the way.'

Ilya watched the two of them slip away into the darkness. He took a deep breath and let it out. He'd deliberately lost the two men trailing him once inside the park so he could have a few moments to speak with Jonas, but he was prepared for a confrontation – in fact, he welcomed it.

Joley's distance had left him edgy and surly inside, his body demanding hers. The more she refused to speak to him, the more he whispered to her, seducing her day and night with his voice. It was a powerful tool, the one he could always fall back on when all else failed. Hunting would let him expend a little of that excess energy.

The trees weren't wide enough to hide his shoulders, and he preferred not using the heavier brush because there was more chance to make noise. He dropped low and moved with care toward the sound of approaching footsteps. A shadow lengthened and grew across the grass, as the man approached. He wore all black. He had two guns out and ready, holding them sideways. Joley would have laughed and said the man watched too many movies. It made Ilya want to smile to think of her, and somehow just the thought of her made him warm.

He stayed prone waiting for the man to come to him. As the shadow approached, he heard the soft hum of a radio and stiffened. The man was communicating with someone else. Ilya spoke several languages and manipulated sound easily. He could talk with perfect accents and imitate voices exactly after one hearing. His pitch was so perfect that when using audio scanners, it was impossible to tell the difference between his voice and whoever he was copying.

He let the man move past him. Rising up, Ilya covered the man's mouth and shoved a knife deep into his kidney. The guns dropped to the ground, and Ilya retrieved the radio, slipping it into his ear. He heard the buzz of voices. Not one more man after him, but several. They'd sent a team to kill him, and that told him they knew his reputation. This wasn't some idiot crew member of Joley's thinking he could protect himself by grabbing a couple of buddies and trying to off the bodyguard. This was a professional hit.

Nikitin had too many enemies. He was a highly intelligent man, and if Interpol knew a war was shaping up for Nikitin's turf, then so did Nikitin. Unless Ilya's cover was blown, the Russian mob boss would never order a hit on him. And Ilya doubted if anyone could unravel his cover. Aleksandr had known him most of his life, and he hadn't known for certain until they'd crossed paths recently and Ilya had allowed him glimpses into his real life.

Being alone for so many years had become wearing, and after a while, undercover agents really began to believe their own cover stories. He had wanted Aleksandr and Jonas Harrington to figure out who and what he was. If there was one man in the world he trusted, it was Aleksandr, and now that he'd come to know Jonas, he was beginning to believe there might be second man he could trust. So if his cover wasn't blown, then who wanted him dead – and why?

The attackers had spread out in a loose line. Ilya had taken out one in the center, but there were men on either side of him, working their way across the park. One appeared to be giving the others instructions. The voice was speaking English perfectly. There was no hint of an accent, other than New York. Not European, certainly not Russian. The man he'd killed had also been American.

He pushed through the grass on his belly, rolled a few feet and came up on a second man. This one was much larger than the first. Ilya rose up like a monster, using the same method, taking him from behind, covering his mouth and sinking the blade into flesh. His opponent was enormously strong and wrenched forward, trying to tear out of Ilya's grip. He fired his weapon, making it no longer necessary for silence.

Ilya caught the man's head in both hands and wrenched, breaking the would-be assassin's neck. He crouched beside him, retrieving his knife and wiping the blade on his enemy's shirt. Having shoved the knife into his belt, he pulled his gun and proceeded to run in a straight line toward the next man. Two down. He was certain there were six of them. The other four burst into a furious round of hissing out questions and orders while he gained several yards on them.

He was adept at throwing sound and made certain to make noise to his left. A volley of shots rang out. He fired at the flash, heard a grunt followed by a thud. Ilya dropped to the ground when he heard the body fall. Immediately more gunfire broke out. The earpiece nearly burst as the leader shouted at the others to stop firing, warning them they might hit one another.

Two men nearly came together over the top of him; he rolled to fire off a shot as one fired simultaneously. The bullet kissed his arm hard enough to knock him back, taking a chunk of flesh with it. That would leave DNA he didn't want on scene. Cursing, he rolled and came up on his feet. The man who'd shot him was down, the bullet having taken him between the eyes. The second was on him, swinging a gun at Ilya's head.

He ducked, just not quite fast enough. The metal scraped across his cheekbone as Ilya jerked his head out of the way. He kicked hard, aiming for a kneecap, striking just above his target. The man grunted, staggered, his leg buckling. Ilya caught him hard with a roundhouse kick to the head, driving him to the ground. He followed through with a kick to the trachea, stomping hard. The man's eyes went wide and the gun slipped out of his nerveless hand.

Ilya hastily tore his shirt and wrapped the wound on his arm to prevent throwing more droplets of blood around the crime scene. Four down. He had two to go and he had to kill them. He couldn't leave anyone alive, since he had only spotted the first two after him. He didn't know if anyone had seen Jonas Harrington and Aleksandr Volstov, but if they had, his cover was blown and Joley was a dead woman for certain.

He retrieved the fallen's man's gun, the one that had struck his cheek, ripping his skin. He couldn't leave that on scene either. That would have to be dismantled and gotten rid of far away from here. Tucking it into his belt, he began to move again.

The others were more cautious in the sudden silence. One swore, the other told him to shut up. Ilya slipped into the trees close to the playground. He could see childhood toys, a swing, a slide, a merry-go-round. Not that he'd ever played on such things. He'd climbed cargo nets over two stories high and scaled the walls of buildings, but he'd never even sat in a swing. His life had always been like this – hunted or hunter.

He waited, calm, not feeling the pain in his arm or face. The only thing that mattered was sound and movement. The wind was soft, rustling through trees, lifting the leaves to show glimpses of silver when the moon managed to break through the clouds. In the distance he heard traffic. In his ear, with the earpiece, he heard heavy breathing. A twig snapped a few yards to his right. He slowly lowered his body, keeping close to the brush to conceal his outline, turning toward the sound, waiting. Just waiting.

It occurred to him then that he'd spent most of his lifetime waiting in the shadows for someone to make a wrong move. He was done after this assignment, done with undercover work and living a solitary, cold existence. He was through killing people. He wished the killing mattered, that it bothered him, but he had been closed off to emotion for too long to resurrect guilt now. Undercover work, or taking out someone who lived beyond the arm of the law, was simply a job, and he had a code he tried never to deviate from, one that he could live with in a world of violence. He had a couple of triggers and his bosses knew it. The mistreatment of women and of children. He had seen too much as a child and wouldn't tolerate it, so he was often sent on the jobs

271

demanding cleanup rather than arrest. Like the one he was on now.

The branches of a bush swayed against the wind. Another twig snapped. Loud. Too loud. He turned fast, felt the knife slice across his ribs as he slapped it down and away from him. A second attacker had come up behind him. The only reason the strike hadn't hit home was because Ilya was blurring his image a bit and his assailant hadn't seen him until he was right up on him. He'd swung a knife instead of firing his gun.

Ilya kicked the man's gun arm, smashing through bone, moving inside to whirl the attacker in front of him, facing the swaying bush. Bullets spat out and thunked into his human shield. Ilya dragged the deadweight with him until he had relative cover. He dropped the body, dove for the ground and crawled rapidly into thicker brush. The moment he was clear, he tore a strip from his shirt with his teeth and bound his wound.

He waited in silence again. Minutes ticked by. The shots were bound to have attracted someone's attention. He didn't have the luxury of patience. He began to work his way toward the remaining man. He could still hear heavy breathing, this time rasping, as the air burst from lungs overtaxed with anxiety.

The last attacker decided to make a run for it. He began to withdraw, backing through the brush, cracking small branches and crunching dry leaves. Ilya pinpointed his position and rolled toward him fast, coming up firing several shots in rapid succession. The attacker hunched over on the ground. Ilya crawled close, still covering him. A finger on the man's neck found no pulse. Ilya spent a few minutes looking for the knife that had scraped his ribs, retrieving it so he could leave a relatively clean scene behind.

He glanced at his watch and swore. Joley's performance was nearly over. The feeling of doom inside him hadn't lessened. The danger he'd sensed hadn't just been this hit squad. He had to get back to Joley fast.

Ilya isn't in the arena. Joley could barely focus. She was worried, worried enough that she'd reached out telepathically and tried to connect with him. He hadn't answered. Uneasily she glanced around at the band. Ordinarily, Staples Center in Los Angeles was another of her favorite performance venues, but this time, she felt overwhelmed instead of energized by the thought of performing that night.

She had a bad feeling. Her stomach churned with a terrible dread she couldn't shake.

'Come on, Joley, get dressed. We've got to go on in a few minutes,' Logan said, glancing at Tish for help.

Tish sent Logan a quick quelling look and flashed Joley a bright smile. 'Logan can watch the baby while I help you.'

'Ten minutes, Tish,' Jerry reminded her.

Joley realized they were all treating her carefully. She knew they thought her arm, which was swollen and bruised but healing fast, was much worse than it was. Only Tish and Brian knew the truth. She was pining away for the wrong man. He talked to her at night when she couldn't sleep. She wanted to beg and plead with him to come to her, but she'd remained silent. If she expected Brian to stay away from Nikitin and Denny to stay away from drugs and women, and Logan to toe the line with Tish, then she expected the same high standard of herself.

'It's amazing how you've just fallen right back into taking care of all of us,' Joley said as she pulled open the door to the large room she'd been given to get ready. She preferred her own bus, it helped calm her down, but she'd come directly from the hotel, so she used the suite the center set aside for their performers.

'I forgot how much I loved to travel with the band,' Tish said, shoving a long narrow box to the back of the table so she could set Joley's makeup case there. 'Who sent the flowers?'

'Are there flowers?' Joley's heart leapt. Maybe Ilya had sent them. If he had, she'd do the right thing and throw them away. Or maybe that wouldn't be right. She wouldn't want them to go to waste. 'Let me see. Is there a card with them?'

Tish dragged the box back to the center of the table and handed the card to Joley while she lifted the lid. Joley bent over her shoulder, ripping open the small card. She glanced at the card, hoping it was from Ilya.

Die bitch

The two words were typed in black bold letters across the white linen card. Tish shoved Joley back and dropped the lid. The box spilled out a dozen long-stemmed blackened roses and a grotesque decapitated doll cut into pieces.

'Okay, that's totally sick,' Tish said.

Joley looked around the room. 'Maybe it wasn't meant for me. I'm pretty sure I'm not a bitch. Well, at least most of the time.'

Tish moistened her suddenly dry lips. 'This is crazy, Joley. Who would do this?'

'I don't know, but they have really poor taste in flowers.' Joley sank down into a chair and looked up at her friend. 'I think I'm done with this life. Really, Tish. I can't deal with the crazies or the paparazzi anymore. Did you see the headlines this morning? There's pictures of me on the ground splashed all over the papers and the Internet. One picture looks as if I'm crawling. The headlines say I'm drunk – too drunk to stand or perform. There's a shot of Brian looking worried and a headline saying he wants intervention to try to save me. They shoved me, Tish, onto the ground and then took the photographs. I wasn't drinking, Brian was worried because he thought I might be hurt. One of them reached down like he was going to help me up, but instead he asked me a question.'

'I know it's hard right now,' Tish said. 'But you're also upset over other things and that's making it worse.'

'You mean Ilya.' Joley pushed her head into the heel of her hand. 'He isn't here. I know something's wrong. I feel it. He isn't here.' The last came out forlorn. 'I didn't realize how much I depended on his presence.'

Tish used a napkin to push the box of dead flowers to the back of the table and replace the lid. 'I'll get the security people to turn that over to whoever takes care of it. In the meantime, Joley, you need makeup. You can't go perform like that.'

'I don't want to go on tonight.' Joley turned around and put her head back so Tish could apply the makeup. 'Maybe we should say I'm sick.'

Tish studied her face. 'Are you?'

Joley sighed. 'I don't think so. I just feel off. Tired. Exhausted.'

'You aren't sleeping again.'

'No. I could sleep when he was there. Why is that? If I don't trust him, why would I be able to fall asleep with him when I can't with anyone else?'

'Hold still.' Tish frowned as she applied eyeliner. 'You're on the pill, right?'

Joley nearly fell off the chair. 'Where did that come from? Of course I'm on the pill. Lissa must be putting babies in your brain. I'm just tired, and sick of the whack jobs following me everywhere threatening to kill me because they love me so much.'

'I don't think whoever sent the flowers feels that way about you. "Die bitch" doesn't seem very loving to me.'

Joley shoved both hands through her hair. She was still back on Tish's unexpected comment implying she might be feeling sick and miserable because she could be pregnant. She was on the pill and she'd just had sex a few days earlier. Tish was nuts. Sheesh. She struggled to bring her mind away from Ilya, sex and babies and keep the focus on whoever had sent her the dead flowers. 'I got a weird phone call on my cell the night we left Red Rocks. Jerry gave me a new cell and number. But Ilya kept that number and phone in case they called back. He said sometimes if they hear your voice it's enough to keep them from escalating.' Joley leaned forward to apply lipstick. 'How much time do I have?'

'You've got to hurry, hon.' Tish patted Joley's hair and nodded her head in satisfaction. 'Your hair looks great. Very healthy and lots of shine.'

'That's nice to know. I don't feel shiny. Where're my clothes?' Joley looked around. 'I thought I hung them outside the closet. I don't know where my brain is tonight.' Thinking of Ilya. Worried about him. Worried about the pressing dread that wouldn't go away. She hopped up and stalked across the room to the little clothes closet built into the wall.

Joley yanked open the closet door impatiently. Tish gasped. There was nothing left of the outfit Joley had planned to wear onstage. It hung in shreds, long thin tails of glittering material. Her special jeans, covered in a dazzling rainbow of rhinestones, were in worse shape.

She moistened her lips and blinked up at Tish. 'They don't much like the clothes I wear either.' Tears burned behind her eyelids. 'I'm not going to let them make me cry.' But she wanted to cry – not for the flowers or the cut-up doll, or even her stage clothes – although it was her favorite outfit – she wanted to cry because Ilya wasn't there and she was terrified for him.

The dread that had been building for the last hour, making her heart race and her palms sweat, was only growing stronger, and it had nothing to do with what was happening to her.

'You're on in five minutes, Joley. What are you going to do?'

'I'll be going casual tonight.' Her chin went up and her eyes glittered with anger. 'Because – screw them, Tish. No one's going to scare me off performing. If and when I quit, it will be because I want to, not because I let them beat me. Whoever this sick person is, they can just go buy a ticket and watch me, because I'll be giving the performance of my life out there tonight.'

'Good for you, honey,' Tish said. 'Let's do it. Jerry and I will see to this mess, you take care of giving those people who came to see you the show of their lives.'

Joley had to run to catch the band. She nearly missed the huddle. Brian raised an eyebrow at her casual garb, but it didn't seem to matter at all to their audience when they took the stage. She joked about her elegant attire and showed off her running shoes as she skipped across the stage, flashing her famous smile. Her voice was in good form, and she delivered every note as if she was having the time of her life. Her joy in her music carried the crowd to a new high, and they went through the roof, yelling, clapping and stomping for more. And she gave them more, finishing up with several of the audience's shouted requests before ending with her latest, very popular single.

Joley waited until after the performance, when they were back in the suite, before she told the band members about the flowers and her clothes. 'Sorry about not dressing up.'

'It didn't seem to matter,' Denny said. 'We rocked the house tonight.'

'Yeah, we did,' she agreed. 'We're leaving for Anaheim in the morning, right? We have one more show before we hit northern California and we're almost home, boys.'

She would be so happy to get home to Sea Haven and her sisters. In the meantime, she wanted to see Ilya, just to make certain he was all right. She'd looked for him when she'd come offstage, but he wasn't there and event security had escorted them from the stage. With a sigh, Joley walked through the parking lot toward her bus, looking around for her bodyguard. She'd be grateful to get inside where she could collapse and close her eyes and concentrate on trying to reach him through their telepathic connection.

Steve came toward her from the front of the bus. She waved stopping him. 'Hey, Steve. I needed to ask you about something. I got this box, narrow, like for long-stemmed roses, but it had dead flowers in it and a chopped up doll. They were in the dressing room along with my clothes, which someone had shredded. Did you happen to see anyone, or have anyone ask you to, deliver the box to my dressing room this afternoon?'

'What are you accusing me of, Joley?' he snapped. 'You think I brought you dead flowers and cut up your clothes?'

His aura bothered her, the colors swirling in muddy grays and darker greens and browns. She talked to Steve all the time, but usually they were separated by tinted glass or the partition in the bus. His aura indicated he was agitated, nervous – upset even.

Joley frowned. 'I wasn't accusing you of bringing the box into the room, Steve, I was asking if you'd seen anyone, or if they'd asked you to drop it off. You've been with me for years. Why would I think you'd want to bring me some dead flowers? Sheesh, if you had a beef with me, I'd assume you'd tell me.'

Steve shrugged, visibly calming. 'I don't know, Joley. I guess everything is making us all a little on edge. Where's your bodyguard tonight? I thought he'd be with you. I wasn't happy when Jerry gave me the word he was hiring him, but I haven't exactly been doing that job for a long time. You never ask me to do anything but drive, and I've gotten in the habit of just taking you or the band anywhere you want to go.'

'I'm comfortable with you, Steve,' Joley said, 'and I sure don't want you to have to fling your body between mine and a bullet. Or a dead flower.' She flashed him a small grin. 'Besides, if you were always hanging with me, how would you ever drive the boys to the parties?'

'You knew about that?'

'Sure. I thought it was a great idea. Jerry told me a few years back that if I was tucked safe in my room or on the bus, you were willing to make certain the boys wouldn't try to drive drunk – that you'd get them safely back. I thought it was wonderful. If Jerry hurt your feelings by hiring Prakenskii, you should have told me. Besides, it's a temporary thing.'

'And he doesn't appear to be here to do his job.' There was satisfaction in Steve's voice.

Joley sighed. She was getting used to people – especially men – not liking Ilya. He was too dominant, and made men uneasy. 'He was supposed to be here. Maybe Nikitin held him up. He's here in LA.' Joley started again for the bus.

'Yeah, I know. I drove Brian to see him this afternoon.' Steve remained where he was.

Joley stopped and looked back at him. 'Brian? Before the show?'

'Yes, he asked me to take him to the hotel and I did. Shouldn't I have?'

'Oh no, it was okay. I just seem to be out of the loop lately. You know I'm not all that fond of Nikitin's parties. The last one everyone went to was a big mess.' She took a step back toward Steve. 'In all the times you drove the band to his parties, did you notice underage girls there?'

He sighed. 'I tried not to see anything, Joley. I like my job. I just do the driving.'

She nodded and turned back to the bus with a

little wave. 'What time are we pulling out tonight?'

'Jerry said he wanted us on the road by five this morning. You can probably catch some sleep before we get moving. That's what I'm going to try to do.'

'Sounds good.' Joley waved again and hurried across the lot to her bus.

She stopped abruptly as she neared her home away from home. A photograph was stuck to the door. It was a picture of her standing in the parking lot talking to Tish. Tish and she each had a bullet painted into the center of her throat. She pulled the picture off and stared down at the words pasted from a magazine onto the glossy print.

Back off the girl or you're both dead.

The girl? The missing girl? She glanced around, her fingers on the door handle. Where was Ilya? Her stomach was dropping out of her body and her heart pounded like it might leap out of her chest. She was getting an awful lot of notes lately. She yanked the door open.

'Joley! Wait. I need to talk to you about those flowers. Hang on a second.'

She turned at the sound of Jerry's voice. His familiar face was a relief. She let out her breath and started toward him, wanting someone else to see the threat, not only to her, but to Tish. The flowers were nothing in comparison. She'd taken several steps when thunder crashed in her ears, and it felt as if a freight train slammed into her.

Chapter Fourteen

The explosion rocked the ground and sent the bus walls bursting outward in all directions, including up into the sky. The concussion blasted Joley off her feet, picking her up as if she were a paper doll and hurling her forward through the air. She landed hard, her ears ringing, lungs fighting for air, pain streaking through her body while burning debris rained down around her.

Stunned and uncomprehending, Joley raised her arms to try to cover her head as shards of glass pierced her skin. Splintered wood, paper and materials fell all around her. Her vision blurred, eyes burning. She barely realized what happened as she fought for breath. She'd hit the ground so hard it had knocked the wind out of her. Panic rose sharp and fast. She couldn't breathe, she couldn't get air, and fiery embers and sharp glass rained down on her.

Joley! Breathe, damn it, take a breath. Protect yourself.

She felt hands on her, lifting her rib cage, but they weren't Ilya's hands, and she fought, doubling her fist, striking out blindly, kicking to fight her way free. Someone was trying to kill her – that much registered, and she fought wildly.

I can't see. There was panic in her voice, in her mind, filling her when she should have been worried about breathing. Where are you? Because he had to come. If he was there, the world would be right again. He would keep her safe. He had to come. She kicked out blindly, swinging her fist, crying when she didn't connect.

'Joley! Stop it.'

Hard hands tried to hold her down. Her ears were ringing so loud the voice was distorted. She didn't recognize the touch. It wasn't him. It wasn't Ilya.

I'm coming, lyubimaya moya. *Take a breath. Breathe for me.*

The hands pinned her to the ground, and something rubbed across her face and eyes. She forced air through her lungs. No matter what, Ilya would come for her. If someone was trying to harm her, they'd never get away with it.

'Let me look, Joley. There's blood everywhere. Stop fighting.'

This time she recognized the voice of her manager, Jerry. She wiped at her face, blinked rapidly and looked at his blurry face through stinging eyes. Her hands were covered in blood. Shocked, she stared at the mess around her, the dust settling to the ground, her ears still ringing from the explosion.

She was barely aware of her manager crouching beside her, wiping at her face again. 'Are you all right, Joley? Answer me. Should I call an ambulance?'

She could barely see, her vision blurry, but she peered around her at the debris that had been her trailer. Smoke and dust littered the air, while splintered furniture and her belongings were scattered around her.

'Joley!' Brian rushed to her, followed by Denny. 'Are you hurt? Is she hurt, Jerry? There's blood all over her. Get an ambulance. Get one now, Denny!'

She blinked up at him, shock in her eyes. 'My God, Brian. This has something to do with that girl's disappearance. It does.' She tried to think, but her brain seemed scrambled, thoughts bouncing so fast she couldn't catch them. She caught a glimpse of Steve off to the side, staring as if dazed at the wreckage.

'She's in shock,' Jerry said.

She shook her head, although she was certain he was right. She was cold – too cold – and she couldn't stop shaking. Even her teeth chattered. 'No, I'm not. And I don't need an ambulance.' She wiped her face and stared down in surprise at the blood smearing her hand. 'It's a small cut, nothing serious.' She hoped it was true.

'You're bleeding from your leg and arm, too, Joley,' Brian said.

She hurt, but in so many places she couldn't process it all. Her hands were trembling. The ringing in her ears was so loud it sounded like a swarm of angry bees. She pressed her hands to her ears in an effort to stop it. 'It's nothing, small cuts.' They didn't feel small. She couldn't quite move, her, body refusing to obey her, and that was terrifying. *Where are you*? He had to come; she didn't know what to do.

'The cuts aren't small,' Jerry protested. 'And you're losing blood all over the place.'

'This is crazy, Jerry.' Joley peered around her,

more dazed than coherent, her body shaking involuntarily. 'Brian, look at this, look at my bus.' She couldn't get her mind to work. She tried to stand, but her legs wouldn't hold her up.

Brian kept a hand on her shoulder, keeping her still. 'Stay there, Joley. The police are swarming the place, security's everywhere, and they'll be sending in a doctor to look at you, so just sit still until someone gets here and clears you.'

'This is about that little girl who went missing. That's what the bomb was all about – getting us to back off trying to find out who she was with. Someone put this on my bus.' She still had the picture clutched in her hands and she held it up.

'That's crazy. It's only drawing more attention to her disappearance.' Brian pressed a cloth to her forehead. Ignoring her wince, he pressed hard. 'And why go for you? You have nothing to do with it. Jerry maybe and me, certainly. We're the ones asking questions, not you.'

She pushed harder at his arm. 'That hurts.'

'You're going to need stitches, so just sit there until we get a doctor in here.' Brian scratched his head. 'Joley, this doesn't make sense. Why bother warning you to back off and then try to kill you? How stupid is that?'

Joley could barely think with her ears ringing, the throbbing cut at her temple and the way her heart squeezed hard and painful in her chest. She was really afraid now. Someone wanted her dead. She should have gone into the bus, would have if Jerry hadn't called out to her.

Sirens wailed and voices grew louder. Joley stiffened, feeling energy surging toward her aggressively.

Joley! Answer me. Are you all right?

The voice in her head trembled with anxiety, but held a firm, commanding note, pushing at her mind to obey instantly. Finally, Ilya Prakenskii, and he was close. Her heart leapt, began pounding a welcome. Adrenaline surged. She clenched her teeth against the need to run to him and fling herself into his arms. She hated weakness in herself, and Ilya was a huge weakness. Cameras were everywhere now. If she turned to him, it would be all over the tabloids, but she wanted to – needed to – be held by him.

Joley. There was a tinge of fear this time, and God help her, she found that small note thrilling.

The voice swore, and the surge of energy grew darker. Someone behind her screamed, and she turned to see Ilya mowing people down as if they were cardboard figures, his glittering blue eyes locked on her, his face grim. He looked like an avenging god, breathtaking, power in motion, his masculine body moving with fluid, lethal grace. The paparazzi, the gathering crowd, even his own security people were knocked flat as he came for her.

He took her breath away. The sheer beauty and energy of him, as if he was power personified, as if he understood the very force of nature and somehow was part of it. Men moved out of his way until he flowed past like the wind of death, holding their breath to keep from taking a chance that they might draw his attention.

Joley couldn't stop the way her body rose and her feet began to run. Her vision blurred again, and this time she was afraid she was crying. She'd been fine – *fine* – in control – until she saw him. Now she couldn't get to him fast enough.

His arms closed around her and he dragged her against his chest. He was so strong – a rock, hard and unyielding, when she needed an anchor to cling to. She knew she was safe. Flashes went off around them, and Joley huddled closer to him, keeping her face buried. Sobs shook her body, and no matter how hard she tried she couldn't stop crying. And the press was already there.

I'm getting you out of here.

He didn't ask. Ordinarily that would have made her crazy, but she didn't want to have to think. He just said trust me and had her in his arms, cradling her close to his chest. Her head hurt and her ears were ringing and her world had just gone up in smoke. She circled his neck with her arms and pressed her face there, accepting his protection.

'Brian,' Ilya snapped. 'I'm taking her somewhere secure.'

'She needs to go to the hospital,' Brian called in desperation.

Joley stirred as if she might protest, but she could feel Ilya's absolute resolve and she didn't have the energy to argue with him. Ilya was always a force to be reckoned with, and right now she wanted to just curl up and cry, so she allowed him to take her over.

She felt the brush of his mouth on the top of her head, the strength in his arms, the shift of his muscles as he took her through the crowd to a waiting car. The door of the Town Car was open and he slid in, an easy, fluid move, never once jostling her. The door slammed closed.

'Go,' Ilya ordered. 'Hurry.'

'They're going to follow us, Ilya,' Joley warned. 'The reporters. They won't stop.'

'They're giving chase,' the driver confirmed,

glancing in the rearview mirror.

'I don't want anyone to see me like this,' Joley protested, without lifting her head. She could live with the tabloids falsely portraying her as a partying, hard-living rock-and-roll icon, but she couldn't bear for anyone to see her vulnerable.

'Go to the house,' Ilya ordered.

Everything in her stilled. Joley pulled away – or rather tried to. Ilya's arms remained around her like steel bands.

'Nikitin's house?'

'No. My house. I do have one or two when needed.' He caught her chin in his fingers and lifted her face so he could examine the cut. 'You'll need stitches.'

For the first time she really looked at him. There was an angry scrape along his cheekbone, a bloody gash at his ribs and a bloodsoaked cloth wrapped around his upper arm. 'Oh my God. *Ilya*. Oh my God.' She tried to kneel up on the seat to examine him. 'You're hurt. You need a doctor worse than I do. What happened? Tell me. And tell the driver to take us to the hospital.'

She touched his raw cheekbone with gentle fingers. 'I'm not Libby, but I can help. Where else? Your side. Your arm.' Blood soaked through the makeshift bandage on his upper arm, and more spread in a widening patch at his side. 'Ilya, this doesn't look good.'

'Shh, *laskovaya, moya*, the driver will get us somewhere safe and we'll take care of everything. You've got a concussion and you're in shock. Lie quietly.'

He settled her back in his arms, holding her to him, his heart still stuttering from the close call.

Someone was going to die over this. Threats were a nuisance, but trying to kill Joley was a death sentence.

'You look like you've been in a war,' she said softly. 'Tell me what happened.' She brushed at her head several times, smearing more blood, wincing, and repeating the action.

Ilya pulled her closer, wrapping his arms around her to stop the involuntary movement. He nuzzled the top of her head, feeling the tremors inside his body that never showed on the outside. Joley was far more to him than sex. There was no getting around his emotional ties to her. He might not like them, but they were there, and he was man enough to realize he was no longer the same and never would be. His comfortable world of detachment was gone for all time. Joley had managed to creep inside him and twist herself around his heart so tightly, there was no shaking her loose.

'You look like you've been in a war as well, Joley,' he murmured. 'Let's just get to a safe house and we'll sort it all out.'

She needed the sound of his voice desperately. The ringing in her ears was so loud, and fear clawed and raked at her stomach – fear for her – for him.

'You have a home? Here?' She thought of him as a loner, a lone warrior who moved restlessly through the world. No friends. No family. Never in one place long. She couldn't imagine him with a home – or a family. Shifting in his arms, she glanced at the front to try to glimpse the driver, but the tinted window had already slid smoothly into place, preventing her from being able to see, and later identify, his face.

She shifted again, her legs moving restlessly. She

reached for the door handle, but Ilya caught her wrist and brought her hand to his chest.

She should have been afraid, but she felt safe – protected even. Her head throbbed terribly, the cuts and scrapes burning, and she was having trouble reining in her scattered thoughts. The urge to get out of the car was strong, as if she had to run, but Ilya lessened the need by his comforting presence.

Her world was upside down. She couldn't begin to sort through everything – the accidents, the threats, the missing teenager. Her bus had been blown up, and the paparazzi followed her through the streets to catch a photograph of her with blood running down her face. It wasn't like her condition mattered at all to them, just getting a photograph to show the world that she was injured. She moved restlessly again, the urge to run strong.

'Not exactly a home,' Ilya said, soothing her with his voice, 'but it will do for now and you'll be safe enough there. No reporters are going to get within miles of it.'

'They always do, Ilya.' She didn't want him to leave her, but she had to be honest. 'If you have anything at all to hide – if you don't want to be photographed with me – you should take me to a hotel and just let me out of the car.'

His ice-blue eyes flickered, and just for a moment she caught her breath at what she saw there – raw desire, smoky need – and something else. Affection? Love even? That couldn't be, but there was enough concern in his eyes to melt her heart and give her hope when she shouldn't dare to hope.

'Are you trying to look out for me?'

His voice nearly curled her toes. For one moment all the pain was gone and she felt safe and loved and wrapped up in velvet. She sighed and made herself be strong.

'You value your privacy, and . . .' It had to be said. She rarely asked him about his lifestyle, or the things he did, other than when she was censuring him, but a man in his kind of work couldn't afford to be splashed all over the tabloids. 'Your life might depend on it. If they photograph you even once with me, the reporters will be relentless. They'll uncover every secret you've ever had. It would be better to drop me off at the hospital and disappear. You got me out of there and I'm grateful to you.'

And she was. She would have hated for the tabloids to get pictures of her so vulnerable, but more than that, she didn't want to make Ilya's life any harder or more complicated than she already knew it was. 'There's no reason to risk everything, Ilya.'

'They won't find us. The driver will have a diversion.'

'He can do that?' She glanced at the tinted partition. 'I'll have to lure him away to work for me. And I've got to call my sisters and let them know I'm all right and where I'll be.'

She was chattering too much, something she did when she was nervous, and right now she was very nervous. Her beloved bus was gone. Dean Walters had been murdered. She had cuts and bruises everywhere, and her head hurt so bad she could barely think. But she knew one thing for certain – she was with the only person in the world who could make her feel that he could keep her absolutely safe.

'Better wait,' Ilya said, and took her cell phone out of her hand. 'We can't take any chances until we're safe inside the gates without the reporters hounding us.'

Joley bit back a protest. What difference did a few minutes make? 'My head really hurts, Ilya.' Her hand went to the door handle again as the urge to move, to keep moving drove her. It was more than pain in her head; there was a roaring, as if her mind couldn't be still when she needed calm most. The noise made it impossible to think.

'I know, *laskovaya moya*. Another few minutes and I'll take care of it.'

He pressed his hand to the cut on her head. That was the one he was most worried about. The ones on her arms and legs were from glass shards or flying metal. They hurt and a couple might need a stitch or two, but the one on her head was larger and she was obviously still dazed. She was attempting to stay focused by chattering, but she kept trying to move, to get out of the car, to brush at her head, and she didn't even realize she was doing it.

His heart ached with love for her. She was courageous, looking out for his safety when she should have been weeping in his arms.

'That hurts,' Joley said, trying to pull away.

'I know, *devochka moya*. I need to slow down the bleeding. It will help get the healing started as well. Relax for me and just let me take care of things.'

He kept his hand pressed to her forehead, palm over the cut, warmth moving from his center to her head. Colors spun for a moment, many different ones, spinning in an ever tightening circle until white light burst through, taking all the colors and turning them into flashes of heat.

She had forgotten that he possessed all the talents, just as Elle, her youngest sibling, did, and healing was among them. She knew from experience, watching Libby, that a cut as deep as the one she had wouldn't magically disappear, but he certainly helped slow the flow of blood and took away a great deal of the throbbing. Even the ringing in her ears was better.

'I think I was in shock.'

Joley tried to sit up, but Ilya tightened his hold. 'Stay still. Relax. Breathe. Let me take care of you for a few more minutes, at least until my heart slows down.' He nuzzled the top of her head. 'You scared me this time.'

'I didn't blow up my bus,' she pointed out.

'Who did you make angry this time?' he asked.

She found a small smile forming, and the coldness inside receded a little. 'You can compare notes with my security people. They think I'm a nightmare.'

'They're right. And don't think I won't be talking to them. What the hell were they doing holding a line instead of getting you the hell out of there? One explosion doesn't mean there's not going to be another. And if you were the target, they should have secured your protection before anything else.'

There was an edge to him, not his voice, but his melody, his aura – she felt it and shivered. She was astonished that he could hold her the way he was when he had his own injuries.

'Just let it go, Joley,' he murmured softly. 'Relax and let me take care of you.'

But who was going to take care of him? She closed her eyes and inhaled him. He smelled of blood and sweat, but also that strange, male musk she found so enticing about him.

'You can't go to sleep on me,' Ilya warned. 'We're pulling through the gates now. No one knows about this house, not Nikitin, not anyone. I'm going to have my driver contact the police to send a detective out to interview you after I take care of your wounds. Then you can rest.'

'He can't see you,' she protested. 'No police, Ilya. I'll go down to the station after I take care of my head.' Her aching head. Even with his healing energy, her brain was shaken.

He carried her from the car, once again disregarding his own wounds, sheltering her against his heart as he crossed open ground to the door. Once inside, he carried her into an enormous tiled bathroom and set her on the sink.

'This is going to hurt, Joley.'

'I know. But I can always sew you up next. You did my arm and it's healing fine.'

'I have a little experience with wounds.'

Joley was certain that was an understatement. She'd seen his body and the various scars covering him. He had three more to add to his collection.

He washed the gash on her forehead carefully with a fiery liquid that had tears running down her face, but she held still for him. She breathed in deeply as the room began to spin and the edges of her vision blurred.

'Talk to me.'

Ilya tried to infuse more healing warmth into the wound before he began the tiny stitches necessary to close it. 'Tell me what happened, Joley. Then I'll tell you about my evening.'

She pressed her hand to his chest, right over his heart. 'Promise?'

He bent to brush a kiss on top of her head before resuming the small even stitches. 'Hold still, *devochka moya*, I don't want to leave a scar.'

'It's not going to scar, not when you're using healing energy,' she said, but she gasped and the tears streamed down her cheeks. 'First there were the flowers.'

He stiffened. 'Someone sent you flowers?'

Her hand was still on his chest and it puffed out aggressively. She smiled through her tears at his male reaction. 'Yes. Long-stemmed dead flowers along with a decapitated doll. The torso and legs of the doll were chopped in several pieces. It was very ugly.'

He paused and looked down at her face. 'Where were the flowers?'

'In the dressing room at the arena. And I'd hung my clothes on a little hook on the closet door, but when I looked around I didn't see them right away.'

He sighed. 'But you didn't leave the room and get security.'

'Are you going to let me tell you? Sheesh, Ilya. I couldn't remember for certain if I'd put the clothes in the closet. I thought maybe I'd just thought about hanging them on the hook.' She tried to hold still, but her forehead burned so bad she squirmed. 'Someone had shredded the outfit into thin tiny scraps of material. My favorite outfit.' Her voice rose to a wail.

Ilya immediately stopped and let her breathe through the pain. 'Almost finished with this one. You're doing fine.'

'You weren't there.' She spoke accusingly even though it didn't make sense to. She'd told herself she'd been relieved when she finally crept out of the hotel like the coward she was and he hadn't been there to guard her. She'd ached to see him, yet at the same time, she was terrified she'd just throw pride away and let him rule her from dusk until dawn without love, without caring. Only for the incredible sex he admitted he'd been trained for.

'I know, *lubov moya*. I'm sorry. You have no idea how sorry. I had an important meeting and should have been back in time.' He bent to kiss her again, this time on the corner of her frowning mouth. 'A couple more stitches should do it.'

She held still, sucking in her breath and counting to herself until he grunted in satisfaction and covered the area with another antiseptic. 'I'm giving you a shot, Joley. You need antibiotics. I have them in my field kit.'

'I hate needles.'

'I know. And you're being very brave.' He gave her the shot quickly and then sponged the blood and tears from her face. 'You'll have to take off your clothes.' He turned from her to run water in the bathtub. 'I need to go over the rest of you and stitch up anything too deep or use a butterfly bandage. I'll get you a robe to wear so at least you'll be clean.'

'I'll take a shower.'

Ilya frowned. 'I can't let you do that, Joley. You obviously have a concussion. I wouldn't want you falling down. I'll get you clean.'

She frowned up at him. 'I'm not going to let you give me a bath. I'm not a baby.'

'Right now you're my baby, so don't argue with me.' There was the merest hint of steel in his voice. His hands went to her shirt.

She caught his wrists. 'Ilya.'

'It's all right, Joley. You're not well. Let me take care of you. Tell me what happened after you found your clothes shredded. What did you do?'

She lifted her chin, trying to ignore the way he was so careful to keep from hurting her as he cut off her shirt. It was stained with blood, and she'd never

296

be able to wear it again, but it made her cry anyway. Which was silly, but she couldn't stop, especially when he dropped the rags to the floor, leaving her exposed in her lacy bra.

He drew her close to his body, pressing her face into his shoulder. 'You're safe with me. You have to remember, Joley,' he stroked caresses down her hair, 'I'm very partial to your body. I'll be very careful.'

'I know you will. It's not that. This is two outfits today destroyed. Two of my favorites.' Which was idiotic, she could care less about her clothes. Her tears had nothing to do with ruined clothes and everything to do with danger and death swirling around her and putting everyone she loved in jeopardy. 'I don't know how you live like this.' She couldn't stop weeping or shaking, no matter how hard she tried.

She felt so vulnerable, standing there nearly naked with tears she couldn't stop and her body trembling. His hands were warm and strong, and he simply unclipped the bra and tossed it after the shirt. His fingers skimmed down the sides of her breasts, sliding to hook her hips. Her body jerked and a sob escaped. Joley pushed her knuckles into her mouth.

He framed her face with his hands. 'I'll buy you a couple of outfits. Nicer ones. Ones you'll love. Come on, *lubov moya*, stand up and let's get the jeans off you. You have a nasty cut on your leg as well. You're exhausted. Don't think about what we're doing. Tell me what you did when you found your clothes shredded.'

She swallowed hard and tried not to shiver as he hooked her jeans and boy-short panties, dragging them over her thighs and urging her to step out of them. He lifted her into the bathtub.

'I gave the performance of my life. I rocked the house. I wasn't about to let someone scare me off.'

Her teeth chattered as Joley sank down into the heated water. Whatever he had put into it stung, letting her know where the cuts on her body were. She crossed her arms over her breasts and swayed. Her head pounded so hard she bit down on her lip to keep from moaning. Ilya crouched down beside her, sponging her off with a soft washcloth, rinsing the blood so he could see how deep the cuts were.

Most were superficial, he saw with a sigh of relief. She did look a little worse for wear with her arm torn from the earlier accident, although he could see it was healing fast. Her head was by far the worst cut, followed by the gash in her leg. It was long, but shallow, not really needing stitches he saw now that he could examine it. A bandage would do the trick, and with the smaller cuts and bruises he just laid his palm on them, summoning healing energy and decided he'd apply a topical antibiotic cream.

'That's my woman. Now tell me about the bomb.' He dried her shivering body off gently with a towel and wrapped her in a robe. He dropped his voice to a hypnotic, mesmerizing tone. 'The pain will lessen in a moment.'

Joley sank into the chair by the mirror, her legs too wobbly to hold her up. She drew her knees up, resting her feet on the seat of the chair, and watched as he casually pulled his shirt off. He had such a beautiful body. She wished her eyes would focus just a little better. He had a really ugly slice down his ribs, obviously from a knife, but it looked fairly shallow.

'Here, let me see.' She beckoned him closer with

her finger. She had recognized the compulsion in his voice; he could spell-sing, although not as well as she could. She hadn't thought of that with her brain so jumbled, but she could do no less for him.

Ilya hesitated but stepped closer when she started to get off the chair. 'It's nothing, really, Joley. I'll shower and wash the wounds thoroughly in a few minutes.'

Joley ignored his statement and touched around the wound lightly with her fingertips. He felt that touch vibrate through his body like an electrical current. As tired as he was, as fearful as he'd been for her, his control wasn't nearly as good as he'd have liked. He didn't want to react physically when she needed comfort and care most, but it seemed he had no control over his body. He felt the blood pooling hot and insistent in his groin.

'Joley, maybe you'd better not . . .'

'Shh,' she cautioned and leaned forward to brush a kiss along the ragged edges.

He'd thought the pads of her fingers were sensual, but her soft lips were a thousand times worse. He cursed and caught her wrists. 'Tell me about the bomb.'

She looked up at him with slightly glazed eyes. He couldn't help himself – he leaned down and kissed her upturned mouth, running his tongue possessively along the seam until she opened for him. He allowed himself the luxury of losing himself in her, just for a moment, to celebrate that she was alive. He'd known fear as a child, but had lost it along the way as an adult – now it was back because for the first time in his life, he had someone to lose.

He lifted his head and brushed her mouth twice more. 'Come on. Let's get you into the living room.

The detective should be here in a few minutes. I'm going to shower and stay out of sight. I have to fix my arm. Can you handle him alone?'

She nodded, her eyes enormous, pupils still somewhat dilated.

He carried her into a large, sunken living room and laid her on the couch, arranging the pillows around her and covering her with a blanket. 'Don't get up when he comes in. Just stay right there. He knows you're waiting for him and he'll let himself in.'

'How do you know that?'

'Because it's my job to take care of details. Tell me about the bomb.'

She frowned, trying to remember. 'There was a photograph pinned to the door of the bus.' She looked around a little helplessly. 'I had it. I don't think I dropped it.'

He'd taken it out of her hands and put it on the bureau beside several of his weapons. 'It's safe. Keep going.'

'It was a picture of Tish and me, but someone had drawn in bullets on our throats and they cut out letters from a magazine, which I personally find hokey. It said to back off the girl. And then I started to open the door, but Jerry called to me and I turned, and then the bus exploded.'

'You did good, Joley. Tell that to the cop. I'll be in the other room. Try not to mention me if you can help it.' He was already moving fast. The detective was coming up the walkway. A small strobe light flashed, indicating his presence. Ilya left her there, trusting that he had reinforced the command enough with his voice that, even in her slightly dazed state, she would obey.

The hot shower felt good on his tired body. It was difficult to sew up his arm when chunks of flesh appeared to be missing, but he managed, although the stitches weren't nearly as small and precise as the ones he'd done for Joley. He closed the wound as best he could, gave himself a shot of antibiotics and attended the other scrapes. He was exhausted by the time he heard the detective leave.

Exhausted, he set the alarms for the perimeter of the house and then the house itself. Flicking off lights, he carried Joley to the bedroom. She was very drowsy. He would have to wake her up every hour to make certain she was all right, but for the time being both of them could rest. He removed the bulky robe and just pulled a blanket over her body, grateful that he was tired and needed to sleep. Hopefully he could get through the night without going crazy lying beside her.

He stretched out, and then turned on his side to curl his body around hers. He thought he could control her movements, at least minimize them, but she was restless and kept batting at the wound on her face. Each time he caught her hands, it jerked the hell out of his arm, sending pain crashing through him. He cursed the fact that drugs didn't work any better on him than they did on her, and finally, to keep her from hurting herself, he used a soft scarf to tie her wrists together and to the headboard.

Joley murmured a protest, but turned into his body for warmth and eventually slept fitfully. She responded each time he woke her and talked to her, but readily went back to sleep when he left her alone. He drifted off, dreaming of her.

Chapter Fifteen

Joley knew she was dreaming again. She'd had so many erotic dreams, her fantasies getting darker, but much more pleasurable each time. As always it was Ilya with her, because only Ilya saw deep inside her and only Ilya mattered to her. She could barely breathe when he was near, her thoughts and body filled with urgent need.

She was naked, cool air on her bare skin as she lay stretched out on the bed. Ilya stood above her, his features carved and sensual. He was stark naked as well, his body rippling with muscle, his heavy erection already thick and hard. She could see his chiseled body, the defined muscles covered with old scars and new, raw wounds. He looked like a wild Cossack, a warrior, the pagan godlike beauty of his face stamped with lust and sin.

Her breath caught in her lungs and lay trapped there, so that she heard her own ragged gasps. She wet her lips and tried to move, her legs stirring restlessly as her body reacted to his presence with a rush of heated liquid. She could feel her thighs tingle and her nipples harden under his heavy-lidded stare. Her arms were a bit uncomfortable held over her head so that her breasts thrust upward toward him. It took a moment for her to realize that a soft scarf wrapped around her wrists held her hands tied to the headboard.

In her dream, the thought of being his captive added to the already smoldering fire in her body. She burned for him, and it was so unfair. He stood above her looking hot and sexy, his hand casually stroking his heavy erection with a near mesmerizing circle, until he was impossibly thick. She couldn't tear her gaze from the sexy sight of him, the pearl of moisture on the broad head. His eyes were filled with lust, his hunger raw and edgy. She loved the look on his face, harshly sensual, his body hot and hard and so ready for her.

She moved her hips, pushing them toward him in invitation because in a dream, she could enjoy the fantasy, glory in the dominating look on his face, the possession in his eyes. He lowered himself to the bed beside her, one hand sliding up her rib cage to cup her breast, his thumb grazing her nipple so that she jumped and the breath left her body in a strangled gasp. His shaft lay thick and heavy against her bare thigh, the heat radiating up from that single spot like a slow wash of molten lava.

'I love the way you look right now, Joley, helpless and so mine,' he whispered. 'So soft, all gleaming skin, wet for me, needy, your eyes begging me to take you. You're mine, aren't you? Tell me. Say it. I want you to acknowledge just this once who you belong to.'

His voice was low, rough, demanding even. The commanding sound added to the thrill. She was so susceptible to sound. His lips whispered across hers. His tongue licked the corner of her mouth, a sensual rasp that nearly threw her into a climax as his fingers tugged at her nipple in a rhythmic melody. Every nerve ending in her body went on alert. She gasped again and arched into him. She was his. She wanted to be his.

'Of course I belong to you.' Dreams and fantasies were safe, and she could have everything she wanted without the risk of giving too much of herself. Right here, now, she could show him how much she loved him, how much she truly was his, because he would never know it any other way than in her dreams.

His hand brushed back the hair from the cut on her forehead, and he leaned in to brush right above it with his lips, fingers tender as he touched her. His palm shaped her face, moved down her neck to her shoulder and then slid over her breasts. She shivered beneath his touch, a broken cry escaping when he leaned over her body and took her breast into his mouth. Hot heat raced from breast to belly as he suckled, his tongue flicking and teeth scraping.

Ilya had meant to slide the scarf from her hands, but Joley lay stretched out before him and it had been so long – too long. The sight of her lush body – flushed with arousal, waiting for him, open to him, a priceless treasure, a gift he could explore slowly – had him torn between wanting to sink his body into hers and pound unmercifully or go slowly, drawing her to new heights so that she pleaded with him for more.

Her skin was like satin, warm and alive and so soft she felt exquisite beneath his stroking palms. Her thigh felt smooth and enticing against his pulsing cock, and her legs moved against him with restless pleading. He inhaled her fragrance, all woman, the scent of her driving him toward the edge of his control.

The full curve of her mouth tempted him again, and he swallowed her soft moan as his lips took hers, tongue stroking deep to tangle with hers. She tasted even better than he remembered, all honey and spice, a flavor supremely Joley. He lifted his head to take in the picture of her lying there, stretched out across the bed, hands bound, breasts thrust toward his mouth, the flat, exquisite belly and tiny curls at the junction of shapely legs. She was an offering sending another shaft of pleasure rocketing through his body.

He dropped one hand to her leg and ran up the smooth skin to her thigh. The pads of his fingers skimmed the cuts with gentle care, infusing a rush of healing warmth even as his hand parted her thighs. Her body welcomed him, already damp and needy with pleading.

He took her mouth again, that beautiful mouth he always fantasized about. So full, so soft, and inside, a velvet heated secret treasure of sensation he could lose himself in easily. His tongue traced her full lower lip, teased her upper one and claimed each corner of her mouth. He nibbled and teased, taking his time, drawing moans from her. All the while he watched as arousal deepened her color and brought her nipples to harder peaks. For him – all for him.

He reveled in the way she gave herself up to the hot need, allowing it to consume her. His hands slipped over her narrow rib cage to her heaving breasts, cupping them, kneading the soft flesh, pushing them together so he could flick first one nipple and then the other with his tongue. She gasped and arched closer to him, crying out when his mouth closed over one hard bud, sucking it in and flicking back and forth with his tongue until she wailed. He bit down and she cried out brokenly.

'That's what I want, *lubov moya*, burn for me.'

One hand slid down her flat belly, exploring the muscles bunched so tight there before slipping lower. He plunged two fingers deep into her hot, wet channel while his mouth closed around her other breast.

Her hips came up, riding his hand, liquid heat flowing along the living silk as her muscles tightened around his fingers in a stranglehold. She moaned, and pushed her breast deeper into his mouth, her head tossing back and forth on the pillow. He suckled hard, tongue tormenting her, his fingers all the while plunging into her, first hard and fast, then slow and easy, so that she tried desperately to relieve the tension building and building. He loved every frantic cry, every involuntary movement of her hip as she twisted and writhed to get more.

'On, no, *lubov moya*, not yet,' he whispered softly and began licking over her soft skin, all that wonderful expanse of gleaming satin that was his alone. He took little nips, watching her skin flush with need. So soft. So warm. He teased her belly button and scraped his teeth over her mound.

Joley went wild, pleading with him. She heard herself, shocked by the need and lust in her voice, in her cries to take her. She blinked, focusing, and saw his wicked smile, the demon in his eyes, as he lowered his head again. The need in her was destroying her, consuming her completely, the fire too hot, threatening to burn her alive.

She'd never seen anything more sensual than Ilya in that moment. This was no dream man, but a very strong flesh-and-blood man. He parted her thighs, his hands spreading her legs, palms warm and rough

306

as he positioned her exactly the way he wanted her, open to his hungry gaze. For a tension-filled moment, while she breathed raggedly and her body pulsed and ached with terrible need, he stroked her inner thighs, moving his fingers against her wet, heated flesh.

She would have done anything for him in that moment. Her body screamed for his. Tremors ran through her and her breath caught in her throat when he slowly lowered his head and his tongue slid across her soft lips in a long, curling rasp and then stabbed deep. She opened her mouth wide, but no sound emerged. Nerves jumped in her thighs, and she couldn't stop the way her hips arched and thrust upward toward his greedy mouth.

He licked and sucked and feasted, his tongue as wicked and sinful as his fingers, driving her nearly insane with the wealth of sensations pouring into her. His mouth moved over her clit, and the small growling noise, as if he were a prowling tiger, vibrated right through her, pushing her higher. She cried out again and whispered his name brokenly.

Ilya moved up her body, unable to stop himself, holding her thighs apart, positioning himself between her legs, watching the arousal on her face, the deep red on her breasts, his marks of possession coming up on her soft skin. She whimpered as he dragged her legs over his shoulders and leaned into her, the broad head of his cock seeking the warmth of her tight channel. He waited a heartbeat, his eyes on her face. She was so beautiful, so hungry for him, dazed with pleasure.

He surged forward, sinking in to the hilt in one fast, hard stroke. Her slick, hot feminine channel clamped down on him as he threw her into an orgasm. Muscles constricted, hot silk winding tighter and tighter, rippling with life around him, squeezing and milking until she had him gasping with the fiery streaks tearing through his body. She writhed under him, increasing the fiery sensations so that lightning sizzled and hissed through his bloodstream.

He plunged again, a deep, hard stroke causing those tight muscles to drag over the thick length of him. He swore as another bolt of lightning streaked through his body, from his toes to his head. Electricity crackled in the air around them, leaping from his skin to hers.

Joley watched the harsh lines in his face deepen with lust as he stretched her impossibly, filling her to the point of madness. His hips began a rhythm that left her breathless, unable to do more than keen in a thin, ragged voice as the tension in her grew and grew. Fiery heat engulfed her, spreading like a storm through her body, but centering deep, where the torturous pleasure bordered on pain. There was no release, only the continuous building of need – more need – more hunger – more of everything.

It was wrong. This was wrong. She lay stretched out, her hands tied, allowing him to command her body, to do whatever he wanted, and she loved the control he had over her, craved the edge of fear and pain that made the music all the sweeter as he built the song between them with his hands and mouth and body.

Joley began to fight, sobs welling up. She was just giving herself to him, surrendering everything she was again. What was wrong with her? She was sinking further and further into that dark place inside of her, and if she kept it up, she'd never be free.

'This is wrong. There's something wrong with me.' Because she liked having him take her over and rule her body. She wanted to be screaming out with pleasure; she didn't care if he tied her up or made her crazy – she wanted to be with him any way she could have him. 'This isn't right.'

It took a moment, with the blood roaring in his ears and pounding in his groin, for him to realize she was really in distress. Ilya froze, still buried deep in her body, thick and hard and feeling the silken walls encasing his shaft. She wanted him. Her body couldn't lie, yet her distress was genuine. The more she struggled, the more her body tightened around his, until he wanted to give himself up to the loss of control and just drive into her over and over until he was a part of her, imprinted forever deep inside of her, until she recognized fully that they belonged together and only he could give her the things she craved.

He forced his body to remain absolutely still. '*Lubov moya*, what is it?' His voice was gentle, as tender as he could manage when he was at the height of his need. 'Tell me what's wrong and we'll fix it.'

'Look at me – at us. This isn't love. I'm tied to the bed and letting you do anything you want – begging you to take me. I don't want to be like this. I don't. I want love, Ilya, not just sex. This is sex.' She wasn't making sense, the words tumbling over one another, her chest heaving as she sobbed, pushing her hard nipples into the heavy muscles of his chest. She'd promised herself – *promised*, but not only was she under him, she was pleading with him for more.

Ilya immediately braced himself over her with one arm and reached above her head to her wrists with the other. 'You're not tied up, Joley. Stop struggling, *laskovaya moya*, and let me get this. It's just looped over your wrists. I was tired last night and afraid you'd open those stitches.' He slipped the scarf from her wrists and took each to his mouth, pressing kisses there. 'See? You're fine. I would never do anything to you that you didn't want.'

She forced herself to be honest with him. She owed him that when she could feel his body stretching hers to the limit, when he was pulsing deep inside of her, breathing hard to control himself, when she had not only encouraged him, but *begged* him to take her.

'That's the trouble, Ilya. I do want this. I want anything I can get from you. I'm terrified of losing myself, of losing who I am and what I stand for. I barely know you, and I'm willing to let you do anything to my body. That's not love. It's obsession with sex. I swore I'd never do this, that when I was with someone it would be because he loved me and I loved him. I'm sorry. I'm so sorry. I know this is my fault. I can't pretend it's yours. I wanted you – I still do.' How could she possibly deny that, when her body was rippling around his, demanding he continue? 'I think I'm going insane.'

Ilya framed her face and brushed kisses over her, catching her tears on his tongue. 'You aren't insane, Joley. This was meant. My mark is on you. What do you think that means? Do you think it would work on just anyone? You were born for me. Me alone. To love, to cherish, to protect, to bring you pleasure. I was born for you for those same reasons.'

She stopped thrashing and fighting beneath him, lying still, tears running down her face, but she was listening to him and there was hope in her dark eyes.

'Great sex is about total surrender, Joley,' he whispered and shifted his body just a little, sending a streak of fire scorching the sensitive knot of nerves deep inside of her. He pressed deeper. 'It's giving yourself wholly to another person.' He kissed the corner of her mouth, a soft brush of his lips that made her heart want to melt. 'In order to do that, you have to truly trust your partner, and trust is a priceless gift.'

Joley couldn't close her eyes and savor the sensations rushing through her body because it was too important to watch his face – his eyes, those amazing blue eyes as deep and as turbulent as the sea she loved so much. He moved slow and easy, sending flames dancing over her, but leaving her needing more. The slow buildup was nearly worse than the wild, passionate tango he played for her.

His mouth moved against hers. A soft enticement. 'Do you know what I believe love is? It's the same. It's total surrender – giving yourself to your partner, putting their needs and desires above your own and trusting them ...' He nuzzled her throat. '*Trusting* that person, Joley, to do the same for you. Isn't that what we're doing here? Tell me, *lubvo moya*, because that's what I thought we were doing – loving one another.'

His voice was pure sin, whispering over her body, sliding past every fear, every guard, and wrapping her heart in warmth. She wanted desperately to believe him, but ...

'Tell me you do not feel love in my touch, Joley,' he continued and bent to brush her throat with his mouth. 'Tell me this doesn't feel like love to you.'

He pulled back, almost leaving her body, and she wanted to sob for his return. When he surged deep in a fast, hard stroke, he took her breath, sent her stomach flipping and the heated muscles in her sheath melting into a pool of need.

'You don't know me, Ilya. How can you love me?'

The small, forlorn note in her voice tore at his heart. 'I've been in your mind every night for nearly a year. We've talked for hours, all night sometimes. I know everything I need to know about you to know I love you. And I can learn the rest, because I'm going to have a lifetime for learning.'

His mouth settled on her, a long, slow, almost lazy kiss, while his body began a rhythm similar to his stroking tongue. He kissed her thoroughly, with all the tenderness a man as rough as Ilya could manage. When he lifted his head, he braced himself over her.

'Put your arms around me, Joley. Want me as much as I want you.'

Her body clenched around his, tightened and gripped, holding him to her as her stomach muscles bunched and her breasts ached. 'You know I want you.'

He shook his head. 'Not sex, Joley. Want *me*. The man. Your man. Want to spend your life with me, want to be my best friend, my lover, my everything. Put your arms around me and give yourself to me.'

She stared up into his blue eyes. The pupils were wide and dark with a need that tugged at her beyond anything she'd ever known. What did she know about him? She'd lived around Jonas too long not to recognize the signs of a man with a code. She'd spent too much time in Ilya's mind, piecing together all the memories and seeing glimpses of colors behind the darkness of his aura. He had to be working undercover, and that kind of a life molded and shaped men into something altogether different.

She searched his eyes for a long time, looking for truth. 'How do I know what's real about you and what isn't?'

'I can't answer that, Joley.'

She moistened her lips and tried to be strong, when everything in her ached to hold him close, to comfort him. 'You have to give me something, Ilya. You're asking me to trust you with more than just me. I love my family. Several are in law enforcement. I would be trusting you with their lives as well. I need more than my body's absolute trust in you.'

He was silent a long time, his body still, but locked with hers. 'Joley, you've been around Jonas long enough to suspect what I do. I've spent my entire life training for or living undercover.'

'If you lived that long undercover as a hit man, as someone who runs in violent circles, how do you know who you are?' The thought was terrifying, because when she looked at his aura and listened to the strands of his song, there was more blood and death, more darkness than light, and it was so blended, so mixed together, she couldn't tell what the truth was and what the lie was.

He sighed and pressed his forehead to hers. 'Do I know what's real and what isn't? Not anymore. I live the way I have to in order to survive every minute of every day. Do I do abhorrent things? Yes. Do they bother me? No, not anymore. The lines blurred a long time ago. You are the only thing real in my life – the only thing for absolute certain. *You*. If you don't save me, I'm lost. I've known that from the moment I heard your voice. I didn't realize I was drowning in the blood until your voice came over the radio and everything in me went to pieces.'

If you don't save me, I'm lost. She heard the echo of those words in her mind. His voice was low, unemotional, but so soft the sound stroked over her skin and wrapped her heart in velvet. There was a plea – yet it was the stark truth. Ilya wasn't making a bid for sympathy, he lived his life in black and white and shades of gray.

'I can only give you who I am, whatever that is, Joley, but I can promise you'll never regret it. I'll never betray you. I'll always put you and your needs before my own.' He kissed the tip of her nose, slid his tongue over the curve of her lower lip. 'Even when you don't know what you want, like right this moment.' His hands shifted, cupped her breast, thumbs rasping over her nipples until she wanted to cry out to him for more.

Joley slipped her arms around him and arched her body closer. 'Then I'm glad my music touched you, Ilya.'

He bent his head to the twin peaks, lapping and nuzzling with his hot mouth, teeth tugging and hands claiming. Each strong pull of his mouth sent a wash of liquid fire sizzling over his thickened cock. 'I want to hear your screams again, Joley. I need to hear them and feel your body milking me dry.' He braced himself over her.

She swallowed hard as he began to move again, long, slow strokes that sent sizzling fire streaking up and down her body. She gasped and clung to him, trying to be careful not to jar his injured arm.

'Your music saved my life, Joley. It changed my world.'

'You've changed mine,' she admitted. 'I've never felt like you make me feel.' Beautiful. Wanted.

Needed. Sexy. More than sexy. And so hungry for him. She loved his body – the hard, defined muscles, his enormous strength, the things he could do just by looking at her, let alone touching her.

Every time his body thrust into hers, she felt stretched and full. She was burning alive, from the inside out. He began to pump into her hard and fast, building the aching need until she felt almost desperate for release. She reached for it – that perfect explosion of her body – but he pulled back, slipping her legs through his arms so he held her open for him and gave his body better leverage.

'Ilya.' She gasped his name in a plea. 'What are you doing?' Because she needed him, needed release from the terrible tension he'd built so fast.

'Marry me, Joley.'

His face could have been carved out of stone, a vision of carnal lust, but his eyes – his eyes were alive with love – unmistakable love. Her body pulsed around his; she couldn't stop the involuntary writhing under him, desperate for the release only he could provide.

'Marry you?' She echoed the word almost blankly. Shocked. It was the last thing she'd expected.

'Say it. Promise me. I need to know you love me the way I am.'

Her body shook, trembled with the aching tension. She could barely think straight. 'Are you sure, Ilya? Are you really sure that's what you want, because marriage for me is forever.'

He surged into her, another hard and fast stroke that forced a small scream from her sensitized body. He stretched her out on a rack of tormenting plea-sure as he changed his pace, pushing through her tight, swollen muscles with excruciating slowness.

'Forever then, because there is no divorce for a woman with that mark on her palm.'

She arched her hips, trying to force his penetration. 'Yes then. Yes.'

He lost what ragged control he had, plunging into her over and over again, his rhythm fast and hard and utterly devastating. He buried the long, full length of himself completely, driving deep with each stroke into her tight, silken channel. She screamed as every muscle in her body tightened, as her very bones seemed to contract, as every cell and nerve focused on one spot. His hips thrust harder, his arms locking her in place. Her muscles convulsed around him, rippling up and outward, sending shock waves of pleasure rocketing through her. Her body clamped down hard on his, taking him with her so that his hoarse cries echoed around hers.

Ilya collapsed over her, laying his head over her shoulder, fighting for air for a few moments, and then he rolled, taking her with him so that she blanketed his body with hers.

Joley lay as limp as a rag doll over the top of him, her head on his chest, listening to the steady beat of his heart. 'I'm exhausted.'

'How's your head feeling?'

'I forgot about it. It must be better.'

'No nagging headache.'

She laughed, she couldn't help it. 'That's funny.' She kissed his chest and throat, nibbled on his chin and then lay back down again, as if that was all the strength she could muster.

'Why's that funny?'

Joley lifted her head again and studied his face. 'Poor baby, you really don't know, do you?

Supposedly men say women use headaches as an excuse not to have sex. I personally don't know any women who do that, but it's a standard joke.'

'I've never had that happen.'

She bit him.

'Ouch!'

His hand came down on her buttocks, but it didn't have the desired effect. Joley just wiggled and gave him a sassy grin. 'Feed me. I'm starving. I haven't had anything to eat for days. We can call for takeout or something.'

'The reason to have a house is to have a kitchen.'

She wrinkled her nose and slowly sat up, straddling him. The movement caused a delicious aftershock. She waited for it to subside before sliding off of him. 'I thought a house was for privacy and lots of places to make love.'

'I see your point. Your idea is better than mine.'

'Only if there's no food in the kitchen. I really am starving.'

'Go take a shower and I'll whip something up.'

She sat on the edge of the bed. 'You mean it? You can cook?'

'You'll see.'

Joley didn't wait to hear any more. She was really hungry, and a shower would help to revive her. Now that he'd mentioned her head, it was hurting a little, but she'd never admit it, not when he might toss her on the floor, or against the wall, or maybe the kitchen table. It all sounded good to her.

It didn't take long to shower and find every bruise and sore spot on her body from the explosion, but none of it seemed to matter. She was happy. She was with Ilya and he said he loved her. He made her feel loved. He made her feel so beautiful and sexy she didn't mind wrapping herself in a robe and finding her way to the kitchen.

He'd pulled on a pair of jeans. They were only partially buttoned, leaving his body, so defined with muscle, for her to enjoy. She sank into a chair at the table, drew her knees up and watched him as he moved around the kitchen with sure, purposeful movements. This side of him fascinated her.

'Ilya Prakenskii, all domestic.'

'One of us has to be,' he pointed out, flicking her a small grin.

The flash of his white teeth sent a small, thrilling somersault sliding through her stomach. She loved making him happy. And he was happy. His melody was joyful, bright colors shining occasionally through that dark shield he always wore. She saw it for what it was now, a cover to keep him safe.

'Fine. I'll admit I'm not great in the kitchen. Hannah loves to cook and bake, and she totally rocks at it. I can make tea though.'

'Tea?' His eyebrow shot up. 'We're going to have sons, Joley, lots of them. I don't think tea is going to be a big hit on the menu.'

She rubbed her chin on her knees and eyed him warily. 'Now it's sons. Are you obsessed with having children or something? Because this isn't the first time you've brought the subject up. And I don't like the sound of that word "lots"'

He stirred the spaghetti sauce. 'In the interests of disclosure, I'm just warning you so you can't ever say you weren't prepared.'

She put on her fiercest scowl. 'I've disclosed to you that I haven't a clue how to take care of a baby. I'm an artist. I sing onstage and travel around the world. I can hold them, but the entire baby thing is

318

just plain scary. Do you have any idea what it takes to be responsible for a child? I made myself read parenting books, and no way am I trying that.'

'I haven't a clue what it takes, Joley. I'll be relying solely on you and your experience.' He blew on a spoonful of sauce and tasted it.

'What experience, you crazy man? I have no experience.'

He added oregano. 'Sure you do. You were raised in a family. You have good parents, a pattern to follow, and we'll just go by what they did.'

'You make it sound so easy. Do you really want children, Ilya? Is it that important to you?' She sighed. 'If it is, give me a few years and I'll give it a try.'

He glanced at her over his shoulder, and his smile had turned into a knowing smirk. 'A few years? You think we should wait a few years?'

She shrugged. 'We haven't even got to the marriage part. We're at the getting to know you part.'

He stirred the sauce again, and she could see from his profile that he was still smiling. 'We're past the getting to know you part. That was this past year. Now we're at the we'd better get married fast part.'

Joley wrinkled her nose. 'You aren't making any sense. We don't want to rush into anything. We have plenty of time to work everything out.'

'You said you'd marry me.'

She nodded, biting down on her lip. She had said it – and she'd meant it – but that had been in the heat of the moment. Now she wanted to be a little more cautious. 'I did say I would, but I was thinking of a long engagement while you got to know my family and maybe figured out what kind of work you wanted to do. Because you're not going to be working undercover anymore, right? Not with a wife and family. You have a lot to think about.' That sounded very well thought out and intelligent.

'As long as you're touring and making appearances, I'll be working your security.'

He flashed one look at her – the kind that sent tremors down her spine and made her all too aware of the dangerous man she'd committed herself to. He didn't really argue. She'd realized that about him. He would try a short discussion and then he did things his way, expecting everyone to fall in line with his orders. Joley didn't mind that in the bedroom, but he wasn't going to just dictate the rest of her life to her.

'Has it ever occurred to you that I might worry about you, Ilya? That I don't want to take chances with your life? Most of the time I need security for normal reasons, just to get through a crowd, but once in a while there's a real threat. The last person I want in jeopardy is you.'

He turned and faced her, looking so incredibly sexy he took her breath away.

'I have no experience with anyone wanting to look out for me. Not even as a small boy.' He flashed a small grin at her. 'This will be interesting, learning how best to react when you talk this way to me.'

She held her breath. 'How do you feel like reacting?'

'Honestly?' He put pasta onto two plates, added the spaghetti sauce and two pieces of warm bread. He put one dish in front of her and the other on the side of the table facing her. 'I want to sweep the counter clean and put you on it and feast on you in thanks.'

The low, wicked voice sent a flood of damp heat between her legs. 'That's a good reaction.' She tried to keep her voice steady as she twirled pasta onto her fork. 'I do need a little fuel and then you can do whatever you want.'

The blue eyes glittered at her and her heart jumped.

'Why don't you untie that robe for me?' he suggested.

'It wouldn't be very sexy if I dropped spaghetti down the front of me,' she pointed out. 'And you're making me so nervous I just might.'

His white teeth flashed again, and this time he looked like a wolf. 'If you dropped spaghetti down the front of you, Joley, I'd be more than happy to use you for a dinner plate.'

She laughed, happiness warming her. 'Okay, just stop right there and behave yourself. I'm getting this image that just is so wrong.'

'Really?' His eyebrow shot up. 'I've got a very erotic one. Want to try it?'

Chapter Sixteen

'Woo hoo, Joley!' Rick said as they entered the suite. 'You were on fire tonight. We were all so worried about you after the bus blew up; we thought for certain we'd have to cancel, but no, you just keep rockin', girl!' He picked her up around the waist, lifting into the air, and swung her around.

Joley caught a glimpse of Ilya's face before she lost sight of him in the mad spinning. A secret grin tugged at her deep inside. He definitely didn't share well with others.

Keep smiling, lubov moya, you think this is funny having another man touch you? The edge to his voice held a warning.

It's not another man, it's Rick. She felt sassy, ecstatic! She had given another great performance in spite of every threat. Only two more shows and she would be home.

Precisely. There was a bite in his voice.

Just like that her body stirred to life. She put her hands on Rick's shoulders and stepped back. 'Crazy man, but seriously we all rocked. I wasn't the only one out there exposed, we all were, and I'm so glad we made the decision to go on tonight together.'

'No one is going to dictate to us whether or not we perform,' Denny said.

'Damn straight,' Logan agreed.

She couldn't help herself, she glanced at Ilya standing by the door. He didn't look uncomfortable, he never did. Just – hot. Sexy. His eyes shifted around the room, but she knew he saw her. Watched her. The thought was arousing.

Leo ruffled her hair. 'Well the lights caught that bandage just right and highlighted the bruises and we're going to get so much publicity – all good – because you are the ultimate pro, baby. No one can touch you.'

Joley laughed. 'Well, I'm hoping not. I felt a lot safer with all the heightened security. I noticed everyone has to have a picture on their IDs.'

Jerry nodded as he handed her an ice-cold bottle of water. After a grueling two-and-half-hour performance under hot lights, she was tired and sweaty and coming down from an adrenaline high. 'We made sure you were totally protected, Joley. And it's going to stay that way. You don't go anywhere without a bodyguard, and when you're getting through a crowd, I want security lining that rope to ensure your safety.'

'You've been talking to Jonas, haven't you?' she said accusingly, and flung herself onto the couch beside Tish. She leaned over to kiss the baby's hand. 'Hello, little angel. You're so perfect. She's so beautiful, Tish.'

'Jonas called me,' Jerry said hastily. 'And you okayed keeping him in the loop.'

Joley laughed again. 'Jonas out of the loop would be Jonas sitting on top of me. There's no such thing as keeping him out of it. He sort of steamrolls his way wherever he wants to be.'

All the while she was rubbing her palm up and down her thigh. He was only a few feet away, the crowd separating them, but they could have been alone the way her body felt. Ilya. Her Ilya. Wickedly she brought her palm to her mouth, breathing warm air on the center. Her lips brushed back and forth, feather-light. There was something very sensual about sex in a roomful of people when no one else had a clue. It was wicked and exciting and very naughty.

She felt him jump in her mind. *Knock it off.* The voice was a growl. A rasp. She found it sexy and too hot to resist.

Her eyes collided with his. The blue had gone to a molten sea, turbulent and wild. She let her gaze drift lower and was more than satisfied at the obvious bulge in the front of his jeans. She grinned and gave a small salute before responding to the teasing from the band.

'Well, boys, since I have no bus, and you're all pulling out tonight for Sacramento, I think I'll just put my feet up here and relax.'

Brian threw a crumpled up program at her. 'Not funny, little Miss Diva. You get to take a plane.'

Joley started to contradict him. She was thinking of making the ten-hour drive with Ilya, but she hadn't checked with him. Instead she licked the center of her palm twice with wicked intent and pressed another kiss there before taking a drink of the ice-cold water.

I will retaliate.

Hmmm. I think I'm pretty safe with all these people around. Her body grew hot just thinking about how she was tormenting Ilya. The palm thing was going from the con side of her list to the pro side very quickly. Glancing around the room to make certain no one was watching her, she took another long, slow lick, curling her tongue around the center, envisioning his hard, thick erection in her mouth. She heard his swift intake of breath in her mind, and she smiled secretly, holding her palm against her heart.

Keep it up, Joley, and I'll throw you over my shoulder, carry you into your dressing room and put you on your knees so you can put that mouth to really good use. His voice was dark with arousal and the threat of wicked, sensual punishment. A shiver of excitement went down her spine. She actually felt her nipples harden and her womb clench in anticipation. Belonging to Ilya was exhilarating.

Some perverse, wicked part of her wanted him to do just that. *Really? Would you like my mouth around your cock right now? Me kneeling in front of you? Maybe you really are into bondage and you like the image of me with my hands tied behind my back, helpless while you slide down my throat. Sounds kind of kinky but exciting. I might like it.*

His low, telepathic groan was harsh with arousal, sending hot flames licking over her skin and spreading like a firestorm through her bloodstream.

Tish leaned close to her. 'Does your hand hurt?'

Around them, the room was alive with everyone pouring drinks, toasting, laughing, happy with the success of the show. Ilya stood only feet from her, his blue eyes burning with hunger, yet never once did he shift his position or stop the restless search of the room. A part of her wanted to shake his control, but mostly she was just happy. She sat beside Tish and felt grateful that she was back.

Things had always been good when Tish was around.

'My palm itches a little.' She closed her fingers around the center to hold Ilya to her there. 'Tish, I did want to say, whatever is happening with you and Logan, this is the way it was meant to be. All of us together like this, a family. You brought us here. All your work, your belief in us, all those posters you made, the website you created, you even designed our first cover on the CD we sold at bars. This is your success as well as ours.'

As if confirming what Joley had said, Logan spun around, his eyes bright with success. 'Tish, come here, honey.' He held out his hand to her.

Tish pressed Lissa closer to her. 'Don't leave when the others do. Stay, just a few minutes so we can be alone. I need someone to talk to.'

'Sure, but right now, let me hold the baby. Logan looks like he wants attention.' She was shamelessly playing matchmaker, but she was happy and she wanted Tish to be happy as well. She held out her arms for the baby.

Tish hesitated, confirming Joley's suspicion that she was hiding behind the baby. Reluctantly Tish gave Lissa to her and stood up. Joley watched her cross to Logan's side. She didn't pull back when he wrapped his arm around her and held her close, but she didn't lean into him either. Body language suggested that Tish was conflicted, and it wasn't difficult to guess what she wanted to talk with Joley about.

You look good with that baby. When you have mine, you'll have to sit naked with all that beautiful soft skin, with our child in your arms, at your breast, and I'll just watch until it's my turn.

She sucked in her breath. Her breasts ached,

sending little sneaky curls of heat radiating from her nipples to her feminine sheath. Muscles rippled and her body softened, went damp. Her breath left her lungs in a little rush. More than the words and the erotic images he thrust into her mind, it was the sexy sound of his voice. The tone played over her skin like caressing fingers, or worse, a stroking, sinful tongue.

No babies. I told you that. They're fine asleep, but I'm not so good with them when they're awake. You'll just have to be content with suckling all by yourself. She felt very daring teasing him. If she could have, she might have taken another long, slow lick of her palm, but she wasn't all that adroit at holding babies and she was afraid she might disturb Lissa.

'Hey you,' Brian said softly, dropping into the vacated seat beside her. 'How are you feeling? They escorted you in so late that I didn't really get much of a chance to talk to you about what happened. Let's see your head.' He swept back her hair and whistled low under his breath. 'Black and blue and swollen. That looks nasty.'

'It hurts,' Joley confirmed, stealing a quick glance at Ilya before meeting Brian's eyes. 'How 'bout you? Are you doing okay?'

'I went to see Sergei,' Brian said in a rush. 'I had to. If he was the one who ordered that bombing, I had to try to stop him.'

Joley shook her head, glanced around and lowered her voice even more. All around them, the band, their women and friends partied, but she and Brian were isolated by secrets. 'You shouldn't have gone, Brian, it's too dangerous.'

He slipped his finger into the baby's hand and

watched her curl tiny, soft fingers around it. 'I don't know what to think – what to believe. He swore – looked me right in the eye and swore – he would never harm you because you're my family and he knows that. He said he had loaned Ilya to you now, when he needed him most, to make certain nothing happens to you – that he did that for me. And God help me, Joley, I believe him.'

Joley pressed her cheek against the baby's face. She ached inside for Brian. She knew what loneliness was. And she knew heartache. Brian was a good man and he deserved to be happy. He'd sacrificed any relationship to keep their band going, and now, when he'd finally found someone he could love, it was the wrong person. She wished she could find a way to help him. 'Brian, you know I love you very much,' she whispered softly. 'You're an amazing person. I'm sorry about Nikitin. I really am.'

'You're wrong about him. You could be wrong. I know he was once involved in the mob. He was born into it, but he's worked hard to become a legitimate businessman.'

'I wish I could say I believed that, but it just isn't true.'

'How do you know? You're obviously falling for his bodyguard. Did he tell you that?'

Alarm bells went off. She sat up straight and tried not to look frightened. 'No, of course not. My family is in law enforcement. I told you that. I had them double-check, but I think you can dig up the facts yourself, Brian. I'm not saying that to hurt you. If I thought for one moment there was a chance this was all a mistake, I'd totally be on your side, but you know better. Deep down, you know better.'

'People change, Joley.'

'I know they do, Brian.' She couldn't stop the flick of her gaze to Ilya.

Do you need me, lubov moya?

She moistened her lips. She didn't want Ilya to draw Brian's attention. *No. Please don't let him even notice you. He's searching for someone to blame and I don't want it to be you. He's still talking to Nikitin, and Nikitin is trying to convince him that he's just a misunderstood businessman. I don't want Brian to think you've given me any information.* She nuzzled the baby again to keep her gaze from straying to her bodyguard.

'I'm just saying maybe Sergei was into some things he shouldn't have been . . .'

'Brian, maybe you're right, you could be right, but until you know, you can't be with him. It's too dangerous on so many levels. Finish the tour. I'll ask my family to help, and we'll quietly investigate him, not to put him in jail or anything, but to make certain it's safe for you.'

Brian ran his fingers through his hair several times. 'I hate being so alone, Joley. I can't live like this anymore. With Sergei, half the time we just talked, just laughed together. We didn't have to go out, party, any of that, we were just quiet together and that was enough.'

She wanted to weep for him. 'Come to Sea Haven with me after the tour. There's something about the town, the people, all of it. The sea is wild there and the sunsets are beautiful. I'd love to have you stay with me. The big house is mostly empty because all my sisters are treacherous wenches and they're getting married. Every last one of them with the exception of my baby sister Elle. She's the only one left with a brain.'

He reached over and took Lissa out of her arms, cuddling the baby close to his chest. 'I've always envied you your family, Joley. Do you know how really lucky you are? We always had money, but I preferred to hang out with Denny, Logan and Rick and the others, anywhere but home. Alcohol was a huge problem. My mom died in her early forties, but it didn't slow Dad down at all.'

Which was why he chose not to drink much, only a rare glass of cognac on a special occasion. She knew all the band members had known one another from childhood and were close. She knew Brian considered the band his family. Would it change everything if they knew he was gay? She hoped it wouldn't, but she knew it often did. Brian looked so sad and alone. All around them his friends partied and laughed, happy about the show they'd put on and deservedly so, but they didn't notice he was apart from them.

Ilya kept his eye on Joley even as he noted all the others in the room, their position, what they were doing, who they were talking to and how close they were to Joley. He was in a good position to get to her if need be, and an even better position to use a weapon. His instincts were on alert, but as always, it was impossible to tell if it was because there'd been threats and attempts on Joley, or because a threat was looming.

Whatever she was discussing with Brian upset her. She looked – and felt – as if she wanted to cry. He wanted to pull her into his arms and shelter her, hold her close and comfort her. She had a good heart and was fiercely loyal to her friends. Ilya wished he could tell her Sergei Nikitin was a good man, but he'd ordered more killings, more torture, and run every kind of operation, from human trafficking to laundering money. While it was true he appeared to have genuine feelings for Brian, if Brian became a threat, Nikitin wouldn't hesitate to kill him just like he'd kill anyone else who threatened him. Violence was Sergei's way of life.

Joley rubbed the baby's hand over her cheek, and deep inside Ilya, something hard and cold warmed and melted. He couldn't wait to watch his child grow in her belly, to lie on the bed with her, waiting the nine months for a life they created together to be born. Joley didn't believe she was the type of woman to be a mother, but she would be fiercely protective, yet fill their lives with love and joy and laughter – all the things he'd never had. Their home would be a sanctuary of laughter and love. It would be Joley who would show them all how to live.

People began to drift out, hugging, laughing, and Ilya stayed to one side, invisible as the band and their friends left.

Brian stood and dusted his clothes off, meticulous as always, walking with Joley over to Logan and Tish. Tish took the baby back with obvious relief. Brian clapped Logan on the back and walked out with Denny. Ilya was very aware that Brian knew exactly where he was at all times, while the others didn't pay any attention at all.

In the end, only Tish, Logan and Joley remained. The two women said something to Logan; he hesitated and then left the suite as well. Silence followed. Tish looked at him, and he knew the moment Joley crossed to his side what she was going to say. The knots in his stomach hardened.

'I'm sorry, Ilya, would you mind stepping out of

the room, just for a few minutes? I promised Tish we could talk alone.'

'I don't like it,' Ilya protested, uneasy with the idea of Joley out of his sight.

She smiled at him, that dynamite smile that tugged on every heartstring and made his blood surge hotly. 'You can stand right outside the door, in fact stand in front of it with your gun out.'

Ilya had a strong desire to throw her over his shoulder like a primitive caveman and carry her to his lair somewhere safe. Glancing over her head, he saw Tish's anxious face. She held the baby close to her, but her shoulders were stiff, her lips pressed together tightly. He nodded, took another glance around the room and stepped into the hall, leaving the door open behind him. He wasn't happy when Joley closed the door.

'I wasn't certain we'd actually get a chance to be alone,' Joley said. 'Without the bus, I'm kind of stuck without a place of my own.'

'Logan wants us to stay together and he wants me to legally adopt the baby with him.' The word came out in a rush, tumbling over one another. 'I can't do that and then turn around and lose both of them again. I can't, Joley.' Tish nuzzled her chin against the baby's head. 'I know you all think I'm really strong, but when I walked in on Logan and that woman, I felt shattered, utterly, absolutely shattered. I was so broken I didn't know if there was any way to ever put me back together again. I've loved him since high school. Maybe grammar school. I've never even looked at another man. His betrayal was so devastating, I came close to suicide.' Now her voice was a mere whisper and tears swam in her eyes. 'I'm ashamed of that, but it was so close, Joley.'

'You should have called me,' Joley said, fear gripping her. 'We all love you, the entire band. It was horrible after you left and has been ever since. I would have helped you through it, so would all the guys.'

'I couldn't call you. I couldn't see any of you. My emotions were all over the place. Part of me blamed all of you, because of the alcohol and drugs. My mother was ill and needed me at home, so I had to stop traveling with the band. I thought Logan would stay away from trouble, but . . .'

The baby in her arms stirred a little and Tish shifted her to pat her back and keep her asleep. She glanced around for the diaper bag. 'I think I left her diaper bag in the dressing room. I need to check her in case she needs a change.'

'I'm not making excuses,' Joley said, following her into the large dressing room, 'but it's hard on the road, you know that. It's lonely and isolating. Drinking is a way to be numb, and I would have considered it as an option myself more than once if my body chemistry was different. Logan always loved you, Tish. After you left, we thought we'd lose him. He went crazy, life didn't matter much to him. Drugs, drinking . . .'

'Women,' Tish supplied bitterly, glancing over her shoulder at Joley as she snagged the bag. 'Believe me, I tried not to read the tabloids, but it was compulsive behavior.' Lissa squirmed, and Tish handed Joley the changing pad to put on the makeup table.

Joley smoothed the pad and pulled diapers and wipes from inside the bag. 'That, too. That's how he got involved with Lucy. He stayed drunk. We finally did an intervention and told him he was out if he

333

didn't pull his life back together. Unfortunately, or fortunately, depending on how you want to view it, Lucy was already pregnant. She'd tried twice to slice Logan up with bottles when she was angry with him, and then as soon as she found out about the baby, she threatened to cut it out of her stomach. We got the lawyers on it and went the legal route. She didn't want the baby, but she has problems with reality.'

'I feel sorry for her,' Tish said, kissing Lissa and putting her gently on the pad. 'I would give anything if Lissa was mine and Logan's child, yet she can't enjoy what she has because she's too ill.'

'If she stays on her meds she does fairly well,' Joley said. 'She makes much more rational decisions when she's on them, but she just won't take them.'

'If I stay any longer taking care of Lissa, I'll be lost,' Tish admitted as she took the little pink outfit off so she could change the diaper. 'I can barely think straight around Logan, but I can't lose myself again like that. It was terrifying to be so depressed, so out of control. Maybe that's why I feel so bad for Lucy. I've had a taste of what depression can do to a person and it's horrible.'

'Do you honestly believe Logan would make that mistake again?' Joley slipped her finger into Lissa's little hand. 'You're so good at this mom thing. Look at you, Tish, changing that diaper like a pro. I'd be freaking out if it was me. She's too small.'

Tish sent her a small grin. 'It took me a while, but I was better than the guys. They're so cute with her, all of them, big bad boys, all fighting over who gets to hold her. It's so funny.' She sighed. 'Right now, Logan's saying everything I want to hear, because he wants me to stay with him. We were never divorced, but I don't want him to be with me because he needs me for the baby. Our relationship wasn't strong enough to sustain being away from each other a few weeks.'

'Tish . . .'

She shook her head. 'I made all the excuses for him already, but military men and women are apart. Pilots. Lots of couples are apart for long periods of time.'

'He was weak. It cost him a huge price, Tish. You didn't answer me. Do you honestly think he'll ever make that same mistake again? He nearly destroyed himself after you left. I was there. I saw him.'

The lights flickered and dimmed. Joley frowned. 'They can't be finished breaking down the set this fast. Surely they're not closing the building.' She turned around to peer out the dressing room door into the larger suite. The lights were off, except the mood lighting over the bar. She was aware of Tish wrapping the baby in a blanket and lifting her into her arms.

Something heavy banged against the outside door. Startled, she looked over at it.

Joley. What the hell is going on?

A chair was stuck under the door handle, effectively blocking the door to the suite. The couch had been pushed up against it as well. Joley caught sight of movement, someone ducking back behind the bar.

Ilya. We're in trouble. Someone's in the room with us and they've barricaded the door. I can't see, but I'm willing to bet they've done the same with the other entrance.

Stay calm, Joley. I'm coming.

The fear subsided a bit, as fast as it had risen. The absolute confidence in his voice calmed her. He would come and nothing would stop him.

335

She caught Tish's hand, preventing her from entering the suite. 'Stay back, hon. We've got company and they barricaded the door from the inside.'

'The baby, Joley. What about the baby?'

Joley caught Tish's hand. 'It's all right. We'll be all right. Ilya and Logan will come for us. We know the dressing room is clear because we've been here all this time and whoever put the chair against the door is out there. So I want you to stay to the back of the room with Lissa. If they come in here, they'll have to get through me to get to you and the baby.'

Tish clutched the baby tighter to her. 'Will your cell phone work in here?'

She'd called Ilya, and that was her secret weapon. No one could possibly know they could speak telepathically. 'Ilya knows, he's coming for us.'

'You know who's out there, don't you, Joley?'

Ilya? It's Lucy, the woman you took down in Dallas. If she's off her meds, she can be very violent and she's tried to kill the baby before.

Does she have a gun?

'Tell me, Joley. I know you suspect someone,' Tish insisted.

Joley sucked in her breath, weighing whether or not to tell Tish the truth as they moved together deeper into the dressing room. Her fingers tightened around Tish's hand. 'It's Lucy, Tish, the baby's biological mother. I'm just guessing, but she's probably responsible for the flowers, doll, phone call and my clothes. My best guess is, in her twisted and demented mind, she believes the tabloid articles and thinks I've stolen Logan and the baby from her.'

'She didn't want the baby. She tried to kill the baby before she was even born and again right afterward in the hospital. She's not supposed to come anywhere near the baby.' Tish's voice trembled with fear. She pulled her hand away from Joley and hugged Lissa tighter to her.

'Did Logan mention she attacked him in Dallas just before we entered the building for the sound check?'

Tish made a small sound of assent. 'He said she'd been arrested. And she violated a restraining order. The judge specifically said she couldn't go near him.'

'Well her mother must have bailed her out, because she's back. I caught a glimpse of her right as I noticed the door was barricaded. She's dressed as a crew member and she ducked back behind the bar, but it was her. And in all honesty, I've never found that restraining orders do much good on people like Lucy. She wants me dead.'

Tish put a hand on Joley. 'Because she thinks you're with Logan and the baby, but as soon as she sees me, she'll know. I was in the bus when those pictures were taken. But she knows I'm his wife. She sent me a few threatening letters telling me to give him up. That was a while back, but they were ugly.'

Joley didn't want to point out that Lucy had to have just now seen Tish holding the baby; that would just frighten her more.

There was sound of glass shattering, the overpowering smell of whiskey and then a slow, deliberate tread that came closer and closer. Tish gasped and clutched Lissa tighter. The baby began to cry.

'Do you have formula for her?' Joley asked. 'Go sit down over there where you're out of the sight of the doorway and feed her. We just need to buy a couple of minutes.'

Tish nodded and ducked back into the smaller alcove, sinking into the chair there and hastily pulling a bottle from the bag to keep the baby quiet.

The sound of humming became loud. Lucy stood framed in the doorway dressed in trousers and shirt proclaiming she was a crew member. Around her neck hung an ID badge with a picture of a man on it – John Dylan. Joley recognized his photo immediately. Lucy kept humming as she looked around the room.

'Hi, Lucy,' Joley said to greet her. 'I didn't know you'd come to the concert. It was a great show. Did you enjoy yourself?'

Lucy's lashes fluttered. A cunning, crafty expression crossed her face. 'Don't pretend to be my friend. I know what you did.'

Joley deliberately looked as innocent as possible. 'I have no idea what you're talking about Lucy.'

Lucy bared her teeth like a wild animal. 'I have friends. You think I don't have friends who tell me what's going on? I know you stole Logan from me. He wanted me and you were jealous – so jealous you crawled into his bed. That bitch of a wife of his thinks you're her friend, just like you're pretending to be mine, but I know the truth.'

Joley shook her head. Lucy took a couple of steps to Joley's right, and in her hand, beside her thigh, were the jagged remains of a whiskey bottle. Her fingers were wrapped around the neck of the bottle, and she began to tap it against her thigh.

'Lucy, be careful. You're going to cut yourself,' Joley cautioned her.

She had to keep her body between Lucy and Tish, and Lucy taking steps forward didn't give Joley much room.

'Do you think I care?' Lucy demanded, brandishing the bottle. 'When I'm finished with you, your face will be in shreds.'

'Like my clothes, Lucy? You tore up my clothes, didn't you?'

Joley was aware of a muffled sound coming from just beyond the darkened interior of the suite. Ilya had to be making his way in. She just had to keep Lucy focused on her and he'd be there.

Lucy tossed her head. 'Strutting around in front of him in your whore clothes. I know all about you, Joley. You pretend to be so innocent, but you can't stand it when you aren't getting all the attention. That's why you didn't want to have Logan's baby. You insisted I carry the baby so you wouldn't have to ruin your figure. You had me impregnated with your child.' She stepped even closer as she lowered her voice, biting out each word between her bared teeth. 'I knew you'd done it before *he* told me, and I tried to kill the brat, cut her out of me so your bitch seed wouldn't take root.'

'Who told you that, Lucy? Because it isn't true. Lissa is your child.' She had to convince her just in case Lucy managed to get past her.

'Lissa?' Lucy snarled the name. 'I told Logan he couldn't call her that. He'll see what happens when he tries to leave me.'

Joley kept her eyes on the middle of Lucy's chest so she could see her entire body – shoulder movement, foot position, the telegraphing of the attack before it came. She stayed on the balls of her feet, slightly to the side to present less of a target. Both arms were loose, one across her body, so she could bring it up fast and block if need be, one up under her chin, so she could use it to strike. She knew Ilya was close, she could sense him moving into the outer room now. He'd gotten through the barricade Lucy had placed against the far door.

Lucy lunged at her, her fist striking out, bottle rushing at Joley's torso in an arc. Every defense was an offense, and Joley timed hers to catch the arm solidly as she swung her own up in a block, knocking the forearm hard to push the broken glass to the outside, delivering a front kick to Lucy's stomach and doubling her over. Joley followed the kick in and slammed her arm down hard on Lucy's back, driving her to the floor. Lucy crumpled, sprawling at the last moment, trying to recover and swinging wildly with the broken bottle to keep Joley away from her.

'You bitch,' she screamed. 'I'm fucking going to cut out your heart.'

A hand dropped on Joley's shoulder. She whirled around swinging, but Ilya caught her, locking her close. 'Everything's fine, *lubov moya*. Please go over to Tish and let me handle this.'

'She's ill, Ilya, please don't hurt her,' Joley said.

'Of course not.' Ilya kept his gaze on Lucy, who slowly climbed to her feet.

Lucy didn't even look at Ilya or acknowledge that he was in the room. She could see only Joley. She straightened her shoulders. 'Do you think that hurt? That didn't hurt.' Deliberately she made a slow cut across her own arm. 'You see that?' Blood dripped. 'I don't feel pain. I refuse to feel pain. You're the wimp bitch Logan thinks he's going to run away with, but I don't let anyone steal my man.'

Joley knew that backing up often brought an attacker forward. She didn't look at Ilya; certain he was ready, she simply took a tentative step back, putting herself in a vulnerable position. It was difficult to move fast when backing up.

Lucy lunged again, this time striking upward toward Joley's throat. Ilya stepped to the side of her arm, blocking her with his body while he took control of her wrist, his grip merciless. Lucy went insane, kicking and screaming, trying to throw herself over backward, but Ilya held her in a grip of steel. She turned and tried to sink her teeth into his shoulder. He shifted his feet, swinging Lucy into an arc and taking her to the floor, facedown.

Joley rushed to Tish, wrapping her arms around her and the baby. 'It's safe now. You're safe.'

Logan, along with several security guards, burst into the room. Logan's face was ashen. 'Tish. Baby, are you all right? Ilya called me and told me. Are you all right?' He dropped to his knees in front of her and pulled her into his arms.

'Are you crying?' Tish touched his face. 'We're safe. We're both safe.'

'I thought I'd lost you again. I wouldn't have survived this time, Tish. Thank God you're okay.' He rained kisses on her upturned face, careful not to smash the baby.

For the first time since they had broken up, Tish kissed him back.

Joley sank back on her heels, trying not to shake, waiting for Ilya to finish helping put Lucy in handcuffs.

Ilya's eyes met hers. She felt tears clog her throat. Her body trembled. He crossed the distance to her and simply took her into his arms, pressing her against his solid strength, one hand stroking a caress down her hair while the other locked her against his chest.

'Hopefully they'll get her the help she needs,

341

Joley. You were wonderful.' He brushed kisses over her temple. She'd scared him to death, but at the same time, the determination, the look on her face as she protected Tish and the baby twisted her even deeper into his heart. 'It's over, now, *lubov moya*. Let's give a statement and get out of here.'

Joley nodded and went with him, careful to keep the appropriate space between them so the paparazzi wouldn't suspect he was anything more than her bodyguard. She knew – and accepted – that he was everything ... and that meant she would do whatever it took to protect him.

Chapter Seventeen

Joley was very subdued with her family as they gathered together in a hotel room in Sacramento. She sat alone in a high-backed chair, looking young and fragile, her eyes downcast as Jonas ranted at her. Ilya wanted to gather her into his arms and hold her. He also wanted to smash Jonas in the face. Instead he waited for a sign, anything at all from Joley to tell him how she wanted her family handled, but she just looked at the floor. If she didn't give him an indication soon, he was going to have to throw her brother-in-law out the door – and there'd be some satisfaction in that. Jonas was making it clear that he believed he was in charge.

'You know better, Joley. You could have been killed. Tish and the baby could have been killed. What were you thinking?' Jonas demanded.

'Jonas,' Sarah cautioned.

'Get over it already,' Kate muttered under her breath.

'Would you like some tea, baby?' Hannah asked her sister, glaring at her husband. The suite had a large kitchen, and Hannah had already taken it over.

Jonas glared right back. 'I'm trying to keep you alive, Joley. You've been raised around security. You know what it means, and you certainly have had experience with what can happen when someone tries to kill you ...'

Ilya stirred. 'That's enough. It was my fault, not hers. I walked out of the room and it wasn't secure. We handled it. *She* handled it. She kept Lucy from getting to Tish and the baby and she stalled to give me time to break into the room.'

Joley flicked him a small look and his stomach tightened. She might *look* fragile and suitably chastised, but Jonas was only annoying her. Her dark eyes smoldered with fire, and that one telling flash lit a blaze in his belly. *You're so damned sexy when you're pissed*.

She nearly choked, but he felt her laughter in his mind, and it connected them back together when he'd been feeling apart from her. The Drake family was large, and they had no trouble talking to one another, giving their opinions and backing each other up. Watching them together had made him feel a little lonely, which was odd. He preferred being alone, but this was Joley's family and he needed to learn to become part of it, because a huge part of her heart lay with them and she would never be truly happy if he wasn't comfortable with them.

'We're just lucky she handled it, aren't we, Ilya?' Jonas demanded. 'Because you fucked up and she nearly was killed.'

'Don't say "fuck,"' Hannah said. 'You said you'd clean up your language.'

Ilya coughed to cover the sudden laughter welling up. A pained expression crossed Jonas's face at his wife's reprimand in the middle of him dressing Ilya down. Family dynamics could be a lot more fun than Ilya had first thought.

'Laugh it up,' Jonas hissed at him, but it was clear Hannah had taken the starch out of his attack. He sighed. 'Joley, I know you're sitting there rolling your eyes while you're trying to look like you're listening, but you have to take your protection seriously.'

'I'm serious,' Joley said. 'I thought we were safe in the suite.'

'Your bodyguard stays with you at all times.'

Joley crossed her arms over her breasts and looked mutinous, but before she could say anything, Ilya made his stand. This was her family, the people she loved most in the world, and whether or not they wanted to accept him into their circle – they were going to have to.

'Joley and I are getting married after the tour.'

Everyone in the room froze. The silence stretched. Joley kept her chin on her knees, her lashes hiding her expression. Ilya simply didn't care. He'd had enough of Jonas scolding them as if they were small children, and he wanted to make it very clear that Joley was under his protection – and more – that he belonged there as more than the bodyguard. They could deal with him on equal footing.

'Married?' Sarah finally echoed. She moved closer to her fiancé, Damon, as if he could change what Ilya had said.

Damon shifted slightly and took her hand.

The teakettle whistled, and Hannah waved her hand toward the kitchen. 'Joley?'

I don't think they believe me, lubov moya. He injected humor and warmth into the caressing tone of his voice, deliberately stroking her with sound.

345

Joley shrugged. *I think you're right.*

Ilya kept all expression from his face as he teased her. *Maybe I should tell them I ate spaghetti off your stomach last night and licked sauce off your breasts.* He'd done more than that – a lot more than that. *Do you think they'd believe me then?*

No, they'll just think all the tabloid stories are the truth.

'Joley,' Hannah repeated. 'Are you really thinking of getting married?' There was a little hitch in her voice and her gaze shifted for a moment to Ilya.

Joley nodded. 'I'm not into big weddings. I thought we'd just run off, get it done and then sort of tell Mom and Dad after.'

'Before,' Ilya corrected.

'After,' Joley said.

'We will tell them before we are married and give them the opportunity to join us,' Ilya said. *I will not be hidden from your parents as if you are ashamed of me.*

Her gaze jumped to his face. 'Ilya. Never. How can you think that?' She was so upset she forgot the others hadn't been privy to their exchange. 'It has nothing to do with you. I just can't seem to do anything right and I've given up arguing with my father.'

Everyone erupted into speech at the same time.

'No!' Sarah said firmly. 'Absolutely not.'

Libby shook her head. 'Joley, you haven't thought this through.'

Abbey stepped directly in front of Ilya. 'Mr. Prakenskii, do you kill people for a living?'

The room fell silent again, and Joley hissed, a long, angry note escaping between her teeth. *Don't answer. Don't say anything. She's using her gift of truthspeaking on you.*' She leapt up and pushed between her older sister and Ilya. 'How dare you? Did you ask Damon that question? Or Matt? What about Jonas? Did you ask him? Or Tyson? You have no right to do that to him.' Furious, she glared at her family. 'I'm done here.'

She turned on her heel, yanked open the door and walked out, slamming it behind her.

Ilya faced her sisters and their men. 'She wanted you to be happy for her. She wanted to share something special with you. I would have given you any information about myself freely had you asked. It wasn't necessary to embarrass her.' He followed Joley out into the hall.

Joley walked briskly toward the elevators. She was furious – *furious* – with her family. It was always the same. Joley, the one they all had to look out for because she couldn't make a decent decision to save her life. None of them had lost their minds over Damon or Matt. Or Jonas. What the hell was that all about? Jonas was bossy and he worked undercover even when he promised he wouldn't. What kind of a husband was he for Hannah?

Ilya caught up to her and took her clenched fist into his hand, stopping her. 'They were objecting out of love for you, Joley.' His thumb slid over her bare knuckles in an attempt to ease the tension out of her.

She was going to cry. She could feel the tears burning behind her eyes, and that made her even angrier. 'I didn't question if Hannah was out of her mind when she chose Jonas. I supported her decision. Maybe I teased her a bit, but I wanted her happy and it was obvious that Jonas made her happy.'

She had always been so careful in her choice of men because she knew she had a weakness for the dangerous ones. She'd laughed about it, joked about it, never once hid it from her sisters, and she'd made certain she stayed away from them. Her family should have trusted that she knew what she was doing.

'Is it possible that all of you knew Jonas and had accepted the man he is already?' he asked gently. 'I watch you all when he's raking you over the coals, and you might roll your eyes and sigh, but you let him have his say because you know he's afraid for you. And when he's afraid, he's angry.'

'Don't defend them. They don't deserve it.'

He brought her hand to his mouth and kissed her clenched fist before pulling her into the refuge of his arms. 'You had the same fears, *laskovaya moya*. It is a legitimate question after all. I went to a great deal of trouble to create my reputation.'

'Jonas and Aleksandr are standing in that room. Aleksandr is Abbey's fiancé. She could have asked him privately what he thought, not tried to embarrass you in front of my entire family.'

'I don't embarrass so easily, Joley.' He nuzzled her neck, holding her close in an effort to still the tremors running through her body. 'But I love you all the more for wanting to defend me.' A sound alerted him, and he whirled around, thrusting Joley behind him as a door opened. Hannah came down the hall toward them.

'Joley, Ilya, come back inside.'

Joley looked stubborn. 'I'm really angry,' she said. 'I'd better not.'

Hannah reached them and drew her sister into her arms, although Joley remained stiff. 'You're hurt,

348

baby, that's not the same thing. And you have every right to be upset. I'm happy for you and so is Jonas. He says Ilya is a good man.'

'By agreeing to marry him, *I* said Ilya was a good man. I know I've always been attracted to the wrong sort of men, so why would I marry someone I wasn't certain of?'

'You're right, Joley. Everyone is very sorry. Please come back and we'll have some tea.' Hannah smiled up at Ilya. 'Joley is very loved and we're all a little overprotective of her.'

Ilya nodded his understanding. He felt very protective of her as well, and sometimes felt her family didn't protect her enough. Joley thought of herself as tough, but she was very sensitive and vulnerable. He slipped his arm around her waist. 'Let's go have some tea.'

Joley scowled at them, but she'd never been able to resist Hannah. She followed her sister back to the room. *You're uneasy. We don't have to go in.*

He looked down at her. She surprised him sometimes. *It isn't your family. I need to go soon. My gut tells me there's a problem with Nikitin, and I'm rarely wrong. I need to be there. In any case he texted me a summons, and you don't say no to Nikitin.*

She stiffened and threw him a quick shake of the head. *No, you can't go. I've heard about the Russians when they get upset.*

His expression didn't change, but she had the impression of a brief smile in her mind. It warmed her as nothing else could.

I am Russian, lubov moya.

Joley stepped very close to him, as if shielding him from her waiting family. They were all on their feet watching soberly as she stepped in front of him. His heart reacted with a curious melting. She looked regal to him, regal and beautiful, and in that moment whatever tiny bit of him he'd held in reserve was gone in an instant. He was completely, utterly hers.

'I am going to marry Ilya Prakenskii. I'm in love with him and I want to spend the rest of my life with him. None of you have to agree with my decision, I'm not asking you to, but I expect you to treat him with respect, the same way you treat every other man in this family.'

She wasn't asking. She was stating, and staring her sisters down while she did it.

Hannah reacted first. To Ilya's dismay, she put her arms around him and hugged him. 'Welcome to the family. Please forgive our former rudeness, we were just very shocked. Joley normally communicates with us, and she failed to tell us she was even contemplating marriage.'

Sarah nodded. 'She's been rather opposed to it.' She still eyed him warily, as if he might have cast a spell on her sister.

Jonas stuck out his hand. 'Why so quick? You'd think you were in a hurry. Mom and Dad are going to want to be there.'

'I want to be there, too,' Hannah said decisively.

'We all do,' Libby added. 'Joley, you can't run off and get married without your family.'

Hannah waved her hand, and a tray floated in with tea in mugs and a platter of fresh-baked cookies.

'It's just better,' Joley said. 'Once we're married, he'll have to quit his job.' She took a cookie and a mug of tea and went over to Abbey, who was huddled on Aleksandr's lap in the corner. 'Here, have some tea, it's good for you, and let's declare a truce.'

Abbey broke into a smile and took the mug. 'Accept my apology.'

'Done.' Joley flashed Ilya a smile. 'He can't work as Nikitin's bodyguard if he's married to me. He'll be splashed all over every tabloid around the world and there goes his career.'

'Is that why you think we're getting married immediately?' Ilya asked. He took a mug as the tray floated passed him.

Hannah looked up, her gaze sharp and focused. 'Your magic is different from ours, close, but different. The mark on Joley's palm, can that be removed?'

'No man would remove his mark from his woman,' Ilya said and took a sip of tea. 'I can't stay long, so make your questions count if you need to know something.'

The slight smile faded from Joley's face. 'They don't need to question you.'

'Actually,' Hannah interrupted, 'I have a question. Are you the seventh son of a seventh son?'

Joley whirled around, sending hot tea streaming out in a half circle. Ilya lifted his hand, and the liquid remained in the air, then refilled the mug.

Joley glared at her sister. 'Why in the world would you think that?'

'His magic works differently, yes, but not that much different, and he has all the gifts, not just one or two, and his gifts are highly developed. It makes sense.'

Joley raised her chin and glared at Ilya. 'We'll it might make sense, but he's not. You're not, so don't even pretend. It's not funny. Do *not* give them ammunition.' She sank gracefully onto the floor and

351

sipped at her tea. 'You aren't funny, Hannah, to even think of that.' She sent Ilya another warning look. *You aren't, so forget teasing me.*

'I don't understand,' Matt, Kate's fiancé, said. 'What difference does it make?'

'None!' Joley said. 'None whatsoever.'

Kate cleared her throat and took the plunge. 'If Ilya is the seventh son of a seventh son and his line works anything like ours, then he's destined to produce sevens sons with all the gifts.'

Joley shuddered. 'Well, he's not.'

Ilya grinned at her. 'The cookies are very good, Hannah. You'll have to give me the recipe.'

Jonas nudged Joley with his foot. 'You look a little pale there, Joley. Maybe you're protesting a bit too much.' He lifted an eyebrow at Ilya. '*Are* you the seventh son of a seventh son? You know, Joley, I've never forgotten that little pro and con list you made for Hannah when I was trying to convince her I should marry her.'

'She did that?' Ilya asked. 'She's still doing it. She has a list for me.'

Joley narrowed her eyes and looked down her nose at both men. 'The cons are stacking up fast, Ilya. I wouldn't get too smug. Siding with them and teasing me goes on the con side.'

'Being the seventh son of a seventh son might just go there, too,' Jonas said.

'Stop saying that!' Joley put down her mug and clapped her hands over her ears. 'I'm not listening to any of you until you start to make sense.'

She might not be listening, but she was looking around the room at her family. Every sister was staring at Ilya with a shocked, apprehensive expression. There wasn't the humor Jonas seemed to find in the situation, and Joley's stomach began to tie into little knots. Her gaze jumped to Sarah's face. Sarah, who often knew things. Joley's mouth went dry. Sarah simply stared at the floor, impossible to see what she was thinking – and that was a bad omen. Joley looked up at Ilya. *You're not.*

Ilya bent and brushed a kiss on top of her head. *I told you not to rely so much on your birth control.*

If she'd been pale before, she went white now, blinking up at him, her stomach going from hard knots to a roller coaster. She could feel the blood draining from her face down her body until she was dizzy – actually dizzy. She shook her head. 'I'm going to throw up. I am. I'm really going to throw up.'

Ilya calmly crouched beside her and laid a hand against her abdomen. The rolling immediately ceased. Joley shoved him backward, hoping to knock him on his butt, but he kept his balance.

'You're not funny. I'm not having children, let alone seven of them. Sheesh. Everyone can just quit looking at us that way. Ilya hasn't a clue about his family, he's making it up.' She flashed him another smoldering glare. *You'd better be making it up, because the sex wasn't that great – nowhere near, in fact.*

Then I'll have to work on it, won't I?

No amount of great sex will make me sign on for having seven sons. I mean it, Ilya. I wasn't ever going to get married, I'm certainly not going to produce seven sons. Have you seen a pregnant woman? Swollen ankles. Labor pains. Water retention. Labor pains! No way. Are you out of your freaky little mind?

He took her hand, the one with his mark, and

353

kissed her palm. 'We'll be fine. I can't stay, *lubov moya*, I have a job to do. Have a great performance this evening. Joley, you stay with security at all times. Change your dance patterns, stay away from the edge of the stage.'

'I can't do that. I can't be thinking about where I am on the stage while I'm working.'

'You're going to have to. And the moment you're done, you get back to your hotel room until I'm there to escort you to the next concert.'

She made a face at him.

His expression hardened. 'Jonas and Aleksandr are going to make certain you do as I've said. Whoever put that bomb on your bus wants you dead.'

'They've arrested Lucy. Jerry called me this morning and told me they found parts she'd used in her hotel room when they searched it.'

'Lucy Brady is not capable of making a bomb that sophisticated, Joley,' Ilya said. 'She was set up. Someone used her to get to you.'

'Nikitin?' Sarah asked.

Ilya shook his head. 'Nikitin has his own reasons for wanting Joley alive right now. I can't see him for this. We've got another player mixed in, but it sure isn't Lucy.'

'When she was threatening me with the bottle, she referred to "he" several times. At first I thought it was Logan, but that didn't make sense now that I really think about it,' Joley admitted. 'But I have no clue who she might have been referring to. I can ask . . .'

'You don't ask anyone anything at this point,' Ilya said. 'You go out on the stage, do your job and get back to cover as soon as possible. I want your word.'

Joley looked mutinous.

He shrugged. 'You can always cancel tonight if you'd rather. It's your choice. Going onstage isn't the best of ideas when someone is trying to kill you.'

'You can't stop me.'

'The last time I looked, I was a lot bigger and stronger than you.'

His voice was absolutely mild, not a hint that he was angry, or even getting close to getting upset, but there was resolve as well, an implacable determination that made it very clear to her that if she didn't agree, he wasn't above using physical force.

Joley took another sip of tea, waiting for the flickering flames to die down a little in her stomach so she could look at him without wanting to throw something. 'I really don't like being told what to do, Ilya. I'm an adult, quite capable of making my own decisions.'

'Then as an adult, make the adult decision to be safe. Give me your word now, Joley or I'll be hauling your ass back to my place and you won't be leaving there until I feel it is safe.'

She inhaled sharply. 'I don't like threats.'

'That wasn't a threat. I don't make threats.'

Her breath hissed out between her teeth. 'I don't like being treated like I'm not quite bright, that I can't get that there are safety issues.'

'I don't think that at all. I know you're bright, Joley. It's just that you think more about other people than you do yourself. So give me your word, because I know you'll never break it and I don't want to have to worry about you.'

'Fine then. I'll do whatever.' She didn't like the little thrill she'd gotten when he said he knew she was bright, or the way his voice had caressed her when he told her she thought of others, because she just capitulated when she should have made it clear she would follow security for herself, not for him.

With my child growing inside of you, it would be good to take extra precautions.

She snatched her hand away from him. 'That's not funny. Run, you coward. You can't know who your brothers are or how many you have or even if you're the youngest. I'm not buying into that. Go away and be careful. I'll kick your ass if anything happens to you.'

Ilya stood. 'Did you get the information I asked for, Jonas?'

Joley grabbed his hand again. 'What information?'

Later, Joley, when we have no one around.

She wanted to protest, but his life was dependent on secrecy, so she just nodded and blew him a kiss he didn't deserve as he followed Jonas and Aleksandr into the kitchen.

'John Dylan seems to be turning up quite often,' Ilya said. 'Lucy Brady had his ID. He claimed she stole it when he took a break and removed it, then left it on the table in the room where they were eating lunch. Most of the crew sleep during a performance because they have to work again breaking down the set and equipment right after. He says he went to bed and didn't notice he didn't have his ID.'

'Bullshit,' Jonas said. 'They know where their ID is at all times, especially during heightened security. The crew protects their band. They're like a family. Why would he even take it off in the break room?'

'He said he broke the chain and was fixing it when someone called him out of the room.' Ilya shrugged. 'It's plausible, but not probable. But he wasn't anywhere near that bus, not for a moment, which is a little suspicious in itself. He can account for every moment of his time and has witnesses.'

Jonas's eyebrow shot up. 'Every moment?'

'Yes. He was questioned along with other members of the crew, and he had his entire day mapped out. Everything checked out just like he said, right down to when he used the can.'

Jonas and Aleksandr exchanged a long look. 'No one can do that, Ilya.'

'Exactly. He's in this up to his ears, but he has an accomplice,' Ilya said. 'Dylan was also with Dean when Joley saw them with the teenagers, and several of the crew told me he spent a lot of time with Dean, but when I questioned him he said he barely knew him.'

'Dylan isn't in any way connected to the Russian mob other than maybe if Dean was working with them to feed them an occasional groupie. He's got connections here in the States,' Jonas supplied. 'He's a nephew of a man named Dominic Dylan. Have you ever heard of him?'

Ilya shook his head. 'Should I have?'

Jonas tapped a manila folder. 'Here's what we have on him. He's been making a name for himself. He's got a big family, lots of siblings and cousins, and he's spreading his net. He went to jail for tax evasion, but they suspected him of everything from arms dealing to running a human trafficking ring. Are you starting to see a connection here?'

'He wants Nikitin's front line,' Ilya said. 'He's looking to take over his business.'

Aleksandr nodded. He'd worked for the Russian police for years and then Interpol, and still had the connections. 'That's what we suspect. The DEA has

357

been keeping an eye on him for a long time. Homeland Security has their hand in as well. We stepped on a few toes getting that information and we called in a few favors owed. Dominic is bad news. He has a large organization, has mobilized a lot of gangs, mostly from being inside, and his particular plague has spread like wildfire.'

'Do you think he had Dean killed?' Ilya asked.

'If the kid was working for Nikitin, bringing him the girls, then yes, I have to say, that's a good bet,' Jonas said. 'He made it look like a Russian hit to throw suspicion on Nikitin – or you. My guess is, John Dylan took professional pride in showing his uncle he knew how to do a solid hit.' Jonas glanced at the door and lowered his voice even more. 'Is it possible the bus was meant to take you out? Had anyone seen you with Joley? Could someone have connected you and put you there?'

'Brian knew. Her driver, probably. It's possible Brian voiced his concerns to the other band members. Certainly Tish knew, and if she did, Logan probably did.' That hadn't been discreet of him. He could have gotten her killed.

He had known from the beginning that getting involved with her would be dangerous to both of them. He shook his head at his own stupidity. He'd been thinking with other parts of his anatomy rather than his brain. 'Yeah. Others knew.' He hated to admit it, hated making such an amateur mistake. In his entire career he'd never made such a selfish, risky error. He couldn't blame it on Joley and the spell she cast over him. The ultimate responsibility was his.

Aleksandr tapped the folder. 'This man, Dominic Dylan, is a huge arms dealer, Ilya. He's been photographed with Kolochek and the German, Heinzman. They only talk to the top men in the business. Word on the street says Dylan wants a bigger piece of the pie. Human trafficking brings in tremendous revenue, as you well know. Anyone who has done their homework knows they have to get rid of you to get to Nikitin. Without him, that branch goes down here in the United States and creates a vacancy.'

'And Dylan wants to fill the vacancy.'

Jonas nodded. 'That's what we think. So the hit could have been on you, and Joley could have been a by-product. Whoever put the bomb there really didn't give a damn who they killed as long as they took you out. It makes more sense. They create a problem for your girlfriend by using Lucy, feeding her anything that would make her believe Joley was her enemy.'

'Great distraction,' Ilya said. 'And it was. I was very focused on Joley and asked Nikitin for a few days off to help her out.'

'They may still come after her to keep you off balance. We'll have our own people all over her tonight, Ilya.'

'I've got to put Nikitin somewhere safe. I've spent three years on this investigation and I'm not blowing it. No way does Dominic Dylan take over the human trafficking market. I'm shutting it down for good on this end. What about Elle? Is she out?'

'As far as we can tell, she's not investigating Nikitin. If your paths have crossed, she may be working to nail Dylan, but she didn't respond to Jackson's calls,' Jonas admitted, referring to his deputy. 'He's pretty pissed. He doesn't get like that often, but when he does, it isn't something anyone wants to witness. We don't know exactly who she's working for. Have you asked Joley? Elle's the loner of the family, keeps everything close to her. If anyone really knows what she's up to, it would be Joley.'

Ilya sighed. 'Even to me, I doubt if she'd betray her sister's confidence. And if she does know, she keeps it buried deep. As much as I'm in Joley's mind, I've never seen a reference to anything Elle's doing.' He glanced at his watch. 'I've got to go. I've got a bad feeling that Nikitin is in trouble tonight. You keep close to Joley. If you think, even for a moment, that she's in danger, just get her out, don't wait for her permission.'

Jonas shrugged. 'You don't have to worry on that score. I'm used to her being upset with me. She gets over things fast.'

'That's good to know, because when she finds out I'm not teasing her about the seventh son of a seventh son, I have a feeling she'll be really angry.'

Jonas drew in his breath. 'That's not right, Prakenskii, you can't do that to her. Are you sure?'

'I don't know much about my family, but I do know I'm the seventh-born son. I don't know if the Drake sisters have exactly the same fate we do, but essentially the seventh carries all the gifts and his partner is destined. In my bloodline, all partners are destined, but they don't seem to have the birth control problems the seventh runs into.'

As he spoke, Ilya walked back into the main sitting room. He reached out his hand to Joley. She let him pull her to her feet. He caught a glimpse of her surprised expression as he tipped her face up to his and took possession of her mouth. There was no hesitation on her part; she kissed him back, melting into him, giving herself to him the way she always did.

You're coming back to me. Don't say good-bye.

I'm not saying good-bye. He tried to be reassuring, but he was saying good-bye. In his business, there were no guarantees, and he had a bad feeling about the night. *I'm saying, no matter what, I love you with every breath in my body.* His hand slipped over her hip to press between their bodies, to feel her flat stomach where his child would grow. He wanted that. Wanted everything from her in the same way he had given everything of himself, body and soul, to her.

I love you, too. Joley clung to him, holding him tight. *Ilya, if there's a chance something can happen to you, don't go. Stay here. I won't perform. I'll stay with you.*

The enormity of what she was offering made him soft inside when he needed to be steel. With great reluctance, he lifted his mouth from hers. 'Please stay safe, Joley.'

'You too, Ilya.'

She didn't cry. And she didn't try to stop him. He was proud of her for that. He lifted a hand to her family and slipped out the door, looking back at her face once before he went out. He wanted to memorize every detail. Feel her bone structure on his fingertips. He wanted to know that if he died this night, her face would be his last memory.

Chapter Eighteen

Nikitin had always preferred to rent houses, even if he was only staying one night. He liked upscale neighborhoods, and he'd move in and make himself at home for however long he could stay. Ilya had noticed a difference in him the past year. He'd gone from surly and mean to a much more mellow and happy man. That didn't matter, however, when it came down to his job. Nikitin carried hundreds of deaths on his shoulders and had no compunction about ordering the torture and killing of entire families if anyone stood in the way of building his empire.

Ilya drove through the neighborhood slowly. As usual, he'd chosen a car that would fit in. He drove past the house Nikitin was renting, not too slow, not too fast, careful to not to draw attention. There were three men standing just inside the gate, bending over a fourth man. At first glance the three men looked like Nikitin's guards, but they weren't men he recognized, and the one on the ground was Eddie, a solid man Nikitin often used for intimidation at his front entrance.

Ilya parked his car down the street and moved into

the shadows as he made his way back to the house. The three intruders were inside the gate, which meant he had to go over the wall without being seen. He walked beside it, running a gloved hand along the brick until he found a small indentation he could work with. He jumped, caught the indentation with the toe of his shoe and went over the wall, landing in a crouch on the other side. He waited, orienting himself to the layout.

A low, mocking laugh was followed by a grunt as the taller of the men dragged Eddie up by his hair and shoved him against the wall. 'You're gonna die,' he said harshly, and kicked Eddie in the stomach. 'But we're gonna have us some fun first.'

The other two men laughed.

'You should have stayed in Russia,' one with a barbed wire tattoo across his arm added.

The third pulled a club from under his coat. 'Guess you picked the wrong boss.'

Ilya broke into a sprint as they closed in on Eddie, forming a loose semicircle. Eddie spat on the ground in front of them defiantly, his eyes bright with rage.

Ilya came in fast and silent, grabbing the bat as it swung toward Eddie's head. He kept turning as he yanked it from the man's hand, swinging at the taller man's hand as he pulled a gun. The club struck him hard enough to break bones and the gun went flying. The tall man swore as he stumbled back.

The man with the tattoo punched at Ilya's open ribs, brass knuckles glinting in the light spilling from the porch. Ilya blocked the shot with his forearm, continued his forward spin going inside and slammed his elbow with full force against the man's sternum. He dropped like a stone, clutching his chest and gasping.

Cursing, the first man, who'd pulled the club, drew a knife and lunged. Ilya stepped into the attack, slamming a brutal fist into the exposed wrist with a short, chopped blow. The knife fell to the ground. Ilya brought up his knee hard into the man's crotch and then turned, shooting the same leg out to slam his foot into the ankle, shattering bone and knocking him to the ground.

'Hell, Ilya, you didn't give me a chance to help out.' Eddie picked up the gun the taller one had dropped. He walked to where he was still rolling on the ground moaning. He put the gun to his attacker's head and pulled the trigger.

'How many?' Ilya asked.

'I didn't get a chance to count, but it looked like a fuckin' army to me,' Eddie answered and shot the second and third man. 'They went around to the back, but they're wiping everyone out where they find them.'

Ilya ignored the statement, already moving across the lawn to the house. He put his hand on the doorknob and turned slowly. The door was unlocked, which meant the assassination team was already inside. He listened in an effort to get a sense of where everyone was and what was happening. There was a brief murmur of voices. Footsteps. The gun Eddie had picked up had a silencer, so the team was probably similarly equipped. They didn't want a visit from the local police. Neither did he. He bent to pull a knife from his boot, indicated the need for silence from Eddie, and slipped inside.

The living room was empty. The television set remained on, playing the local news channel. Beside the couch, on the small end table, a cut crystal glass sat half-filled. A second glass was on the coffee table, beside several magazines. Nikitin hadn't been alone when the intruders broke in. The secret silent alarm Ilya always set up for Nikitin would have gone off, giving the Russian time to make it to the safe room they always meticulously set up when they occupied a house, whether it was for one night or ten.

With his gloved hand, Ilya lifted the glass and took a small sniff. Cognac. The good stuff. He shook his head as he replaced the glass. Nikitin only drank cognac with one person. Brian Rigger, lead guitarist for Joley's band. She would be so upset if Brian didn't make it out alive. Damn his stupidity. He'd been warned to stay away. There was a part of Ilya that understood. Brian, and Nikitin for that matter, had been every bit as lonely as Ilya had been, and he hadn't been able to stay away from Joley, even though it put both of them in jeopardy. But having Brian there was an unexpected complication.

He did his best to protect Brian, hastily wiping prints from both glasses and any surface he could find that it seemed likely Brian had touched. It was the best he could do when time was short and the enemy was too close.

Ilya began a cautious tread down the hall. Overhead, he could hear footsteps as the assassination squad searched the rooms above him. Eddie caught his sleeve and indicated up the stairs. Ilya shook his head. No one else was ever privy to Ilya's plan to extract Nikitin should there be trouble. If there was a traitor, there would be no chance that he would know where Nikitin would be.

In the first bedroom, a man lay faceup, blood soaking into the carpet from his slit throat, eyes open and staring at the ceiling. Ilya cleared the room, found no target and went to the next one. It was the pool room. Four of Nikitin's soldiers lay dead. One was draped over the pool table with a gun in his hand and the back of his head gone. A second was at the sliding glass door, as if he'd run, a gun inches from his hand where he'd fallen. The third man had been shot first, dead center and never saw it coming. He was slumped just inside the door, a glass of wine soaking the carpet along with his blood. Overturned furniture showed that the fourth man had managed to put up a struggle. He'd been shot several times and lay a few feet to the side of the pool table.

They'd been surprised, which meant either they hadn't noticed the strobe going off – which was difficult for Ilya to believe – or someone inside was a traitor – and that was more likely. 'You have any idea how many soldiers we had here tonight, Eddie?'

Hopefully Nikitin had noticed his personal alarm and done exactly as Ilya had instructed – gone without speaking to anyone and hidden. That had probably saved his life. Had the traitor known where he was, certainly he would have given the information to the hit team.

'Hell, Ilya.' Eddie wiped his mouth with his sleeve, shaking a little after seeing his friends dead. 'Pavel Demidov was here, too, along with Ivan and Klaus.'

Continuing down the hall, Ilya peered quickly into the kitchen. Ivan and Klaus lay on the floor in pools of blood, with two men standing over them. One was a stranger and the other was Pavel Demidov, Nikitin's trusted bodyguard. Ilya was certain he was privy to the workings of the human trafficking ring, the one

Nikitin had been careful to keep Ilya away from. This assignment was the one time that Ilya's reputation for protecting women and children had hindered him. Nikitin often sent him on errands, or just out of the room so he could talk to this man – Pavel Demidov. He had found his traitor.

The man with Pavel started to turn, and Ilya threw the knife, spinning as he did so and yanking the gun from Eddie's hands to fire three rounds into Pavel's left eye. Both men dropped, and Pavel's gun hit the tile with a clamor. Ilya waited a heartbeat, listening, and then handed the gun back to Eddie. 'Make certain they're dead, but don't make a sound. And collect their weapons. We may need them. Get my knife, wipe it on his shirt and give it back to me.'

He wasn't about to leave his weapon on scene, or risk leaving evidence if he could help it. He'd always been a ghost at a kill sight; he couldn't afford to let this one be any different.

Eddie nodded and hastily bent over the bodies while Ilya made his way to the den. The door stood wide open as if in invitation. The room had obviously been checked and dismissed. A small gas fire lit it and threw flickering light over the deep wood panels. He moved around the desk toward the small closet. The door stood open there as well, several coats hanging. The closet was very narrow, barely allowing the hangers to fit between the back wall and the front.

Ilya stepped inside and knocked in the prearranged pattern. The back wall was a false steel panel Ilya had designed to fit most standard hall closets. The one in this house by the front door had been too large, but the den unexpectedly had a smaller room which served their purposes perfectly. Staying behind that thin steel panel with its wooden front required endless patience, nerves of iron and the ability to stand for long periods of time.

Ilya didn't hurry, although Eddie hissed a warning at him. He didn't want to make a sound as he stealthily pulled the false back away to reveal Nikitin and Brian flattened against the wall. Both men were soaked with sweat, and Nikitin held a gun, rock steady in his fist.

'Let's go,' Ilya said softly. 'Stay close to the wall. Make no noise.'

Nikitin indicated to Brian to follow Ilya to the door of the den. Brian was trembling almost uncontrollably, but he did as Ilya said, sliding one shoulder along the wall, maintaining contact and staying as close to the bodyguard as possible.

At the door, Eddie handed Ilya the knife and dropped back to guard the rear. Ilya slid the knife into his boot and pulled his gun. There was no silencer on the barrel, so once he fired, he'd bring everyone down on them, and they were severely outnumbered. He hoped they'd make it out clean, but he needed the firepower just in case.

He made his way back toward the kitchen. They'd have to go out the back to avoid the stairs, but no self-respecting assassination team would leave the back open as a means of retreat. They would be walking into their enemies' hands.

He heard Brian gasp when he saw the carnage on the kitchen floor. Glancing back with a hand signal for silence, Ilya glimpsed Brian shoving his hand against his mouth, his stomach obviously rebelling.

Nikitin put his hand on Brian's back. 'Don't look. Just follow Ilya out. You'll be all right,' he said encouragingly, his voice a whisper. 'Prakenskii is the best.'

Ilya glanced at Brian's white face. Beads of perspiration stood out on his forehead, but he kept moving, trying not to look at the blood and gore on the floor.

Brian swallowed hard and nodded. He reached up and, for one moment, clasped Nikitin's hand. Ilya looked away, feeling he'd caught a sad, intimate moment that was too private for witnesses.

He heard movement and held up his hand, signaling the others to stop. He continued forward, to the back door. Behind him, Brian crouched down against the counter, Nikitin blocked his body with his own, and Eddie placed himself in front of his boss. No one moved, no one breathed.

Ilya listened for movement again, trying to get a sense of how many he was up against and where they were. Again he held his hand up to emphasize that no one move. He had to risk drawing fire in order to get positions. They couldn't wait; the rest of the team that had been searching upstairs in the house would be coming in behind them. They'd be caught in a squeeze trap, with no way out.

The door was a no-win. Once he was through it, every gun would be on him. They expected the door to be used. Ilya went from a crouch to a sprint, leaping and going through the window feet first, gun firing in the direction of the voices he'd heard. He landed and rolled, watching for the flashes of return fire even as he scrambled for cover.

He knew the exact layout of the backyard. It was essential in his business to be familiar with any potential battlefield in or outside a house. It was three feet to the relative cover of brush and an additional two feet to the large boulders placed artistically around the waterfall that flowed down a small stream into a large pool.

Four flashes and a long howl told him he was facing at least five. He felt it then – that stillness in him – the trained warrior taking over. No emotion, only the killing machine that had been developed at such an early age. His vision changed – widened – then tunneled as he saw targets. Systematically he took them out. Dylan was losing soldiers tonight.

He shot one after another, using kill shots, no mercy, kill or be killed. There could be no mistakes, no mess-ups, not when so many innocent lives were at stake. He wasn't trading one human trafficking ring for another. If he could shut the ring down before they managed to get started, he would do it.

He fired fast – one, two, three, four, five. The fifth shot took out the man who had been wounded. Ilya cleared the area in less than forty seconds and was back to the kitchen, yanking open the door and signaling the others into the night.

'They're coming right behind us,' Eddie warned as they ran for the nearest car. 'I heard them running down the stairs.'

Ilya slid his hand along the visor, dropped the keys into Eddie's hand, grabbed him by the collar and thrust him into the car behind the wheel. He spun around and fired several shots at the door to keep what was left of the assassination squad back.

'You're driving, and do exactly what I say when I say it. Brian, backseat with Sergei. Stay down at all times, and I mean down. They'll be coming after us.' He slammed the door behind Nikitin and dove into the front passenger seat. 'Go. Get moving.'

Eddie shoved the gear into reverse and stomped his foot on the gas pedal. Tires screamed, and they swerved, straightened, and crashed into the gate. The gate crumpled and burst open, so that they emerged backward onto the street, hit the curb, jumped the sidewalk and then Eddie got control and managed to put the car in gear to go forward. Bullets rained on them, hitting the windshield, the doors and the sides of the car.

Ilya leaned over and stomped his foot over Eddie's. The car fishtailed down the street with Eddie cursing every inch of the way. Ilya didn't let up at the corner, forcing Eddie to run the stop sign and shoot them in a wider turn into oncoming traffic before he straightened them out again.

Ilya glanced over his shoulder. 'Everybody all right?'

Nikitin nodded. He kept one hand on Brian's back, holding him down. 'Who are these fuckers?' the Russian boss demanded, his face tight with anger.

'None of Tarasov's family could have orchestrated this move against you. A couple of the cousins were left alive, but they don't have the balls to try to take you out.' Ilya didn't want to give up the information on Dylan before he was certain he got the names and locations of Nikitin's network of human traffickers.

Ilya tossed his phone to Nikitin then steadied his gun with his other arm, waiting. It wasn't easy to shoot out of a moving car the way they portrayed on television. 'Pavel Demidov was a traitor. Whatever he knew of your operation, the competition knows. They'll try to kill everyone. You're going to have to call your people and tell them to get undercover fast. He'll have exposed them all. I need time to find out who's behind this.'

Nikitin glanced behind them at the two cars moving through traffic at high speed. 'Just get me out of this, Ilya, and I'll . . .' He abruptly switched to Russian to finish his sentence, saying, 'I'll kill every one of them and their families. Find out.' He kept his hand on Brian's back, his body shielding the guitarist, who had been pushed to the floor.

He was furious. Ilya could hear it in his voice. Nikitin was many things, but he wasn't a coward. He would never tolerate an attempt on his life without brutal, bloody retaliation. There would be a bloodbath the likes of which few had ever seen the moment Nikitin knew who was trying to kill him. And from the way Nikitin was covering Brian, it would be worse for whoever was trying to kill them, their bad luck to catch Brian in the cross fire. Nikitin's feelings for the man had to be real, and that made him all the more dangerous, because if it was true – Brian was probably the only person in the world Nikitin had genuine feelings for.

Ilya needed him to make those calls. He needed numbers – and names if possible. Pavel Demidov had always been Nikitin's right-hand man in the human trafficking operation. Ilya didn't dare even glance at the Russian boss. He needed to appear concerned only with keeping him alive, but inside, everything stilled. It was now or never that he would get the information they had waited so long for.

Nikitin flipped open the phone, and while Eddie took the car screaming around another corner, weaving in and out of traffic, the Russian made his calls, warning his associates one by one to lay low, put everything on hold, until they could find and remove the threat to their network.

'Coming up on our left,' Ilya warned Nikitin calmly. 'Eddie, don't evade. Sergei, stay low. Just keep up the speed, but hold the car steady until I say otherwise, then you're going to pull hard to the left.'

Eddie nodded his understanding.

Ilya watched the big Cadillac barreling down on them, the calm, centered place inside of him seeing every target, every detail of the night itself and the traffic around them. A small pickup truck swerved, suddenly aware of the drama taking place on the highway, recovered and hit the brakes to allow the Cadillac to move into position. Gun hand braced, Ilya centered on the driver, ignoring the guns flashing, and very deliberately squeezed the trigger.

'Now, Eddie, clip it hard.'

Eddie swerved into the larger vehicle, bounced off, recovered and kept going. The driver of the Cadillac slumped over the wheel, the deadweight of his foot on the gas. With their car sideswiping the caddie, the larger vehicle spun out of control, slamming into the guardrail, breaking through it at high speed.

'They're gone,' Nikitin said, looking back, satisfaction in his voice.

'Get down.' Ilya hissed the order between his teeth. 'Eddie, take the exit and head down toward the river.'

'My concert's in an hour,' Brian said. 'Sergei, I have to be onstage in an hour. Everyone's going to be freaking out.'

There was silence. Ilya glanced back at Nikitin and saw the stunned look on his face. He was used to violence, Brian wasn't, and in that moment, Sergei realized how shocked Brian really was. 'It will be all right,' he promised.

'Why are they doing this?' Brian asked. 'I don't understand why they're doing this, Sergei.'

Nikitin rubbed his back, all the while looking out the window, watching the other car fishtail down the exit ramp after them. 'I don't know, but we'll find out. Just stay down where you'll be safe. I don't want anyone to see you.'

Ilya didn't point out that Pavel Demidov had known Brian was in the house, and since he had, then chances were good Dominic Dylan had been told at the very least that Brian was a good friend, or worst case scenario, that he was Nikitin's lover. Nikitin had always been discreet about Brian. Ilya had guessed at the relationship for a number of reasons. Nikitin had been different since he'd met Brian, definitely mellower and much happier. His aura had changed, and around Brian, sexual colors had grown stronger.

'Okay, Eddie, start slowing down. Stay ahead enough to keep them from getting a good shot, but make sure they follow us.'

The road ran along the fast-moving river. It had rained often and hard, and the river was swollen, threatening to breach the banks. In some places the road had a bit of water across it where the current splashed up over the sides.

'They're on us, Ilya,' Eddie confirmed, glancing in the rearview mirror. 'Not tight, but they're coming, about a curve or so back.'

'We want a clear stretch without any witnesses or bystanders that can get hurt,' Ilya said. 'We should be coming up on a turn that will take us under the bridge. They'll lose sight of us. Slow down, let me out, and keep going.'

'No, no, that's not a good idea,' Nikitin objected. 'We shouldn't separate.'

'I'll take out the other car without a risk to you or Brian. Eddie can take you up the road to the exit back to the freeway. You should be able to see from up there. If I take out the car, come back and pick me up; if not, get clear.' He tapped Eddie on the shoulder. 'Here. Pull over right here.'

Eddie shot a quick questioning glance over his shoulder at Nikitin, but he was already stomping on the brakes. Ilya bailed out of the car almost before it stopped moving. It was ironic that he was saving the life of the man he knew he would eventually have to kill. Nikitin had no compunction about killing his enemies, and there would be no quitting undercover work until he was dead. At the same time, Ilya wasn't going to allow Dylan to take over the trafficking network. He knew eventually someone would step in and fill the void once he'd taken down Nikitin, but he hoped to slow things down for a long while.

He shoved a clip into his gun, checked his other and waited. He found a spot on higher ground where he had a clear view of the driver's side of the vehicle. He'd have to take him out first. That was imperative. With the driver dead, the car would be a hazard. The others would have to bail or ride it out and try to survive a crash into the river.

Above the roar of the water, he could hear the powerful engine as the car rounded the bend and accelerated. The driver held it steady in his lane, making the target easier than anticipated. Their attention was on the road, trying to find Nikitin's car. Windows were rolled down, arms and heads hanging out. Ilya concentrated on one target. He steadied his arm and took the shot, drilling the driver through his left eye.

The windshield fragmented, and the car slewed back and forth; then as someone tried to grab the wheel, it abruptly turned, spun and slid into the rapid current of the river. The car tipped forward, drawn into the powerful current. Water poured into the windows. Ilya heard a shout. Someone fired a wild shot. The car began to be dragged downstream, still sinking.

Ilya made his way down the slippery slope and walked along the embankment. A head popped up, and without hesitation he took the shot. If any of these men lived, and they knew about Brian, the guitarist was dead. He kept his eyes on the body. It was torn loose from the car and carried away, the water rolling over and over the limp form.

A second man emerged, coming up out of the water like a geyser, spewing bullets, aiming wildly, spraying the shore even as he fought to stay afloat. Dirt flew into the air all around Ilya's feet, splattering his jeans as the bullets came close.

Ilya shot the man twice, a quick one-two as the river swept the bobbing head away. The bodyguard was certain he'd killed the shooter, but he raced along the bank to make sure. The body turned facedown, tumbled and churned, a red stain spreading, and then it was pulled under.

Ilya waited, watching the surface of the water. No one could hold his breath that long, but if it had been Ilya, he would have gone out through an open window and swum downstream, letting the current carry him before sticking his head up and chancing it getting blown off. He began to jog along the riverbank heading downstream, reloading as he went and watching both sides of the bank as well as rocks the fourth man might be able to cling to.

Movement caught his attention. At once he dropped to the ground. Bullets spat around him, one actually going through the sleeve of his jacket. He felt the kiss, the heat, and then he rolled, stretching out in a two-handed grip to steady his shot as he fired back. The gun bucked in his hand, feeling familiar, part of him, his aim natural. Where he looked he shot, and the bullet traveled true, striking his target.

He watched the man fall back into the river. He knew his opponent was dead; he knew exactly where the bullet had hit. He turned and began to jog toward the freeway exit. Within minutes, he saw the car driving in reverse back toward him.

Nikitin grinned at him as he slid into the car. 'Well done.'

'Get us out of here, Eddie,' Ilya said. 'We have to clean this mess up. You rented that house, Sergei, and your prints are everywhere. I did my best to get rid of Brian's, but I had no way of knowing everything he touched.'

'He'd only been there a few minutes when the strobe went off.' Nikitin took his hand off Brian and allowed him to sit up. 'If you wiped the glass and the couch, we should be good.'

Brian pressed an unsteady hand to his mouth. 'No one knew I was going there. I had the taxi let me off several blocks away.'

'Good, that's good, Brian,' Ilya said, praising him to steady him.

'Why is this happening?' he asked again.

Ilya didn't want to take any chances with Nikitin's patience – or the fact that Brian had witnessed a battle between two warring factions of the underworld. 'Sergei must have mentioned to you that he was born into a family in Russia that controlled certain aspects of business. They don't want him getting out. He's been legitimate for some time, but a few powerful people fear his knowledge.' It was Nikitin's standard story, and it was what Brian wanted to believe. Believing it now might save his life.

Out of the corner of his eye, Ilya saw Nikitin visibly relax.

'I've tried to tell you,' Nikitin said. 'I know it looks bad, but there's little I can do about the family I was born into.'

'We have to go to the police. These people tried to kill you, Sergei. What if there are more of them?'

Nikitin handed Ilya's phone back to him. 'Don't worry. This isn't the first time. We don't want the police involved, because these are the kinds of people who buy off the police.'

Ilya tucked his cell phone safely into the inside pocket of his jacket. He deliberately glanced at his watch. 'Can you perform tonight, Brian? If you can't, say so. Everything has to be exactly as if you never were a part of this. Not only you, but everyone around you would be in danger, and especially Sergei. Can you handle performing?'

Brian swallowed hard. 'Will you be there?' he asked Nikitin.

Ilya flinched at the raw emotion in Brian's voice. He didn't want Eddie to have a clue about Brian's relationship with Nikitin. It was too late. Far, far too late. Nikitin flicked a single glance at Eddie, and it was enough to let Ilya know Eddie was a dead man. In spite of his loyalty, in spite of the fact that he'd helped save both Brian and Nikitin, the Russian boss wouldn't take any chances with his relationship being made public.

Brian had no way of knowing what kind of a man Sergei Nikitin really was and what he was capable of doing. Murder was second nature to Nikitin. He'd grown up making hits when other boys were playing ball. He'd learned torture before he ever went on his first date. As with Ilya, there had been no childhood, and violence had become his way of life.

'I have to make certain Sergei is safe, Brian,' Ilya said. 'Until we know who is trying to kill him, we can't take chances with his life.'

Brian nodded. 'That's right. You're right. Maybe you should get out of town, Sergei. Leave tonight. We have one more gig to play in San Francisco and then we're finished with the tour.'

'Where do we go?' Eddie asked.

'We have to switch cars. This is full of bullet holes. Then we take Brian to the Arco Arena if he thinks he can put on a show.'

'Yes, yes, if it will help,' Brian agreed. 'Of course.'

'You have to act as though nothing happened. You have to be normal, Brian,' Ilya reiterated and pulled a cell phone from inside his jacket. His hand slid over the other one, the one with the special chip that had sent every number Nikitin called to Ilya's bosses. They'd be moving on the information, matching numbers with names in order to set up raids.

The two phones were identical, just in case Nikitin wanted the phone destroyed. Ilya would have cooperated fully. He wanted the original phone for evidence, but if not, they still had the numbers.

He spoke briefly into the phone then turned to Eddie. 'Take this next exit, Eddie. A car will be waiting at the McDonald's parking lot. We'll ditch this one in the parking garage just next to it.' He glanced back at Brian. 'You don't have any blood on your clothes, do you? Or your shoes?'

Brian shuddered, but inspected his clothing. 'No. I'm fine.'

'Good. You're doing great.'

Nikitin nodded. 'I'm sorry this happened. It comes with the territory. At least you know I was telling you the truth.'

Brian took a deep breath as Eddie pulled into the parking garage and found a dark corner on the second level. 'You don't lead a boring life, Sergei.' He made an attempt to smile.

Ilya pulled open the door. 'Don't touch anything. Eddie and I will wipe the car down. Stand over there, where I can see you, but no one can approach you.'

Ilya worked vigorously, wiping the steering wheel, seats and door handles in the front seat, while Eddie wiped down the back and floor.

'Let's go. Brian, walk normally, we're just looking for a Big Mac,' Ilya instructed. 'You're recognizable, so hunch a little and keep your head down so no one sees your face. You're doing fine,' he added as he herded the men through the parking garage and out onto the street.

Darkness had fallen. If they were going to get Brian to his performance, they would have to hurry. Ilya wanted him gone. He didn't want to give Nikitin an opportunity to regret protecting Brian, or to figure out that Brian was an intelligent man who would sooner or later realize Nikitin was no legitimate businessman.

Ilya glanced down at the guitarist as they walked, noting his aura, and everything in him went still. Brian did know the truth. The shakiness, the trembling, his fear, had nothing to do with the attempt

380

on their lives, and everything to do with his knowledge of what and who Sergei Nikitin really was. Brian's melody was sobbing, wailing, every note drawn out in utter and real despair.

He rested his hand briefly on Brian's shoulder, the merest of touches, but sending healing warmth and encouragement to him, a small salute that the man was holding up under the worst circumstances. Brian kept his head down, stumbled a little, recovered and kept walking.

The car was waiting right where Ilya had instructed. Nikitin didn't ask who had put it there, but if he had, Ilya had a ready answer. He covered every detail – that was how he stayed alive.

The Arco Arena was already filled with cars and a crush of people. They drove around the top where the buses were parked, and Brian slid from the car.

'You can do this, Brian,' Ilya said, keeping his gaze steady.

Brian nodded. 'Don't worry. I won't let you down.'

'I know you won't,' Nikitin said.

Brian lifted his hand and turned and walked away.

Some of the tension that had coiled in Ilya's stomach drained away. 'Let's go, Eddie. Take us to the safe house.'

'Do you have any idea who those fuckers were?' Nikitin asked.

'Not Tarasov,' Ilya said. 'Someone here in the U.S. How much did Demidov know about your operation?'

'Everything. He knew everything. He's been with me for years.'

'So how did they get to him? Money wouldn't have done it. What did they use to turn him against you?'

'I don't know,' Nikitin said, 'but I'm going to find out.'

Chapter Nineteen

'What the hell were you doing out there, Brian?'
Rick demanded, throwing a towel on the low-slung
couch. They were in the suite at the Arco Arena,
surrounded by some of the crew, a few friends and
girlfriends. 'You played worse than an amateur.
Joley covered for you time after time. You were
lagging. You forgot which song you were playing.
Shit. It was crap tonight.'

Brian swung around, his expression going from
upset to furious instantly. 'You know what, Rick?'
Brian shouted back. 'Fuck you and your opinion. I
don't see you playing the kind of music I play.
You're all safe back there on your bass, playing off
my lead.'

Rick took several aggressive steps forward.
'Lead? Is that what you think you were doing tonight? You couldn't pick up the beat. You were all
over the place tonight. It was my bass that saved
your ass more times than I can count.'

'Then you can fucking take over.' Brian picked up
his guitar, swung it over his head and smashed it
repeatedly against the floor.

There was a shocked silence. Brian was the

mellow one, the diplomatic one. The band counted on him for stability.

The baby started to cry, and Logan put his arm around Tish and pushed her toward the door. He held it open. 'Everyone out. You too, Jerry. Just the band stays.'

The members of the crew, Rick's girlfriend, and Jerry went out. Logan shut the door firmly, stood in front of it and crossed his arms.

Joley took what was left of the guitar from Brian's hand. He jerked away from her and paced across the room. He was trembling. His melody and aura was so sorrowful she felt weighed down, drained. A hopeless, shattering despair ate at her, and she knew it was coming from him.

Brian flung up both hands. 'I'm out. How 'bout that, Rick? I'm gone. You fucking play the guitar if you're so damned good at it.'

Rick puffed out his chest. 'You think I can't? Hell, I could play better than that any day of the week.'

'Stop!' Joley stepped between them. 'Everyone has a bad night. All of us have had them. Flu, hangovers, losing a girlfriend – all of us have had accidents and lost our mikes, pulled wires, come on. This is crazy. Everyone's on edge here. We've been on tour for months. We're tired and need a break.'

'We're all tired, we all need a break. But we're not fucking throwing a tantrum,' Rick snapped.

'That's exactly what you're doing,' Logan said. 'Shut up, Rick. Can't you see something's wrong? What the hell's going on, Brian?'

'Nothing. Nothing at all.' Brian couldn't control the rush of adrenaline, the buildup of aggressive energy. He was looking for a target, pacing back and forth, his fists doubled up.

383

Joley had a bad taste in her mouth. She knew. It had to be Nikitin. Brian wouldn't look at her, wouldn't meet her eyes. He'd gone to see him again, and this time something had happened. He knew the truth about the man he'd grown to love. She felt sick for him.

Denny leaned against the door, watching his friend with worry in his eyes. 'Dude. Don't blow us off. We've been your family. You've never been upset like this. I've never seen you angry. Not once in all the years we've been hanging together.' He spread his hands out in front of him. 'Whatever it takes, man, it's yours. Whatever you need. You've always been there for us, we're not walking away from you now.'

'Really? Really, Denny?' Brian's eyes glittered with anger. His face was flushed red, his hands balled into two tight fists. 'I'm your friend? Your family? What the hell are you going to say when I tell you I'm fucking gay? Yeah, man, that's right, I'm a fucking fag.'

'You say it like that again, Brian,' Joley snapped, 'and I'll slap your face.'

Brian stood in the center of the room, his chest heaving as he fought for air. He looked defiant, ready to fight. His challenging gaze fell on Rick.

Rick glared right back. 'Shit, man, that's what this is about? If coming out of the closet was going to make you play like an asshole, why the fuck didn't you wait until after the tour was over.'

'I ...' Brian's mouth opened and then closed; he stared at them in shock. 'You ... *knew* about me ... about ... How long?'

'Hell, Bri, of course we knew.' Logan shook his head. 'We've known each other since grammar

384

school. Did you really think you were that good at keeping a secret?'

'You never said anything,' Brian said. He was still breathing hard, trying to assimilate what they were saying. He was stunned, staring around the room in astonishment at his friends.

'What was there to say? You never brought anyone around, not that it would have mattered, and then we figured you were careful because of the paparazzi. If you didn't want it splashed all over the tabloids, neither did we.'

Brian looked at each one of the band members. 'I can't believe this. All this time you knew and never said anything?'

Denny shrugged. 'It wasn't our business. What's the big deal, man?'

Brian shoved both hands through his hair several times. 'I thought it would change everything between us if you knew.'

'Why the hell should we care what you do, Brian?' Denny asked.

'I don't believe this. Weren't you afraid the tabloids would make up a bunch of stories about us traveling together?'

'They make up shit all the time,' Leo said. 'What the hell, Brian? You've known us since we were five. Did you really think it would make a difference to us?'

Brian shook his head. 'I told my old man after my mother died and he told me he never wanted to see me again. Hasn't anyone ever wondered why I never go home?'

'Your old man's a drunk, Brian,' Rick pointed out. 'Screw him. You never liked your family anyway. You slept on my couch half the time and on

Denny's the other half.'

'Well, shit,' Brian said and sank down onto the couch. He stared around him in a kind of dazed confusion. 'I *really* don't believe this.' He flashed the beginnings of a faint grin. 'I ruined my fucking guitar for no damned reason.'

Rick toed the wreckage. 'Waste of a damned fine Gibson Les Paul.' He sat down beside Brian. 'Next time you decide to come out of the closet, Bri, smash a cheap guitar instead. This just makes me wanna cry.'

Brian managed a faint smile. 'You all knew?' He repeated. 'You all discussed it? Talked about me?'

Denny snorted. 'Hell yeah, we talked about you. We talk about everyone, why should you be any different? But, no, if you think we sat around talking shit, it was never like that. I'd beat the crap out of someone who talked shit about you. Any of us would.'

Brain rubbed his hands over his face again and shook his head, obviously dazed by their reaction. 'I don't know what to say.'

'You can say you need a new guitar before tomorrow night,' Joley said with a quick grin. She'd never loved her band members more than at that moment. But she could see the raw pain still swirling around Brian. In spite of what he'd revealed, in spite of everyone's reaction, he wasn't all right. He was struggling to maintain. She had to find a way to distract the attention from him. 'The next time you have a secret, try not to go all Jimi Hendrix on your guitar. Of course, if you really wanted to do it right, you could have smashed your guitar onstage. Then we could have gathered up the pieces, autographed them and sold them as souvenirs.'

She redirected the conversation, all the while keeping watch on Brian. The anger had drained away, but the dark moody colors still swirled around him and his melody was sad and lonely, as if his heart were breaking.

Talk gathered around them, the band members teasing Brian about breaking his guitar into tiny matchsticks and selling the pieces on eBay. Brian took the teasing in his normal good-natured way, but while his mouth was smiling, there were shadows in his eyes, so she stayed with the band, being there with him, with them, laughing and teasing in a way she hadn't done in years.

Eventually, as the others drifted out and made their way to the hotel, she sat down beside Brian. 'Are you all right?'

He shook his head. 'It hurts, Joley. I've never hurt like this before. Not even when my father disowned me.'

'What happened?'

'Someone tried to kill Sergei tonight. I was with him. If it wasn't for the bodyguard, Prakenskii, we'd all be dead.'

Joley inhaled sharply and reached out. Ilya didn't answer her. She closed her fingers over the mark on her palm and pressed her hand to her heart. 'Is everyone okay?'

Brian glanced at her sharply. 'You mean the bodyguard? He just about killed everything that moved, but he got us out alive. I have to take back everything I said about him. He didn't hesitate to come into that house after us, when we were completely surrounded. I thought we were dead, Joley. I really did.' He hung his head, scrubbing his face with his hand, over and over, as if he could wipe away the memory.

Her heart pounded hard. She tried to still it by taking deep breaths. 'But everyone's okay?'

'Yeah. After a car chase and a shoot-out.'

'And then you came here and performed.'

A ghost of a smile touched his mouth. 'Not very well, apparently.'

Joley answered his smile with a teasing one of her own. 'I don't know. After all that, I'd say you did pretty well.'

The smile faded from Brian's face, and he looked as if someone had ripped out his heart. 'He's a mobster, Joley. Prakenskii tried to cover for him, and I knew he was doing it for my protection.' The words stumbled over one another fast, coming out in a rush, as if all the air in his lungs was bursting out with the revelation. 'Prakenskii was worried Sergei would hurt me if he guessed I knew the truth.'

She bit at her lip, frowning. 'How did you find out?'

'You mean aside from all the dead bodies? Bodyguards aren't like that. Prakenskii is a machine, Joley, cool and without emotion; he didn't hesitate to pull the trigger, not one time. There were so many of them, and he killed them all. Sergei and the other guy, Eddie, took it all as if it happened every day – and for normal people that's just not the case. And then, when we were in the car, Sergei told Prakenskii he would kill the people who attacked us and kill their families.'

'He said that in front of you?' She tried not to let her alarm show.

'He spoke in Russian. I know he thought I wouldn't understand, but I've been studying Russian for the last year. It was supposed to be a surprise for him . . .' He trailed off, tears swimming in his eyes.

388

'It doesn't matter. Businessmen don't say they're killing not only their enemies, but the families of their enemies. I knew right then.'

Joley put her arms around him and held him close. 'I'm sorry, Brian. I'm really, really sorry.' She didn't like the crazy thoughts swirling around in his head. 'Come back to the hotel with me tonight, Brian, and we'll just talk for a while.'

'I don't want to intrude.'

'Don't be silly, you wouldn't be intruding. Say you'll come. Steve can drive us both back together. And if you don't want to hang with my family, you can call it an early night.'

Brian looked around the empty room. 'I loved all this. The music – the life – all of you.' He spread his hands out in front of him. 'Now it seems so empty.'

'Because you need someone to share it all with,' Joley said. She stood up and tugged at his hand. 'You know you shouldn't be alone, Brian. I may not be Nikitin, but I love you, and I'm always here for you. Come on back with me. You can sit in a corner and read a book if you don't want to talk. I'll spoil you with gourmet chocolate,' she added, using a clear bribe.

He managed another laugh and toed the wreck of his guitar. 'I can't believe I did that.'

'Me either. That was your favorite guitar.'

Brian put his hand in hers and they walked out of the room. Jonas and Aleksandr shot her an inquiring look as they stood and closed ranks around Brian and Joley.

'Everything okay?' Jonas asked.

Joley nodded. 'It's all good.'

They walked through the halls until they came to

the exit. Security was everywhere, and a few lifted their hands when Joley flashed them a smile. Steve stood beside the car waiting as they came over.

'I'm sorry I held you up,' Joley greeted. 'We got talking.'

Steve shrugged. 'It's my job. No big deal.'

Jonas opened the door for her. 'We'll follow behind you in the other car.'

'That's dumb. There's plenty of room and no need to take two cars. Just tell the other driver you're coming with us,' Joley protested. Steve started the car and at once warm air began to fill the interior. Joley hadn't realized she was cold until that moment. 'And hurry up because I want to get back and have a hot cup of tea.'

Jonas nodded and shut the door. Steve put the car in gear and began to pull away.

'Wait. Wait for my brothers-in-law,' Joley said, leaning forward in her seat. 'They're coming with us.'

A smoky window went up between the front and back seats. At the same time, the locks snicked into place.

'Steve. What the hell are you doing?' Joley demanded as the window continued to rise between them. 'We need to wait for Jonas. Steve, damn it. What are you doing?' She knocked on the window. When there was no response, she tried the doors. The lock wouldn't respond. 'Great.' She slumped back in her seat. 'This is just great.'

Joley pulled her cell phone out of her pocket and flipped it open to call Jonas. 'Shit. No service. He must have a jamming device in the car with us.'

Brian's eyebrow shot up, and in spite of the situation he laughed. 'A jamming device? You sound like a spy. Are there jamming devices? And if so, how do you know about them?'

Joley flung herself back against the seat. 'This is such bull, Brian. My own driver-slash-bodyguard is kidnapping us. And my bodyguard brother put us in the car. And my bodyguard boyfriend is off playing with his friends. Sheesh.' She crossed her arms across her chest and kicked the front seat hard, right in the middle of Steve's back. 'And when he stops this car, I'm kicking his ass.'

Brian laughed again. 'You're so crazy, Joley. Most women would be scared at this point. Hell, if I hadn't seen a dozen dead bodies today, I'd be scared, too.'

'I'm tired and mad. Really mad. We've been working for months nonstop. I'm one show away from going home. Sea Haven is about four hours from here, Brian. That's it.'

'So what are we going to do?'

She scowled and drove the toe of her shoe deep into the middle of the back of the driver's seat a second time just for emphasis. 'I have no idea. But these idiots are messing around with the wrong woman. My sisters are not going to be happy about this.' Joley looked around her. 'All right. What do we have back here that can be used as a weapon? We just have to buy ourselves a little time. Jonas and Aleksandr will be following. Ilya will come, and my sisters are going to be a force to contend with. Give me a minute and let me see if I can reach any of them.'

But it was Ilya she called first. She closed her eyes, blocked out everything around her – all sounds, all thoughts – and concentrated on him. Her palm itched, and she ran her fingertip over the mark, as if she could physically touch him.

Ilya. I'm in trouble.

She felt him moving through her mind, and then there was warmth. *That's nothing new.* The faint note of humor caressed her with a soothing touch. *The word just came in to Nikitin that the kidnappers want a meet. They're using you and Brian, who apparently is with you, as a bargaining chip to work out a deal. Nikitin would never have shown up for you. They don't know it, but they're holding a winning hand with Brian.* There was that same reassuring warmth. *Don't worry, I'd show up for you, but as Steve's involved, they probably expect that.*

Joley sent him an impression of haughty disdain. *I wasn't in the least bit worried.* She sobered with a little sigh. Everything was falling into place now. All the clues had been there; she just hadn't read them. *I talked to Steve the evening the bus blew up. He asked where you were. He was coming from the bus and we talked for a minute, but it was a bizarre conversation. Do you think he's the one who planted the bomb?* The thought made her angry. She'd known Steve and trusted him. She *liked* Steve. How had she missed that he would betray her? Some psychic she was. She hadn't known her best friend was gay, and she hadn't realized Steve was in the employ of people trying to kill her.

Magic isn't science, Joley. You rely too heavily on your gifts. People are different, and they can be a multitude of things – not all bad, not all good.

She didn't want a lecture, she wanted help. Nikitin and whoever his rival mobster was might have a small army with tons of firepower, but she had her family – her sisters. And she had Ilya. The combination was unstoppable.

She reached for her closest connection with absolute faith. *Hannah?*

We're here, honey. We feel it. We'll be waiting.

She wasn't afraid. Deep inside she felt centered and calm, definitely in control. Already she could feel the energy building around her as her sisters united. She flashed a reassuring smile at Brian and tapped her fingers against the back of his hand. 'We'll be all right. If they mention Nikitin to you, act like you don't know anything.'

'You think these are the same people who tried to kill him earlier?'

'I think they have to be. And I think Steve planted the bomb that blew up my bus, so don't think he's going to have any loyalty toward us. Ilya will come for us.'

'I've seen him in action. He inspires confidence.'

Joley nodded. He did that. She was amazed how safe she felt, how reassured. She'd always had that with her family. Having Ilya only made the feeling more so. Whatever differences they had to work out, trust was no longer one of them, because she knew he was coming for her – nothing would stop him.

The ride was long. North on the freeway for what seemed an hour and then west toward the coast. They drove through a series of twists and turns. They were definitely off the highway and running along a narrow, winding road that led to the foothills. She recognized the area.

Bear Valley. They're taking you on the road to Bear Valley. Hannah's voice was soothing and calm in Joley's mind. *We're not far behind you. Jonas picked us up. We're tracking your energy.*

All people left a specific trail behind, a part of their aura, their song, the same as fingerprints, and

393

Joley knew each sister could find one of the others if she ran across that energy trail.

Ilya? She couldn't help reaching out to him. She wanted to feel the warmth of his touch, the comforting caress of his voice.

We were sent a map to follow. He's distraught, Joley, genuinely distraught.

You know it's a trap. They have cover everywhere. This is heavy brush country, lots of trees, and they'll have the advantage of knowing the terrain. They chose it.

You worry too much. It will be all right.

She wanted the reassurance, and his voice, that amazing voice, provided it. She believed in him, which was almost shocking to her. She believed in her family and never thought anyone could come close to making her feel safe in the way they did, but Ilya had slowly inserted himself into her life until she found herself believing. And now that belief was so strong, she had no doubts he would find a way to rescue her.

Joley stared out the window into the night, watching the lights of cars flashing past. For Joley, marriage was sacrosanct. In her profession, marriage often ended up in a quick and easy divorce. She didn't want that. Her parents had a long and happy marriage, and her ancestors had done the same. One by one her sisters had found men they felt were true partners – best friends, astonishing lovers. Joley had never believed that would happen to her. She had always believed the bond of her sisters would be all that she had, and she'd been determined to make that enough – until Ilya. He was everything. Her heart, her soul, and he certainly commanded her body. She knew what love was, and she had finally made that sacred commitment with every fiber of her being.

The car slowed, and Joley let her senses flair out as much as possible, trying to send impressions of movement or heat or anything that might help Ilya. Her sisters would be somewhere safe, and no one would ever know they'd been there, helping in the battle, but Ilya would be on the front line and she wanted him to have every advantage.

'Look for guards on your side,' she hissed to Brian.

Jonas let us out a few miles away from you. We're going to high ground so we can command the wind, Hannah informed Joley.

They were coming up on a cabin. Steve parked the car and they sat for a few minutes. He slowly lowered the glass between them. 'Don't do anything stupid, Joley, and you might get out of this alive.'

'Maybe I will,' she said, 'but you won't.'

Brian kicked her ankle. 'Don't provoke him.'

'You haven't seen provocation yet,' she answered, tossing her head in defiance, not bothering to lower her voice.

Steve opened the door and reached in to pull Joley out.

She slapped his hand away. 'Don't you touch me, you miserable slug, slimy, worthless, traitorous piece of shit.' She put all the contempt she could muster into her voice – the one weapon that none of them had even considered. She let him feel her disgust, allowed her voice to influence, not only him, but everyone within hearing distance to look at Steve the way she did. 'You have no honor. If you would turn on me after being my friend for years, you would turn on anyone. No one can trust you.'

Steve reddened visibly, her voice leaving him exposed not only to the others, but to himself. He shifted his feet and stepped back.

Joley shot him a look of utter disdain and climbed out on her own, carrying herself as regally as possible. She looked him up and down and stepped past him, going straight to the cabin and the men waiting on the porch. She flashed a cold smile at John Dylan, who half sat on the railing, swinging one leg, arms crossed over his chest.

'If you'd wanted a meeting, John, you might have just said so at the hotel or the arena. It's a little on the chilly side here.'

Brian trailed after her, and just as he reached the porch stairs, the man behind him shoved him. Brian stumbled and fell into her. Joley staggered, recovered her balance, turned and in one precise move, snapped out a front kick, catching the guard square in the chest. She wanted the attention centered solely on her, especially now that John Dylan was present. Nobody could guess at Brian's relationship with Nikitin.

Dylan stepped up to her and slapped her hard, rocking her backward. She tasted blood in her mouth, but she refused to flinch. She just stood there, staring him down.

What the hell just happened? The voice was utterly cold, white-hot but arctic-cold, the voice of death.

Joley shivered. There was that underlying fury, the volcano beneath the ice cap. *I kicked one of Dylan's guards, so Dylan slapped me. John Dylan is here and everyone is deferring to him. Looks to me like he's in charge.*

She could feel Ilya making an effort to tamp down

his fury. *Stay away from that son of a bitch. I'll be there in another couple of minutes. Aleksandr and Jonas will take out as many guards as possible to give us a clear escape route. Just don't provoke him.*

Brian took her arm, drawing her against him.

'Now that I have your attention,' Dylan sneered, 'where's your friend, the bodyguard?'

She smirked. 'You mean the one you're all so afraid of?' She embedded the suggestion in her voice, as well as amplifying their fears. 'What do you want, Dylan?'

'In a few minutes you'll find out.' He pulled out a pack of cigarettes, offered Brian one, and when he declined, Dylan pulled one from the pack and lit it. 'Sorry you got mixed up in this, Brian, you weren't part of the deal. You just were in the wrong place at the wrong time. You never should have gotten in the car with her.'

The wind shifted slightly, coming in from the west. It tasted of salt water, as if blowing off the ocean that was behind several mountains. Joley lifted her face to the cool breeze and inhaled the scent of sea. Around them the branches of the trees rustled, murmuring softly, the leaves flashing silver in the night. She heard the faint sound of feminine voices rising in an age-old chant. Soft. Insistent. Musical. She recognized the surge in power surrounding her like a protective cloak.

'Car coming,' Steve announced.

'Shoot the bodyguard the moment he steps out of the car,' Dylan ordered. 'Grab them.'

They're planning to shoot you on sight, Ilya, Joley warned, ignoring the man who grabbed her arms and yanked them behind her back. *Turn around. Get out of here.*

Dylan caught at Brian as the car swept up to the house, using his body as a shield, and dragging him backward toward the door of the cabin. Joley was thrown facedown over the railing, a gun pressed to the back of her neck, a hard hand against her back.

The car rolled slowly toward the cabin. The guards began to shoot, the bullets drilling holes into the vehicle until it looked like a sieve. Joley could see it coming toward the porch at the same steady speed.

Don't move.

It was all the warning she got. The gun suddenly shifted, pointing away from her. She felt the guard jerk. He was flung back and away from her. Blood spattered across her back and arms. The gun clattered to the floor.

Now. Toward the trees.

Joley leapt onto the railing and jumped off of it, sprinting toward the tree line. Around her the wind whirled and screamed, creating a mini-cyclone. Branches broke off from the trees above her head, hurtling toward the porch, knocking men down. Ilya came out to meet her, the gun bucking in his fist, spitting death, laying down a covering fire as he yanked her behind him.

'Go! Get down.'

Deliberately, Ilya fired three shots into Steve's throat, sending him over backward.

'Brian. They've got Brian,' Joley said as she raced deeper into the trees and shrubbery.

Ilya aimed over Brian's head and squeezed the trigger, but at the last moment, Dylan went through the door.

'No! Hold your fire.' Nikitin grabbed Ilya's gun arm. 'You might shoot Brian.'

'You shouldn't even be here. They want you dead, I told you that. Get to cover,' Ilya snapped.

In the distance they heard the crack of a rifle, then another shot. Jonas and Aleksandr were protecting their escape route. The wind tore at the house, whirling around it, loosening boards and rattling the windows. It increased in strength, vicious, finally ripping boards loose so that they flapped. Shingles flew from the roof.

Nikitin pulled out his gun, speared Ilya a fierce look and ran toward the cabin. Ilya swore and ran after him. Twice he shot one of Dylan's soldiers as they reared up in front of Nikitin. The Russian made it to the porch in spite of the wind and kicked at the door. Ilya grabbed his shirt and jerked him to the side as bullets splintered the door from the inside.

Sergei Nikitin was no coward, he never had been. He was used to giving orders and expected his men to obey him. He was going in after Brian, which told Ilya more than anything else that his feelings for the guitar player were absolutely genuine, because Nikitin never took an unnecessary risk.

Ilya took a breath and summoned energy to him, tapping into the Drake sisters' combined strength, gathering the wind so that it pulled back for a moment and then slammed into the door with the force of a battering ram. The door buckled and crashed to the floor, and the wind swept inside.

A volley of shots poured out of the room, the flashes bright in the darkness. Ilya waited for the sudden silence, sent another blast of wind ahead of him and rolled in behind it, going to the left, at an angle from the gunfire. He tried to track Dylan, but the man had already moved. Brian began to struggle violently, kicking and hitting until he broke free and

399

made a dash for the window, obviously intending to dive out of it.

Ilya couldn't get a clear shot at Dylan, who had overturned furniture to provide cover. He saw Dylan's gun sweep up and track Brian. Heart in his throat, he rolled to get a better angle. Nikitin ran at Dylan, firing round after round. Most of the bullets thunked harmlessly into furniture, but the distraction forced Dylan to turn the gun from Brian to Nikitin. The two mobsters exchanged a ferocious storm of bullets until Ilya aimed, squeezed the trigger and shot John Dylan through the heart.

The wind retreated, leaving behind silence. The room smelled of blood, gunpowder and death. Brian turned slowly, his fingers still clutching the windowsill. Nikitin lay on the floor, the gun still in his hand, blood pouring from several wounds.

Brian dropped to the floor and crawled to Nikitin, taking his hand. 'Don't.' He rocked himself. 'Don't go.'

Nikitin glanced at Ilya, who shook his head. 'Get him out of here.' He tried to say more words, but blood choked his throat, poured out of his mouth. He coughed, tried to clear his throat. 'Don't let any of this touch him.' More blood streamed.

'I'll take care of it,' Ilya promised.

Nikitin looked up at Brian, and, as their eyes locked together, he died.

Chapter Twenty

The sea crashed and foamed, spraying over rocks and up into the darkened sky in white bursts, the sound loud, but familiar and comforting. Joley walked along the captain's walk, pacing slowly back and forth, knowing one of her ancestors had traced exactly the same path – waiting, watching, hoping for her man to return home from the perils of the sea. She felt a kinship with that woman from long ago; she knew what it was like to wait and watch and worry. She knew what it was like to love someone else with every breath in her body. She desperately wanted Ilya to escape unscathed from his dangerous job and return to her.

Ilya had been away, tying up the remnants of his operation for three long weeks. The first week, she and the band members had spent with Brian, helping him through the first rush of terrible grief. Now he was staying with Logan and Tish, living quietly and trying to come to terms with what he wanted to do in the future.

Joley had returned to her family home and tried very hard to fit in again, but without Ilya, her world, even the sanctuary of the Drake house, was gone.

She concentrated on the ocean, watching the way the endless waves rose and fell. At night the water appeared black and shiny, with sudden bursts of silver as it foamed against the rocks.

She ached, inside and out, worried about Ilya, afraid for him. He'd gone after Sergei Nikitin's human trafficking network, determined to shut it down. With Nikitin gone, his front line would scramble and hide, so Ilya had very little time to catch them before they disappeared into the shadows where they preferred to live. Working undercover for so long had made Ilya a loner, rarely using or even having a backup, or checking in as regularly with his bosses as he should. Jonas had told her what little he could, but Ilya preferred being alone and didn't often give much information. Bottom line – she had no idea where he was or even if he was safe.

Joley sighed and leaned on the railing, the wind blowing her hair from around her face. She inhaled the salt air, tasted the sea spray, felt restless and empty. *Where are you*? She would wait as long as it took for him to come to her. It was two in the morning. She accepted that there would be another night without sleep. She missed Ilya so much that she could barely go into the house anymore. She wanted to stay outside, close to the sea, where the wind could carry her news of her man. *Where are you*?

She pulled her cloak closer around her and continued her lonely vigil. Deep inside, her stomach churned like the wild sea, her brain refused to quiet, wave after wave of anxiety crashing through her mind, conjuring images of every conceivable injury or death that could befall Ilya. What if he never returned to her? So many women before her had stood in this very place waiting for a man who never came home, and they never knew where his ship had gone down. That could happen. He would just disappear and no one would ever know.

Where are you? She pressed a hand to her stomach. She needed peace. She needed Ilya. *Come home to me. Just come home.*

The wind tugged at her hair, teasing her with small fingers of awareness over her skin. She inhaled and caught a faint scent. Everything inside of her went still. Fear held her paralyzed for a moment. Her mind might be playing tricks on her. She turned slowly and walked to the rail, looking down away from the sea and for the first time toward the path leading up to her house. She had refused to allow herself to look – to hope – to believe he would really be there.

In the distance, emerging out of the dark and the few tendrils of fog, she made out a man with wide shoulders and a long stride. Joley would recognize that walk anywhere. In the night he was a dark shadow, moving with stealth and power. As he approached the gates, she held her breath. The Drake home had power of its own, and the padlock was on those high gates. The house would protect any Drake woman from a threat if need be. Ilya never even broke stride, although he had to have seen that the iron gates were locked. He would know those ancient symbols of protection, yet he walked, head up, his strides covering ground fast.

Joley's heart began to beat too fast – too hard. Her legs went weak so that she clutched at the rail. Tears burned in her eyes and blurred her vision. She felt a lump rising in her throat, choking her. Ilya. *Her* Ilya. At that moment she couldn't speak or move, not even to call out to him, absolute joy bursting through her.

The padlock simply fell from the gates, and they swung open. The creak was loud in the silence of the night as the metal parted in the middle and welcomed him inside. Ilya kept walking up the winding path, through garden still overgrown with flowers in the dead of winter. Behind him the gates closed, clanking hard, and the padlock leapt from the ground, back to its place to guard the entrance.

Joley dropped her cloak and ran. She waved her hand and the door opened for her. She raced down the hall and took the stairs two at a time. The house was dark and cold, mirroring the way she felt inside. She hadn't been able to bring herself to light a fire or even make a cup of tea, but the darkness didn't hinder her, she knew every step of the way to the front door and she sprinted, her heart bursting.

The door swung open before she even managed to send it a command, and he was there. On her front porch. Real. Solid. *Alive*. Joley leapt on him, so that he had no choice but to catch her in midair. She wrapped her legs around his waist, her arms around his neck, sank her face into the hollow of his shoulder and burst into tears.

He buried his face in her silky hair and just held her on the porch while the wind whipped around them in a joyous frenzy and the waves climbed higher and higher as if dancing in their delight.

Ilya carried Joley inside and kicked the door closed behind him. At once a fire sprang up in the fireplace. Candles on the mantel lit one by one, lending the room an amber glow. The mosaic beneath his feet seemed to come alive, swirling with colors and shooting stars. He swore for a moment that he heard whispers, feminine voices welcoming him home, but when he looked around, they were completely alone.

Ilya let Joley's legs slide back to the floor, but he caught the nape of her neck and turned her face up to his. He had never in his life had a home, but when he walked through the gates, and the door to her house had swung open, and Joley had been there, her face lit up like Christmas morning – he had known. He was home.

Emotion overwhelmed him, robbed him of speech, leaving him without words to tell her how much he loved her. He brought his mouth to hers, slowly, inch by inch, watching her face – her eyes. Watching the way she loved him back. He had dreamt of this moment, feeling the soft silk of her mouth, warm and tasting of that long-ago honey that had been so good. The dream didn't come close to the reality. He sank into her arms, into her kiss, and knew he was truly home. She held nothing back; she simply melted into him, her body soft and pliant, sensual with promise.

Joley couldn't stop her tears, and he tasted them, too, his lips wandering over her face, memorizing the shape and feel of her.

'I was so scared,' she whispered, linking her fingers behind his neck. 'Please never go away like that again.'

'I have no intention of ever leaving you, Joley. I handed in my resignation and walked away.'

'What happened? Were you able to take the network down?'

'The bust covered four countries and netted us sixteen major players. I found your missing teen and we brought her home. She was traumatized, but she was alive and HIV-free, luckier than some of the others.'

'Thank God!'

Ilya kissed her again, a long, slow savoring of her,

pulling her closer, needing to feel her warmth. 'How is Brian?'

Joley pulled off his jacket, needing to inspect him for injuries. She almost dropped it on the floor, but something made her go and hang it in the entryway closet beside her coat. The two jackets looked as if they belonged together. 'We're all taking turns watching over him, and hopefully he'll come to terms with his loss. It makes it so hard for him because he can't really talk about Nikitin to anyone and have them understand why he might have fallen in love with a monster.'

She turned her head and stared at him – drank him in. She still could barely believe he was really there.

Ilya swept her into his arms, cradling her close to his chest. 'Tell me where the bedroom is.' He was already going up the stairs.

She just pointed and nuzzled his neck, much more interested in the scent and texture of him than their destination.

The walls were covered with pictures, and as they passed, the photographs rustled softly and two wall sconces glowed with light.

Joley's bedroom faced the sea. There was a large window, already open, the sheer curtains billowing, like ghostly dresses, with the wind coming off the ocean. Her bed lay beside the window, giving her a huge view of the sea. Ilya put her down beside the large four-poster bed and tugged her shirt over her head. Joley kicked off her sandals as his hands went to the waistband of her jeans. He unzipped them and tugged, taking her panties as well. She held his arm while she stepped out of them. The moment he unhooked her bra, the cold air shaped her nipples into twin hard peaks.

She stood with the moonlight spilling over her soft skin, her dark eyes luminous, her silky hair tousled from the wind.

'You're so beautiful,' he said, his breath catching in his lungs. He unbuttoned his shirt with one hand, reaching out with the other to cup her breast, his thumb sliding over her nipple, watching her reaction. 'I missed you.'

She leaned into him for another kiss. She couldn't get enough, would never get enough. She ached with missing him. His arms slid around her, and he simply lifted her, kissing her the entire time, even as he laid her on the bed. The darkened shadow on his face rubbed erotically against her sensitive skin. When he raised his head, she felt bereft. He sank down beside her and removed his shoes.

Joley couldn't take her gaze from him, afraid that if she did, he might disappear. She wanted to inspect him for injuries, and the moment he shed his clothes, she came up on her knees and ran her hands over him. Of course there were fresh bruises, scrapes and a couple of raw-looking gashes.

His hand slid over her bare bottom, shaping the naked cheek lovingly as he brought his mouth down to the hollow of her shoulder. She went still, the breath leaving her lungs in a rush. She slid her arms around his neck and pressed close, still shaken by his absence – by his return – tears burning behind her eyelids even while her body was soft and aching with need.

He lifted her hips. 'Put your legs around me, *lubov moya*.'

She was almost afraid to – she wanted to have him deep inside, yet she didn't want anything to interfere with this time, this moment when the love was so overwhelming she could barely breathe.

He whispered to her in Russian, bit gently at her earlobe, her neck, kissed her upturned mouth again. 'Lock your ankles, Joley.' This time there was that edge of command to his voice, and it brought a rush of damp heat, a small thrill in her stomach.

She raised her legs obediently and sank down on his thick length, impaling her body. He was larger than she remembered, forcing his way through the tight velvet folds, stretching her impossibly. She was slick with liquid heat and the sensation of pleasure washing over her, but love was also there in abundance. She felt surrounded by her deep commitment and emotion for this man, she felt lifted by it, but most of all – complete. She felt his ragged gasp, the heat and raw honesty in his whisper of love.

Ya lublu tebya.

I love you. The three words meant everything. She was a spell-singer, and her world was sound. She knew truth when she heard it. She tightened her arms around him, holding him closer, wanting to share the same skin, wanting to crawl inside the shelter of his body and have them be as close as they could to each other.

'I love you, Ilya, more than anything,' she answered, meaning it, knowing he heard sound in the same way she did.

Around them their colors swirled and merged like the notes of their song. It no longer frightened her. Ilya was part of her – the best part – and he felt the same way about her.

His lovemaking started gentle, so incredibly tender she felt tears run down her face. Each stroke was slow and easy as his hands shaped and memorized her body. She felt as if he was worshiping her, the sweet pleasure washing through her in gentle waves. As his hips maintained that same gentle rocking, the tension began to rise, to build, until she couldn't think, until she was desperate for him to pick up the pace. She tried to force it, writhing and moving her own hips, but no amount of squirming or eventual pleading could change his tempo.

Heat became an inferno; around them she heard the notes of their song catch fire as passion sizzled and burned through her veins. That slow burn grew hotter and brighter, threatening to consume her. She threw her head back, absorbing the sheer erotic magic of Ilya.

Tongues of fire began to lick along her breasts, her belly, deep inside where that relentless stroke of velvet-encased steel continued to drag over sensitive nerves, until she heard her own sob and her body clenched and spasmed and began to coil tighter and tighter. Each stroke was precise, driving deep, a hard, thick piston that only tightened the stranglehold her body had him in. When it came, her orgasm rushed, overtook, consumed them both, throwing them into an explosive series of waves, roaring through their bodies, taking Ilya with her, her feminine sheath like hot silk gripping hard, forcing him to submit and surrender.

She cried out his name, dropped her head onto his shoulder as she collapsed, kissing his neck, her arms holding him tight.

'If you didn't understand what I just told you, I am in love with you,' Ilya said. He didn't mean just what he'd told her when he was speaking Russian, he meant what he'd said with every beat of his heart, every stroke of his body. He remembered her fears of his wanting only sex from her, and he wanted to lay them to rest forever.

'I understood perfectly.'

He felt her lips curve against his neck and knew she was smiling. He laid her back, careful of her smaller body as he blanketed her, holding her close to him, unable to break away yet. He wanted to feel the beat of her heart, hear her soft breath, feel the silk of her hair and the satin of her skin against his. She was soft, all woman; she was – everything.

'Listen to that, Ilya,' she said softly.

'What am I listening to?' He was listening to her song, almost purring like a contented kitten. He would never hear that song enough.

'The sea. Earlier, before you were here, the waves were wild and crazy. I could hear the roaring and crashing against the rocks.' She pressed a hand to her stomach. 'Inside I felt the same way, moody and stormy and all on edge. And then you came home. The sea is at peace.' And so was she. Deep inside, everything had become calm and still and at peace.

He looked at her instead of the inky water. Her heart leapt. His eyes, his beautiful eyes, often so like the turbulent sea in the midst of a wild coastal storm, were as serene as the clear skies after a storm passes. She could see his colors; the dark shadow was still there – and it probably would always be second nature to Ilya to hide who he was – but she could see the colors swirling beneath the darkness, light and happy and tranquil. His music was soft and sensuous, a blend of notes that made her heart melt and her world right.

'You make everything in me still and relaxed, Joley. You make my body and heart sing. I swear, when I saw you coming toward me, the rest of the world fell away and I knew I was home. It didn't matter where, just as long as I was with you.'

Joley smiled and kissed him again, a long, lingering kiss that stole his breath. 'Look at the sea, Ilya. The ocean is so enormous and beautiful. Especially at night, it just sweeps everything bad in your life under those pounding waves and takes it out to somewhere in the middle of all that vast space, leaving life good.'

His smile was slow and heart-stopping. She got another kiss, and then he braced himself above her to look out the window at the continually moving water. 'It is beautiful, Joley,' he agreed. 'I had hoped we could buy the property next to Jonas. There's twenty acres for sale, a huge home with enough bedrooms for our sons, but we're not on the ocean. You have to look over the tops of the trees to see it in the distance.'

There was a small silence. 'You were looking at property? When? How?'

'Jonas sent me a link on the Internet. I had to do something while I was traveling, so I went through my e-mail. It sounded perfect, but now that I can hear the sea, maybe we should be closer.' He lowered his body over hers again, bending his head to kiss her. It was difficult resisting her, the shape and texture of her curves when she melted the way she did each time he sank into her.

'I hadn't thought that far ahead,' she admitted, running her hands up and down his arms. It was necessary to touch him, to feel every inch of his skin. 'But I'd love to live close to Hannah.'

'Our children can play together.' He rolled over to lie beside her, one hand massaging her stomach.

'There you go with the children again. Get over it

411

already. We're not having children for a long, long time.' But she was already a *little* enticed by the prospect of letting him see a real childhood by watching their son grow up in a loving home.

'Really?' He bent his head and kissed her stomach, his dark hair falling across her skin and tickling her. 'I don't know that I'd call eight months a long time, but I guess by the end of it, most women think it's a very long time.'

Joley couldn't help but immerse her fingers into that wealth of silky hair as he pressed his ear to her stomach and then rubbed another caress over her. 'You are so insane. I told you, I'm on birth control.'

'Does birth control work for Elle?'

She frowned and, with her fingers curled into his thick hair, yanked to bring his head up. 'I am *not* Elle.'

He flashed a small grin. 'No, but I am – well – the masculine version of her, and I'm feeling life here in your womb. I felt it the first time I ever made love to you.'

Joley gaped at him. It wasn't true. A baby? She put her hands on her belly. Could she be pregnant with a baby? *His* baby? That little boy with dark curls who would never hide in a corner trying to make himself small? She imagined Ilya carrying the child on his shoulders, laughing. Ilya needed to laugh; he needed to see a childhood the way it was meant to be. Secretly, she thought she might like the motherhood thing – with *one* child – but there would be no admitting it to him.

'You'd better be wrong. That would be like a fate worse than death. I'm not having seven children. Do you know how many times I'd have to be in labor?'

He nuzzled her stomach. 'Not if we did it two at a time.'

She sat up, pushing his head away from her. 'Did I say I missed you, because if I did, I was sadly mistaken.' She pointed across the room. 'Go over there and sit down.'

He grinned at her, unrepentant. 'I think we should have at least one girl, too. I want to find her trying to get out of windows when she's been naughty at school.'

Joley groaned. 'Don't wish that on us!' She wrapped her arms around him and pulled him back to her. 'Seven sons, for real? You'd better be really good at the daddy role.'

'I'll do my best,' he promised, nuzzling her neck, 'but I intend to be dynamite at the husband role.' He kissed her several times, unable to stay away from her soft mouth. 'And thank you for the way you lit up the house when I returned, the fire in the fireplace, the candles – it was so beautiful and made me feel unlike anything I've ever felt. It was perfect.'

Joley's hands smoothed through his hair lovingly. 'I didn't do that,' she whispered, knowing the truth. 'The house recognized you and welcomed you home.'

Turn the page for a special preview of

DARK CURSE
by Christine Feehan

Available in September 2008
from Berkley Books!

Available soon
from Piatkus Books!

'Lara, let's get out of here,' Terry Vale said. 'It's getting dark and there's nothing here. Look below us. There's caves crisscrossing the entire mountain. Take your pick.'

Lara Calladine didn't bother looking away from where she was scanning the mountainside for the smallest crack that might signal the presence of a cave. She wasn't wrong – not this time. Power surged and crackled the moment she set foot on the upper slopes of the mountain. She took a deep breath and pressed a hand over her pounding heart. This was *it*. This was the place she had spent her life searching for. She would recognize that flow of energy anywhere. She knew every weave, every spell, her body absorbing the gathering power so that veins sizzled and her nerve endings burned with the electrical current building inside of her.

'I've got to go with Terry on this,' Gerald French agreed. 'This place gives me the creeps. We've been on a lot of mountains, but this one doesn't like us.' He gave a nervous laugh. 'It's getting dicey up here.'

'No one says "dicey,"' Lara murmured, running her hand along the face of the rock about an inch from the surface, looking for threads of power.

'Whatever,' Gerald snapped. 'It's getting dark and there's nothing here but mist. The fog is creepy, Lara. We've got to get out of here.'

Lara spared the two men an impatient glance and then surveyed the countryside around them. Ice and snow glittered, coating the surrounding mountains with what appeared to be sparkling gems. Far below she could see castles, farms and churches in the distance despite the gathering dusk. Sheep dotted the meadows and she could see the river running, filled to capacity. Birds cried overhead, filling the sky and dive-bombing toward her, only to break off abruptly and circle again. The wind shifted continuously, biting at her face and at every bit of exposed skin, tugging at her long thick braid, moaning and wailing all the while. Occasionally a rock fell down the slope and bounced off the ledge to the hillside below. A trickle of snow and dirt slid near her feet.

Her gaze swept the wild countryside. Gorges and ravines cut through the snowcapped mountains, plants clung to the sides of the rocks and shivered naked along the plateaus. She could see the entrances to several caves and felt the strong pull toward them as if they were tempting her to leave where she was to explore. Water filled the deeper depressions below, forming a dark peat bog and beds of moss, which were a vivid green in stark contrast to the browns surrounding them. But she needed to here – in this spot, this place. She had studied the geography carefully and knew that deep within the earth, a massive series of ice caves had formed.

The higher she climbed, the smaller everything below her looked and the thicker the white mist surrounding her became. With each step, the ground shifted subtly and the birds overhead shrieked a little louder. Ordinary things, yes, but the subtle sense of uneasiness, the continual voice whispering, warning her to leave before it was too late, told her this was a place of power. Although the wind continued to shriek and blow, the mist remained a thick veil that shrouded the upper slope.

'Come on, Lara,' Terry tried again. 'It took us forever to get the permits, we can't waste time on the wrong area. You can see nothing's here.'

It had taken considerable effort this time to get the permits for her study, but she had managed the usual way – using her gifts to persuade those who disagreed with her that, with the universal global warming, the fate of the ice caves was unknown and needed immediate attention. More than that, microbes – extremophiles – not only survived within the caves, but thrived in extreme conditions. The hope was that the microorganisms that lived and reproduced far from sunlight and traditional nutrients could aid medical science in the fight against cancer or even produce an antibiotic capable of wiping out the newer superbugs emerging.

Her research project was fully funded and, although she was considered young at the age of twenty-seven, she was acknowledged as the leading expert in the field of ice-cave study and preservation. She'd logged more hours exploring, mapping and studying the ice caves around the world than most other researchers twice her age. She'd also discovered more superbugs than any other caver. NASA, one of the leading researchers of the extremophiles, was one of her biggest supporters.

'Didn't it strike you as odd that no one wanted us in this particular region? They were fine giving us permits to look virtually anywhere else,' she pointed out. Part of the reason she'd persisted when no caves had been mapped in the area was because the department head had been so strange – strange and rather vague when they went over the map. After studying the area, the natural geographical deduction was that a vast network of ice caves lay beneath the mountain, yet the entire region seemed to have been overlooked.

Terry and Gerald had exhibited exactly the same behavior, as if they didn't notice the odd structure of the mountain, and both men were superb at finding ice caves from the geographical surface. Persuasion had been difficult, but all of that work was for this moment, this cave, this find.

'It's here,' she said with absolute confidence.

Her heart continued to pound with excitement, not at the find, but because walking had become such a chore, her body not wanting to continue forward. She breathed away the compulsion to leave and pressed through the safeguards, following the trail of power, judging how close she was to the entrance by how strong her need to run away was.

Voices rose in the wind, swirled in the mists, telling her to go back, to leave while she could. Strangely, she heard the voices in several languages, the warning much stronger and insistent as she made her way along the slope searching for a crack, for anything at all that might signal an entrance to the caves she knew were there. All the while she kept her senses alert to the possibility that monsters might lurk beneath the earth. But she had to enter – to find the place of her nightmares, the place of her childhood. She had to find the two dragons she dreamt of nightly.

'Lara!' This time Terry's voice was sharp with

protest. 'We have to get out of here.'

Barely sparing him a second glance, Lara stood still for a long moment, studying the outcropping that jutted out from smoother rock. Thick snow covered most of it, but there was an oddity about it that kept drawing her gaze back to the rock. She approached cautiously. Several small rocks lay at the foot of the larger boulders, and strangely, not a single snowflake stuck to them. She didn't touch them, but studied them from every angle, carefully observing the way they were arranged in a pattern at the foot of the outcropping.

'Something out of place,' she murmured aloud.

Instantly the wind wailed, the sound rising to a shriek as it rushed toward her, blowing debris into the air so that it shot at her like small missiles.

'It's the rocks. See, they should be arranged differently.' Lara leaned down and pushed the small pile of rocks into a different pattern.

At once the ground shifted beneath them. The mountain creaked in protest. Bats took the air, pouring out of some unseen hole a short distance from them, filling the sky until it was nearly black. The dark crack along the outcropping split wider. The mountain shuddered and shook and groaned as if alive, as if it were coming awake.

'We shouldn't be here,' Terry nearly sobbed.

Lara took a deep breath and held her palm to the narrow slit in the mountainside, the only entrance to this particular cave. Power blasted out at her, and all around she could feel the safeguards, thick and ominous, protecting the entrance.

'You're right, Terry,' she agreed. 'We shouldn't.' She backed away from the outcropping and gestured toward the trail. 'Let's go. And hurry.' For the first time she was really aware of the hour, the sun setting, the gathering darkness spreading like a stain across the sky.

She would be coming back early morning – without her two companions. She had no idea what was left in the elaborate ice caverns below, but she wasn't about to expose two of her closest friends to danger. The safeguards in place would confuse them, so they wouldn't remember the location of the cave, but she knew each weave, each spell, and how to reverse it so that the guards wouldn't affect her.

Ice caves as a whole were dangerous at all times. The continual pressure from overlying ice caps often sent great frozen chunks of ice blasting out of the walls, like rockets being fired, capable of killing anything they struck. This ice cave held dangers that far outweighed natural ones, and she didn't want her companions anywhere near it.

The ground shifted again, throwing all of them off balance. Gerald grabbed her to keep her from falling and Terry caught at the outcropping, fingers digging into the widening crack. Beneath their feet, something under the ground moved, raising the surface several inches as the creature raced toward the base of the rocks Lara had realigned.

'What is that?' Gerald shouted, backpedaling. He thrust Lara behind him in an effort to protect her as the dirt and snow spouted into a geyser almost at his feet.

Terry screamed, his voice high-pitched and frightened as he tipped over backward and the unseen creature raced toward him beneath the earth.

'Get up! Move!' Lara called, trying to get around Gerald's sold bulk to throw a holding spell. As he swung around, Gerald's backpack knocked her off her feet and sent her rolling down the steeper slope. Her birthmark, the strangely shaped dragon positioned just over her left ovary, suddenly flared into life, burning through her skin and glowing red hot.

Two dark-green tentacles burst from the snow-covered ground, slick with blood, the color so dark it nearly was black. They emerged on either side of Terry's left ankle. The sound of bubbling mud rose, along with a noxious, putrid stink of rotten eggs and sulfur, so overpowering the three of them gagged. The bulbous ends of the tentacles reared back, revealing coiling snake heads, and then struck with brutal speed. Two curved, venomous fangs clamped through Terry's skin nearly to the bone. Blood dripped into the pristine snow. The small gap in the ground began to widen into a larger hole a few feet from Terry. At once, the tentacles retreated toward the hole, slithering across the surface, dragging Terry by his ankle. His screams of fear turned to pain and terror.

Gerald flung himself forward, gripping Terry under his arms and throwing his weight in the opposite direction. 'Hurry, Lara!'

Lara scrambled to the top of the slope. The mist whirled and thickened around her, making it difficult to see. She spread her arms as she ran, gathering energy from the darkening sky, uncaring of her companions, knowing she was Terry's only chance at survival. She hadn't used the knowledge inside of her, the wealth of information her aunts had shared with her – indeed, she hadn't been certain it was real – until that moment. Power flooded her. Her mind opened. Expanded. Reached into the well of knowledge and found the exact words she needed.

'It's too strong.' Gerald dug his heels into the

earth and held on to Terry with every ounce of strength he possessed. 'Stop wasting your energy and help me, damn it. Come on, Terry, fight.'

Terry abruptly ceased screaming and began to fight in earnest, kicking with his free leg in an attempt to dislodge the two snake heads.

The vine threw more tentacles out, the greenish-black stems writhing hideously, looking for a target. The teeth sank deeper into Terry's ankles, sawing at flesh and bone in an effort to keep their prey.

Lara flung herself forward, lifting her face to the sky as she muttered the words she found in her mind.

I call forth the power of the sky. Bring down lightning to my mind's eye. Shaping, shifting, bend to my will. Forging a scythe to sharpened steel. Hot and bright the fire be, guide my hand with accuracy.

Lightning zigzagged across the sky, lighting the edges of the clouds. The air around them charged so that the hair on their bodies and heads stood on end. Lara felt electricity snapping and sizzling in her fingertips and focused on the thinner space between the long, thick bodies and the bulbous heads of the snake-vines.

White light streaked across the short distance and pierced the necks of the creatures. The smell of rotting flesh burst from the vine. Both severed bodies dropped limply to the ground leaving the teeth, with the heads attached, still sunk deep into Terry's ankle. The rest of the tentacles reared back in shock and then burrowed beneath the dirt and snow.

Terry grasped one of the heads to pull it out.

'No!' Lara protested. 'Leave it. You don't know if the teeth are barbed. We have to get out of here right now.'

'It burns like acid,' Terry complained. His face was pale, nearly as white as the covering of snow, and beads of sweat dotted his forehead.

Lara shook her head. 'We have to get off this mountain now. And you can't take chances until I can look at it.'

She took his arm and signaled to Gerald to grab his other one. They steadied Terry between them and began to hurry from the slope to the well-traveled path off to their right.

'What was that?' Gerald hissed, his eyes meeting hers over Terry's head. 'Have you ever seen a snake like that before?'

'Was it two-headed?' Terry asked. Anxiety made him hyperventilate. 'I didn't get all that good a look at it before it struck. Do you think it's poisonous?'

'It isn't attacking the central nervous system, Terry,' Lara said. 'At least not yet. We'll get you back down to the village and find a doctor. I know a few things about medicine, I can treat you when we get to the car.'

The mountain rumbled ominously, shivering beneath their feet. Lara glanced up at the swirling white mists. Above them, spiderweb cracks appeared in the snow and began to widen.

Gerald swore, renewed his grip on Terry, and started sprinting along the thin, winding trail. 'It's going to come down.'

Terry gritted his teeth against the pain radiating up from his ankle. 'I can't believe this is happening. I feel sick.'

Lara kept her eyes on the mountain behind them as they raced, dragging Terry every step of the way. 'Faster. Keep moving.'

The ground shifted and rolled and small fans of

snow slid in artful patterns toward the slope below them. The sight was dazzling, hypnotic even. Gerald shook his head several times and looked at Lara, puzzled, slowing down to gaze at the undulating snow. 'Lara? I can't remember what happened. Where are we?'

'We're about to be creamed by an avalanche, Gerald,' Lara advised. 'Terry's hurt and we've got to run like hell. Now move it!'

She put every ounce of compulsion and command into her voice that she could muster on the run. Fortunately both men obeyed, concentrating on getting down the steep slope as quickly as they could and asking no more questions. The safeguards protecting the cave were not only lethal, but they confused and disoriented any traveler stumbling across them. The warning system was usually enough to make people so uneasy they left the area, but once triggered, the safeguards fought to erase memories or even kill to protect the entrance to the cave.

It was the place she had been looking for. Now she had to survive in order to come back and discover the long-buried secrets of her past. Gerald stumbled and Terry screamed as one of the snake heads slammed against a particularly dense pile of snow and ice, shoving the teeth further into his flesh.

Lara felt the mountain tremble. At first there was silence, and then a distant rumbling. The sound increased in strength and volume until it became a roar. The snow slid, slowly at first, but picking up speed, churning and roiling, rushing toward them. Lara forced back panic and reached into the well of knowledge she knew was deep inside of her. Her aunts had never appeared human to her, but their voices had been, and the immense wealth of information they had collected over centuries had been stored in Lara's memories.

She was Dragonseeker, a great Carpathian heritage. She was human, with courage and strength of the ages. She was mage, able to gather energy and use it for good. All of her ancestors were powerful beings. The blood of three species mingled in her veins, yet she belonged in none of those worlds and walked her chosen path – alone, but always guided by the wisdom of the aunts.

She felt strength pour into her, felt the crackle of electricity as the sky lit up with lightning. Looking over her shoulder once more, she sent a command to the wilds of nature to counteract the protection guard the dark mage had used on the mountain.

I summon thee, water ice, fit to my hand, provide me with shelter as I command.

The snow stopped movement abruptly, sprayed in air, frozen in place, curled over their heads like a giant wave motionless in mid-air.

'Run!' Lara shouted. 'Go, Gerald. We've got to get off the mountain.'

Night was falling and the avalanche was not the worst they might face. The wind had stilled, but the voices remained, shrieking warnings she dared not ignore. They gripped Terry and half ran, half slid down the steep slope. Above their heads, the heavy mantle of snow formed a wave, cresting over them, motionless like an ominous statue.

Terry left behind streaks of blood as they skidded over the icy surface. They were sweating profusely by the time they made it to the bottom. Breathing heavily, they paused, looking around for their car. It stood out like a sore thumb. In this particular area of Romania, most of the locals used carts with tires pulled by horses. Cars weren't a common sight at all and, as small it as it was, it looked far too modern in a place centuries old.

Gerald dragged Terry through the meadow to the where the car was parked beneath some naked branches. Lara turned back toward the mountain, let out her breath and clapped her hands together three times. There was an odd, expectant pause. The wave rolled, snow dropped. The mountain slid, raising a cloud of white into the air.

'Lara,' Terry gasped. 'You have to get these teeth out of ankle. My leg burns like hell and I swear, something's crawling inside of me – inside my leg.'

He sprawled on the small backseat, his skin nearly gray. Sweat soaked his clothes and his breathing came in ragged gasps.

Lara knelt in the dirt and examined the hideous heads. She knew what they were – hybrids of the dark mage, bred to do his bidding. She'd seen the beginnings of them in her nightmares. The snakes injected a poisonous brew, including tiny microscopic parasites, into their victim's body. The organisms would eventually take over Terry's body and then his brain, until he was a mere puppet to be used by the dark mage.

'I'm sorry, Terry,' she said softly. 'The teeth are barbed and have to be removed carefully.'

'Then you've seen this before?' Terry gripped her wrist and held her close to him as she crouched beside the open door of the car. He was sprawled across the back seat, rocking in pain. 'I don't know why, but the fact that you know what they are makes me feel better.'

428

It didn't make her feel any better. She'd been a child, dragged into a laboratory. The sights and smells had been so hideous she'd tried to forget them. The stench of blood. The screams. The grotesque tiny worms in a putrid ball, wiggling in a frenzy, consuming blood and human flesh.

Lara took a deep breath and let it out. They didn't have much time. She needed to get Terry to a master healer who could handle such things, but she could slow down the deterioration.

Gerald looked around him, then back up at the mountain, now quiet and still. White mists swirled, but the voices were gone. Overhead the clouds grew heavier and darker, but the mountain looked pristine – untouched – certainly not as if anyone had climbed it and been attacked.

'Lara?' He sounded as puzzled as he looked. 'I can't remember where we were. I can't remember how these snakes attacked Terry. Don't snakes need warm weather? How did this happen, and what's wrong with me?'

'It doesn't matter right now. What matters is getting these teeth out of Terry's leg and getting him to the inn where someone who knows what they're doing can help him.' Someone with healing skills, more than medical skills. If they were in the vicinity where she had been held as a child, then it stood to reason that someone knew how to treat a mage wound.

She closed her eyes to block out the sight of Terry's gray face and Gerald's anxious one. Deep inside, where that wealth of knowledge lay, she found her calm center. She could almost hear the whisper of her aunts' voices, directing her as the information flooded her mind. The curved fangs had a barb at the tip.

Severed head that now does bite, fangs be removed with heat and light. Draw the poison that would remain, holding the harm, stop the pain.

'There might be someone much better at taking these out,' Lara said. 'We can get you to the inn fast and the couple that owns it might be able to find someone for us who has dealt with this before.'

Terry shook his head. 'I can't stand it, Lara. If you don't take them out now, I'm going to rip them out. I really can't stand it.'

She nodded her understanding and reached beneath her jacket for the knife on her tool belt. 'Let's get it done then. Gerald, get in the back seat on the other side and hold Terry's shoulders.' More than anything, she didn't want Gerald positioned where some of the tainted blood might spatter on him. The tiny microorganisms were dangerous to everyone.

Gerald obeyed her without question and Lara studied the first snake head. The hybrid was part plant, part living animal, and all frightening. It was meant to take over a person, no matter what the species, and bring them under the dark mage's control. It hadn't been just Carpathians and humans he had tortured, but his own people as well. No one was safe, not even his own family, as Lara could attest to.

She closed her eyes and swallowed hard, slamming the door on memories that were too painful, too frightening to remember when she had such a complex task before her. She had rarely used her healing abilities on anyone else in the last few years. In her childhood, she'd made the mistake several times, traveling with gypsies. She'd knit broken bones. Healed a wound from a blade that would have killed a man. Removed harmful bacteria from children's lungs. At first people would be grateful, but inevitably they would come to fear her.

Never show that you are different. You must blend in wherever you are. Learn the language and the customs. Dress the way they dress. Speak as they speak. Cloak who and what you are and never trust anyone.

She liked Gerald and Terry – very much. They'd worked together for several years, and she'd been careful never to intrude on either of them or to show them that she was different in any way. That had been a difficult lesson she'd learned repeatedly, every time she was kicked out of the family taking care of her.

'Lara.'

Terry's pleading voice forced her thoughts to the task at hand. She steadied herself and gave him a reassuring nod. They were used to her being the leader in caving, and it was natural to look to her now. She took another breath and let it out, pushing down the revulsion that was welling up.

The words to the healing chant rose out of that same bank of knowledge and she repeated them under her breath as she slid the razor-sharp knife beneath Terry's skin and found the barb.

Kunasz, nelkul sivdobbanas, nelkul fesztelen loyly.
Ot elidamet andam szabadon elidadert.
O jela sialem jorem ot ainamet es sone ot elidadet.
O jela sialem pukta kin minden szelemeket helso.
Pajnak o susu hanyet es o nyelv nyalamet sivadaba.
Vii o vermin sone o verid andam.

The ancient Carpathian language came easily; it was one she'd known since childhood. She might be

431

rusty, having never used it other that to murmur to herself before she fell asleep, but the words, spoken in a chant were always soothing to her.

As she whispered the healing words, she blocked Terry's pain. The tooth was wicked and nasty. It curved into the skin, growing wider, digging deep, and at the end was a small barb, curving in the opposite direction. She had to slit the skin carefully to allow the points on either side to become loose enough to slide out without further damaging Terry's leg.

At first she used her human sight, blocking all other ability to see until she had the barb out. Only then did she allow herself to look with the eyes of a mage. Tiny white worms writhed and burrowed, swarming to the cells to reproduce as quickly as possible. Her stomach lurched. It took tremendous effort to shed her awareness of her own thoughts and physical self and become a blaze of healing white light, which she then poured into Terry's wound to burn the organisms as quickly as she found them.

The wormlike creatures tried to hide from the light, and given the chance, they reproduced quickly. She tried to be thorough, but Terry squirmed and moaned, distracting her, all at once reaching down to his other ankle, trying to yank the remaining snake head free.

She found herself abruptly back in her own body, disoriented and panic-stricken. 'Terry! Leave it. I'll take it out.'

She was too late. He screamed as he yanked at the foul snake head, tearing it loose from his ankle. The barb ripped through his skin and muscle. Blood sprayed the back of the car and shot across the seat, splattering Gerald's chest.

'Don't touch the blood with your hands!' Lara yelled. 'Use a cloth. Get your jacket off, Gerald.'

She clamped both of her hands over the wound, pressing hard, ignoring the burning pain as the blood coated her skin, burning to the bone. She fought past her own fear and panic to reach for the cool, centered place inside of her, calling healing light, burning white-hot and pure, to counteract the acid of the snake blood. The way her birthmark was burning there had to be vampire blood mixed in the foul brew.

Gerald ripped his jacket open and threw it away as the material smoldered with a grayish smoke. He rubbed at his face and eyes, slapping his palms down his face and chest to rid himself of the sensation of things crawling on him.

Terry grew quiet as Lara sent healing light streaking through his body to the gaping wound in his leg. The bleeding slowed to a trickle and the tiny worm-like creatures retreated from the spreading heat Lara generated. She cauterized the wound, destroying as many of the parasites as she could before bathing her hands and arms in the same hot energy.

'Did you get any blood on you, Gerald?'

He shook his head. 'I don't think so, Lara. It felt like it, but I wiped my hands and face and there aren't any smears.'

'Once we get Terry to a healer, take a shower as soon as you can. And burn your clothes. Don't just wash them, burn them. Everything.'

She backed out of the seat, helping Terry to swing his legs out of the way of the door so she could close it and rush around to the driver's side. Terry's coloring was terrible, but more importantly she didn't like the way he was breathing. Part of it could be shock, the shallow, too-fast breathing of panic, but she feared she hadn't stopped the parasites from assaulting his body. He needed a master healer immediately.

She drove as fast as she could over the narrow, pitted mountain road, sliding through some of the sharper turns and bumping over the muddy holes. Dirty water sprayed into the air as the car fishtailed through mud and snow, throwing up debris in its wake. All around them the peaceful countryside seemed in sharp contrast to the terror of the snake heads that had been embedded in Terry's ankle.

Haystacks and cows surrounded them. Small thatched houses and horse-drawn carts with huge tires gave the impression of stepping back in time to a much more slower paced and happier time. The castles and abundance of churches lent the area a medieval look, so that one expected knights on horses to come charging over the hills any moment.

Lara had traveled all over the world searching for her past. She remembered little of her journey from the ice cave, and once the gypsies had found her she'd traveled all over Europe. Passed from family to family, she'd never been told where they found her. Coming to the Carpathian mountains had been like coming home. And when she had entered Romania, she *felt* home. This place was still wild, the forests untamed and the land alive beneath her feet.

The car slid around another corner and they were out of the heavier forest and into the peat bogs. The trail narrowed even more, winding on solid ground while the smell of the bog permeated the air around them. Trees swayed and drooped under the heavy weight of snow. Lights in the distance heralded farms, and for a moment she thought to stop at one of the nearest ones for aid. But Terry had been bitten by a hybrid, a mage-bred snake carrying vampire blood. Healing a mage wound was difficult enough, but a hybrid with vampire blood – that required skills far beyond her knowledge or that of a human doctor.

There one hope lay with the innkeepers. The couple had been born and raised in the area and had lived their entire lives there. Lara couldn't imagine that they wouldn't have some knowledge of the danger lying beneath the mountain. Over time it became difficult to tamper with the same memories. And there had been something about that inn – something that had drawn Lara to it. A suggestion of power, as if perhaps there was subtle influence at work, pushing tourists and visitors to the area to want to stay at the homey, friendly inn.

Lara had allowed herself to be susceptible to the flow of power because it was the first time since the dragon had shoved her onto the upper cavern ledge that she had encountered the light delicate touch of flowing energy. She had forgotten what it was like to bathe herself in the crackle of electric power, to feel it surrounding her, flowing through every cell until her body hummed with it. The inn and the entire village gave off the amazing feeling, although it was so subtle she had nearly missed it.

'Lara,' Gerald called from the back seat. 'My skin is starting to burn.'

'We're almost there. Go in and take a shower, first thing.' She didn't want to think what Terry was suffering. He was very quiet, other than making a soft moaning sound. 'Gerald, when we get to the inn, we'll need to talk to the owners and ask right away who the village healer is.'

'The owner's name was Slavica and she seemed very nice.'

'Hopefully she's very discreet as well. She certainly seems to know everyone.'

'Wouldn't it be better to ask for the nearest doctor?' Gerald asked.

Lara tried to sound casual. 'Sometimes the local healers know so much more about plants and animals in the area. Although we've never encountered this particular species before, it's a good bet the villagers have and the local healer probably knows exactly what to do to extract the poi—' She broke off and hastily changed her description. 'Venom.'

Lara drove the car up the twisting road to the inn on the edge of town. It faced the forest with its long porch and inviting balconies. She parked as close to the stairs as she could get and raced around to help Gerald get Terry out.

Shadows lengthened and grew as the clouds overhead thickened with the threat of snow. The wind howled and the trees swayed and rustled in protest. Lara glanced around her with sharp, wary eyes as she opened the door to the back seat and reached inside for Terry.

'I'll come back for the snake heads to show the innkeeper. Don't touch them,' she cautioned.

Terry was nearly deadweight as he hung between them. Gerald had to practically carry him as they stumbled through the snow. The walkway was clear, but they took a shortcut, tramping across the front slope to get to the porch faster.

A tall, dark-haired man opened the door for them and reached to help. Even under the dire circumstances, Lara found him handsome, compelling even.

'Don't get the blood on you,' she warned. 'It's highly venomous.'

The dark-haired man's gaze swept up to her face and froze, locking on her. For one moment there was shocked recognition in his eyes and then it was gone as he got his shoulder under Terry to relieve her of the weight.

Lara whirled around, back toward the car. 'Get him inside and ask the innkeeper to find a healer. I'll get the snake heads.'

She rushed back down the steps, crossing the distance to the car in a run. As she yanked open the door, her birthmark, the one shaped like a dragon, began to burn hot against her skin.

There was only one thing that brought forth the dragon's warning. Vampire. And he had to be close. She closed the door and looked carefully around her, one hand sliding beneath her thick red cloak to find the knife on her belt.

tion of a dangerously influential admirer. He's pursuing the elementally gifted beauty for his own wicked purpose. And he's willing to go to deadly lengths to make it happen.

Safe Harbour

One of seven daughters in a line of extraordinary women, Hannah Drake has been the elusive object of affection for Jonas Harrington for as long as the young man can remember. If only the stunning super-model was driven by a passion other than her career. But Jonas isn't the only one with desires for Hannah.

From the shadows has emerged a vengeful figure who stalks the beauty with one terrifying purpose: to strip her of all she is and destroy her. Only one man was destined as her protector. Now, out of a storm of danger, Jonas must guide the woman he loves from a sinister darkness that threatens not only Hannah, but the entire Drake family.

D0696542

My Lady

in Time

Angie Ray

JOVE BOOKS, NEW YORK

TIME PASSAGES is a registered trademark of Berkley Publishing
Corporation.

MY LADY IN TIME

A Jove Book / published by arrangement with
the author

PRINTING HISTORY
Jove edition / February 1998

The Putnam Berkley World Wide Web site address is
http://www.berkley.com

ISBN: 0-515-12227-0

A JOVE BOOK®
Jove Books are published by The Berkley Publishing Group, a member of
Penguin Putnam Inc.,
200 Madison Avenue, New York, New York 10016.
JOVE and the "J" design are trademarks
belonging to Jove Publications, Inc.

PRINTED IN THE UNITED STATES OF AMERICA

10 9 8 7 6 5 4 3 2 1

*For Dan and Mike and Jeff and Millie
I never suspected when we were kids
that you could grow up to be so great.
I love you.*

*And with many thanks to:
Sandra (Paul) Chvostal
Barbara Benedict
Colleen Adams
Vickie (Bruce) Bashore
and Jeanette Baker*

*Your support, wisdom, enthusiasm, friendship,
and restraint in not using the "B" word when critiquing
have meant a lot to me.*

My Lady

in Time

Chapter 1

DEREK SINCLAIR STOOD back in the shadows where the lights from the house and pool area couldn't reach him and seriously considered lighting a cigarette.

Oh, he knew that to do so would draw the wrath of the well-dressed, well-heeled, well-bred crowd attending the Sinclair Import/Export Company's private and very exclusive dinner party. Simex Co., always a health-conscious employer, had hired only nonsmokers since its inception—even before most of the cities in Southern California had prohibited smoking in the workplace. The guests—all of whom spent a good part of their six-figure incomes on making sure that they had the healthiest, most perfect bodies money could buy—would be outraged if he polluted even a small portion of their smoggy oxygen supply with cigarette smoke. Charles would be especially pissed off.

Derek stared across the dark lawn to where his older brother was standing at the far end of the pool. Charles Sinclair, president and C.E.O. of Simex Co. since their father's death, had been dubbed "The Terminator" by some of the former employees whose companies he had acquired. He was one of the most respected—and most feared—men in town.

A wry smile curled Derek's lips, and he reached into the pocket of his tux for his pack of cigarettes. It would do Charles good to be pissed off. Big Brother was always too much in control.

He flicked a match against a tree trunk, the smell of sulphur biting his nostrils. As the small light flared, he saw Charles turn slightly.

Automatically Derek drew back farther into the shadows of the pine trees. As much as it might benefit Charles to be pissed off, it wouldn't do Derek any good at all. He'd already had one run-in with his brother this evening—all over a harmless flirtation with the wife of a potential investor. Lynette White, a bosomy redhead, had a reputation for knowing her husband's employees—at least the young male ones—better than he did. Derek had been about to ask her if she would like to dance when Charles had intervened, telling Lynette in his Perfect Host voice that her husband was looking for her. At the same time, he'd directed a Terminator stare at Derek.

Lighting the cigarette, Derek inhaled deeply, drawing the pungent, soothing smoke into his lungs. He'd learned long ago that caution was the better part of valor as far as dealing with Charles was concerned. He'd slipped away while Charles was escorting Lynette to her husband, and he'd just as soon avoid him for the rest of the evening.

As if Charles had heard Derek's thought, he frowned and looked around.

Shit. Derek froze, the cigarette dangling from his lips, as the cold gray gaze searched the shadows where he was standing, then continued on without giving any sign of seeing anyone hidden there.

Derek exhaled on a long sigh. Smoke swirling around his face, he took a step backward—only to bump into something warm and soft.

"Oh!" a breathless voice exclaimed.

Turning, he automatically reached out to steady Lynette White, who was teetering on her four-inch spiked heels. "I beg your pardon," he said, his gaze irresistibly drawn to the front of her low-cut, gold lamé dress. "I hope I didn't hurt you."

"Oh, don't apologize," she said in that same breathy voice, her lashes fluttering up at him. "It was my fault. I wasn't looking where I was going. I wanted to see the horses and someone said I should go this way to the stables. I love horses."

Derek didn't comment on the fact that she'd chosen a tortuous and shadowy route to her destination. Nor did he ask how she'd managed to escape from her husband's zealous guard. He merely tapped the ashes from his cigarette, his gaze traveling from her big hair to her big breasts. "Do you?"

"Mmm-hmm. I've heard all about the famous Sinclair studs." She turned, her breasts brushing against his arm, and smiled up at him. "I'd love to take a tour."

Derek considered the invitation in her eyes and hesitated for a fraction of a second. He thought about Mr. White and his reputation as a jealous maniac. He thought about Charles and his innumerable warnings and threats. He thought about the potential deal the two men were negotiating.

And then he dismissed them. In his opinion, husbands, brothers, and business should never interfere with pleasure.

He dropped his cigarette and ground it out with his heel. "I'd be delighted to serve as your tour guide," he said, offering her his arm.

Her lashes swept down, a catlike smile curving her lips, and she placed her long, French-manicured nails on his sleeve. Pressing close against him, she allowed him to lead her down a rose-bordered path to a long, low building a short distance away.

The shadowy stable was another world—a very different world from the perfumed, noisy, glittering one outside by the pool. Here, everything was dimly lit and quiet—except for a few shifting hooves, swishing tails, and muffled snorts from the animals. The smells were different, too—horse and manure and hay. The odor was a bit strong and not exactly conducive to romance, but Lynette didn't seem to mind, although her nose did wrinkle as she stared around the stable.

As if sensing her disdain, one of the Thoroughbreds snorted loudly right behind her. Looking nervously over her shoulder, she teetered on her high heels again and clutched Derek's arm.

"Perhaps you would like to see the trophy room," he said smoothly, guiding her to a door at the back of the stables.

"Oh, yes," she said with obvious relief.

Derek opened the door and flipped a switch. The light here was much brighter than in the stables and illuminated the gold and silver medallions, plates, and trophies that lined all four walls.

Lynette gasped. "Are these yours?"

Derek glanced around at the glass cases enclosing the trophies. There was no sign of the one fourth-place ribbon he'd won in dressage when he was eight years old. His father had barely spared it a glance while admiring Charles's gold first-place trophy. "Nope. They all belong to Charles."

She seemed mesmerized by the gold and silver. "They must be worth a fortune."

"Very likely." Bored, suddenly, he flipped off the switch and stepped back into the dimly lit stables. "Come on, we'd better get back to the party."

"Wait!" She put her hand on his arm again and pouted seductively. "Surely, there's no rush."

She stood very close to him. The heavy musk of her perfume obliterated even the strong earthy odors of the stable. He felt the curve of her breast pressing against his arm, and his body reacted automatically. His boredom faded as quickly as it had bloomed. "I suppose not," he said.

Her mouth curved sensually. "You must have trophies of a different nature." She moved in front of him and slipped her arms around his neck.

"That's true." Her lips beckoned and he focused his gaze on them. Lowering his head, he murmured, "I'm an expert at one sport in particular. . . ."

But before he could demonstrate exactly how expert, a querulous voice called from outside the stable, "Lynette? Lynette? Are you in there?"

Lynette snatched her arms from around Derek's neck and

stepped back, her smile changing into a disgruntled scowl as she turned to face the bent old man who appeared in the doorway. Derek's smile faded, too, when he saw the tall, dark figure standing behind the old man.

"Here she is, Mr. White," Charles said, his level gaze focused on Derek. "I told you there was no cause for alarm."

"That's a matter of opinion." His eyes sharp and suspicious, the old man glanced back and forth between Derek and Lynette. "I didn't expect to find my wife with your brother. *Again*."

"I'm certain he was only showing her the stables," Charles said. "Weren't you, Derek?"

"Yes, of course," Derek lied smoothly. "Mrs. White expressed an interest in seeing the Thoroughbreds."

Mr. White's forehead creased into a thousand fierce wrinkles. "Lynette hates horses."

"You're mistaken, Gerald," Lynette said, smoothing her dress down over her hips. "I adore them."

A few hundred more wrinkles appeared on Mr. White's forehead. "No, you don't. I distinctly remember you saying you thought they were the smelliest, stupidest animals alive after you fell off the pony ride—"

"That was only because I was angry." She smiled, but it didn't reach her eyes. "I really do love horses."

"Hmmph." His lips pinched, the old man turned abruptly to Charles. "After considering the matter, I've decided that I don't wish to invest in your company. Come along, my dear," he said to Lynette. "I think it's time we left."

"Yes, Gerald," she murmured. She cast a longing look at Derek as her husband, clutching her tightly around the waist, dragged her off.

Derek, aware of his brother's gaze still on him, turned toward one of the stalls. Black Sin, an ebony stallion, snorted softly. "That was unfortunate."

"Unfortunate?" Charles's voice was steely. "White's investment was critical for our expansion plans. His withdrawal means a setback of at least several months. I would say it's more than *unfortunate*."

Derek stroked the stallion's neck. "I had no idea he was so important."

"You might have realized it if you had attended the board meeting last week where the expansion plans were discussed."

With a crooked smile, Derek glanced at his brother. "Was there a board meeting? I must have forgotten."

"Did you also forget that you promised to escort Eleanor to the party this evening?"

"Actually, I don't remember promising any such thing. I remember you making a statement that I would escort Eleanor, but I never agreed to do so. So you see, I'm quite innocent of abandoning the poor girl."

Charles's eyes grew colder. "That 'poor girl' is your fiancée. I doubt she would be very happy to find you flirting with a redheaded bimbo."

Derek's easy smile didn't falter. "Did you propose for me, big brother?"

"Don't be ridiculous," Charles snapped.

"Then as far as I'm aware, Eleanor and I are not engaged," Derek said.

Charles stepped closer. Although only an inch or two taller, and barely three years older, he could, on occasion, be quite intimidating. Derek maintained his calm facade, but it was more difficult than he liked to admit—even to himself.

When Charles spoke, his voice was low and menacing. "We discussed this, Derek. We agreed that you need to settle down and be more responsible. You also agreed that marriage to Eleanor would be ideal."

"Did I?"

Charles focused a familiar stare on him. "Yes, you did. Dammit, you're not going to talk your way out of this one the way you usually do. I'm fed up with having to drag you out of messes like that one last year—"

"I told you," Derek interrupted. "There was no way that baby was mine. The blood test proved—"

"I don't care what the blood test proved. The lawyers cost a fortune, the papers had a field day, and the bad publicity soured the New Morality, Inc., deal for us—"

"If it's publicity you're worried about, it's probably better that we didn't do business with them—remember the baby turned out to be the boss's and the woman ended up claiming sexual harassment? The women's groups were all in an uproar. They boycotted everyone involved with New Morality, Inc.—"

"That's not the point, and you know it. The point is you've caused more trouble for Simex Co. than you're worth. Sooner or later, you're going to ruin us, and I'll be damned if I'm going to sit around and wait for that to happen. You'll propose to Eleanor tonight, or else . . ."

"Or else what?" Derek asked flippantly. "You'll ground me?"

"No," Charles said, his face colder than any futuristic android's. "I'll fire you."

Derek's smile slipped. He knew his job at Simex had been created for him because he was one of the family; and he knew that any Joe Blow off the street could wine and dine and play golf with the company clients just as well as he could. The job was a dream—all play, no work—and the money wasn't bad, either. True, he got a little bored at times, but he could usually find some way to amuse himself. At least he wasn't a company drone like Charles. Derek wanted to enjoy life. Marriage, with all its attendant responsibilities, was not the way to do it. Especially not marriage with Eleanor—a nice enough woman, but a touch too bossy for his tastes. Too much like Charles, as a matter of fact.

"Well?" Charles demanded. His gaze was like a narrow beam of red light aimed at Derek's forehead.

"Has it ever occurred to you that she might not agree to marry me?" Derek asked.

"You needn't worry about that. Eleanor is ambitious—she will see the benefits of marrying into the family."

Was that supposed to be an inducement? Stalling for time, Derek said, "Maybe you're right, maybe this marriage would be a good idea. Unfortunately, there's a problem."

"A problem? What kind of problem?"

"An insurmountable problem." Derek scrambled to think of one. "Eleanor is in love with someone else."

Charles snorted. "Eleanor in love?" he scoffed. "I don't believe it. With whom?"

Derek cast about in his mind for some likely candidate. No one strong-willed enough to deal with Eleanor occurred to him. Except, perhaps, for . . .

"You, of course," he said blandly.

Charles's eyes widened an infinitesimal amount—a huge display of emotion for him. "You're crazy—"

"No, you are." Derek took his last cigarette from his pocket and stuck it between his lips, although he didn't light it. "Haven't you ever noticed the way her eyes follow you?"

"No, I haven't. You're making this up." Charles made no comment about the cigarette—the only sign that Derek's comment had thrown him for a loop. "I have to get back to our guests—and so do you. We'll continue this discussion after the party."

"I would like to," Derek said. "But I was just about to leave. I promised Mrs. Jabrowski that I would run those papers over to her house tonight."

Charles's eyebrows snapped together. "She can wait until tomorrow."

"Do you think that's wise?" Derek arranged his features in an expression of concern. "You know how she is. She likes to feel the upper echelons of the company are catering to her whims. You know that, Chuck."

"Don't call me Chuck. I'll run the papers over to Mrs. Jabrowski myself as soon as the party is over. As for you . . . I've changed my mind. Stay away from the party. I don't want you causing any more trouble. You can spend the night at Nan's."

"At Nan's?" Derek arched an eyebrow. "Don't you think I'm a little old for a baby-sitter?"

"That doesn't alter the fact that you need one," Charles said rudely. "But that's not why I want you to stay there. I spoke to her today and she wasn't feeling well. She wants someone to stay with her. I was going to ask Eleanor, but you'll do just as well."

"I'm sorry, I can't. I have a date tonight," Derek said, mentally reviewing the names in his address book. Perhaps

Samantha—no, he'd never been able to get to first base with her. Maybe Karen—yeah, Karen was always up for a good time. Or maybe he could even try Lynette. . . .

"Dammit, Derek, can't you even show a little concern for the woman that practically raised us? Must you always be so selfish?"

Derek's eyes narrowed. Then he laughed, although there wasn't much amusement in the sound. "You sound just like Dad. He'd be real proud of you, Chuck. Fine, I'll stay at Nan's cottage. I'm fond of the old lady."

"Thank you."

Charles was always gracious when he got his way, Derek thought, watching his brother stride away. But at least he'd forgotten about Eleanor—

Charles paused at the door of the stables and turned back. "Oh, and by the way—you're not going to weasel out of this marriage, Derek. We'll discuss the matter tomorrow in my office at ten o'clock sharp. I suggest you be there."

Derek, hiding his chagrin, nodded affably.

As soon as his brother's back was turned, however, Derek's smile vanished. Damn Charles and his infernal persistence. Even the real Terminator had never pursued its goal with such single-minded determination.

"Your brother sounds serious," a voice said from behind him.

A bit startled, Derek turned to see a slightly stooped figure with a broom in his hands, barely visible in the shadows. It was Ray Guise, stablehand for the Sinclairs ever since Derek could remember. The old man was blind, but his blindness had never prevented him from doing his job. He had an extraordinary ability to croon to a recalcitrant stallion or a restive mare and have either one eating out of his hand within minutes.

Derek tossed his unlit cigarette aside. "Charles is used to having his own way," he said a trifle bitterly.

Ray smiled. "Not unlike his brother."

Derek glanced at the old man sharply, then laughed. "You're right about that."

"It's a shame you should have to waste your night visiting a sick woman," Ray said casually, stroking his thin silver mustache. "How about I go and check on her for you?"

"I thought she'd forbidden you ever to set foot in her house again."

Ray shrugged. "She was upset because she caught me flirting with Debbie Zangan."

Derek's brows rose. Deborah Zangan was the 80-year-old chairwoman for the local Friends of the Philharmonic Orchestra. "And Nan objected?"

"Of course," Ray said. His sightless blue eyes narrowed. "Someday she'll learn she can't have everything."

Derek bit back a smile. For two senior citizens, Ray and Nan had the most volatile relationship he'd ever seen. "I'd better do it myself," he said, leading Black Sin out of the stall. "Charles might decide to check up on me to make sure I've obeyed his orders."

A few minutes later Derek was bent low against the stallion's neck, riding bareback across the rolling green lawn toward the small cottage at the far end of the estate.

Yeah, he would check on Nan himself. But once he'd done so, there was no reason why he couldn't call Lynette and ask her to meet him later at his apartment.

There was, after all, a limit to self-sacrifice.

"Nan?"

Derek tapped at the door more loudly, but still there was no response. He tried the doorknob and found it unlocked. "Dammit, Nan," he muttered under his breath. She'd be lucky if she didn't get robbed and murdered one of these days.

He opened the door and stepped inside. The tiny cottage was dark and quiet. "Nan?" he called out.

He groped for the light switch and flicked it on. Dim light filled the room. There was no sign of anyone. He headed for the door at the far end of the room and opened it a few inches. "Nan?"

"Derek?" a weak voice croaked.

"Nan!" He threw open the door, allowing a shaft of light

to stream through and illuminate the bed against the far wall. He strode forward to stare at the elderly white-haired woman huddled under a quilt. "Are you sick?"

She coughed, a weak, wheezing sound. "I'm fine," she gasped. "I've never been sick a day in my life."

Frowning, Derek studied the frail figure in the bed. He hadn't really believed Charles's story, but Nan definitely did not look well. Her hair, usually coiffed and sprayed into helmetlike perfection, lay limp and tangled against the pillow. Her skin had a slight grayish cast, and her lips looked dry and parched.

Unsure what to do, he grasped her hand. In spite of the warm spring night, her fingers felt cold and stiff. "Never?" he asked lightly, hiding his dismay. "I seem to remember you claiming sick headaches every day for a week."

She glared up at him. "I never claimed any such thing! That was the last of those silly women your father hired to be your nanny when he decided I was too old. You were horrible to her."

Derek smiled. "I was, wasn't I? But I don't regret it. Dad finally gave in and hired you back."

"Hmmph." He could see she was trying not to smile. "I actually was enjoying my retirement. It was very restful."

"Restful? Sounds boring to me."

The smile peeked out. "*You* might think so, but it wasn't. I had much more time for my spinning."

Derek glanced at the old spinning wheel in one corner of the room. It had two parts—the wheel which was mounted on a small three-legged bench, and an elaborately carved pole that had a mass of some fluffy fibers wrapped around the top. The wheel part sat crookedly, one leg that had been replaced a little shorter than the others. "Why don't you let me buy you a new wheel, Nan? I'm sure there are better ones available."

"I like this one. I've tried others and the thread is never quite as fine." Her voice took on a quavering note again. "Although I don't like it when it spins by itself."

Derek, about to tuck the blanket around her narrow shoulders, paused. "The spinning wheel turns by itself?"

She nodded. "Every night. Sometimes I can't sleep at all. I think that's why I'm not feeling well."

Derek stared down at her. "Perhaps I should take you to a doctor. I think you're sicker than you realize."

She grimaced, deep lines fanning out about her eyes. "I don't like doctors. But you may be right—maybe I am sick after all. Will you stay here tonight in case I need you?"

Shit. Derek thrust his hands into the pockets of his pants. He really had not intended to stay for the whole night. He had plans for the evening—plans that involved a particular big-breasted redhead. "I'm terrible in sickrooms, Nan. I wouldn't know what to do if you needed help. Why don't you let me get someone else—like Ray. He offered to sit with you."

"Ray!" Nan half sat up in bed, and a flush rose in her cheeks. "I wouldn't have that lying, cheating muckraker in my house for all the wool in Tibet!"

"All right, Nan." Alarmed by her vehemence, Derek pushed her gently back against the pillow. "It was just a suggestion. What have you got against him, anyway?"

"Hmmph." She lay back down, but the flush remained in her cheeks. "He's only interested in his own selfish pleasure. He's been that way ever since I met him, and I have no intention of dying an old maid because of his fear of commitment. If he doesn't settle down and ask me to marry him soon, I'm going to find another man who will."

"Oh?" Derek's lips twitched. "I'm sure they'll be beating down the doors for you, Nan."

She looked at him a trifle suspiciously. "Hmmph. All men need to be married. Including you."

"I'm not getting married any time soon," he responded, a little more emphatically than necessary.

Nan frowned. "Why not? What have you got against marriage?"

"Nothing at all." Except that he was really getting tired of the subject. "I'm only twenty-seven, Nan. Too young to settle down." He smiled, but he could see she still looked troubled.

"I worry about you. Your life seems so empty."

"What are you talking about? I'm busy all the time."

"Are you? Does that fill the emptiness?"

"Nan, I assure you, my life is not empty," he said firmly.

She made a harumphing noise, but she didn't argue anymore. "You'll stay with me, won't you, Derek?"

An image of Lynette's breasts flickered in his brain, then disappeared. "Okay," he said resignedly. "I'll stay."

She smiled. "Thank you, Derek. You may sleep on the sofa," she said. "Oh, and one more thing—"

"Yes?"

"Will you take the spinning wheel with you so it won't keep me awake?"

"Yeah, sure."

"Thank you, Derek." Her voice grew fainter. "You're very sweet . . . you always were a good boy. . . ."

She drifted off to sleep, and he stood by the bed a moment, staring down at her.

You always were a good boy.

With a shake of his head, he crossed over to the spinning wheel. Taking care not to break the delicate thread that connected the two parts, he picked up the pole with one hand and the wheel with the other. He carried them into the other room, wondering why she alone had never seemed aware of his numerous faults.

She should talk to Charles. Big Brother would soon set her straight.

Derek set the wheel down in the corner by the linen closet, pricking the palm of his hand on the spindle as he did so. Cursing, he sucked on the spot as he wandered over to the hideous purple and green plaid couch.

He studied its sagging cushions with a jaundiced eye. He knew that Nan was very proud of the fact that she had purchased it at a swap meet and reupholstered it herself. As a prospective bed, though, it had its drawbacks.

Sighing, he gathered sheets and a pillow from the linen closet and made up the couch. His tux was covered with horse hair, he noticed as he stripped down to his boxer shorts. It would never be the same, he thought wryly.

He turned off the light and lay down, but the couch was a good six inches too short for his six-foot frame. He twisted and turned, trying to get comfortable. Finding a halfway tolerable position, he closed his eyes. He was actually more tired than he'd realized. A full night's rest might not be a bad thing after all. And the dark silence of Nan's cottage was rather soothing—

A sound like a motorcycle revving its engine echoed through the room.

His eyes snapped open and he half sat up on the sofa.

The raucous sound came again from the direction of Nan's room. Derek's mouth curved and he lay back down. How could he have forgotten? She'd always been a ferocious snorer. Sometimes when he'd had trouble sleeping as a child, he'd crept downstairs to her tiny room by the kitchen and laid down on the floor by her door. The sound of her snoring had instantly put him to sleep. It had been a comfort to him.

Closing his eyes, he listened to the noise for several minutes. Strange how it wasn't as soporific as when he was a child. He'd grown accustomed to silence while he slept. Silence and the comfort of a warm female body curled up next to him.

Your life seems so empty.

He shifted on the couch. Turning over, he punched the cushion. His life wasn't empty. He had everything. Money, women, and a red '65 Ford Mustang. What more could a man want?

A cigarette, maybe. Yes, definitely a cigarette. He wished he hadn't thrown his last one away in the stables. That had been a stupid thing to do. He should have put it back in the pack if he wasn't going to smoke it.

He turned on his side and closed his eyes again. But the wanting was changing into craving and the craving into desperate need. How could he possibly go to sleep without a cigarette?

Abruptly he rose to his feet. He groped through the darkness to the bathroom, where a pink shell nightlight glowed softly. Looking in the medicine chest, he found some sleeping pills. The date on the bottle had expired, but he swallowed a couple anyway.

Back on the couch, he stared up through the darkness at the ceiling, waiting for the pills to take effect.

After several long minutes of painful wakefulness, he got up again, made his way to the tiny kitchenette, and opened the refrigerator door. A bright shaft of light streamed out of it, nearly blinding him. Blinking, he peered in at the contents.

Rabbit food. Lettuce and tomatoes and carrots, but no sign of what he was searching for. He was about to close the door when he spied two bottles in the back. Sighing in relief, he pulled one out. Nan almost always had some homemade strawberry liqueur on hand. It wasn't whiskey, but it should at least alleviate the discomfort of the couch. He poured the liqueur into a glass and quickly drained the sugary-sweet wine.

A warm, pleasant glow enveloped him. Surprised, he stared at the innocent-looking bottle. It packed quite a wallop. Either that, or the sleeping pills had suddenly kicked in.

He poured another glass. Charles wouldn't approve of his methods, he thought a trifle fuzzily, but hell, Charles disapproved of everything he did.

Too bad he'd never been able to fool his father or Charles the way he had Nan. They had always seen through him, to every weakness, every flaw, every fear. He had tried to measure up, but somehow he'd never quite been able to.

He drained the second glass of liqueur even more quickly than the first. The glow became a haze.

He stumbled a little as he made his way back to the couch and sat down. Hell, he didn't care what they thought of him. Dad was dead, and as for Charles—Derek was damned if he was going to marry anyone just to please his uptight brother. He didn't care about the job. He didn't care about anything or anyone. Except—as Charles so often reminded him—himself. . . .

A soft whirring noise, barely discernable between the muted roar of Nan's snores, interrupted his rambling thoughts. He frowned. His brain was spinning, just like Nan's wheel.

The whirring grew louder. And faster. It wasn't inside his head, he decided. It was coming from somewhere else. It almost sounded like . . .

Slowly he turned.

A soft shimmer lit up the dark corner by the linen cupboard. The spinning wheel turned quickly, propelled by the woman sitting there.

The *glowing* woman sitting there.

Chapter 2

GLITTERING IN THE radiant light that surrounded her, she wore a long blue dress that fitted tightly against her full breasts. Golden hair rippled down her back, the strands held back from her face by a thin gold band and partially concealed by a transparent veil. Her profile was composed of a squarish jaw, a small straight nose, and downswept thick dark lashes. At her throat was a pendant, and slung low across her hips a jeweled belt with a key ring on it. One slender hand, almost hidden by the voluminous sleeves of her dress, spun the wheel while the other twisted a thread of bright, blinding gold.

He blinked, but the vision did not disappear.

She turned, her lashes lifting until he found himself staring into a shadowed pair of midnight blue eyes. Her image wavered for a moment and he held his breath. Was he dreaming?

"My lord," she said in a soft, sweet voice, the motion of her fingers never ceasing. "I am Lady Allison of Pelsworth Castle. If you will do a small favor for me, I will reward you richly."

His ears perked up. Reward him richly? His gaze swept

over her again, lingering on her round breasts. God, this was too good to be true—a dream where he was going to have great sex. "Are you a dream?" he asked, a trifle hazily.

"No, I'm a ghost."

Her response sounded a bit clipped. He looked up to see the red lips were smiling. But—was it his imagination?—the blue eyes seemed to be snapping.

"Sorry." Ghost, dream, what did it matter? He was damn well going to enjoy himself. He smiled his best smile at her, the one that Nan—or any other woman for that matter—had never been able to resist. "I've never met such a beautiful ghost before."

Her fingers fumbled on the string a moment, then quickly recovered. She smiled back. "Will you help me, kind sir?"

He sat up on the couch, the action making his head spin. He waited for the whirling to stop before he asked, "Help you how?"

"'Tis rather a long story." She glanced down at the thread. "I married a man I didn't love."

"Marriage sucks," Derek said earnestly, thinking of Eleanor . . . and Lynette.

"Sucks?" The ghost frowned. "I am not familiar with this usage, but from your tone I gather that you do not think highly of marriage. I must agree."

"Why did you marry this guy then?"

"I . . . because of my father. It seemed a good match at the time."

Her father had forced her into it, Derek guessed, reading between the lines. He nodded in sympathy.

"My marriage was not a happy one," she continued. "Wilfred was a small, weak man, not worthy of his title. He lost the king's favor and all that my family spent hundreds of years building." She stopped the wheel and fingered the gold thread. "Death, when it came to me, was almost a relief."

Derek shifted uncomfortably on the couch. She sounded so tragic. What kind of dream was this anyway? He wanted to get to the sex part. But apparently, he was going to have to play along if he wanted to get to the good stuff. "That's very sad, but it must have happened"—he glanced at her strange dress—"a long time ago. How could I help you?"

"I am determined to change the past." She looked at him directly. "I seek a chivalrous gentleman to agree to go back in time."

Derek almost laughed. "Oh, is that all?"

She nodded.

She actually seemed serious. "What could a 'chivalrous gentleman' do once he was there?"

"Prevent my marriage to Wilfred, of course. Then he will not have a chance to ruin the castle."

"Sounds like a good plan," Derek said. Actually, he thought the idea sounded half-baked. Even if the marriage could be prevented, how could she be sure the fate of the castle would be changed? "But what if it wasn't Wilfred's fault? What if you still lose the castle?"

"That will not happen. I will wait for my True Love. He will come soon. After I married Wilfred, I met a knight, Sir Boris. He is my sweetest, most perfect knight. He is brave, courageous, chivalrous, and he worships the ground I walk on."

"He does?" Dudley Do-Right in armor, Derek deduced. Everything was becoming clear now—she had a lover. The castle was just an excuse to dump this Wilfred guy.

She nodded. "Yes, he does. I believe he may be my True Love. If I marry him, then I am certain we will live happily and all will be well with the castle."

"Yeah, right." Sounded like she was in for a major dose of disillusionment. "I still don't see how I could prevent your marriage to Wilfred."

"By announcing to my father that *you* are my True Love."

Derek stared at her uneasily. He didn't want to say something so stupid even to a dream woman who promised him great sex. "How would that help?"

"There is a family legend that says the Pelsworths must marry only our one True Love. My father is . . . very superstitious. If he believes you might be my True Love, he will not allow me to marry Wilfred."

"But surely your father wouldn't believe a complete stranger was your True Love."

"You must say you had a vision—that an angel told you to remind him of the promise he made to her on her deathbed. He will believe you then, and he will not sign the betrothal papers. Wilfred's nature is such that he will perceive this as a great insult, and I am certain he will withdraw his offer."

"He sounds like a real wimp."

"A wimp? What is that, pray tell?"

"Never mind." This dream was getting weirder and weirder. "How would I travel through time?"

"I need only bring you onto my plane of existence. Then it is a simple matter to take you to the past."

"Your plane of existence? But you said you were a ghost. Are you saying I would have to be *dead*?"

She shook her head. "No, no. A dead man is of no use to me. I can send you back while you are asleep."

"I see." Traveling through time while asleep sounded a helluva lot better than doing it dead. Especially since he was already asleep. "And would I return the same way?"

"No, that would not be possible." She touched a pendant at her throat. "I will give you this magic emerald, however. It can transport you back through time. As your reward, I will let you keep it."

He glanced at the jewel, then looked again. The dark green stone glowed with a curious brilliance as if a fire burned in the heart of it. Unable to look away, he stared at the emerald. It glowed brighter, almost as if it were alive. As if it were trying to tell him something.

He tore his gaze away. "What year are we talking about here?"

She gave the wheel a spin and started twisting the thread again. "The year of our Lord 1498."

"Fourteen-ninety-eight! That's over five hundred years ago! That's practically the Stone Age. I'll bet people were still living in caves."

She stiffened. "We most certainly were not! We lived in castles and fine houses, not these little hovels." She glanced around the room disdainfully. " 'Twas a wonderful time, full of gaiety and excitement. We had festivals and holidays every month, with dancing and games. We rode and hunted and hawked and there were magnificent feasts and jugglers and troubadours. We had beautiful books with beautiful pictures and the most wondrous stories imaginable."

"I didn't think anyone could read back then," he said, admiring the sparkle of her eyes, the slight flush in her cheeks, the rise and fall of her breasts as she spoke passionately about all this "excitement" of the past—most of which sounded like pretty dull stuff.

"That only shows your ignorance. Many nobles were well educated. And my grandparents, who were lord and lady of Pelsworth Castle when I was a child, allowed the priest to teach reading to any that desired to learn. They were brave and kind and good. I lived like a princess. Grandmama let me sit next to her at tournaments and give my favor to the knights. Everything was perfect. We had no troubles, no worries. Everyone was so happy—"

She broke off, biting her lip. He watched, fascinated by the way her small white teeth pressed into the lush redness and the way her slim dark brows drew together. A tiny wrinkle marred the smoothness of her forehead. Then the wrinkle disappeared and she smiled, looking directly at him. Her eyes were so dark a blue, they'd probably appear black when she was making love. . . .

"Men were chivalrous and honorable. They would never deny a lady's request. A man would die for his honor and for the love of his lady."

Her last words jarred him from his pleasant fantasy.

Love and honor.

Not exactly his two strong suits.

His lips twisted. She was looking at him expectantly, he saw. The way Charles and their father had looked at him when asking him to attempt some impossible feat. He'd seen that look often—and the way it changed into disappointment when he failed.

Suddenly he felt very tired. He was beginning to suspect that this was one of those trick dreams, where you thought you were going to have sex but something kept preventing it. He pressed his fist against his forehead.

"My lord?" The wheel slowed and her fingers grew still. "Please, my lord, will you not help me?"

Derek stared into her pleading eyes for a long moment before shaking his head, "I'm sorry, sweetheart, but I'm not playing along any longer. I'm not the hero type."

She held out a hand to him. "Please, my lord! Is there aught else you want? Perhaps more jewels? I can arrange that—"

Shaking his head again, he lay back on the couch, trying to stifle a yawn, his eyelids drooping. She didn't understand that he was on to her. She wasn't going to have sex with him. When she found out he couldn't help her, she would leave him high and dry. "Sorry. Jewels don't tempt me."

"Then what *would* tempt you?"

The edge in her voice pierced his daze enough to make him open his eyes again. She had risen from the spinning wheel to stare at him, determination written all over her face. He groaned silently. He really was tired, and she didn't seem like the type to give up easily. He didn't want to spend all night arguing with her.

"Listen, unless I get my 'reward' right now, I'm going to sleep. And I'm not talking about any stupid jewels."

She drew back, the sparkle fading from her eyes. "Then what do you want?" she asked coldly.

"What do you think?" he asked impatiently.

"A kiss?" she said hesitantly.

He laughed. "Yeah, right." He glanced at her tight expression. "No? Ah, well." He yawned again. "I hope you will excuse me then, my lady ghost, but it's late and I'm tired. It was a pleasure meeting you."

His eyes drifted closed, shutting out the view of her outraged face. A few seconds later he was fast asleep.

Clenching her fists, Allison crossed the room to glare down at the man lying on the strange piece of furniture, no longer bothering to hide her anger and disgust. What impudence! She would sooner kiss a wild boar than this drunken sot.

He obviously had no idea how to behave with a lady. He'd made no apology for his unshaven, undressed appearance. Perhaps he'd thought to impress her with his manly form, but there was little in his long, lean frame to be impressed by. He did not have the powerfully muscled arms and barrel-like chest of a knight—he looked more like a scholar or a priest. Or at least he would have if it weren't for the impertinent gleam in his eyes.

How she had kept her temper with his bold gaze, she did not know. 'Twas obvious he was no stranger to women. She would never even have considered asking such a blatant rogue for help, if she weren't so desperate. . . .

But she was desperate.

Restlessly she paced around the room. Over five hundred years desperate. In all that time she'd never been able to find anyone to agree to her request. And she was determined—yes, determined—that this time she would not fail. Even if she had to kiss a drunken, snoring sot.

She stopped at the spinning wheel and sat down. Setting the wheel into a spin, she twisted a gold thread. The familiar motion of the fibers gliding through her fingers soothed her anger and helped her think more clearly.

It wasn't as if she had never kissed such a one. In truth, she had experienced much worse—marriage to Wilfred had been full of foul, slobbering kisses and other painful intimacies. And even though she had sworn never to subject herself to such shame again, she could not pass up this opportunity.

After all, opportunities did not come along very often—only every hundred years or so. There had been the man with the ruff around his neck. He'd agreed to help after he'd fought some "armada," but he'd never returned. And there'd been the man in the bright scarlet uniform who had promised to help her as soon as he got back from "putting down those upstart Colonials," only he had never returned, either. Then there'd been the man who'd gone off to fight the "Nazis." At least his spirit had had the courtesy to stop by and apologize for letting her down.

That last one had been over sixty years ago. She did not mean to wait that long again. Too much was at stake. Much more than her own happiness.

For a moment her fingers faltered on the thread as she remembered that last horrible day, when the soldiers had attacked. The pounding footsteps, the echoing screams, the smoke of burning buildings, the clank of swords and armor. The bitter taste of blood and betrayal. All had been lost—her life, her family's honor, the castle. . . .

No. Allison's fingers tightened on the golden thread. No. She would change what had happened. Whatever it took, no matter what indignity she must endure, she would see it changed.

Stopping the wheel, she stood up and approached the strange bed, to look at the man again.

Her gaze traveled over the sun-lightened cropped hair. She studied the way his lips curled upward even in sleep. 'Twas not an unpleasing face. There were no pockmarks from disease, no unsightly scars from battle, no worry lines from fear and anger and despair. He had the visage of a man who had led an easy life, with little or no responsibility.

This was the man she must rely on to save Pelsworth Castle?

She sighed. In truth, she could not afford to be particular. If 'twas a kiss he wanted, then a kiss he would have. She would give him a kiss that would befuddle his wits and leave him begging to do whatever she wanted.

If she could hide her revulsion.

She tightened her lips. She could. And she would. She had to.

Taking a deep breath, she set her chin firmly and bent down.

Chapter 3

LIPS SOFTER THAN down pressed against Derek's. He smiled in his sleep. What an incredibly pleasant dream. Her mouth felt so real. He parted his lips and licked hers.

He heard a slight gasp, but paid no attention. He wrapped his arms around her, hauling her down to sprawl on top of him. She gasped again, pulling back, and reluctantly he opened his eyes.

His breath caught.

Her hair streamed down around him in a fall of silvery-gold, like the "angel hair" Nan had used to decorate her room at Christmas when he was a child. He'd been fascinated by the silken threads of spun glass. She'd always warned him not to touch it, that it could cut. . . .

He grabbed a fistful of the shining hair in his hand.

A slow sigh escaped him. Nan had been wrong. It was soft. Softer than he would have believed possible.

Groaning, he pulled Allison sideways, turning so that she lay beneath him on the narrow couch, and plunged his tongue into her mouth. He felt her breasts pressed against his chest and the beating of her heart. He was momentarily confused. She was a ghost, wasn't she?

She felt so solid, so warm, so real in his arms. He could feel the slightly itchy wool of her dress, the tickling tresses of her hair, and the keys at her waist pressing against his hip. She smelled of cinnamon and cloves, and she tasted like wine and honey. Sweet. Spicy.

He knew she was a dream, an alcohol-induced hallucination, no doubt conjured up in his brain for some weird Freudian reason. But hell, that didn't mean he couldn't enjoy himself.

He leaned down to kiss her again, only to pause as she made a little gasping noise. Blinking, he tried to focus on her face.

Her dark blue eyes looked huge, wide with . . . dismay? Distrust? Fear? Before he could quite decide, her lashes swept down.

He frowned. "What's wrong?"

Her eyes flew open again. "Wrong? Nothing is wrong."

"Then why do you look like that?"

Her brow wrinkled. "Like what?"

"Like . . ." He pushed her hair away from her face, his fingers lingering in the silken strands. "Like a martyr about to be tortured."

Color rose in her cheeks. "I don't know what you mean."

"Don't you?"

"No." Her flush deepened. "I am not a harlot."

She sounded defensive, as though she expected him to argue with her. As if he would be so stupid. "Who said you were?" he asked. He took her hand and stroked her palm with his thumb. "After five hundred years, you deserve a little pleasure."

She turned her face away. "There's no pleasure in it," she said, a trifle bitterly.

Ah. So Wilfred had been a disappointment in bed. And her lover, Sir Boris, too, apparently. An odd anger filled Derek at the thought of wimpy Wilfred and boring Boris making clumsy love to Allison. "Wilfred and Boris ought to be shot."

She stiffened and her gaze flew back to his. "Why do you say that?"

"They caused you to exist for five hundred years thinking that sex is unpleasant." He brushed his knuckle against her cheek. Her skin was satiny soft. "If it had been me, you would have enjoyed it."

"You are very arrogant, my lord."

"Because I think I could have taught you to enjoy sex?" He kissed the soft hollow of her throat, caressing the delicate curve with his tongue.

"Because . . ." She appeared to be having difficulty speaking. "Because you seem to think that is the most important thing between a man and a woman."

"It is the most important thing." He traced his fingers down the soft wool of her dress to the narrow span of her waist and the curve of her hip. "Let me show you, Allie. Let me show you what you've missed. Let me show you how good it can feel."

Her eyes were wide and dark in her flushed face. "I don't even know you."

"What better way for a woman to know a man?" He moved his fingers back up to brush against the side of her breast. He heard her breath catch. The small sound sent the blood racing through his veins. He moved his hand to cover her breast.

"No," she gasped. "There's more than . . . than mere lust."

"Is there?" He caressed her breasts gently, watching the nipples swell under the fabric of her dress. "Like what?"

"I . . . there is trust. And respect and honor. And love."

He glanced up and saw the purity of her face, the innocent curve of her lips. An odd tightness squeezed inside his chest. "Love doesn't exist."

"I thought that, too." Her hands gripped his shoulders. "And I married a man I didn't love. It cost me everything. Now I know I should have waited. Love *does* exist."

"Perhaps in your time. In your world. But not here. Not now. I'm no knight in shining armor, Allie. I can't give you what you want. All I can give you is this. . . ."

He kissed her again, and this time Allison didn't try to pull away. She wanted to prove him wrong, to prevent him from making the same mistake she had . . . but of course she couldn't. She barely knew him. She could only give him this one kiss and hope that somehow, some way, it would make him understand.

Strangely, she felt no revulsion. His mouth was passionate, yet surprisingly gentle—nothing at all like the rough, brutish kisses she'd suffered five hundred years ago. In fact, this kiss was surprisingly pleasant.

Perhaps Derek Sinclair was not the complete cad she'd thought. Perhaps there was a good side to him. When she'd first seen him, drunk and crude, she'd had no remorse for not telling him everything. But now, a niggling guilt trickled through her. Perhaps she should tell him exactly what he would be facing. . . .

Her lips parted. But before she could say anything, his tongue slipped inside.

The impulse to speak faded rapidly. Sensation flowed from her mouth and spiraled lazily down through her body to her toes and back up again. She shivered with delight. How persuasive he was. How tempting.

His mouth nibbled at her throat and his fingers traced the neckline of her dress. She supposed she should stop him now. He'd had his kiss. But an odd languor was creeping over her, making it difficult to speak. She really didn't want him to stop. It felt too good.

He slipped his hand inside her dress and cupped her breast.

She gasped. His thumb brushed against her nipple, and suddenly the languor changed into a heat that expanded and swelled and made it difficult to think too clearly.

He pushed her skirt up her leg and fingered the knitted hose she wore. At her knee he traced her garter, teasing the soft skin around it. His mouth moved to the neckline of her gown, and his fingers moved up to her flanks and farther. . . .

The heat burst into flames. Arching her back, she pressed up against his mouth and hands. Kissing the upper curves of her breasts, he slipped his fingers between her thighs. The tension in her rose higher. "Please . . ."

"I will, Allie, I swear I will. I'll show you how to make the world explode with pleasure beyond imagining."

She could see his eyes, dark and intense, as he moved away from her for a moment to take off his strange-looking braies. Then he was above her again, kissing her forehead, her cheeks, and her neck.

"I'll show you what it's like to live for the moment and nothing else." He traced his tongue along the madly beating pulse in her throat. "I'll show you how to forget about Wilfred, your castle, about everything. . . . "

The words made no sense. Forget about what? Forget about her castle? Her castle? Her . . .

The castle. Dear heaven, *no!*

What was she doing? She had promised him a kiss, nothing more—

His lips moved to her mouth, kissing her even more deeply. His hands stroked and teased her breasts. His knee nudged apart her legs.

Her heart pounded. Heat poured through her. Good Lord, how could he do this to her? She'd never thought . . . she'd never dreamed . . . oh, she must keep her wits about her! She must remember her purpose . . . she must . . .

"My lord . . ." She made a slight gulping noise.

"Hush, Allie," he murmured, trailing kisses from her lips to her ear and back again. He took her hand in his, holding it tightly, his thumb caressing the palm in a soothing, circular motion. "I won't hurt you. I promise."

He lied. She knew he lied. And yet . . . "My lord!" she said, pulling her hand away and pushing at his chest.

Derek, hearing the protest in her voice, closed his eyes. Was she going to refuse him now, at this point? He didn't know if he could bear it if she did. He wanted her so much. He wanted her so much that he was shaking with it. "Yes?" he asked through clenched teeth, the blood pounding in his groin, sweat breaking out on his brow.

"Will you come?" she gasped.

His eyes flew open. He looked down into her face. Her eyes were black, as black as he'd thought they'd be, her mouth red and swollen from his kisses. Desire and relief flowed through him. He smiled. "Oh, yes," he whispered huskily. "I'll come."

He lowered his mouth to hers. Kissing her hungrily, passionately, he plunged forward.

Into nothingness.

Chapter 4

DEREK GAGGED. SITTING up on the pile of hay, he spit out a mouthful of straw and looked around in confusion.

What the devil had happened?

One second he was in Nan's cottage having a great dream, the next he was unpleasantly wide awake and . . . where?

He rubbed his forehead with his fist. Those pills and Nan's liqueur must have been stronger than he realized. He must have left her apartment, driven out to this barn, and passed out.

Damn. He should've been more careful about those pills. He'd meant to keep an eye on Nan. He hoped she was okay. He'd better get to a phone and call her. If he was in a barn, then there must be a house nearby. Only . . .

Reaching down to scratch where the straw was poking him in the ass, he caught sight of his hairy legs. His *naked* hairy legs. Where the hell were his clothes?

He peered around the barn—a shack really. Sunlight filtered through the chinks in the rough wooden planks and cast a soft glow over the piles of hay. An antique plow of some sort sat in one corner and a few rags lay in another, but he saw no sign of his shirt or pants.

Now what? No one in their right mind would let a naked

man into their house to use the phone. They were more likely to call the police.

Shit. If Charles got wind of this, Derek would be in serious trouble. He was going to have to come up with something to keep Big Brother from finding out.

His gaze fell on the pile of rags again. He stood up, only to nearly keel over. His head swam. Placing his hand against the wall for balance, he brushed the dusty straw off as best he could. Then, with slow shaky steps, he walked over to the corner. The rags were rough linen and none too clean—in fact, they stank—but they were better than nothing, he decided.

He had just managed to twist them into a sort of loincloth when he heard the pounding of hooves. Someone was coming, thank God. He wouldn't have to go searching for a telephone after all. He walked slowly to the door just as two horsemen rode up.

Two horsemen in armor, with shields and swords.

Derek gripped the doorframe, his brain reeling.

Wavering images flashed before him—Allison begging him to go back in time; Allison asking, *Will you come?* and his answer—*Oh, yes. I'll come.*

No. It couldn't be. There had to be some other explanation. Some logical explanation. He must still be asleep—

One of the couldn't-really-be-knights nudged his horse forward. For a moment, Derek's gaze rested on the yellow dun stallion. He'd never seen a breed quite like it. Similar to an Andalusian, it had a shortish muscular neck, strong shoulders and magnificent quarters, but he'd never seen an Andalusian as big as this—seventeen or eighteen hands at least.

He became aware of a sharp pain in his hand. Loosening his grip on the rough wood, he saw a splinter had pierced his palm. Automatically he plucked out the sliver of wood. Blood welled from the small wound.

Okay. Maybe he wasn't asleep. These guys must be actors.

The shorter man opened his mouth, revealing a row of crooked, brownish teeth, and asked a question, his voice harsh. Derek could barely understand the words, the accent and inflection were so strange.

"What art thou doing here, knave?" the man repeated more loudly. "Art thou a thief?"

The guy didn't sound like he was acting. Was someone playing a joke on him? Derek looked around, half expecting to see Phil, the practical joker from accounting, jump out from behind the bushes.

But there was no sign of Phil. Uneasily, Derek looked back at the two knights. They *looked* real. And so did the swords they were carrying. Very real. And very deadly.

Without conscious thought Derek said, "I'm here to speak to Lady Allison Pelsworth."

The two knights stared at him, apparently struck dumb by his words. Then they began talking to each other in low voices, glancing at him every so often. The second knight, taller than the first, but uglier, with his pitted face and greasy beard, appeared to be arguing with his companion. With his gauntleted hand, Greasy Beard made a slicing motion across his throat.

Uh-oh. Apparently he'd said the wrong thing.

Derek took a cautious step backward. Then another.

The men stopped arguing and looked at him. Greasy Beard put his hand on the hilt of his sword.

Derek turned tail and ran.

His heart pounding in his throat, he headed for the thick underbrush surrounding the small clearing. He heard a shout from the men behind him, then the thundering sound of horses' hooves.

The ground shook below his feet. Steel scraped along steel. The horses' hot breath blew on the back of his neck. Derek heard the whistle of wind as the sword descended.

The blade struck his back with the force of an airplane propeller, knocking him flat. Pain burned along his shoulders before his head hit a rock and everything went black.

When Derek came to, the world was upside down.

His head throbbing, he watched the dirt road bobbing above him for a few seconds. An upside down man walked along it, dressed in a long gown and carrying a staff and a bundle on his back. Upside-down children, playing along-side the road, stopped to point and stare as Derek passed.

He closed his eyes tightly. God, his head hurt. The rest of him hurt, too. His feet and his knees and the palms of his hands. And his back . . .

His eyes flew open. His back. Dear God, was he dead?

He craned his neck to look over his shoulder, but he really couldn't see anything. He was fairly certain he wasn't dead, though. Being dead wouldn't smell like horse, leather, and sweat. Judging from the dull throbbing of his back, Greasy Beard must have used the flat of the blade, not the point, to strike him. He was still alive.

He looked at the road again. The world wasn't upside down, he realized. *He* was.

He was alive all right . . . alive, trussed like a turkey, and slung facedown over the back of a horse of a smelly me-dieval knight.

Turning his face into the warm, rough hair of the horse's hindquarter, Derek groaned and closed his eyes again.

Drifting in and out of consciousness, he didn't open them again until he heard a shout.

He lifted one eyelid a crack. What he saw made him lift the other one, too.

They had reached a bridge which crossed a river, and there, on the other side, on a hill under a leaden bank of clouds, loomed a castle.

An upside-down castle, but still a castle.

Derek stared at the monstrosity. Massive gray stone walls loomed ominously at the end of the road. Towers, with nar-row slitlike windows, rose from four corners, reaching up toward the sky. The entire structure was surrounded by more stone walls as if warning off all who approached.

Even the sun seemed intimidated. It hid behind the clouds, not daring to send so much as one ray of sunshine to lighten the gloomy battlements. The only touches of color he could see at all were the blue and gold pennants above the towers—but they hung limply, forlornly, as if ashamed of their brightness amidst so much gray.

Derek had never seen anything so bleak, so *gloomy* in his entire life.

The knights joined the steady stream of humanity approaching the castle. Moving quickly to the side of the road, people watched the spectacle passing through their midst. Men stared and shook their heads. Women whispered and clutched their shawls. Children pointed and giggled. One small boy threw a dirt clod.

Derek barely felt the dirt showering down his back. The throbbing in his head had intensified, and he was seriously afraid he might vomit.

To his relief, he reached a gate in the outer wall without completely humiliating himself.

Once inside, they crossed a large field, then passed through another, much larger stone gate, with a portcullis and high arch. Beyond that was a courtyard of sorts, with pigs rooting in the dirt, and chickens and geese squawking and running to escape the horses' hooves. Buildings lined the inner walls. He could see and smell smoke coming from the chimney of one of them.

Four boys, who had been sweeping the dirt, dropped their brooms and ran up to hold the horses as the knights dismounted. "Where is Lord Pelsworth?" the short, stocky knight asked.

"In the hall, Sir Everard," one of the boys replied. "At Lady Allison's betrothal feast."

Lady Allison. Derek closed his eyes again. He wasn't sure if he was glad or sorry to hear her name. The ridiculous thought that had occurred to him earlier wormed its way back into his brain and refused to go away.

All of this was *real*.

Greasy Beard made a harumphing sound. "I say we kill the varlet anon. There be no reason to disturb the feast."

To Derek's relief, Sir Everard shook his head emphatically. "We must consult His Lordship, Sir Jarvis."

Grumbling, Sir Jarvis dragged Derek off the horse. Dizziness immediately assailed him. Swaying, unable to gain his balance with his feet bound, he fell forward.

Sir Everard caught him by the arm in the nick of time.
Making a noise of disgust, Sir Jarvis knelt and cut the rope
binding his ankles, then prodded him toward the building at
the back wall. "To the hall, varlet. We shall see what His
Lordship wishes to do with you."

Through a haze of pain, Derek considered his situation.
Okay, so maybe—just maybe—all of this was real. If it was,
it shouldn't be hard to fix everything. In a few seconds he
would see Allison and get this mess straightened out. Obviously, she had misunderstood him. When he had said he
would come, this was *not* what he'd meant.

The two knights escorted him into a smoky, dimly lit hall
that smelled of roasted meat and lavender and thyme. Derek
had a vague impression of a crowd of people sitting on
benches at long tables, eating with their fingers and talking
gibberish, before Sir Jarvis shoved him. Derek stumbled forward, almost falling on his rear. Laughter broke out. Annoyed, he glanced around to glare at the man, but as he did
so, he caught sight of a familiar face.

Allison.

Seated at a table on a dais, she was dressed in an elaborate blue gown embroidered with silver thread, her hair concealed by a close-fitting cap that framed her countenance.
She looked slightly different than he remembered. Maybe it
was the effect of the candlelight, but her cheeks were
rounder, her chin softer. She looked much younger. Well,
she *was* over five hundred years younger. He remembered
how she'd looked when he'd last seen her—her hair and
dress in disarray. Her lips red with his kisses. Her breasts
swelling under his hands. . . .

He shook his head. This was not the time to be thinking
about sex. His first priority was to return home. Now.

The only problem was, how could he do so with all these
people around? He needed to talk to Allison in private.

Catching her gaze, he jerked his head slightly toward the
door.

She stared at him a moment, then calmly looked away.

Annoyed, Derek frowned. The message was loud and

clear. She wasn't going to help him until he did what she'd asked.

He watched through narrowed eyes as she ate daintily from her plate and sipped from a silver cup. Nonchalantly she leaned over to speak to the large, hairy brute sitting on her left, then rinsed her fingers in a little bowl of water.

Derek's annoyance slowly gave way to appreciation. How calm she was, how cool. The lady obviously knew how to get what she wanted. He had to admire that. Even if it did mean he was going to have to make that ridiculous claim about being her True Love.

Sir Everard stepped forward and spoke to the elderly man seated at Allison's right. "Lord Pelsworth, we found this man in an outbuilding. We believe he is a thief."

By listening carefully, Derek was able to understand Sir Everard, in spite of the knight's thick accent. Turning his attention to the front of the room, he studied Lord Pelsworth. He had a thin gray beard, gaunt cheeks, and bloodshot blue eyes that studied Derek with a marked lack of interest.

So this was Allison's father. What had she said about him? Oh, yes. That he was forcing her to marry Wimpy Wilfred. And that he was very superstitious—he would not sign the engagement papers if her True Love made an appearance.

Derek hesitated. He should speak now, he knew, but the thought of trotting out that drivel about True Love in front of all these people was enough to make him queasy again. He would look like a damn fool saying all that crap—especially since he was wearing nothing but a diaper. Was he supposed to propose, too? Surely not. The thought of a proposal—even a fake one—made him wince, no matter what century it was.

He couldn't do it.

He *refused* to do it. She was going to have to find someone else to make an ass of himself. And so he would tell her, as soon as he could get her off by herself—

"Hang him."

For a moment Derek thought he must have misunderstood Lord Pelsworth. No one showed much of a reaction to the gruesome words. The spectators all turned their attention back to their plates, and Lord Pelsworth picked up a golden goblet, turning to the man sitting on the other side of Allison. "And now, I propose a toast—"

Sir Jarvis grabbed Derek's arm. The grin on his face told Derek more plainly than words that he hadn't misunderstood anything.

Derek pulled his arm from the knight's grasp and stepped forward. "Wait!"

Sir Jarvis grabbed him again. Without expression, Sir Everard seized his other arm. The two knights started to drag him away.

"Wait!" Derek cried again, unable to believe this was happening. "I am not a thief! I have an important message for Lady Allison!"

He was beginning to panic when he saw Allison put her hand on Lord Pelsworth's sleeve and whisper something. The old man hesitated, then shrugged and held up his hand. "Hold, Sir Knights."

The two men stopped.

"Did you say you have a message for my daughter?" Lord Pelsworth asked.

Derek, his heart starting to beat again, straightened and glared at Allison. She could have spoken up a little sooner. Feeling a sharp nudge, he transferred his glare to the two thugs. Were they what passed for law enforcement in this day and age? They gave new meaning to the phrase "police brutality."

"Well?" Lord Pelsworth demanded.

Derek cleared his throat and faced Allison. She looked at him rather expectantly, a small smile on her lips.

Derek knew when he was beat. "I am here in answer to a vision." Fixing his gaze on a point above her head, he said tonelessly, "I am Lady Allison's True Love."

For a moment his words echoed through the cavernous room. No one spoke or moved. Even the flickering candles seemed to grow still.

Then, as if shown a sitcom cue card, everyone in the hall

burst into laughter. The men howled. The women tittered. Sir Jarvis brayed like a donkey and slapped his thigh.

At least Allison had the decency not to laugh, Derek thought sourly. Her father wasn't laughing, either, nor the Bluto look-alike sitting on her other side. Meaty with thick black hair growing on his neck and the backs of his hands, he leaped to his feet.

"My lord!" the brute bellowed, a dark flush rising in his cheeks and his nostrils flaring to reveal more hair. "I will not tolerate this insult! Say the word and I will thrash this miserable worm to a pulp."

Lord Pelsworth, his mouth a tight line, ignored the brute and stared coldly at Derek. "Do you think we are fools to believe such a story?" He looked at the guards. "Take him away and hang him."

"Wait!" Derek shook off the guards, frantically trying to remember exactly what Allison had told him to say. "I can prove it. In my vision, an angel came to me—she told me to come here to Pelsworth Castle to find Lady Allison, my True Love. The angel said to remind you of the promise you made to her on her deathbed—"

Lord Pelsworth clutched his cup and grew pale.

"Permit me to skewer this knave," the hairy brute begged.

"No." Lord Pelsworth rose to his feet also, still clutching the cup and staring at Derek as if he were a ghost. "I wish to hear more of this man's tale. Pray be seated, Sir Wilfred."

For a second, the name didn't register. But when it did, Derek did a double take. Sir Wilfred?

This was Wimpy Wilfred?

The man stood almost six feet tall and was nearly as wide. He was as burly as a grizzly bear, and he had almost as much hair. It appeared to cover nearly every square inch of skin not concealed by his clothing. He looked more like Bigfoot than the wimpy little guy Allison had described.

Derek glanced at her suspiciously.

She wasn't even looking at him. She was whispering to Wilfred. Whatever she said appeared to have a soothing effect on the brute—at least, he sat down and contented himself with glaring malevolently at Derek.

Lord Pelsworth remained standing, his gaze never leaving Derek. "What is your name, stranger, and from whence do you hail?"

"Derek Sinclair," Derek said distractedly, his gaze still on Allison. Why had she lied about Wilfred? "I'm from Los Angeles, California." She turned to look at him with a strange expression on her face. As if she was angry about something. Did she dislike the way he'd made the announcement? Well, that was just too damn bad. She shouldn't have forced him to speak in front of all these people.

"Caf-i-lornia?" Lord Pelsworth frowned. "I've never heard of this place. Is it in Spain? What is your position there?"

Spain? Derek tore his gaze away from Allison. Oh, shit. What year was this? Fourteen-ninety-something, she had said. America had barely been discovered. Was it even called America yet?

"California is, um, an island off the coast of Italy," he said, just to be on the safe side. He would be long gone before anyone could check out his story. "I am known as, ahem, Sir Derek Sinclair of California. After I had the vision, I set sail at once for England."

"Ah, Italy." Lord Pelsworth nodded his head wisely. "That explains your strange speech."

Wilfred brought his heavy fist down on the table, causing the cups and platters to rattle. "A cock-and-bull story if ever I heard one. Look upon him, my lord. 'Tis obvious the knave is no knight. Please, I beg of you, allow me to punish his lies and run him through."

"We must not be hasty, Sir Wilfred." Pelsworth drank again from his golden goblet. "I shall think on this matter. In the meantime, Sir Derek, you must consider yourself our honored guest. Lady Anne! Show Sir Derek to the Great Chamber and have a servant bring him a tray of food. Oh, and find him some suitable attire."

A slim, dark-haired woman rose from one of the tables and curtsied. She approached Derek, smiling, fine lines fanning out around her bright, dark eyes.

Derek hesitated, then allowed himself to be led away. He

would have preferred to get the emerald from Allison immediately, but it was clear she had no intention of leaving the feast. He supposed he would have to be patient. She must be planning to come to his room later where they could speak privately.

And maybe pick up where they had left off? Hmm. If she did, he was going to have to say no. With his pounding head and aching body, all he wanted was to go home and go to bed. He really didn't want to spend a moment longer here than necessary. Allison not withstanding, he found the Middle Ages completely void of charm.

"This way, sir." Lady Anne led him to the opening in the carved wooden screens at the end of the hall and passed through it. Derek paused and glanced over his shoulder. Allison was leaning toward Wilfred, her hand on his arm.

Frowning, Derek followed Lady Anne.

She led him to a door which opened into a circular room with a spiral stone staircase, steep, dark, and narrow. As he climbed, the various parts of his body throbbed painfully. He hobbled after Lady Anne, wondering how long it would be before Allison brought him the emerald.

At the second floor Lady Anne led him through a room that had a few books lined up on a shelf.

"This is the library," she told him, before continuing into the next room. The murky light from the windows illuminated the room's sparse furnishings—some wall hangings, a bed, a chest, a three-legged stool, and not much else. There was a door at the far end.

"Where does that lead to?" Derek asked, nodding toward it.

"Lord Pelsworth's bedchamber," Anne replied. "This wing is the family apartments. Lord Pelsworth shows you great honor."

"Mmm," Derek murmured. Maybe it was a great honor, but the layout of the rooms was definitely strange.

A young girl came in, carrying a basin of water, some clean rags, and—blessedly—a pile of clothes.

Glancing at him sideways, she put the things on the lid of the chest, bobbed a curtsy, and hurried out.

Lady Anne showed no such shyness. "Please sit down, Sir Derek, and I will tend to your scrapes."

She spoke simply and clearly, her accent less thick than the others. Relieved he could understand her without difficulty, Derek sank onto the stool, glad to be finally off his feet. "Are you related to the Pelsworths?" he asked.

"No, I am merely an old friend of the family's." She dipped one of the rags in the water and wrung it out. "I've lived here most of my life, though," she added, dabbing at his back.

"Ouch!"

"I beg your pardon, Sir Derek."

He winced as she pressed the cloth against another graze. "That's okay," he muttered.

She continued to dab and press. "Your speech is very strange. Where did you say you are from?"

"California."

"California." Her brow creased and she stopped dabbing for a moment. "There is something very familiar about that name . . . ah well, it will come to me." Her fingers moved up to his hairline. "You've caused quite a commotion, Sir Derek, claiming to be Lady Allison's True Love."

"Have I?" Derek gritted his teeth as she prodded the bump on his temple.

"Yes, indeed. Everyone was quite amazed by your claim. Not everyone believes in the Legend."

Derek studied her a moment, wondering if she was one of the skeptical ones. "The Legend?"

"That the Pelsworths must marry for Love. 'Tis unlikely you would have heard of it so far away in California."

"Actually, now that you mention it, I do remember hearing some sort of story. Doesn't the Legend also say something about an emerald?"

Her eyebrows lifted. "You've heard of the emerald? The family does not speak of it overmuch for fear of thieves."

"Most understandable." Was that suspicion in her eyes? He changed the subject smoothly. "Do you think Lord Pelsworth will honor my claim and refuse to sign the betrothal papers to Wilfred?"

"The contract is already signed."

"Oh? Does that make a difference?"

"Certainly. 'Twill not be easy to break the contract. I think Lord Pelsworth may be persuaded to do so. I am not sure about Sir Wilfred, though." She applied some ointment to his back. "He will not be pleased. It has long been his wish to acquire Pelsworth Castle."

There was a tap at the door. The servant girl entered again, this time with a tray. She placed it on the chest, casting sideways glances at him the whole time. She blushed when she met his gaze.

"Is there aught else you need, my lord?" the girl asked, peeking at him from under her lashes.

Derek glanced at the unappetizing food on the tray. "I could do with a cigarette."

"A what?"

"A cig—" He stopped abruptly. Damn. Fourteen-ninety-something. Had anyone brought tobacco to Europe yet? Probably not. It was highly unlikely cigarettes even existed.

The realization made him angry. Where was Allison? She'd better hurry her sweet little ass up here. He was damned if he was going to go without cigarettes while she partied the night away.

He looked at the servant girl, who was still waiting for an answer. "Some light would be nice. It's dark in here."

The girl hesitated, her gaze flying to Lady Anne. Derek saw the dark-haired woman was looking at him rather oddly. But all she said was, "Light the fire and the rushlights, Tilly."

Tilly nodded and hurried over to the fireplace, where she spent several minutes coaxing a fire to life. She then lit what looked like some sort of bulbous plants and placed them in brackets on the wall. They provided a soft glow, but not much in the way of real light.

The girl was looking at him for approval, however, so he smiled and said, "Thank you, Tilly."

She blushed a violent shade of peony and fled the room.

Surprised, he glanced at Anne. "What's the matter with her?"

"Likely she's thrilled by the romance of your declaration. Doubtless half the castle maids will be in love with you."

"Oh?" Perhaps the Middle Ages had a good side after all . . . but no. He was determined to return home immediately. Where the hell was Allison? Surely she could have found some excuse to join him by now.

"Lady Anne, would you be so kind as to ask Lady Allison to see me for just a few moments?"

Anne studied him with bright dark eyes. Their expression was somehow very familiar.

"It's vital I speak to her," he added.

" 'Tis late, Sir Derek. Tomorrow would be better."

"Please, Lady Anne. I, um, yearn with all my heart to speak to my True Love." So he could tell her what he thought of her little trick, manipulating him into agreeing to come here. "I yearn to hear her sweet voice." So he could hear her explain why the hell she'd made Wilfred out to be as threatening as Bullwinkle in a tutu. "I yearn to see her loveliness once more tonight before I go to sleep." So he could get the emerald and go home and have a cigarette. "At least ask her."

Anne continued to gaze at him. He arranged his features into what he hoped was an expression of lovelorn eagerness.

Her eyes seemed to grow brighter. "Very well. I will do as you ask."

"Thank you, Lady Anne. You are as kind as you are beautiful."

She laughed. "Save your flattery for Allison. She will appreciate it more than I."

She left and Derek gingerly felt the bump on his forehead. Shit. He might have to go to the doctor's when he got home. But first, he was going to put some clothes on.

Shivering, he stood up. The room didn't spin, so he walked over to the pile of clothing. Thank God. He couldn't wait to be rid of the smelly, ragged loincloth.

He picked up the item at the top of the pile. Made of wool, it was kind of baggy and had a drawstring around the middle.

He looked at the garment doubtfully, then down at the loincloth he wore, then back.

Sighing, he stripped off the loincloth.

The underwear was itchy. Manfully, he ignored the discomfort and picked up the next item of clothing . . . a pair of yellow woollen hose.

His lips tightened. "Tights," he muttered. "They expect me to wear yellow tights?"

He pulled them on, but there was no elastic to hold them up. Clutching the waist to prevent them from falling down, he looked at the rest of the clothes.

The loose shirt was tolerable at least, but there was a tight padded jacket—of green velvet!—that went over it. Leather strings tied it together at the front. Worse was to come, however.

A belt of linked silver squares and, not one, but *two* purses. One of them had beads, long silk tassels and loops to slide the belt through. He put it aside. He absolutely refused to wear anything that looked like a ladies' evening bag.

The other small, padded purse was embroidered with green and yellow silk, but at least it didn't have beads and tassels. It didn't have any loops, either, but he noticed some eyelet holes. He could tolerate it, he supposed, especially since the jacket and tights didn't have any pockets. He attached the pouch to the belt, using the leather strings that lay in a pile next to the clothes. There were eyelet holes in the hose and jacket also, he realized.

He spent a frustrating half hour tying all the pieces of clothing together, the task made doubly difficult by the growing darkness. But at least the tights stayed up when he was done, even if they did sag a little around his knees.

The only problem now was the gap at the front of the tights. Taking a closer look, he saw more eyelet holes. Reluctantly, he picked up one of the leather strings and tied the gap together. The tights were now *really* tight, uncomfortably so. How could the men here stand the discomfort? But he supposed the tights were better than the smelly rags. He just hoped he wouldn't have an urgent need to take a piss before he got home.

The calf-high boots wouldn't have been bad, but they were at least a size too small.

He was looking at the last item of clothing, a flat round cap with a feather pinned to it, when the door opened. He looked up eagerly.

Anne stood in the doorway.

"Oh, hello again, Lady Anne," he said, looking behind her. There was no sign of Allison. "Where's Lady Allison?"

"She is still at the feast." Anne smoothed her skirt. "She cannot leave."

Derek bit back an obscenity. Forcing himself to smile, he said, "I suppose I will have to curb my impatience then. Thanks for your help, Lady Anne."

"You're welcome, Sir Derek." She stared at the purse on his belt and seemed to hesitate a moment. But all she said was, "Rest well."

As soon as the door closed behind her, Derek's smile gave way to a scowl. This was unbelievable. How much longer was she going to make him wait?

He was half tempted to go downstairs and demand she give him the emerald at once. Caution dictated, however, that he not do anything foolish—these medieval people were way too quick with their swords and nooses as far as he was concerned.

But where was she, dammit? He'd done what she asked—so why the hell was she playing games with him?

Restlessly he turned and walked over to the tray. It held a piece of cheese, a chunk of bread, and a bottle of wine. His stomach growled. He hesitated a moment, then picked up the bottle and took a couple of swigs. It was more sugary than he was used to, with a sour undertaste, but he supposed it would have to do. He gnawed on the bread. The texture was grainy, but the taste wasn't bad. The cheese, however, was sharp enough to bring tears to his eyes. He decided to leave it.

Once he was finished with the meager meal, he looked around the room. There was nothing to entertain him, so he went and sat down on the bed. He sank about twelve inches into the mattress.

He lay back and was immediately cocooned in softness. It was like lying in a huge marshmallow.

Staring up at the canopy, he waited.

He wished he had a cigarette. He wouldn't mind waiting quite so much if he could just have a smoke. After all he'd been through, he really needed one. He needed one desperately. It had been over twenty-four hours—no, over five hundred *years* since he'd had a cigarette. He couldn't wait much longer—

The door opened.

Derek sat up, but it was only another servant, carrying an armload of wood. With a nod to Derek, the man carried it through to the room beyond Derek's.

Derek lay back down.

A few minutes later the door opened again.

Another servant entered, this one with an old-fashioned warming pan.

Over the next hour a constant stream of servants trekked through his room to the one beyond. Derek began to get annoyed. What if he had been trying to sleep? Hadn't these people heard of privacy?

At one point Derek got up and looked in the other room— it was a bedroom, similar to the one he was in, only a little more richly furnished.

At least another hour passed before Derek heard laughter outside his room. He jumped in the bed, pulled the blanket up to his chin, and closed his eyes, pretending to be asleep. The door opened and he heard footsteps crossing the floor.

"Good night, Sir Derek," Lord Pelsworth slurred, before entering the other bedroom.

Derek opened his eyes and got out of the bed.

Allison must have been waiting for her father to go to bed. Surely she would come now.

But the minutes ticked by, and except for one or two more servants, no one entered the room.

Another hour passed and everything became silent except for the occasional howl of a dog.

Unable to wait any longer, Derek cracked open the door again. The door creaked a little, but there was no other sound. He opened the door farther and looked out.

The "library" was dark and still.

Frowning, he opened the door all the way, so the rush-lights cast a dim arc of light into the other room.

Quickly he grabbed one of the rushlights and hurried to the stone staircase. He hesitated, remembering that Anne had said that this was the family wing—Allison must be in a room nearby. But was she upstairs or down? Mentally flipping a coin, he went up.

The first room on the third floor had tapestries on the walls, a loom, and two spinning wheels. Derek walked to the door at the far end and put his ear to the panel.

From within, he could hear a soft snoring.

Quietly he opened the door. The snoring came from a large bed against the wall. He tiptoed over and held up the rushlight.

In the bed he found the snorer—Anne, her shiny dark hair covered by a cap. Next to her lay an old woman with gray hair and a young girl with a round, plump face.

Ok-a-a-ay. The sleeping arrangements around here were definitely weird.

Derek lowered the rushlight and proceeded to the next room.

Inside, a glow from the rushlights along the wall illuminated the room. His gaze went directly to the huge, canopied bed. Heavy red velvet drapes concealed its occupant. He stuck his rushlight in a bracket and walked to the bed. Reaching forward, he pulled back one of the swaths of cloth.

His breath caught. Allison, her lashes dark against her cheeks, lay fast asleep within, like a princess in a fairy tale.

He pushed the drape farther back, and the light from the rushlights sent a gleaming sparkle of gold along the waving tresses of her hair cascading across the pillow. She lay on her side, and the light played softly on her face, illuminating the silken roundness of her cheek and the hollow of her throat. He could see intricate embroidery at the neckline of her nightgown and one linen-clad arm thrown out to the side of the blanket. A small hand peeked out from lace-edged cuffs, the ringless fingers long and slender.

He stared at her, an odd sense of disorientation making him feel dizzy for a moment. He remembered, suddenly, in vivid detail, how she had felt in his arms last night. How smooth her skin had been. How sweet her scent. And as for her breasts and thighs . . .

He closed his eyes and drew in a deep breath. He must have hit his head harder than he'd thought to be thinking about sex again.

"Get the emerald and get the hell out of here, Sinclair, before you do something really stupid," he muttered to himself.

Leaning forward, he gently pushed her onto her back and placed his hand over her mouth.

Her lashes fluttered upward.

"Don't scream," he whispered. "It's just me. Derek."

In the dim light her eyes were a deep dark blue. He could smell a faint scent of cloves from her hair. He could feel her lips soft and moist against the palm of his hand and the exquisite silkenness of her cheek under his fingers.

God, he wanted her. In spite of his aching head and battered body, in spite of his determination to return home without delay, he still wanted her.

His resolve to leave as soon as he had the emerald faltered. Perhaps he would stay long enough to finish what they'd started last night. Just an hour. Or two.

Sliding his fingers up into her hair, he bent forward, his gaze fastened on her ripe red mouth. Her lips parted. She inhaled deeply.

And then, she screamed loud enough to wake the dead.

Chapter 5

DEREK JUMPED BACK, the shrill, ear-piercing shriek almost deafening him. "What the hell—?"

Another scream worthy of Frankenstein's bride made him clap his hands over his ears. The throbbing in his head returned full force. "Dammit, Allie, what the hell's the matter with you? Shut up or someone will—"

The door flew open, banging against the wall. The three women from the other room came in. Two of them took one look at him and started screaming, also. The old one had brought her pillow and started hitting him over the head with it. On the third blow the seams split and feathers flew through the air.

Choking on the swirling feathers, his ears ringing from all the screaming, Derek raised his arms to protect his head and inched toward the door.

But just as he reached it, two men in chain mail charged through and seized him, dragging him back into the room. Derek grimaced as several new bruises were added to his collection.

His grimace deepened when, a moment later, Lord Pelsworth appeared in the doorway, dressed in a voluminous nightgown, a cap hanging over one ear, and brandishing a sword.

Oh, great, Derek thought. Just what he needed—Allison's father catching him in her bedroom.

"What is the meaning of this?" Lord Pelsworth demanded, lowering his sword when he saw Derek.

The women finally stopped screaming. They turned to look at Derek accusingly, waiting for his answer.

Derek coughed up a feather. "Just a little misunderstanding—"

"This man sneaked into my room and tried to ravish me!" Allison cried, clutching the bedcovers to her chest. "You must hang him at once!"

Derek's head whipped around. An unpleasant suspicion belatedly crept into his aching brain.

She *did* remember him . . . didn't she?

"Draw and quarter him, Father!"

No, apparently not.

Derek groaned. Her accent was stronger than it had been in the future, but there was no misunderstanding her words. She didn't remember him. How could that be? He remembered her. But maybe there was a weird logic to it after all—how could she remember him when she wouldn't meet him for five hundred years?

Of course she couldn't remember him. If she could, then she would remember everything else, too, and she would know not to marry Wilfred. She wouldn't have needed Derek's help at all.

He wished he'd thought of that before.

He brushed a feather out of his eye. Really, he didn't give a damn whether she remembered him or not as long as she gave him the emerald. But would she?

"Father, please listen to me! You must castrate him. As a warning to all other would-be-ravishers."

Shit. The only thing she was likely to give him was a knife in the back—or somewhere even less pleasant. He'd better figure out a way to placate her and Lord Pelsworth. Fast.

Unfortunately, his aching brain was as sluggish as the

stock market during a recession. "Forgive me," he interrupted Allison's continued exhortations for his execution
and/or dismemberment. "I can explain. It is, er, the custom
in California to visit the bride in her bedchamber after a declaration has been made. It gives the couple a chance to get
to know each other better—"

Allison made an incredibly rude snorting sound. "You expect us to believe such a tale? Father, this man is obviously
an adventurer. He hoped to ravish me and force me into marriage."

Derek stared at her coldly through the still-swirling feathers. "I would never rape a woman." Belatedly remembering
his role, he added, "Especially not my True Love."

She snorted again and rolled her eyes. "Boil him in oil,"
she beseeched her father. "He cannot be trusted."

Lord Pelsworth frowned. "I am inclined to trust a man
who has had a holy vision." He tugged at his beard. "But
perhaps 'twould be wise to be a trifle cautious. Guards, take
this man to the dungeon. He can spend the night there. I will
decide in the morning what to do with him."

Derek didn't know whether to laugh or cry. A dungeon. It
needed only that to make this hellish day complete.

He made no resistance as the guards dragged him through
the door, scattering a crowd of nightgowned spectators

At least in the dungeon he would have time to think, time
to come up with a plan to get back home.

If he was lucky, he might think of one before his True
Love had him executed.

Allison watched the man leave, knotting her fists in the
blankets. The impudent villain! How dare he come here,
claiming to be her True Love? And how dare he come to her
room to manhandle her? He was a charlatan, a rogue, no
doubt looking for some way to enrich himself.

"Father," she implored, "you must hang him."

Lord Pelsworth, who had been staring thoughtfully at a
floating feather, frowned. "You are too quick to judge, Allison. He may be telling the truth."

"Please, Father. He comes here with no servants, no

money—no clothes even!—and claims to be a knight from some land no one has ever heard of. 'Tis obvious he seeks to advance his position in the world with this unlikely tale."

"And yet, he knew about the promise I made to your mother."

"A lucky guess, no doubt. He is a nobody."

"It matters not who he is if he is here to fulfill the Legend."

Allison sighed silently. She knew her father would likely prove stubborn on this point. "But, Father, how can he be my True Love? I have no feelings for him whatsoever—except dislike."

"You must become better acquainted with him before you decide whether or not he is your True Love. Perhaps if he stays with us for a while as our guest—"

"Our guest! You can't mean to give hospitality to that rogue! Sir Wilfred will be grossly insulted."

"Sir Wilfred will have to abide by my decision, as will you," Lord Pelsworth said coldly.

She opened her mouth to protest, but seeing the obstinate look on his face, she changed her mind. Instead, she bowed her head. "Yes, Father."

His gaze softened. "'Twill work out, you'll see. 'Tis a shame he has no title here, but he will somehow make his fortune. The Legend promises it."

"Yes, Father," she repeated. "Does this mean you will be extending your stay here?"

He immediately averted his gaze and shuffled his feet. "No, I cannot. I would like to, but I must visit our other properties. I have spent too much time here already."

"But, Father, there is much that needs your attention. There is a petition from one of the tenants, and the servants are fighting—"

"Don't worry your head about such things, Daughter, I'll deal with them. You concentrate on falling in love with Sir Derek."

With a pat on her shoulder, he left quickly. As soon as the door shut behind him, Allison's meek expression gave way to a scowl. Rising up on her knees, she yanked at the bed curtains.

Fall in love with Sir Derek, indeed!

How could her father believe that trickster, that rogue for a moment?

Oh, this Derek Sinclair was a bold one, she had to admit—look how he had stood there in the hall, filthy, nearly naked, but tall and straight as he met her gaze. For a moment, something about him had piqued her interest— long enough for her to ask her father to hear the man's story. How she regretted her folly now!

And he . . . had he no shame? Apparently not, for he had continued to stare at her without flinching. How dared he look at her like that? Boldly. Familiarly. As if he knew some secret about her. As if an angel really had come down from heaven and told him something.

Allison sank down on her knees, her fingers sliding along the material of the bed curtains. How *had* he found out about the deathbed promise? She had been crouching outside the door when her mother made her father make the vow; but she would have sworn no one else could have heard.

Not that it mattered. She didn't doubt the scoundrel had his methods. Perhaps it *had* been a lucky guess. Obviously, he was bold enough to try to bluff his way through anything. True Love . . . ha!

Flopping back on the bed, she sank into the mattress. He should have been whipped just for that impertinence. And then to come to her room! What amazing boldness! She'd been terrified to be wakened by a hand over her mouth.

But then she'd recognized his voice—'twas an oddly compelling voice, deep and melodic, even with his strange manner of speaking. It had sent ripples over her skin. From fear, undoubtedly. Although she hadn't been afraid. From shock, perhaps. Fortunately, she'd recovered her wits quickly and screamed.

He'd seemed surprised by that. What had he expected? To be welcomed with open arms? Had he truly thought she'd heed his command?

Don't scream. It's just me, Derek.

She turned on her side and stared through the darkness. How odd. What could he have meant? He had sounded as though he expected her to know him.

Now that she thought about it, if he had intended to ravish her, he'd chosen an odd way to go about it.

Restlessly she yanked the covers up to her chin and closed her eyes. It didn't really matter what he had meant. All that mattered was that he had jeopardized everything she'd worked so hard to attain. . . .

Oh, why hadn't she let Wilfred skewer him? If only she hadn't been so squeamish at the thought of a little bloodshed! Now she had to think of a way to get rid of him herself.

But how?

His image rose before her mind's eye. He had not been ill looking. He was tall and slim, with fine brown eyes, regular features, and hair lightened by the sun. He had no battle scars, no marks from disease. But he had grimaced over his few minor scrapes as if they were mortal wounds! And he claimed to be a knight. 'Twas obvious he was no such thing—he was too smooth, too pampered. His hand over her mouth had given further proof of his coddled existence—it had been soft and free of calluses. No knight ever had such beautiful hands. She'd noticed them earlier—the nails were clean and looked cut, not chewed or broken or torn. She doubted he'd ever done a day's work in his life—

She sat up suddenly, staring through the darkness.

A day's work . . .

She hugged her knees to her chest. It just might work. She would have to talk to her father, convince him 'twas necessary, but she was certain she could do so. She had to.

Smiling, she lay back down.

By this time next week—if not sooner—Derek Sinclair would go running back to California.

With his tail—and his other parts—tucked firmly between his legs.

Chapter 6

DEREK LAY VERY still, his head aching with a dull throb, and a sour taste in his mouth. He had been awake for several minutes now, but he hadn't opened his eyes. He couldn't quite bring himself to do so.

He was certain yesterday had been nothing but a nightmare. An unusually realistic one, yes. But still just a nightmare.

He was definitely swearing off the booze—he'd never touch another drop. Charles had preached time and time again about the evils of liquor, but Derek had always ignored the lectures. Now he was willing to concede that his brother had a point. Alcohol did strange things to one's brain. Alcohol was bad news. Alcohol was—

The scraping metal of a key turning in a lock interrupted Derek's thoughts. Without thinking, he opened his eyes.

Greasy Beard—Sir Jarvis—stood in the doorway of the dungeon cell. "Get up, you!" he ordered.

Derek groaned and closed his eyes. God, he needed a drink.

"Are you deaf or just stupid? I said get up! His Lordship is waiting to see you."

Reluctantly Derek opened his eyes again. He wasn't re-

ally surprised by what he saw. The smell of dank stone and
filthy straw, the feel of itchy wool against his skin, and the
hard pallet under his back had already told him what he
would see. He just hadn't wanted to admit the truth.

He was insane.

Sir Jarvis, obviously not too strong in the patience department, made a movement as if to pull out his sword.

"Okay, okay," Derek muttered, forcing his protesting
body to a vertical position. "Keep your pants on."

He must be insane, he thought as he limped toward the
door. The only other alternative—that he was in a dungeon
somewhere in England in the Middle Ages—was completely ludicrous. Yesterday, with his head screwed up from
alcohol and pills, ghosts and time travel had seemed the
most logical explanation. But today, without the influence of
the drugs, he couldn't buy it.

He followed the guard up the stairs, trying to make sense
of what was happening. He wished he had a cigarette. It had
been, what? Nearly thirty-six hours since he'd had one? No
wonder he was having trouble thinking clearly. He hadn't
gone this long without tobacco since the time Charles had
insisted he undergo hypnotherapy to quit.

Hypnotherapy . . .

No. Shaking his head, he followed the guard across the
courtyard and into another building. It was too farfetched to
think this was all some kind of quit-smoking program. Even
Charles wouldn't go to such lengths.

Sir Jarvis stopped abruptly. Derek looked up to see they
were in a room where Lord Pelsworth was eating breakfast
with Allison, Lady Anne, and Sir Wilfred.

Sir Wilfred, hunched over his plate, glared at him. Lady
Anne, in a red dress that contrasted beautifully with her
shining black hair, smiled encouragingly.

To Derek's surprise, Allison appeared to be ogling his
crotch, but when she saw him looking at her, she hastily
turned up her nose and looked away.

Derek stared at her, automatically noticing the way the
fur-trimmed green gown hugged her figure. He remembered
her glowing image in Nan's apartment. He remembered her

claim that he could travel through time on "her plane of existence." He remembered the hot, intense passion that had flared between them.

Was he insane?

"Ah, there you are," Lord Pelsworth said testily. His eyes were even more bloodshot this morning and his skin had a greenish hue. There was no food in front of him—just a silver goblet. "I hope you slept well."

Derek's gaze flickered back up to Pelsworth's face. Was the old man joking? "Well enough," he said expressionlessly.

"Excellent, excellent." Pelsworth waved his hand at an empty seat. "Please sit down and break your fast with us."

On the off chance that he wasn't insane, he decided to play along with Lord Pelsworth.

As Derek moved toward the empty seat next to Anne, he caught Allison staring at his crotch again, a small smile curving her lips. Derek's brows rose. She was bolder than he'd thought—

"Sir Derek . . ."

Derek turned his gaze to Lord Pelsworth. "Yes, my lord?"

"Is it the fashion in California to wear your codpiece on your belt?"

"My cod—?" Derek stopped abruptly, then sat down hastily. "Yes, it is."

"Hm. How odd. I wonder if 'twill become the fashion here, also."

"My lord," Wilfred growled. "This is not the time to be discussing fashion. Have you made a decision about this varlet, or not?" He put what looked like an entire roast in his mouth and swallowed it whole without chewing. "I hope you have decided to hang and quarter the cur," he added.

A servant placed a round, flat piece of bread on the table in front of Derek, along with a huge leg of mutton and a tankard of ale, but Derek's appetite had suddenly dwindled. If this was real, he'd better get the emerald from Allison—before he became raven bait.

"No, I don't believe that would be prudent," Lord Pelsworth said. "I cannot discount Sir Derek's claim. We must allow him time to become acquainted with Allison. Two months should suffice to determine whether or not he is her True Love."

Wilfred's face reddened. "Two months? What am I to do in the meantime? Twiddle my thumbs while this cuckoldy knave is a pampered guest in your home?"

Calmly Lord Pelsworth drank from his goblet. "What you choose to do is your own concern, but I assure you, Sir Derek will earn his keep."

Derek, chewing a piece of the stale bread, paused. Earn his keep? What the hell did that mean?

But before he could swallow the bread and ask, Wilfred jumped to his feet and placed his hairy hands on the table. Leaning forward threateningly, he snarled, "If you do not rid the castle of this knave at once, I will be forced to break the betrothal agreement."

Pelsworth shrugged. "Do what you must."

"The king shall hear of this insult!" Wilfred shouted, blasting the entire table with his sour breath before he stormed from the room.

"My goodness," Anne said, taking a bite of a pear. "Sir Wilfred seems a trifle upset."

Allison rose to her feet, a tense look on her face. "Don't worry, Father. I will talk to him. I think I can convince him not to write to the king—"

"Small matter if he does," Lord Pelsworth said, drinking from his goblet. "I have already written the king."

Allison stared at him, her face growing pale. "You've done what?"

"Written to the king. He will have to approve the match with Sir Derek, naturally. I explained the situation to him."

"You did?" Allison sank back into her seat, her hands clenching the wooden arms of her chair. "Has the messenger already left?"

"Yes, at dawn." Lord Pelsworth frowned. "Why?"

"I was but curious."

Her voice sounded normal enough—but her eyes were dark with . . . shock?

Derek sipped his ale, watching her closely over the rim of

the cup. Her lips were white, and her fingers trembled
slightly as she picked up a morsel of food.

He set down his cup and took another bite of the bread,
chewing thoughtfully. Judging from her expression, Allison
was not happy about the letter. But why?

"Sir Derek," Lord Pelsworth said, apparently not noticing
his daughter's distress, "as soon as you're finished, Jarvis
will take you to Sir Drogo."

Derek swallowed the bread. "Sir Drogo?"

"The master of arms. Did I not explain? As my daughter
pointed out to me earlier this morning, it would hardly do to
treat you as a guest for the next two months if you are a
fraud. I am certain you agree."

Derek directed a narrowed stare at his True Love, all cu-
riosity about the letter vanishing. "Of course. I only wish
there was something I could do to repay you for your hospitality." He took a bite of the leathery mutton.

"There is," Lord Pelsworth said. "Allison thought—and I
concurred—that if you are truly her True Love you would
not object to sharing some of the duties of the castle's
knights."

Lord Pelsworth beamed jovially. "Therefore, as soon as
you are finished eating, Jarvis will take you to the yard to
join the knights in their daily practice at arms."

Derek choked on the bite of mutton. Practice at arms?
Wasn't that fighting with spears and swords and axes and
things? There was no way in hell . . .

He cleared his throat. "I'm afraid that won't be possible.
The order of knighthood I belong to is a peaceful one. We
don't carry weapons. We believe fighting is morally wrong."

Lord Pelsworth frowned. "Anyone with such a cowardly
belief is definitely not worthy to be my daughter's husband
and shall be hanged immediately."

On the other hand, perhaps this wasn't the time to take a
moral stand. "You, ah, misunderstand me. We choose fighting as a last resort, but of course we believe in being prepared against our enemies. Unfortunately, I have been busy
with other matters and am sadly out of practice."

Lord Pelsworth waved his hand. "Fear not. You may prac-

tice with the squires whilst you rehone your skills. Sir Drogo
will whip you into shape in no time."

"Wonderful," Derek said, his voice hollow.

A servant came in and approached Allison. Derek glanced
at her and saw she was watching him closely, a small smile
on her face, before she turned to the servant.

Apparently she had recovered from her distress, Derek
thought dryly. She looked altogether too smug. Had she en-
gineered this little surprise in an effort to get him to leave?

If only she knew that he would leave if he could—and
gladly. But he couldn't. Not without the emerald.

He took another bite of mutton, eyeing her consideringly.
She looked almost prim this morning in her long sleeves and
covered hair. An image of how she'd looked last night in her
bed with her hair loose and her nightgown slipping off her
shoulder flashed through his head. Her room would be a
good place to start searching. Maybe tonight. Only this time
he would persuade her to be silent—

"By the way," Lord Pelsworth said, pouring himself some
more wine. "If you are found in Lady Allison's bedchamber
again, your head will be cut off. You understand?"

Derek met the old man's suddenly perceptive gaze. "Yes,
my lord."

Derek returned his attention to his mutton, taking care not
to look at Allison again, even when she murmured something and left the room with the servant.

He could start his search somewhere else. Surely the castle had some place for valuables—a vault or something. He
would look there first. If he was lucky, he'd find the emerald and be home in the wink of an eye.

If not, he'd have to sneak into Allison's room and risk getting his head chopped off.

The thought made his stomach churn a little. He swallowed a long deep drink of his ale, even though it was warm
and had a pine taste, as if someone had decided to flavor it
with a Christmas tree. But at least it settled his stomach a bit.
He wasn't going to think about head chopping right now. He
was going to think about searching the castle. Getting the
emerald might take a bit longer than he would have liked,

but he would just have to make the best of it. It wouldn't hurt to stay here a *few* days. Hey, knight practice might even be kind of fun—riding horses, waving a sword around—no problem. And besides, he'd been wanting to get in shape. He'd let his tennis club membership lapse a few months ago. This might be just the thing to lose that flab he'd noticed around his waist. Heck, he might even quit smoking. This whole thing might actually turn out to be good for him.

After all, a few days in Knight Boot Camp wouldn't kill him.

Chapter 7

H<small>E WAS DYING.</small>

Standing in the grassy field outside the castle gate with the other men several hours later, Derek swung the sword at the wooden post—a "pel"—and tried not to wince. It seemed like he'd been swinging for an eternity. Sweat was running down his face and his back underneath his armor, he was out of breath, and his arm was on fire. Tennis elbow was nothing compared to this.

He hadn't expected knightly exercise to be, well, so *difficult*.

He hadn't expected he would have to march, carrying a sack of rocks on his back, around the castle walls—"to improve one's endurance," Cuthbert, one of the squires, had explained. By the time Derek had made the circuit, he'd been wheezing and gasping for air.

Nor had he expected to be required to do a series of somersaults and handstands "to improve one's balance," according to Cuthbert. The somersaults had made his headache worse, and while trying to do the handstands, he'd landed on his back more times than he cared to count.

He *had* expected the armor to be uncomfortable. But he

hadn't expected it to be pure torture. It quickly heated to ovenlike temperatures. It clanked and squealed when he walked. And it made going to the bathroom damned difficult.

He supposed he should have guessed how bad it would be when Cuthbert was helping him put it on. There were more pieces than Derek realized, and they all had to be buckled on or tied to the "arming doublet"—a sort of leather jacket with strings in strategic places. It had taken over an hour, and Cuthbert seemed surprised when Derek didn't know what a "sabaton" or a "greave" was. "We call them, er, sneakers and shin guards in California," Derek improvised.

" 'Sneakers,' " Cuthbert mused. "It seems an odd name. One can hardly sneak in sabatons."

Derek glanced at him. About sixteen, with curly blond hair and earnest blue eyes, the boy looked confused. "It's a joke," Derek explained.

"Oh," Cuthbert said blankly.

At first Derek had been surprised at how lightweight the armor was. But now, after three hours of unrelenting exercise, he felt like he'd been entombed in a lead coffin. The ill-fitting armor pinched and rubbed, and the cold wind whistled up under the helmet. He'd tried leaving the visor up—most of the squires had theirs raised—but his kept falling down. He was nearly blind from trying to peer through the narrow slit, and even worse, there was no ventilation. He felt—not to mention sounded—like Darth Vader.

He was definitely dying.

The only good thing about the morning was it had proved to him absolutely and irrefutably that he was *not* insane—being insane could not possibly be so excruciatingly and unrelentingly painful.

Doggedly, he swung his sword at the pel, panting heavily within the confines of his claustrophobic helmet. The sword was weighted to make it heavier than a "normal" sword—which he considered quite heavy enough—in order to "develop one's muscle strength."

He couldn't believe Sir Drogo hadn't called a break yet.

Derek was weak from hunger—and no wonder. That breakfast was not something he wished to experience again.

Nor was the garderobe—an evil-smelling closet with a hole and a pile of straw next to it. He'd stared uncomprehendingly at the straw for a moment until it dawned on him what it was for.

He shuddered at the memory, swinging a little less forcefully at the pel as he did so.

"Sir Derek! Is that how a knight of California attacks a foe? If so, 'tis a wonder every man, woman, and child hasn't been butchered by your enemies. You must leap in to make your thrust, and out, to avoid a return blow. You must vary your blows—strike the 'head,' 'sides,' and 'thighs,' of your target. You cannot just stand there swinging your sword like a ladies' fan!"

Several of the other men sniggered, and Derek glared through the slit of his visor after Sir Drogo's retreating black-clad figure. The old knight had a craggy face and bushy white brows over piercing green eyes that had seen right through Derek's claims of being out of practice. Sir Drogo had assigned him the most basic of "exercises"—*and* made him the butt of several caustic jokes.

If the old man ever wanted to take a trip into the future, he'd make a fine Marine drill sergeant. Or an excellent sadistic dictator for a Third World country.

Derek thrust his sword at the post with a little more vigor, wishing it were Sir Drogo, and wondering how the hell he was going to get out of this mess. It was too bad Charles wasn't here. He was always useful in a jam.

Briefly Derek wondered if Charles was worried over his disappearance. Nah. Probably not. Derek had cut out on unpleasant situations before. When he went home in a few days, he'd probably have to endure a tongue-lashing from Big Brother. But it would almost be worth it, just to be home again. . . .

"Halt!" Sir Drogo cried out.

Thankfully Derek lowered his sword. It was about time. He started to bend down, wanting to sit for a moment, but

Cuthbert nudged him and nodded toward the castle gate. Derek turned.

A company of knights cantered through the stone gate of the castle and across the field where the squires were practicing. In front rode Sir Wilfred and a woman—Allison.

Derek tensed. "Where are they going?"

"Most likely to London. Sir Wilfred is one of the King's guards."

"And Allison is going with him?"

"Oh, no. She is probably just riding to the outer gate with him."

Sure enough, the cavalcade stopped at the smaller gate, and Allison spoke to Wilfred. He appeared to hesitate a moment, then nodded. Turning his horse, he raised his hand. The horsemen proceeded forward, through the gate, and out of sight. Allison stayed where she was, watching them go, a frown on her face.

Derek wondered what she'd said to Wilfred. Had she tried to placate him over the broken engagement? If Wilfred was a personal guard to the king, he might have influence with the monarch. It was probably smart of her to keep relations with the burly knight as pleasant as possible.

After the last wagon had passed through the gate, Allison turned her horse and rode toward Sir Drogo.

Derek pushed back his visor and held it up so he could see her better. She didn't appear to have much of a seat, although it could be because she was riding sidesaddle. The dress she wore was becoming, however—the dark blue gown was tighter than the others he'd seen her wear, and emphasized the bouncing of her breasts very nicely.

Hearing a deep sigh, Derek glanced over at Cuthbert. The boy was gazing at Allison, his heart in his big baby blue eyes.

Derek turned his attention back to Allison. She had stopped by Sir Drogo. As they exchanged a few words, her gaze traveled over the squires. For a moment, her gaze met Derek's.

Without smiling or sign of recognition, she looked away.

Derek released the visor and it snapped shut with a *clank.*

Through the slit, he watched her ride past, haughty as a queen. He glared after her.

He'd endured a lot on her behalf. He'd made a fool of himself, making that stupid claim to be her True Love. He'd nearly gotten hanged and/or run through while waiting for her brutish fiancé to break the engagement. He'd suffered pain and abuse and countless other discomforts. The least she could do was treat him with a little common courtesy. He was tempted to go after her and pull her down off that horse and—

Derek took a deep breath—or at least as deep as he was able to inside the helmet. There was no point in being angry at her. Anger was such an unproductive emotion—he'd learned that when he was thirteen and his father died. It was better not to feel anything—

"Sir Derek!" a voice roared.

Jumping, he turned to see Sir Drogo bearing down on him.

"What do you think this is, Sir Derek? A woman's gossip circle? Cuthbert, are you so proficient with the broadsword you think you may stand around like a moonling all day? Continue your exercises! 'Tis to be hoped the castle need never rely on the two of you for its defense—judging from your performances, the village children could overwhelm you with a few sticks and stones."

Sir Drogo stomped away to yell at some of the other men. Derek glared after him, then turned and thrust his sword. It hit the pel with a satisfying *thunk*. "That old tyrant. I'd like to—"

"Please, Sir Derek." Cuthbert stepped forward, thrust his sword, then nimbly leapt back. "Sir Drogo is right. We must be strong and brave. You know what the chivalric code says about always being prepared to defend your lady."

"Mmm." Derek yanked his blade from the post. No, he didn't know. What's more, he didn't want to know. He just wanted the hell out of there.

He wanted that emerald.

Chapter 8

SHE COULDN'T BELIEVE a week had passed, and he was still there.

From her vantage point on the battlements, Allison watched the men at their practice, her attention focused on one man in particular. He swung at the pel, his sword hitting the wood post several heartbeats after the others. He moved gracelessly and handled the sword awkwardly, his ineptitude plain for all to see. Even the youngest squire, Cuthbert, was more skilled than he.

Allison turned away and continued along the battlements. She'd come up to spy on the men, to see if Derek Sinclair was still amongst them. To her vast disappointment, he was.

She didn't understand it. Every day, when she rode out and saw him slogging away, she thought surely he couldn't endure much longer. But now a whole week had passed, and he was still there. Why didn't he leave?

She should just be patient, she knew. It was unlikely that he would persist in his wild story much longer under Sir Drogo's stern tutelage. She should go about her duties, pretending to be totally unaware of the varlet. As lady of

Pelsworth Castle, she had a position to uphold. Her position required that she be calm and dignified at all times.

Oh, Anne might say she was a trifle *too* calm and dignified, that she had forgotten how to enjoy herself, but Allison brushed off such petty criticisms. She had many responsibilities that demanded all of her time and attention. She could not waste her energy on unimportant things like pleasure—or Derek Sinclair.

She would ignore him, she told herself firmly as she descended the tower stairs.

A small frown knitted her brow. Actually, she'd already tried to ignore him. It wasn't easy though when everyone kept talking about him.

In the evenings, when she went to the tapestry room to spin, all her ladies would be speaking of some bizarre thing he'd told them about—hamburgers and pizza (some kind of food, from what she could gather); and football and TV (which sounded like the most mindless entertainment she'd ever heard of); and cigarettes (some herb that life wasn't worth living without). And when she went to the servants' hall, or the kitchens, the maids would be giggling and whispering about some peculiar request he'd made—for matches (a magical lighting device); for ice (at this time of the year!); and for Pepto-Bismol (whatever that was).

Somehow, in spite of how busy Sir Drogo kept him, Derek Sinclair had managed to meet every female in the castle.

Frowning, she stepped into the courtyard. As if they'd been lying in wait, three men rushed up to her.

"My lady!" the steward cried, wringing his hands. "The pantler and butler are fighting again! You must come at once!"

"But, my lady!" the bailiff said, picking up one of the documents he'd dropped. "You promised to speak to your father about the petition from the Wyatt family this morning. The matter is quite urgent. Their rent is now almost a year in arrears and your father still hasn't made a decision."

"My lady, obviously you are quite busy," the priest said. "I will take but a moment of your time—I merely wished to

remind you that Lord Pelsworth agreed to contribute toward
the cost of repainting the village church, and he still hasn't
paid. And"—he lowered his voice—"there is another matter
I must speak to you about. In private."

"Yes, yes, yes," Allison said, glad to be distracted from
her thoughts of Derek Sinclair. "Larkin, I saw a peddler on
the road when I was up on the battlements. Have the butler
go greet him and find out if he has any wine to sell. And tell
the pantler that I will be inspecting the cupboards this afternoon. Perhaps that will keep the two of them busy. Renfry,
put the petition in the library. I will read it as soon as I am
able. And Father Gregory, walk with me to the wardrobe
keeper's office, and I will have him make that contribution
anon."

As soon as she and the priest had moved away from the
other two men, Allison said, "Now what was the other matter you wished to discuss?"

His mouth drooped in an expression of gloom. "I am
sorry to report this, my lady, but the village laundresses have
been making overtures to some of the men again."

"Hmm," Allison said. The laundresses' lack of morals
was an ongoing problem at the castle. "I will speak to the
women and make it clear that I will not tolerate such behavior."

"I fear it will do little good to speak to them," Father Gregory said. "But I thought perhaps you could speak to Sir
Derek."

"Sir Derek!" Allison's brows drew together. "Why would
I speak to him?"

"It seems he is the object of the laundresses', er, affections. I thought if you could ask him to be less, ahem,
friendly to the laundresses, then all might be well."

Allison could not trust herself to speak for a few moments. "I will see what I can do," she said, trying to control
her expression.

Father Gregory glanced at her a little uneasily as they entered the wardrobe keeper's office. "I don't mean to imply
that he is *encouraging* them."

Oh, no, Allison thought sourly as she directed the

wardrobe keeper to pay Father Gregory. The laundresses didn't need any encouragement. How dare that knave come here claiming to be her True Love, then cavort with the laundresses?

"I don't believe he seeks them out at all," Father Gregory continued anxiously as the wardrobe keeper counted out the coins. "In fact, most of the time I see him, he is alone. He is very interested in Pelsworth Castle. Why, a guard found him in the dovecote a few days ago, and I, myself, discovered him in the crypt under the chapel just yesterday. Apparently he likes to explore."

To explore—or to spy?

For a moment Allison's blood ran cold. But then, just as quickly, she rejected the thought. If the king were to send a spy, surely he would have chosen someone more intelligent. The king would not have picked someone so foolish as to wear his codpiece as a purse.

Bidding the wardrobe keeper and Father Gregory a good day, she left and headed back for the courtyard. She was being ridiculous, she thought, seeing phantoms where none existed. She had enough problems already without creating more.

Outside, she glanced heavenward, seeking some warmth, but there was none to be found. Instead, the skies were cold and leaden. The grayness seemed to press down on her, enveloping her, suffocating her.

She took a deep breath. Sometimes she wondered what it would be like to be a child again, free of care and full of joy. Sometimes, she thought she would give almost anything to experience that happiness again. . . .

She gave herself a mental shake. Those days were gone forever. She had responsibilities now. Responsibilities that precluded such fantasies as True Love.

She sighed. The stranger might not be a spy, but he was an annoyance that she didn't need. She would have Sir Drogo speak to him.

As for herself, she had every intention of keeping as far away from Derek Sinclair as possible.

* * *

Wanting the emerald and actually getting it were two very different things, Derek had discovered.

A week after his arrival in the Middle Ages, he took off his helmet after a vigorous workout, hobbled into the shade, and collapsed.

Or at least, he tried to. Full armor did not lend itself to collapse. Awkwardly he bent down, then put one hand on the ground to support himself while he lowered the rest of his body onto the grass.

He couldn't take much more of this. Even putting as little effort into his "practice" as possible, he ached in every muscle, every bone, every cell of his body. Not only from the blows he'd taken in the "matches" between the squires—accompanied by howls of laughter from those watching—or from the relentless exercise with ax, mace, sword, great sword, flail, and lance. No, this pain went far deeper than that. His toenails hurt—from the ill-fitting shoes; and his skin—from the unbearably itchy wool hose; and his rear—from using straw for toilet paper. He hated everything about the Middle Ages—the food, the sponge baths, the "practice". . . .

As he pulled off his gauntleted gloves, a servant girl—Marjorie—approached and handed him a cup. He smiled automatically and took a sip. Shuddering, he stared down at the contents with loathing.

And most of all, he hated the warm piss they called beer.

A short distance away several of the squires sat in the shade, also. They gulped their beer thirstily, smacking their lips as though it were nectar of the gods. One of them glanced at him, then whispered something to the others. They burst into laughter.

Derek ignored them. He didn't care what a bunch of snot-nosed Medieval brats thought—

"Excuse me," a voice interrupted his thoughts. "May I sit here?"

Derek looked up to see Cuthbert standing before him. "Sure. There's plenty of room," he said a bit wryly.

Cuthbert sat down. "You must pay no attention to those

blockheads. They have no perception, no wit, or they would treat you with the respect you plainly deserve."

Derek glanced at the boy in surprise. "Thanks, Cuthbert. I really appreciate that."

"You need not thank me. As Lady Allison's True Love, you are worthy of respect, no matter how incompetent you appear."

Derek winced. Tact was obviously not the boy's strong suit.

A small cough drew Derek's attention. Sir Percival, the chief herald, had taken his place near the group of men and was preparing to speak.

Derek groaned silently. The beer might be the worst thing about the Middle Ages, but this man came a close second. Every time the squires took a break, the herald lectured them on "knightly behavior."

"Be kind and generous," Sir Percival intoned, "to those in distress. . . ."

If Sir Percival practiced what he preached, he would stop right now. It hadn't been so bad at first, when Derek could barely understand what the man said. But his ear was growing more and more accustomed to the speech of the Middle Ages, and now the endless lecturing—not to mention Percival's high-pitched, droning voice—was beginning to wear on his nerves. And his poor nerves didn't need any more abuse. They were already struggling under the torture of nicotine withdrawal.

"And know no fear. . . ."

Know no fear? Who'd this guy think he was fooling? Everything about the Middle Ages was scary. Gloomily Derek stared at the pigs rooting around the castle walls. They were scary-looking pigs—small, with black hairy skin and mean eyes. The cow being led down the road by a farmer was scary looking, too. It had a curly, multicolored coat and long horns. None of the animals looked—or tasted—the way they should. What little meat he got was always tough and gamey.

"You must speak only the truth. . . ."

The truth was everything here was strange—even the horses. They were very different from the fast, responsive Thoroughbreds with deep bodies and generous quarters that he was used to—although he doubted any Thoroughbred would allow a creaking, clanking man in armor to repeatedly jump on and off it as Derek was required to do. The medieval "warhorse" was steady and strong, but not speedy, with a shorter, broader back and thicker, more powerful legs.

At least the warhorses were prized and well cared for. Others were not so lucky. He'd been angry at first at the condition of some of the horses—until he'd seen their owners. The people, thin and sickly, looked even worse than their animals.

The nag pulling a cart down the road toward him now was more fortunate than most—it at least appeared well fed. Its owner looked like a peddler of some sort, with pots and pans hanging from the sides of his cart and a cask in the back. Derek wondered if it contained beer. *Real* beer.

"You must champion what is good and right. . . ."

There was nothing good or right about the beer here. God, he wanted a real beer. A cold and frothy beer. And he wanted to know what was going on in the NFL. The teams should be signing their draft choices by now. Now that the salary cap was in place, the teams would undoubtedly be dropping some of their high-priced players. He wanted to know who had gotten the boot.

"And the knight shall be patient and content. . . ."

He was definitely losing patience. How much longer would he be stuck here? He'd already been here six days—or was it seven? There were no calendars in the castle for him to check. Nor any clocks. Only bells that rang every couple of hours for no purpose that he could determine.

"Be loyal to God and the church. . . ."

Church. Dear God. Derek closed his eyes, shutting out the sight of the girl with a flock of geese, the farmer with a cow, and the peddler's cart. Church was a torture in and of itself. The priest droned on and on—in Latin no less. There were no pews—everyone stood to sing or knelt to pray. He'd

never known anyone could pray so much or for so long. His
knees still ached from kneeling on the cold stone floor of the
chapel. The only entertainment was to watch Allison, and
that wasn't particularly amusing. He could usually only see
the back of her head, covered by a close-fitting hat—a
"caul" Cuthbert had told him it was called. When he *did*
catch a glimpse of her face, she looked nauseatingly pious.
Perhaps because *she* had a cushion to kneel on.

"Be just and pure. . . ."

And speaking of entertainment . . . there wasn't any. He'd
never met such a pack of gloomy people in his life. He'd
commented on this fact to Cuthbert who had informed him
that the people there prided themselves on being pious and
hardworking.

"Yeah, I'll say," Derek had muttered.

"Although, 'twasn't always so," Cuthbert said, a thought-
ful look on his face. "I have heard that before the old lord
and lady died, Pelsworth Castle was known as one of the
merriest places in England. Everyone must still have gotten
their work done, though, because the Pelsworths have always been prosperous."

Pelsworth Castle—merry? It was hard to imagine. Although he did think the mood of the castle had improved in
the last few days since Lord Pelsworth had left. Everyone
seemed more relaxed after his departure. Except, perhaps,
for Sir Drogo. The man was a slave-driver. He also had an
eye like a hawk, making it difficult for Derek to slip away
and search for the emerald.

Derek was confident, however, that he would eventually
find it. For the most part, these medieval people were amazingly trusting. The women were especially friendly and
forthcoming. Except for Allison.

Not that he saw much of her. He caught glimpses of her
around the castle—always with one or another of the servants—and he saw her riding out every afternoon, but she
never so much as glanced in his direction after that first day.
He could never resist looking at her, however, even though
the sight of her, so calm and cool, annoyed him more often
than not.

He saw no sign of the distress that had been so apparent when her father told her about the letter to the king. He wondered about that occasionally. Why had she been so upset? Was she afraid the king would refuse to allow the engagement to Wilfred to be broken?

He'd asked the ever-informative Cuthbert what he thought about it one day when they saw her riding out the gate with Sir Everard and Lady Anne, but Cuthbert had seemed confused by the question. So Derek had changed the subject and asked where she was going.

"She visits the village and various tenants on the estate," Cuthbert had answered absently, staring after her in a lovelorn fog. "And she bathes in a pool upstream from where the two rivers join."

Derek's ears had immediately perked up. "Oh?"

Cuthbert must have heard something in his tone, because he'd given him a slightly worried look. "You must never go there, of course."

"Of course," Derek echoed.

Cuthbert, apparently satisfied with Derek's halfhearted agreement, returned his gaze to Allison's retreating figure, his face taking on a fatuous expression that was becoming increasingly familiar.

"Lady Allison is so dedicated to the welfare of everyone who belongs to the castle." He sighed worshipfully. "She never has a thought for herself. She is always helping those in need. She is so beautiful. So warm."

Beautiful, yes. Derek had to agree with that assessment. But as for warm . . . well, suffice to say he'd seen warmer ice cubes.

"She is so kind. So generous. So wise."

Derek tried not to gag.

"If only I could kiss the hem of her gown, I would die happy—"

Derek snorted.

Cuthbert looked at him in surprise. "Do you not agree?"

"Yeah, sure. Kissing her . . . hem is a dream of mine, too."

Listening to Cuthbert's goddess-worship had made Derek wince. The boy's adoration made him want to sit the lad down and explain to him that women were women, not goddesses, saints, or angels. Most certainly not angels.

Derek glanced sideways at Cuthbert, who was now listening with shining eyes to the herald's instruction.

"And protect your lady. . . ."

What would the boy think of Lady Allison if he knew that she had a lover waiting in the wings? Derek stared down at his mace. If only the man—what was his name? Oh, yeah, Boris. If only Boris would show up and claim Allison. Then perhaps he, Derek, could quit this damned knight stuff and go home. *If* he could get the emerald.

"Honor is your most precious jewel. . . ."

Derek took another small sip of beer, grimaced, then set down the cup. He'd discovered from the servant girl, Tilly, that a "treasury" for valuables did indeed exist, in one of the storerooms under the main gatehouse. He'd sneaked down there yesterday and found the door—locked, of course. He'd studied the large keyhole a moment, then tried to pick it. Unfortunately, lock picking wasn't one of his skills.

Upon further questioning, Tilly had informed him that Allison had the only key, and she wore it on the ring at her waist at all times.

He was going to have to steal it from her, Derek thought, idly plucking at the grass. Unless he could somehow make her remember her promise.

Perhaps if he told her who he was, it would prompt her memory. It was a long shot, granted. But at this point, he was willing to try just about anything. He really needed to talk to her. . . .

A woman in a blue dress walked past the guard at the postern gate and approached the peddler. The peddler, gesturing expansively, held up a frying pan. The woman shook her head and pointed at something else.

Derek was on his feet in a flash, unaware of the fact that he'd knocked over his cup of beer.

"Sir Derek?" Cuthbert said inquiringly. And then: "Sir Derek! Where are you going? No, you can't, the rest period is almost over! Wait! Come back. . . ."

Derek paid no heed.

Cuthbert watched him sprint across the yard toward the postern gate, then sighed and righted the cup.

People from California were very strange.

Very strange indeed.

"Ah, you have a remarkable eye, my lady," the peddler said, handing her the bolt of fabric. "'Tis the finest silk from India, brought here with the greatest of difficulties. 'Tis worth a fortune—"

Allison touched the material, then arched her brows skeptically. "It feels like coarse Italian silk to me."

"My lady! You wound me! I assure you, 'tis the most rare, most highly sought after—"

"Yes, yes, I'm sure," Allison interrupted him. She was beginning to be sorry that she'd decided to come out and look over the man's wares. She wasn't in the mood to tolerate a cheating peddler. She already had one scoundrel interfering in her life; she didn't have the patience to deal with another. "Tell me, do you have medicines?"

"Of course!" The peddler handed her another bottle. "This is a wondrous potion. One sip drains black bile and ill humors from the body and fosters a pleasant temperament."

Allison looked at the bottle with more interest. Wilfred had departed from the castle in a black humor, indeed. She'd managed to calm him down before he left, but it might be prudent to take further measures. The potion might prove useful when he returned.

She pulled the sliver of wood out of the bottle and sniffed. "It smells of spirits."

"Does it?" The peddler sounded surprised. "Well, I know the priest who concocts these potions often uses spirits as a base, but then he adds special herbs and spices to give the elixir its unique properties. It also begets sweet slumber and pleasant dreams."

"Is that so?" Allison murmured. She didn't believe the peddler for a moment, or she might have bought the potion. She'd had trouble sleeping lately—she was plagued with nightmares. 'Twas all the fault of that rogue, Derek Sinclair. She'd barely seen him since the day of his arrival—and she planned to keep it that way—but for some reason she'd dreamed of him every night. If only she could control her sleeping mind as well as she could her waking one. . . .

"Ah, good morning, my lady! Lovely day, isn't it?"

Allison stiffened, unable to believe the boldness of the villain. He swaggered toward her in a way she would have thought impossible in his dented, mismatched armor, his light hair darkened with sweat at his hairline, and his brown eyes gleaming in a way that made her stomach clench in anger.

Pretending deafness, she set down the bottle and perused the peddler's other merchandise.

The peddler glanced uncertainly from her to Derek.

"Don't mind her," Sinclair said to the peddler in a confiding voice. "She's a bit hard of hearing."

Allison's head snapped around. "There is naught wrong with my hearing," she said sharply. "'Tis your heathen accent that is difficult to understand."

"Oh?" he replied, lounging against the cart in a casual, disrespectful manner. "I am finding it easier and easier to understand yours."

She stared at him coldly, ignoring the whiteness of his teeth against the brown hue of his skin. "The men are returning to their practice. Should you not join them, Sinclair?" She refused to give him the title he claimed. If he were a knight, she would eat her best caul.

"There's no rush." He picked up a few small items from the other side of the cart. "Hmm. These look interesting. What are they?"

"They are very rare, very precious relics," the peddler said. "That one is a tooth from Apollonia, patron saint of tooth disorders. 'Tis very helpful if you have a toothache. The thorn encased in glass is from a wreath worn by Dympna, patron saint of lunatics. I sold a similar one to a man whose wife had gone mad. It cured her instantly."

"I can't use either of those." He cast a sidelong glance at Allison that made her fume. "At least not yet. What about this one?"

"Ah, that is a toe bone from Saint Christopher. It protects travelers from all harm."

Allison could listen no more. "I have no doubt 'tis a fake." She stared at Derek pointedly.

He looked amused, the rascal.

"Oh, no, my lady," the peddler protested. "'Tis a genuine relic brought back from the Holy Land at great expense."

Sinclair turned the bone between his long fingers. Allison noticed with some small satisfaction that his hands were no longer so pretty—they were covered with scratches and half-healed blisters.

"I've sold hundreds to ladies whose lovers are about to go on a long journey," the peddler added. "And I've never had any complaints."

"Hmm," Derek said. "I might be able to use one of those. What do you say, Lady Allison? Will you buy me one as a betrothal gift?"

"Only if you promise to go on a long journey."

He laughed, the wretch. "Is that any way to talk to your True Love?"

"You are no more my True Love than this peddler here."

Derek looked at the fat old man with food in his beard. "Oh?"

Allison flushed, but managed to keep her nose in the air.

Derek sighed exaggeratedly. "You are hard-hearted, Lady Allison. I see you every day, riding by and at dinner, but you never so much as glance my way."

"I am sure I have never noticed you," she lied. In truth, she was always conscious of his stare. Once, at dinner, she'd accidentally glanced in his direction. He had stared so intently, she hadn't been able to look away. It had taken the snarling of the dogs fighting over a bone to break the spell. She hated the way he stared at her.

"How odd," he said softly. She felt a light touch on the nape of her neck. "I always notice you."

She whirled to face him. Which was a mistake, because he was much too close. So close, she could smell the scent of him—leather and beer and sweat. But it wasn't an unpleasant smell. He didn't have the stale aroma that most men had—he was amazingly clean. Even his hair looked clean. The sun, peeking through the clouds, shone on the blond highlights. He must have spent a lot of time out of doors for it to be so light. He was as brown as a Spaniard—or a peasant. His skin had a darker hue than she was accustomed to see on a gentleman. In the hall, when he'd first come, she'd noticed that he was an even brown color all over, from his face, down to his chest and stomach and . . .

"Have you noticed me now?" he asked.

He was smiling as if he already knew the answer. She stuck her nose in the air, determined not to add to his already overweening conceit. "There's not much to notice."

"I'd be glad to show you more—in private."

She opened her mouth to make a sharp reply, then closed it again. She would not allow him to make her lose her temper. She was the lady of Pelsworth Castle. She wasn't going to stand in front of the gatehouse exchanging insults with this varlet. She would be calm and cool at all times, and once she saw how indifferent she was to him, he would realize that it was pointless to stay.

"You are wasting your time here." She looked him up and down with her haughtiest stare. "I will never marry you."

He smiled crookedly. "I hope not. I have no desire to marry."

Disconcerted, she stared at him. "Then why are you here?"

"Because you asked me to come and prevent your marriage to Wilfred."

Allison gasped. "You lie! I have never met you. And I *want* to marry Wilfred."

Derek frowned. "You do? But what about Boris?"

"Boris?" Allison was confused.

"Your lover."

"I have no lover!"

"Oh, that's right—you haven't met him yet. But when you do, you're going to want to marry him instead of Wilfred."

"What are you talking about? I have no intention of marrying this Boris, whoever he is."

Derek shrugged, his armor squeaking a little as he did so. "That's fine by me. It's none of my business if you want to have your cake and eat it, too. But I'm not going to wait around while you try to find some other poor sap to propose."

"Have my cake . . . ? Some other poor sap . . . ?" Allison stared at him. "Now I understand. You're insane!"

"No. At least I don't think I am." He stared into her eyes as if watching for something. "I'm from the future."

Allison couldn't help herself—she gaped at him. "Are you trying to say you are some sort of magical being? You *are* insane."

"Perhaps. Or perhaps I dreamed about a ghost that looked exactly like you, who begged me so prettily to come back in time and prevent her marriage to Wilfred." He frowned. "I've been meaning to talk to you about him—he's hardly the Bullwinkle clone you made him out to be."

"Bullwinkle clone?" she repeated, dazed.

He rubbed his chin, which was dark with a week's worth of stubble. "I suppose you thought I wouldn't come if I knew what I was up against."

He met her gaze. Whatever he saw there, made him shrug. "Never mind. Believe what you like."

"I most certainly will! I want you to leave at once!"

"I wish I could, but I can't. Not until you give me what I came for."

"And what, pray tell, is that?"

He hesitated. "I can't tell you."

"I see." At last this conversation was beginning to make sense—he had made up this insane story to distract her from discovering his true purpose. Did he really think she would fall for such a trick? "Well, Sir Derek, your 'trip through time' has been wasted. I will not give you anything, and I *will* marry Wilfred, just as I planned. You will not last long here." She gazed at him insultingly.

His eyes narrowed for a moment, but then he laughed. "You're right about that. Come on, Allie. Admit that I'm doing you a favor. I would think breaking up your engagement to Wilfred would be worth almost any price. You cannot want to marry the brute."

"I *do* want to marry the brute, er, Wilfred. He is very strong. And manly." She looked down her nose at him.

Derek raised his brows. "I suppose so . . . if you like the dancing bear type."

Caught unawares, Allison choked back a laugh at the apt description. She frowned haughtily to cover her lapse, but he didn't appear to have noticed it. He was frowning, too, his fingers tapping on his leg armor.

"Is that why you were so upset about your father's letter to the king?" he asked after a moment. "Because you were afraid the king would *agree* to breaking your betrothal?"

Reminded of her father's letter, Allison lost all desire to laugh. She glanced at the peddler. He was pretending to straighten the wares on his cart, but she could see his ears perked in their direction, no doubt hoping to hear some tidbit of gossip.

"I do not know what you are talking about." Hoping to distract Derek from the subject, she turned to the cart and picked up the nearest item. "Ah, here is something more suited to you, Sir Derek—a deck of cards. Do you have cards in California? They are particularly favored by the lazy and idle."

Derek's lips twitched, but he said nothing. He still watched her curiously—and much more closely than she liked. Fortunately, the peddler drew his attention with a vociferous protest.

"My lady, I must object! Even the king plays cards. And this is a particularly fine deck. See how carefully the court cards are painted. Notice, too, the fine detail of the coins, cups, swords, and batons." He turned to Sir Derek. "I assure you, you will not find a finer deck in all of England."

"I'm sure I won't," Derek agreed. "Unfortunately, I have no money."

The peddler looked crestfallen. Before he could say more, Cuthbert rushed up. "Sir Drogo has summoned the men, Sir Derek! We must go at once."

Derek nodded absently, inspecting the pictures on the cards. "These are amazing. The suits are so different. I really would like to buy these."

"Don't be foolish, Sir Derek," Cuthbert said. "Sir Drogo has forbidden playing cards."

"Oh, has he?" Derek glanced at Allison. "I want them just as a souvenir, I assure you."

Allison restrained a snort. Did he honestly expect her to believe that? "I feel 'tis my Christian duty to buy you something that you need much more than cards, Sir Derek." She picked up St. Dympna's thorn for lunatics and held it out to him. "I will pray that 'twill wreak a miracle and restore some small measure of your wits."

As soon as the words left her mouth, she regretted them. She'd wanted to put him in his place, to show him what she thought of him. But instead of looking insulted, he gazed at her with a warm gleam in his eyes as though she'd offered some intimacy.

She started to lower her hand, but before she could do so, he grasped it with his own. She tried to pull away, but he held on, his fingers warm and strong.

"Sir Derek, we must *hurry*," Cuthbert reminded him.

Derek nodded, but made no move to release her hand. "I still want to know about that letter."

She stiffened. "I told you—"

"Yeah, I know. You don't know what I'm talking about." His gaze searched hers. "I don't think you're telling me the truth."

"Sir Derek! Cuthbert!" Sir Drogo stormed up before Allison could reply. "Back to training at once!"

"Of course, sir," Derek said, not looking away from Allison. He stared at her a moment longer, then shrugged.

Stepping back, he made a flourishing bow, still holding onto her hand. "Thank you for your gift," he said. Impervious to her attempts to free herself, he lifted her fingers and pressed his mouth against them. "I'll treasure it always."

She gasped and opened her mouth to berate him, but he was already gone, whistling insolently as he strolled back to the training yard.

She wiped her hand on her skirt, trying to eradicate the tingling warmth that radiated from the spot he'd kissed. Oh, he was a smooth one. But not smooth enough. He had revealed his true purpose here—he wanted something from her. Gold or some favor most likely. Obviously, he had made up the story about being her True Love merely to gain access to the castle. As far as his tale about being from the future—that was pure rubbish.

"My lady," Sir Drogo said from beside her, his voice gruff. "I hope those varlets weren't bothering you."

Allison glanced at the peddler, who was straightening his already straight wares. She forced herself to smile. "No, not at all." Taking Sir Drogo's arm, she led him a few steps away from the cart and the nosy peddler. "Tell me, how fares Sir Derek?"

"Not well," Sir Drogo said bluntly. "He is a shirker. He makes next to no effort. 'Tis my belief he's had no training with weapons whatsoever. And at the rate he's going, it will take ten years for him to acquire even the smallest prowess. Furthermore, he cannot endure the sight of blood. I have never known a man so squeamish. The smallest wound in any of the men makes Sir Derek turn as pale as an infant's backside."

"Then he cannot possibly be a knight." Ha! Allison smiled in triumph. Sir Drogo's analysis confirmed all her suspicions. She would write her father; tell him that Sinclair was a fraud and a liar—

"'Tis unlikely. Although . . ." Scowling, Sir Drogo tugged his beard.

Allison stopped smiling. "Although what?"

"He does ride," the old knight admitted.

Allison frowned at this unwelcome news. "Does he ride well?"

"Amazingly so." Sir Drogo shrugged. "So his tale of being a peaceful knight could be true."

"But you said 'twas unlikely."

He shrugged. "'Tis hard to say. One thing is certain, however. Riding skill alone would not save him in a battle."

"No, it would not," she agreed, her frown deepening. How unfortunate that he could ride. It gave him just enough credibility to make his tale possible.

She shook her head. She would still write to her father. But in case he refused to believe Derek was a fraud, she would have to continue her efforts to rid the castle of the trickster.

She pasted a worried frown on her face. "Dear me, I hate to think what would happen to him if we were ever attacked and there was blood all over the place. Perhaps you should take him hunting. 'Twill help inure him to the sight of blood and make him more manly."

"Very well, my lady. I will arrange it as soon as possible." With a bow he departed, and she entered the courtyard through the postern gate, feeling very pleased with herself.

That jackanapes Sinclair would soon regret his impudence with her. A nice, bloody hunting expedition would drive off the stranger with his soft stomach, soft hands, and soft ways. It would make him sorry that he'd ever come here with his flirtatious manners and outrageous tales. The gall of the lunatic to say she would take a lover—she would never do such a thing. And to imply she didn't want to marry Wilfred . . .

She looked across the crowded courtyard. Everyone bustled about, happy and busy, the picture of contentment. No one in that courtyard would ever guess at the dark undercurrents that were swirling about them, threatening to destroy them all. . . .

Feeling suddenly dizzy, Allison hurried past the kitchen and inside the well tower. With trembling hands she drank a dipperful of the cool water. It tasted bitter and metallic against her tongue.

Of course she wanted to marry Wilfred.

Dear heaven, she *must* marry him.

Chapter 9

HELL. THIS WAS hell.

There could be no other explanation, Derek thought a
week later as he stared into the mean red eyes of a wild
boar. He hadn't gone back in time—he'd died and gone to
hell.

The vicious-looking animal pawed the dirt and tossed its
head, razor-sharp tusks glinting in the sunlight. In response
Derek lifted the boar-spear to a more threatening angle, hoping he was doing it right and wishing he'd made some excuse to avoid going on this hunting party.

"Hunting helps knights train for war," Cuthbert had explained that morning when Sir Drogo announced the
planned excursion. "It gives us a chance to prove our
courage by facing dangerous animals."

Really, he had no interest in proving his courage, Derek
thought, eyeing the boar warily. It made a high-pitched
squealing sound that sent shivers down his spine. He definitely should have made an excuse. But the idea of the out-
ing had been appealing—especially after the drudgery of the
past week.

It had rained every day. He had thought, when he first saw

the rain, that Sir Drogo would call off the practice. But when Derek had suggested as much, the old knight looked at him scornfully.

"You think our enemies are going to care if 'tis raining when they attack? Do you have a brain inside that head of yours, Sir Derek?"

Slogging in the mud, Derek hadn't been sure. His brain felt numb. Wavering images, like mirages, rose before his eyes. Pizza. Real beer. Cigarettes . . .

He'd spent the whole week sinking in a quagmire of mud, being sprayed with flecks of water every time he struck the rain-soaked pel. Was it any wonder that the idea of riding outside the castle in the sunlight had been too tempting to resist?

If only the sight of blood didn't make him sick.

He had thought maybe he could endure it, but unfortunately, traveling through time had not eradicated his weak stomach. When the hunters had found a boar and set the dogs on it, the resulting sights and sounds of flesh ripping, blood spraying, and guts spilling onto the dirt had made his stomach lurch violently. Fighting nausea, he'd slipped away from the others, planning to return to the castle to take a well-deserved (as far as he was concerned) rest.

If only he hadn't gotten thirsty. If only, upon catching sight of a stream, he hadn't gotten off his horse and slaked his thirst with the cool water. If only he hadn't apparently managed to choose this ugly little porker's favorite watering spot. . . .

Sweat trickled down Derek's forehead, but he didn't dare lift a hand to wipe it away. He stood as still as possible, spear raised, thankful that he'd managed to grab it before his horse bolted. He hoped the boar would decide somewhere in its piggy brain that a human wasn't suitable prey.

The boar raised its ugly snout in the air and snorted malevolently. It tossed its head, slashing the air with its savage tusks.

Derek held his ground.

It pawed the dirt violently and squealed fiendishly.

Derek stood firm.

It lowered its head and charged.

Derek dropped the spear and ran.

He could hear the vicious pig's demonic squeals coming closer and closer. He ran faster—but the boar was even quicker. A sharp pain tore through his lower calf. Fear—and adrenaline—surged through him. With a superhuman effort, he leaped . . . and caught hold of a low-hanging tree branch.

Swinging his legs around the limb, he pulled himself up.

The boar squealed in fury. It trotted around the tree trunk, trumpeting its frustration shrilly. In a frenzy it butted its head against the trunk repeatedly, sending chunks of wood flying. Derek held onto the branch for dear life.

Finally, with a squeal of disgust, the boar butted the tree one last time, then trotted off in search of new prey.

Derek didn't move. He lay on the tree branch, his cheek pressed against the rough bark. Gasping for breath, he waited for his heartbeat to return to normal.

Dear God. What he wouldn't give for a cigarette right now.

He eyed the leaves of the tree. Hadn't he heard that some people made cigarettes out of leaves? Maybe he could . . .

No. Derek closed his eyes. He was losing it. Definitely losing it. He wanted to go home. He *needed* to go home before he was a complete nut case—or dinner for a possessed pig. He would do anything if he could just go home. Hell, he'd even marry Eleanor—

The sound of hoofbeats made Derek freeze, then slowly open his eyes.

On the path some distance away, were three riders—Sir Everard, Lady Anne . . . and Allison.

He stared through the leafy branches at her. He hadn't seen her at all in the last few days, but he found himself thinking about her a lot—more often than he liked. He couldn't seem to help himself.

He kept remembering things from when he'd talked to her by the peddler's cart. How she smelled, for example. She had smelled so damned good. In the last few weeks he'd become inured to the earthy aroma of everyone around him—and indeed, he was aware that in spite of the sponge baths he took two times a day, he was probably smelling a bit ripe himself.

So it had come as something of a surprise to find that Allison had such a sweet scent. Such an incredibly enticing scent.

He recognized it vaguely from when she was a ghost and when he'd gone to her room that first night. But it hadn't struck him so strongly there. At the cart, however, everything inside of him had responded to that scent. He wasn't sure why. Maybe because nicotine wasn't dulling his sense of smell anymore. Or maybe because it was the first time he'd been able to observe her up close when his head wasn't pounding.

He'd noticed something else, too—she was smaller and more delicate than he'd thought. Her head barely reached the top of his shoulder. And when he'd lifted her hand, he'd been surprised to see how small and slender it was in his grip.

It was her tart tongue that made her seem taller and sturdier. He actually rather liked her tartness. She wasn't at all the sweet helpless maiden he'd first thought.

A horse neighed, startling Derek from his thoughts. The riders were on the path directly below him. He grew still, watching them as they passed.

Sir Everard rode a little ahead, his gaze searching the path for possible dangers. Behind him, Lady Anne chatted with Allison, although the older woman appeared to do most of the talking. Allison listened and responded occasionally, but mostly she seemed deep in thought.

She was close enough now that he could see she was wearing the tight-fitting dress again. The gown hugged her figure, down to her waist and hips. God, he'd love to get inside her panties.

But she didn't wear any, he remembered. That night in Nan's cottage, when he'd pushed Allison's skirts up her thigh, there had been no impediment to his searching fingers, no underwear of any kind. . . .

Derek's groin throbbed . . . but then his leg throbbed even harder. Reminded of his recent trauma, he waited until the riders rounded a bend in the path, then sat up on the tree branch to inspect his calf.

The boar's tusks had torn right through his boot. The wound on his leg, however, was not as deep as he'd thought—in fact, it was barely a scratch. He paled, however, at the sight of a thin line of blood. No doubt about it—he'd come within inches of being seriously injured.

He leaned back against the tree trunk and closed his eyes again. How could he have just been thinking about sex when he'd barely escaped being killed by the Demon Pig? Life in the Middle Ages was definitely affecting his brain.

A wry smile curved his lips. Reaching into the purse—a plain leather one—on his belt, he withdrew St. Dympna's glass-encased thorn.

Allison had surprised him when she'd suddenly given him the thorn and offered to pray that it would restore his sanity. He would have thought she was much too serious to show such a sassy sense of humor. But perhaps she hadn't always been so solemn. From what she'd said at Nan's cottage about her childhood with her grandparents, it sounded as though she'd once been happy and carefree. She'd certainly changed.

Derek's smile faded. She was a tough one to figure out. First she claimed she wanted to break her engagement to Wilfred; and yet now she said she had no desire to do so. What the hell was going on?

He wasn't sure. But one thing was obvious. He needed to stop thinking about Allison and concentrate on the emerald. It was clear there was no chance of her remembering him. Therefore, he was going to have to steal the jewel. But how?

She wore the key to the treasury constantly. Presumably she took it off at night while she slept, but he wasn't eager to venture into her room and risk losing his head. He had to find another time when she might take off the key. Like when she was taking a bath . . .

He straightened. What had Cuthbert said? That she took a bath in a stream in the afternoon?

He jumped down from the tree and silently set off down the path the trio had taken.

* * *

He had trouble finding the place where they'd turned off the path until he heard a loud sneeze. Through the trees, he spied Sir Everard wiping his nose and blocking a narrow passage between two outcroppings of rock. Skirting the spot, Derek crept through the thick underbrush and up one of the outcroppings.

The sound of the water and feminine voices grew louder and louder until Derek reached the top of the rocks. Pushing aside a branch, he saw a small pool, fed by a thundering waterfall, and screened by bushes. There was no sign of Allison, but he saw Anne folding a red cloak and setting it on a flat rock next to a pile of clothing, a small pair of boots . . . and a ring of keys.

Derek glanced at the keys, then at Anne. How to get the key with her there?

As if in answer to his question, a light voice called out, "Anne, would you please bring me the soap?"

"Yes, my lady." Anne walked around the thick bushes that shielded most of the pool—and Allison—from Derek's view.

Once Anne was out of sight, Derek hurried down. He slipped a few times, scraping himself painfully on the sharp rocks, but fortunately distance and the noise of the waterfall screened the sound of his descent.

He moved through the bushes toward the rock more carefully, aware that he was close enough now that they might hear any noise he made.

Reaching the rock, he picked up the key ring and slipped off the biggest key of the bunch, taking care not to let any of them clank against each other.

He was about to turn and sneak back up the hill when he heard a splash.

He hesitated a moment. Every day Sir Percival pounded it into the squires' heads that knights were always courteous, honorable, and chivalrous. So Derek knew that no knight would ever spy on a lady in her bath.

Thank God he wasn't a knight.

Carefully, quietly, he pushed through the bushes until he could see the pool.

Anne sat quietly on the bank, sewing. Standing under the waterfall was Allison.

Derek breathed in. The water streamed down over her and rose in a mist around her, making her look like some medieval water sprite. He caught a glimpse of small, rather squarish shoulders; of a narrow, curving waist; and of full, rounded buttocks with a dark cleft between.

Derek breathed out, then in again. He remembered stroking those shoulders and the curve of her waist through her dress at Nan's cottage. He remembered pushing her skirt up her leg and cupping those buttocks against him. God, it had felt good to hold her like that. But now he wished he hadn't been in such a hurry. He wished he'd taken the time to undress her and look at her.

He leaned forward against a branch, trying to see better. God, he wanted to see her. He wanted to know if she had large pink nipples or small brown ones, if her stomach was rounded or concave, if her thighs were dimpled or lean, if the hair at the juncture there was full or fine.

If only she wasn't facing the other way. If only the waterfall didn't conceal more than it revealed. If only she would turn around. . . .

She reached up and pulled her hair forward over her shoulder. Half turning, she began to soap her back.

"That's it, Allie," Derek breathed, leaning forward. He could see just the beginning of the curve of her breast. "Turn just a little bit more. . . ."

She turned just enough to lift one foot and place it on a rock. Her hair draped her breast as she leaned forward to soap her leg.

"Yes, Allie." He leaned farther forward, his heart beating faster. "Yes, that's it. C'mon, just a little bit—"

Cra-a-a-ack!

The branch snapped with appalling loudness. Anne immediately turned in his direction, searching the bushes with keen eyes.

"Who's there?" she asked sharply. "Come out, or I'll call the guard."

Cursing, Derek raced away through the bushes. He wasn't sure what the penalty for spying on Allison in her bath was, but considering the enthusiasm of these Medieval people for chopping off heads, he wasn't about to wait around and find out.

Reaching the rocks, he climbed them as quickly as he could, Anne's cries of "Guard! Guard!" spurring him on to superhuman speed and strength.

What a damn fool he was, he thought as he sprinted through the forest, gasping for air, but not daring to slow down. He shouldn't have lingered. As soon as he'd gotten the key, he should have run.

A muffled snort interrupted his thoughts. For a moment, he froze, thinking the boar had returned.

But for once luck was with him—it was his horse, grazing on a small patch of grass.

He vaulted onto the hunter, grabbed the reins, and dug his knees into the horse's sides. He streaked out of the woods and across the meadow, riding low against the horse's neck. Reaching the road, he slowed his mount to a sedate trot and joined the throng of people that constantly seemed to be coming and going to the castle. He glanced back at the forest, then turned his head sharply away as he saw Sir Everard burst out of the trees on foot.

Keeping his face averted, Derek entered through the gate. Once he'd handed his mount over to a stableboy, he headed immediately for the storerooms under the main gatehouse.

He reached the treasury door without incident. Still breathing heavily from the exertion of escaping the knight, Derek inserted the key in the lock and turned it.

He paused, exhilaration filling him. He'd done it! Now he only needed to find the jewel and then finally—*finally* —he would be able to go home.

Pushing the door open, he looked inside.

The room was pitch black.

Cursing the lack of electricity, Derek glanced about the gloomy cellar for a lantern or candle. There was none.

It took him another five minutes to go to the kitchen, get a lantern, and return to the treasury. Once inside, he carefully closed the door behind him and held the lantern aloft.

A jumble of riches met his gaze. Chests of every size and description filled the room. Bolts of silk and velvet were stacked in one corner, silver plate and candelabra filled shelves in another. Large jars lined the wall. He removed the lid from one, and the smell of pepper wafted upward. Fighting an urge to sneeze, he checked the others and found cinnamon, nutmeg, and cloves.

Abandoning the jars, he tried one of the chests. To his relief, it wasn't locked. He opened it and saw gleaming gold. Pausing a moment, he studied one of the coins—it had a figure of an angel slaying a dragon on one side and a ship of some kind on the other.

Returning it to the chest, he quickly rummaged through the coins, searching for jewels, but there weren't any. He opened another chest and found it full of parchment and vellum. He pulled them out and looked underneath—but still no sign of the emerald.

He looked through the other chests and found more of the same. Frantically he searched the room again, checking each of the chests thoroughly, but to no avail. There was no sign of the emerald. Which could mean only one thing.

The jewel must be in her room.

Derek groaned.

But then he took a deep breath. He couldn't stop now. He'd already risked this much. Besides, what better time to search her room than now, when she wasn't in the castle?

There was no time to waste, though. Hastily he left the treasury and gatehouse and crossed the courtyard to the southeast tower. He climbed the circular staircase and walked through the tapestry room, nodding to the two servants brushing the wall hangings as if he had every right to be there.

He entered the next room and halted abruptly. A man with black curly hair and a pencil-thin mustache was sitting in the window seat, strumming his lute softly. Derek cursed. Ready to give up, he opened his mouth to make some excuse and leave, then paused when he realized the man hadn't even looked at him.

It was Rafael, the minstrel, Derek realized. Cuthbert had pointed him out at dinner one day. "He is in love with Lady Anne," Cuthbert had said. "She will not consider him, however, because of his blindness."

Derek hesitated. But then, remembering the boar and the muddy training yard, he set his jaw and moved forward.

Although he'd never done any lock picking as a teenager, he'd had plenty of practice sneaking out of the house. Silent as a shadow, he tiptoed across the room, keeping a wary eye on Rafael. He had just reached the door when the minstrel suddenly stopped playing.

Derek froze. In spite of his blindness Rafael appeared to be staring straight at him. The light blue eyes flickered, and for a second Derek thought it was all over.

But then, with a shrug, the minstrel turned his gaze away and started playing again.

Quickly Derek slipped into the room and shut the door, exhaling on a long sigh of relief. That had been a close one. He didn't want to take a risk like that again.

He glanced around the room. He hadn't noticed anything except the bed on his first visit, but now he saw it contained very little in the way of furnishings—the bed, a chest at its foot, a chair, some wall hangings, and a spinning wheel. He stared at the wheel a moment. It looked exactly like the one in Nan's apartment. Maybe it was even the same one.

That must have been what attracted the ghost to Nan's cottage, Derek thought briefly, before returning his gaze to the chest.

Smiling, he stepped forward, only to freeze when he heard a voice in the outer room. "Good day, Lady Allison, Lady Anne! How beautiful you both sound today!"

Shit! How had they managed to get back to the castle so fast? He must have spent more time in the treasury than he realized.

Panic-stricken, he glanced around the room. There was no place to hide—except under the bed.

He dived underneath just as the door opened.

"Take yourself elsewhere, minstrel, and quit bothering my lady," Anne said coldly, before shutting the door firmly.

A masculine laugh floated through the door.

"Anne," Allison said in a gentler voice than Derek had yet heard her use, "you shouldn't be so cruel to him."

"Oh?" Anne replied. "And I might say the same to you of Sir Derek."

"Sinclair!" Now it was Allison's voice that was cold. "That pestilent knave. The sooner he is gone the better."

Derek saw her feet approaching the bed. He held his breath, a vision of himself with a noose around his neck floating through his head. But then she turned, and he heard the soft rustling of the mattress above him as she sat down.

He rested his forehead on his hand and closed his eyes, letting out the breath he'd been holding slowly and quietly.

"How can you say that?" Anne said. "Don't you find him attractive?"

The vision of a noose faded. His ears perking up, Derek opened his eyes again. Allison's feet dangled in front of him.

She made an unladylike snorting sound and one foot rose out of sight. "Has the man cast a spell over you? Can you not see he is a base, beggarly good-for-naught?" There was a *thump* as her riding boot landed on the floor. The other foot rose, and a moment later the second boot fell to the floor. "I am certain he was the one spying on me at the pool."

Spying was becoming something of a habit, Derek thought wryly as he stared at her feet, which were now covered only by thin stockings. Her feet were small and narrow, her ankles trim. He remembered noticing them that night in Nan's apartment when they'd very nearly made love. The stockings had been fastened at the knee with buckled garters—but he hadn't paid much attention to the stockings or the garters. He'd been too busy admiring the smoothness of her thighs—and the sweet secrets above. . . .

"Oh, Allison," Anne said. "It was probably nothing but an animal."

"An animal named Derek Sinclair," Allison muttered, putting on a pair of soft slippers.

Derek frowned.

"I like him," Anne said. "He makes me laugh. And he's taught the men to play a very diverting card game called poker."

"A card game! But where did he get the cards?"

"From the peddler who spent the night here last week."

"But Sinclair had no coins. How did he pay for them?"

"Cuthbert said Sir Derek taught the peddler poker and several other games in exchange for the cards. He also taught the man to do something called 'shuffling.' I saw Sir Derek do it, Allison, and 'twas truly amazing. He could make the cards arch and fold together and spread out like a fan—"

"Ha! He is obviously a trickster, not a knight. Sir Drogo told me he barely knows a mace from an ax."

"But he must be noble to have learned to ride so well. Have you seen him? He rides like a centaur."

"He was probably a stableboy."

"He doesn't act like one. He must be wealthy—he is quite extravagant. He thinks nothing of burning twenty candles in a room at night or asking for salt or sugar or rare and expensive fruits. He claims they are common in California."

"You sound as though you've spent a good deal of time with him."

"Not much. But he does tell the most amusing tales—"

"Tales! Lies, you mean. I did not tell you this before, but now I see I must—he claims to be from the future! Have you ever heard anything so ridiculous?"

Anne didn't reply.

"Anne? Anne!" Allison's voice was incredulous. "Surely you cannot believe him?"

"No, of course not. Although . . . How did he know about the deathbed promise? *I* didn't even know about that."

"Father probably said something whilst in his cups."

"That is not very likely. I have never heard your father mention your mother."

"Honestly, Anne! You think 'tis more likely that Derek Sinclair traveled through time?" Allison jumped up and walked to the chest at the foot of the bed. She took something out of the chest and began pounding it. "It doesn't matter how he knew or where he came from. He could have come down from Mount Olympus for all I care. He means nothing to me."

"I can see he doesn't affect you at all." Anne's voice was dry.

The pounding slowed. "Oh, Anne. I suppose I am a trifle overwrought. 'Tis just that I am a little tense. I haven't been sleeping well of late."

"Oh? Perhaps I should fix a sleeping draught for you then, before you beat that flax to death."

"Thank you, but I don't want a sleeping draught. I want to be rid of Sir Derek. I only hope my father hurries home."

"Lord Pelsworth has been gone little more than a week— he never returns so quickly."

"Usually, no. But I sent a messenger after him with a letter saying that I have proof Sinclair is a fraud. He should be arriving any day now."

"Come now, Allison. Ignorance of weapons is hardly proof."

"I know. I only hope my other plan works."

"Plan? What plan?"

"Sinclair is squeamish about blood. I asked Sir Drogo to take him hunting, and they went today. I am hoping the beetle-headed knave will not be able to endure it."

Under the bed Derek stiffened. Why that little—

"Allison, you are cruel."

"Bah! 'Tis Sinclair who is cruel to me. His game has jeopardized my marriage to Sir Wilfred."

"You truly prefer Wilfred to Derek?"

Allison hesitated, then said firmly, "Wilfred is strong. He will protect Pelsworth Castle, something Derek could never do. Now come, Anne. Supper is waiting. Let us go eat before this topic sours my stomach."

Derek's stomach was already sour—she had gone too far. Silently he began enumerating her sins. She had tricked and lied to him, heaped abuse and insult upon his head, and caused him to suffer deprivations and indignities—

A knock sounded at the door. Derek heard the door open and a voice say, "My lady! The butler and pantler are fighting again!"

Allison sighed. "Again, Larkin? I'll be there at once. Anne, you'd better go ahead without me. I'll eat later."

"But, Allison, your supper will grow cold—"

"I've eaten cold suppers before—and dinners and breakfasts, also. I think 'twill be a miracle if I ever am able to eat an entire meal in peace."

"Hmmph. You should not allow those knaves to impose upon you so—"

"Please, Anne, I haven't time to argue. I must go before someone is seriously harmed."

Derek heard her put the flax in the chest and a clicking noise, then saw her slippered feet hurrying out the door. He paid little attention, though. He was still intent on cataloging his sufferings. He spent hours every day training under a sadistic fiend; he had to face Demon Pigs and brush his teeth with a twig. He hadn't had a cigarette for an eternity—

"Sir Derek?"

Derek grew still.

"Sir Derek?" the soft voice came again. "Are you coming out?"

Damn. How had she known? He must have made some noise. He rolled out from under the bed and rose to his feet, facing Anne's speculative gaze.

"What were you doing under there, Sir Derek?"

"Admiring Allison's ankles," he said, brushing himself off.

"Oh? And is that what you were admiring at the bathing pool earlier?"

He glanced at her warily. Her expression was stern, but there was a sparkle in her eyes that made him decide to brazen it through. "There were other things more interesting to admire there."

The sternness vanished, and she chuckled. "Allison is right about one thing. You *are* a bold one. But I still like you, even if you do claim to be from the future."

He smiled wryly. "I suppose you think I'm insane, also."

"Perhaps." She stared at him searchingly. "But then, I have seen some strange things, so perhaps not."

He looked at her hopefully. "Then you'll help me?"

She appeared to consider the matter. "I detest Wilfred. I am certain he beat his first wife to death. I would much rather Allison marry you."

"Whoa, wait a minute. I meant help me return home, not help me marry Allison. I never said I would marry her. All I agreed to do was stop her marriage to Wilfred."

Anne frowned. "But I thought you loved her."

"Well . . ." Derek shifted uncomfortably under her penetrating gaze. "I find her attractive, but I'm not cut out for marriage."

"You and every other man," Anne muttered. "But perhaps . . ." Her gaze turned speculative again and she gave him the once-over.

Derek didn't like that look. It reminded him of the way Nan sometimes looked when she was plotting something for his own good. "Perhaps what?"

"Never mind. So why haven't you left?"

Meeting her dark, compelling gaze, Derek opened his mouth to tell some story. But to his astonishment, the truth came tumbling out. "I need the Pelsworth emerald. Unfortunately, Allison is not being cooperative about giving it to me."

She drew in a sharp breath. "The Pelsworth emerald. Of course. What a fool I've been—"

Derek, annoyed at himself for being so indiscreet, glanced at her warily. "You know about its magic powers?"

Her gaze became inscrutable. "Yes, indeed. So you need it to return home?"

"Yeah." Since he'd already revealed the truth, he saw no point in dissembling. "And pardon me, but I don't intend to wait any longer." He strode over to the chest and tried to open it. It was locked.

"Why am I surprised?" he asked the ceiling.

"The emerald is not in the chest, Sir Derek. It is too valuable. Allison keeps it well hidden."

"Oh?" Looking over his shoulder, Derek smiled persuasively. "You'll tell me where, won't you?"

She almost smiled back before she recovered herself and frowned sternly, crossing her arms over her chest.

"It's in this room somewhere, isn't it?" he persisted.

Her eyes flickered, then she turned slightly away. "I really don't know, Sir Derek. But I think I could convince Allison to tell me. If . . ."

Derek felt a sense of foreboding. "If?"

"If you will help me."

"Help you do what?"

"If you leave now, Allison will simply renew her betrothal to Wilfred. You must stay until she finds someone else to marry."

"But that could take years!"

"I doubt it will take so long. In fact, I would guess it won't take more than a month. Will you stay that long? Just until Saint Swithin's Day?"

Derek's mouth tightened. Another month of enduring the Middle Ages? He didn't know if he could stand it. But then again—did he have a choice? He was certain the emerald was here in this room, in the chest most likely—the flicker in Anne's eyes had been very revealing. But he wasn't eager to try to steal another key and sneak in here again to search. Especially not at the risk of losing his head.

He glanced at Anne. He sensed her offer was prompted by some ulterior motive—but what? Did she hope he would fall in love with Allison and marry her himself?

The idea was laughable. But he wasn't going to tell Anne that. He'd let her play her matchmaking game. Then, when the month was up, he'd take the emerald and leave.

"Very well," he said. "I agree to your bargain. I will stay one more month—until Saint Swithin's Day."

"Excellent." Her eyes stared into his, and he had a sudden uneasy feeling she knew exactly what he was thinking. Restraining the urge to shift under her gaze, he kept his expression relaxed and his stance casual.

To his relief, she nodded and smiled, apparently satisfied

with what she saw. She turned as if to leave, then paused. "Oh, and one more thing."

Derek could not prevent himself from tensing this time. "Yes?"

"You had better spend more time with Allison."

"Spend more time with her?" he repeated warily. "Why?"

"If you don't, Lord Pelsworth will not believe that you are her True Love and he will throw you out of the castle." Casually she added, "There are outlaws in the forest. And wolves. And boars."

Boars! Derek shuddered. If he was thrown out of the castle, he would be adrift in the Middle Ages with no chance of returning home. "All right. I'll spend more time with her. But if I acquire the emerald myself before the month is up, the deal is off."

She arched her brows. "Surely you don't intend to try to come in here again? 'Twould be very foolish of you, Sir Derek. You could lose your head—or something equally precious."

"Yes, yes, I know," he said a bit curtly. He was getting tired of these threats to his head and various body parts. "Do we have a deal or not?"

She hesitated, then nodded. "Come to the tapestry room in the east wing tonight after supper."

"The tapestry room?"

"Yes. Allison spends most of her evenings there with her ladies. Spinning and weaving."

Spinning and weaving. Wow. This would be exciting.

But in spite of his silent sarcasm, he nodded.

Anne opened the door a crack and peered out. The plaintive notes of a lute floated into the room.

Anne frowned. "Has that layabout not left yet? Wait here while I get rid of him."

She went into the next room and planted herself, arms akimbo, in front of Rafael. "Have you nothing better to do, sirrah?"

He smiled up at her. "How haughty you sound, Anne. Surely you're not still angry at me."

"Of course not," she said snootily. "'Tis impossible to be angry with one so lacking in wits. I can only feel the deepest and utmost pity for you."

He laughed. "Pity? Well, if that's what you want to pretend you feel for me—"

"Oh, go away."

He rose to his feet, towering over her. "Do you think I don't know what you're up to, my sweet?" he whispered. "'Twill never work. This Derek is a scalawag if I ever saw one." In a louder voice he said, "Farewell, Sir Derek. Have a care for the wiles of women."

Derek watched the minstrel stroll away, still laughing. Hell. It seemed like half the castle knew he was in Allison's room. It would be a miracle if he got out safely.

Anne reentered the room, slamming the door behind her.

"What did he mean by that?" Derek asked.

"Nothing," Anne said. "He is an idiot."

Derek studied her flushed cheeks. "I don't think so," he said slowly.

Anne shrugged impatiently. "Forget about that wretch. Just remember—"

"Yes, yes. The tapestry room." Derek nodded. "I'll be there."

Chapter 10

DEREK STRAIGHTENED HIS green velvet doublet and checked his codpiece to make sure it was tied on correctly. He gave his hose a good yank in an effort to dispel the wrinkles at his knees, but without much success. With a shrug he turned his attention to the polished piece of metal which served as a mirror, eyeing the nick on his chin where he'd cut himself shaving. No safety razors here.

"Hey, Sir Derek!" one of the squires huddled in a circle on the floor called out. "Will you not join our game?"

Derek glanced over at them. They were playing five-card stud—twos and one-eyed knaves wild. "Not tonight, Simon," he said. The cards had proved an excellent way to relieve the tedium of the evenings—but tonight he had something more stimulating in mind. "You'll have to play without me."

Satisfied that he hadn't grossly marred his chin, Derek set off across the courtyard for the southeast tower, a spring in his step. In spite of the day's unpleasant hunting experiences and the two-hour workout Sir Drogo had given him as punishment for abandoning the hunting party, Derek felt remarkably chipper. The exhaustion that usually beset him at the end of the day had magically evaporated earlier. He was actually looking forward to the evening, and to spending time with Allison.

It had occurred to him shortly after he left her room earlier that she might wear the emerald some evening. If she did, he would swipe it first chance he got. But even if she didn't wear the jewel, spending time with her might prove profitable in another way—he might be able to penetrate that cold surface she showed to the world. He knew—probably better than anyone—the passion she hid. With a little persistence he would be able to unmask it and get her into his bed. Hell, if he had to stay here a whole month, he deserved a little pleasure.

Whistling, he took the stairs two at a time.

In the tapestry room Allison looked hopefully at Sir Drogo. "Has he left?" she asked, her fingers growing still on the spinning wheel.

"No, my lady," Sir Drogo said, his craggy face grim. He stood stiffly in his black attire, clearly uneasy in the tapestry room with the ladies all staring at him and whispering behind their hands. Ignoring them, he continued, "He did disappear halfway through the hunting expedition, for which he was punished, but he is still here."

"I see." Disappointed, she gave her spinning wheel a hard turn. Derek Sinclair was persistent, she had to grant him that. Now she would have to think of a new plan. But what?

"There's something else you should know, my lady," Sir Drogo said. "I believe the men are ignoring curfew. In the yard they are so tired, they can scarce keep their eyes open."

"What could they be doing?" Allison asked, glancing up from the thread she was spinning. She lowered her voice. "You don't think they are visiting the village laundresses, do you?"

"Possibly. But whatever they are doing," Sir Drogo said darkly, "I am certain Sir Derek is behind it. The man is a troublemaker. I am going over to the squires' quarters right now to see what is toward."

"An excellent idea, Sir Drogo," Allison said approvingly.

Sir Drogo left and she continued spinning, hoping the old knight would catch Derek Sinclair at something. She was certain he was the one who had spied upon her this afternoon at the pool—no one else would have dared. If only Sir Everard had caught him, her problem would have been solved.

"Oh, dear, oh, dear!" a worried voice said. Allison looked over to see Lady Humfrey, the plump blond wife of Sir Everard, clutching the shirt she was sewing. "Sir Derek will not get in trouble, will he?"

"If he does, 'twill be no more than he deserves," Allison replied, giving her spinning wheel another hard turn.

"Oh! How can you say so?" Emmeline, Lady Humfrey's fourteen-year-old daughter, carded her wool slowly. "He loves you so much."

Allison barely restrained herself from rolling her eyes. The girl, a younger version of her mother, was an incurable romantic. "It might appear so, dear, but in truth, he's nothing but a rogue."

"But an extraordinarily fine rogue," said the lady seated at the loom—Lady Mountford. "'Tis rare to see a man so handsome."

Allison stiffened a little at the woman's words. Lady Mountford, a widow in her late twenties, was well-known in the castle—and three shires around—for her wandering eye. "I do not agree. Personally I find little in Sir Derek to attract any woman."

Lady Mountford's sensual smile drew attention to the small dark mole just above the corner of her mouth. "You'll understand better after you are wed, Lady Allison."

"I like him, too," wheezed Lady Ursula, huddled next to the fire with her embroidery. "He apologized for frightening Emmeline and me that night in your room. He has a nice deep voice, and although his speech is strange, he speaks very clearly."

Since Ursula was over sixty and nearly deaf, this was a high point of recommendation with her.

Allison looked around the circle of women in disbelief. Had he bewitched them all? Even Anne, sitting in a corner with her own spinning wheel, her black eyes bright and merry, did not support her. Although after Anne's defense of the man earlier, Allison didn't know why she should be surprised. The older woman kept glancing toward the door as if she were expecting someone.

Allison could contain her incredulity no longer. "Are you all mad?" she demanded. "Can you not see that he is a charlatan, a ne'er-do-well, a flap-eared knave—"

"Good evening, Lady Allison," the warm, deep voice of the flap-eared knave said from behind her.

A fiber slipped through Allison's fingers, causing a lump on the thread. Not stopping the wheel, she slowly turned her head to see Derek Sinclair lounging in the doorway. What was *he* doing here? "Sir, it's past curfew for the squires," she said in freezing accents.

He smiled at her. "It is, isn't it? Sir Drogo made some mention of it when I passed him on the stairs a few moments ago."

"Did he not order you back to the men's quarters?"

"I believe he meant to, but when I explained that you were expecting me, he allowed me to proceed."

Allison over twisted the thread and a few more lumps formed. "You dared tell such a lie?"

Derek smiled lazily. "A man in love will risk all to be with his lady."

The avidly listening ladies giggled. They were gazing at Sir Derek with varying degrees of warmth, from innocent admiration to outright lust.

Derek swept them a flourishing bow. "Besides, who wants to sleep when there are so many charming ladies still awake?"

The "ladies" giggled like harlots.

Allison could barely contain her disgust at their gullibility. Could they not see he was up to something? Knowing it was her duty to protect her ladies, she stopped the wheel and directed a stern gaze at Derek. "Why are you here?"

"To gaze upon your beauty."

The ladies sighed.

Fortunately, Allison was not so easily beguiled. "I tell you now, Sir Derek, you are wasting your time. Please leave."

"What kind of man would I be to give up so easily?" He looked around at the ladies. "Lady Allison is terribly hard-hearted. Will not any of you help me?"

"Lady Allison, you must not be so cruel," Lady Humfrey said. "You must let him stay."

A chorus of "Let him stay!" and "Don't be cruel!" echoed throughout the room. Even little Emmeline stared at her beseechingly.

Allison met Derek's gaze.

"You're not afraid, are you?" he asked softly.

"Certainly not." She straightened her back. She never backed down from a challenge—especially not from a villain like this one. "In fact, I am glad you are here. You were hunting today, were you not? By any chance did you see some loathsome varlet lurking about in the bushes?"

She watched him closely, but his expression did not change. "No, I'm afraid not," he said. "What was this loathsome varlet doing?"

"Spying upon me."

"Spying! That does not sound very chivalrous. It couldn't have been anyone from here, I'm sure."

"I must agree. No one from *here* would stoop to violating a lady's modesty. No one from here would do something so low, so dishonorable. It must have been someone from some *other place*. It must have been some *cur*, some *rascally knave*."

His eyes gleamed. "You should try not to think about him, my lady. It appears this knave has a very unsettling effect on you."

"I would never allow such an insignificant person to unsettle me," she snapped, then was immediately vexed at herself for doing so. She removed the bobbin from the spinning wheel, even though it was only half full, and put a new one on, to give herself time to regain her composure. This was ridiculous. She had no intention of spending the evening bandying words with this lout. It was time to put an end to his pretensions. "Thank you for your concern. Now I hope you will excuse me, but I am very busy and must concentrate on my work."

Turning slightly away, she turned the wheel and concentrated fiercely on twisting the thread.

There was a moment of silence. Then, from underneath the screen of her lashes, she saw him walk over to sit with the other ladies.

Allison was momentarily nonplussed. Then she grew angry. She doubted he had any interest in her—obviously he had a roving eye—but she would think he would at least *pretend*.

She watched from the corner of her eye, catching only snatches of what he was saying to the ladies that had them all laughing hilariously. He lounged carelessly in his chair and he smiled a lot—showing off his even white teeth, she thought sourly. He was freshly shaven, and without the stubble, she could see the slight gauntness that had hollowed out his cheeks and put shadows under his eyes. Those eyes still gleamed, however, with the same knowing impertinence that made her long to put him in his place.

He was not the least bit attractive, she thought, spinning her wheel faster and faster. Although the other ladies did not seem to agree—especially Lady Mountford, who gazed at him like a wolf over a juicy piglet. She fawned all over him with a lack of discretion that was utterly appalling.

Allison tried to concentrate on her spinning, but the giggles and laughter from the other side of the room made it more and more difficult. She endured it as long as she could—two or three minutes at least—then said coldly, "Sir Derek. Would you please be quiet? 'Tis difficult to concentrate on one's work when you are so noisy."

"You sound like my brother," he said. "All he thinks about is work, too."

"You have a brother?" Lady Humfrey asked, her double chin bobbling with surprise. "I thought your family was all dead."

"My parents are. And my other brother probably is. He ran away when he was fourteen and we haven't heard from him since."

"How terrible!" Lady Ursula's voice quavered, and the lines in her face deepened. "I lost my sister when I was young. I grieve for her still."

To Allison's surprise, Derek patted the old woman's hand, looking sincerely sympathetic. "I was four when Rick left. I barely remember him."

"At least you have your other brother," Anne commented from her corner. Her dark eyes sparkled.

"Yes. Although we don't get along too well. He likes work too much." Derek slanted a glance at Allison. "You would like him."

"I am sure I would. You would do well to follow his example," she said.

"And you would do well to follow it less," Derek responded promptly. "Is it true you don't allow anyone in the castle to celebrate holidays and festivals?"

The ladies grew still, their eyes widening.

Allison could feel their gazes upon her. All of them, even timid little Emmeline, had complained at one time or another about the lack of celebrations. How had Derek Sinclair managed to hit upon such a sore spot?

She bit back a defensive retort and answered as calmly as she could, "No, it's not true. We celebrate both Christmas and Easter."

"But there are festivals every month, aren't there? I heard that Pelsworth Castle once had a reputation for being a merry place."

"Times have changed, Sir Derek," she said coldly. "There is no time for foolishness when there is work to be done. And now I must ask you to leave. You are turning my ladies' heads with your attentions."

"Are you jealous, my lady? Don't be. If I could, I would devote all my attentions to you. It's only that it's difficult to do so with so many chaperones present." He turned to the goggling women. "Perhaps you could leave us alone."

"They most certainly could not!" Allison said angrily.

"Hmm. This does present a problem." He smiled at the ladies. To Allison's disgust, they smiled back like mindless geese. "Perhaps if you ladies would turn your backs."

Allison rose to her feet. "This is ridiculous—"

Her protest was drowned out by the scraping of chairs as the women all turned to face the wall.

Derek stepped to her side and took her hand. "Hush, Allie. I won't hurt you."

His thumb was brushing intimately against her palm. She started to pull away, but then, staring down at his hand holding hers, she grew still.

The motion of his thumb against her palm was strangely familiar. As were his words. Her eyelids drifted half closed as she tried to grasp the fleeting memory.

A tingling warmth spiraled from her hand, up her arm and down to her belly. The sensation tugged at her, teased her, frustratingly familiar.

She gazed up into his eyes, searching the brown depths for some clue. "You cannot deceive me," she said, but her voice was weak. The warmth inside her belly increased. "You want something from me."

His eyes darkened. "You're right, I do." He stepped closer and looked down at her intently. "Ever since I first saw you, I've wanted you. I can't stop thinking about that night in Nan's cottage. About how sweet you were." His gaze seemed to focus on her lips. "How sweet you tasted . . ."

His mouth was barely a whisper away. His words made no sense. She tried to move, to step back, but somehow she couldn't. It was as if she were under a spell. . . .

The door opened, slamming against the wall.

Allison jumped back. Turning, she saw her father, still wearing a travel-stained cloak, entering the room.

Coming to her senses, Allison hurried to his side. "Father! I did not hear the trumpets . . . no one told me that you . . . oh, Father, thank heavens you have come!"

He looked at her in a rather disgruntled manner. "How could I not after your letter? I trust the matter is as important as you claim."

"Yes, yes it is. I . . . that is . . ." She took a deep breath, then pointed her finger at Derek. "This man is a fraud! Sir Drogo told me he has no knowledge of weaponry. No knight could be so ignorant."

Lord Pelsworth turned to look at Derek with raised brows. "Well? Is this true?"

"It's true I'm not familiar with all your weapons," Derek said. "We have different ones in California."

The two men gazed at each other, communicating in some silent way. Then Lord Pelsworth half-smiled and nodded. "That explains it then." He started to turn away.

"Father!" Allison cried, dismayed by his unceremonious dismissal of the charge. "You cannot believe him!"

"Why should I not?"

"He told me himself that he doesn't want to marry me—that he came only to break my engagement to Sir Wilfred."

"Lady Allison, you must have misunderstood me," Derek said with what to Allison was blatantly false sincerity. "It is my fondest wish to marry you."

Angrily she snapped, "Did I also misunderstand you when you said you were from the future?"

"I was merely teasing you, dear heart. You must not take everything I say so seriously."

"Allison doesn't have much of a sense of humor," her father said. "You'll have to forgive her."

Allison glared at the two men in impotent rage. Restraining an urge to scream at the both of them, she tried once more, giving the one argument that might sway her father.

"He cannot possibly be my True Love—I do not care for him at all. He repulses me."

"It did not appear so when I entered this room."

Allison flushed bright red. "I . . . he caught me unawares. I could not believe his boldness. No true knight would ever treat a lady thus."

Derek stepped forward. "I'm afraid I haven't much of a way with the ladies."

Angrily Allison muttered, "Methinks you have too *much* of a way."

Derek's eyes gleamed, but his voice, when he spoke, sounded repentant. "I humbly beg your pardon for anything I may have done to offend you."

Ha! But Allison didn't voice her skepticism. Instead, she

said, "Father, such a mannerless lout cannot possibly be my True Love."

Lord Pelsworth frowned. "Now, Allison, you haven't given him enough time—"

"Lady Allison is correct," Derek intervened smoothly.

Caught off guard, Allison looked at him in astonishment.

Lord Pelsworth also appeared surprised—and dismayed. "But . . . but Sir Derek! Surely you haven't changed your mind?"

"No, of course not. But above all, I wish to be worthy of your daughter. If only . . . but no. It is impertinent of me to even think such a thing, let alone suggest it."

"What?" Lord Pelsworth demanded. "Suggest what?"

Derek appeared to hesitate. "That Allison teach me the customs and manners of courtship in your country." He ducked his head. "Forgive me. It is my love that makes me so bold."

Allison couldn't believe her ears. The impudence of the creature!

"Boldness is not necessarily a bad thing," Lord Pelsworth said.

"Father!" Allison laid her hand on his sleeve. "You can't be serious. He already receives training in chivalry from Sir Percival—"

"I'm afraid the herald's instruction does not include the finer points of courting a lady," Derek said.

"True, Sir Derek, true," Lord Pelsworth said.

Allison could barely contain her outrage. "Father—"

"Hush, Daughter." He patted her hand as if she were seven instead of twenty. "I think Sir Derek's suggestion is an excellent idea. . . ."

"Father, no—"

"Therefore, 'tis my wish that, starting tomorrow, you begin instructing Sir Derek in the Art of Courtly Love."

Chapter 11

DEREK CROUCHED BEHIND the bush, watching as Allison stood in the waterfall, washing herself. He leaned forward. The branch broke, and Allison turned around.

"Who goes there?" she called.

Derek stepped out of the bushes. "It's me."

Fortunately, Anne and the guard had disappeared. Pleased, Derek smiled at Allison.

She smiled back and began swimming toward him through the water. As she approached the bank, the water grew shallower, and her shoulders appeared to his view. Then the tops of her breasts. Slowly she came forward. The water grew shallower still. The peaks of her nipples were just barely hidden by the water. She stepped forward and—

"Sir Derek, wake up! You'll be late for training!"

Allison's image wavered. Derek turned his head away from the insistent voice. "Go 'way," he mumbled. "'msleepin'." He concentrated on Allison's image, but the voice spoke again.

"Sir Derek, you must wake up!"

Allison faded. "Don't go," Derek begged.

"I'm not going anywhere until you get out of bed! Sir

Drogo is in a rage after catching the men with the cards last
night. He's ordered everyone into the yard in full armor."

Annoyed, Derek opened one eye just far enough to see
Cuthbert's worried face. "I'm not going to training," he said
very distinctly. "Now go away." He closed his eye again.

"Not going! But why?"

Derek sighed. "Because today, I'm 'training' with Allison. She is going to instruct me in the Art of Courtly Love.
Now, for the last time, *go away.* "

There was silence for a few moments, then the sound of
retreating footsteps.

Derek exhaled. Now where had he been? Oh, yeah. Allison
had been just about to come out of the water. He concentrated
on remembering the picture. It remained elusive at first, but
after a few minutes reality receded and the mists of sleep returned. His dream world reappeared, hazy and tenuous, then
slowly gaining substance and coming into focus. Ah, yes. She
was beckoning him to come into the water. Quickly he
stripped off his clothes. Not looking away from Allison's smiling face, he ran down to the bank and dived into the water—

"AAAAAAAAAAAAAAAAAAAAAAAAhhhhhhhhhhhhhh-
hhhh!!!!"

Yelling, Derek jackknifed up in bed as the ice-cold water
hit him. Still gasping, he opened his eyes to see Sir Drogo
tossing a now-empty basin onto the floor.

"On your feet, Sinclair!"

Automatically Derek obeyed. Shivering, he wiped the
hair from his eyes and glared at Sir Drogo. "What the hell
was that for?"

"Dare you ask, Sir Slugabed?" Sir Drogo roared. "Practice began a quarter hour ago."

Derek grabbed a towel and dried himself off as best he
could. "Haven't you heard? I'm supposed to spend the day
with Allison learning courtly manners."

"You are mistaken," Sir Drogo said coldly. "Your instruction in manners with *Lady* Allison will take place after your
training."

Derek frowned. "But Lord Pelsworth said—"

"Lord Pelsworth left early this morning. Lady Allison and

I decided that your practice cannot be neglected. You will go to her *after* I'm done with you."

Derek's eyes narrowed. She'd done it to him again—

"You might also be interested to know that Lady Allison confirmed that *you* were the one who purchased the cards I discovered the squires playing with. I have confiscated the deck, and for your punishment, all of you will spend extra time in the yard today. Cuthbert will be here in a moment to help you into full armor."

Derek groaned silently. Most days Sir Drogo was content to let them practice in half-armor or even just the arming doublet.

Sir Drogo smiled sadistically.

"As soon as Cuthbert's done with you, get your arse into the yard. Perhaps a few laps around the castle in full armor will cure you of your slothful ways. . . ."

Derek spent a miserable day in the yard. Sir Drogo worked him longer and harder than everyone else. Derek even had to stay two hours after the others had been excused!

He'd jogged innumerable laps around the castle, attacked the pel with a great sword, and ridden at the quintain, struggling to hit its arm without taking a blow in return. He'd been so tired, however, he was unable to avoid the quintain's vicious arm as it swung around and hit him squarely in the back time after time.

He'd expected to be excused with the others when it grew dark, but no. He'd had to polish the armor, carry the swords to the blacksmith to be sharpened, unsaddle the horses, and brush them down.

When Drogo finally dismissed him, Derek was so exhausted, he could barely stand. His legs were like jelly from jogging in full armor, his arms ached from hefting the leaden sword, and his back and legs were a mass of bruises from his repeated falls. He could hardly wait to get out of the tin suit and fall into bed.

Wearily he returned to the squires' quarters and asked Cuthbert to help him remove the armor.

Cuthbert shifted his feet. "Sir Drogo said you were to

wear the armor this evening as well—including your helmet—so that you will become more accustomed to it. And
Lady Allison sent a message that you are to go to the tapestry room immediately."

Allison—damn. He'd forgotten about his "lessons." He
supposed he couldn't back out now, after the fuss he'd made
about wanting to be "worthy" of her, but *God,* he was tired.
Maybe the lesson would be a short one.

His eyes half closed, he trudged across the courtyard to
the southeast tower.

The steep, narrow stairs that circled up to the tapestry
room looked more daunting than Mount Everest in a bliz-
zard. He lifted one foot onto the bottom stair and groaned.
He wondered how many years until escalators would be invented. He lifted his other foot onto the bottom stair.

The weight of the armor on his feet, shins, knees, and
thighs made the ascent especially difficult. By the time he
reached the top of the stairs, his legs were quivering like
overcooked rigatoni. Ignoring the pain, he pushed up his
visor and entered the tapestry room, his gaze falling immediately upon Allison.

". . . and I shall take a flitch of bacon to the newlyweds.
Perhaps that will help. But if it doesn't—"

She broke off abruptly as her cool, midnight blue gaze
met his.

The visor slammed shut. Cursing silently, he pushed it up
and stepped forward, armor clanking, his weariness fading a
little as he remembered last night's near kiss. "Good
evening, my lady."

"Good evening, Sir Derek."

Her voice and eyes were cool, but Derek wasn't deceived.
Last night her eyes had been dark with passion beneath the
half-closed lids. Her voice had quivered with desire when
she spoke, and her lips had parted as his mouth approached
hers. For all her aloofness, she wasn't as indifferent as she
pretended. She would have kissed him, he knew, if her father hadn't come home at exactly the wrong moment.

God, he wished they hadn't been interrupted. If only he'd
had her somewhere private. Like her bedroom.

"Are you ready to begin your lessons?" she asked.

"Yeah." Derek smiled at her, silently admiring the curves displayed by her low-cut gown. If he could get her alone, it would be a simple matter to slip the dress off her shoulders and reveal her breasts. . . .

"Very well," she said, her voice even cooler. "Your first lesson is: You must do whatever your lady bids."

Visions of her naked in his arms, pleading with him to take her, filled his brain. His visor slipped down, and he hastily pushed it up. "I'll gladly do whatever you want," he said huskily.

She smiled. "Good." She turned to her spinning wheel, then paused. "Oh, dear. I've left my basket of wool downstairs in the family dining room. Will you fetch it for me, Sir Derek?"

His smile dimmed. Fetching a basket of wool wasn't exactly what he'd had in mind. The memory of those stairs was almost more than he could bear. But she was smiling at him—sweetly, encouragingly, *promisingly*. Hell, he'd do anything if she'd just continue smiling at him like that.

Even brave Mount Everest.

The basket of wool was exactly where she'd said it would be. Derek grabbed it and headed back for the tapestry room.

He paused at the bottom of the stairs, looking up to where they disappeared into darkness, his weariness returning fourfold. With a sigh he trudged up them.

He made it back up the stairs. He returned to the tapestry room and handed Allison the basket.

She smiled again. "Thank you so much, Sir Derek. Now, please, sit down . . . oh! This wool is cotted—see how 'tis matted at the end? I cannot use such poor quality wool. Sir Derek, would you please go and get some more? 'Tis in the storeroom under the main gatehouse."

Derek, holding his visor up, swayed on his feet a little. "Couldn't you spin some other time?"

"Our stores of thread are low. Please, Sir Derek."

Something in her voice pierced the fog of exhaustion clouding his brain. He stared at her suspiciously, but her angelic expression didn't change. Now that he thought about it, smiling so sweetly was completely out of character for her. With a curt nod he left the room.

This time the trip took longer. He went down the stairs and outside to the courtyard. It had started to rain. He slogged through the mud to the gatehouse and down more stairs to the storeroom. Once inside, he had to find the wool. He grabbed a healthy supply of what looked to him like wool, and tucked it into his breastplate to keep it dry. Then he went upstairs, slogged back across the courtyard, climbed the tortuous tower stairs, entered the tapestry room, and gave the wool to Allison.

Too tired to push up his visor, he sat down. He had barely done so when she exclaimed in an increasingly familiar way, "Oh!"

He tensed a little. "Yes?"

"This is mohair, not wool. Could you please—?"

"No, I could not," he snapped. He might have been slow to catch on, but that didn't mean he was completely stupid. There was no way in hell he was going to run around on ridiculous errands all night.

"Oh!" Her eyebrows rose. "That settles everything then."

Derek peered through the slit. "What do you mean?"

"If you were really my True Love, you would want to please me. You would perform any task I set willingly. Since you are not willing, that proves you are not my True Love. I will write my father, and you can leave at once—"

Derek lifted the visor so he could see her face more clearly. Her eyes had a gleam that in his fatigue he hadn't noticed before. Not only was the conniving little witch trying to torture him into leaving Pelsworth Castle, but she was actually *enjoying* doing so.

"Never mind," he growled, standing up again. "I'll get the damn wool. Is there anything else you would like me to do while I'm getting it?"

"No, I don't *think* so."

He fixed a steely gaze on her. "Please take your time. Are you *sure*?"

She tapped a finger against her squarish chin. "Yes, I'm quite sure."

Grimly he sallied forth once more. The trip seemed longer than ever. The rain hadn't let up. He dragged himself across the muddy courtyard and into the storeroom. He grabbed handfuls of fluffy stuff from several baskets to make certain he got some that pleased her. He made his way back across the courtyard. Then there were the stairs.

He groaned.

But he managed to climb them once more, spurred on by the thought that this was the last time he would have to do so tonight.

He hobbled into the tapestry room and gave Allison the wool. He limped over to a chair and started to sit down.

"Sir Derek . . ."

Derek froze, his rear end a scant two inches from the seat. "Yes?" he said through clenched teeth.

Allison fluttered her eyelashes. "I am terribly embarrassed to ask you . . ."

"Yes?"

"But right after you left, Lady Humfrey reminded me that I had promised to ask Rafael to come play for us." She smiled. "Would you please—?"

"*Yes!*" His reply was half-growl, half-shout. He stomped out of the room. Outside the door he yanked off his helmet. He had thought Sir Drogo sadistic. Lady Allison Pelsworth could give lessons to Saddam Hussein.

He had to search half the castle before he found the minstrel in the kitchen, flirting with a laundress.

"Your presence is requested in the tapestry room," Derek said through gritted teeth.

For all their sightlessness, Rafael's eyes were remarkably expressive, and right now they were full of masculine sympathy. "Women are hell, aren't they?" he said.

"I've always associated women with heaven, myself—until now." Derek glowered in the direction of the tapestry room.

Rafael laughed. "There's still time to escape your fate."

"My fate?"

"Most men can't seem to resist." Shaking his head, Rafael picked up his lute. "Love . . . it never should have been invented."

Derek frowned. "Love has nothing to do with it."

Rafael smiled in a pitying manner and strolled toward the door.

Gritting his teeth, Derek followed.

Allison tended her duties the next day, finding them less tedious than usual. But that could have been because her mind was only half on her work. The other half was preoccupied with coming up with a new way to make Derek Sinclair suffer. It took some thought, but by the time he entered the tapestry room that evening, she had the perfect plan. Since running up and down the stairs and through the mud in full armor had not induced him to depart, she had decided to try something a little more subtle.

The harp.

Although some court gentlemen enjoyed playing the harp, most of the ones she'd met couldn't abide it. Her own father, according to a story told by Anne, had once thrown a harp—and the minstrel who'd been hired to teach him—through the window into the courtyard. The harp—and the minstrel—had never been seen again.

She watched Sinclair anxiously, hoping she hadn't underestimated him.

She hadn't.

"You want me to do *what*?" he asked incredulously.

She smiled in satisfaction. "Learn to play the harp. 'Tis important for a gentleman to have accomplishments, Sir Derek. And I do so love music."

"You want me to learn to play the harp?" he said again, as if to make absolutely certain that he hadn't misunderstood.

"Yes. 'Tis very pleasant to be entertained whilst we are at our work. Anne will teach you."

Anne came to his side. "Don't worry, Sir Derek," she whispered. "It isn't difficult."

Derek didn't care how easy it was. There was something . . . *effeminate* about playing the harp. It was a stupid instrument, as far as he was concerned, all sweet and frothy. "I am not going to play a damn harp," he said, glowering in Allison's direction.

"Please, Sir Derek. Remember our bargain. And remember what will happen to you if Lord Pelsworth thinks you don't love his daughter."

"I know, I know," he muttered. "I'll be boar bait."

He picked up the harp.

Allison hid a smile as she watched him from the corner of her eye. His reaction was all she could have hoped for. Happily, she hummed in time to the spinning wheel.

Her humming faltered, however, as Derek began to play.

Anne showed Derek the basic chords and showed him the correct fingering, but he was amazingly inept. Anne explained slowly and patiently and showed him the notes to play over and over again, but somehow he could not seem to grasp the simple tune. Mischord after mischord croaked from the harp.

Allison tried not to wince when he played a particularly sour note. She'd never known a harp could sound so terrible. The noise was beginning to give her a headache. Perhaps making him play the harp had not been such a good idea after all—

Glancing up from her thread, she saw Derek watching her. As her gaze met his, he twanged a wrong note, the sound reverberating loudly through the room. She could not prevent her wince.

The corner of his mouth curled upward.

Allison stiffened. He played another wrong note, his gaze never leaving hers, the amusement in his eyes plain.

Seething, she looked down at her thread. So, he thought to flout her in this manner, did he? No doubt he thought she would not be able to tolerate his abominable playing and she would excuse him.

How little he knew her.

Derek twanged at the harp more loudly, but she had herself under control now. "You must not be discouraged if you're a trifle . . . slow," she said kindly. "I will not think the less of you for it."

His fingers grew still on the strings. Then he plucked three wrong notes at the same time, meeting her gaze challengingly.

"You're improving, Sir Derek," she said sweetly.

A tiny frown knit his brow.

"I think that's enough for tonight," Anne said hastily. "'Tis late and time for bed. We will continue tomorrow, Sir Derek."

Still frowning, Derek left the room.

And in her own bed a short time later Allison fell asleep, a smile on her face.

Derek played even more horribly the next night.

He twanged the harp mercilessly, smiling at Allison the whole time.

She spun steadily, smiling back as though he played with heavenly perfection.

Her ladies, however, showed no such endurance.

After about half an hour of the unrelenting cacophony, Lady Anne rose to her feet. "I can teach you no more for now, Sir Derek. You must practice. Good night." Without further excuse, she left.

Lady Mountford stood up, smoothing her gown over her hips. "Lady Allison, forgive me, but I promised Sir Jarvis that I would attend him this evening. Please excuse me." She glided from the room.

Barely had she left, than Lady Humfrey rose also. "I . . . I must go, too. I, er, promised to trim Sir Everard's mustache for him."

"And I, uh, need to wash my hair," Emmeline said. She almost ran from the room after her mother.

Lady Ursula, dozing by the fire, started awake as the door slammed behind Emmeline. "Eh?" She glanced around the room in confusion. "Where did everybody go?"

"Apparently they had other things to do this evening," Derek said.

"Hmmph," Ursula said. "You can never rely on these young women." She looked at Derek. "Why don't you play a song for Allison and me?"

His gaze met Allison's. "Gladly," he said and twanged the harp.

To his disappointment, she merely returned her gaze to her thread.

Grimly he continued playing, wondering if she would ever give in and tell him to stop. He looked at the obstinate lines of her square jaw. It was amazing that such a small woman could be so stubborn. Didn't she ever get tired of being so contrary?

He played as badly as he could, intent on annoying her, but she appeared oblivious. She continued to spin, stopping only once when the chaplain came in.

Derek played more quietly—although not more skillfully—wanting to hear what the man said.

"My lady, I have distressing news to report," Father Gregory said. "The almoner has been pilfering the leftovers from the dinner table instead of distributing them to the poor. I also have reason to believe that he has been keeping the alms bestowed upon him."

"I see." Allison frowned. "And what does he say to these charges?"

"He denies them. He says the grooms and servants have been stealing the leftovers."

"I wish you to investigate this matter further, Father Gregory," Allison said. "If the servants or grooms are stealing, they must be let go. But the almoner must be let go in any case—'tis his responsibility to make certain no one steals the leftovers. If there was a problem, he should have reported it."

"Yes, my lady," Father Gregory said. "I shall take care of the matter. Thank you, my lady."

The chaplain left, and Derek stopped twanging the harp to look at Allison more closely. For the first time he noticed the paleness of her face and the faint shadows under her eyes. He frowned. "You look tired."

Her gaze flew to his, then back to her spinning. "'Tis a busy time of year. The sheep were just sheared and the wool must be cleaned, or sold, or traded. The haymaking has begun and must be finished quickly before harvest time. 'Tis nearly time for rents to be collected and the yearly accounts to be reviewed—"

"Doesn't Lord Pelsworth handle all this?"

"My father spends very little time at Pelsworth Castle."

Her shoulders seemed to sag a little. "He is not familiar with all the details of these situations."

Derek stroked the harp strings idly, forgetting to twang the notes. "He shouldn't dump everything on you, though."

"I do not mind." She gave a small smile. "I am glad to serve Pelsworth Castle in this way. 'Tis my life."

Derek's frown deepened. "No wonder you're so grim. You need to learn to have some fun."

Her smile disappeared. Her back straightened, and a slight flush rose in her cheeks. "I have all the 'fun,' as you call it, that I need," she said sharply. "I am having 'fun' this evening, listening to you play the harp."

"Oh, are you?" His fleeting sympathy vanished at her sharp tone. "Then forgive me for stopping and depriving you. I will remedy that immediately." He slashed his fingers across the strings of the harp in a jangle of notes.

She bared her teeth. "That is quite beautiful."

His smile was equally vicious. "I'm glad you think so," he snarled.

They both had headaches when they went to bed that night.

She could not take much more of this.

Allison sat in the tapestry room the next evening, spinning and trying to appear unaffected by Sinclair's horrible playing.

It wasn't easy. She couldn't believe anyone could make such a terrible noise on a harp. She had thought he wouldn't be able to keep it up this long. She didn't know how much longer she could bear it. She glanced at Anne and Ursula, the only two of her ladies that hadn't made an excuse to desert the tapestry room.

Anne, as usual, appeared amused, her dark eyes sparkling. Allison looked at her pleadingly.

Tiny lines fanned out from Anne's eyes, but to Allison's relief, she turned to Derek.

"Sir Derek."

Derek continued to play.

"Sir Derek!" Anne repeated.

Perhaps he'd gone deaf from his horrible playing, Allison thought. 'Twould serve him right if he had.

Anne rose to her feet and tapped Derek on the shoulder. He jumped a little and turned to look at her. Allison saw him reach up and pull what looked like a small wad of wool from his ear.

Her eyes narrowed.

"Yes, Lady Anne?" Derek asked.

"I think you have learned this piece and need not practice anymore."

"Well . . ."

Allison saw him glance in her direction. Quickly she dropped her gaze to her thread, pretending to be intent on her task.

"What do you think, Lady Allison?" he asked.

She shrugged as if the matter was of complete indifference to her. "I enjoy the music, but whatever Lady Anne says," she said airily.

"My goal is to please *you*, Lady Allison. If you enjoy the music, I will continue playing until you ask me to stop."

So, he was determined to make her surrender completely. Allison squared her shoulders. She would never give in to this rapscallion. Never—

He twanged the harp.

"No!" she blurted out. "I wish you to stop!"

"If you insist, my lady," he said blandly. "Although I find I enjoy the harp so much that I wouldn't mind playing for you every evening."

"That will not be necessary," she said hastily, the thought making shivers run down her spine. "That is, 'tis very kind of you to offer. . . ."

He smiled—a wide, white smile so full of triumph, that Allison had to clench her fists to prevent herself from slapping him. Smiling as sweetly as she could, she said, "But I think 'tis time to move on to your next lesson."

To her intense satisfaction, his smile vanished. Her own smile widening, she cast about in her mind for some distasteful task for him to perform.

"When I was at court," she said in a sickeningly sweet tone, "there were many poems composed to my beauty."

She didn't mention that most of the poems had been composed by the court poets—or that most of the other men
were more likely to write a poem to one of their hunting
dogs than to a lady. "There were ones about my eyes, my
hands, my brow, my neck, my lips, my nose, my breasts—"

"Your *breasts* ?"

She ignored the interruption. "You must also compose a
poem."

"Me? You want me to write a poem?"

She nodded serenely. "One that expresses your love and
admiration for me."

Derek stared at her, the glow from his victory with the
harp completely dissipated. No. Absolutely not. He opened
his mouth to refuse. But before he could do so, he caught
Anne's eye upon him.

But I don't know how to write poetry, he argued silently.

You must learn, her stern gaze seemed to say.

But I hate poetry—

Too bad.

I won't do it—

You must. Or else . . .

He groaned silently. If he refused, he might get kicked out
of the castle. He might get eaten by lions, tigers, and boars. Or
whatever. But that might be preferable to writing poetry. . . .

"Sir Derek?" Allison asked. "Will you do it?"

Fuming, he turned to her. Must she look so damn smug?

"I'll do my best, my lady," he snarled.

Yeah, he'd do his *best,* he thought as he stalked out of the
room.

He couldn't wait to see how she liked it.

Chapter 12

IN THE TAPESTRY room the next evening the ladies were all aflutter. Allison, pretending to be intent on her spinning, listened to their conversation.

"I cannot wait to hear Sir Derek's poem," Lady Humfrey said, her small plump hands busily stitching a pair of braies for her husband. "I'm sure it will be wonderful."

Emmeline, putting tufts of wool in the carder on her knee, sighed rapturously. "I think it's so romantic. I hope someone will write poetry to me someday. Mama, did Papa ever compose a poem for you?"

Lady Humfrey shook her head sadly. "Unfortunately, your father does not have a gift for poetry. Not many men do."

"Husbands especially," Lady Mountford commented from her place at the loom.

"Your husband never wrote any poetry to you?" Emmeline's round blue eyes were disappointed.

"No. But many other men have." A sensual smile curved Lady Mountford's lips, and she put down her shuttle to smooth her bright green dress against her waist and hips. "I am looking forward to hearing Sir Derek's efforts."

"As am I." Lady Anne, her black eyes sparkling, turned

her spinning wheel quickly and efficiently. "He seemed very enthusiastic last night."

Allison directed her gaze back to her own spinning, biting back a smile at Anne's remark. *Enthusiastic* was the last word Allison would have chosen to describe Derek's expression last night. *Horrified* was much more accurate.

She laughed silently. She hadn't seen such a look on a man's face since one of the laundresses propositioned Cuthbert in the middle of the courtyard. Allison, who had been standing nearby when the laundress whispered in the boy's ear, had heard him mumble something about the chivalric code demanding that he remain pure, before he'd fled.

As Derek would no doubt soon flee. . . .

The door opened, and the women looked up eagerly.

"Good evening, ladies," Derek Sinclair said, entering the room.

Allison studied him covertly, noting his swaggering walk as he came forward, the confident smile on his lips, and the glint in his eye. A small frown knit her brow. He appeared entirely at ease, not what she'd expected at all. She'd expected clenched teeth and glares and reluctance. Instead, he appeared positively cheerful.

"Are you ladies ready to hear my masterpiece?" he asked.

"Yes!" cried a chorus of female voices. The noise woke Lady Ursula, who had been dozing by the fire, her embroidery in her lap. She sat up and looked around, blinking.

Derek struck a pose. "My poem is called"—he paused dramatically—"'Ode to My Lady's Elbow'!"

The excitement in the ladies' faces faded a bit.

"Ode to *what*?" Lady Ursula asked.

"'Ode to My Lady's Elbow,'" Derek repeated. Ignoring the lukewarm expressions around him, he cleared his throat. Then, in thrilling accents, he recited:

> *"My love doth grow and grow*
> *At the sight of my lady's elbow.*
> *It bends, it points,*
> *It props, it shoves,*
> *'Tis truly the uniquest of joints.*

Men everywhere grieve,
When it's encased in a sleeve,
But uncovered, it never disappoints.
Oh, my love doth grow and grow,
At the sight of my lady's elbow."

Finished, he looked around expectantly.

The room was silent.

"A very interesting first effort," Lady Anne finally said.

"Very clever the way you rhymed *joints* and *points*," Lady Mountford commented.

Lady Ursula looked confused. "Did you say men grieve when it's in a sleeve?"

Emmeline giggled.

Lady Humfrey coughed to cover up the noise. "'Tis a fine poem," she said loyally. "Very, er, expressive of your strong feelings for Lady Allison."

"Yes," Derek said, looking directly at Allison. "It reflects the depth of my respect for her exactly."

Allison met his gaze for a moment, then looked down at her spinning wheel, struggling to control her expression. The varlet! How dare he make mock of her by writing that . . . that drivel? 'Twas obvious he'd done it on purpose, too—the gleam in his eyes revealed as much.

So why did she want to laugh?

He was a scoundrel. An amusing scoundrel, she had to admit, but still a scoundrel. She had expected he would have given up by now. Between his daily practice in the yard and the "lessons" with her, she would have thought he would have fled back to that heathenish place he claimed to be from. He was proving more stubborn than she would have believed possible.

She hadn't enjoyed herself so much in years.

"Well, my lady?" His deep voice was full of mocking challenge. "What do you think of my poem?"

Allison looked up at his boldly smiling face. She returned a sweet smile. "'Twas wonderful. So wonderful, in truth, that tomorrow we shall move on to your next lesson."

His smile faded. "My next lesson? What is it?"

"You will find out tomorrow," she said serenely.

He bowed, and turned to speak to Lady Anne. But every so often, he glanced sideways at her, his expression full of apprehension.

Allison pretended to concentrate on her spinning, but once again she was struggling not to laugh.

Derek staggered into the yard the next morning, yawning, his eyes half-shut, dragging his sword behind him. For the first time in a week Sir Drogo had told them not to wear armor, but Derek barely noticed the difference.

He hadn't slept well last night.

He'd been disappointed by Allison's lack of reaction to his poem. But that wasn't what had made him toss and turn all night. No, it was wondering what devilish new "lesson" she would conjure up for him to learn tonight.

It couldn't be too bad, he tried to reassure himself. What could be worse than being treated like a lackey, playing a wussy harp, or writing poetry that "expressed his love and admiration" for Allison? Nothing.

If only she hadn't had that gleam in her eye. . . .

He noticed several of the squires standing in a huddle by the pels, whispering. They grew silent as he approached. After he passed by, he heard a buzz of conversation and several snickers and chortles. Derek paused for a moment. Then, stoically ignoring them, he lifted his sword and struck the post.

A moment later Cuthbert joined him. Derek started to greet him, then noticed the younger man was sporting a black eye and a swollen lip.

"What the devil happened to you?" Derek asked.

Cuthbert's good eye grew fiery with indignation. "That troublemaker Oswald was reading a ridiculous poem to the squires behind the chapel this morning. He claimed that *you* had written it. Of course I had to defend your honor. As if you would ever write anything so idiotic as an 'Ode to My Lady's Elbow'! It was the worst thing I've ever heard! Something about love that 'doth grow and grow' whenever the fellow catches sight of Lady Allison's elbow. An infant

could have done better. The gall of Oswald to suggest that
you had written such pap!"

Derek winced. "Er, Cuthbert . . . I appreciate your defense
and all, but the truth of the matter is I *did* write that poem."

Cuthbert stared at him. "You did?"

Derek nodded.

After a few moments of silence Cuthbert said, "Well . . .
that is . . . oh, there's Sir Drogo. We'd better get to work."

For the rest of the day Derek endured the sniggering looks
and laughs of everyone in the castle. He pretended to be unaware of their laughter at his expense, although it wasn't
easy, especially when Oswald cried out at the dinner table,
"Sir Derek, what do you think of *my* elbow?"

Through the roars of laughter, Derek seethed silently. He
never should have written that stupid poem. He'd done it to
punish Allison, but somehow, his plan had backfired.

Oh, she must be feeling satisfied with herself. She probably thought she had won. Well, she hadn't. He would never
surrender to Lady Allison Pelsworth no matter what agony
she subjected him to. . . .

At the end of the day he marched into the tapestry room,
steeling himself to face whatever torture she had in store for
him.

She looked up and smiled.

He stopped, immediately suspicious. He didn't like that
smile. He didn't like it at all.

She patted the seat beside her. "Come sit here, Sir Derek."

Warily he complied.

"You're doing remarkably well," she said, her voice as
sweet as double-fudge chocolate chip cookies. "You have
made such wonderful progress, I think it is time to take the
next step." She smiled again. "You must serenade me."

Disbelief flowed through him. "Serenade you?"

"Yes, serenade me. The poem you wrote will sound de-
lightful set to the tune you've learned to play on the harp."

No. There was no way he was going to make such a fool
of himself. No way in hell—

He caught Anne's stern eye—no, her *evil* eye—upon him,
reminding him of his fate if he refused.

He was beginning to suspect Anne was a witch.

He looked around the room, seeking deliverance. Everyone nodded encouragingly—except for Rafael. Derek almost hadn't noticed the minstrel sitting in a shadowy corner, an odd smile on his lips. Derek looked at him hopefully, but the other man didn't speak.

Derek sighed. As the Borg would say, resistance was futile. "Very well."

Allison smiled blindingly. "Then go."

"Go where?"

"Outside, beneath my window."

"What, you mean serenade you *now*?"

She nodded.

"But it's raining."

"A true courtly knight must be willing to brave the elements for his lady."

Gritting his teeth, Derek took the harp and went down to the courtyard. The rain poured down on him, plastering his hair to his scalp and soaking his woolen hose. He looked at the wall in front of him. There was a vine growing up to the window of the tapestry room. He supposed next she would expect him to climb up the vine like some damn Romeo.

What the hell was he doing?

He was doing whatever the hell was necessary to get back home. To get back home, he had to have the emerald. To get the emerald, he had to stay in the castle. To stay in the castle, he had to pretend to be Lady Allison's True Love. How had everything gotten so complicated?

Taking a deep breath, he opened his mouth and started to sing.

"My love doth grow and grow—"

A dog howled.

Derek stopped. The dog stopped howling, also. The rain beating down on his head, he tried again.

"My love doth grow and grow, every time I see—"

The dog howled louder. Another joined in.

Determinedly Derek kept singing. Unfortunately, the dogs were drowning him out. His fingers kept slipping on the harp's wet strings, and his hose were sagging around his knees. Frustrated, he stopped again.

As the last howl died away, he heard another sound. A quickly muffled sound, but still clearly recognizable.

It was a giggle.

Something snapped inside him. The frustrations and humiliations of the past week boiled and ignited, sending his temper skyrocketing. Tossing the harp in the mud, he grabbed the vine, and scaled it as though he were Romeo, Robin Hood, and Spiderman combined.

Lady Allison was laughing uncontrollably as he climbed through the window. Her ladies were giggling, also, but he barely noticed them. He stalked toward Allison, a fire in his brain and murder in his heart. She rose to her feet and backed away, still laughing. He followed.

She darted around the spinning wheel and the loom, and he went after her. Gasping with laughter, she stopped behind a chair. He knocked it aside, grabbed her, and hauled her up against his chest.

Her laughter died away.

The ladies, their eyes wide, stopped giggling, also. Without looking away from Allison, he snarled, "All of you—out."

They didn't hesitate. They scurried out the door.

Allison stared up at him. He reached up and tore the caul from her head. Burying his fingers in the hair at the nape of her neck, he held her still and kissed her.

The kiss went on and on. The fierceness of his mouth softened slightly as her resistance lessened and he absorbed the sweet scent and taste of cinnamon. He became aware of the silkiness of her hair in his fingers and the soft curves pressed against his chest. His grip on her hair loosened and his hand curved to cradle her head. He kissed her more gently, his hand running over her, pulling her closer and closer, wanting to imprint himself upon her. He stroked her buttocks and hip and waist, caressing her, slowly moving his hand upward. He cupped her breast, rubbing his thumb against her nipple through the layers of cloth. She made a small noise, but he paid no attention.

"Allison . . . dear heaven, Allison . . ."

"Ahem . . ."

Cursing, Derek turned his head to see Rafael still sitting in the shadowy corner, a cool smile on his face.

"I beg your pardon," he said, shifting his lute on his lap. "Would you like me to leave, also?"

"Yes," Derek growled.

"No!" Allison tore away from him. The front of her dress was wet from where he'd pressed her against him, and speckles of mud streaked her face. She raised shaking hands to her hair. "I . . . I . . . please excuse me." She hurried out the door.

"Thanks a lot," Derek snapped.

Rafael laughed. "You're welcome. Although I can see you don't appreciate the favor I've done for you. Let me introduce you to a girl I know—a fine peasant wench. You won't lose your heart to her."

"I have no intention of losing my heart to anyone—especially not to Allison, if that's what you're implying. The only thing she'll get from me is my body—which I'd be only too happy to share with her." Derek raked his fingers through his wet hair. "So in the future, do me a real favor and mind your own business."

"Are you certain that is your wish?"

"I am."

"Very well." Rafael sighed loudly. "But I warn you—take care, or you *will* lose your heart. And then you will be lost—forever."

He sauntered out of the room, and Derek glared after him. Rafael's warnings were becoming tedious—and they were totally unnecessary. Derek would have the emerald in a couple of weeks. There was no time to fall in love, but there *was* time for a brief, passionate affair.

And he planned to enjoy every minute.

Chapter 13

THE NEXT DAY dawned bright and clear. In the training yard Derek rode at a gallop toward the quintain. At precisely the right moment he swung. His sword hit the dummy's shield with a solid *thwack!* and the opposite arm swung around. With a quick pressure on the reins, Derek evaded the retaliatory blow. Pausing at the edge of the course, he pushed back his visor. It stayed up—he'd gotten up early and had the armorer tighten the bolts—and he glanced over at Sir Drogo.

The old knight's jaw had dropped. Seeing Derek looking at him, he quickly snapped it shut. "Harrumph. Not bad, Sir Derek. If you ever meet a ten-year-old in battle, you may be able to beat him. Next!"

Smiling in satisfaction at these high words of praise, Derek trotted his horse to the next obstacle. For the first time since coming to the Middle Ages, he was actually enjoying the workout. It had almost been worth the torturous practice to see that look on Sir Drogo's face.

Now, last night's kiss . . . *that* had nearly been worth the knightly training, the beer, and giving up cigarettes combined. That kiss had been fantastic. It had been amazing. It had been fireworks, chocolate with whipped cream, and "Stairway to Heaven" all rolled into one.

That kiss had been . . . different. He supposed that after nearly a month of celibacy, it was only natural that his senses had been keyed up. But it hadn't been just that. There had been something about *her* —about Allison.

Derek hit a series of posts with his sword, then rode back to the beginning of the course, where several squires waited to take their turns. He took his place at the end of the line, his thoughts returning to Allison.

She was a peculiar woman. She seemed so cool and distant. But she'd fought fiercely in the battle of wills between them, and it was obvious that surrender did not come easily to her. Last night's kiss was a perfect example.

She'd resisted at first. He'd felt her straining against his hold on her hair, pressing her lips tightly together under the onslaught of his. But gradually, her resistance had lessened, and her lips had softened. She hadn't been particularly skillful. In fact, he would guess she had no experience at all. So initially, her mouth had been shy and uncertain. But she had caught on quickly. And then, instead of straining away, she had been straining toward him, against him, into him, and she'd been kissing him back with an intensity that had nearly blown his mind.

Damn Rafael for interfering. And damn himself for not making certain everyone had left the room. He wouldn't make that mistake again. The next time he kissed Allison, he would make sure that they were completely alone. . . .

"Next!" Sir Drogo called.

Derek rode the course again . . . and then again. The day grew hotter, the workout more intense, but his high spirits did not falter. By the time Sir Drogo called a halt, Derek was breathing and sweating heavily, but he felt better than he had since he arrived in the Middle Ages.

He washed quickly, but thoroughly, wondering how Allison would greet him tonight. Would she be cool? Would she claim that he must learn to stand on his head or spin or weave or accomplish some other ridiculous feat?

Or would she forgo the games and just come into his arms?

He tugged on his hose to eliminate the wrinkles around the knees, then hurried toward the southeast tower. He bounded up the stairs and opened the door to the tapestry room.

The ladies stopped sewing and greeted him enthusiastically. Smiling automatically, he glanced around the room. There was no sign of Allison.

"She is with Father Gregory," Lady Anne said when he asked where Allison was. "She said to tell you that she has fallen behind in her other duties and therefore will not be able to continue your lessons."

Derek grew still for a moment—then he laughed out loud.

"You find something amusing, Sir Derek?" Lady Anne asked.

"Mmm," Derek murmured noncommittally. He did find something amusing—but he wasn't about to tell anyone that Allison was running scared. Did she really think hiding from him would stop the inevitable? "Please excuse me, ladies, I also have other duties to attend to."

Whistling, Derek returned to the squires' quarters, where Oswald and Kenrick sat on their pallets polishing armor—punishment for their poor performances in the yard earlier. They glared at him as if it were his fault. Which maybe it was since he'd celebrated the morning's victory over the quintain by drinking multiple toasts at dinner with all the squires.

Ignoring them—and the pile of armor that awaited him on his own pallet—he glanced around the room. Cuthbert sat in a corner, plucking the strings of Derek's harp, a dreamy look on his face. A short distance away the other men were playing with crudely made dice. "Hey, Sir Derek, join us!" cried Simon.

"No, thanks," Derek said. He was an expert at the games between men and women, but he still needed to think a little about his strategy.

It wouldn't do to frighten Allison off. In fact, it might be wise to give her a day or two to lull her into a false sense of security.

He walked over to where Cuthbert sat in the corner. "I need a vacation," he announced.

"A vacation?" Cuthbert looked up from the harp. "What is that?"

"It's where you take off for a day and do whatever you damn well please."

Cuthbert looked shocked. "But you can't do that. Sir Drogo would flay you alive."

"Not if I was sick," Derek said.

"Sick?" Cuthbert repeated stupidly.

"Yes, sick." Derek was beginning to get impatient. "Haven't you ever played hooky?"

"Hook—"

"Never mind." Derek sighed. "Tomorrow morning you're going to be ill."

"But I feel fine."

"I know, you idiot. But if you tell Sir Drogo you're sick, he'll let you stay in bed. And then we can go swimming."

"Swimming? I don't know. . . ." Cuthbert looked doubtful.

"Sounds like a great idea to me." Simon had abandoned the dice game and wandered over to listen. "Can I come, too?" he asked, a glint in his hazel green eyes.

Derek rubbed his chin. "I don't know if that would be a good idea."

"Please? I know some laundresses."

Derek opened his mouth to say no. But then he paused. What the hell was he thinking? Women were all the swimming expedition needed to make it perfect. It didn't matter that they weren't Allison—

Cuthbert looked aghast. "What are you thinking, Simon? Sir Derek is Lady Allison's True Love. He has no interest in other women."

"I don't know why being Lady Allison's True Love should interfere with Sir Derek having a little pleasure now and again," Simon said.

Yeah, Derek agreed silently. Especially since Lady Allison most certainly was *not* his True Love.

Cuthbert frowned. "You forget. The Pelsworths' True

Loves always practice fidelity. Not to mention that Lord Pelsworth would probably have Sir Derek hanged if he was caught with some wench."

"Well, there's no reason why the rest of us should suffer," Simon pointed out, grinning wickedly. "Is there, Sir Derek?"

Derek hesitated. The idea of everyone else frolicking with the women while he played the part of virtuous True Love wasn't too appealing. Still, he'd enjoy the swim—and he could always think about what he would do with Allison once he had her in his bed.

"Of course not," he said generously. Sitting down on his pallet, he picked up a piece of armor and started polishing in a desultory fashion, imagining several scenarios involving Allison and himself.

He was so involved with his pleasant fantasies that he didn't notice Simon whispering to the other squires.

"I'm sorry to say, Lady Allison and Lady Anne, that all the squires are ill." Sir Percival brushed an insect off the shoulder of his orange doublet, then tightened his hands on the reins of his horse. "Apparently they ate some bad meat at supper last night. The servants and knights are having to take over some of the squires' chores, which is why Sir Everard is not available to escort you today. Sir Drogo and I are here in his stead. But there is havoc in the castle, and 'twould behoove us not to tarry. Which is why I recommended that we take this shortcut through the woods . . . Lady Allison! Watch out for that branch."

Allison obediently ducked her head, not to avoid the branch—which she would have had to stand on her horse to reach—but to avoid the huge plumes in Sir Percival's hat. She'd been dodging the plumes ever since they'd left the castle, and already she was exasperated enough to want to snatch the hat from the herald's head and toss it under the hooves of her palfrey.

But no sooner did she have the thought than she felt guilty for her meanness. She was tired and edgy today, but she shouldn't take it out on a good man like Sir Percival. It was only that she'd slept poorly last night. Sleep had been elusive after the tension of the evening—the tension of waiting. And waiting. And waiting.

She didn't know what she had expected. That Sir Derek would seek her out, perhaps. That he would come and taunt her for being a coward. That he would drag her off and continue that kiss. . . .

That kiss.

Dear heaven, that kiss. How had he dared to kiss her so? How had he dared to hold her so closely, so tightly? He'd been wet and muddy, and he'd smelled of earth and rainsoaked wool. His chin had been damp and scratchy against her face, his hands hard and callused on her skin. How had he dared to touch her hips and waist and breasts so intimately?

She should have had him whipped for his impudence. Only somehow, she hadn't been able to bring herself to do so. So she had made an excuse to avoid him. And she'd waited for him to come and find her.

But he hadn't. And last night she'd tossed and turned, plagued by an odd disappointment.

She didn't know why exactly. Except that there was a tingling warmth deep in the pit of her stomach that refused to go away. The same warmth that assailed her every time he was near. What was it about him? Perhaps it was just that he reminded her of the old days, when everyone had been full of joy and laughter—

"Yes, there are many important tasks awaiting my return," the herald said, once they'd passed the dangerous branch. "I must check my roll for mistakes. One never knows when a careless clerk might have written down the wrong name or made a mistake on the coat-of-arms. Did I tell you that I once caught a clerk painting the background of a shield red instead of green? Think of the confusion such an error could have caused! Alas, if only the squires were not ill, they could help me. But perhaps they will be recovered by the time we return. If that rascal, Derek Sinclair, wasn't also afflicted by the illness, I would suspect that he somehow poisoned the men. I do not like that man. He does not listen when I am lecturing on chivalry, and his behavior infects the others. It even affects the dogs. For some reason they have begun to howl every time they see him. Yesterday I could not even conduct my lesson, the howling distracted me so."

Allison glanced at Anne, then hastily looked away, trying not to smile. It was true—the dogs *did* howl every time they saw Derek. And really, she couldn't blame them. Derek's singing had truly been awful—even worse than his dreadful poem. She hadn't laughed so much in ages.

A loud burst of masculine laughter rang through the trees.

Startled, Allison pulled back on her reins as feminine squeals and giggles joined the laughter. The sounds came from around the corner, where a bridge crossed the river.

Sir Drogo frowned. "Wait here, ladies. Sir Percival and I will investigate." He spurred his horse forward. Sir Percival, rather timidly, followed suit.

Allison looked at Anne.

"Do men really expect women to obey the ridiculous orders they give?" Anne asked, her eyes sparkling, before she rode after Sir Drogo.

Smiling a little, Allison followed.

She rounded the corner to see a group of men and women bathing in the river . . . although it looked as though some of them were doing more than just bathing. Allison's faint smile disappeared. Her shock increased when she saw Cuthbert—dear, sweet, innocent little Cuthbert!—staring with awe at the magnificent bosom of a naked girl who was casually washing herself. Simon had his arm around another girl and was tipping up her chin for a kiss. And Derek . . . Derek! What was he doing here? He was supposed to be ill, not swimming across the river with the most amazing speed she had ever seen—

"You men!"

Allison tore her gaze away from Derek as Sir Drogo crossed the bridge, roaring at the squires. Hastily, not wanting to be caught spying, she backed her palfrey into the shadows and thick underbrush. Anne quickly followed suit.

On the other side of the river, Sir Drogo wheeled his horse around to face the men. "Out of the water! At once!"

A mad scramble ensued. Squealing women ran naked into the forest. Panic-stricken men dashed out of the water and lined up on the bank. They stood at stiff attention—presenting Allison with a very fine view of a row of round white buttocks. She glanced down the line, her gaze pausing at one particular behind. It was firm and muscular, and as white as the others, but strangely, the skin above and below was a rich, smooth brown. . . .

"What the devil is the meaning of this?" Sir Drogo demanded.

Derek stepped forward and cleared his throat. "In California, swimming is recommended as a cure for stomach ailments. And, ahem, it has worked! We are all pretty well recovered."

Sir Drogo glared at Derek. "Do not take me for a fool, Sinclair, and do not compound your sins by lying. First the shirking, then the cards, now this! All of you, back to the castle immediately, and stay there until I decide what your punishment will be."

When they didn't immediately move, Sir Drogo roared, *"Go!"*

The men obeyed.

Allison watched as they ran down the path past her hiding place in various stages of undress, some hopping as they tried to put on their hose and shoes without pausing.

Allison looked at Anne.

Anne looked at her.

Anne made a choking noise.

Allison began to gasp.

She clapped her hands over her mouth to restrain the sounds erupting from her throat. Tears streaming down her face, she tried not to burst out laughing.

"Allison, stop!" Anne moaned. "I'm going to laugh if you don't stop making those noises."

Allison doubled over. She was certain that if she couldn't laugh she would explode—

Fortunately, the sound of men's voices distracted her before she did.

She looked up, wiping her cheeks, to see Derek sauntering down the path. He wore his hose and a loose shirt, but his doublet was slung casually over his shoulder as he strolled back toward the castle.

Simon slowed down to let Derek catch up to him. "I don't care what our punishment is," she heard Simon say. "I haven't had so much fun in ages."

Derek smiled. "C'mon. We'd better hurry. There's no point in angering Sir Drogo further."

Soon all the men were out of sight.

As Allison and Anne emerged from the trees, Sir Drogo and Sir Percival rode up. "That Sinclair!" Percival exclaimed, the plume in his hat quivering. "The man is a troublemaker."

"I doubt he meant any harm—"

"My lady," Sir Drogo said. "I recommend that Sinclair be imprisoned in the dungeon for a week with only bread and water."

"A week?" she repeated, dismayed. "Don't you think a day or two would do as well?"

Sir Drogo's bushy white brows drew together in a frown. "This is a serious matter, my lady. We must maintain discipline."

"Yes, of course," she said, biting back another protest. What was she thinking, to be defending Derek?

A week of imprisonment, with nothing but bread and water was doubtless what he deserved. He had caused more trouble in his short time here than anyone else had in years. He wouldn't be so quick to flout Sir Drogo's authority—or hers—after his sojourn in the dark and dirty dungeon.

But somehow, as Allison continued down the path with her companions, the thought did not make her as happy as it should have.

Chapter 14

THE NEXT FEW days were busy ones for Allison, and she was glad of it. Working so hard kept her mind off Derek—and off the niggling guilt that plagued her for subjecting him to such misery.

She tried to shrug it off, but at odd times, she found herself thinking about him and about how he must be suffering. When the servants lit the candles in the evenings and she sat listening to her ladies laugh and chatter, she imagined him sitting in the dark, alone and despondent. When she lay on her soft bed, cocooned in warm blankets, she imagined him huddling in a corner of the dank dungeon, shivering and perhaps even coughing as the cold air settled in his lungs. When she ate pheasant and sweetmeats and drank good wine, she imagined him growing thin and pale, and the light in his eyes fading and growing dim.

It had to be done, she told herself over and over again.

But as the days passed, thoughts of Derek continued to haunt her—even though she had other things to worry about. Everyone in the castle seemed afflicted by odd ill humors. The knights got drunk; the ladies shirked their sewing. The stableboys slept on the job; the maids cleaned sloppily. The pantler and the butler quarreled endlessly; and the squires missed morning prayers to go swimming.

By the third day of Derek's imprisonment, Allison's nerves were stretched to the breaking point, and she thought that if she was called upon to deal with one more petty infraction, she would take her vows and go live in a convent.

Father Gregory cornered her shortly after midday when she was in the dovecote, helping the cook choose some birds for tomorrow's dinner.

"The men did not attend chapel this morning again. Upon a search, I discovered several of them in a hayloft with the laundresses!" he said, puffing slightly from the climb up to the small room in the top of the southwest tower. "I cannot believe they would be so imprudent as to endanger their immortal souls for the sake of mere pleasure! You must do something, my lady, before their souls are completely lost—"

Thinking longingly of the peaceful life of a nun, Allison promised to look into the matter, then hurried down the stairs and across the courtyard to the smith's shed before the chaplain could say more.

"Good morrow," she said to the smith. "Cook needs some pots and ladles repaired. Will you attend to it?"

"Aye, my lady, but I must clean this chain mail first. The squires have been neglecting their duties, and it has rusted. Rust is extremely difficult to get rid of. I have to scour it with sand and vinegar—"

Allison murmured something, then headed for the kitchens, only to be waylaid by the steward.

"My lady! My lady! The ladies still haven't finished embroidering the linens for the beds and our supplies are dangerously low! I have begged and pleaded with them to work faster, but they seem to make no progress at all."

Allison sighed. "Don't worry, Larkin. I shall take care of the matter."

And she would, she thought as she climbed the stairs to the tapestry room. As she always took care of everything. It was part of being lady of the castle. But, oh, how wonderful

it would be to forget about all the problems, to have no responsibilities, to have a care only for herself. . . .

She opened the door, hearing a scuffle as she did so. Pushing the door all the way open, she saw all her ladies, their
faces rather flushed, sitting at a table in the middle of the
room, their embroidery on their laps.

"Good afternoon, ladies." She glanced at the table, wondering where it had come from. "Larkin informed me that
the embroidery of the bed linens still isn't finished. I must
ask all of you to work a trifle harder or we will be sleeping
on bare mattresses."

The ladies nodded vigorously. "I will go get some more
linens right now," said Anne.

"I will help you." Lady Mountford followed quickly.

"Hmmph. It seems I am out of gold thread," said Lady
Ursula. "I will go find some more."

Lady Humfrey dug through her sewing basket. "Dear me,
I have lost my thimble. I must have dropped it in my bedchamber." For all her plumpness, she made a nimble exit.

"I, uh, better help my mother find her thimble," Emmeline said, rising to her feet.

Allison stopped her before she could escape like the others. "Emmeline, what is toward?"

"Toward?" The young girl avoided her eyes. "I know not
what you m—"

Before she could complete her sentence, her sewing basket tipped and a stream of small square pictures fell out.

Allison stiffened. "Aren't those the playing cards that Sir
Drogo confiscated from the squires?"

"Uh, yes, I believe so. I wonder how they got into my
sewing basket?" Emmeline hurriedly picked them up. "If
you will excuse me, my lady, I'd better go—"

"Emmeline," Allison said sternly, holding her hand out
for the cards. "Have you and the others been playing cards?
Is that why the embroidery isn't done?"

Reluctantly Emmeline handed them over. "I'm sure none
of us realized—we were so caught up in the game, you see.
'Tis called Hearts, and we are having a special competition.
The winner receives a prize."

"A prize?"

"Yes. A kiss from Sir D—" Emmeline broke off, but it was too late.

"From Sir Derek?" Allison asked severely.

Emmeline bit her lip, then nodded. " 'Twas Lady Mountford's idea. 'Tis all in fun."

Allison's eyes narrowed when she heard Lady Mountford's name. " 'Twill not be fun if we have no bed linens."

Emmeline looked sheepish. "I'm sorry, Lady Allison. We'll work late until the linen is all embroidered. Do not worry."

Do not worry? Allison bit back a sharp reply as Emmeline hurried away so quickly, she didn't even close the tapestry room door. She would love not to worry. She would love to sit around playing card games and winning kisses from Sir Derek. . . .

Her stomach turned a little somersault as she remembered what it was like to be kissed by Sir Derek. She banished the memory quickly. She could not allow herself to be influenced by a kiss. She could not allow herself to be influenced by a completely irresponsible, extremely annoying, impossibly attractive rogue—

"My lady!"

Allison turned to see Sir Drogo standing in the doorway.

"My lady, I am concerned. The squires are not doing well. This is the worst bunch I've seen in twenty years. I am afraid Sinclair has been a bad influence. These last several days have been particularly bad. Something must be done."

Allison looked down at the cards in her hands. Sir Drogo was right. Something must be done.

"I will take care of it," she said firmly.

An hour later Allison was ready to take care of it—or Derek Sinclair, to be more precise. She entered the cellar beneath the northwest tower and approached the guard at the entrance to the dungeon. "Good morrow, Simon," she said to the guard, feeling unaccountably nervous. "I wish to visit the prisoner."

Simon's hazel eyes flickered, but he only said, "Yes, my lady."

She felt a trifle uncomfortable under his gaze. Did he think it odd that she was visiting Derek Sinclair? This was business, she reminded herself sternly. She had no reason to be embarrassed. She was here for the sake of the castle, nothing else.

Simon unlocked the trapdoor and lifted it, only to have it slip through his fingers. It slammed down, the noise echoing through the cellar.

"I beg your pardon, my lady," he said, lifting it again. He took a torch from the cellar wall and led the way down the steep stairs, holding the light aloft so she could see.

To Allison's surprise, she could hear the faint notes of a harp being played. "Does Sinclair have a visitor?" she asked.

"Er, I don't believe so." He coughed, then said in a rather loud voice, "Watch your step here, my lady."

Allison avoided the uneven place on the stone as they rounded the bend in the stairway, her nervousness increasing. She hadn't spoken with Derek since the night he'd kissed her. She wasn't sure what he would do or say or think when he saw her. He might think she'd come because she wanted to see him. He might think that she'd come because she wanted him to kiss her again. . . .

She squared her shoulders. That was *not* why she was visiting him. She was visiting him out of a sense of duty, nothing more. And so she would tell him if he dared suggest anything else.

They reached the bottom of the stairs. Shivering a little, Allison wrapped her cloak more tightly around herself as they approached the cell. She was glad that she'd thought to bring it. The air down here was definitely cooler.

Through the wooden slats of the grille, Allison saw Derek lying on a low cot, apparently asleep. She could no longer hear the harp music—she must have imagined it, she decided.

"Wake up, Sir Derek!" Simon said. "You have a visitor."

Derek rose to his feet, taking care to arrange the blanket

on the cot. Allison was surprised by his neatness—and by the thick, soft-looking blanket. Apparently she needn't have worried about Derek being cold after all—Sir Drogo was more generous with prisoners than she would have expected.

In fact, Allison thought as Derek approached the grille, it appeared she needn't have worried at all. Derek looked remarkably hale and hearty—and the light in his eyes had not diminished one iota.

"Good afternoon, my lady."

Seeing the glint in his eyes, she stiffened.

"I would not think it's a good afternoon for you," she said a bit waspishly.

He laughed. "How could it not be good when such a beautiful lady is visiting me?"

The mockery in his voice annoyed her. She wanted to turn on her heel and leave, but she restrained herself. She wasn't leaving until she'd done what she came to do. She turned to the guard. "Would you please leave us?"

Simon shifted his weight from foot to foot, then nodded. He lit the torch that was in a wall bracket by the cell, then quietly left. The torch sputtered and flickered, and Allison frowned at it. 'Twas burnt nearly to the quick. She noticed the ring of keys hanging on a nail below it, before she turned back to Derek.

He stood by the grille, his eyes glinting even more brightly.

"I'm flattered, my lady. Here it's been so long since I've seen you, I thought you must be avoiding me. Now I see you were waiting for an opportunity for us to be alone together."

She flushed. "What I have to say I wish to say in private."

"Oh? Now I'm all agog. Please speak."

"I am glad you can still make jokes," she said, trying to sound disdainful. "But how much longer will you be able to endure this? It cannot be pleasant."

He rubbed his nose. "Dungeons are not usually pleasant places."

"Exactly. So I have come to make you an offer."

"Oh?"

"Agree to leave Pelsworth Castle and I will have you released."

"That's very kind of you. But I'm afraid I must decline."

She clasped her hands beneath her cloak, trying to ignore the foolish relief she felt at his refusal. She made herself speak sternly. "Sir Drogo plans to keep you in here another four days. Are you certain you don't wish to reconsider? When you are released, you will have to work harder than ever. And neither Sir Drogo nor I will tolerate any more episodes like the swimming incident. I shudder to think what effect it will have on poor little Cuthbert. I couldn't believe my eyes when I saw him with that wench—"

"Wait a minute." Derek straightened from his lounging position a few feet away. "You *saw* Cuthbert with that wench?"

Allison, aware that she had blundered badly, stammered, "I . . . I couldn't really see much, I was in the forest. . . ."

"What *did* you see?"

"Hardly anything, I assure you. 'Twas entirely inadvertent. Sir Drogo and Sir Percival were escorting Lady Anne and me when we came upon you at the river. We immediately averted our gazes, of course—"

"Lady Allison, do you know what this means?"

His voice was stern, and she looked at him half fearfully. "No, what?" she asked in a small voice.

"It means you were *spying* on me."

"Spying?" she repeated uncertainly. "No, I told you—"

"I know what you told me, but it doesn't alter the facts. I can't believe you would do something so *low,* so *dishonorable.*"

She looked at him suspiciously. "Sir Derek, you are being ridiculous—"

"Ridiculous! How can you say that when *my modesty has been violated*?"

"Oh, you are impossible." She turned away to hide her twitching lips. "I see I am wasting my time here. Send word if you change your mind about my offer."

"Tell me one thing, Allie." He stood at the grille, smiling at her. "Did you like what you saw?"

"No, I did not," she said as haughtily as she could. But then she ruined it by asking the question she'd been longing to ask ever since she'd seen him in the river. "Sir Derek . . . how did you learn to swim like that?"

"Like what?"

"Like . . . like a bird skimming across the water. I have never seen anyone swim in such a way."

"Everyone in California swims like that." Before she realized what he intended, he reached through the slats of the grille and drew his finger down her cheek. "I'd be happy to teach you, if you like."

Belatedly she drew back, her foolish heart beating rapidly. "No, thank you," she said coldly. "I doubt you will be here long enough to teach me anything."

"Oh, I expect I'll get a chance to teach you *something,* Allison."

Depraved images of what he might teach her popped into her head. Sternly she banished them. "Sir Percival was right—you are a bad influence. I warn you, I will not allow you to further corrupt anyone in this castle—not the squires, nor my ladies, either."

"How have I been corrupting your ladies?"

"That look of false innocence does not become you, Sir Derek. I know all about the game called Hearts and the 'prize.' " She patted her purse where the cards were safely stowed. "There will be no more such wickedness."

Derek's gaze traveled from her purse up to her face. "You have the cards?"

She nodded.

"Perhaps I'll teach you something right now, Allie. How about if I teach you to play five-card stud?"

She made a scoffing noise. "I have no interest in learning a card game."

"What if I make a bargain with you? You play five-card stud with me, and if you win, I'll leave Pelsworth Castle. If I win, you release me."

Allison paused. She truly had no interest in cards, but his offer sounded tempting. It would be a small matter to release him a few days early if he won. But if *she* won—all her worries would be over. "How is this game played?" she asked, suspecting some catch. The game likely required great skill.

"We both get five cards," he said. "Whoever has the best hand wins the round. The hands are ranked by how difficult they are to get. A straight-flush—five cards of the same suit in numerical sequence—is the best hand. The others are four of a kind, full house, flush, straight, three of a kind, two pairs, and one pair."

Allison listened carefully. It sounded easy enough—and appeared to be nothing more than a simple test of one's luck. "How does one win the game?"

"The players bet chips on each hand. If a player runs out of chips, he—or she—loses."

"But we don't have any chips."

He pulled a small bag out from under his pillow. "I have some."

"Where did you get those?" she asked.

"The last occupant must have left them here."

Suspiciously she glanced at him, but his expression was bland. "Very well," she said. "But you must tell me the order of the hands again."

He did so, adding a few more details about dealing and betting, then proceeded to whip out a small table and stool from under his bed. He set them up by the grille and split the chips into two piles of fifty.

This was the most well-furnished dungeon cell she'd ever seen, she thought. Glancing around, she saw another stool by the wall under the flickering torch. She pulled it in front of the grille.

Derek dealt two cards facedown. Allison reached through the grille and picked hers up. It was the two of cups. Hesitantly she put a chip into the pot.

Derek did the same and dealt the next two cards faceup. Hers was a four of cups. His was an ace of batons. He threw a chip onto the table.

Allison followed suit and waited eagerly for her next card. A ten of cups appeared before her. His was the king of swords.

Two more chips went into the pot, then two more, after he dealt her the seven of coins and himself the knave of swords.

Allison's last card was the two of batons. She stared at it gloomily, then looked at the knave, queen, king, and ace resting before Derek. He could have a straight. Or a pair. Any pair would beat her pitiful twos.

Her chances seemed small, but she went ahead and bet another chip. Derek called her, and they both turned over their concealed cards. Derek's was the five of batons.

"I won!" she crowed, raking the flat wooden chips into her lap.

Smiling, Derek nodded and dealt another hand. This time her first two cards were eights. Excited, she raised her bet to two chips.

Her excitement increased when on the fourth card, she received another eight. She looked at his cards. He had nothing so far—only a knave, six, and three, all of swords. Recklessly, she bet ten chips.

He called and dealt two more cards.

Hers was the five of coins, his the five of swords. Silently, she gloated. 'Twas impossible for him to beat her—unless he had another sword. But that was not very likely. She put ten more chips in the pot.

"I'll see your ten and raise you twenty," Derek said coolly, pushing the rest of his chips into the pot.

Allison's excitement faded. He must have another sword after all. A pox on him. "I fold," she said reluctantly.

Without comment, he reached out to rake in his winnings.

"Wait," she said. "You must show me your card."

"You folded. I don't have to show it," he replied.

She looked at him suspiciously. "But how do I know if you have a sword or not?"

"You don't."

"But you might be lying!"

"Lying? I never said I had a sword."

"But . . . but you raised the bet."

"So?"

She stared at him. The torch flickered and dimmed, then brightened, revealing the glint in his eyes quite clearly. "I want to see that card," she said adamantly.

He looked at her a moment, a small smile playing about the corner of his lips, then turned over the card. It was the queen of cups.

"You cheated!" she cried. "I had three eights. I would have beaten you."

Derek smiled. "It's called bluffing, Allie."

"But . . . but . . . that's not fair!"

"All is fair in love and poker," he said, dealing the next hand.

Fuming, Allison picked up her card. She should have known he would try some trick. Well, she wouldn't fall for it again.

Her cards were lackluster this time, but his were equally so. In fact, she thought, studying his four upturned cards, her pair of tens would certainly beat anything he could possibly have. She bet the rest of her chips.

"I call," he said. "And I raise you five."

"But I don't have any more chips," she said.

He shrugged. "You fold then?"

"Sir Derek," she protested indignantly. "This is clearly unfair. I will win this hand."

He appeared to consider her words. "Hmm. Very well. I'll give you five chips for your hat."

Her hands flew to her caul. "Are you insane? My caul is worth much more than a few wooden chips."

"I'll give it back when the game is over," he promised.

She hesitated. She didn't want to give him her caul, even for such a short period of time.

Her lips tightened. Even less did she want to let him win so easily.

She took off the hat and handed it to him through the grille. He laid it gently on his cot and gave her the five chips.

She called his bet and won the hand. Her delight was tempered however, by the knowledge that she had come very close to losing. More than ever, she was determined to beat him.

The next hand she had an ace in the hole. Derek dealt another card, faceup. It was an ace, also. Her heart pounding, she bet a chip.

Derek matched her bet and raised her ten.

She put in another ten, and he dealt her a card.

Another ace.

Derek had a three and a six of coins showing. She put in another chip.

He called her and raised her ten.

She bit her lip. She only had seven chips left. "Sir Derek, will you accept my cloak in lieu of three chips?"

He nodded.

She hung her cloak on one of the slats of the grille. He left it there, and dealt her a card.

It was another ace.

Allison was so excited, she could barely contain herself. Four aces! He would need a straight flush to beat her, and that was impossible.

She looked at his cards. A three, a six, and a seven, all coins. Hmm. Perhaps it wasn't *impossible*. But it was highly unlikely. She was certain to win the hand—if she didn't have to fold. She glanced down to see what else she could wager.

"Sir Derek, will you take my belt for five chips?"

He pursed his lips. "I'll take your belt and your boots," he said.

She looked at him a trifle askance, but went ahead and slipped off her boots and belt, taking care to put her purse and keys on the floor by her stool.

Derek put ten chips on the table and added another ten.

"I'll take your hose and garters," he said casually.

Allison stiffened. "My hose and garters! Absolutely not!"

"You're folding then?" He reached out as though to take the pot.

"No! Wait!" She nibbled at her lip. Really, her hose and garters were no great thing. Her legs would still be covered by her gown. She hesitated a bit more, then said, "Very well," and leaned over to remove them.

Conscious of his gaze on her, she made sure to keep her legs decently covered with the skirt of her gown. She fumbled underneath it for the buckles of her garters, then slowly pulled them and her stockings down her legs. Blushing a little, she put them on the table.

Derek dealt the last card.

She received the five of cups and he received the four of coins.

Allison looked from her cards to his. The only way he could win was if he had the five of coins.

What were the chances of that?

But she had nothing left to wager—except her gown.

His brown eyes had little flames in them, reflected from the flickering torchlight. "I'll take the gown, Allie."

She stared at him, unable to look away. "No."

"Yes." He cleared his throat. "That is, of course, unless you want to fold."

Allison hesitated. She still had her kirtle on underneath—but that was all. She knew she should refuse. A small, shrill voice in her head warned her the game had gone too far. And yet, somehow she couldn't quite bring herself to stop it.

The kirtle *did* cover her completely, she assured herself. And the flickering torchlight was very dim. And besides, she couldn't stop now—not when she was so close to victory.

Ignoring the shrill little voice, she turned her back. She undid the laces at her bodice and slipped the gown off.

Derek was sitting very still. He didn't move even when she hung the gown next to the cloak.

His gaze made her squirm a little on the stool. "Are you going to play?" she asked, lowering her lashes.

"Yes. I call, and I raise you twenty."

Slowly Allison looked up and met his gaze. His eyes were very dark. Her heart thumping, she looked back down at the cards. She knew what he wanted. He wanted her to take off her kirtle.

"No," she said.

"Oh, c'mon, Allie." His voice was low and a trifle husky. "What's the big deal? Neither one of us has any modesty left to violate."

She was suddenly aware of how isolated they were and of the shadowy intimacy of the dungeon. And of the keys hanging below the sputtering torch. And of the narrow cot behind him in his cell.

"No," she said.

"Allie . . ." His voice was soft and persuasive. "There is a locked grille between us. There's nothing I can do to you."

"No."

"Then you fold? If you do, I win, and you must release me."

"I . . . I'll have the guard release you."

"No, the agreement was that *you* release me. The keys are right there under the torch. Release me, or take off your kirtle and finish the hand."

Allison stared at him. The torchlight shone on the planes of his face. The usually pleasant smile on his lips was gone. He looked . . . dangerous. She couldn't release him. Not when he looked like that. Not when she felt all warm and shivery in the pit of her stomach.

Slowly she untied the string at the neck of her kirtle. It slipped down over one shoulder. Reaching up, she took hold of the neckline and tugged. The kirtle slipped down. . . .

The torch sputtered and went out, casting the dungeon into darkness.

Derek cursed.

Her heart pounding, Allison reached blindly for her dress and cloak. She caught a fistful of wool and silk, but the silk caught on something.

The "something" tugged at the gown, pulling her closer to the grille. A hand touched the bare flesh of her waist.

With a little squeal, she released the gown and jumped back, her heart pounding.

"Allie . . ."

"Please, do not speak to me," she said, her voice shaking. "I don't know what I was thinking . . . I was caught up in the game. . . ."

"Allie, we can still finish—"

"No! Give me my clothes."

"The game's not over. I said I'd give them back to you when it's over."

"It is over. We cannot see."

"Simon can get a new torch—"

"No. I do not want to play with you anymore. You do not play fairly. Now, give me my clothes."

"Come and get them, Allie."

His voice was dangerously seductive. She bit her lip, trying to decide what to do.

"C'mon, Allie. I'll give them to you. Just come a little closer. . . ."

She had to get out of here. But she couldn't leave without her clothes.

"Allie?"

Cautiously she reached out, groping on the floor.

"Allie? I know you're there. I can smell you. Have I ever told you how sweet you smell? Like cinnamon and cloves . . ."

She tried to block out the sound of his seductive voice. She found her keys and purse, and picked them up as quietly as possible. But where were the rest of her clothes? She hesitated, wondering if she should go closer to the cell.

"Of course, the way you smell is nothing compared to the way you taste. I want to taste you, Allie. Not just your mouth, but all of you. Your breasts, and your belly, and the sweetness between your thighs . . ."

She took a deep shuddering breath. She didn't dare go any nearer. Her cloak would have to suffice.

Wrapping the cloak tightly around herself, she groped her way through the darkness to the stairs.

Derek listened as her bare feet ran quickly up the stairs. A few moments later he heard the creak of the trapdoor as it opened, then slammed shut.

He drew a deep, shuddering breath, then groped his way over to the cot and sat down, pulling out the harp he'd hidden under the blanket. Idly, he plucked the strings in the darkness, his thoughts on the woman who'd just left.

God, what had he done to deserve such torment? If the torch had lasted just a few seconds longer . . . but perhaps it was for the best. He'd nearly lost control there for a few minutes. He'd been completely caught up in the game and the intensity of his desire for her.

He laughed, a bit wryly. Had a man ever had such bad luck as he did? A few more seconds and he would have won the game. Then she would have had to let him out. And once the cell door was open, he would have been alone with Allison—with a *naked* Allison. What would have happened next would have been inevitable.

He sighed. He supposed he shouldn't complain. He was making much faster progress with her than he'd expected. He just needed to be patient. He was sure she would succumb soon. All the signs were there.

She'd spied on him at the river—that was definitely a good sign. And she'd been curious enough about his swimming to ask about it—another good sign. She'd wanted to accept his offer to teach her to swim, he could tell.

He wouldn't mind giving her a few lessons. It would be very pleasant to have her in the water with him, his hands against her wet skin. . . .

He sighed again. It was damn difficult being patient.

Footsteps sounded on the stairs, and Derek's fingers grew still on the strings. Had Allison decided to return for her clothes? Quickly he gathered them up and put them under his blanket along with the harp.

But to his disappointment, it was only Simon.

"Did Lady Allison notice anything amiss?" the squire whispered theatrically.

"I don't believe so," Derek replied.

Simon grinned widely in relief. "Thank goodness! I was afraid she heard you playing your harp. And she looked rather strange when she came up."

"Oh? In what way?"

"She had her cloak wrapped around her like a shroud. And she sounded a trifle breathless, as if something had frightened her."

"Maybe she saw a mouse."

"Hmm. Perhaps so." Simon unlocked the grille and opened it. "Here's your supper."

Derek took the tray a little reluctantly. He must have grown accustomed to the constant exercise—without any, he still felt full from the dinner Lady Mountford and Emmeline had sneaked in earlier. But he didn't allow his lack of enthusiasm to show. "Thanks, Simon. How's everything going?"

"Not well. Sir Drogo is still giving everyone extra chores as punishment for going swimming, and several of the squires blame you."

Derek shrugged. He hadn't forced any of them to go. "That's too bad. Here, let me get my candle. I had to put it out."

Simon lit the candle. "Is there anything else you would like? More blankets? More food? Another book?"

"How about a woman?"

Simon frowned. "I don't know . . . but I suppose I could arrange something. I think Clarice might—"

Derek laughed. "No, no. I was only joking. I'm keeping myself occupied with the books and harp." He really had no interest in the buxom kitchen maid. He wanted Allison. She was becoming something of an obsession with him. Other women seemed dull in comparison.

"Your harp playing has improved tremendously," Simon said. "I'm sure Lady Allison will be most pleased when she hears you."

Simon left, and Derek opened the packet of food the man had brought.

Inside was a leg of mutton, an apple, and a honey cake. He took a bite of the cake. It was sweet on his tongue. Almost as sweet as the taste of Allison's mouth . . .

Derek shook his head and retrieved the harp. Really, he shouldn't be torturing himself like this. He should stop thinking about her—at least for now. It wasn't healthy for him to be so obsessed with her—especially when he would be leaving as soon as Anne gave him the emerald.

Lying back, he strummed the strings of the harp. After a few minutes, he unconsciously began to sing along.

"My love doth grow and grow. . . ."

Chapter 15

FOUR DAYS LATER Allison sat in the library, staring at her father. "The king is coming *next week?*" she repeated numbly.

Lord Pelsworth drank from his cup. "Yes. I came here as soon as I received the letter."

"Does he say why?"

"Not exactly. He said something about the Flemish ambassador's trip to London being delayed, so he had decided to pay us a visit."

"I see." Her lips felt stiff. The king—he must have received her father's letter. And he must be coming to . . . to what? To find out if her father was mad? To seize the castle and throw her father into an asylum?

"Wilfred is coming, also." Lord Pelsworth frowned. "Although I don't know why. He sent a messenger ahead saying he would be here tomorrow."

Wilfred. Somehow, she had almost forgotten about him. Had he lodged a protest with the king over the broken betrothal? Was the king coming to order that she marry Wilfred?

A royal decree would solve a lot of her problems. Her father would not be able to refuse. She would be married to Wilfred—as she'd planned and hoped for so long.

Her heart felt like an anvil in her chest. She should be happy—but if she was honest with herself, she'd admit the idea of marrying Wilfred had lost much of its appeal. Because of Derek.

In the last few weeks he'd been here, he'd made everything more exciting. She never knew what he might say or do next. He'd distracted her from her problems with the king, her father, Wilfred. . . .

He'd distracted her, yes. But now it was time to face those problems.

"I had best make preparations," she said quietly. She left the library and went downstairs, bumping into Sir Drogo, who was on his way up.

"My lady! I beg your pardon."

"No, 'twas my fault." She gave him a strained smile. "Is all well? How fares your prisoner?"

"I was just coming to tell you—he was released an hour ago." Sir Drogo frowned. "Spending a week in the dungeon does not appear to have affected him at all. He appeared remarkably cheerful."

"Did he?" Allison looked down at her hands folded tightly before her. "I have news, also. My father just informed me that the king will be arriving next week."

Sir Drogo's bushy eyebrows lowered. "I see." He glanced at her. "'Tis said King Henry is not an unfair man."

"Yes." But would his fairness continue when he had heard everything?

She didn't know.

She only knew that it was more imperative than ever that she get rid of Derek Sinclair.

Derek was savoring his first breakfast outside the dungeon when he received the message to go to the chapel. He went inside the building to find Lady Allison waiting for him.

Derek hid his surprise—he had not caught even a glimpse of her since his release yesterday evening—and smiled.

"Lady Allison! I'm flattered. It's an odd choice for a tryst—but very clever. I doubt anyone will interrupt us here."

She flushed, but her voice was cold as she said, "I chose this place in the hopes that God would keep you in check."

"How optimistic of you."

"Please. I didn't summon you to bandy words about. I wish you to leave. And I am willing to give you fifty gold sovereigns if you will agree to do so."

His brows rose. Fifty gold sovereigns was a veritable fortune in this time, he knew. She must have been even closer to surrender in the dungeon than he'd thought to show such desperation.

"No, thanks. I'm not leaving until I get what I came for." He started walking toward her. "And I think I'm very close to finding it."

She stood still, staring at him with wide eyes as he approached. He took her chin in his hand.

She looked up at him. "Don't be a fool, Sinclair. Wilfred is expected to arrive today. He will find some excuse to kill you, I know it. Is that what you want?"

"All I want," he whispered against her lips, "is you—"

His mouth touched hers. She pulled away, but at the same time, reached up and placed her hands on his chest. "Sir Derek, please. I'm begging you. You must leave before the king arrives. Or 'twill be disastrous for us all."

A frown appeared between his brows, but he did not release her. "I heard the king was coming. Why are you so afraid of him?"

Allison bit her lip. "The king has never liked our family. My grandparents supported the Yorkists during the wars. Henry tried to confiscate our property on grounds of treason, but since we were supporting the rightful king, he could not get the bill of attainder through Parliament. But now he looks for any excuse. I am certain he would love to declare my father mad and appoint himself my guardian, thereby taking control of Pelsworth Castle. By breaking my betrothal and condoning you as my 'True Love,' my father may have played directly into the king's hands."

She looked at him beseechingly. "So you see? You must leave before he arrives."

"And if I do, you'll resume your engagement to Wilfred?"

She nodded. "He is high in the king's favor. If I marry Wilfred, there is even a possibility that the king will revoke the heavy taxes he has demanded from our family to prove our loyalty. The taxes are crushing Pelsworth Castle. Leave and everything will be well."

Derek frowned. If he left, everything wouldn't be well. What was it Allison's ghost had said about Wilfred?

He lost the king's favor and everything my family spent hundreds of years building.

Marriage to Wilfred had ruined Allison and her family—and she had somehow ended up dead.

A hard, cold knot formed in his stomach. He hated to think that could happen. In spite of all the torment she'd put him through, she didn't deserve a fate like that. In different circumstances he would have liked her a lot. He would have liked teasing her and trying to coax a smile out of her as he seduced her into his bed. He would have liked teaching her to enjoy life.

But it was impossible. Anne was giving him the emerald on Saint Swithin's Day, and he was leaving—the same day the king was due to arrive. There was nothing he could do.

Or was there? He didn't have to tell Allison he would be leaving. Perhaps acting as her "True Love" until the king came would somehow prevent her from renewing her engagement to Wilfred. It was worth a shot—and what could it hurt?

She placed a hand on his arm. "Will you leave? Please?"

He looked down at her hand, then up into her eyes. "No," he said. "I'm sorry, Allie, but I can't."

"Why not?" Her hand tightened on his arm. "You will gain nothing by this mad imposture. If Wilfred doesn't kill you, the king undoubtedly will. He hates pretenders. If you are wise, you will leave now. There is nothing for you here."

He tipped up her chin. She had incredibly beautiful eyes. He felt as though he could look into them for a million years. "Nothing, Allie?" he murmured.

She opened her mouth to respond, but before she could do so, the door crashed open behind her.

Wilfred stood in the doorway.

Inwardly cursing, Derek stepped back from Allison.

Wilfred looked suspiciously between the two of them. "What is the meaning of this?" he bellowed.

"Lady Allison was offering me some spiritual guidance." Derek glanced at the big, hairy hand grasping the hilt of a knife, then looked up to meet Wilfred's gaze. "She's very good at that kind of thing."

With a gap-toothed snarl, Wilfred pulled the knife from its sheath and advanced.

Before he could reach Derek, however, Allison stepped between them. "Sir Wilfred, remember where you are."

With a rumbling growl, Wilfred returned the knife to his belt, but his eyes gleamed a feral red in the dim light. "I will tolerate this no longer, Lady Allison. I insist that you choose between us."

The chapel was very silent after Wilfred's pronouncement. Allison was aware that Derek had grown very still, watching her with an odd look in his eye.

"Yes, Lady Allison," he said. "Choose."

She wished he would stop looking at her like that. Hadn't he been listening to what she said? She couldn't choose him. She hesitated, images flashing before her eyes—images of him telling the ladies to turn their backs; of his clumsy fingers fumbling on the harp strings; of his ridiculous "Ode to My Lady's Elbow," and the dogs howling while he sang beneath her window. Oh, how she had laughed—until he climbed up the vine and kissed her. The blood had sung in her veins then. As it had sung in the dungeon when he'd tempted her nearly to the breaking point. At those moments she felt the same thing she'd felt when she'd first seen him standing in the hall—a shock of awareness, a sense of connection, a sense of recognition almost. And she'd felt a flicker of something that she'd thought had died long ago— a flicker of hope.

She wished . . . She wished . . .

Oh, 'twas impossible what she wished. She couldn't choose Derek Sinclair. 'Twas foolish to even think of it.

Avoiding Derek's gaze, she stepped forward and placed her hand on Wilfred's arm.

Wilfred hauled her up against him and smiled triumphantly at Derek. "She's made her choice, Sinclair. Now leave Pelsworth Castle and go back to California."

Derek flicked a glance at Wilfred, then returned his gaze to Allison's face. For some reason, she could not quite meet his eyes. "Oh, I'll go. But not until I'm ready to do so. Good night, my lady." He sauntered out the door.

Growling, Wilfred took a step as if to go after him.

"Let him go," Allison said. "He will be gone soon enough."

" 'Twill be none too soon for me," Wilfred muttered, then turned to glower at her. "What were you doing with him? I couldn't believe my ears when Sir Jarvis told me that he'd seen you and that varlet come in here. Do you care for the weakling?" He grabbed her arm, squeezing so tightly that she was sure she would have bruises in the morning.

"Of course not," she said coolly. "He means nothing to me."

Wilfred refused to let go of the subject. "Then what were you doing?" he asked again.

"I was trying to bribe him to leave, if you must know." She tried to pull away. "Please release me."

He ignored her request. "I don't like the way he looks at you. And I don't like the way you look at him. I suggest you direct your gaze elsewhere."

Her mouth felt dry. "If that is what you desire."

"It is. But that's not all I desire."

He took her in his arms and covered her mouth with his, pressing until she cut her inner lip on her teeth. His coarse beard scratched against her skin and the sourness of his breath filled her nostrils.

She pushed at him. "Please, Wilfred. You're hurting me."

His grip tightened, making her wince in pain. "I will be patient for now with your maidenly ways," he said. "But you'd best prepare yourself—once we're married, you'll find out what 'tis like to be with a *real* man."

She was almost fainting when he finally released her. "Excuse me, Wilfred," she said as calmly as she could. "I must make sure there is lodging for you and your men."

Once outside, she began walking across the courtyard. But as she walked, her feet began to move more and more rapidly until she was almost running away from the chapel and the man she intended to marry.

Standing in the long line for breakfast the next morning, Derek waited for his bread and ale, still oddly angry at the memory of what had happened in the chapel the night before.

He hadn't really expected her to choose him. She had made it clear that she wanted to marry Wilfred. And yet, there had been some small part of him that had wanted her to choose him—to admit what was between them. To admit that she wanted him as much as he wanted her.

Damn Wilfred. And damn the king. Why did they have to come just now? Everything had been going so well. Just a few more days, and Allison would have given herself to him, he was sure.

Now, it might be too late. She had withdrawn again and he might never get another chance. He might never have the chance to make love to her.

And he wanted to. God, how he wanted to. He wanted her so much he ached with it. He would give anything to spend just one night in her bed. He would give his life, his heart. . . .

Derek stopped abruptly, causing someone behind him to bump into him. "Sir Derek! Please move forward!" Cuthbert said indignantly.

"Sorry, Cuthbert," Derek muttered. He stepped forward again, but he was still stunned by what he had been thinking.

What the *hell* was the matter with him to be thinking romantic drivel like that? The Middle Ages must be scrambling his brain. The Middle Ages and all that chivalry crap the herald kept spouting.

He was going home in less than a week. He wasn't going to lay down his life or his heart for anyone. Most especially not for a woman who had chosen another man—no, a big hairy ape—over him.

"Sir Derek, 'tis your turn," Cuthbert hissed, giving him a nudge.

Derek stepped forward and took his trencher and ale, then made his way to a spot in the shade. Cuthbert sat next to him.

"I can't wait until Saint Swithin's Day," Cuthbert said as he tore off a hunk of the bread. "'Twill be most exciting to see the king. I pray that he will rule in your favor, although some of Sir Wilfred's men were boasting that Sir Wilfred would wed Lady Allison anon."

Biting down hard on his bread, Derek pictured a coarse black beard and rotten teeth. How could Allison even consider marrying that Neanderthal? Couldn't she see what a brute he was?

Apparently not.

Well, that was just fine. If she wanted to marry Wilfred and end up losing her precious castle—not to mention her life—that was her business. He'd done his best to dissuade her from the engagement. He was through sticking out his neck for her—

Two knights came and sat a short distance away from Derek and Cuthbert. One, in his late twenties, had what appeared to be a permanent case of acne. "This visit should offer some fine entertainment," he said.

"Aye." Glancing at Derek, the other man—remarkable mainly for the rancid odor emanating from him—said in an overly loud voice, "I can't wait to see this simpleton who claims to be Lady Allison's True Love."

Cuthbert stiffened and started to rise. Derek placed a hand on the boy's arm. "Ignore them, Cuthbert."

Cuthbert frowned. "Didn't you hear that rascally knight insult you? Surely you don't intend to let that pass?"

Derek glanced at the two knights, both Wilfred's men. There were also several other of Wilfred's men standing with pseudo-casualness nearby. The air of anticipation about them made their mission plain—they wanted to beat the shit out of him.

He drank some of his ale. "Such petty remarks are beneath my notice," he said. Especially when objecting meant that in all likelihood he would get his teeth kicked in.

"I have heard of the simpleton," said the pimple-faced knight. "He calls himself Sir Derek. Perchance, did you see him practicing yesterday?"

"Aye! Tell me, Baldwin, have you ever seen such a weak swing?"

"Nay, Harvey, I have not. But what can you expect from a man—if he is a man—who claims to be from a place called 'California'?"

Derek kept eating at a steady pace, pretending deafness.

"I heard he wrote a poem," the odoriferous Harvey said. "The stupidest poem anyone has ever heard. An ode to Lady Allison's *elbow*. Tell me, Baldwin, have you ever seen a *lady's* elbow?"

"All the ladies I know keep their arms decently covered. Only sluts show their elbows."

"You're right, Baldwin. It follows then, doesn't it, that Lady Allison is a slut."

Derek stiffened, but then forced himself to relax. He wasn't stupid enough to get in a fight over a few insults. Self-preservation, that had always been his motto. He wasn't about to change it now—

"Myself, I would call her a whore. That ice queen facade doesn't fool anyone. I've heard stories that she'll wrap her legs around any man—"

"Sir!"

Oh, *shit*. Derek looked up to see Cuthbert, his face red, springing to his feet. "I must ask you to take back your remarks or suffer the consequences!"

The two knights stared at him in astonishment. Then they burst out laughing. "The little rooster is going to challenge us, Harvey," Baldwin said, wiping the tears from pimpled cheeks. "Shall we accept? Or shall we just squash him like a bug?"

"Let's squash him. Bugs deserve nothing better."

Double shit. The little fool. Derek hesitated a moment, then set aside his trencher.

Stepping over to Harvey, Derek tapped him on the shoulder. "Excuse me. Don't you think it's a little unfair for two fully trained knights to attack a child?"

"I'm not a child," Cuthbert sputtered.

"Hey, look, it's the California man," Harvey said, looking Derek up and down. "Baldwin, have you ever seen such a pretty face?"

"No, I haven't," Baldwin answered. "Personally, I don't think any man has a right to look so pretty."

Derek saw the swing coming. Instinctively he blocked it and punched Baldwin in the face.

Baldwin stepped back, his hand rising to cover his nose. He glanced at his fingers, which were covered with blood, then up at Derek. "You will pay for that, California man."

Before Derek could move, Harvey and another of Wilfred's men seized his arms and held him tightly. Glancing over, he saw that two others held Cuthbert.

Smiling evilly, Baldwin approached Derek. "You're going to regret that, California man."

The first blow was like a sledgehammer to his ribs. Pain exploded through Derek like shards of scrap metal. White spots danced before his eyes while everything in between grew dark.

Hazily Derek saw the fist draw back, then come at him again. It connected with his cheek, just below his right eye.

The white spots grew smaller and the darkness spread.

Then everything went black.

Allison was checking the new linen, when Wilfred entered the storeroom.

She concentrated on folding a length of the material. "Good morning, Sir Wilfred."

"Good morning, my lady." He smiled, showing the crenellated row of his teeth. "Please come with me. I have arranged some entertainment for you."

"Entertainment?" She looked at the piles of cloth around

her. "I really don't have time for amusements right now. I must inspect all of this cloth—"

He took hold of her arm. "It will not take long."

Reluctantly she allowed herself to be dragged along to one of the towers and up the circular stairs to the battlements. Standing on the narrow walkway, she looked out at the training yard—where a circle of Wilfred's armed men stood. In the center several men appeared to be fighting. She glanced at them, then looked again.

One of them was Derek.

And he wasn't really fighting. He was being beaten. Two of Wilfred's men were holding his arms, while a third pummeled him. Derek sagged limply, apparently unconscious. Even from this distance she could see the blood running down from his mouth.

Shock held her immobile. For a moment her vision grew hazy.

"Well? What do you think?"

Wilfred's voice cleared the haze. She became aware that he was watching her very closely.

He suspected . . . what? She wasn't sure, but she knew that to show any distress would be disastrous. Feeling sick, she forced herself to pretend indifference. "Is this your entertainment? It seems rather uninteresting to me. 'Tis clear that Sir Derek is no match for three of your men."

"True," Wilfred said. "Usually I wouldn't waste the effort. But 'tis important that he understand that you are mine."

Allison's chest felt tight. She could hardly breathe. She wanted to scream at Wilfred that she would never be his. She wanted to scream at him to stop the beating now.

But again she forced herself to speak calmly and unemotionally. "I'm sure he understands by now. Do you intend to kill him? Father will not be pleased."

Wilfred hesitated. "I suppose I've made my point." He raised his hand to his men.

They released Derek and stepped back, allowing him to fall to the ground.

"Yes," Allison murmured, sick with fear and disgust. "I think you have, indeed."

Through a fog of pain, Derek became aware that the beating had stopped. He lay on the ground, his face in the mud, feeling as though he were going to die. He hadn't experienced this much pain since Brandon, the bully in eighth grade, had beaten him up.

"Sir Derek! Sir Derek! Can you hear me?"

Derek opened his one good eye to see an uninjured Cuthbert peering down at him.

"Sir Derek?"

"I'm okay," Derek mumbled. He started to close his eye again.

"Sir Derek, please get up! You cannot just lie there."

Derek sighed. With superhuman effort, he sat up, only to feel nausea rise in his throat. Rolling over, he retched violently.

"Is anything broken, Sir Derek?" Cuthbert asked when Derek had finished.

Weak from the vomiting, Derek gingerly prodded his ribs. Surprisingly, nothing appeared to be broken. He was just bruised . . . in about every place it was possible to be bruised.

Groaning, he shook his head and closed his eyes.

"I will leave you then."

Cuthbert's stiff voice made Derek reopen his eyes. He looked at the younger man, surprised to see that Cuthbert was frowning. "Is something wrong?"

Cuthbert hesitated, then blurted out, "You didn't defend Lady Allison's honor!"

Derek stared at him incredulously. "Are you crazy? Those two goons were itching for an excuse to beat the pulp out of me. Couldn't you see that? If you hadn't taken the bait, they would have gotten tired and left."

"But it is your duty to defend the honor of your lady."

"Not when I'm about to get the shit beat out of me."

Cuthbert's usually pleasant expression tightened into a look of grim disapproval. "I see."

"Do you, you ungrateful, brat?" Derek snarled. "I just saved your hide. If I hadn't intervened, *you* would be the one lying here puking your guts out."

"I wouldn't have minded. The satisfaction of knowing I had defended my lady would have made the pain as nothing. Chivalry demands this."

"Chivalry, my ass," Derek snapped.

Cuthbert looked shocked to the core. "But . . . are you saying . . . Sir Derek, don't you believe in chivalry? Don't you believe that one must always be honorable and true? Don't you believe that one must always defend one's lady?"

Slowly Derek turned to look at the boy. There was a hint of hope in the boy's eyes, like a kid asking if the Easter Bunny really did exist even though all his school friends had told him it didn't.

"No," Derek said coldly. "I don't."

Without waiting to see Cuthbert's reaction, Derek turned and limped toward the squires' quarters.

God, he was sick of the Middle Ages. It wasn't enough for a man to get beat up here—oh, no. He had to listen to whining nonsense about chivalry and defending a lady's honor.

He couldn't take much more of this. Thank God he had only one more week to go—although at this point, he wasn't sure he could even tolerate that. He had to get out of here—soon.

He wanted to go home.

Derek was still seething later that day when he and the squires were ordered to wait on the dinner table.

The sight of Allison sitting next to Wilfred did nothing to improve his temper.

He served the platters of food in cold silence, ignoring the guffaws from Wilfred's knights as they pointed out his bruised and battered face. Allison, he noticed, didn't so much as bat an eyelash at his appearance when he approached Wilfred's side with a bowl of soup. Wilfred grinned at him, then possessively placed his huge hairy paw on Allison's thigh.

The dull haze that befogged Derek's gaze turned bright

red. His fingers tightened on the bowl of soup. The pressure caused the bowl to shoot upward through his fingers and go flying in a graceful arc—right onto Wilfred's lap.

Wilfred leaped to his feet with a roar. He approached Derek, his eyes as red as his face, his lips drawn back over his teeth in a snarl, his sword raised over his head.

Derek stumbled backward and tripped over a stool as Wilfred brought the weapon down. Acting on pure instinct, Derek grabbed the stool and brought it up, deflecting the blade. The force of the blow splintered the stool into a thousand pieces and caused Wilfred to lose his grip on the sword. It flew to the floor.

With surprising quickness, Lord Pelsworth seized it. "Cease!" he cried. "Are you no better than two dogs fighting over a bone? Both of you leave at once. Your rudeness has insulted everyone at this table."

For a moment Wilfred didn't move, and Derek thought the other man was going to ignore Lord Pelsworth. Then he stepped forward, close enough for Derek to smell his sour breath.

"You're fortunate that I don't wish to offend the old man right now. But beware, California. One day soon I will carve my initials on your dead carcass, serve your entrails to my dogs, and put your head on a pike over my door so the ravens can pick the eyes from your head and the flesh from your skull."

With a final lethal glare, Wilfred turned and stalked from the hall.

Derek followed more slowly, walking past the rows of trestle tables and their whispering, staring occupants. He kept his gaze straight ahead, trying to keep his face impassive.

Once outside in the courtyard, however, he leaned against the stone wall, his skin clammy, his hands shaking. Over and over again, his brain replayed the image of Wilfred's sword arcing down toward him.

He'd almost been killed.

Dear God, what was he doing here?

It had almost seemed like a game to him, living here in

the Middle Ages. He had laughed and joked his way through the inconveniences and discomforts, knowing that he'd be going home fairly soon. He had never really thought that he could *die* here.

Pushing himself away from the wall, he started walking toward the southeast tower. As he walked, he was conscious of the dirt and the geese and pigs rooting around the courtyard for scraps of food. He'd grown accustomed to the smells, but now the stench of stagnant water, unwashed bodies, animals, and shit struck him anew.

What was he doing here in this primitive time risking his life—and for what? So that Allison could marry her "True Love"? He didn't even believe in love. And neither, apparently, did she.

He took the circular stairs two at a time. Clearly, she wanted to marry Wilfred. And if that was what she wanted, then as far as he was concerned, she could damn well have the brute. He was sick of this barbaric place where there were no laws to speak of and life was cheap. Where men judged you on stupid things like whether or not you defended a lady's honor.

He strode through the tapestry room and outer chamber, ignoring a servant girl who gave him a startled look.

He wanted to go home. He couldn't wait any longer, not even another week until Saint Swithin's day when Anne had promised to get him the emerald. All it would take was Wilfred or one of his men sticking a knife in his back and he would be dead. *Dead.* He wanted to go home, and he wanted to go *now*.

He stopped at the door to Allison's room.

He stared at it a moment, then threw the door open.

Her room was shadowy, in spite of the light from the windows. He strode over to the chest at the foot of the bed. Anne had said the emerald wasn't in the chest, but Derek didn't believe her. He pulled his knife from his belt and inserted it into the lock, twisting until he felt it give way. After removing the knife from the ruined lock, he lifted the lid and looked inside.

The chest was full. He started pulling out the contents and

throwing them aside—dresses, hosiery, gloves, a few books, a small tapestry, the bundle of flax . . . but no emerald.

Angry, frustrated, he sat back on his heels and looked around the room, his gaze passing by the spinning wheel, the tapestry on the wall, the chair. . . .

His gaze returned to the tapestry.

In a flash he was on his feet and across the room.

Pushing the wall hanging aside, he saw a niche with a box inside it.

Derek grabbed the box. It was locked, but he quickly dealt with it as he had the chest. Holding the box with one hand, he lifted the lid with the other.

A bright glitter met his eyes.

Triumph flowed through him. He pawed through the jewels, ignoring the priceless ropes of pearls, the ruby-studded rings, the sparkling diamond tiaras. He was interested in only one jewel—the emerald.

But it wasn't there. Disbelievingly, he dug through the contents of the box again. It must be there. It *must*—

The door opened behind him.

Turning, he saw Allison in the doorway. She looked from the chaos on the floor to the ropes of pearls dripping over the sides of her jewelry box. Then she looked into his face. She didn't say anything, she just looked at him.

For a moment he couldn't move. Then, coming to his senses, he dropped the box, sending jewels scattering across the floor, and grabbed her, kicking the door shut at the same time. "Where is it?" he demanded fiercely. "Where is the emerald?"

"The emerald?"

"The Pelsworth emerald. I want it, and I want it now."

"The Pelsworth emerald," she repeated slowly, realization dawning in her eyes. "So that is what you came here for. You are nothing but a thief."

"Call me what you like, but that emerald is mine. I have more than earned it—"

He paused as voices sounded outside the room. Quick as a flash, he put his hand over her mouth. "Tell me where the emerald is."

She shook her head, her eyes scornful.

Desperate, furious, he pulled the knife from his belt and placed it at her throat, removing his hand from her mouth at the same time. "Tell me now, Allison," he hissed.

"No."

Allison felt the blade press against her throat as she stiffened. She should be afraid, she knew. But she wasn't. She was too angry to be afraid. She faced him unflinchingly.

"Go ahead and kill me, you varlet."

A dangerous light flickered in the cold brown depths of his eyes. "Don't be a fool, Allison. Is a bit of green glass worth your life?"

"No, but my self-respect is. Something you obviously know nothing about. What kind of coward threatens a woman?"

His nostrils flared. His eyes narrowed. She felt the knife press against her flesh.

For a long moment the room seemed to pulse. The rush-lights flickered and sent dancing shadows across their faces. The silence enveloped them, cocooning them from time and place and reality.

With an oath, he flung the knife away, hauled her into his arms, and kissed her.

The room whirled in a dizzying arc, and she closed her eyes. But then, as abruptly as he had seized her, he released her. Without a word and without a backward glance, he strode from the room.

She stared after him, shaken, confused, and angry. Trembling, she knelt down and picked up the jewels he'd dropped on the floor.

So he was nothing but a thief. A thief come to steal the Pelsworth emerald. She didn't know why she felt so disappointed. She'd always known he was a plaguey cur. She'd been a fool to ever think anything else.

Slowly she put the jewel box back in its niche, then began picking up the things he'd pulled from the chest. He had shown his true colors tonight. He'd covered her mouth with his hand and held a knife to her throat, trying to force her to give him the emerald.

She should have been afraid—but she hadn't been. She knew him too well. He was all bluff and no action. He would never have the courage to kill anyone, let alone her.

She picked up the bundle of flax and stared at it. Her mother had given it to her, telling her it was the finest flax from Holland. Her mother had been saving it, planning to spin it into thread when Allison's father returned. Allison remembered how her mother had told her stories of him—how kind he was, how gentle, how brave. Her mother had never said a harsh word about her beloved "Sebastian"—even though he had left her alone and pregnant. "He promised to marry me when he returned from the wars," her mother had said. "And then you, he, and I will always be together."

Allison had believed her—and she had believed that her own "True Love" would show up one day. Even after her father's betrayal and her mother's death, Allison had still believed. It wasn't until years had passed, and the situation at Pelsworth had deteriorated to a point that she'd known she must take some action, that she had finally given up all hope.

Allison fingered the flax. She should begin spinning it—there was no point in waiting.

An image of Derek flashed into her brain. Derek, the irresponsible, laughing knave. And yet, there was something about him. Something that made her heart yearn . . .

Her fingers tightened on the flax. Ah, she was a fool. If she couldn't find true love, she could at least marry sensibly. By wedding Wilfred, she would restore her family to the king's favor. She must marry Wilfred and forget about Derek Sinclair.

He was nothing but a thief and a coward.

Chapter 16

ALL THROUGH THE next day and the ones that followed, Derek waited tensely to be dragged into the courtyard and executed.

But as the week progressed and nothing happened, he began to realize that Allison, for whatever reason, had decided not to tell about his attempt to take the emerald.

At the end of the week, swinging his sword at the pel, he felt an odd combination of relief, frustration, and anger. He was relieved that his head was still on his shoulders. He was frustrated that Allison hadn't given him the emerald. And he was angry at himself for threatening her.

God, how had he sunk so low?

He had been like a man possessed. He remembered the scorn in her eyes—and he knew he deserved it.

This last week he'd seen her only from a distance, talking to various people, never so much as glancing his way. But every time he saw her, he wished he could see into her brain, see what she was thinking. Why hadn't she told her father what had happened? He had broken into her room and threatened her. God, that had been a stupid thing to do. And then, to add insult to injury, he had kissed her.

She must despise him now, and he couldn't really blame her. But maybe it was just as well. Everything had gotten out of hand. He'd only wanted a brief affair before he took the emerald and went home, nothing else. But sometimes when he was with her, he almost wanted to stay. . . .

A sudden heavy clout on his head made his ears ring.

"Pay attention, Sinclair! What if I were your enemy? You would surely be dead!"

Derek rubbed his aching head and glared after Sir Drogo. Almost. But not quite.

From the corner of his eye, Derek saw Cuthbert frowning at him disapprovingly. Ignoring him, Derek made a half-hearted thrust. The boy had barely spoken to him since the incident in the yard, but Derek didn't care. The opinion of the idealistic little fool meant nothing to him.

Thank God he wouldn't have to do this much longer. Tomorrow was Saint Swithin's Day, the day Lady Anne had promised to give him the emerald.

Tomorrow he would go back home.

By the next morning Derek had himself firmly under control. He rose early and went searching for Anne. He found her in the kitchen, the smell of baking gingerbread redolent in the air.

"Lady Anne, I've come for the emerald." He spoke in a whisper so the kitchen maids, tearfully chopping onions on the wooden table in the middle of the room, wouldn't hear.

Pushing a floury strand of hair back from her forehead with her forearm, Lady Anne frowned. "I don't have it."

Derek froze. "You promised," he said through gritted teeth, following her as she walked to another table and stirred a bowl of brown-speckled batter.

"I promised to help you get it. And I have."

"Oh? How is that?"

"Lady Allison will be wearing it at the feast today. You need only get it from her." She stuck her finger in the batter and tasted it.

"Oh, is that all?" he muttered. He liked Anne, but there were times he'd like to strangle the woman.

She grinned, then abruptly set down the bowl, sniffing the air. "Is the gingerbread burning, Clarice? If it is, you careless girl, you shall be whipped. . . ."

Derek left the kitchen, frowning.

How the hell was he supposed to get the emerald from Allison?

The question revolved in his brain as he sat in the hall a few hours later, watching Allison and waiting for the feast to begin.

She wore an elaborate green gown, embroidered with gold and silver thread. Covering her hair was a close-fitting jeweled caul and on her fingers priceless rings. And nestled between her breasts was the Pelsworth emerald.

What did Anne expect him to do? Run up to the head table, shove the king aside, and grab it? He eyed the guards standing at attention behind Henry. He might have tried it if he wasn't certain one or another of the king's guards would strike him down before he got anywhere close.

Trumpets blew, announcing the beginning of the feast. Sir Percival approached the table and presented an elaborate silver saltshaker to the king. Henry inclined his head.

Derek watched the ceremony thoughtfully. He hadn't been too impressed by Henry VII at first—the king was rather pale and grim-looking with straggly graying hair hanging around his face. But upon closer inspection, Derek had noticed the shrewd eyes, with a cold, rather calculating gleam to them. Earlier, Lady Humfrey had told him that the king often made notes about people in a notebook. "His friends, his enemies, his ideas, and his thoughts—all are listed in his little black book," she'd warned him.

The original blacklist, Derek thought wryly as the pantler approached the table. Henry VII of England was not a man he'd care to cross.

The pantler cut the upper crust from the top of a round loaf of blue-tinted bread and offered it to the king. More servants carried trenchers to the other diners. Derek eyed the pink-hued bread placed before him for a moment before turning his gaze to Allison.

She looked pale and nervous. And no wonder. Her whole life would be determined by what the king said.

So far, however, Henry had said nothing about Allison's betrothal. At the moment the king was talking to Lord Pelsworth about someone named Perkin Warbeck.

"Warbeck's attempted escape was ill-advised," Henry said as a servant placed a basin on the table and poured water over the king's hands. "He was captured within a week and returned to the Tower. But I like not these traitors and impostors who claim to be king. And I like those who support them even less. I demand loyalty from my subjects."

"Our family has always been loyal to you since you were crowned king," Lord Pelsworth said, washing his hands and drying them on a towel.

"Oh?" Henry nodded to the butler, who had approached with a bottle of wine. "Why then do you seek to break the betrothal of your daughter to Sir Wilfred, one of my most loyal and trusted men?"

The butler poured the wine into a golden goblet carried on a tray by another servant.

"Unfortunately, 'tis necessary," Lord Pelsworth replied. "My daughter's True Love has appeared."

"Her True Love?" Henry's expression was cold and disapproving as he watched the cupbearer taste the wine. "What madness is this?"

Allison, nodding at the butler to serve the rest of the guests, grew even paler. But her voice was steady as she said, "Sire, you have heard of the Pelsworth Legend?"

The king frowned. "No, I have not."

"It says that if the Pelsworths marry their True Loves, good fortune will follow," Allison explained.

"Sounds like a passel of superstitious nonsense."

Allison looked like she wanted to agree with him, but all she said was, "Nonetheless, 'tis true that the Pelsworths have always enjoyed great good fortune—at least until my father's time." She glanced at her father, who sighed loudly.

"In my foolishness," Lord Pelsworth said, "I ignored the Legend and did not marry my True Love. Since then, disaster after disaster has befallen my family. I vowed on my sacred honor that Allison would marry none other than her True Love."

Henry's frown deepened. "Then why did you betroth her to Sir Wilfred?"

"My daughter assured me she had tender feelings for Wilfred. But then another man arrived here claiming that he was Allison's *true* True Love."

"A man with no money or connections," Wilfred growled.

"Sir Wilfred makes an important point," Henry said. "No matter what the Legend says, Lord Pelsworth, Lady Allison cannot be permitted to marry a nobody. She can find True Love with Wilfred as well as any other man."

"Sir Derek is not precisely a nobody," Lord Pelsworth said. "He comes from California, an island off of Italy. 'Tis an incredibly wealthy land. And think how it might benefit England, sire, if we could form an alliance with this kingdom."

Henry stroked his chin. "Incredibly wealthy, you say?"

"Majesty!" Wilfred burst out. "Sinclair's claims are highly doubtful. No one else has visited or even heard of this land he talks of. As for Sinclair himself—'tis clear that he barely knows one end of a sword from the other."

Henry looked at Pelsworth. "Is this true?"

Pelsworth shrugged. "Sir Derek says the island is a peaceful one and the men do not learn fighting skills."

Henry frowned. "That would never do. Whoever marries Allison must be able to protect Pelsworth Castle and defend me against traitors."

"Sir Derek could be trained to be an English knight," Pelsworth argued.

Wilfred snorted. "The man is more suited to be a jester than a knight. 'Twould take years."

"Hmm," Henry said. "Where is this man?"

Derek rose to his feet and bowed. "Here I am, sire."

"Come forth, Sir Derek."

Derek did so, and Henry looked him over, his gaze lingering on the fading bruises on his face. "Tell me about this land of yours," he commanded.

"It's a very rich land, sire," Derek said. "Full of gold and rich farmland. The people are well-educated—they are scientists, engineers, and businessmen."

"Your speech is very strange. What language do they speak in this land of yours?"

"Er, American. It's a fairly new language, similar to English."

"I see. And what is the position of you and your family there?"

"We have trade agreements with China, Hong Kong, and Japan. What you would call the Indies, I believe."

"You know of a sea passage?"

"No, not personally. But there are ships that go from our harbors to there."

Henry's eyes lit up. "Now that I think on it, I would not go against the Pelsworth Legend—I believe we must give this Sir Derek a chance—"

"Sire, you cannot believe this varlet's preposterous tale!"

Henry frowned at Wilfred's protest. "Naturally, I will send an envoy to California to verify Sir Derek's claims—and to negotiate a trade agreement. If all goes well, then I will grant an estate to Sir Derek, and I will approve his marriage to Lady Allison."

"But, sire!" Wilfred's face was almost purple with rage. "What about Lady Allison's betrothal to me?"

Henry waved him to silence as Father Gregory gave the blessing for the feast. As soon as the priest was finished, however, he said, "You have served me well, Sir Wilfred. I cannot discount your claim. Therefore, 'tis my command that we have a tournament to settle the matter—but not until after the trade agreement is signed. We would not want California to refuse to sign just because one of her knights was killed by one of ours. The tournament shall be next year at Saint Swithin's Day."

Lord Pelsworth frowned. "But that gives Sir Derek only a year—he has had virtually no training in weapons. 'Twould take at least five years for him to attain anywhere near the skill of Sir Wilfred."

"If Sir Derek is what he claims, True Love will find a

way." Henry glanced at Wilfred. "In the meantime, Sir Wilfred, you will return to London with me. With so many conspiracies afoot, I need all my guards about me."

Wilfred didn't look too happy at this pronouncement, but even he did not dare to protest again.

Henry, on the other hand, looked more cheerful than Derek had yet seen. He watched as the king rose to his feet.

"I propose a toast!" he said, holding up his golden goblet and directing an almost jovial smile around the hall.

"To California!"

Chapter 17

ALLISON WAS THANKFUL when the parade of subtleties was over and the last of the pastry sculptures eaten. The musicians began playing for the dancing, and she went out on the floor. At the first opportunity, however, she edged to the back of the hall until she could slip behind the screens at the far end.

She took a deep breath. She needed just a few moments alone, a few moments to regain her composure.

The day had gone better than she possibly could have hoped. Although the issue of her marriage still had not been settled, at least nothing terrible had happened—yet.

A heavy footstep sounded behind her. Turning, she saw Wilfred approaching.

She straightened and forced herself to smile. "Sir Wilfred! Did you come to ask me to dance? I found it a trifle close in the hall, but I am much recovered now." She took a step toward the screens.

Wilfred blocked her. His breath heavy on her face, he asked, "Why did you not tell the king that you preferred me?"

"I could not make my father look like a fool," she said.

"He *is* a fool—an interfering old man."

Allison stiffened. "Please don't speak about my father in that manner."

"I will speak of him in any manner I choose. I grow weary of these games, Lady Allison. You will marry me, or else. . . ."

"There is no need for threats, Sir Wilfred," she said with all the dignity she could muster. "I have already agreed to marry you."

He watched her with a narrowed gaze. "Make certain you do not forget it." Abruptly he turned and walked back into the hall.

Allison—scared, angry, and in despair—did not follow.

Derek looked around the crowded floor in frustration. He had seen Allison just a few minutes ago, but the procession of dancers had blocked his view and now he'd lost her. He did, however, spy Anne and Rafael over by the screens at the end of the hall. They appeared to be arguing.

They both grew quiet as Derek approached, however.

"Good morrow, Sir Derek," Rafael said, before Derek said anything.

Wondering how the blind minstrel always knew who was nearby, Derek said, "Good evening, Rafael, Lady Anne. Have either of you seen Lady Allison?"

"Er, no," Lady Anne said, averting her eyes.

"You haven't forgotten our agreement, have you, Lady Anne?" Derek asked, a touch of steel in his voice. "You agreed to help me obtain a certain item."

"Yes, yes. And I will. But are you *certain* you still want it?"

"Of course I still want it."

"Oh. Well, I think she's dancing. Let me see if I can find her—"

"I believe I heard her voice behind the screens just a few moments ago," Rafael interrupted. "And then I heard her footsteps running up the tower stairs."

"How could you possibly know they were Allison's footsteps?" Anne said, glaring daggers at Rafael.

"She has a very light footstep, almost soundless," he said. "Sir Derek's have a slight unevenness, as if his shoes are too tight. And you, my dear Anne, your footsteps are as sweet as . . . a lumbering elephant's."

"They most certainly are not!" she cried indignantly.

Rafael laughed.

Derek murmured his thanks—which he didn't think either of the two heard since they had started arguing again—and took off up the stairs.

At the top he slowed down, moving as quietly as possible to Allison's room. He eased the door open silently and saw her sitting by the window, staring out.

He stood in the doorway for a moment, watching her, an odd longing whispering through his blood.

His fingers tightened on the door. He wasn't staying here any longer. He was going to take the emerald and leave. Nothing—*nothing*—could make him stay in this place.

His mind firmly made up, he stepped forward.

"Good morrow, my lady."

She turned, looking startled. The emerald rested between her breasts, winking and gleaming in the luminous light of the long summer's eve. For a moment its fiery green brilliance held him mesmerized. He walked toward her, stopping only a few feet away.

He held out his hand. "Give me the emerald."

Without a word she slipped it over her head and handed it to him.

He closed his fist around it, but he looked at her, not the jewel.

She looked so proud, standing there, with her shoulders held back, no sign of fear in her face or stance. Her eyes stared back at him, flashing with a brilliance to rival the emerald, full of scorn.

He glanced down at the emerald. He had it. He was going *home*. Home to pizza, beer, and cigarettes. Home to hot sun and smoggy skies and football. Home to his '65 Ford Mustang, his Jacuzzi, and his nice, easy job. Never again would he have to march around the castle in full armor. Never again would he have to play the harp or write poetry. Never again would he see Allison. Haughty, obstinate, aggravating, contradictory, challenging, beautiful, sexy Allison . . .

He turned the emerald in his fingers. Strangely, for all the emerald's inner fire, it felt amazingly cold in his hand.

He looked back at Allison. "Before I leave," he said, "you owe me one final kiss."

"I most certainly do not, you cowardly thief."

Her blatant contempt angered him. "You're right. You don't." He shoved the emerald in the purse on his belt and grabbed her around the waist, pulling her up against him. "For everything you've made me suffer, you owe me a helluva lot more than that."

Her eyes blazed, but before she could respond, his mouth covered hers.

She resisted at first. She was stiff and unresponsive in his arms. But slowly, gradually, she relaxed, and soon she was responding with a passion that made his own flame even higher, the fire threatening to consume them both.

He tore the jeweled caul from her head and buried his fingers in her loosened hair. "Allie, Allie," he murmured in her ear, his fingers pulling impatiently at the strings of her bodice. He wanted to undress her, to see all of her. He wanted to touch her breasts and belly and thighs. He wanted to make love to her, just this once, to remember her by, and so that she would remember him, always and forever.

He picked her up and laid her on the soft mattress. Moving over her, he kissed her deeply, still pulling at the strings of her dress. The laces at the back were tight, making it impossible for him to do more than loosen the bodice.

By this time, however, he was beyond caring. His entire body was aflame. He pushed the heavy brocade of her dress up her legs. If he didn't have her now, he wouldn't be able to bear it, he would go insane, he would die—

A shout sounded from the tapestry room.

Derek grew still, listening. He could hear the clank of armored footsteps coming straight toward the door of Allison's room.

Shit.

He yanked her bodice up over her breasts just as several knights burst through the door. Two of them stopped, but the third, Sir Drogo, strode forward.

"On your feet, varlet!"

Derek glanced at him, then back at Allison. The corner of his mouth lifted. "You're saved again."

She blinked up at him, her eyes dazed and as black as midnight. Her hair was tousled and her dress awry. There was a small red mark on her neck where he had kissed her.

His gaze grew intent. "Allison . . . come with me."

The dazed look vanished, replaced by horror. She lashed out angrily, "Go with you where? To the gibbet? Because I assure you, you villainous lout, that's the only place you're going! Let me up!"

The mad impulse to take her with him faded. Hell, what was he thinking? Charles would kill him if he brought home a medieval lady. He smiled ruefully. He couldn't take her with him—but damn if he wouldn't miss her. "Ah, well. Goodbye then." He released her and took the emerald out of his purse. "I won't forget you."

She scrambled to her feet. "No, you won't forget me, I'll make certain of that. Guards, seize this man!"

Sir Drogo waved the two knights forward. They approached.

Still smiling, Derek shrugged and stood up, holding the emerald.

Now that he had the jewel in his grasp, now that it all was almost over, he could look back at the last few months with something approaching fondness. What an amazing time he'd had. He'd experienced the Middle Ages first-hand— he'd eaten medieval, slept medieval, nearly been killed medieval. He'd even almost made love medieval.

He looked at Allison. God, he wished . . . but no, it was impossible. He tightened his fingers around the emerald. "Take me home."

Nothing happened.

The guards were closing in.

Derek's smile faded. "I wish to be back in Los Angeles in my own time," he said.

Still nothing happened.

He looked at Allison. She stood by the bed, watching him

with a scornful smile. "You didn't *believe* those stories about the emerald being magic, did you?"

For several long, shocked seconds he could only stare at her. Then, as the meaning of her words sank in, a shimmering red haze rose before his eyes, growing brighter and brighter until it almost blinded him. He took a step toward her, but the knights grabbed his arms.

With a hoarse shout he attacked them, twisting and kicking like a wild man.

Until one of them clouted him on the head and for the second time that week he sank into merciful oblivion.

Chapter 18

DEREK WOKE UP to find himself once again in the dungeon, lying on the straw pallet. There was a dull ache in his head, but it was nothing compared to the despair in his heart.

He was never going home. He would never drive his red '65 Ford Mustang down Pacific Coast Highway with the hot Santa Ana winds in his hair. He would never watch another sunset over the Pacific. He would never sit in a Jacuzzi, he would never watch another football game. He would never see Fourth of July fireworks or have another Thanksgiving dinner. He'd never hear Nan snore or see his brother again.

God, he wished Charles were here. Charles had always saved him from awkward situations in the past. Derek had never appreciated that until now. Now there was no one to save him.

What would he do? Where would he go? He couldn't stay here. Wilfred would kill him if he did. If Lord Pelsworth didn't hang him first for taking the emerald. Allison was probably urging her father right now to execute him.

Allison. He still couldn't quite believe she'd lied to him about the emerald. How could she have been so cold, so calculating as to lure him back here with no way to return? He'd actually thought she cared for him. What a fool he was. He could still see her scornful smile. He'd been furious, but now his anger was gone and the reality of his situation was staring him in the face.

He was stuck in the Middle Ages for the rest of his life. Forever.

God, he couldn't bear it. There was nothing for him here. Nothing. Thank God they would be hanging him soon. He would rather be dead than stay here. After everything that had happened, death would be a relief.

Closing his eyes, he allowed the darkness to take him.

Over the next several days Derek drifted in and out of consciousness. He wasn't sure how much time had passed when he was awakened by an insistent voice.

"Sir Derek? Sir Derek!"

Derek raised his eyelids a crack to see Lady Anne standing on the other side of the grate. He closed his eyelids again.

"Forgive me for not rising, Lady Anne," he mumbled. "I'm not feeling too well."

"Sir Derek, listen to me! Lady Allison told me what happened, and I have to tell you . . . the emerald *is* magic. But it works only for the Pelsworth family." She paused. "All you need do is marry Allison and you will be able to use its magic."

Derek laughed weakly, then coughed. "Is *that* all I need do? Why should I believe you?"

"I am very familiar with the powers of the stone. Even Lady Allison doesn't realize what it can do. But I swear to you, it *can* take you home."

Derek wished she would go away. He was tired, more tired than he'd ever been in his life, and listening to her made his head ache. "Even if what you say is true, it makes no difference. In order to marry Allison, I would have to beat Wilfred in a tournament."

"I am certain you could do so, Sir Derek, if you trained for the next year—"

"You must be joking. I could never be a knight." Didn't she *know* that? Wasn't it obvious?

"You might if you tried. You have improved much since your arrival—"

"All I've done since my arrival is to perfect the art of getting by doing as little as possible. Even Cuthbert can beat me in any match of skills. Besides, I don't want to be a knight. Knights are full of honor and chivalry and all that crap."

"But—"

"No *buts*. I can't do it. It's impossible. Now, I hate to be rude, but I am very tired, Lady Anne. I hope you will excuse me." He turned his back to her and let blessed sleep encroach upon his consciousness.

Soon the pain would be gone, he thought sleepily. Soon it would all be over.

Allison sat in her room, spinning on the old wheel that had once belonged to her mother. She liked to come in here and spin, sometimes, away from the constant demands of the castle. It soothed her somehow. And after this last terrible week, she needed soothing.

The king had finally left, but in a way, his departure had not made her life any easier. On the contrary, without the constant demands his presence created, she had more time to think and more time to remember what had occurred right here in this very room.

She still could barely believe what had happened. How could she have been so lost to all common sense? How could she have let him kiss her like that, touch her like that? Dear heaven, if a servant hadn't seen him going into her room and mentioned it to one of the knights, Allison actually might have let Derek Sinclair make love to her.

Oh, she could not bear to think about it. She wished she could forget it. But how could she when every night she dreamed of him kissing her in exactly the same way?

She wished the dream would go away. It had been plaguing her ever since his arrival, but this last week it had been more vivid, more intense than before. Now, she could see the room they were in—the strange furniture and objects scattered about. She could see him lying on a strange narrow bed. And she could see herself bending down to kiss him. . . .

It seemed so real. Sometimes she found herself thinking that perhaps it was real. That perhaps his story was true after all. That he really was from the future.

She gave the wheel a hard spin. Oh, what utter nonsense. He was nothing but a liar and a thief. He'd heard the stories of the magic emerald and thought to steal it. She hoped he stayed in the dungeon forever—

"Allison? Oh, Allison, there you are! I'm so glad I found you—you must do something about Sir Derek!"

With a sigh Allison looked up to see Anne in the doorway.

Allison returned her gaze to her spinning. "There is nothing I can do—and nothing I *want* to do, either."

"Allison, how can you say that?"

"Because 'tis true. He has caused me no end of trouble. He has nearly broken my betrothal to Wilfred, caused dissension and dissatisfaction among the squires, and jeopardized my father's position with the king. And for what? All so he could steal the Pelsworth emerald."

"Allison, I think you judge him too harshly—"

"Too harshly! Anne, you know how precarious our situation is. Do you have any idea how difficult it was to explain to Henry why my 'True Love' was inhabiting the dungeon?"

"Bah! You had a ready explanation."

"That the order of knighthood Derek belongs to in California requires that he spend this week of the year in a dungeon as penance for his sins? You call that a ready explanation? 'Tis a wonder the king didn't have us all dragged into the courtyard and hanged for our lies." Allison spun the wheel faster. "I have not the least bit of sympathy for Derek Sinclair."

Anne put her hands on her hips. "Allison, don't be a fool. You love him. Why won't you admit it?"

"Because 'tis not true."

"Oh? Then why did you not tell your father about Derek trying to steal the emerald? And why didn't you remind him of his order that Derek be executed if he was found in your room?"

"I doubt it would have done any good," Allison said. "My father is as blind as Rafael as far as Derek Sinclair is concerned. He would have found some excuse not to carry out his threat."

"But, Allison—"

"Anne, what is it you want me to do? Order his release?"

"No. Lord Pelsworth already did that before he left. But Derek refused to leave the dungeon."

Allison frowned. "He did? But why?"

"I believe he has lost his will to live. Go to him, Allison, and tell him you love him."

Allison stared down at the twisting, turning thread between her fingers. A tightness squeezed at her chest. "I can't," she said quietly. "Don't you understand? How could I love a man who is so irresponsible? How could I take a husband like that? I need someone who is strong—not someone who will be a burden to me. Oh, Anne, don't you think I would like to seize this chance for passion and happiness? I would. Sometimes I lay awake at night hurting with how much I want it. But how could I abandon Pelsworth Castle and the people here? How could I be happy knowing I'd hurt so many others? I can't love him. I *can't*."

Anne was silent for a long moment. "He will change," she finally said. For once, her dark eyes did not sparkle.

Allison laughed humorlessly. "How can you know that? How could *I* take such a risk when so much is at stake?"

"But, Allison, he has refused food. He grows weak. If you don't do something, he will die."

"He looked perfectly healthy when he came out the last time. I am sure you must be exaggerating, Anne."

"I swear I am not."

Allison hesitated. She didn't want to see Derek. She didn't want to hear taunts about her last visit to the dungeon. She didn't want his mocking eyes reminding her of her weakness every time he kissed her. She didn't want to be tempted to forget about everything and everyone else but him. . . .

But as lady of the castle, 'twas her responsibility to see to the well being of everyone in the castle.

"Very well," she said unwillingly. "I will speak to him tomorrow. But if you're lying to me, Anne, you're going to spend a week in the dungeon yourself."

Chapter 19

Reluctantly Allison descended the northwest tower stairs. She suspected that Anne had exaggerated Derek's condition to make her visit him, and she was not looking forward to making a fool of herself—again.

In the cellar she was surprised to see no guard—only Rafael, seated on a stool that was tilted on two legs so he could lean against the wall.

He stopped playing the lute and straightened on the stool when she stepped forward. "Lady Allison? Is that you?" he asked.

"Yes, 'tis I," she replied. "I was just going to visit Sir Derek. Lady Anne thinks my visit will help him recover from his ill humors."

"Ah, does she?"

Allison smiled a little. "You sound skeptical. I confess, I agree with you. But Anne insists that Sir Derek is in love with me. She thinks that the mere sight of me will miraculously make him recover."

Rafael stroked his chin thoughtfully, a slight crease between his brows. "She may be right."

"That the sight of me will make him recover? I doubt it."

"No, that's not what I meant," he murmured.

"I beg your pardon?"

"Never mind." He turned his sightless eyes toward her and smiled. "May I accompany you? A dungeon is an unpleasant place for a lady to venture alone."

She stared at him a little uncertainly. For all his blindness, he seemed extraordinarily perceptive. She did not really understand him—or the relationship between him and Anne. At times she was certain they were in love. But at the same time it seemed as if they were engaged in some mysterious battle of wills that only the two of them understood.

Whatever was going on between them, Allison didn't quite trust the minstrel. But all the same, she saw no reason to refuse his offer. She lit a candle and took his arm.

They descended the steep stairs without speaking. At the bottom, Allison approached the cell, but Rafael hung back a little, keeping to the shadows.

At the cell grate Allison took a deep breath and peered in, bracing herself for some remark.

None was forthcoming.

She held her candle higher, tilting it so that its light fell directly on Derek.

She gasped.

He lay on his back, his mouth half open, his breathing shallow. Under layers of dirt, his skin was pale and his face thin. He looked barely alive.

"Derek!" Her heart began to pound with a slow thumping dread. Was he already dead? "Derek!"

His eye opened a crack.

She almost sagged in relief. "Sir Derek, I wish to speak to you."

"I don' wanna speak to you," he mumbled and turned over so that she could only see his back.

His action shocked and frightened her. "Derek! Please! I . . . I'm sorry about this. I didn't realize you were ill. Come with me, and I'll have Anne tend to you."

He didn't respond.

Sharp fear pierced her. What had happened to him? What had happened to his impudence, his brashness?

A sob caught in her throat. He meant nothing to her. He was irresponsible, a troublemaker. He had done nothing but infuriate her ever since he arrived. But that didn't mean she wanted him dead.

"Derek! Can you hear me? Answer me!"

Still no response.

She bit back a sob. Dear God, what could she do?

"Make him angry," Rafael whispered from behind her.

Allison had forgotten his presence. "What?" she asked distractedly, trying to see if Derek's rib cage was moving. He seemed so still—

"Make him angry," Rafael said again. "It is your only hope of reaching him."

"No. I can't."

"You must. You *must,* Lady Allison. Or he will die."

Or he will die.

The words rang in her ears. She gripped the slats of the grille and pressed her forehead against the smooth, cool wood. She inhaled deeply and forced herself to speak.

"Perhaps it would be better if you did die."

She hardly could believe that it was her own voice speaking, she sounded so cool and mocking.

"How much simpler things would have been if my father had just hanged you that first day you arrived."

She saw him stiffen and turn slightly toward her.

"But I suppose hanging is too good for the likes of you. Starving to death is much more suitable for a knave like you. A knave with no honor—"

With a snarl he leaped toward the door, his hands reaching through the grate. She jumped back, frightened, barely evading his grasp. His fingers curled around the slats instead. "Don't speak to me of honor, *Lady* Allison," he snarled.

Trembling, she stuck her nose in the air. "Why not? You are no knight. You are not even a man."

He looked at her with burning eyes. "I was man enough to make you respond to me."

Color burned high in her cheeks. "A moment's folly. I was curious, nothing more. I never cared about you."

He stared at her. "You bitch. You selfish, lying bitch. You never cared, did you? I had a life—a damn good life, and you stole it from me. You were willing to do whatever it took, weren't you? You were willing to use your body to entice me, to drive me half insane with passion, just so you could get what you wanted. All you cared about was saving your own ass. All along you've been trying to get rid of me—because I'm of no use to you now, am I? You got what you wanted. What do you care that it has nearly destroyed me? I've worked like a dog, had the shit beaten out of me, and nearly been killed by your precious Wilfred, but so what? What do you care, *Lady* Allison?"

Her hand crept to her throat at his wild, incomprehensible words. "I don't know what you're talking about—"

"Oh, I know you don't. Because you've always tried to hide from the truth, haven't you? You've never wanted to show any weakness, any vulnerability, because you are afraid to feel anything. You've been satisfied to live your life in an ivory tower, pretending that you're above it all, while the rest of us mere mortals struggle to please you. You're a cold, selfish bitch and you care for no one except yourself."

She stood very, very still for a long moment. Then, without a word, she turned and walked away.

She rounded the bend in the stairs, stopping when Rafael stepped out of the shadows.

"Excellent, Lady Allison," he whispered. His sightless light blue eyes glowed in the candlelight. "I believe you have worked a miracle."

"Have I?" Allison asked, her voice sounding strange even to her own ears. "Please excuse me." She hurried past the minstrel. Once out of the dungeon, she ran across the courtyard and up the stairs to her room. She slammed the door behind herself and leaned against it, closing her eyes.

She stood there for several long moments. Then, like a sleepwalker, she slowly crossed the floor to the chest at the foot of her bed. She opened it and took out the flax her mother had given her. She had combed the flax recently, making it as soft and fine as silk, then tied the fibers into neat bundles.

The door opened and Anne rushed in. "Sir Derek has asked for food!" she cried excitedly. "You did it, Allison, you did it!" She rushed out again.

Allison stared down at the flax.

She'd done it. She'd saved Derek. But at what price? He hated her now. Her dream of finding love with him was now really and truly dead.

Stiffly she carried several of the bundles over to the wheel in the corner and sat down. She wrapped the fibers around the distaff and drew a thread around the wheel and onto the bobbin. Twisting the fibers, she began to spin.

And as she spun, tears poured down her cheeks.

Derek bit into the bread and chewed, even though the taste of the food made him gag after his long fast. But he didn't care. He was determined to eat. He was determined that he wasn't going to die.

He wouldn't give her the satisfaction.

He still couldn't believe what a fool he'd been. How could he have been so stupid to think there was something special about her? How had she managed to worm her way under his skin to the point that he'd even asked her to go back with him? She was nothing but a lying, deceitful little bitch, and he wished to God he'd never fallen for her wiles.

But he had.

Now, whatever it took, whatever he must do, he would win that tournament and he would marry her. And once they were wed, he would leave this accursed place and return home.

But before he left, he would make her pay for what she had done. She would pay.

She would pay very dearly indeed.

Chapter 20

THE TWO MEN circled each other, their faces hidden by their helmets. The massive knight in black silver-edged armor stumbled a little, his clumsy movements bespeaking his exhaustion as he lumbered around his light-footed opponent.

The other man, although an inch or two shorter and more slender, appeared more than a match for the Black Knight. This man's armor was plain and had obviously been made up from several suits of armor, but he moved with a grace and precision that was rare. The swift thrusts of his sword battered the Black Knight, denting the expensive armor and causing the huge man to sway at times from the force of the blows.

The Black Knight retreated farther and farther across the field until he bumped into the quintain. With a last burst of energy, the Black Knight swung.

The other man darted out of reach, and the massive knight's blow struck the quintain instead of its intended target. The quintain, adorned with a ragged yellow doublet and matching cap, spun around and glanced off the Black Knight's helmet.

The watching crowd laughed uproariously.

"I beg your pardon," the smaller knight said, his voice deep and clear in spite of the helmet. "Two against one is a most unfair fight. Allow me to reprimand this base Yellow Knight."

He hit the quintain, then quickly ducked as it swung around. The Black Knight, however, was not so nimble. The quintain caught him squarely on the front of his helmet.

He teetered a moment, then toppled to the ground with a crash.

A mixture of groans and cheers rose from the watching crowd. Simon turned to the freckle-faced squire standing at his side. "Pay up, Oswald. I told you our man would win. He hasn't lost a match for this last two months and more."

"Neither had Sir Rufus," Oswald said gloomily, handing over a silver coin. He glanced over at the winner of the contest. "'Tis incredible that a man could improve so much. Why, a mere ten months ago he could barely hit the quintain."

"Ten months ago he was a different man," Simon informed him loftily.

The two squires strolled off to where a crowd of men, including Lord Pelsworth, surrounded the victorious knight.

"Well done!" Lord Pelsworth cried. "Well done, indeed, Sir Derek!"

Derek pulled off his helmet and shook back his wet hair. Looking at Lord Pelsworth and the others crowding around him, he laughed, full of triumph and exhilaration.

He had never known how good it felt to be respected and admired by other men. To know that he had the power to fight against any one of them. That he had the strength, no matter what, to survive.

The last ten months had been an agony of hard work such as he'd never known. He'd learned to wield the ax, mace, sword, and lance. He'd trained from dawn till dusk—and even into the night—in furnacelike heat and freezing cold.

He'd trained when it rained, when it sleeted, when it snowed.

There were times when he'd thought he couldn't take any more, that he would break. But every time, he'd only had to think of Allison and the way she had stolen his life, of her mocking voice telling him that he was better off dead, to give himself the will to go on. He had sworn she would pay, and nothing, *nothing,* would prevent him from keeping his vow. Not exhaustion, not pain, and certainly not her feeble attempts to apologize. Did she really think she could get off so lightly for everything she had done by a simple apology?

He had soon disabused her of that notion.

He had avoided her at first, after he'd left the dungeon nearly a year ago. He had just walked away whenever he saw her approaching, ignoring the way she would bite her lip and the way her eyes would grow dark with hurt.

This had worked for nearly a month, until one day she stopped him as he was about to enter the chapel.

"Sir Derek," she said, her hand on his arm. "I want to apologize. I never meant—"

"Lady Allison," he interrupted, his voice as hard and cold as the knot inside his gut. "Take your hand off my arm."

Obeying instantly, she drew back, her face growing pale. She had not approached him again.

Every once in a while, however, he would see her looking at him. Her sad dark eyes only made him more furious. How did she dare to look at him like that? As if he was the one who had wronged her?

But he had ignored her sad looks and carried on with his daily routine. He attended mass every morning, and for the first time in his life he prayed—he prayed for God to give him the strength to carry out his revenge.

The desire for revenge was like a fire in his belly. The initial flames had died out, but the embers were still there, banked, hot, and smoldering. Hatred had etched into his brain like acid—and it burned deeper and deeper every time he saw her.

As if drawn, his gaze turned to where she stood at the edge of the field, near the walled gardens. Dressed in a simple blue gown and a bibless white apron, she carried a bowl as if she'd been involved in some task and stopped to watch. Although he could not see her face from this distance, he could picture it clearly—as beautiful as always, perhaps even more so. She looked more like she had as a ghost— paler, her face a little thinner. But he was no longer enticed by her beauty. Now her beauty was only a reminder of what a fool he'd been.

Without any sign that he had seen her, he turned his back, and focused his attention once more on the admiration of the crowd around him.

Allison fought to keep her face impassive as he turned away from her. She would not let anyone know that his cold-ness bothered her; she would *not*.

"Ahhh." At Allison's side Anne sighed. "What a fine fig-ure of a man. His hard work has certainly paid off. I think such constant exercise as he has subjected himself to these last months would have killed another. One must admire his dedication."

"One must do nothing of the sort," Allison said coldly. "Come, Anne, we must gather the herbs. I have no interest at all in Sir Derek."

"Oh?" Anne's voice was skeptical as she followed Allison into the walled herb garden. "Then why do your eyes follow him whenever he is about? Why do you rise so early in the morning and go up on the battlements to watch him at his practice? And why did you tell Sir Drogo that you were wor-ried that Derek might become ill with so much exercise and ask for the training to be cut back?"

Allison knelt and picked a sprig of valerian. "I look at Sir Derek no more than anyone else. I go up on the battlements to be alone for a while. And as for expressing my concern about his health to Sir Drogo—I would have done the same for any of the men. The welfare of the people here is my re-sponsibility."

"Is that the only reason?" Anne looked at her searchingly. "What happened between the two of you?"

"How many times must I tell you? Nothing happened."

"I do not believe you. Everything had been going so well—"

"You were imagining things. I have disliked him since the day he arrived, and nothing has changed since then—except that he is even uglier now."

"Ugly? You think he is ugly?"

"Certainly. That bump on his nose does nothing for him. And that hideous scar on his chin is repulsive."

Anne looked surprised. "What man-at-arms doesn't have a few scars? Actually, he's lucky not to have lost an eye or an ear. The nose and the chin are unfortunate—if only he had let me tend them immediately instead of insisting on finishing the fight . . . ah, well. At least you must admit some admiration for his new prowess with a sword."

"Bah. There is more to a man than his ability to handle a sword."

Anne rolled her eyes. "You are as stubborn as a mule, Allison. 'Tis no wonder the two of you are at odds."

Allison bit back the impulse to defend herself. What was the use? Over the last year she'd tried to apologize to him for her words, tried to tell him that she'd never done any of the horrible things he'd accused her of. But he'd rudely ignored her until her pride took over. Why was she trying to apologize? True, she had said some cruel words, but that was all. He, on the other hand, had caused no end of trouble. He had threatened her with a knife and tried to steal the Pelsworth emerald. If anyone should be apologizing, it was *him*.

She began to treat him as coldly as he treated her, with no outward sign that she cared one way or the other. But inside, in spite of her determination to think of him no more, her misery grew.

She missed his teasing, his laughter. She missed the daily anticipation of wondering what outrageous thing he would do next. For a very brief time he had made her laugh.

But now she never laughed. Nor did he—at least not when she was near. She felt tense whenever he was around, and as the day of the tournament approached, her tension grew. It was becoming more and more likely that he would beat Wilfred. And if he did . . .

She shuddered. She couldn't marry Derek. Not when he looked at her with the cold flame of hate in his eyes. His hatred was so strong, he now frightened her even more than Wilfred did. She doubted Derek would ever strike her as she suspected Wilfred might; but she sensed that Derek had the power to flay her spirit to shreds. She could not bear to be wed to someone who despised her so. Bruises to her body she could endure; the torment to her soul she could not.

Her soul was already in agony.

Every night she dreamed strange dreams. She no longer dreamt of his making love to her. No, she dreamed of an endless search, of begging strangers for help over and over again. The faces and clothes and houses changed, but always she was begging, for what she did not know. But with each refusal, her despair grew greater and greater—

"Do you not think that's enough of the valerian?" Anne asked a trifle dryly. "The flowers are not really very useful."

Allison looked down at her bowl, which was overflowing with the small white flowers. She forced herself to laugh. "Good heavens. My mind was wandering. Will you take this to the stillroom, Anne? There must be something we can do with it."

With a shake of her head Anne took the bowl and left. Allison stood and wiped her hands on her apron, then entered the castle through the postern gate.

Her father, returning from the training yard at the same time, fell into step beside her.

"Ah, daughter. I have not had a chance to speak to you since I arrived home. Have you had any messages from the king whilst I was away?"

Allison stopped at the cistern in the gatehouse and washed her hands. "Yes," she said, not looking at him. "He still has not heard from the messenger he sent to verify Sir Derek's claim, but he wishes to continue forward with the knighting ceremony and the tournament. I also received a letter from Sir Wilfred two months ago saying that the king has given him another estate for his 'loyal service.' "

Lord Pelsworth frowned. "Hmm. I hope Sir Wilfred does not gain too much favor in Henry's eyes—I believe he will make trouble for us when you marry Sir Derek."

Allison dried her hands on a towel. "What if I don't marry Sir Derek?"

"Why would you not? He has beaten Rufus most handily—'twill not be difficult for him to win the tournament." Lord Pelsworth's gaze sharpened as she stepped away from the cistern and walked out into the courtyard. "Daughter, why did you not give your favor to Sir Derek this morning when he fought Sir Rufus?"

"I did not think he would want it, Father."

Lord Pelsworth's frown deepened. "Have the two of you quarreled?"

She paused at the door to the southeast tower. "Yes," she said quietly.

"Then you must apologize at once!"

She bit back an angry retort at his assumption that the quarrel was her fault. "I have tried, but he will not listen. Perhaps he is not my True Love after all."

"Do not say that—of course he is your True Love. I will have a talk with him." Still frowning, he turned and headed across the courtyard toward the northwest tower.

Allison watched him go. What would Derek say to her father's questions? Would he finally tell the truth—that he had no wish to marry her? If he did, her father would most likely ask him to leave.

It was what she wanted.

Yet the thought made her feel strangely like crying.

"You were magnificent, Sir Derek! Rufus never knew what hit him."

"I've never seen such a subtle blow as the one you gave Rufus. Well done, Sir Derek!"

"May I polish your armor for you, Sir Derek, please?"

Simon, in the process of removing Derek's gauntlets, stopped to glare at Oswald. "Sir Derek promised to let *me* polish his armor! You will have to wait your turn."

Sullenly Oswald kicked his pallet.

"Perhaps tomorrow, Oswald," Derek said generously.

Oswald's face brightened immediately. "Thank you, Sir Derek!"

Derek smiled and gazed around the squires' quarters, drinking in the adulation. It was pleasant to be appreciated. A year ago he'd barely been tolerated by most of the knights and squires—now everyone in the castle looked up to him.

He caught sight of a quiet figure sweeping the hearth. Glancing over, he saw Cuthbert.

Derek's smile faded. Everyone except Cuthbert, that was. The boy had never forgiven him for repudiating chivalry. He was the only one in the castle that still cold-shouldered him—besides Allison, of course.

His lips tightening, Derek held out his arm so Simon could unbuckle the vambraces. The boy had no sense whatsoever. He still believed Allison was some kind of angelic saint. Well, Derek would not disillusion him. The boy would find out the truth soon enough. As he, himself, had done.

"Ho, Sir Derek!"

Derek glanced over his shoulder to see a young page approaching.

"Lord Pelsworth requests your presence in the library," the boy said.

Derek frowned, wondering why the older man wanted to see him. Lord Pelsworth had arrived just yesterday, and already Derek wished he would leave. Everyone in the castle seemed more unsettled when Lord Pelsworth was in residence—including Allison. Derek was familiar enough with the goings-on of the castle now to realize that Lord Pelsworth was frequently half-drunk, and that he often gave arbitrary and contradictory orders, confusing and upsetting everyone.

The real head of the castle, he'd discovered, was Allison. The responsibility for everything rested squarely on her shoulders. A year ago he might have felt some sympathy for her burden. Now he felt nothing at all.

Derek would have liked to refuse Lord Pelsworth's request. But he knew he couldn't really ignore an invitation from the man who was, to all intents and purposes, his host. "Tell him I'll be there as soon as I've washed and changed."

The page nodded and left.

Washing and changing took quite a while, so it was some time later when Derek entered the library.

After greeting him and offering him some wine, Lord Pelsworth said, "I am greatly pleased at your progress. I have no doubt you will be able to win the tournament easily."

Derek studied the older man. Pelsworth had aged in the last year. His hair was thinner, his beard grayer, his eyes a more faded blue. He also seemed more obsessed with Allison and Derek's marriage than ever. On his rare visits to the castle, he spoke of little else.

"Your success has helped me come to a decision," Pelsworth continued. "I have decided that after you marry my daughter, I will put you in charge of Pelsworth Castle."

"That is very generous of you, my lord."

Pelsworth frowned a little at this lackluster response, but not for long. "Excellent. 'Tis my wish that you begin taking your meals with Allison and me in the family apartments. We will start with supper tonight."

Pelsworth was watching him very closely, Derek saw. The old man must have noticed the strained relations between Allison and Derek.

Derek knew he must tread warily. He didn't want to give Pelsworth any reason at this late date to decide Derek wasn't Allison's True Love after all.

Cursing silently, he pasted a smile on his face.

"I would be honored, my lord."

The supper was not a success.

Derek made an effort for Lord Pelsworth's benefit, but Allison refused to cooperate. She declined to share his cup and shook her head when he offered her morsels from his trencher. When he spoke to her, she answered briefly, or not at all and turned back to Sir Jarvis who was seated on her right.

Her rudeness infuriated Derek. But aware of Pelsworth's gaze on him, he showed no sign. Calmly he ate his meal as though nothing were amiss.

From the corner his eye, however, he watched Allison broodingly. She had definitely lost weight, he noticed. Her dress hung on her and her cheekbones were more prominent. She laughed and talked to Sir Jarvis, but she barely ate anything. In spite of the proud tilt of her head, she looked frail. She worked long hours, also, he knew. Even longer than he did. It was no wonder she looked so pale. She should get more rest. . . .

Derek turned his attention back to his meal, angry at himself for the thought. He didn't care how thin and tired she looked. She meant nothing to him.

Determined to ignore her, Derek turned to Lady Mountford on his left.

Allison heard him laugh at something the beautiful widow said, but she did not look around. She knew she was being rude, but she couldn't seem to help herself. She couldn't make herself smile and converse with Derek as if everything was well between them. Not when he looked at her with such cold, hateful eyes.

She told herself she was glad he'd given up and turned his attention to Lady Mountford, but in truth, she was miserable. Especially when she saw the crease between her father's eyebrows growing deeper and deeper as he looked back and forth between Derek and her.

It was almost a relief when the steward came to the table and whispered in her ear.

"The pantler and the butler are at it again," Larkin said.

Allison started to stand, glad for an excuse to leave the table.

A hand on her arm prevented her from rising.

She stared at it in astonishment, then up at the face above.

"You cannot leave," Derek said coldly. She continued to gape at him as he turned to the steward. "Tell the pantler and the butler that they may fight as much as they like—kill each other if necessary—when their work is done, but in the future they are not to bother Lady Allison. If they have a problem, they may come to me."

Larkin, looking frightened, nodded and fled.

Allison yanked her arm away. "How dare you!" she hissed.

He spoke in a low, equally vicious tone. "If I must eat with you, I refuse to have my meals disturbed by servants' quarrels. Furthermore, I refuse to have my appetite ruined by watching you pick at your food and grow scrawnier and scrawnier. Now sit down and *eat*. Your father is looking at us."

The authority in his voice made her obey without thinking. But as soon as she had sat down, she was angry at herself. How dare he order her around? And even more, how dare he interfere with her management of the household? She was in charge of Pelsworth Castle—not him.

Allison glared at the delicately cooked beef on her plate. She took a bite, and then another. So he thought she picked at her food, did he? He would be well served if she grew as fat as the cows in the meadow. Scrawny—ha!

Derek, equally annoyed, took a long swallow of his wine, trying to calm his irrational anger. He supposed he shouldn't have prevented her from dealing with the pantler and butler. It didn't matter to him if she never ate a meal in peace. The servants could run her ragged for all he cared. He'd be damned if he interfered again.

With a small flounce, Allison turned to Sir Jarvis.

Gritting his teeth, Derek turned to Lady Mountford.

Neither of the two spoke to each other or so much as glanced at the other for the rest of the meal.

"Sir Derek, please help me! This varlet, Hobbes, won't return my plow!"

"Sir Derek, Wyatt is not telling you the whole story. He promised to pay me for the seed I lent him, but has not done so—"

"My plow is worth much more than your paltry seed!"

"Shut your mouth, you turnip head!"

"Who are you calling a turnip head, you cabbage brain!"

"Cabbage brain! Why, you—"

"Silence!"

The two men immediately shut up. Indeed the whole courtyard seemed to grow quiet. The stableboys stopped sweeping, the servants stopped bustling to and fro, and the maids by the kitchen stopped giggling. Even the chickens stopped clucking.

Satisfied that he had their attention, Derek continued in an authoritative tone. "Wyatt, either pay Hobbes for the seed or the plow will be sold and the proceeds split between the two of you."

"But, my lord, I have no money," Wyatt whined.

"Then you will have to give one half of your crop to Hobbes."

"Half my crop! I've spent months laboring over that crop. 'Tis not fair—"

"Enough! If you don't like my decision, you can go to Lord Pelsworth."

Wyatt shuffled his feet. "Er, no. I spoke in haste. Your judgment is fair. I will give Hobbes half my crop."

The two men left, and Derek continued on his way across the courtyard.

Ever since the argument between the pantler and the butler, people had been approaching him with their problems. Barely an hour went by that he wasn't called upon to arbitrate some disagreement. It should have been annoying, but strangely, it wasn't. There was a certain satisfaction that came from being the one people looked to for help. Reaching the southeast tower, he entered and took the stairs two at a time.

Lord Pelsworth looked up from the book he was reading when Derek entered the library. "Sir Derek, well met! I had begun to think you meant to ignore my summons."

"I beg your pardon," Derek said politely. "Castle business delayed me."

"Hmm. You've been working very hard of late."

"Everyone has, Lord Pelsworth."

"True. I've noticed tempers seem a bit short." The older man closed the book and tapped his fingers on the cover. "Which brings me to the matter I wished to discuss with you. I thought it might be a good idea to have a festival."

"A festival?"

"Aye. At one time Pelsworth Castle was famous for its holidays and festivals. I think 'tis time to resume the tradition. What say you?"

Derek hesitated. He had no desire to cavort at some festival. He needed to concentrate on his practice. "Many would be pleased," he finally said.

"Good. I'm glad you agree. A Midsummer's Eve celebration would be nice. 'Twas my favorite when I was younger. 'Tis a fine opportunity for lads and lasses to make merry."

Derek made no comment.

Pelsworth studied him a moment, then looked at the book he held. "Allison told me that the two of you have quarreled."

Oh, had she? "Even True Loves have a bit of a spat now and again."

Lord Pelsworth frowned. "Going on for a year now?"

"It's nothing. I have been focused on completing my training."

Lord Pelsworth appeared unconvinced. "I think it would be a good idea for you to spend your afternoons with her."

Derek swore silently. "My lord, that would waste valuable daylight hours during which I could be practicing. I must devote all my time to training if I am to beat Wilfred in the tournament—"

"You beat Sir Rufus, who has beaten Sir Wilfred."

"It wouldn't do for me to get careless, though."

"'Twould not do for you to be careless with Allison's affections."

Derek did not answer.

Pelsworth stroked the cover of the book. "I don't know if I ever told you how delighted I am that my daughter will be able to marry her True Love. It has been my greatest wish ever since her mother died."

"Has it?" Derek said expressionlessly.

"Yes, it has. I loved Cecilia, Allison's mother, very much, but I failed her. She died in my arms when Allison was ten."

Lord Pelsworth put down the book and crossed the room to a table where a bottle of wine rested. He poured two glasses and gave one to Derek before taking a long drink from his own. "I swore to Cecilia before she died that I would make certain Allison married her True Love." Setting down the glass, Lord Pelsworth looked directly at Derek. "So tell me truthfully—do you love her?"

Derek's fingers tightened around his glass. He stared at the old man, then looked down at the wine. *Shit.* His throat felt tight as he forced the lie to his lips. "Yes, I love her."

Lord Pelsworth exhaled on a long sigh. "Cecilia would be glad." He paused a moment, then asked hesitantly, "Did she seem happy?"

"Who?"

"Cecilia. When she appeared to you in your vision. Did she seem happy?"

"Oh." Derek swallowed his wine in one gulp. "Yes."

A spark of light entered Pelsworth's usually dull blue eyes. "What exactly did she say?"

"She said that I must come here to Pelsworth Castle," Derek said woodenly. "That Lady Allison was my True Love. And that you had promised her that Allison would marry none other. That was all."

Lord Pelsworth seemed disappointed. "How did she look?"

"She looked . . . very beautiful. Like an angel."

Pelsworth's face grew wistful. "Aye, she was beautiful. Allison is very like her." He put his hand on Derek's shoulder. "You must not make the same mistake I did. You must spend more time with Allison."

"But my practice—"

"You have practiced enough to take on twenty knights single-handedly. 'Tis my wish that you seek out Allison immediately after the midday meal."

Derek knew when he was beaten. "Yes, my lord."

"Excellent." Lord Pelsworth's hand dropped to his side. "I'll inform Allison to start preparing for Midsummer's Eve, and I'll tell her you'll be visiting her this afternoon." The old man beamed. "I'm certain she'll be delighted to see you."

Chapter 21

Derek SAT NEXT to Allison in the tapestry room, watching her pass the shuttle back and forth through the loom. Her slender hands, with their short oval nails, moved quickly, skilfully. They did not hesitate or falter, but kept steadily to their task, and the bluish-white cloth in the loom grew thread by thread right before his eyes.

For the last half hour Derek had watched her weaving, her entire attention apparently focused on her task. He tried not to stare at her, but somehow, whenever he looked away, his gaze was irresistibly drawn back.

Finding himself looking at her once more, he turned away and stared straight ahead. He didn't want to look at her. Looking at her made him angry. The sight of her reminded him of the lie he'd told Lord Pelsworth.

Yes, I love her.

He wished Lord Pelsworth hadn't asked the question so directly. He wished he could have somehow evaded giving an answer. But there had been no way to do so. Not without making Lord Pelsworth suspicious.

So he had lied.

He didn't know why it bothered him. He had lied often

enough in the past—and in the future—for expediency's sake, and it had never concerned him. So why did it trouble him now?

"Sir Derek," Lady Humfrey said, her voice bright. "Tell us how you convinced Lord Pelsworth to hold a Midsummer's Eve festival."

From the corner of his eye Derek saw Allison stiffen, but he ignored her as he turned to Lady Humfrey. She'd acquired some new silver threads in her blond hair in the last several months, but her plump, round face was as kind as ever.

"I had nothing to do with it," he said. "It was Lord Pelsworth's idea."

"He's never cared about having a festival before," Lady Anne said skeptically. She hadn't changed at all in the last year—her dark eyes still sparkled and her smooth, black hair shone like silk. "Why would he now?"

Derek shrugged. He wasn't about to reveal his own suspicion—that Lord Pelsworth hoped the celebration would somehow draw Derek and Allison together.

"A festival sounds very . . . pleasurable," Lady Mountford said, her gaze drifting lazily over Derek.

"Everyone is most excited about it!" Emmeline bounced a little on her stool, almost dropping the sampler on her lap. She had lost some of her puppy fat, but none of her innocent enthusiasm. "Cook told me there will be diviner eggs and destiny cakes, and Rafael said there will be dancing and singing, and Cuthbert thinks there will be a hunt for fern seeds. Oh, I cannot wait!"

"You will have to," Allison said flatly. "There is much to be done. I hope all of you are prepared to work hard."

"I don't mind the work," Emmeline said.

"I hope you still feel that way next week." Allison's voice was repressing.

Emmeline, looking crestfallen, stopped bouncing.

Derek stared at Allison. "Must you spoil even an innocent child's enjoyment?" he asked in a low, angry voice.

All the ladies' eyes—except Ursula's, since she was

asleep by the fire—widened at Derek's question. They looked from him to Allison.

Allison's lips tightened. "Must you interfere in something that is none of your concern? Ever since you came here, you've been causing trouble. Nothing has changed."

Four heads swiveled back toward Derek.

"Hasn't it? It sounds to me like you've got a bad case of sour grapes because no one consulted you about having a festival."

Four faces with identical expressions of half horror, half anticipation, swung to Allison.

"If someone *had* consulted me, I would have told them 'tis a ridiculous idea to hold a large festival a mere two weeks before a tournament. But of course, *some* people know nothing of what it takes to prepare for an event like this."

Four pairs of eyes flew to Derek.

"And *some* people can suck all the pleasure out of anything. Holidays are meant to be enjoyed—if you aren't capable of that, then at least allow the rest of us to do so."

Four mouths formed perfect *O* 's.

"Sir Derek," Allison said coldly. "You are a guest here, nothing more. In the future, I'll thank you to remember I am in charge here, not you, and leave the arrangement of festivals to me." She glanced at the four rapt faces. "Ladies, you are neglecting your embroidery."

Three pairs of hands flew to their needles.

Lady Anne, looking amused, stuck hers in her pincushion. "Tell me, Sir Derek, do you celebrate Midsummer's Eve in California?"

"No, but we have Christmas and Easter and Thanksgiving." He stared broodingly at Allison for a moment, reluctant to give up the argument, but courtesy made it impossible for him to ignore Anne. "We also have the Fourth of July, Halloween, Saint Patrick's Day, and Cinco de Mayo."

"Sink the what?" Ursula asked, waking from her doze for a moment. She drifted off again before Derek could answer.

Derek repeated it anyway. "Cinco de Mayo. It's actually a Mexican holiday, but lots of people in California celebrate it."

"What does it celebrate?" Emmeline asked.

Derek shrugged. "No one really knows. But there are parades and mariachi bands, and everyone eats tacos and tamales and drinks Margaritas."

Lady Mountford looked at him sideways from under her thick dark lashes. "It sounds quite . . . stimulating."

Derek smiled at her. Plainly, Lady Mountford knew how to have a good time.

"It sounds to me as though no one ever does any work in California," Allison said, her voice full of disapproval. "Who grows your food and makes your clothes?"

"Oh, people work," he said, his smile fading. "But a lot is done by machines." He glanced at her loom. "Machines spin thread, weave cloth, and even sew the clothes."

Awe filled Lady Humfrey's round blue eyes. "I've never heard of such machines."

Lady Mountford had no interest in machines. "What are the clothes like?" she asked.

"Men wear pants and shirts. Women wear pants or gowns. Short ones that show their legs."

"How absurd!" Allison exclaimed. "Your stories are too outlandish to be true. Next you will tell us the men wear their codpieces as purses."

The ladies gasped. All except Anne, who made a choking noise.

A slight flush rose in Derek's face. He opened his mouth to make a cutting remark, but Anne, recovered from her fit of coughing, hastily intervened.

"Can a machine weave as well as Allison?" she asked, gesturing toward the loom.

Derek glanced at the cloth on the loom. "Much better," he said.

It was Allison's turn to flush.

"That is hard to believe," Emmeline said innocently, oblivious to the undercurrents. "All the Pelsworth women have been known for their spinning and weaving. Except for the first Pelsworth bride, of course."

"Oh?" Derek murmured.

"Yes, she was a fairy and unused to human endeavors. Hasn't Lady Allison told you the story?"

"No, she hasn't."

"Lady Allison, tell Sir Derek," Emmeline urged. "You know it better than anyone."

"A fairy?" Derek looked at Allison mockingly.

Her mouth tightened. She might not believe the story herself, but that didn't mean she wanted *him* jeering at it. "By agreeing to stay in the mortal world and marry the first Pelsworth, the fairy ensured that all future Pelsworths would lead long and happy lives—as long as they married their True Loves."

Derek's face was full of skeptical amusement. "Then what happened to your mother?"

Allison stared down at the shuttle in her hands. "My father never married her. She died of a broken heart when he returned from the wars with a French bride—an heiress."

To her horror, she felt tears spring to her eyes. What was wrong with her? She'd never cried over the tale before—not even when it was happening.

But the tears wouldn't go away. Unable to bear the thought of revealing her weakness to Derek's mocking gaze, she rose to her feet and left the room without a word.

Derek stared after her, his anger forgotten. "Is that really what happened?"

Anne nodded somberly. "Lord Pelsworth—or Lord Sebastian as he was then—was madly in love with Cecilia. Promising to marry her when he returned, he left for war—and left her with a child in her belly. His parents took Cecilia in and treated her like a daughter. Lord Sebastian didn't return for ten years. When he did, a big feast was prepared. Allison was told that her father was coming home, and she and Cecilia were waiting excitedly when he arrived. But when he stepped out of the carriage, he turned to hand down a woman big with child. His wife. Everyone was shocked."

"I imagine so."

"The sweating sickness hit the castle shortly thereafter. No serious illness had ever come to the castle before—not even the plague. Cecilia and the old Lord and Lady Pelsworth died. Jacquelyn, Lord Sebastian's wife, escaped the sickness, but she died in childbirth a few days later and the babe with her. 'Twas a frightening and tragic time."

"And Allison?"

"Allison . . . changed. Before she'd been a happy child, full of smiles and laughter. But after her mother and grandparents died, she became sad and solemn. Lord Pelsworth managed to have her legally declared his heir—and 'twas not easy—but he was ravaged with guilt. He began to drink too much, and stayed away from the castle as much as possible. Allison had to assume more and more responsibilities. Nothing was ever the same."

"No, I don't suppose it would be," Derek said expressionlessly. Rising to his feet, he bowed to the ladies. "I hope you will excuse me, but I would like to take a few runs at the quintain before dark."

"Certainly." Anne smiled at him. "We all hope that you will win the tournament, Sir Derek. Your victory and marriage to Allison will make everything right at Pelsworth Castle."

Derek forced himself to smile.

Once in the yard, however, he rode at the quintain with a viciousness that sent the watching stableboys scurrying back to their chores.

He'd never promised to save the castle, he thought savagely, wheeling his horse around to make another run. He'd never even promised to save Allison. All he had—inadvertently!—agreed to do was to come back and claim to be her True Love.

Derek charged the quintain again. True Love—what a bunch of crap. The story about Allison's mother proved that. Derek wished he'd never asked about the woman. Allison had answered him coolly enough, but he had seen the glint of tears in her eyes. He didn't want to think about those tears.

He didn't want to think about Allison at all.

Chapter 22

BUT HOW COULD he not think of her, when he saw her every afternoon and at every meal?

Derek made a point of avoiding her as much as possible, but it wasn't easy—especially when Lord Pelsworth seemed determined to throw them together at every opportunity.

"Sir Derek," the old man said one morning at breakfast a few weeks later. "I have a request. Would you please escort Allison this afternoon?"

Derek opened his mouth to refuse.

But before he could do so, Lord Pelsworth held up his hand. "I know you wish to practice. But it would reassure me to know that you are there to protect her in her bath."

Derek stiffened. He stared suspiciously at Lord Pelsworth's innocent blue eyes.

"Father," Allison interjected in a low voice. "I am certain Sir Derek is too busy."

"Nonsense, child."

She picked up her knife, holding it with the point toward Derek. "I don't think it would be wise, Father."

"What? You don't think you can trust your betrothed, Allison?" Lord Pelsworth asked jokingly.

Her expression said *no* very plainly.

Derek picked up his own knife. "I would be delighted to escort Lady Allison."

She looked at him sharply. "I don't think—"

"Hush, Daughter. The matter is settled."

Tight-lipped, Allison glared at Derek.

He leaned toward her. "Don't worry," he said. "You can trust me."

She speared a sausage viciously. "I doubt it."

"I assure you," he said in a low, cold voice only she could hear, "your naked form holds no interest for me."

It was her turn to stiffen. "Fine," she said loudly. "Please be at the postern gate after dinner."

"I will," he told her, his jaw tight.

They ate the rest of their meal in angry silence.

No interest at all.

Derek kept the thought firmly planted in his brain as he sat on a large rock, keeping guard.

He hoped this wouldn't take too long. He really should be practicing. He never should have agreed to come. But he wanted to prove something to her—*and* to himself.

She no longer had any power over him. He had become stronger in this last year. He had purged all his weaknesses in the practice field. The thought of her naked body could no longer drive him half crazy with lust—

He heard a loud splash from the pool.

An image immediately flashed into his brain of her standing under the waterfall. It had been a year, but the picture was sharp and clear in his mind. Her small square shoulders, narrow waist, and—barely visible through the rushing water—the sweetly rounded curves of her buttocks. . . .

He closed his eyes. He disliked her intensely. She had tricked him, mocked him, lied to him—

"Is something wrong, Sir Derek?"

Derek opened his eyes to find Anne watching him with a knowing smile. "Nothing at all," he lied through gritted teeth.

"You're not tempted to look?"

"No."

"Not even to sneak one teensy-weensy peek?"

"No."

"Excellent. Then I may leave her safely in your hands. I must visit Mistress Wyatt, who lives only a short distance away."

"Lady Anne, you cannot go unescorted. Lady Anne . . . Lady Anne! No! Wait—"

He watched in frustration as she walked quickly down the path, her laughter floating back to him.

Clenching his teeth, Derek pulled his harp off his horse and sat back down. Staring straight ahead, he played a grim religious tune.

It didn't help.

He could hear Allison splashing and humming in the water. He remembered when they'd been playing five-card stud in the dungeon and she'd let the kirtle slip over her shoulders—he'd almost seen her then. God, he'd wanted to see her so much. It had been almost an obsession to see her naked. Perhaps because he kept coming so close to doing so. But somehow, he'd never managed to catch more than just a glimpse of smooth flesh and rounded curves.

Even when he'd had her in her bedroom, when he'd almost made love to her, he hadn't seen much more than the length of her slender legs and the upper curves of her breasts. It was all the fault of these damn medieval dresses and the infernal laces that tied the women up tighter than overwrapped Christmas presents. God or the Devil—he wasn't sure which—must have designed those dresses, that much was clear—

"Anne! I'm ready to come out."

Derek's fingers fumbled on the harp strings. "She's left." The words emerged as a hoarse croak.

"Anne? Where are you?"

Derek tried again. "She's left!" he shouted.

There was a long silence. Then, "Oh."

He heard sluicing water, and he imagined her rising from the pool to stand naked on the bank.

"Sir Derek! Where are my clothes?"

Derek caught sight of a bundle by his feet. His heart sinking, he picked it up.

The white cloth wrapped around it fell open, revealing her riding boots and dark blue velvet gown.

"Anne left them with me."

"You expect me to believe that? You must have stolen them while I wasn't looking."

"No, I didn't."

"I don't believe you."

"Believe what you like."

Silence.

"Sir Derek . . ."

"Yes?"

"I need my clothes."

She needed her clothes. His fingers tightened on the bundle and he breathed in deeply. He walked down to the bank of the pool.

She was standing behind a leafy bush—that wasn't quite leafy enough. He caught glimpses of pearly pink flesh, shadows, and curves. He closed his eyes and held out the bundle.

"I cannot reach. You must come closer."

His eyes still closed, he took a step forward. The bundle was snatched from his hand. Turning his back, he folded his arms over his chest and stared straight ahead. He heard the snap of a buckle and a picture flashed into his brain of her bending over, her breasts swaying softly and her rounded buttocks jutting out as she extended one shapely leg to pull on her hose and fasten them to her garters.

Derek swallowed and forced the picture out of his head.

Cloth rustled. Instantly a new picture formed—of her breasts lifting as she raised her arms to pull the kirtle down over her head. He imagined the material skimming down over her hips, past the hair at the juncture of her thighs to swirl softly around her legs.

He heard the slight scraping sound of metal-tipped leather strings being threaded through eyelet holes. He tried not to think of her lacing the kirtle up over her breasts, pulling the material tightly against the sweet curves, but he failed miserably.

He heard the rustle of more cloth, and he imagined the blue velvet gown covering up the tight kirtle, concealing everything that he was aching to see—

"Are you finished yet?" he asked harshly.

"Almost. But . . ." Her voice sounded small.

"But what?"

"I need help with the laces at the back of my gown."

Swearing under his breath, he turned.

She stood with her back to him, her hair in a long wet braid. She pulled it forward over her shoulder, revealing the long row of tiny, crisscrossing laces that held her dress together. They were completely undone to the middle of her back.

His heart thumping with a loud, slow beat, Derek stepped forward.

As he took the strings between his fingers, he became aware of how alone they were. How completely isolated.

If he chose to untie these strings and undress her, there was no one to stop him. No one would interrupt them this time if he laid her down on the grassy bank and made love to her as he'd longed to do so many times. . . .

He shook his head, trying to clear away the unruly thoughts.

The strings were small, and the eyelet holes even smaller.

Every time he poked a string through a hole, his fingers brushed against her. He tried to avoid touching her, but his fingers had grown callused and clumsy in the last year, and he had to rest his hand against her back to steady the string so he could thread it through. She wore the kirtle, so he wasn't touching bare skin, but he could feel the slight dampness of the cloth and the expansion and contraction of her rib cage as she breathed.

He wanted to hurry, but his fingers did not cooperate. They moved slowly, carefully threading the laces through each and every hole, pausing after each one to make certain the strings were tight.

He had to put his hand on her waist to hold her steady while he tightened the strings. He could feel the slight hollow between her hip and stomach through the material of her dress.

He bent forward to see better at a particularly difficult hole. He pushed the thread through, then straightened, turning his face slightly as he did so. His cheek brushed against her hair. The damp strands smelled like cinnamon and cloves.

He tied the laces into a bow at the top, near the nape of her neck. Her hair grew to a small point there, and the skin below looked soft and pink and vulnerable.

Finished tying the bow, he stepped back.

"Thank you," she said. Her voice sounded a bit muffled.

"You're welcome." His own voice sounded strange, too.

They returned to the castle in silence.

"Well?" Anne demanded several hours later as she entered the tapestry room. "What happened?"

Allison glanced up at her, then bent over the shirt she was sewing. "Nothing happened."

"Nothing?" Anne looked disappointed.

"What did you think would happen?"

"Oh . . . nothing. How interesting that he didn't look. It's amazing how much he has changed in the last year. How honorable he is now. And how strong. And brave. He's everything a woman could possibly want in a husband."

Allison pushed her needle through the fine linen cloth. "Do you think so?"

"Yes, I think so!" Anne said impatiently. "When are you going to admit it, also? When are you going to admit that you love him?"

"I most certainly do not love him."

"Yes, you do."

"No, I don't."

"Yes, you do."

"No, I . . ." Her voice trailed off and her eyes filled with tears. "Well, even if I did, it would make no difference. He doesn't love me."

"How can you be so certain? Perhaps if you would stop arguing with him, you would find out he does."

Allison looked down at the shirt on her lap. Was Anne right? Allison didn't know. She only knew that whenever she thought of Derek, she felt an odd combination of yearning and unease.

She remembered his fingers on her laces—he'd seemed to take an inordinate amount of time. It had been difficult to stand still when his hands were touching her all over. She had been so aware of him—of his warm breath against the back of her neck, of the brushing of his cheek against her hair, of the scent of horse and sunshine that clung to him.

His nearness had made her breathless. She'd wanted to turn around and put her arms around his neck. She'd wanted to stand on her tiptoes and press her lips to his. She'd wanted him to kiss her the way he had so long ago. . . .

Oh, she was a weak fool. How could she want such things when she knew he was still angry at her—for real and imagined wrongs? She knew that his hard work this last year was not from a desire to marry her, but for some darker purpose.

She couldn't possibly trust him.

Could she?

That night she had the dream again. She begged the different faces for help and they all said no. But this time, the last one was Derek's.

"Will you come?" she asked.

"Oh, yes. I will come."

She woke with tears on her face. Turning on her side, she stared through the darkness. The dream was so odd. Parts were so real and so clear—and others were hazy and confusing. What did it mean? Why had she been begging for help? It had something to do with Wilfred, "the small, weak man." How well that summed him up. Small of mind and weak of heart. But who was Boris, the "sweetest, most perfect knight"? She knew no such man.

But of course, there was no reason she should. The dream was just that—a dream.

She pushed back the bed curtains and got out of bed. She went over to the window and pushed it open.

The night was clear. The stars shone in the sky. In the distance Allison could hear the rippling notes of a harp.

She'd heard the harp player before. He often sat up on the battlements late at night and played for hours. Sometimes he played slowly, picking out tunes she'd never heard before. At other times he played violently, as if there was a well of anger and hate and frustration inside him that was too much to bear.

But tonight, he played softly, wistfully, tenderly.

She didn't recognize the tune, but the melancholy sweetness of it brought tears to her eyes.

She stood there listening for over an hour until the sound abruptly stopped.

As if awakening from a trance, she closed the window. She stood there for a moment, shivering, then retrieved her keys and unlocked the chest. She pulled out the shirt she had finished just that afternoon.

Allison stared down at the shirt. Even in the dim rushlight, it was beautiful. The linen cloth was strong and even and had a fine luster to it. Every stitch was small and perfect. It would fit Derek perfectly. She would give it to him tomorrow at the Midsummer's Eve festival, and she would try once more to mend matters between them.

She would try.

And perhaps, if he would try, also, they might discover the Pelsworth Legend was true after all.

Chapter 23

SWEAT RUNNING DOWN his forehead, Derek thrust his sword at the pel in the dusky light, stoically ignoring the sounds of laughter and music and the smells of food and bonfires that drifted from the castle courtyard above.

Several of the squires had expressed astonishment at his decision not to attend the Midsummer's Eve festival.

"But 'tis because of you that we are having it!" Simon had exclaimed. "You were the one who insisted to Lord Pelsworth that we should reinstate having festivals and holidays."

"With the tournament only two weeks away, I must spend all my time practicing," Derek had replied stone-faced, not bothering to correct Simon's misconception.

In reality, however, he had not wanted to see Allison again so soon after yesterday.

Not that anything had happened at the pool, exactly. He had done nothing more than tie the laces of her dress.

But something had changed. The ever-present flame of anger that had burned steadily in the pit of his stomach for the last year had flickered for a moment, and he hadn't liked it. For the first time in nearly a year the anger that had sustained him for so long had almost failed him.

He'd gone up on the battlements the night before, intending to let the harsh music of his harp reinforce it. But instead, the music that flowed from the instrument had been soft and full of a yearning that he hadn't even realized he felt.

Derek thrust his sword more forcefully, and the blade sank deeply into the wood. He definitely needed to stay away from Allison. She was too tempting, too seductive. If he wasn't careful, he might start making excuses for her. He might start thinking that it wasn't fair to blame her for stealing his life when she had no memory of what had happened five hundred years in the future. . . .

"What dragon are you slaying tonight, Sir Derek?" an amused voice asked.

Derek turned to see Anne, a cup in her hands, standing behind him. He yanked his blade from the wood. "Good evening, Lady Anne. Is the feast so boring that you decided to come watch me striking a wooden post with my sword?"

"Not at all. Everyone, including myself, is having a wonderful time. In truth, I felt guilty for enjoying myself so much when you were out here working with such dedication. So I decided to bring you a cup of CuckooFoot beer."

From up in the courtyard, Derek heard laughing voices sing out, "Merrily sing cuckoo! cuckoo!"

He removed his gauntlet and accepted the cup. "Thank you, Lady Anne." He took a sip. It tasted rather pleasant, a little like root beer, with a hint of anise. The cool liquid was refreshing after his exercise.

He drank the rest and handed the cup back to Anne. She glanced at the empty cup and then at him. "Are you certain you do not wish to join the festival?"

"I'm certain. I must work."

"Yes, I suppose you must. Although it seems a bit strange when you were just lecturing Allison about learning to take pleasure. Ah, well. At least Allison has taken your advice— she is enjoying the company of our new neighbor greatly. I have never seen her so happy. Well, I had best return. I do not wish to miss the diviner eggs. Godspeed, Sir Derek."

Derek stared after her as she walked back up the slope to the postern gate. Then, with a frown, he turned back to the pel and made a thrust.

What exactly was Allison taking such pleasure in? he wondered. Who was this new neighbor whose company she enjoyed so much?

He tried to imagine her smiling and laughing, but it was difficult. She smiled so rarely. Was it the man who caused her to do so now?

Derek swung his sword again, but the blow had less force. The scent of the smoke from the bonfire smelled stronger, the aroma of cooking food more delicious. He tasted ginger and anise on his lips. The music and laughter grew louder and louder.

With a curse, Derek stopped swinging his sword and set off for the gate.

He wanted to see Allison and this new man.

And if there was any pleasure taking going on, he wanted to make sure he was the one taking it.

After washing and changing into his dark green doublet, Derek slipped into a seat by Lady Ursula, his gaze searching the long rows of tables.

"Sir Derek! 'Tis about time you joined us!" Lady Ursula cried. "Pin this sprig of birch leaves to your doublet and take this Saint-John's-wort. If it is still fresh at the end of the feast, then your lover's affection will endure. If it hasn't wilted or faded by morning, then your love will be vigorous and long lasting."

Derek's gaze stopped at a table perpendicular to the one he was at. Allison sat near the middle, dressed in a blue brocaded gown, a wreath of birch leaves in her hair. She was laughing and smiling at the man at her side, a young, dark-haired fellow, with sharp, narrow features and a pointed black beard. Derek disliked him immediately.

Forcing his gaze away from the couple, Derek took the Saint-John's-wort from Ursula. "And if it does wilt?" he asked her.

"Then your romance will be bleak and short," she cackled. "Ah, look! They're bringing the destiny cakes." Ursula, with a birch wreath set slightly askew on her thin gray hair, looked and sounded as excited as a child. "You missed the diviner eggs, so be sure to take a cake."

Derek watched as several servants carried platters covered by cloths to the tables. Each person reached under the cloth and withdrew a cake while those watching howled with laughter.

"The shape of the cake tells you something about your future," Lady Ursula explained. "Oh, look, Lady Allison has chosen a dragon."

"There must be a dragon in your future," called a voice from one of the tables. "You will need a knight to slay it for you."

"I will slay it for you, Lady Allison," the man sitting next to her declared in ringing tones.

"Who is that man?" Derek asked Lady Ursula, his dislike of the stranger increasing.

She peered at him. "I know him not. He must be a visitor."

At a table opposite Derek, Cuthbert leaped to his feet. "I would be honored to slay it, Lady Allison!"

"No, I will do it!" called another, and then another.

Laughing, Allison said, "Thank you all!" and bit into the cake.

Derek watched her chew and swallow, then lick a crumb from her lower lip. Still laughing, she turned to the dark-haired man. As she did so, her gaze met Derek's.

Her laughter faded, and a blush rose in her cheeks. Her lashes swept down.

Derek could not look away. He had never seen her laugh like that before. He had never seen her look so happy, so carefree. In her rich gown, with the simple birch wreath resting on her streaming hair, she looked utterly gorgeous.

Lady Ursula laughed wheezily. Derek tore his gaze away from Allison to see that she had picked a cake shaped like a baby. "Do you think this means that I am with child?" she asked.

Smiling automatically, Derek reached under the cover and withdrew a cake. It was shaped like a spinning wheel.

Lady Ursula laughed again. "Your fate is plain, Sir Derek—you are to become a spinster!"

The next course was served, an omelette cooked with almonds and raisins, and each guest was given a red rose. Everyone plucked the petals, reciting, "He loves me . . ." "She loves me not . . ."

Derek left his rose on the table and watched Allison. The petals floated around her as she plucked steadily. She stopped when she reached the last one, a smile curving her lips. She looked at him, and this time she didn't look away.

Some silent communication that Derek barely understood passed between them.

"Sir Derek!" Lady Ursula said in his ear. "'Tis time to search for fern seeds. 'Tis said if you find and keep them, you can become invisible at will." She smiled toothlessly at him. "But I think most use the time to slip away with their lovers. You had best hurry, Sir Derek, before someone else is before you."

The sun had set, but there was a bright full moon in the sky. Laughing and chattering, everyone headed for the gates. Derek, catching sight of Allison's long golden hair, followed swiftly, feeling as though he were in the grip of some magical spell.

He caught up to her by the garden wall. Grabbing her hand, he tugged her into the moonlit shade of a sweet-smelling pear tree. He stepped closer, but she didn't speak, and neither did he. The scent of birch leaves and roses clung to her. He noticed a few red petals caught in her hair. Carefully he plucked them out.

"Sir Derek . . ."

"Yes, Allison," he murmured huskily, his lips touching her hair.

"I . . . I want to thank you for convincing my father to hold this festival. I thought it a silly idea at first, but now . . . oh, Derek, 'tis just like when I was a child! The singing, the games, the food—I had forgotten how much I enjoyed them. 'Tis all so wonderful. It makes me think . . . it gives me hope that . . ."

"That what, Allison?" His lips moved to her temple and he felt her quiver.

"That . . . I . . . oh, I have something I want to give you."

He put his hand on the wall next to her head. "What is it?"

" 'Tis a gift. 'Twill take me but a moment to fetch it from my room."

"Let me come with you." He put his other hand against the wall, hemming her in, and leaned closer. "Let's go to your room and you can give me your present there."

With a breathless laugh, she ducked under his arm. "No, you must wait. I'll return in just a few moments."

He watched hungrily as she hurried away and disappeared through the postern gate. Leaning back against the wall, he turned his gaze up to the moon, all of his senses humming.

He could smell the acrid scent of the bonfires and torches, the scent of ripe fruit in the tree above him. He could hear the sound of laughter and running footsteps, the whisper of wind in the branches above. He could feel the hard smoothness of the stone wall at his back, the dew falling gently on his face, the softness of the rose petal he'd taken from Allison's hair in his fingers.

The moon looked bigger and brighter and more beautiful than he'd ever seen it—

"Ah, I recognize that sigh. I do believe you are moonstruck."

The rose petal slipped through Derek's fingers. Slowly he turned toward the mocking voice. "Good evening, Rafael," he said evenly. "Are you enjoying the festival?"

The minstrel's white teeth gleamed in the moonlight. "Oh, yes. But you seem rather lonely. Wouldn't a female companion make your evening even more pleasurable? I know a fine wench—"

"What is your game, Rafael?" Derek interrupted harshly.

Rafael arched his brows. "Game?"

Derek was not deceived. "You seem determined to drive me away from Allison."

Rafael brushed a rose petal from the sleeve of his dark blue doublet. "'Tis nothing personal, Sir Derek. 'Tis only that Anne and I have been debating the matter of True Love for centuries. For what *seems* like centuries," he corrected himself. "I do not like to see any man fall prey to that foolish emotion called love. It gives women too much power." He shrugged. "But if you do not believe me, go to Lady Allison and surrender your heart. You'll find her in the southeast tower room." He started to stroll toward the garden gate, then paused and said over his shoulder, "She's with the man she was sitting next to at the feast." His blue eyes glittered strangely in the moonlight. "Sir Boris."

The minstrel disappeared into the garden, but Derek barely noticed. *Sir Boris?*

He stepped away from the garden wall, the magic of the night broken. What was it Allison's ghost had said that long ago night in Nan's cottage? *I met a knight, Sir Boris. He is my sweetest, most perfect knight. He is brave, courageous, chivalrous, and he worships the ground I walk on.*

Derek's hands tightened into fists.

So. Her True Love had finally appeared. Did she think to marry this Boris *now*, when Derek had been working for nearly a year to marry her himself?

Without conscious thought, Derek strode to the postern gate. He wouldn't allow it. He wouldn't allow her to slip away and fall in love with someone else so easily.

He would make it clear to her—and to this Boris—that she was marrying *him* and no one else.

"Lady Allison, I worship the ground you walk on," Sir Boris crooned in her ear. "My heart nearly sprang from my chest when I first saw you. I will never be happy again unless you tell me that you felt the same."

Allison, leaning as far away from him as she could on the circular stairway where he had cornered her, said, "I'm sorry, Sir Boris. But the only thing I felt when I saw you was concern for your beautiful white doublet and hose. A feast can be very messy, and in truth, I thought I saw a spot of gravy upon the velvet."

Sir Boris paused in his seduction a moment to glance down at the immaculate expanse of his doublet. Then, with utmost chivalry, he declared, "I almost would not care if I could have but one kiss from your beauteous lips."

Allison had to restrain herself from rolling her eyes. Sir Boris was a guest and she did not like to insult him, but really . . .

"I'm afraid her kisses are already spoken for," a familiar deep voice said from behind them.

Joy shimmered through Allison at the sound of that voice. Relieved, she turned to see Derek silhouetted in the doorway. She smiled at him, but the dark tower room hid his face in the shadows.

"Sir," Boris said, puffing his chest out like a roosting pigeon. "You are interrupting. Please go away."

"And if I refuse?"

Derek's voice was low and menacing. Surprised, Allison peered through the darkness at him, trying to see his expression. Surely he would not fight a buffoon like Sir Boris?

"That would not be wise," Boris said, his hand going to the hilt of his dress sword—a harmless-looking blade that Allison doubted had ever left its scabbard. "I might be forced to issue a challenge—"

"Sir Boris, please remember that you are a guest in my home!" Allison interrupted. "As is Sir Derek."

"Sir Derek Sinclair of California?" Boris's chest deflated like a pig's bladder. Apparently he had heard of Derek's prowess with a sword and lance. "I, er, I, ah, I beg your pardon, Sir Derek. I did not mean . . . that is, I, oh, please excuse me! There is a spot of gravy on my doublet, and I must wash it off before the stain sets!"

He stepped toward the door, then stopped, realizing Derek was blocking it. For a few, agonizingly long moments, Derek did not move.

Then, to Allison's relief, he stepped aside and let Sir Boris scurry past.

"Thank you, Sir Derek," she said, laughing a little at Sir Boris's undignified exit. "I thought I would never be rid of him."

Derek didn't respond, and Allison glanced at him with a twinge of uneasiness. She wished she could see his expression.

She approached the doorway where he stood. "I was on my way back to the garden when Sir Boris stopped me on the stairs." She was close enough now that the light from the bonfires outside in the courtyard illuminated his face. The line of his jaw was rigid. "'Twas difficult to discourage him," she explained a trifle uncertainly.

"Especially since you made so little effort to do so."

Allison stiffened. "That's not true. You cannot seriously think I was interested in his attentions?"

"Why wouldn't I? You've never been very particular about your 'True Loves.'"

Anger flared in Allison, and she opened her mouth to make a sharp retort, but then she bit it back. She stepped closer and laid her hand on his arm.

"Derek," she said, her voice low. "Let us not argue. Let us not spoil this night. I want everything to be well between us. Can we not forget the past? I am willing to do so. And . . . and as a token of my good faith, I wish to give you this shirt. I made it myself from my mother's flax."

The speech hadn't come out quite as she'd planned. It sounded awkward and rushed, even to her own ears. Hoping he hadn't noticed, she thrust the shirt at him, the shirt she'd worked on with such painstaking care.

He took it, but did not so much as glance at it. "What about Sir Boris—are you in love with him?"

"In love with him?" she gasped. "Of course not! I've only just met him."

Derek seemed to relax a little. "I'm sorry," he said. "I thought . . . I don't know what I thought."

She smiled tenderly, realizing he had actually been jealous. "That Sir Boris was my 'sweetest, most perfect knight'?" she said teasingly.

Derek froze. "*What* did you say?"

Allison smiled uneasily, vaguely aware that she had revealed something she shouldn't have. "I . . . I mean, I would

never describe him so. Except maybe in comparison to Sir
Wilfred . . ."

Slowly he turned to stare at her, his face as hard as the
stone of the castle walls.

"You remember," he said flatly.

Chapter 24

"No," ALLISON STAMMERED. "That is, not exactly—"

Derek barely heard her pathetic attempts to explain. Fury was boiling through his veins and pounding in his ears. "You remember everything, don't you? My God. Here I made excuses for you, thinking you didn't remember me. But it was all an act, wasn't it?"

"No! I don't know what you mean. I've only had a few dreams about you. . . ."

Her words condemned her more. "I don't care if it was a damned holy vision. What exactly did you dream?"

"I . . . mostly asking people to help me. And you . . . agreeing to come. To save Pelsworth Castle."

"Pelsworth Castle!" Derek said the name with loathing. "You *do* remember. I don't know why I'm surprised. After all, you always made it clear you would do anything for this pile of rocks. You never cared about anything else. I've spent a year in *hell* because of you—you and your precious castle."

"I didn't . . . I don't know . . . I never meant to make you suffer, I swear." She clasped her trembling hands together.

"I'm sorry. I will tell my father you don't wish to marry me—"

"Oh, no, Lady Allison," he said, refusing to succumb to the plea in her eyes. "Don't think you're going to weasel out of our marriage at this late date. You're marrying me, all right. And then"—he smiled cruelly—"and then I'm taking the emerald and leaving you. I'm going home and never coming back."

Her eyes grew wide. "You would abandon me and Pelsworth Castle?"

He laughed harshly. "Why not? I don't care about Pelsworth Castle, and I sure as hell don't care about you."

He turned to leave, then glanced at the shirt clutched in his fist. Deliberately he dropped it to the floor and ground it into the stone with his heel.

Allison, pale and quiet, watched him. She didn't move. She didn't speak.

Her still, blank expression penetrated the haze of anger enveloping him like nothing else could have. He hesitated a moment, a niggling remorse struggling to take hold.

Still silent, she bent and picked up the shirt. For a moment, she stared at the ground-in mud staining the once pristine cloth. Then she draped it over her arm and walked out into the courtyard.

He stood in the doorway, staring after her, feeling oddly guilty. She deserved everything he'd said. So why did he feel like he'd crushed a small, white blossom in his fist?

He took a step after her. "Allison . . ."

She couldn't hear him above the boisterous merrymakers. Reaching the table, she sat down—next to Sir Boris. Smiling, she put her hand on his arm.

Derek's rage returned full measure. His hands tightening into fists, he turned away from the sight. God, what a fool he was. If anything, he'd been too easy on her.

He would not make the mistake of trusting her again.

Allison spent the rest of the festival in a daze. She smiled and laughed as players acted out the story of Saint George and the dragon; she made a wish and set a candle in a paper boat on the fish pond. She danced and chanted with the others as if nothing was wrong. But through it all, Derek's words echoed and reechoed in her head.

I don't care about Pelsworth Castle, and I sure as hell don't care about you.

She felt cold. He was going to abandon her. She would be a woman alone, unprotected by a husband, yet unable to marry. Pelsworth Castle would be like a ripe, juicy peach, ready to fall into the hands of the first unscrupulous knight who passed by.

She couldn't let that happen. Protecting the castle and the people within was her sole purpose in life. She had never looked for love or happiness for herself. It was only these last few weeks, seeing how Derek had changed, that she had begun to hope for something more.

But no. She had wanted too much. Her mother had warned her against that sometimes as a child when she'd been fretting over the absence of her father. "Be thankful for what you have," her mother had always said.

Allison looked down at the shirt draped over her arm. She felt numb inside. But perhaps that was just as well. If she hadn't been numb, she might have cried at the sight of the dirt staining the once beautiful shirt.

It had been foolish of her to hope for something that didn't exist.

It was time to put aside her silly dreams and do what she'd always known she must do. Now, more than ever, it was imperative that she marry Wilfred.

But in order to do so, Wilfred would have to beat Derek in the tournament in two weeks time.

And Allison would have to make certain that he did.

Chapter 25

WILFRED ARRIVED TWO days before the tournament with the news that the king's cavalcade would arrive the next day.

Allison greeted him, but inwardly she was shaken by his appearance. Had his eyes always been so small and mean? Had he always been so big and so hairy? Had his breath always been so sour?

She turned her face away from his kiss, ignoring his black frown. She excused herself, saying she must prepare for the king's arrival. It wasn't until much later, when she saw him crossing the courtyard, that she summoned up the fortitude to speak to him again.

"Sir Wilfred!" she called, lifting her skirts above her ankles to avoid trailing them in the dirt.

About to enter the building next to the stables, Wilfred paused and turned, watching her as she drew close. She released her skirt, instinctively wanting to cover herself from his lecherous gaze.

Pulling her into the shadows, he hauled her up against his sweat-stained doublet and kissed her roughly on the mouth.

She accepted the caress passively, trying not to gag at the sour odors emanating from him.

"So," he said. "Are you ready to become my bride?"

"Yes," she whispered.

"Good. At the tournament, I will beat that weakling, Sinclair."

Allison turned her face away, her chest tight. "That may not be possible."

"How so? My men tell me he has improved, but 'tis hard to believe—"

"Yes, it *is* true," she interrupted. "In fact, 'tis expected he will win the tournament."

Wilfred frowned, his grip on her loosening. "How can this be?"

She took the opportunity to ease away from him. "He has worked like a madman the last year," she said, smoothing the rumpled skirt of her gown. "Some say he is indefeatable. He beat Sir Rufus."

"Sir Rufus?" Wilfred's heavy black brows lowered. "Sinclair has improved that much?"

Allison nodded.

"There still hasn't been any word from the messenger the king sent to verify Sinclair's claim?"

"No. It doesn't matter, though. I have thought it all out. I will give him a tincture that will render him unconscious."

Wilfred's brow cleared. "An excellent idea. While he is unconscious, I will run him through—"

"Run him through! You cannot!"

Wilfred looked at her, his eyes cold and hard. "What is this? Do you harbor some tender feelings for him after all?"

She turned slightly away. "No, of course not. It is just that I cannot bear to have a man's death on my conscience when his only crime is that he claimed to love me."

Wilfred stared at her suspiciously.

Frantically Allison tried to think of a reason that would convince him not to harm Derek. "Besides, the tournament rules forbid it. It would be most cowardly to kill an unconscious man. Everyone would be outraged. Better to have him fall off his horse as if he's fainted from fright. Once he's

off his horse, you will be the winner, and he will be a laugh-
ingstock."

"Hmm." Wilfred appeared to consider this. "Perhaps
you're right."

Allison breathed a little easier. "You must swear to me,
before God, on your honor, that you will not harm him."

"Very well," he said reluctantly. "I so swear."

"Thank you," she whispered. "I must go now. Good night,
Sir Wilfred." She left quickly before he could think to kiss
her again.

Wilfred stared after her retreating form, a cruel smile on
his lips. When she was out of sight, he entered the armorer's,
brushing by Simon who was on the point of leaving.

"Good evening, my lord," the armorer said. "You wish me
to dull the edge of your sword for the tournament?"

Wilfred shook his head. "Make certain that my sword and
ax have a fine edge to them," he ordered.

"But—" The armorer looked at Wilfred's face and
thought better of what he was about to say. "Aye, my lord."

Satisfied, Wilfred went to his bed, and soon was having a
pleasant dream—of Sir Derek Sinclair, lying on the ground
with the blood slowly draining from his body, a sword
through his heart.

The pain was unbearable.

*Blood seeped from the wound in her chest as she crawled
across the floor to her father's side. He lay still and quiet.
She heard the distant sound of her own gasping sobs as she
struggled to cover him with his cloak. It was terribly heavy.
The pain in her chest expanded and increased until suddenly
it exploded into an odd lightness.*

*Everything was fading when she heard more crying.
Looking down, she saw an old woman bent over the two life-
less bodies on the floor. "Allison! Allison! You cannot die.
You cannot!"*

*She tried to comfort the old woman, but she appeared not
to hear. The old woman leaned over the body and took the
emerald. "Right this wrong, Allison," she whispered before*

putting the jewel in its hiding place. "Find your True Love and save Pelsworth Castle. . . ."

"Allison, wake up! There is much to do today!"

Allison woke slowly at the sound of Anne's voice, an unaccustomed sense of dread filling her. It took her a moment to remember why.

I'm taking the emerald and leaving you. I'm going home and never coming back.

The memory, clear and sharp and unwanted, came to her. She buried her face in her pillow. She must stop him. Dear heaven, she must, before he destroyed everything.

"Allison?" Anne pushed back the bed curtains and peered inside. "Are you awake?"

Allison lifted her face from the pillow. Pretending to yawn, she sat up. "Is it morning already, Anne? It seems as though I just fell asleep."

Anne, in the process of opening the window, glanced over her shoulder. "Are you still having trouble sleeping?"

Allison faked another yawn. "Yes, I am. In fact, I wondered if you could make up a tincture of corn-roses for me today. Perhaps it would help."

Anne laughed. "It would help certainly—you would sleep for a se'nnight! I'll brew a nice chamomile tea for you instead."

Allison busied herself with untying the strings of her nightcap. "I prefer the tincture."

Anne's gaze sharpened. "Why? Tell me the truth, Allison."

Allison didn't want to, but she'd never been able to lie to Anne. Throwing the covers back, she said defiantly, "If you must know, I intend to put the tincture in Sir Derek's wine at the tournament tomorrow."

Anne's eyes grew wide. "Why would you do such a thing?"

"Oh, Anne!" Allison's defiance disappeared as quickly as it had appeared. She fought back foolish tears. "I must marry Wilfred—for the castle's sake. I don't want Derek to be hurt—Wilfred has promised not to do so—but Derek must not win the tournament."

"So you intend to sacrifice yourself for the castle, is that it?"

Allison gave her a startled glance. "I don't think of it as a sacrifice."

"How can marrying Wilfred be anything else? Marrying him will not help you or the castle. 'Twill only make everyone miserable. Can't you see that?"

"Can't you see that I have no choice? Derek told me he intends to marry me, then abandon me. He will ruin us all."

"He would never do such a thing!"

"Wouldn't he? A year ago I might have agreed with you, but he's changed. He's ruthless enough now to pull Pelsworth Castle down stone by stone if it serves his purpose." Allison rose to her feet. "If you won't make the tincture, Anne, I'll buy it from old widow Scryven in the village."

Anne hesitated, her brow furrowing. But then she sighed. "I will prepare it. But God help you—and Pelsworth Castle—if you marry Wilfred."

The day was a bustle of activity. Knights and their retinues arrived from all over the country to participate in the tournament. Colorful tents popped up in the fields around the castle. Carpenters hammered at fences to hold the horses and added the final touches to the newly built lists where the jousting would take place. Sir Percival meticulously recorded each new arrival and the coat of arms in his roll. The kitchen fires blazed nonstop as the cooks turned out pies and sweets and every imaginable culinary delight.

Usually, Allison would have enjoyed the excitement. But today, as she went about greeting guests and supervising the preparations, she felt nothing but apprehension. Would everything go as planned? She could not allow any mistakes. Derek must drink the tincture and Wilfred must win the tournament, or the castle was doomed.

By late afternoon Anne still hadn't given her the tincture, and Allison was beginning to grow uneasy. She went in search of the other woman and found her in the Royal

Chamber, directing the maids in the arrangement of the linens and last-minute cleaning.

"Allison!" Anne cried upon seeing her. "Has the king's cavalcade been sighted? We're almost finished here, I promise."

"Yes, he will be here in a moment." Allison paused, watching Anne fluff up a pillow. "Have you prepared the tincture we spoke of?"

"Not yet." Anne put the pillow on the bed and picked up a vase of flowers. "Tell me, Lady Allison, should these go here by the bed or on the mantel or—"

"Anne," Allison interrupted impatiently. "I must have that tincture. When will it be ready?"

Anne's hands grew still on the flowers. "I shall give it to you tonight," she said, her voice resigned.

"Thank you." Allison glanced at the vase. "And I think the flowers should go on the table."

Trumpets sounded from the courtyard. Allison left the Royal Chamber and hurried down the stairs into the courtyard.

The king had arrived.

Chapter 26

DEREK HEARD THE trumpets announcing the king's arrival late that afternoon, but he did not pause in his preparations for the knighting ritual.

The first thing he did was go to the armorer's to pick up the new armor and sword Lord Pelsworth had commissioned for him. To his surprise, the edge of the sword was sharp.

"Watch out for Sir Wilfred," was all the armorer said when questioned. "And take care what you drink."

Frowning a little, Derek headed back to the squires' quarters where Clarice and another maid were pouring hot water into a tub for the ritual bath. Clarice lingered a bit after the other maid had left.

"Beware!" she said in a low voice. "Sir Wilfred means to poison you at the tournament!" Without another word, she turned and disappeared.

Derek stared after her a moment, then shook his head. He washed himself, then dressed in a white shirt, purple cloak, and gold tunic. After gathering up his armor and sword, he headed for the chapel. He was crossing the courtyard when he heard a hissing sound.

It was the pantler. "Take care," the man said. "Be on your guard at the tournament tomorrow!"

It would appear Wilfred had some plot, Derek thought. Shrugging, he entered the chapel and knelt on the floor in front of the altar. Father Gregory said a few words of prayer, then whispered, "Beware of false knights, Sir Derek!"

Derek nodded. Whatever Wilfred had planned made no difference. Derek had every intention of defeating the knight at tomorrow's tournament.

The priest exited through the vestibule, and a few moments later, Simon entered the chapel. He knelt a short distance from Derek.

"Psst. Psssst."

Derek turned to look at him. "Yes, Simon?"

"You are in danger—Sir Wilfred plans to render you unconscious at the tournament and kill you."

"Really? Thank you for the warning. Do you have any idea *how* he plans to do this?"

"I think Lady Allison has some plot."

Derek froze. "Lady Allison?"

Simon glanced at him quickly. "She is probably concerned for your safety."

"Mmhm." So here it was—the final treachery. He should have known she would try something. A slow, hot fury burned deep within him.

He'd seen her only from a distance since the night of the festival. The memory of that night still had the power to enrage him. He wondered how long the "dreams" had been going on, how long she'd known the truth—that she'd lured him back to the Middle Ages with false promises and the knowledge that his chances of returning home were practically nonexistent. Had she known when they'd lain on her bed, kissing and almost making love? Had she known when she taunted him in the dungeon, when he'd been half dead from despair? Had she known these last months when he'd been slaving night and day to become a knight? She'd probably never thought he would survive this long.

How very disappointed she must be.

"Do you know what her plan is?" he asked.

Simon shook his head. "Lady Anne might know. I will ask her."

"Thanks, Simon."

Simon left, and Derek looked up at the cross above the altar. *God, give me strength,* he prayed fiercely, *to defeat Wilfred and deal with Allison as she deserves.*

Night fell, and he continued to pray, but he was interrupted quite often as an amazing number of people felt the need for prayer. They trickled in, one after the other, knelt near Derek, and whispered their warnings.

The grapevine worked just as well in the Middle Ages as the future, Derek thought wryly.

The chapel was dark now, lit only by a single lamp. Outside, the courtyard had grown quiet. Derek stared at his armor. On its shiny surface, he saw the reflection of a movement behind him.

Turning, he saw a woman dressed in a black cloak, her face concealed by the hood. She pushed it back.

"I must speak to you," Anne said.

Derek arched a brow at her.

"Sir Wilfred plans to kill you at the tournament."

"Yes, I know," Derek said.

"You do? Well, I must tell you he also intends to give you a tincture of corn-roses."

"So the rumor mill has informed me. Do you know how he will give it to me?"

"'Twill be in the ceremonial wine."

"And how will Sir Wilfred manage that?"

Anne averted her gaze. "Never mind. Just make sure to watch me. I will signal which cup to take."

Derek nodded, and she pulled the hood forward and left the chapel. When she was gone, he smiled cynically. So Anne was still trying to protect her mistress. Perhaps he should have told her it was useless, that he already knew, but he'd decided to keep silent. He'd confront her later—when he'd figured out a plan.

The door creaked open again. Cuthbert entered, gazing cautiously to the right and to the left.

Derek eyed him a trifle askance. The boy had barely spoken to him since Derek's repudiation of chivalry. Warily he waited.

"Godspeed, Sir Derek," Cuthbert said stiffly. "Duty compels me to warn you that there is a plot afoot to tamper with your wine at tomorrow's tournament."

"Oh?" Derek said. "And who is behind this nefarious scheme?"

"Honor prevents me from revealing the identity—"

"Honor, my ass. It's your precious Lady Allison, isn't it? She plans to drug me and Wilfred to kill me. Tell me, are you still convinced that she is all kindness and generosity?"

Cuthbert flushed, but his eyes still flashed. "I'm certain she has her reasons! You've never understood her. You've never even given her a chance—"

"I've more than given her a chance. She's betrayed me every time."

Cuthbert fell silent. Then he ventured, "I'm certain she has no idea Wilfred intends to kill you. I'm sure she means only to protect you—"

"She has an odd way of doing so." He saw that Cuthbert was about to protest. "Never mind. I don't want to argue with you. Will you help me or not?"

Cuthbert hesitated. "Perhaps I could challenge Sir Wilfred myself." His thin hands clenched and his eyes glowed with a fervent blue light. "I know I am not a match for him, but God watches out for those who are pure of heart and deed. Wilfred will be blinded by the light of Truth, Honor, and Chivalry—God will turn my sword into a flaming harbinger of justice, and Wilfred will cower beneath its power—"

"Let's not count on God for this particular problem, okay, Cuthbert? I think He expects us to use our own wits to resolve things, not go running to Him every time we have a little problem."

"A little problem?" The glow in Cuthbert's eyes dimmed. "I don't think I would call Sir Wilfred a little problem. More like a gigantic problem."

Derek shrugged. "Whatever. But we don't have to bother God." He looked up with a reassuring smile. "I've thought of a plan. And I'm sure Lady Anne will help. . . ."

That same night Allison stood on the battlements, looking over the dark countryside. She didn't come up here very often anymore, although it had been one of her favorite places as a child. Her grandmother had often scolded her, saying the narrow passage for the castle guards was dangerous. But Allison had loved being up so high. She had loved looking out across the fields and forests and knowing that one day they would be hers. She had looked forward to that day with all the excitement of innocence.

She didn't feel innocent now. She felt dirty and corrupt at the thought of the vile thing she planned to do. But do it she must. There was no other way to protect the castle.

"Being lady of the castle is an enormous responsibility," her grandmother had lectured her. "You must always think of the castle's needs, the people's needs, before your own."

Allison had tried to do so. She had just never expected the responsibility to weigh so heavily. It had been difficult at first, when her father retreated more and more often from his duties and obligations. She'd done her best to fill the void, to learn what needed to be done, but inevitably, she'd made mistakes. She'd angered some people and offended others, and it had seemed nothing she could do made everyone happy. She'd cried herself to sleep at nights, missing her mother, her grandparents, wondering how she could ever live up to being lady of Pelsworth Castle.

But she had. Eventually she had earned the people's respect. And along the way she had come to care for the castle and the people within in a way that was more meaningful and more important to her than she possibly could have imagined.

Now she almost hated it for what it was making her do.

How had it come to this? How had it all come down to this single point in time? She had tried so hard to protect Pelsworth Castle, to do what was right. Only somehow, nothing ever turned out the way she intended. Tomorrow would decide the fate of the castle and everyone in it. She could do nothing more.

A step behind her made her turn. Sir Drogo approached.

"My lady, 'tis late. You should be in bed."

"And so should you, sir." She looked at him, seeing as if for the first time, the tall, thin figure dressed in black. His fierce, bony features and beetling gray brows had frightened her as a child, but as she grew, she'd depended more and more on this man and his unwavering loyalty. After her grandparents' deaths, when her father had fallen apart and she was still learning, Sir Drogo had held the castle together almost single-handedly. He had stayed by her side through it all, even the dark days when Henry had tried to bring a bill of attainder against her father, and they'd all been at risk of losing their heads.

"Sir Drogo," she said, her voice husky. "I don't know if I have ever thanked you for everything you've done for my family."

Sir Drogo's brows rose, then descended in a scowl that Allison recognized hid his discomfort. "You need not thank me, my lady. I have always done my best. I know the men have complained at times that I was too strict—"

"No, you were right," she said. "'Twas needed. Everything was in disarray after my grandparents died. Without your help, Pelsworth Castle would have been lost long ago."

Sir Drogo still scowled, but she could see her words had pleased him. "It has always been my pleasure to serve you, my lady. I hope I may continue to do so for many years more."

"As do I, Sir Drogo," she murmured. "As do I."

The day of the tournament dawned bright and clear.

Squires rose early to polish and grease their masters' armor; to array the horses in harness, armor, long cloths, and saddles; and to dress the knights in their armor.

The "lists"—the field where the combat would take place—was ready, enclosed by a fence, where spectators were already lining up at prime positions. Red, yellow, and blue cloth draped the lodges where the lords and ladies would sit. Jugglers, acrobats, and minstrels entertained the gathering crowd, while peddlers, beggars, and pickpockets all plied their trades.

Inside the dimly lit chapel Derek knelt before Father Gregory, listening as the priest said mass over the armor on the altar. Derek didn't understand the words, but the rhythms and cadences reminded him of his harp music. He didn't pray, he just sat quietly, allowing the soothing sound to wash over him.

When the mass was finished, Father Gregory asked solemnly, "Do you, Derek Sinclair, swear now before God and man, to be brave and honorable, to uphold honor and truth, to right all wrongs, to protect women and children, to give aid and succor to those in distress, and to have mercy on the weak and defenseless?"

"I so swear," Derek said in a firm voice.

Cuthbert stepped forward and helped dress Derek in his armor. Lord Pelsworth belted on his sword, buckled golden spurs on his feet, and presented him with a shield painted with a coat of arms—a gold dragon protecting a castle on an azure field.

Derek knelt again and Henry struck him on the shoulder with the flat of his sword. "I hereby dub thee Sir Derek of Pelsworth. Go forth, Sir Derek, and fight bravely."

Derek walked out of the chapel, a strange energy flowing through his veins. He was a knight. An honest-to-God knight. Once, he might have derided the title, laughed at it. But now he felt only pride and a sense of accomplishment. He'd worked for the title, slaved for it, stretched himself to the limits of his endurance. No one could ever take the title from him. He'd earned it.

Outside, he saw Cuthbert, leading a charger richly caparisoned in blue and gold cloth. Derek leaped astride the saddle and nudged the charger toward the cavalcade of knights waiting to enter the lists.

A few minutes later trumpets and drums sounded as the procession moved forward.

First came the heralds, blowing their horns; then the squires, proudly displaying their masters' colors. And then finally the knights—fifty in all—their armor flashing in the sun.

Derek rode around the field with the others to the applause and shouts of the audience.

"Fight bravely and honorably!"

"Bring honor to thyself!"

"Think upon thy lady!"

Some of Derek's heady elation faded. He would rather *not* think of Allison, he thought as he passed the boxes where the ladies were blushing and throwing favors to their sweethearts—a veritable rainstorm of ribbons, belts, and handkerchiefs. The honored knights scooped up the items with their lances and attached them to their helmets.

But how could he not think of Allison when there she sat, looking so incredibly, impossibly, irresistibly beautiful?

She was dressed in an emerald green satin gown, worked with gold thread. A golden caul, encrusted with pearls, covered her hair, and her beringed fingers toyed with the jewel hanging around her neck—the Pelsworth Emerald.

She leaned toward Henry, seated at her side, nodding and smiling as he pointed to something in the procession. Her gaze drifted along the ranks of knights, stopping abruptly as she met his cold stare. Her lips still smiling, she pulled the glove from her hand and tossed it—straight to Wilfred.

Wilfred picked the glove up with his lance and attached it to his helmet—making him look rather like a rooster, Derek thought. Anger churning in his gut, he lined up with the knights in the center of the field. How could she sit there, smiling and waving innocently, when she was plotting such treachery?

He supposed it was a stupid question. Obviously she was a superb actress. Her performance since his arrival here had been nearly flawless.

Lord Pelsworth rose to his feet and held up a hand. Everyone grew silent.

"Welcome all! I bid ye, let this grand tournament, in honor of our good King Henry, begin!"

Derek rode with the rest of the procession off the field, grimly pushing all thoughts of Allison from his mind. He

must concentrate on the tournament for now—but once it
was over, he would deal with her as she deserved.

The knights reentered the field and were directed either to
the north or south side of the field for the opening game.

It was similar to a melee, but instead of the two teams of
knights merely trying to knock the opposing knights off
their horses, the team had to try to spear a ring at the far end
of the field.

Not too different from football.

Derek studied the knights facing him on the other side of
the field. Among them, he saw Harvey and Baldwin, the two
men who had beaten him up a year ago. They kept glancing
at him and whispering to the other knights. Derek had little
doubt as to what they were saying. He was certain Wilfred
had given instructions to his men that, if possible, they
should make sure Derek had a little "accident."

Derek looked around at the men on his own team. He had
spoken to them at length yesterday morning, and he was
pretty sure they all understood what to do. He hoped they
did, at least, or he might be in serious trouble.

In the stands Sir Percival raised a sword. "Sir Knights, be
at your ready!" he cried.

The two teams lowered their lances.

"Sir Knights!" the herald called. "In the king's name—do
your battle!"

The sword descended.

The horses reared and charged. The thundering of hooves
was almost deafening as the two teams rode directly at each
other.

A thunderclap of colliding horses and splintering wood
rang out across the field. Lances shattered, hurling chunks
of wood through the air. The crowd's roar could barely be
heard.

A flank of knights moved in perfect formation to the right,
blocking Wilfred's men. Derek spurred his horse along the
narrow passage left, so close to the fence that the dirt from
his horse's hooves sprayed the people standing there.

Wilfred's men, seeing what was happening, charged to
the end of the line. Quickly the Pelsworth knights broke

ranks, allowing Derek to slip through and charge toward the middle of the field where Sir Wilfred was surrounded by another group of Pelsworth knights.

Derek circled them and charged toward the ring.

A cry went up from the opposing knights as they saw how he had evaded them. They tried to go after him, but the other flank of Pelsworth knights blocked them. Only one of them managed to slip through—Sir Harvey. He raced after Derek.

But Derek had a good lead. He looked toward his goal. One knight stood between him and the ring—Sir Baldwin. Holding his lance steady, Derek charged the massive knight. The blow caught Sir Baldwin squarely on the chest—he went down like a rock.

The clash slowed Derek momentarily. Harvey was right on his heels. Derek nudged his horse with his knees again, urging it forward at a full gallop. He could see the small gold ring glinting in the sunlight.

It would be easier to spear the ring if he slowed his horse. But the thunder of hooves behind him told him that he could not allow himself that luxury. Without any break in speed, he rode straight at the ring, his lance held steady under his arm.

The point of his lance speared the ring. He pulled back on the reins, and his charger reared. Derek held the lance high.

The crowd roared.

But before the trumpeters could blow a signal that the game was ended, Harvey spurred his horse forward, his lance aimed directly at Derek's back.

The spectators' applause turned to cries of horror. The trumpets blew, but Harvey didn't stop his headlong charge.

In a flash Derek wheeled his horse and raised his shield, barely in time. Without pausing, Derek swung his lance around, blocking the charging knight.

The lance caught Harvey across his chest, knocking him from his horse to land flat on his back.

The crowd cheered.

Triumphantly Derek cantered around the field, his lance with the ring raised in the air.

Allison watched him, her pulse still thudding from the excitement of the game. He'd ridden with such skill, such daring, she could not help but admire his prowess. But at the same time, her dread increased. Now, more than ever, she saw that she must carry through with her plan to drug the wine. Wilfred would never be able to defeat him in a fair fight.

The game over, Sir Percival called an intermission so that the field could be cleared of debris and injured knights tended to. Harvey and Baldwin, lurching to their feet, limped off the field, accompanied by the jeers of the crowd.

The victorious knights approached the lodges to claim their prizes and rest before the jousting started. Derek, as the knight who'd speared the ring, was invited to sit in the box during the intermission—next to Allison.

Her heart sank as he removed his helmet and sat down. She took a cake and some wine from the tray offered by a servant and did her best to ignore Derek.

He didn't make it easy.

He spoke to the king across her, laughing when Henry complimented him on his strategy in the game. He was full of life and vitality, and Allison felt sick inside at the thought of what she must shortly do.

She felt even sicker when she saw Wilfred approaching.

He bowed before her, his thick black hair still dripping with sweat. "Lady Allison," he said in a loud voice. "Fear not—I will do you honor in the jousting. This melee is a child's game. There are those who use a coward's guile to win, instead of fighting fairly."

Derek smiled, but his voice was menacing as he said, "Oh, I'll fight you, Sir Wilfred. But when I do, I want to make certain none of your men are around to stab me in the back."

Wilfred turned red with fury.

Ignoring him, Derek rose to his feet. "Now, if you will excuse me, Sire, I must prepare for the jousting."

He strolled away, and Allison watched him go, her stomach twisting.

"Don't worry, my lady," Wilfred whispered. "He will not be so cocky when I've finished with him."

Allison nodded faintly, and he left, also. She couldn't bear this, she thought unsteadily. She wanted it to be over with. She wanted Sir Percival to call the knights for the jousting immediately. . . .

She was forced to wait, however, for nearly an hour. Tension coiled more and more tightly in her stomach until she was almost ill from it. When Sir Percival finally called out, "Bring on the jousts!" she nearly wept with relief.

"Let Sir Everard and Sir Lawrence come forward!" the herald called.

The two knights approached the lodges on foot and drank a ceremonial toast to the king before returning to their respective ends of the field.

From the seat behind her, Allison heard Emmeline say, "There's Papa, Mama! Oh, does he not look splendid?"

"Yes, indeed, dear," Lady Humfrey replied proudly as her husband cantered out onto the field.

The two knights charged each other, and their lances met. There was a crack of wood and Sir Everard fell to the ground. Lady Humfrey and Emmeline cried out, and the crowd groaned.

Allison gripped the arms of her chair as a squire ran out to tend Sir Everard. To her relief, Sir Everard rose to his feet and walked off the field, uninjured.

Other knights, in the matches that followed, however, were not so lucky. Several had bones broken. Others bled profusely. One had to be carried off the field on a stretcher.

Each time one of the Pelsworth men fell, Allison felt a little bit ill. Was it her imagination, or were Wilfred's men overly brutal? As the injuries mounted, Allison's tension grew, and a new worry took hold of her.

How long would it take the tincture to work after Derek drank it? Would he be on his horse when it took effect? What if he fell from his horse and was seriously injured, or even killed? If that happened, how would she ever be able to live with herself?

These and a thousand other questions raced through her brain. She wanted to flee from the lodge and the lists before Derek came to the field. She wanted to hide from the ugly thing she must do to save Pelsworth Castle—

"Let Sir Wilfred and Sir Derek come forward!" the herald cried.

Wilfred and Derek approached the lodge and knelt before the king.

"Rise, Sir Knights." To the servant at the edge of the field, the king said, "Bring forth the wine!"

The servant approached, and Henry announced in ringing tones to the crowd, "This battle will decide which of these brave knights will wed the Lady Allison. To honor them both, she has offered to pour the wine herself."

The crowd cheered wildly.

For a moment Allison couldn't move. Then, she took a deep breath and rose to her feet. She stepped out onto the field and approached the servant who stood in front of the two knights. She glanced at them quickly—Wilfred, grinning, his hairy face dripping with sweat, his eyes small, mean and cruel. And Derek, sweating also but clean shaven, his mouth unsmiling, his brown eyes cold, hard and unforgiving.

Her chest tight, she lowered her gaze, and quickly poured a few drops of the tincture into one of the cups, her sleeve concealing the vial and her action. Then she picked up the flagon of wine. Her hands shaking, she poured it. The servant took the tray and turned to the two men.

To her horror, Derek reached across the tray and took the cup without the tincture.

Quickly she stepped forward and pretended to stumble, knocking against his arm and causing him to spill the wine. Blood-red liquid splashed against his armor.

"I beg your pardon," she said calmly, her nerves screaming. "I will pour some more."

She put the cup on the tray and poured again. Stepping forward, she blocked Derek so that Wilfred could take a cup first. He seized the one with the unadulterated wine.

She turned to Derek. Glancing up, she saw him watching her, a cynical smile on his lips. She grew still.

Dear God. He knew.

Something shriveled inside of her. How had he found out? Guilt and shame and despair filled her. She wanted to run and hide.

But she couldn't. She had to carry through. But how? What could she do now? He would never drink the wine. But he must. He *must*.

Pasting a smile on her face, she lifted the cup from the tray and held it to his lips.

To the watching crowd, it appeared a gesture of favor. They cheered their approval.

The noise became a buzzing as Allison met his gaze. His burning eyes stared straight into hers, full of terrible accusation. For a moment she thought he would refuse to drink. But then he placed his warm hands over her icy fingers, holding the cup steady as he opened his mouth and drank the entire contents.

She returned to her seat, shaking. She should be relieved that he'd drunk the wine. But she wasn't. She almost wished he had refused and the consequences be damned. How he must hate her. How she hated herself.

The two men rode to opposite sides of the field, and wheeled their horses to face each other. They lowered their visors. They charged.

Nausea churned in Allison's stomach.

The sound of wood striking metal rang through the air, making her want to cover her ears. She watched in terror as Wilfred's lance struck Derek's shield squarely in the middle, only to glance off. Derek's lance splintered with the force of his return blow.

"Fairly broken!" cried the crowd. "Well done!"

The recoil as the men struck each others' shields was strong enough to force the horses back on their haunches amid a shower of turf.

Both men held their seats, however. Allison didn't know whether to be glad or sorry as they rode back to their respective starting points. She wanted this to end before Derek was hurt. She looked at him—he was wheeling his horse around to face Wilfred again, apparently unaffected by the tincture. How much longer, she wondered frantically, before it took effect?

Derek grabbed a new lance and charged again.

Wilfred met him at the center of the field.

The thunderous sound of their blows rang out. Both lances splintered this time, sending chunks of wood flying through the air. The spectators, lined up at the fences, ducked and shielded their faces as splinters rained down on them.

"Well struck!" roared the crowd in approval. "A brave course!"

The two knights faced each other for the third time.

Allison could not bear to watch. She closed her eyes as they charged.

The ground vibrated with the pounding of hoofbeats; the clash of wood and metal rang through the air; the crowd cried out.

Her eyes flew open.

Wilfred's blow had broken his lance again—and Derek was reeling under the force of it. He had slid sideways in his saddle and was nearly on the ground. If he fell, Wilfred would win the contest.

For several long moments she watched with the crowd as he struggled to regain his seat. The heavy armor weighed him down, making it nearly impossible to right himself. He strained again and again, until, with a sudden lunge, he pulled himself upright.

Cheers rang out. "Nobly done! Bravely fought!"

Allison slumped back in her chair. Why couldn't he have fallen? Then this madness would be over. Now, with three broken lances, the two men would be forced to fight hand to hand. Oh, why wasn't the tincture working?

The squires ran out to take the horses as the two knights dismounted and drew their swords.

The sound of metal clashing against metal rang out across the field. Derek's sword struck Wilfred's shield time and time again, denting the steel and chipping paint from the image of a black boar on a red field.

Slowly, but surely, Derek drove Wilfred back across the field.

Then, a child darted under the fence, distracting Derek for an instant before the mother caught the boy. Wilfred, taking immediate advantage, struck a blow directly to Derek's breastplate. Derek fell to the ground with a crash, his helmet flying off and his shield falling into the dirt. Mud splattered across the dragon and castle.

His head flopped back, and Allison saw a trickle of blood on his forehead. Her nails bit into her palms. He lay completely still, showing no signs of consciousness.

Wilfred grunted in satisfaction and pulled off his own helmet. He raised his sword over his head.

The crowd gasped as his intention became clear—he was going to cut off Derek's head.

Allison's brain could not accept what she was seeing. The edges of her vision grew blurry. She felt as though she was seeing everything from a great distance, but at the same time, the details remained sharp and clear.

Wilfred's sword seemed to be moving with agonizing slowness as it descended toward its target.

With the blade only a few hand spans away from accomplishing its goal, Derek opened his eyes.

Looking up at Sir Wilfred, he smiled.

Chapter 27

WILFRED'S EYES WIDENED, but he did not stop his downward slash.

In a flash Derek rolled to one side, Wilfred's sword glancing off his armor to strike the dirt with a dull thud. Grabbing his shield and sword, he leaped to his feet, swinging his sword around to land a solid blow to Wilfred's back.

Wilfred staggered forward, his apelike face wearing a stunned expression that made Derek want to laugh.

"You appear surprised," he said mockingly, moving quickly forward to make another thrust. "Did you really think I was stupid enough to drink tampered wine?"

Regaining his wits, Wilfred brought his shield up and blocked Derek's blade. "You should have drunk it," he snarled through clenched teeth. "Your death would have been painless then. But I will enjoy watching you suffer before you die."

Derek's smile did not falter as Wilfred made a vicious thrust. He blocked it easily, feeling no fear, only the elation of meeting his enemy and fighting him on equal terms.

He hammered Wilfred with his sword, striking blow after blow. He was vaguely aware of the sun pounding down on his head and the smell of freshly churned grass in his nostrils; the increasing heaviness of his arms and the sting of sweat in his eyes. But he paid little attention. His entire concentration, his entire being, was focused on one thing—on defeating Wilfred.

Wilfred, sweat pouring down his face, defended himself as best he could, but he was helpless under the onslaught. His face grew gray with fear as he realized he could not possibly beat Derek. Derek heard him gasping for breath, the sound harsh and heavy.

Wilfred stepped back again, just as Derek struck another blow which slipped past Wilfred's guard and caught him off balance. Wilfred fell back, landing hard in the dust, his sword and shield flying from his hands.

In a flash Derek put the point of his sword to the other man's neck. "Yield, Sir Wilfred, before I do the world a favor and kill you."

"I yield," Wilfred said, his voice choked.

Derek lifted his sword, fierce exultation coursing through his veins. A year ago this man's attack had left Derek shaken and afraid for his life. Now Wilfred lay in the dirt, humbled and defeated. Derek felt strong, powerful, invincible. Victory was indeed sweet.

Stepping back, he allowed Wilfred to rise. The defeated knight stalked off the field.

Then a laughing, cheering crowd surrounded Derek, eager hands lifting him up and carrying him triumphantly to the lodge where the king sat.

"You have done well, Sir Derek," King Henry said, smiling. "And your reward is, of course, the Lady Allison's hand in marriage."

With obvious reluctance Allison put her hand in Derek's gauntleted one.

Lord Pelsworth beamed. "I knew you could do it! I have arranged for the marriage to take place one month from today."

"Why wait?" Derek asked, his gaze on Allison's downcast eyes.

Her lashes flew up. He could see the fear in her eyes. He

smiled cruelly. "I have already waited a year, I would as soon wait no longer. With your permission, sire, my lord, I would wed the Lady Allison today, this very moment."

"But . . . but . . ." she stammered.

The king smiled. "True Love is impatient, 'twould appear. You have earned your reward. Summon the priest and let us proceed to the chapel!"

Allison couldn't believe what was happening. Still reeling from the failure of her plan and from Wilfred's treachery in attempting to kill Derek, she numbly allowed herself to be swept along.

She didn't hear a word of the nuptial mass. She mumbled incoherent responses to the vows, but no one seemed to notice or care. It wasn't until it was over and she saw the cruel triumph blazing in Derek's eyes that she began to tremble. She trembled so much that Derek had to put his arm around her waist to prevent her from falling as he escorted her to the hall and the waiting feast.

Allison sat through the presentation of the salt, the cutting of the upper crust from the bread, the washing of the guests' hands, and the testing of the wine. She sat through the toasts and the blessing of the food. She sat through dish after dish of fantastical foods, and entertainment after entertainment.

She ate little, aware of Derek's cold gaze upon her. He played the perfect knight, offering her succulent pieces of meat and sharing his cup with her, but the frozen knot in her stomach only grew larger. It all seemed like a horrible nightmare.

She wished fervently that the feast was over—but then, remembering what would happen afterward, she prayed it would never end.

God ignored her plea.

All too soon the women came and laughingly pulled her upstairs and bathed her and dressed her in a fine nightgown. Still giggling, they sprinkled primroses on the floor and in the bed and left the room.

Barely had they departed than the men pushed Derek inside and slammed the door shut. Their rowdy laughter retreated through the outer chamber and the anteroom to the stairs.

The candlelit room grew quiet as the two newlyweds stared at each other.

Chapter 28

"COME HERE, *WIFE*."

He saw her shiver at his brusque words, but then she straightened her back and all expression disappeared from her face. She walked slowly toward him, stopping just out of reach, standing straight and proud.

Her lack of fear angered him. She should be cowering now, begging for forgiveness. She should be praying that he wouldn't beat her as any other man in this age would most likely do. Instead she stood there, the candlelight casting a soft golden aura over her hair and skin, making her almost seem to glow. She had looked very similar that long ago night in Nan's cottage. Innocent. Seductive.

"Well?" he said harshly. "Have you nothing to say for yourself? No pretty excuses, no more of your lies?"

"Do your worst." She tilted her chin up, causing the light to ripple down the length of her hair. "I expect no more from a false knight like you."

Her audacity amazed and infuriated him. He took a step forward, his booted foot crushing one of the small yellow flowers on the floor. "You dare call *me* false? After what you did today?"

"What else could I do?" she asked fiercely, her hands clenching into fists. "You made it clear you planned to abandon me. How could I marry you?"

"How could you indeed? Much more convenient to have me dead and out of the picture."

Her small white teeth bit into the fullness of her lower lip. "Wilfred promised not to hurt you. I had no idea he intended to break his word."

"Yeah, right. You think I'm going to believe you after all the lies you've told?"

A delicate pink color rose from the scooped neckline of her gown and traveled upward to her pale cheeks. "It's true I have not always been honest with you. But I only did what was necessary to protect the castle—and you."

"Me!"

"Yes, you. If I wanted to kill you, I could have easily poisoned the wine today." She gave a bitter laugh. "If I wanted to kill you, I certainly would have left you to rot in the dungeon a year ago instead of prodding you out of your despair."

He gazed at her incredulously. "Are you trying to make me believe that you said what you did out of *kindness*?"

Her fingers toyed with the bow that primly tied the neckline of her nightgown together. "I know it sounds ridiculous, but Rafael thought the only way to reach you was to make you angry."

Derek's eyes narrowed a bit at the mention of the minstrel's name, but he still wasn't convinced—not by a long shot. "Come on, Allison. We both know that when you lured me back here, you fully expected I would not survive."

"What are you talking about?" Her fingers grew still for a moment. "I didn't 'lure' you here. I never saw you before that day you appeared at my betrothal feast."

He gave a snort of disbelief. "Are you trying to change your story at this late date? You already admitted that you know everything. Your 'dreams,' remember?"

"Why are you so determined to make a fuss about those dreams? I remember parts—I remember a room with strange furniture and I remember . . . kissing a man who looks like you. I remember asking people for help. And I remember seeing . . . my father's and my deaths and an old woman urging me to find my True Love and save the castle. The dreams were very real. But they were only dreams, I never believed them. Except sometimes, you would say something strange, and I almost thought they were. . . ."

He watched her fingers begin worrying the bow again. "You expect me to believe that?"

"Believe what you like."

Frowning, he stared at her averted face. She made it all sound so plausible—could she be telling the truth?

Unexpectedly a memory flashed into his brain—of the shy hesitation in her eyes as she gave him the linen shirt made from her mother's flax. She had offered it to him as though it were some rare and precious treasure. He'd been too angry at the time to pay much attention to her reaction, but now he remembered the blank, still expression on her face as he ground the gift into the floor with his heel.

His frown deepened. He didn't understand her. He never had. He only knew she could make him more furious than any woman he'd ever known. Perhaps because she meant more to him than any woman he'd ever known. . . .

Hell and damnation. What was he thinking? The heavy scent of the flowers strewn about the room must be affecting his brain. She had teased him, taunted him, mocked him, and nearly killed him. It was insane to still want her.

But he did.

Now, here she stood, clad in nothing but a thin nightgown.

Without thinking, he reached out and put his hand on her shoulder. With a cry she pulled away.

She faced him, her eyes angry and defiant, her breasts rising and falling with the force of her breathing.

Derek's gaze dropped to her gown. He stared at the thrust of her breasts against the fabric.

How could he stay angry at her when he wanted her so much?

"Allison," he said. His voice was low and husky, all anger gone from it. "Take off your nightgown."

"No." She crossed her arms over her breasts. "If you're going to rape me, please hurry and be done with it."

Derek frowned, startled by the ugly word. He'd never thought of it in those terms. "Allison, I don't want to rape you. I would never hurt you like that."

She averted her face, not responding.

"I want you, Allison. I've wanted you . . . God, it seems like forever. Remember that time I kissed you in the tapestry room? I could have killed Rafael when he interrupted. You were so sweet. So sensual. I wanted to keep on kissing you forever. I was dying for you, Allie. The smallest thing would have made me happy. Just the sight of you naked would have made me happy. Do you know how I suffered when the torch went out in the dungeon?"

A slight blush rose in her cheeks.

"And then in your bedroom—if it hadn't been for those damn guards, I would have made love to you there."

Her lips parted. He could see a pulse fluttering in her throat.

"Do you remember the pool, Allie? Do you know how much I wanted to look? Do you know what torture it was to help you with that dress, when I wanted nothing so much as to strip it off you? Do you know what an obsession it has become with me to see you naked?"

She didn't answer.

"Allie . . . take off your nightgown."

"No." She hugged herself more tightly.

"Then let me." He stepped closer to her, his hand going to the bow at her neckline.

Gasping, she covered his hand with both of her own, preventing him from untying the bow.

"Allie, can't we put the past behind us, just for this one night? Let me love you just this once, Allie. Tomorrow we can go back to hating each other, but for tonight let's pretend that we don't. Let's pretend that we love each other more than anything else in the world. Please, Allie, let me take off your nightgown."

She hesitated, her gaze searching his face. He wasn't sure what she saw there, but slowly she lowered her hands.

Equally slowly, giving her a chance to change her mind, he tugged at the bow.

She didn't speak, but he saw her breathing quicken as he pushed the nightgown down over her shoulders. It slipped down, catching at her hips.

Derek's breath stuck in his lungs.

Her breasts were round and full, with large rosy pink nipples. Her waist curved inward, the smooth flesh glowing in the candlelight. He dislodged the nightgown, and it fell to the floor. Settling his hands on her hips, he looked at her, feeling light-headed. Her belly was softly rounded above a thatch of light brown, softly curling hair. Her hips were round, also, and tapered down to long, lean flanks, dimpled knees, and small, narrow feet.

God, she was beautiful.

She stood before him, her head high, making no effort to cover herself. Half mesmerized, he slid his hands up over her rounded hips, into the curve of her waist, then up the smoothness of her rib cage to cup her breasts. Glancing up at her face, he saw a faint blush rise in her cheeks, and the midnight blue of her eyes darken.

Deliberately, he leaned forward and flicked his tongue across her nipple.

A slight gasp escaped her lips, but he paid no attention. A sense of urgency surged through him. He lifted her and laid her on the bed. The sight of her lying there, the scent of flowers rising around her, made his senses swim. He began removing his own clothes, his fingers fumbling on the points. Cursing under his breath, he broke the leather strings and stripped off his clothes, before joining her on the bed.

Wherever he touched, there was softness.

He kissed her everywhere, lingering wherever she squirmed or sighed. He kissed the peaks of her breasts, the curve of her waist, and the softness of her belly. He kissed the roundness of her hips and the smoothness of her thighs, paying particular attention to the sweetness in between. He kissed the dimples in her knees, the arches of her feet and the palms of her hands. He kissed the crook of her elbow, the hollow of her shoulder, and the pulse in her throat. Her nipples grew taut and dark red, her skin warm and flushed, under the ministrations of his mouth and hands. He thought he would never get enough of the sweet smell of her, the exquisite feel of her, the delectable taste of her.

He returned his mouth to her lips, kissing her deeply. "Touch me," he whispered against her lips.

Hesitantly at first, but then with increasing eagerness, she ran her hands over his shoulders and chest, her fingers lingering in the rough hair there and brushing against the small flat nipples similar to but so different from her own.

He sighed with pleasure. "Keep going, Allie," he said huskily.

Her fingers traced the line of hair that descended to his navel, then continued lower, hovering for a moment just above him. He held his breath, wondering if she would be bold enough to go all the way, wondering if she knew how she was torturing him.

Her hand closed around him, and his breath escaped in a groan. Her fingers stroked and caressed him until a fireball seemed to explode inside him. Dear God, he had wanted this, wanted *her*, for so damned long. The pent-up strength and fury of his desire roiled through him with the force of a tornado.

Pulling her hand away, he moved over her and parted her legs.

"Derek . . ." She made a slight gulping noise.

"Hush, Allie," he murmured, trailing kisses from her lips to her ear and back again. "It will be all right. I promise. Let me make love to you." He stroked her between her legs.

She gasped and squirmed under his touch. "Derek . . ."

"Yes, Allie?" He poised himself at the brink of her.

"Will you stay?"

He stared down at her. Her eyes were dark, nearly black in the soft candlelight, her mouth red with his kisses. The blood pounded through him, urgent and inexorable.

"Yes," he whispered. "I'll stay."

He lowered his mouth to her and kissed her deeply, passionately. At the same moment he plunged forward.

Into sweet heaven.

* * *

Sometime later, after the glow of lovemaking had dissipated, Derek stared up at the canopy above him. Allison slumbered peacefully at his side, but he was wide awake, sleep eluding him. Extricating himself from her arms, he rose to stand beside the bed.

He gazed down at her for a moment, a crease between his brows. In the dim candlelight she lay on her side, her face flushed, a smile on her lips. She looked relaxed, content.

He supposed he should be content, too. He'd gotten what he'd wanted for so long. His body felt relaxed, satiated.

So why did the rest of him feel so dissatisfied?

He turned and walked over to the window where the morning sun was just peeking through. A glint of green on the sill caught his eye. The emerald.

He picked it up and turned it between his fingers.

He could go home now—but only if he broke his word. He had told her he would stay. He had vowed in the chapel to cherish and protect her. Once, the promises would have meant nothing to him. But something had changed. He had changed.

All of the nonsense about chivalry and honor that he had mocked for so long had somehow taken root inside him.

He could root it out right now. He could break his vows, and go back to the future, back to pizza and beer and cigarettes. He could go back to what he had been before.

But the thought of his old life was strangely unappealing. He didn't want that life. It seemed empty and aimless.

And yet . . . what was there for him here? He could stay with Allison and be lord of the castle. He was certain she would accept him—just as she would have accepted Wilfred or any other man capable of protecting the castle. In spite of their passion, nothing was settled here. Perhaps she'd told him the truth that she didn't remember everything that had happened in the future, but where did they go from there?

He didn't know what she felt for him. Nor did he know what he felt for her. He'd thought he loved her a year ago; but she'd killed those feelings with her words in the dungeon.

But that love had been a shallow thing, an emotion that would have lasted only as long as the two of them faced no hardships. It would have survived only a short while.

Now he felt . . . what? Passion, certainly. But love? How could he love someone who cared more about a pile of rock and stone than she did him?

"Derek!"

The strangled cry made him turn toward the bed. Allison was tossing and turning. Swiftly he crossed the room and took her into his arms. He could feel tears on her face. "What is it? What's wrong?"

"I . . . I had a dream. A horrible dream. I was married to Wilfred, and it was terrible—so terrible. And then the castle was attacked. People were being killed all around me. My father, Sir Drogo, Cuthbert . . . all slaughtered. It was horrible."

"Shh," he whispered. "It was only a dream."

"Are you sure? It seemed so real."

"I'm sure, Allie. Go back to sleep."

She relaxed in his arms, and soon her breathing became soft and even. Derek lay down beside her and stared up at the canopy.

Sleep continued to elude him.

Chapter 29

ALLISON WOKE TO the sound of a lute. She smiled sleepily, wondering if Derek had asked Rafael to play outside their door. She turned to ask him.

He wasn't there.

She sat up abruptly, her feeling of peace vanishing, and looked around the room. Still no sign of him. Where had he gone?

A sudden fear assailed her. He had said he would leave her as soon as they were married. Was that why he wasn't here? Had he left?

Her heart feeling as though it were being squeezed, she got up and peeked out the door. "Rafael, have you seen my husband?"

His brows rose. "Indeed I have. He was summoned by the king. I am to tell you he will return shortly."

Relief flowed through her. "Oh, thank you." She closed the door and leaned back against it. How foolish she was. Of course he hadn't left her. He wouldn't—not after last night.

She smiled dreamily. Last night had been . . . heaven. She

had never known that such passion, such pleasure existed. She couldn't wait to experience it again. . . .

A flash of green from the windowsill caught her eye.

Slowly she walked over and looked down at the Pelsworth emerald lying on the sill.

She stared at it, remembering the dream she'd had last night and the ones before. Derek had implied more than once that her dreams were true—and she'd scoffed at the notion. But somewhere at the back of her mind, she'd always wondered—*could* they be true? Was she having dreams that foretold the future?

It didn't seem possible. And yet, there were so many things Derek had known—about the promise her father had made to her mother. About Sir Boris and about the things she'd dreamt. About the emerald and the stories of its magic . . .

She stared down at the jewel, a frown knitting her brow. She remembered Derek standing in her bedroom with the emerald in his hand, saying, "Take me home."

A shiver coursed down her spine. She remembered the stories her grandparents had told her of the emerald's magic. That was all they had been—stories. And Derek had promised to stay with her—she remembered that clearly.

Her frown deepened. She had better put the emerald away. It wasn't wise to leave such a valuable jewel sitting out.

She walked over to the spinning wheel in the corner and unscrewed the right front leg. She placed the emerald in the hollow there, then carefully screwed the leg back on.

Then, too restless to wait for Derek's return, she summoned a maid to help her dress.

The king and Lord Pelsworth were waiting for Derek in the library, their faces solemn. Derek grew still when he saw the man standing with them.

It was the messenger Henry had hired to find the truth about Derek's claim.

"This man brings disturbing news," Henry said.

Derek braced himself. "Sire, I can explain—"

"Sir Derek," Lord Pelsworth interrupted, "perhaps you should hear the man's news before you say anything."

Derek, his brows raised, turned to the messenger.

The messenger cleared his throat. "I have informed the king that California does indeed exist. However . . . there was a terrible earthquake and it sank into the ocean!"

The king signaled the messenger to leave and laid a hand on Derek's shoulder. "This is distressing news for you. Your home, your people . . . all lost."

Derek shaded his eyes with his hand. "We've heard for years that California might sink into the ocean—although none of us really believed . . ." He made a choking noise. "Will you excuse me, Sire?"

"Of course," Henry said.

With a bow Derek left. He hurried down the stairs and into the courtyard. Once there, he leaned weakly against a wall, trying not to laugh too loudly. But after a while he sobered. What on earth . . . ? Why had the messenger lied?

As if in answer to his question, he saw the man walking by. Derek quickly collared him.

"That was interesting news about California," he said.

The man eyed him a bit warily. "Aye."

"But we both know it isn't true." Derek leaned closer. "So why did you lie?"

The messenger shrugged, then said, "Lady Allison offered a very generous bribe."

"Lady *Allison*?"

The man nodded. "Aye. Lord Pelsworth's wasn't bad, either. Lady Anne's, Lady Ursula's, Lady Mountford's, and Lady Humfrey's—oh, and all the squires', too—their contributions were appreciated, also. Sir Wilfred's offering, however," the man said scornfully, "was extremely pitiful." He straightened his doublet and glanced around a trifle warily. "Speaking of which, I had best be on my way. Sir Wilfred's bribe included a very unpleasant threat."

Derek half smiled. "I will send an escort with you till you are safely out of the shire."

"Thank you, Sir Derek. I will—"

Before the man could finish his sentence, there was a shout. Derek turned to see a pack of mounted men ride through the castle gate, swords drawn.

* * *

The maid had just tied Allison's caul in place when shouts sounded from the courtyard. Allison ran to the window to see chaos. Chickens and geese scattered before the on-slaught of a company of mounted men whose armor and shields bore no identifying marks. Pelsworth knights, buck-ling on their armor, scrambled for weapons. The clash of metal on metal rang out, and screams rose from around the house.

The blood drained from Allison's face. The scene was just like her dream—

Dear heaven, *no*.

She ran down the stairs to the library. As she entered, she saw a knight thrust his sword at her unarmed father. Lord Pelsworth sank slowly to the ground.

"Father!" Allison flew to his side and fell to her knees. Blood seeped from the wound in his shoulder. She tore the sleeve from her arm and pressed it against the deep cut. His breathing grew more shallow.

"My child . . . I am so sorry . . . so sorry for everything. I loved your mother so much . . . I was a fool. . . ."

He grew still.

"Father! Oh, Father, you cannot die. You can't leave me, too." Burying her face in her arms on his chest, she sobbed, tears running down her face.

"You're too late, Lady Allison. The old man is dead."

Shock rippled through Allison at the familiar voice, steal-ing her breath and erasing her tears. Slowly she looked up at the knight as he lifted his visor.

Wilfred's cruel face smiled down at her.

She stared at him a moment, rage and anger sweeping away her grief. "Murderer!" she screamed.

He laughed. "The old man deserved to die. He almost ru-ined my plans."

"What plans? What are you talking about?"

"To take control of this castle—and to kill Henry."

"Kill Henry? Are you mad?"

"Not at all. Perkin Warbeck will reward his supporters richly once he is king. We've schemed to seize power for a long time. This may not be exactly what we planned, but it will do. Especially since I will have my prize after all."

His eyes, hot and lustful, drifted over her.

She rose to her feet. "You cannot be serious."

"Oh, but I am. I'll have to kill you afterward, but I intended to do so anyway."

Without another word, she fled.

With a laugh he was after her.

But his armor and the sword hindered him on the narrow, circular stairs. She raced into her bedchamber ahead of him and slammed the door. She sought to drop the bar into place, but before she could do so, the door was shoved open with a force that sent her flying to the floor.

Laughing, the bloody sword still in one hand, Wilfred fumbled at his mail skirt with the other.

Allison closed her eyes. She would not scream.

She would not scream.

"Excuse me, Sir Wilfred, but I think you've got the wrong room."

Allison's eyes flew open.

Derek stood in the open doorway, a sword in his hand.

She cried out with joy.

His eyes flickered to her. His face hardened, and he returned his gaze to Wilfred.

Wilfred grinned.

"So I am going to get to kill you after all, Sinclair."

"You're welcome to try," Derek said.

Wilfred laughed. "You have no armor, you fool."

Allison's eyes widened as she realized the truth of Wilfred's words. Derek didn't even have a shield.

Wilfred made a sudden thrust.

Derek dodged it, stepping quickly back.

Allison scurried out of his way, into the corner by the spinning wheel, watching with horror as Wilfred thrust again.

Derek blocked it, the sound of clashing metal ringing through the room. With barely a pause, he made his own thrust, slamming his blade against Wilfred's hip.

The blow didn't faze Wilfred at all.

Fear coiled in the pit of Allison's stomach. Derek's movements were quick and skillful, unhindered by heavy armor—but without the protective suit, it would take only one blow to kill him. One mistake, and he would be dead.

Allison stared at him as he blocked another of Wilfred's thrusts. He had appeared in her life out of nowhere, with his laughing eyes and his outlandish tales.

She had thought his presence endangered Pelsworth Castle. But now, seeing Wilfred for what he truly was, she realized Derek had been protecting it. Unwittingly perhaps. Unwillingly, most assuredly. He had almost been killed several times.

And she knew, suddenly, that she couldn't ask him to risk his life again. She loved him too much.

Tears streaming down her face, she grabbed hold of the spinning wheel leg where the emerald was hidden, watching as Derek drew back his sword to make a thrust. "I wish Derek Sinclair back to his own time and place!"

A brilliant light flashed through the room. Instinctively Allison held up her hand to block it. When the light faded, she lowered her hand and looked around. Derek had disappeared.

Wilfred, his sword raised to block the blow that never came, looked around in confusion.

There was no sign of Derek.

Tears rolled down Allison's cheeks. It had worked! He was safe!

For a moment happiness and relief sang through her blood.

The singing changed to dread, however, when Wilfred's gaze fell upon her.

A feral light in his eyes, he raised his sword. "If I can't kill Sinclair, then I suppose I will just have to kill you. . . ."

Chapter 30

Nan's cottage was shadowy and quiet, except for the muffled sounds coming from the two figures entwined on the sofa. There was a groan and a soft sigh.

"Charles . . . oh, Charles—"

A breeze fluttered through the room. It grew stronger and stronger until the couple on the sofa looked up in confusion.

Suddenly a brilliant flash of light lit up the entire room.

The woman let out a little scream and huddled back against the sofa, clutching her gaping clothes. Charles, with an oath, leaped to his feet as a man suddenly appeared in the middle of the room.

The light dissipated, leaving only the firelight to illuminate the man thrusting a deadly looking sword at Charles.

Instinctively Charles grabbed the lamp and held it up to block the sword, catching a glimpse of the man's face as he did so. He froze.

"Derek?"

Derek pulled back the sword barely in time. He glanced around in confusion. "Shit!" he swore. "Little fool!"

Charles stared at him. "Derek, is that you? Where the hell

have you been? Do you have any idea how worried we've been? Must you always be so damned irrespons—"

"Hold your tongue, Charles, before I cut it out of your head."

Charles's mouth fell open. The woman gasped. Derek glanced at her, then did a double-take. "Eleanor?"

For a moment Derek thought she would hide behind Charles, but then she straightened and eyed him coolly. "Hello, Derek. It's nice to see you again."

"And you, also." He was having difficulty forming the words. Their speech sounded alien to him. "I hate to be rude, but I must go."

"Go? Go where? Where have you been?"

Derek ignored Charles's questions. His entire being was focused on only one thing—returning to Allison. He had to get the emerald and return immediately. . . .

The emerald. For a moment despair overwhelmed him. She must have been wearing it when she wished him here . . . but no, he was certain she hadn't been. So how had she caused him to return?

He knew she'd been huddled in the corner by the spinning wheel, but he couldn't remember what she'd been doing. His attention had been wholly focused on defeating Wilfred. But if she hadn't been wearing the emerald, it must have been hidden somewhere nearby. Under a floorboard, perhaps? Behind a brick in the wall? He replayed the scene in his mind—Wilfred's thrust, his own block; then from the corner of his eye, as he drew back his arm, he had seen her reach for . . .

The spinning wheel.

He looked over in the corner. It stood there, looking old and worn. He strode over and upended it. He unscrewed the leg. Out fell the emerald.

He seized it and turned to the couple by the sofa. "Say goodbye to Nan for me."

"Dammit, Derek, what are you talking about? Where have you been? What happened to you? Why are you wearing that outfit?"

Derek smiled crookedly. "I've fallen in love, brother. With a lady five hundred years in the past."

Charles and Eleanor looked at each other.

Derek smiled again. "No, I'm not crazy. I'm sorry I don't have time to explain, but I must return."

"I don't know what the hell you're talking about, but you can't leave yet—"

"I'm sorry, but I must. Take care, and . . ." Derek paused and stared at his older brother. "I love you, Charles. Wish me happy."

Charles stared at him. "You've changed, Derek. Don't go, you must explain—"

But it was too late.

With another blinding flash, Derek disappeared.

Chapter 31

SNARLING, WILFRED STALKED toward Allison.

She stood unflinchingly before him. She didn't care what happened to her. She never had. She only hoped the Pelsworth knights would successfully defend the king and the castle.

Wilfred lifted the sword over his head, and she closed her eyes, waiting for the blow.

She heard a whistling wind, and knew the blade was descending toward her head.

A brilliant flash of light exploded behind her closed eyes, and for a moment she thought she must be dead. But then she heard a great clashing noise and felt an arm around her waist swinging her out of the way. Her eyes flew open.

Derek!

Even as her brain recognized him, he brought his sword down on Wilfred's helmet. The visor dropped, and Wilfred staggered under the force of the blow. He fell to his knees. Derek swung again, banging the flat of his sword against Wilfred's head. Wilfred fell to the floor with a crash.

At the same moment the door flew open, and Henry, Sir

Drogo, and four of the Pelsworth knights burst into the room.

Henry's gaze went from Wilfred's fallen body to Derek. "Is he dead?"

"No, Sire," Derek said. "I thought you would prefer to deal with him yourself."

Henry nodded. "He will make a fine example for other traitors. Sir Drogo, take Sir Wilfred to the dungeon."

Sir Drogo and the Pelsworth knights dragged Wilfred's unconscious body away.

Henry looked at Derek. "Your loyalty will be rewarded." Without further speech, he left.

"Oh, Derek!" Allison threw her arms around him and kissed him with all her might.

The door opened again a few moments later, and Anne and Rafael looked in. Anne looked at Allison and Derek and smiled. The minstrel, cocking his head in the direction of the soft sounds they were making, grimaced.

Derek glanced up. "My love," he whispered to Allison, "as usual, we have company."

Dazed, she looked up, blushing when she saw Anne and Rafael. "Oh, forgive us."

"Don't apologize," Anne said. "I just wanted to tell you, your father will recover."

Allison clasped her hands together. "He's alive? Oh, thank heaven! I thought Wilfred had killed him. I must go to him at once!"

"He is asleep. 'Tis best you don't disturb him."

Allison nodded. "And the others who fought?"

"They are all quite healthy. Miraculously, Wilfred and his men failed to kill a single one."

"Thank heaven! Oh, Anne, I am so happy! Everything is perfect!"

"I'm glad to see you so happy." She cupped Allison's cheek, then turned to Derek. Tears misted her eyes. "And you, too. You always were a good boy."

His brows drew together and he stared at her.

"That's enough of this mushy stuff," Rafael said, pulling Anne out of the room.

Derek stared after them. For a second there Anne had sounded exactly like Nan. . . .

No, it was impossible. Shaking his head, he turned his attention back to a more pressing matter—kissing Allison.

In the outer chamber Rafael shook his head, also. "That was foolish, woman. I believe he suspects something."

Anne shrugged. "I doubt it. And don't try to change the subject. You must now admit that I'm right—True Love *does* exist."

Rafael looked skeptical. "Anne, why don't you give up? All your efforts will never convince me that True Love is anything but a fairy tale. You have interfered too often already—"

"*I* have interfered? Do you think I don't know you were the one who introduced Pelsworth to that French hussy? Are you happy with the havoc *you* wrought?"

Rafael frowned slightly. "I did not expect . . . Pelsworth handled the situation badly. That English witch—that *you* introduced to him—had him firmly under her spell. You see the damage so-called love can cause?"

"Bah. You're blind as usual."

Rafael smiled wryly. "Rather more blind than usual. Haven't you punished me long enough?"

"Not nearly long enough," she snapped.

Rafael laughed. "Sweet Anne, the day is won, the lovers are united—how much more do you want? Now, come give me a kiss."

She tossed her head. "I want everything." But she gave him the kiss anyway.

Later that night, after a fierce bout of lovemaking, Derek lay satiated and content, Allison curled in his arms.

"Derek," she murmured, cuddling closer.

Automatically his arms tightened around her. "Yes, Allison?"

"What was Cuthbert talking to you about so earnestly at supper earlier?"

"He was apologizing for ever doubting me." Derek's lips quirked. "He said he should have trusted me, that he should have recognized the honor and chivalry in my soul even if it was disguised by the superficiality of my words and actions."

She grew still in his arms. "Derek . . ."

"Yes, Allison?"

"I'm sorry about the wine."

"Never mind," he said.

She lifted her head and looked down at him, her hair pooling on his chest. "You knew, didn't you?"

He caught a golden strand between his fingers. "Yes. I asked Anne to replace the tincture with a harmless one."

"I see." Her eyes were dark and shadowed. "Can you ever forgive me?"

"It doesn't matter," he said. "Everything has worked out. No one was hurt."

"But it hurt you, didn't it? I betrayed you." She placed her hand on his chest. "I'm sorry, Derek. I'm so sorry. I was so worried about the castle that I was blind to everything else."

His fingers tightened in her hair. "Then why did you send me away when I was fighting Wilfred?"

She hesitated. "My dreams . . . I knew you hadn't come here willingly. You told me once that I had stolen your life, but I never meant to. I couldn't bear it if you were killed."

His fingers tightened in her hair. "You have given me my life. I barely existed before. I love you, Allison."

"Oh, Derek . . ." Tears welled in her eyes. "I love you, too."

She bent down and kissed him. He kissed her back, and for a long time neither one of them spoke.

It wasn't until she was curled once more in his arms that she said, "But what about your home? My dreams were true, weren't they? You really are from the future."

Derek heard the slight tension in her voice. He kissed her temple. "Nah. I'm from Italy. Your dreams were just that— dreams."

A soft sigh escaped her, and the tension eased from her body. She curled up next to his heart.

"Oh, Derek," she said sleepily. "I'm so glad you came."
"So am I, Allie." His arms tightened around her. "So am I."

Dear Reader—

Derek Sinclair's opinion notwithstanding, there are actually a few people who know that Cinco de Mayo celebrates the May 5, 1862, victory of a small Mexican force over the invading French army. Although this battle was the only victory for the Mexicans in a long string of defeats, it proved a turning point in their war for independence from France.

I love hearing from readers! Please write to me at:

P.O. Box 4672

Orange, CA 92863–4672

If you would like a copy of *"The Secret Diary of Angie Ray; or, The Writing of MY LADY IN TIME,"* or a free bookmark, please enclose a self-addressed, stamped envelope.

Angie Ray